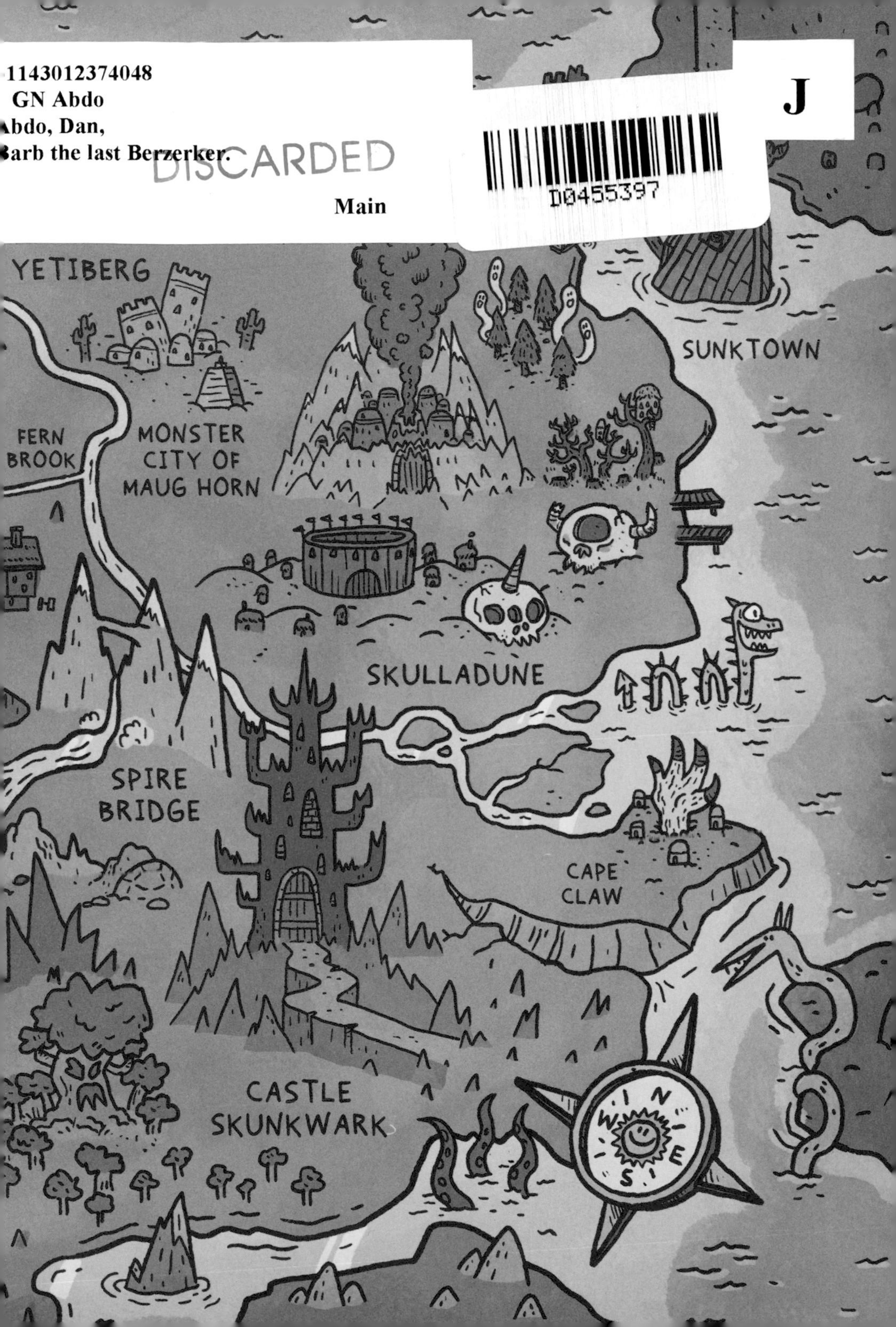
YETIBERG
SUNKTOWN
FERN BROOK
MONSTER CITY OF MAUG HORN
SKULLADUNE
SPIRE BRIDGE
CAPE CLAW
CASTLE SKUNKWARK
N
W
E
S

BARB
THE LAST BERZERKER
BOOK 1

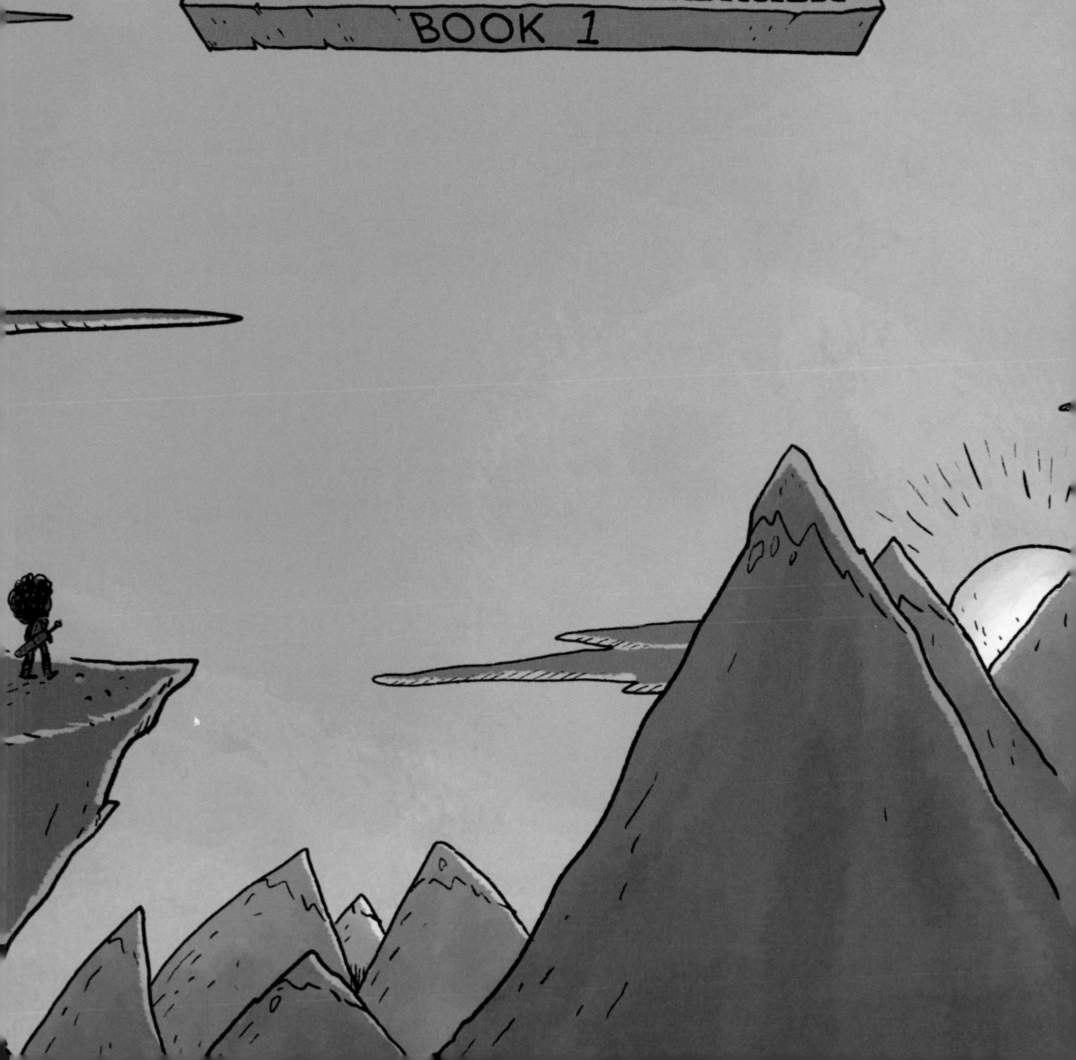

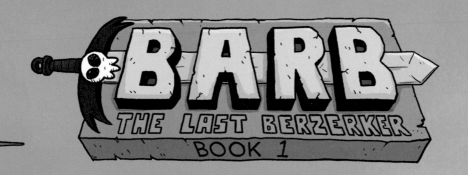

For Harrison, Vivian,
Eloise, and Winona:
the most amazing Zerks
we've ever known.

P.S. Don't let the
"bed slugs" bite!

—D. & J.

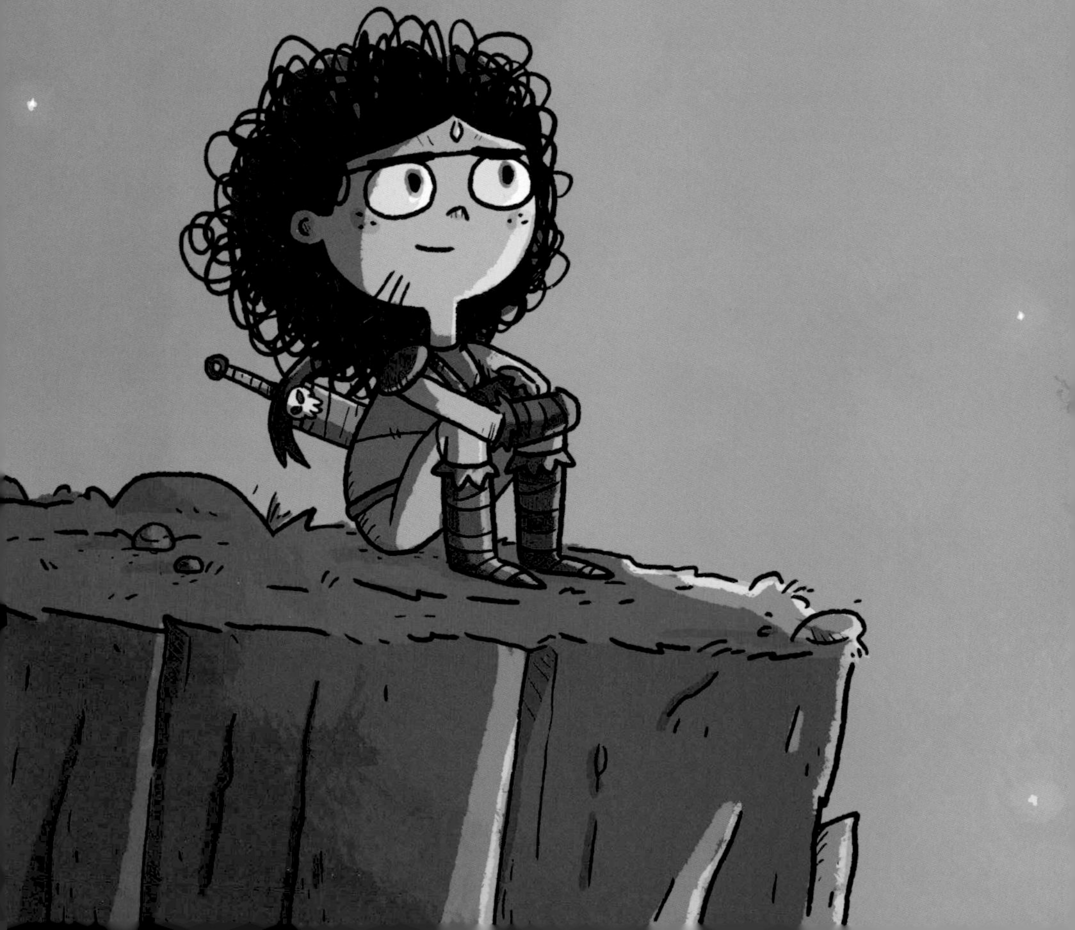

BARB
THE LAST BERZERKER
BOOK 1

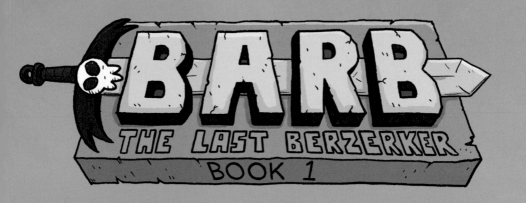

by

Dan & Jason

Simon & Schuster Books for Young Readers
New York London Toronto Sydney New Delhi

SIMON & SCHUSTER BOOKS FOR YOUNG READERS
An imprint of Simon & Schuster Children's Publishing Division
1230 Avenue of the Americas, New York, New York 10020

© 2021 by Daniel Rajai Abdo and Jason Linwood Patterson
Case design by Chloë Foglia and Dan & Jason © 2021 by Simon & Schuster, Inc.

SIMON & SCHUSTER BOOKS FOR YOUNG READERS and related marks are trademarks of Simon & Schuster, Inc. For information about special discounts for bulk purchases, please contact Simon & Schuster Special Sales at 1-866-506-1949 or business@simonandschuster.com.
The Simon & Schuster Speakers Bureau can bring authors to your live event. For more information or to book an event, contact the Simon & Schuster Speakers Bureau at 1-866-248-3049 or visit our website at www.simonspeakers.com.
Interior design by Chloë Foglia and Tom Daly
The text for this book was set in Barb 03-Regular.
The illustrations for this book were rendered digitally.
Manufactured in China
0322 SCP
2 4 6 8 10 9 7 5 3
Library of Congress Cataloging-in-Publication Data
Names: Abdo, Dan, author, illustrator. | Jason (Jason Linwood Patterson), author, illustrator. Title: Barb the last Berzerker / Dan Abdo and Jason Patterson. Description: New York : Simon & Schuster Books for Young Readers, 2021. | Series: Barb the last Berzerker ; book one | Audience: Ages 9–12. | Audience: Grades 4–6. | Summary: Barb and her best friend Porkchop the yeti must save her fellow warriors from the evil sorcerer Witch Head before he destroys the land of Bailiwick.
Identifiers: LCCN 2021009678 (print) | LCCN 2021009679 (ebook) |
ISBN 9781534485716 (hardback) | ISBN 9781534485730 (ebook)
Subjects: CYAC: Graphic novels. | Yeti—Fiction. | Monsters—Fiction. | Wizards—Fiction. | Swords—Fiction. | Adventure and adventurers—Fiction. | Fantasy. | BISAC: JUVENILE FICTION / Comics & Graphic Novels / Action & Adventure | JUVENILE FICTION / Comics & Graphic Novels / Fantasy | LCGFT: Graphic novels.
Classification: LCC PZ7.7.A245 Bar 2021 (print) | LCC PZ7.7.A245 (ebook) | DDC 741.5/973--dc23
LC record available at https://lccn.loc.gov/2021009678
LC ebook record available at https://lccn.loc.gov/2021009679

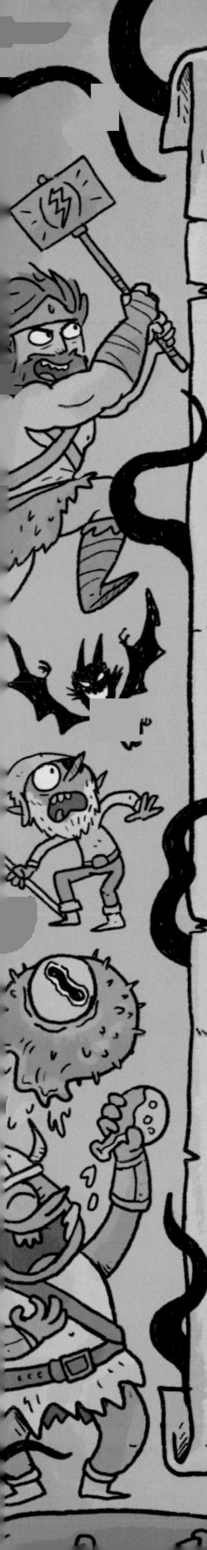

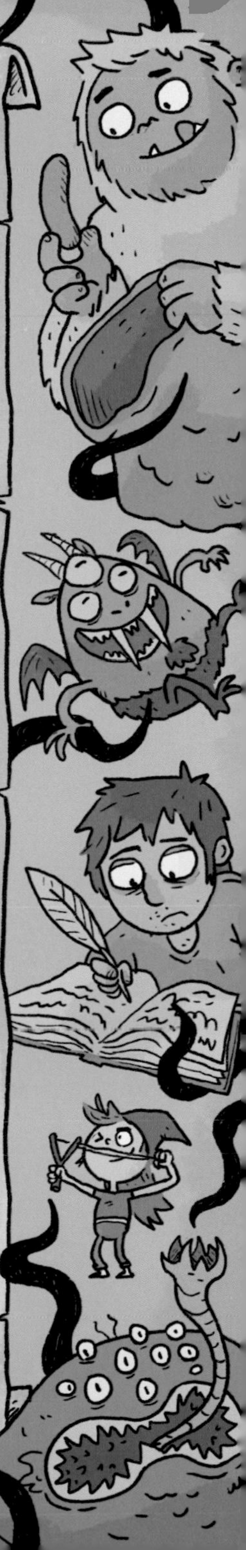

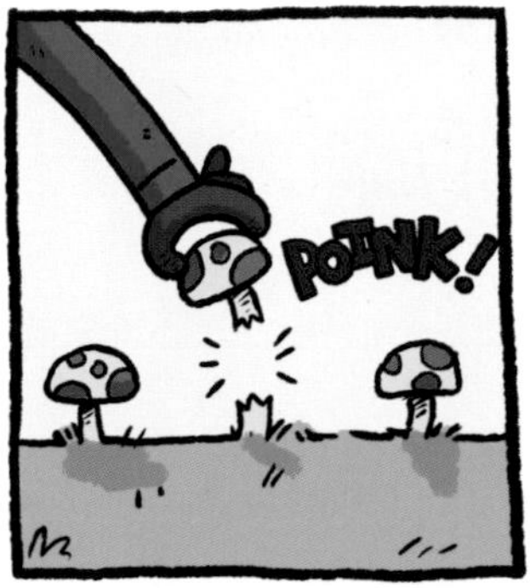
POINK!

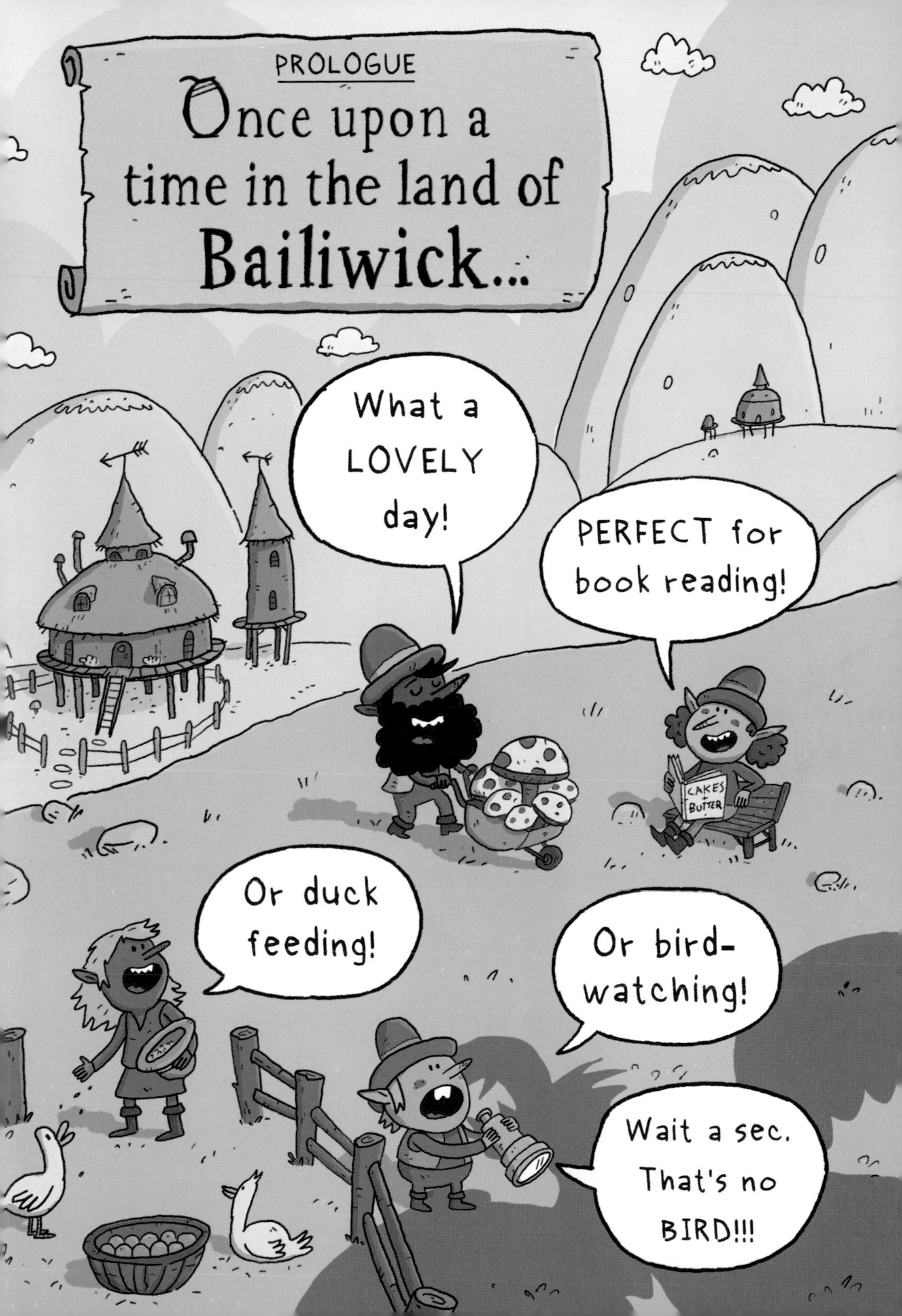
PROLOGUE
Once upon a time in the land of Bailiwick...
What a LOVELY day!
PERFECT for book reading!
CAKES + BUTTER
Or duck feeding!
Or bird-watching!
Wait a sec. That's no BIRD!!!

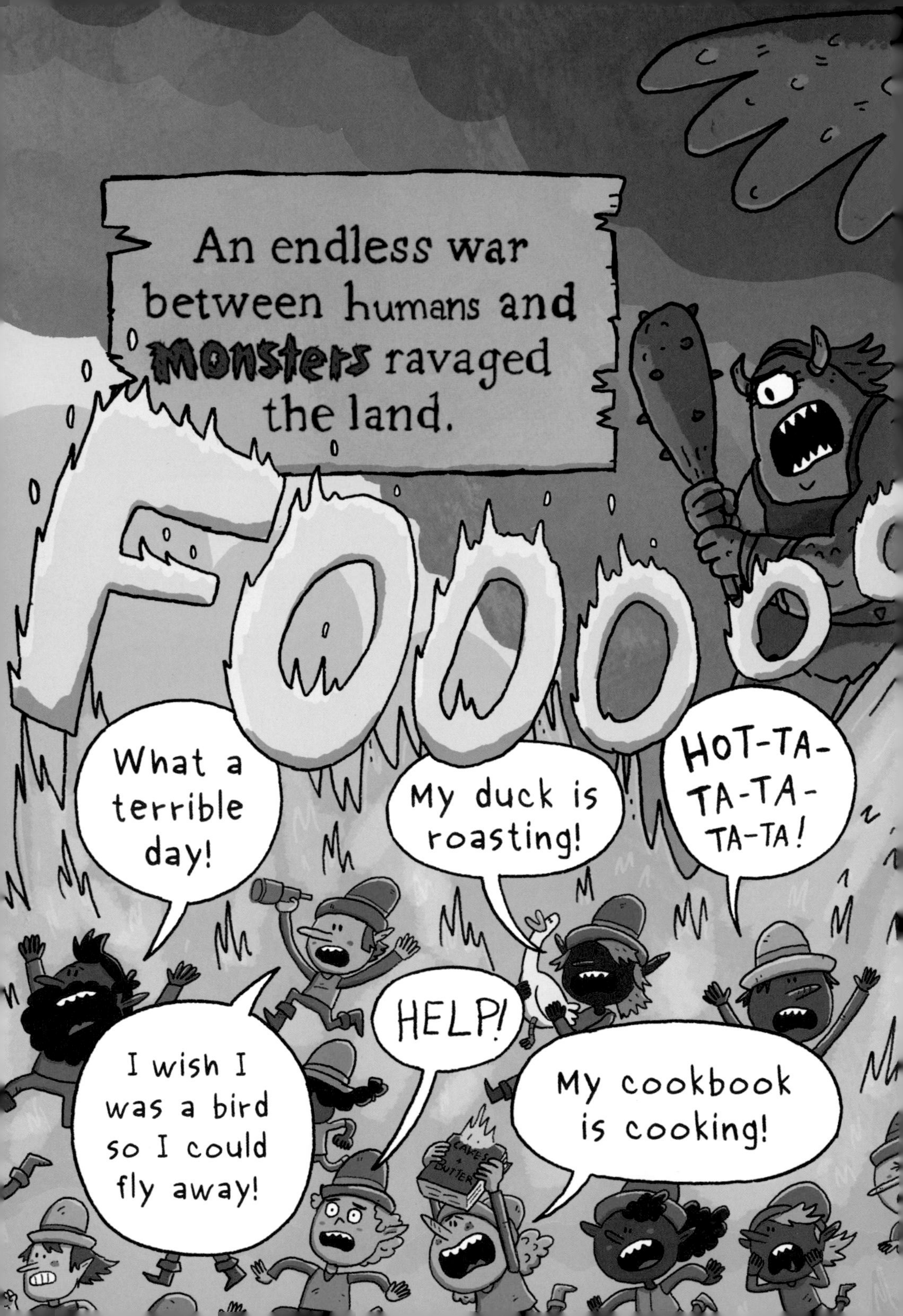

An endless war between humans and monsters ravaged the land.
FOOOO
What a terrible day!
My duck is roasting!
HOT-TA-TA-TA-TA-TA!
HELP!
I wish I was a bird so I could fly away!
My cookbook is cooking!
CAKES + BUTTER

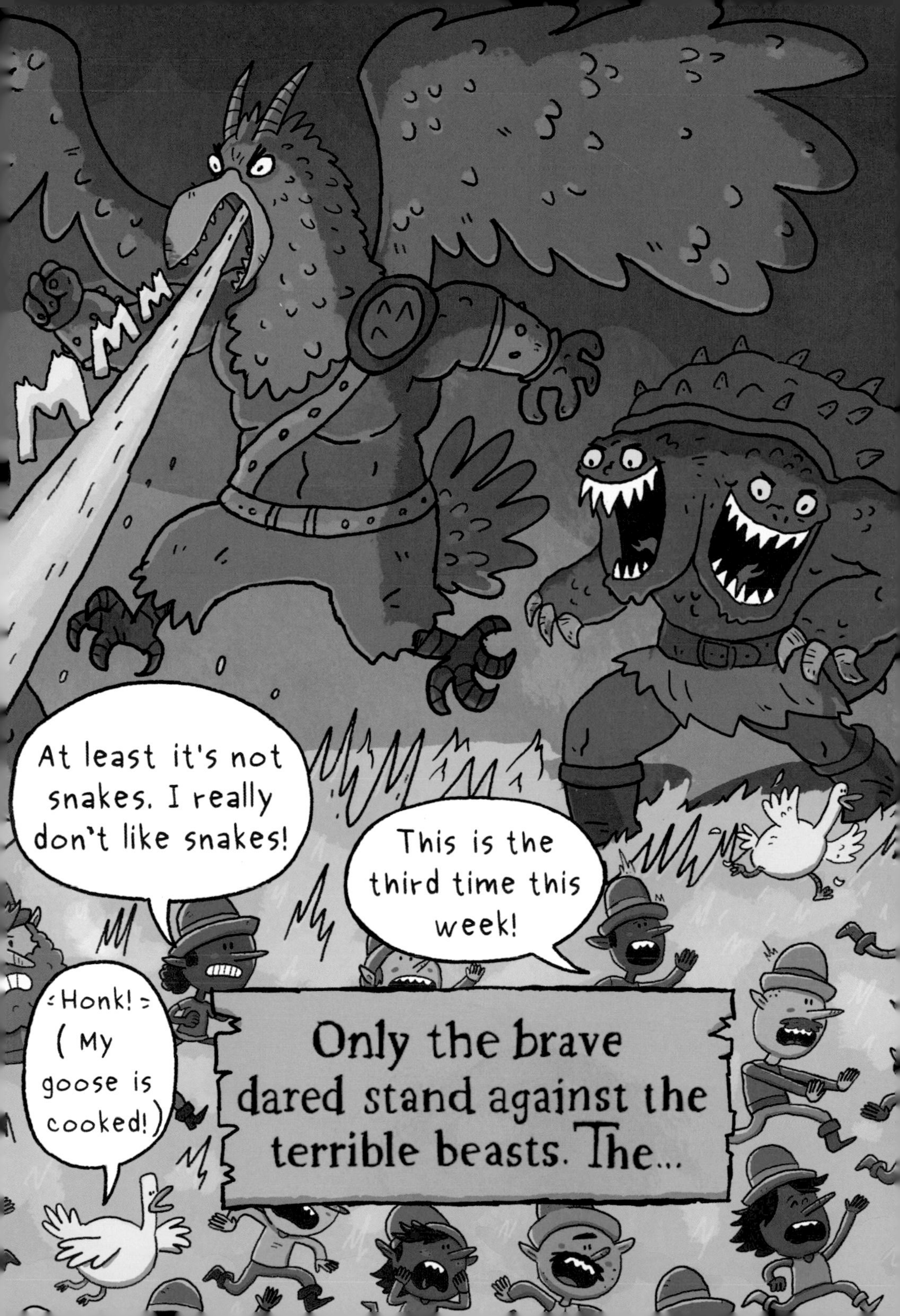

At least it's not snakes. I really don't like snakes!
This is the third time this week!
Honk! (My goose is cooked!)
Only the brave dared stand against the terrible beasts. The...

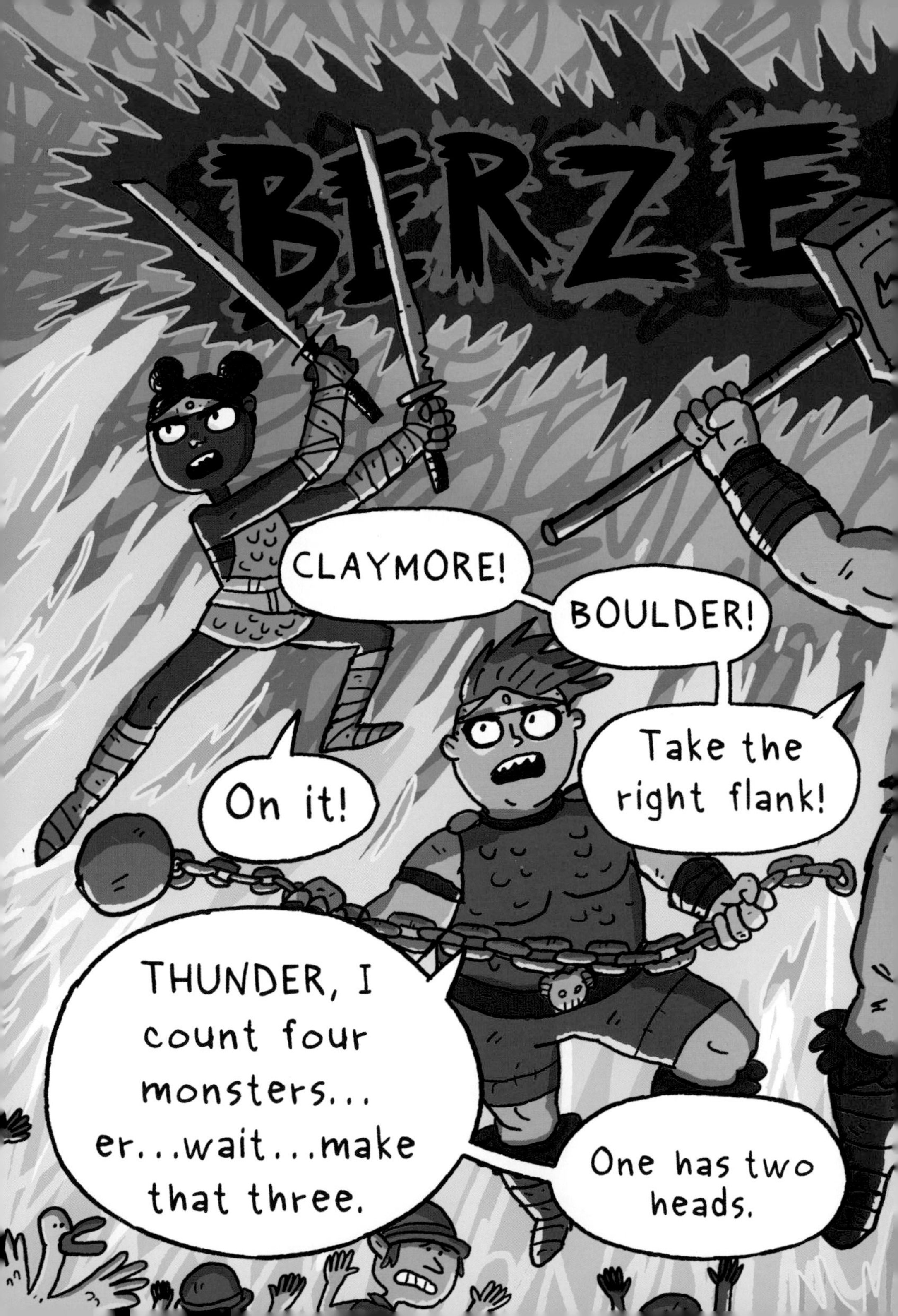
BERZE
CLAYMORE!
BOULDER!
Take the right flank!
On it!
THUNDER, I count four monsters... er...wait...make that three.
One has two heads.

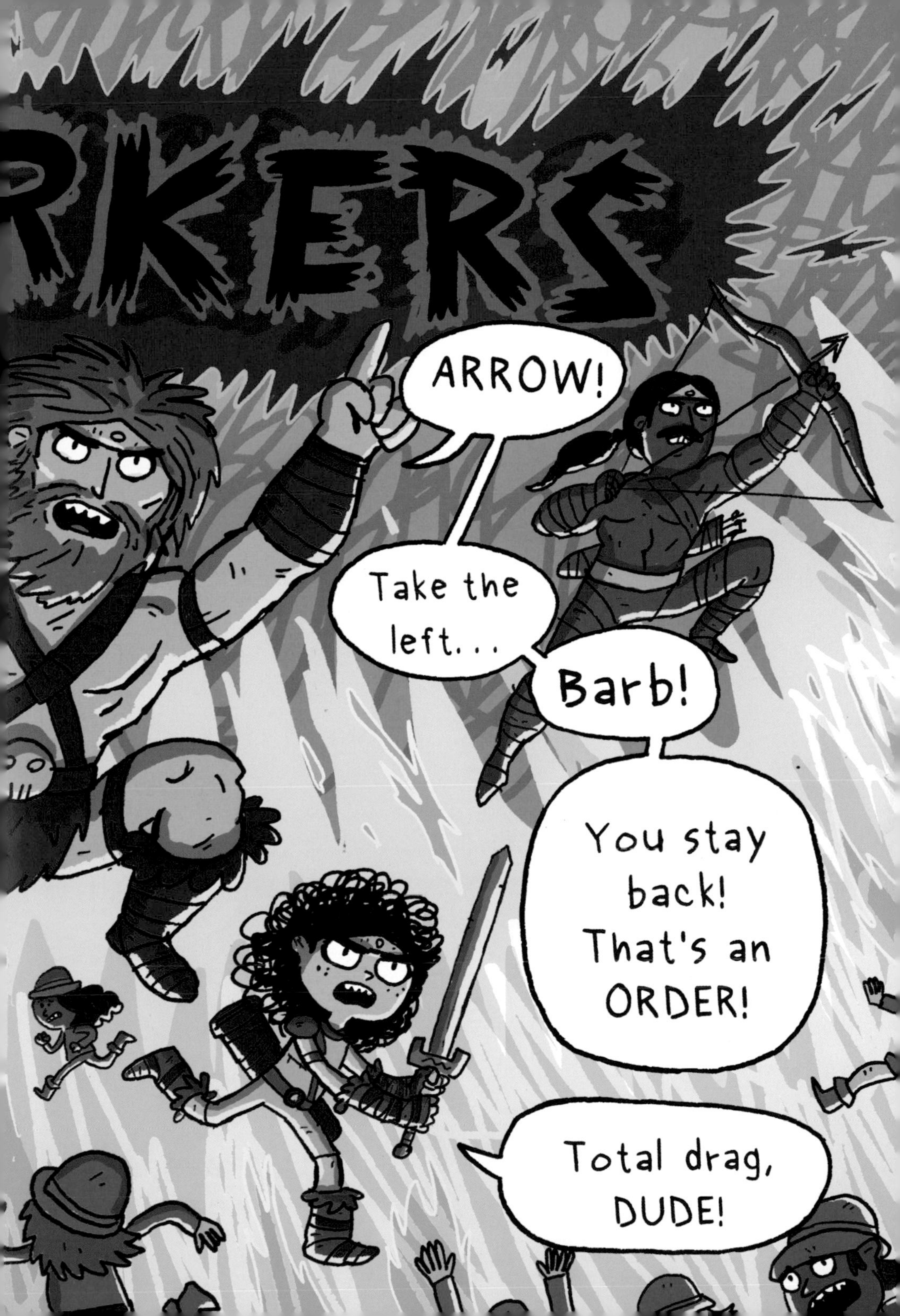
RKERS
ARROW!
Take the left...
Barb!
You stay back! That's an ORDER!
Total drag, DUDE!

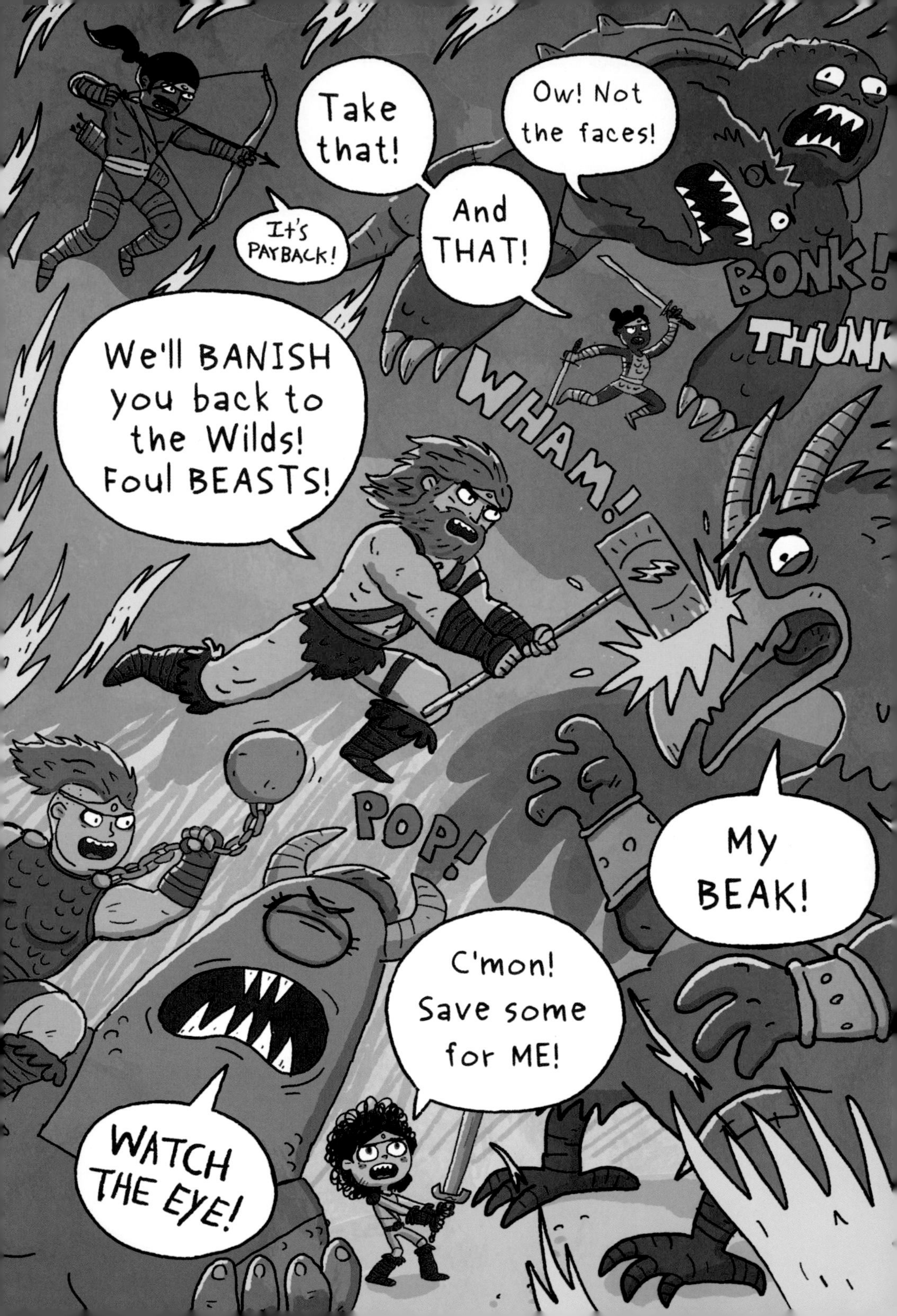
Take that!
It's PAYBACK!
And THAT!
Ow! Not the faces!
BONK!
THUNK
WHAM!
We'll BANISH you back to the Wilds! Foul BEASTS!
POP!
My BEAK!
C'mon! Save some for ME!
WATCH THE EYE!

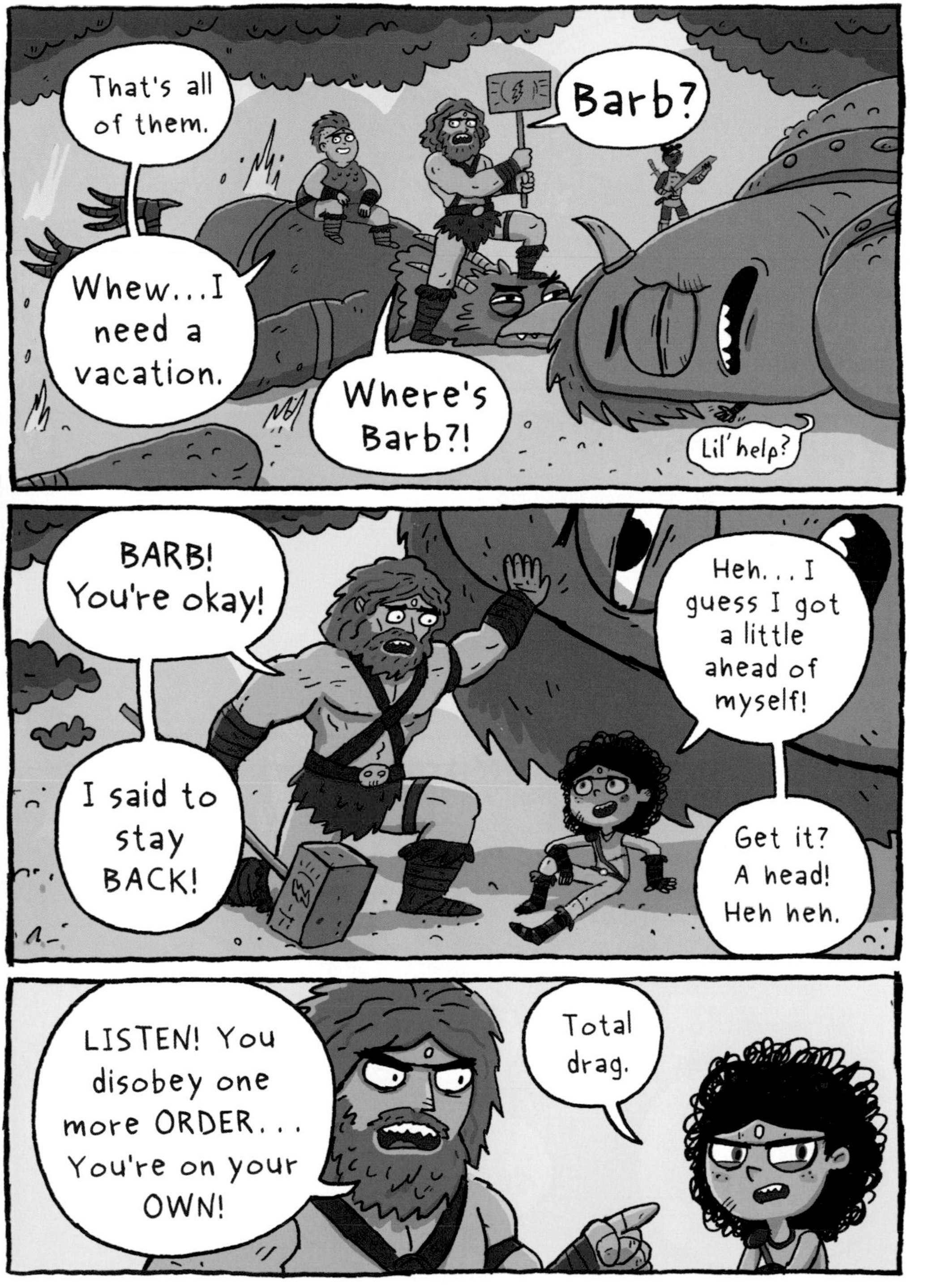

That's all of them.
Whew...I need a vacation.
Barb?
Where's Barb?!
Lil' help?
BARB! You're okay!
I said to stay BACK!
Heh...I guess I got a little ahead of myself!
Get it? A head! Heh heh.
LISTEN! You disobey one more ORDER... You're on your OWN!
Total drag.

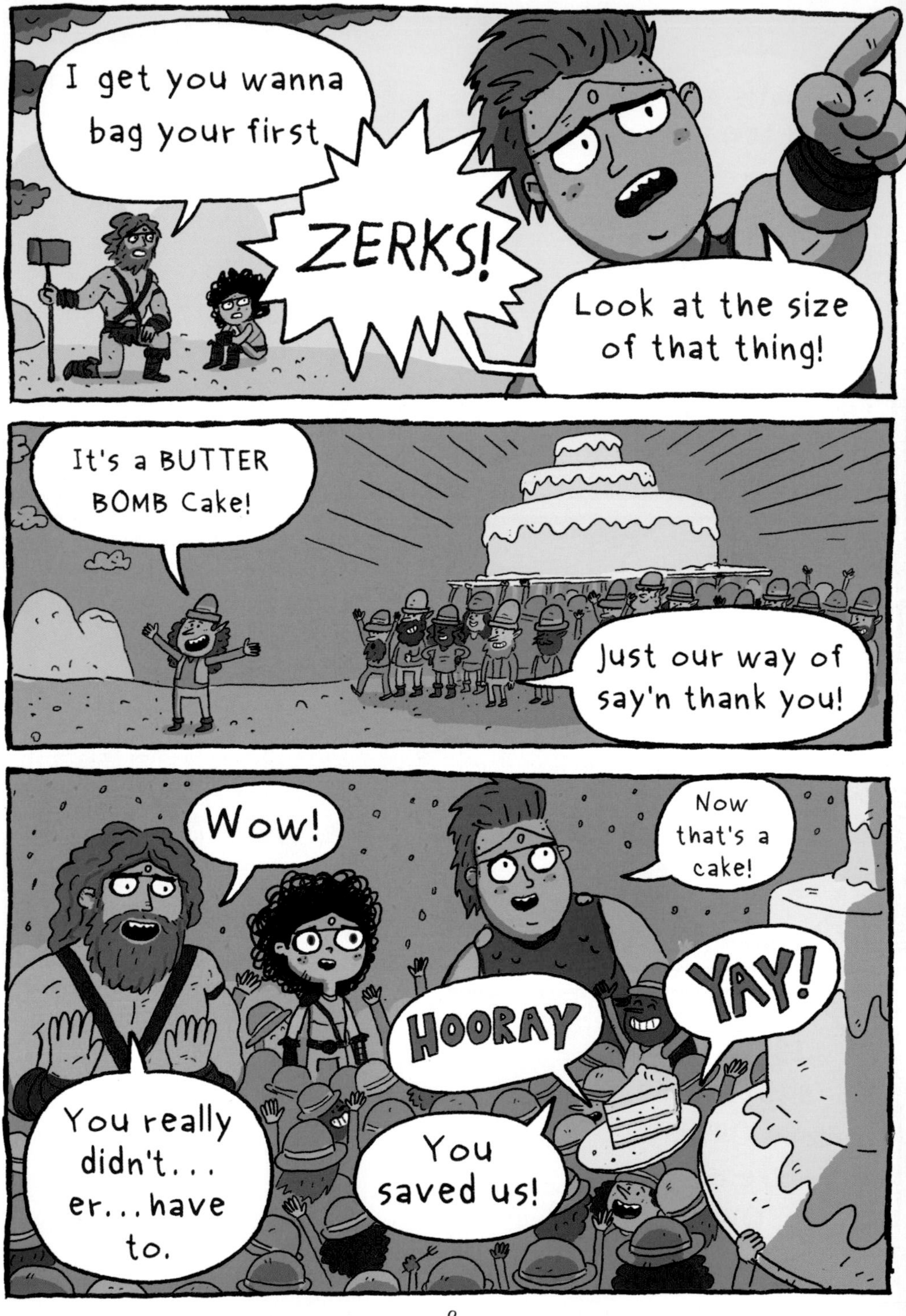

I get you wanna bag your first
ZERKS!
Look at the size of that thing!
It's a BUTTER BOMB Cake!
Just our way of say'n thank you!
Wow!
Now that's a cake!
You really didn't... er...have to.
HOORAY
YAY!
You saved us!

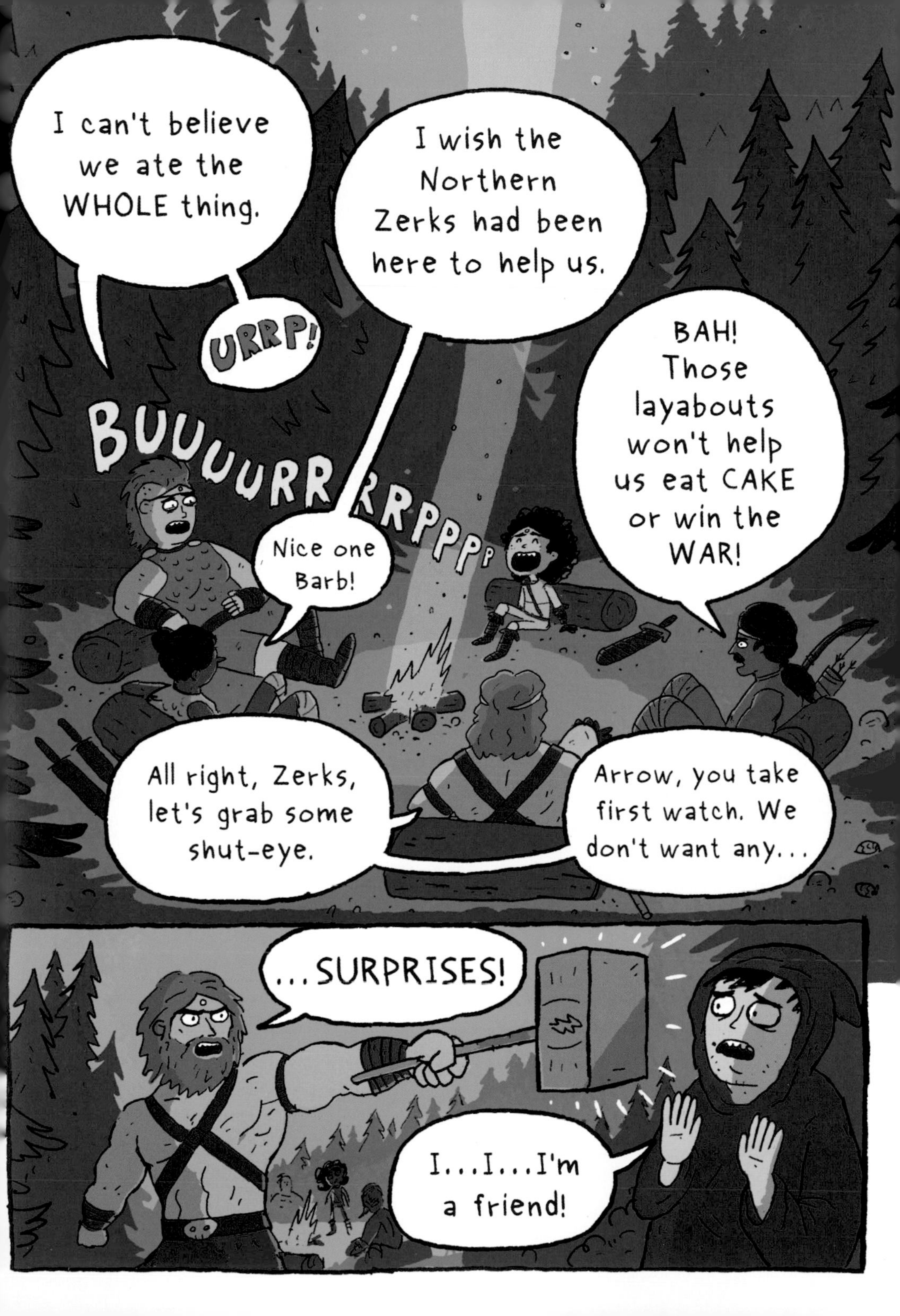
I can't believe we ate the WHOLE thing.
URRP!
I wish the Northern Zerks had been here to help us.
BUUUURRRRPPPP
Nice one Barb!
BAH! Those layabouts won't help us eat CAKE or win the WAR!
All right, Zerks, let's grab some shut-eye.
Arrow, you take first watch. We don't want any...
...SURPRISES!
I...I...I'm a friend!

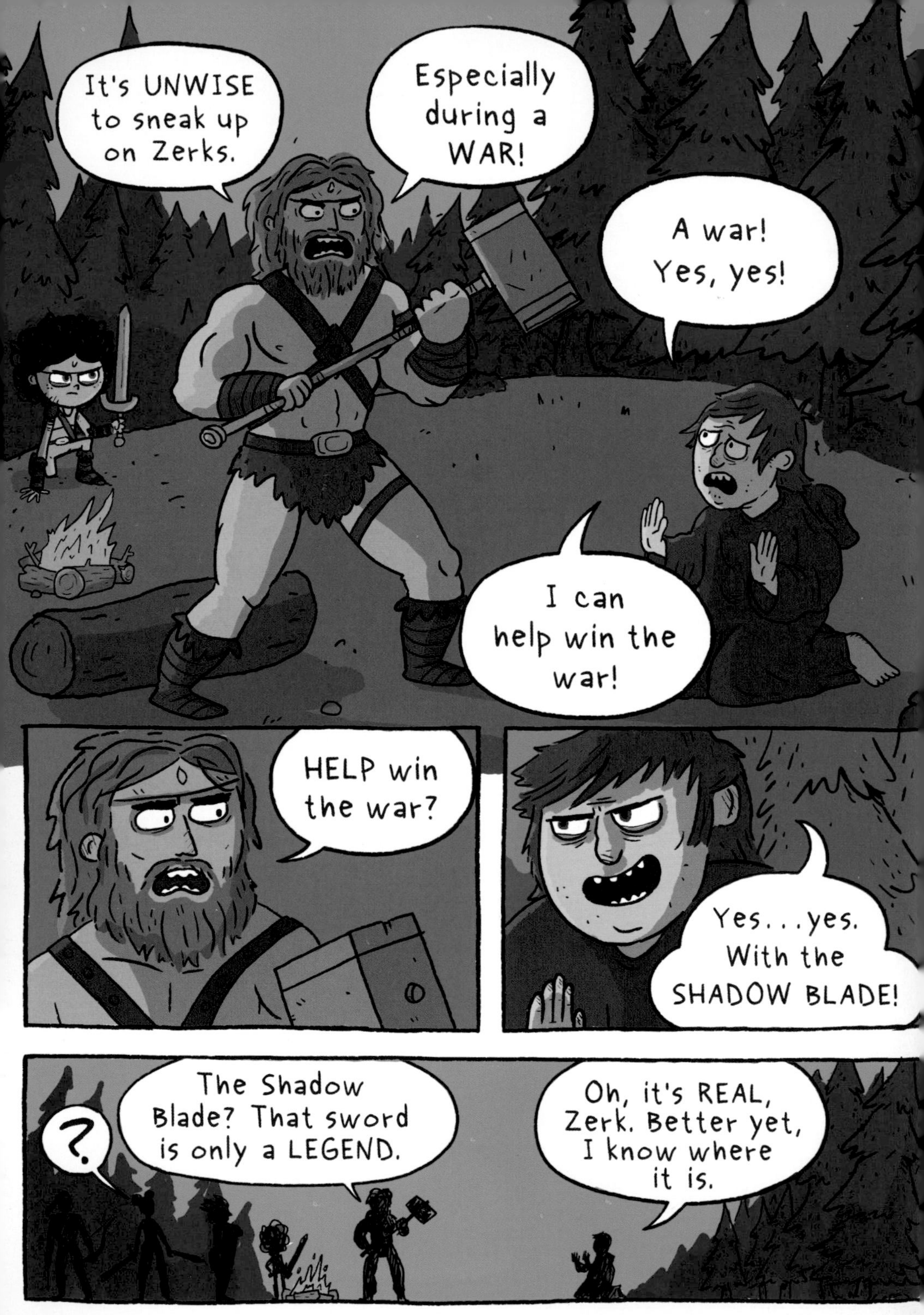
It's UNWISE to sneak up on Zerks.
Especially during a WAR!
A war! Yes, yes!
I can help win the war!
HELP win the war?
Yes. . . yes. With the SHADOW BLADE!
?
The Shadow Blade? That sword is only a LEGEND.
Oh, it's REAL, Zerk. Better yet, I know where it is.

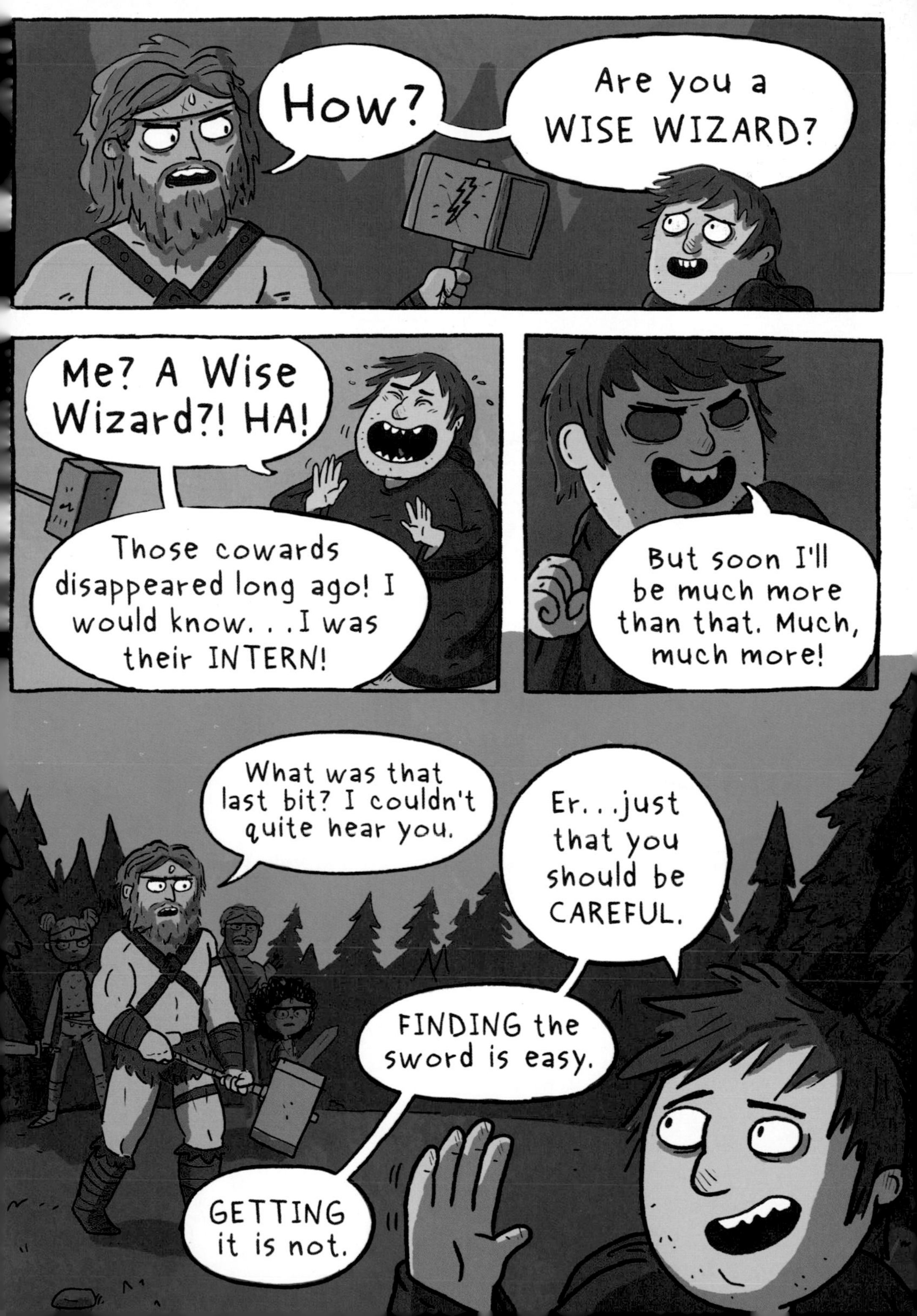
How?
Are you a WISE WIZARD?
Me? A Wise Wizard?! HA!
Those cowards disappeared long ago! I would know. . .I was their INTERN!
But soon I'll be much more than that. Much, much more!
What was that last bit? I couldn't quite hear you.
Er. . .just that you should be CAREFUL.
FINDING the sword is easy.
GETTING it is not.

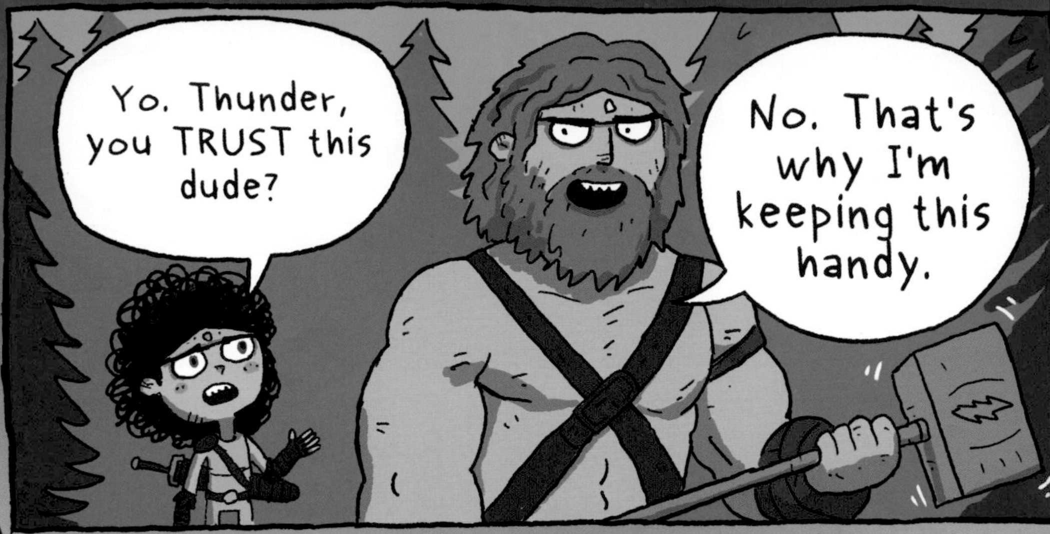
Yo. Thunder, you TRUST this dude?
No. That's why I'm keeping this handy.

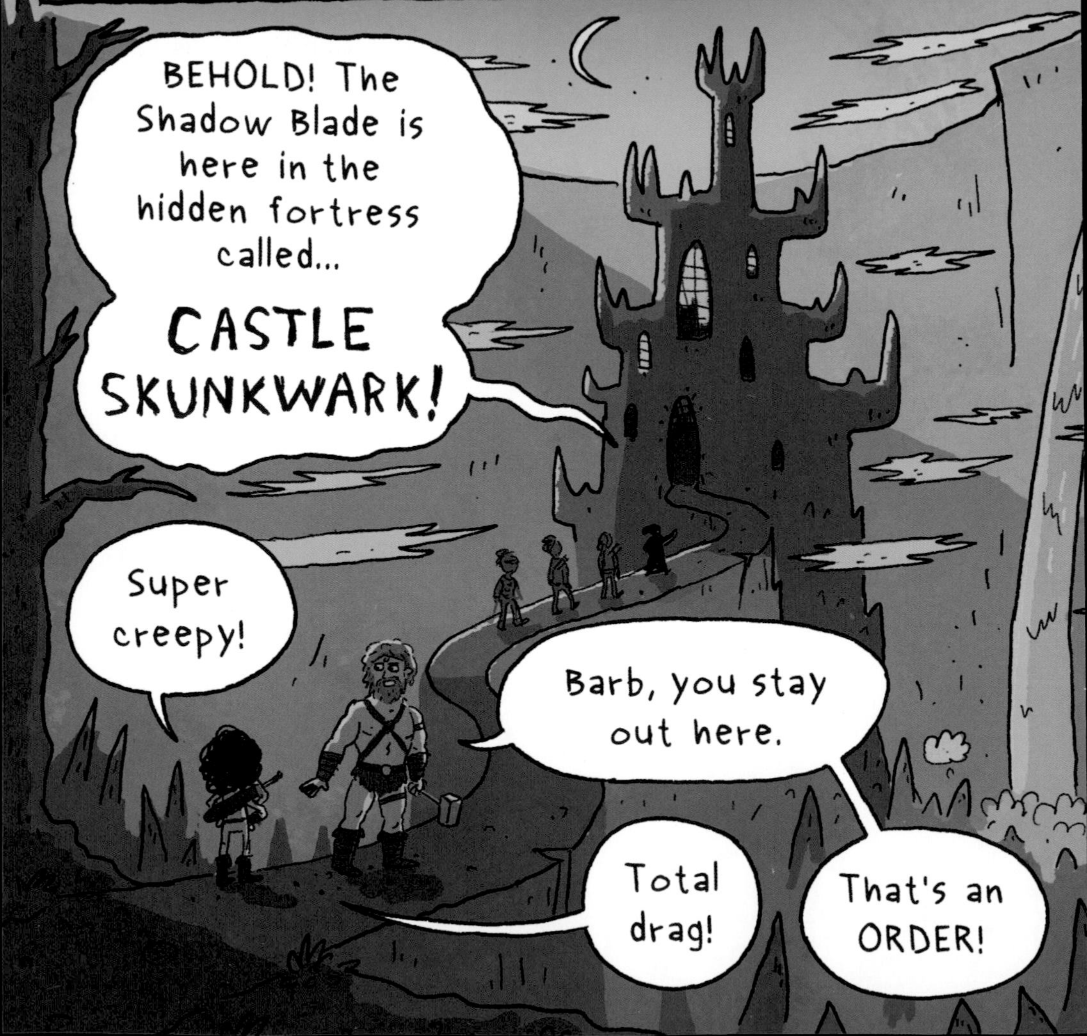
BEHOLD! The Shadow Blade is here in the hidden fortress called...
CASTLE SKUNKWARK!
Super creepy!
Barb, you stay out here.
Total drag!
That's an ORDER!

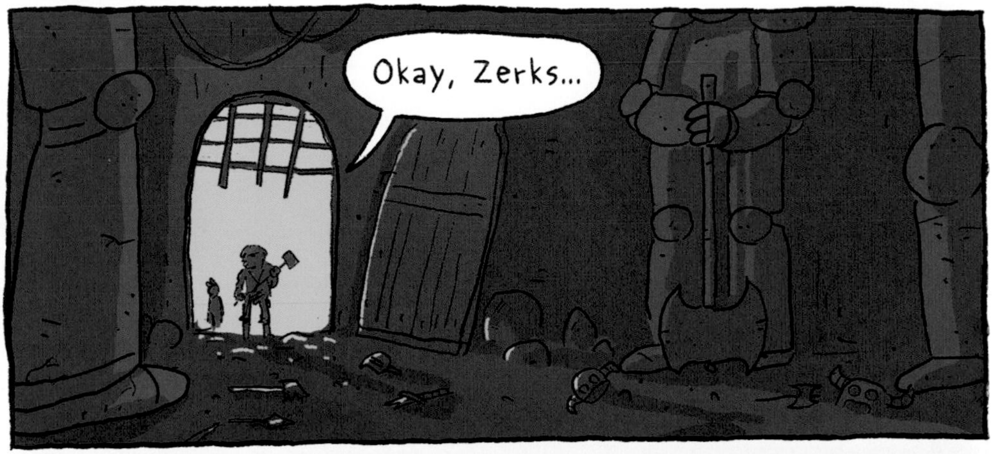
Okay, Zerks...

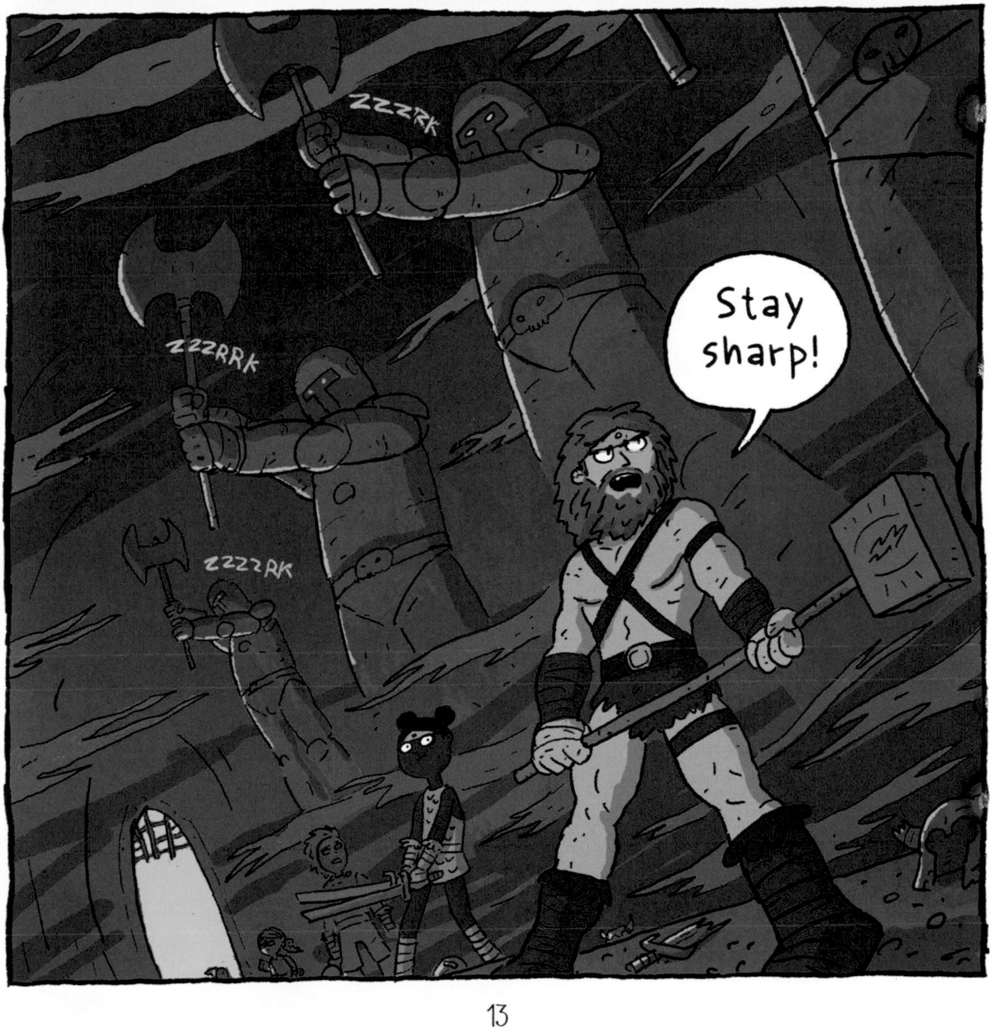
ZZZRK
ZZZRRK
ZZZZRK
Stay sharp!

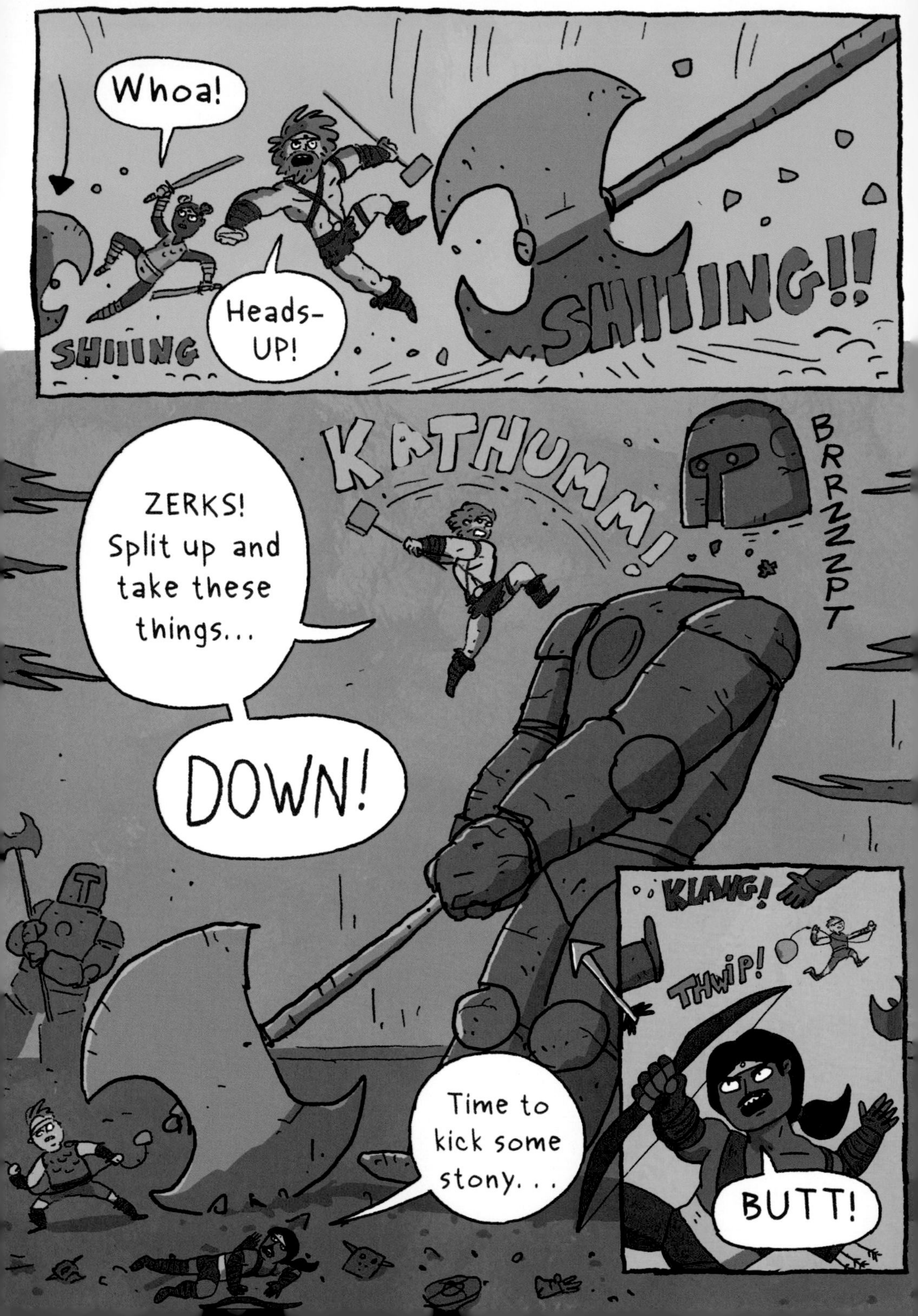
Whoa!
Heads-UP!
SHIIING
SHIIING!!
KATHUMM!
BRRZZZPT
ZERKS! Split up and take these things...
DOWN!
KLANG!
THWIP!
Time to kick some stony. . .
BUTT!

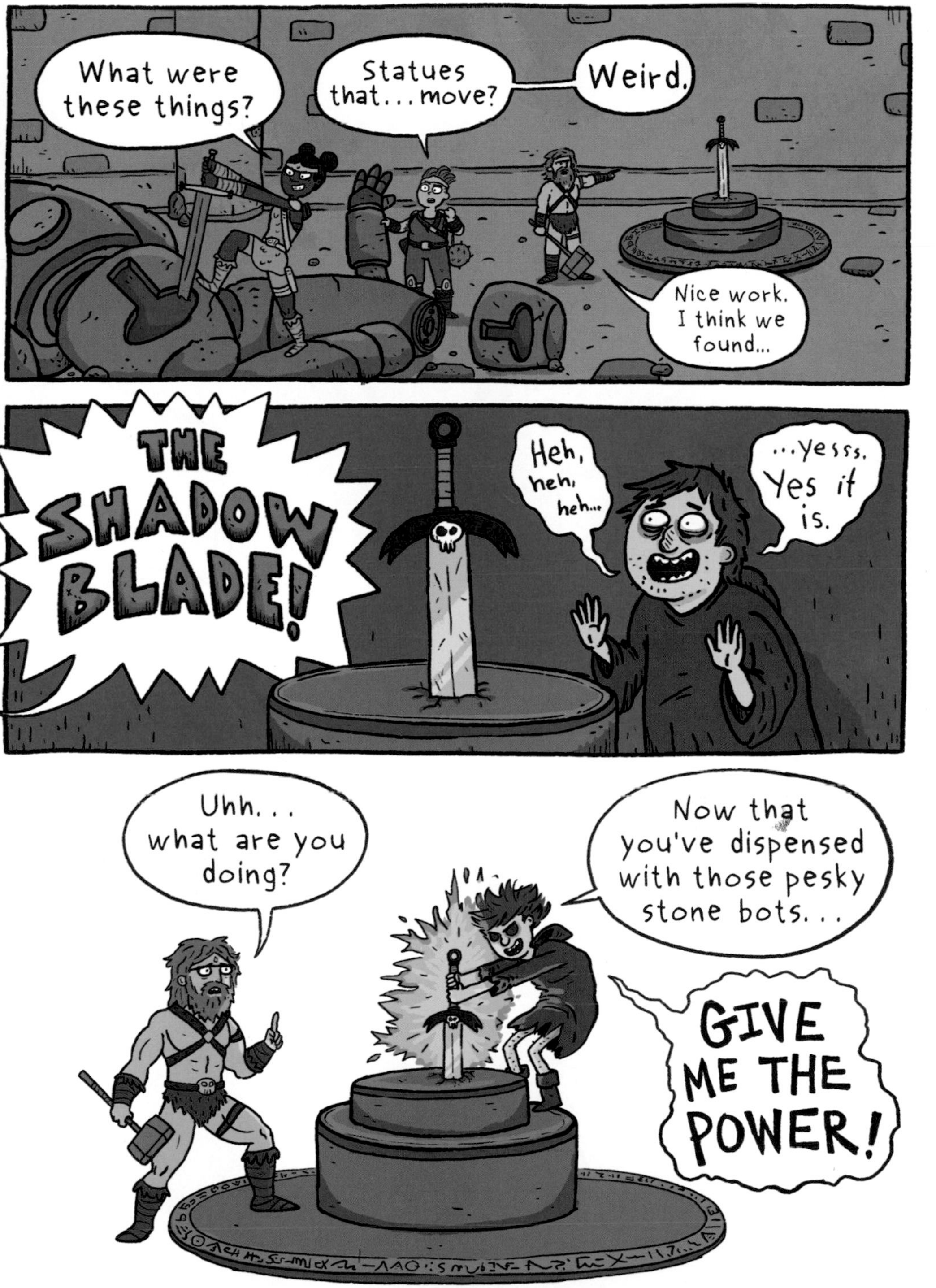
What were these things?
Statues that...move?
Weird.
Nice work. I think we found...
THE SHADOW BLADE!
Heh, heh, heh...
...yesss. Yes it is.
Uhh... what are you doing?
Now that you've dispensed with those pesky stone bots...
GIVE ME THE POWER!

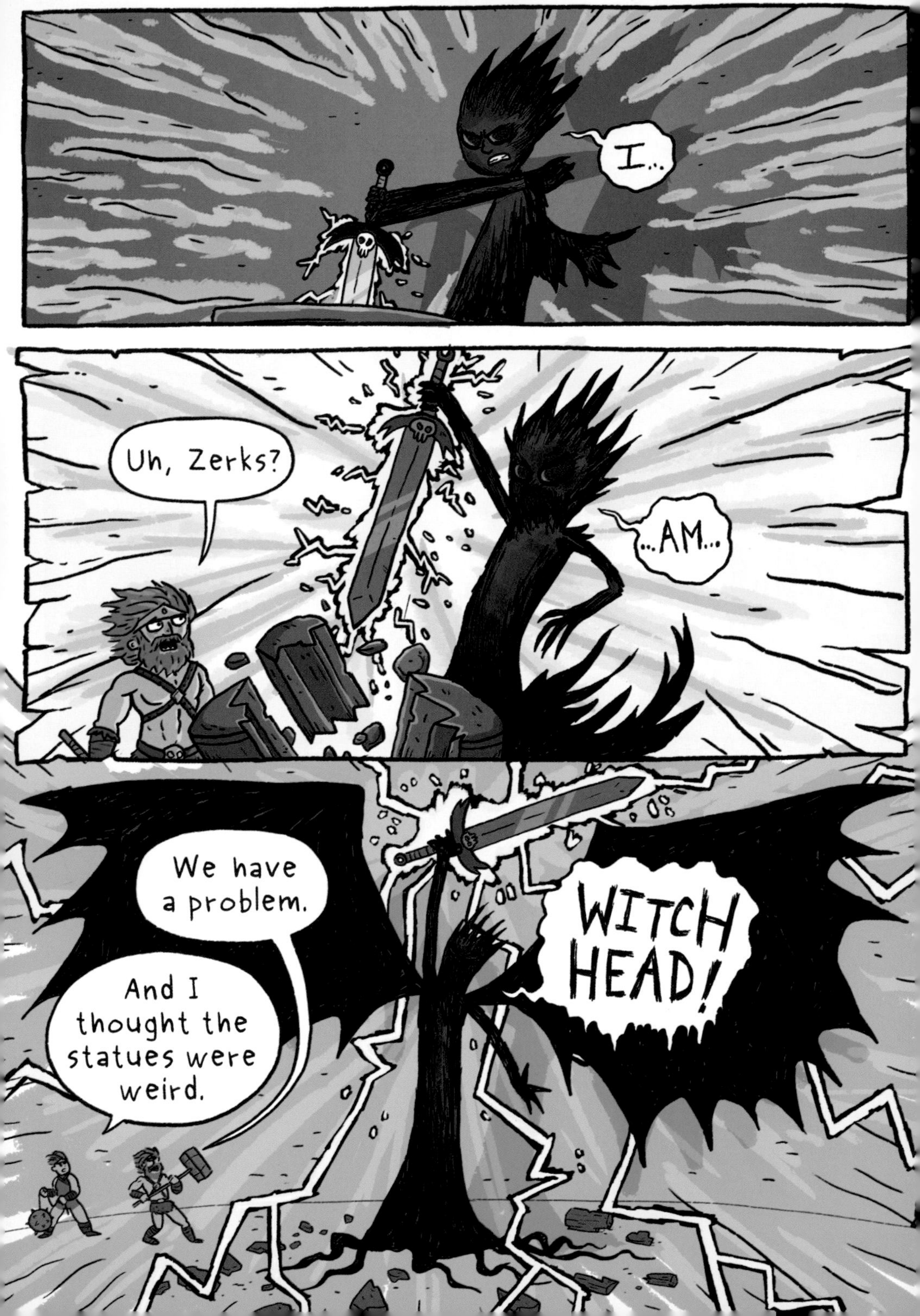
I...
Uh, Zerks?
...AM...
We have a problem.
WITCH HEAD!
And I thought the statues were weird.

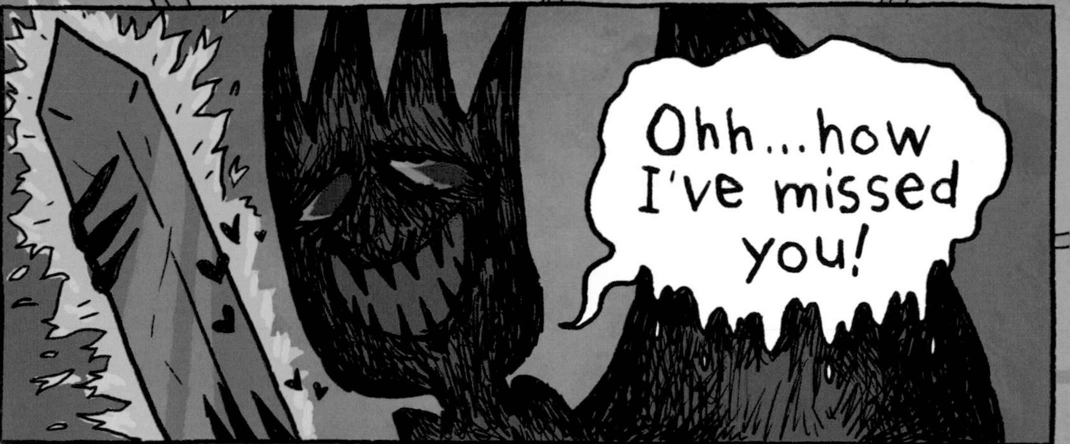
Ohh...how I've missed you!

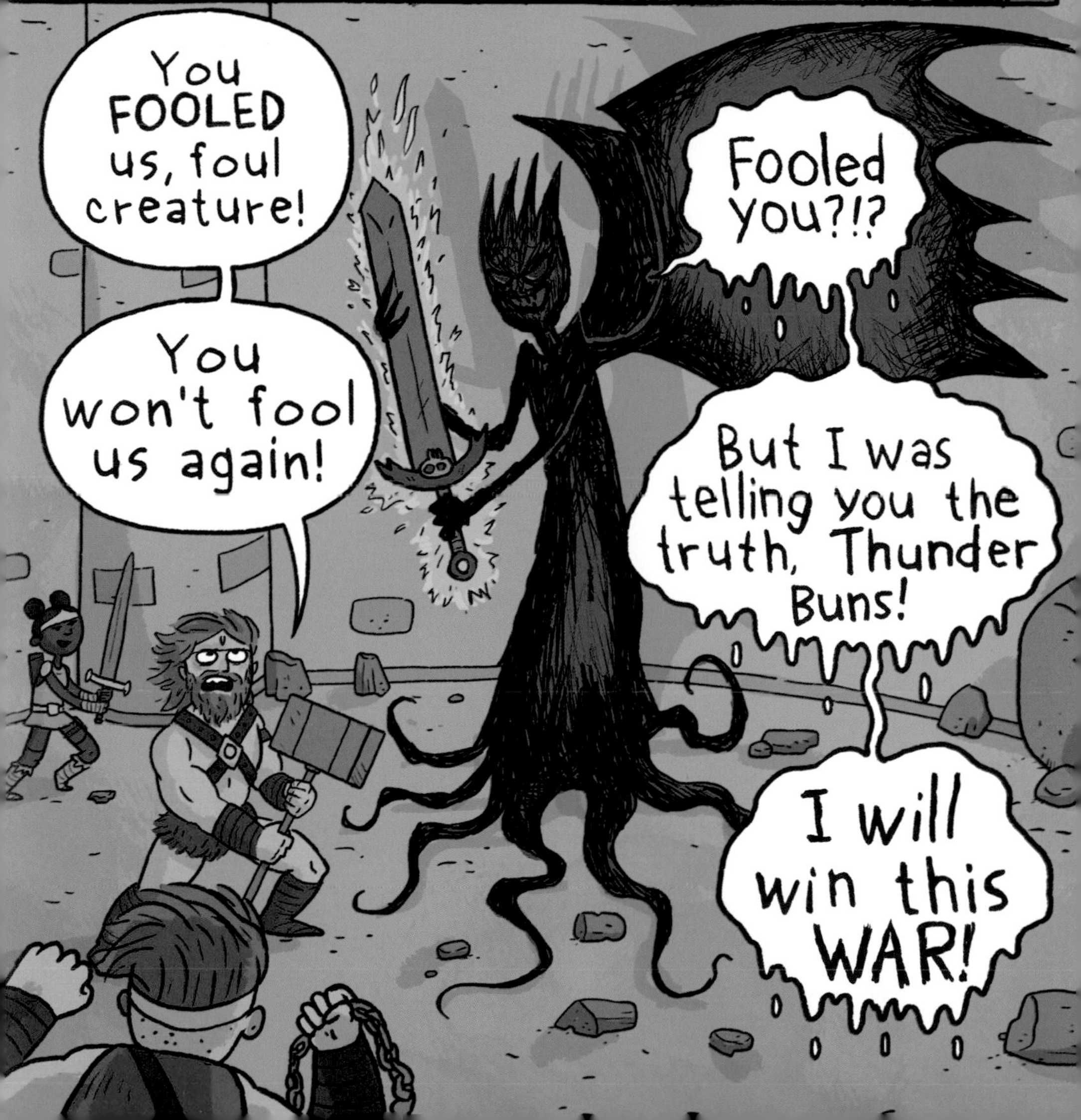
You FOOLED us, foul creature!
You won't fool us again!
Fooled you?!?
But I was telling you the truth, Thunder Buns!
I will win this WAR!

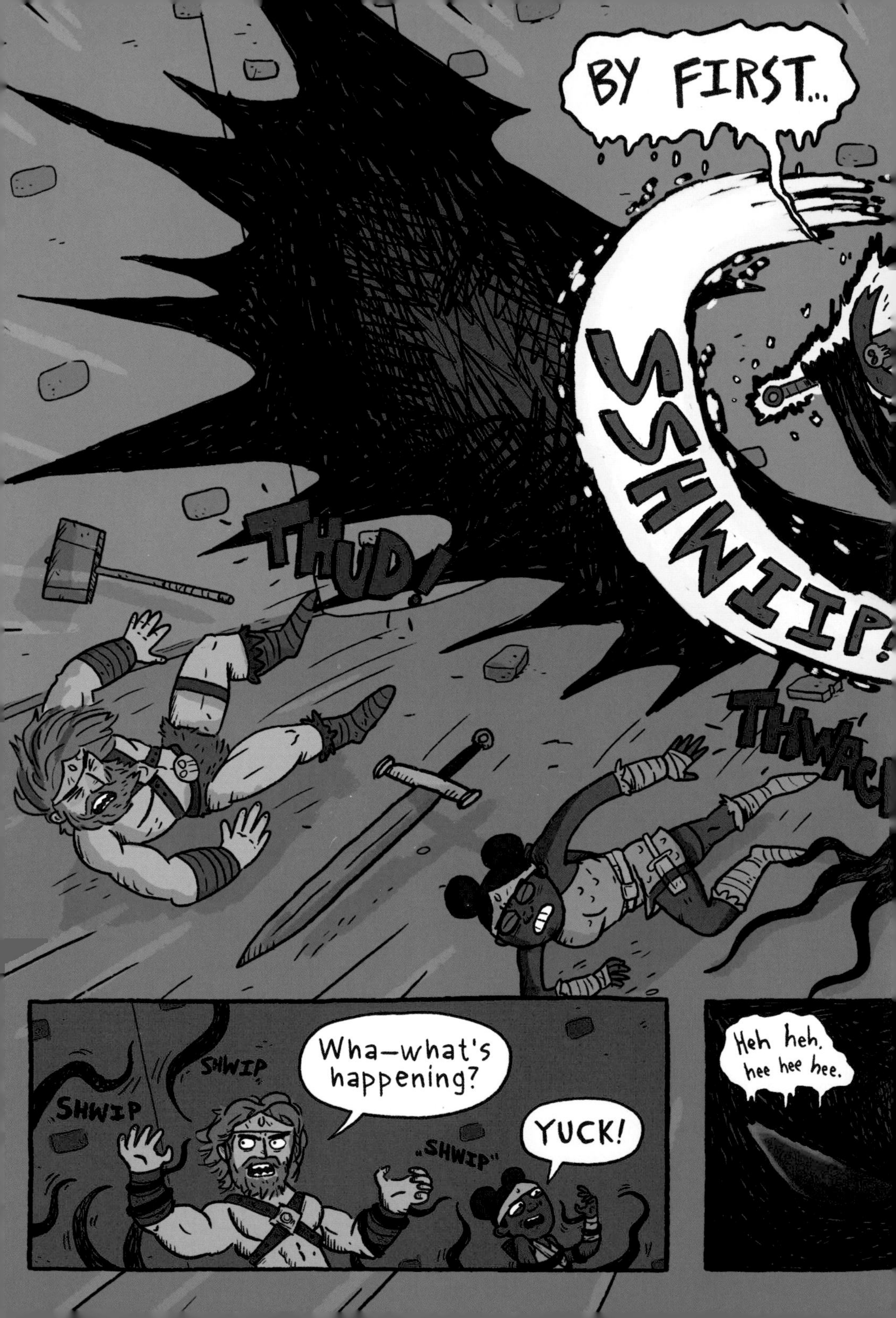
BY FIRST...
SSHWIIIP!
THUD!
THWACK
SHWIP
SHWIP
"SHWIP"
Wha-what's happening?
YUCK!
Heh heh. hee hee hee.

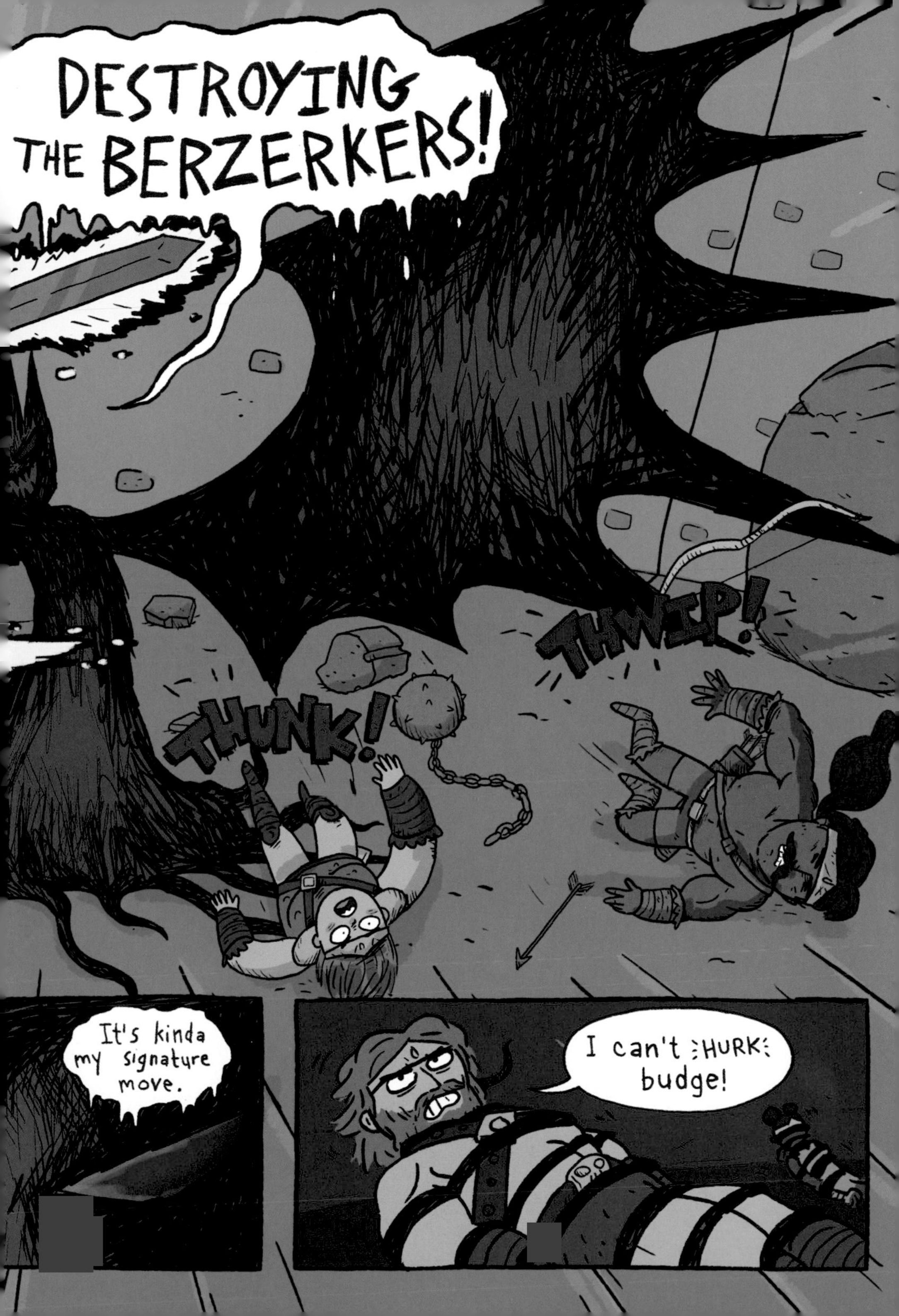
DESTROYING THE BERZERKERS!
THUNK!
THWIP!
It's kinda my signature move.
I can't HURK budge!

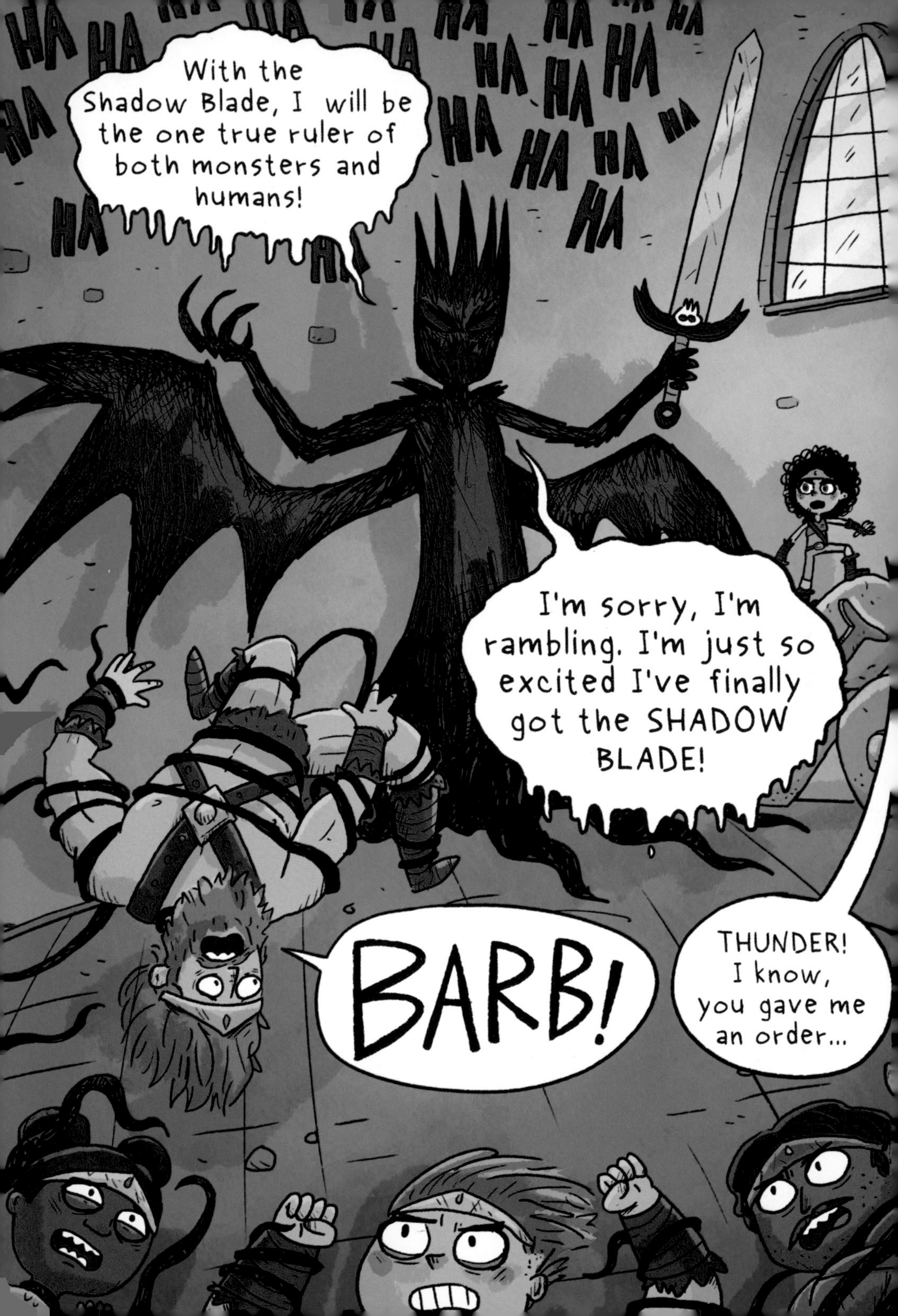
HA HA HA HA HA HA HA HA HA HA HA HA HA HA HA HA HA HA HA HA HA
With the Shadow Blade, I will be the one true ruler of both monsters and humans!
I'm sorry, I'm rambling. I'm just so excited I've finally got the SHADOW BLADE!
BARB!
THUNDER! I know, you gave me an order...

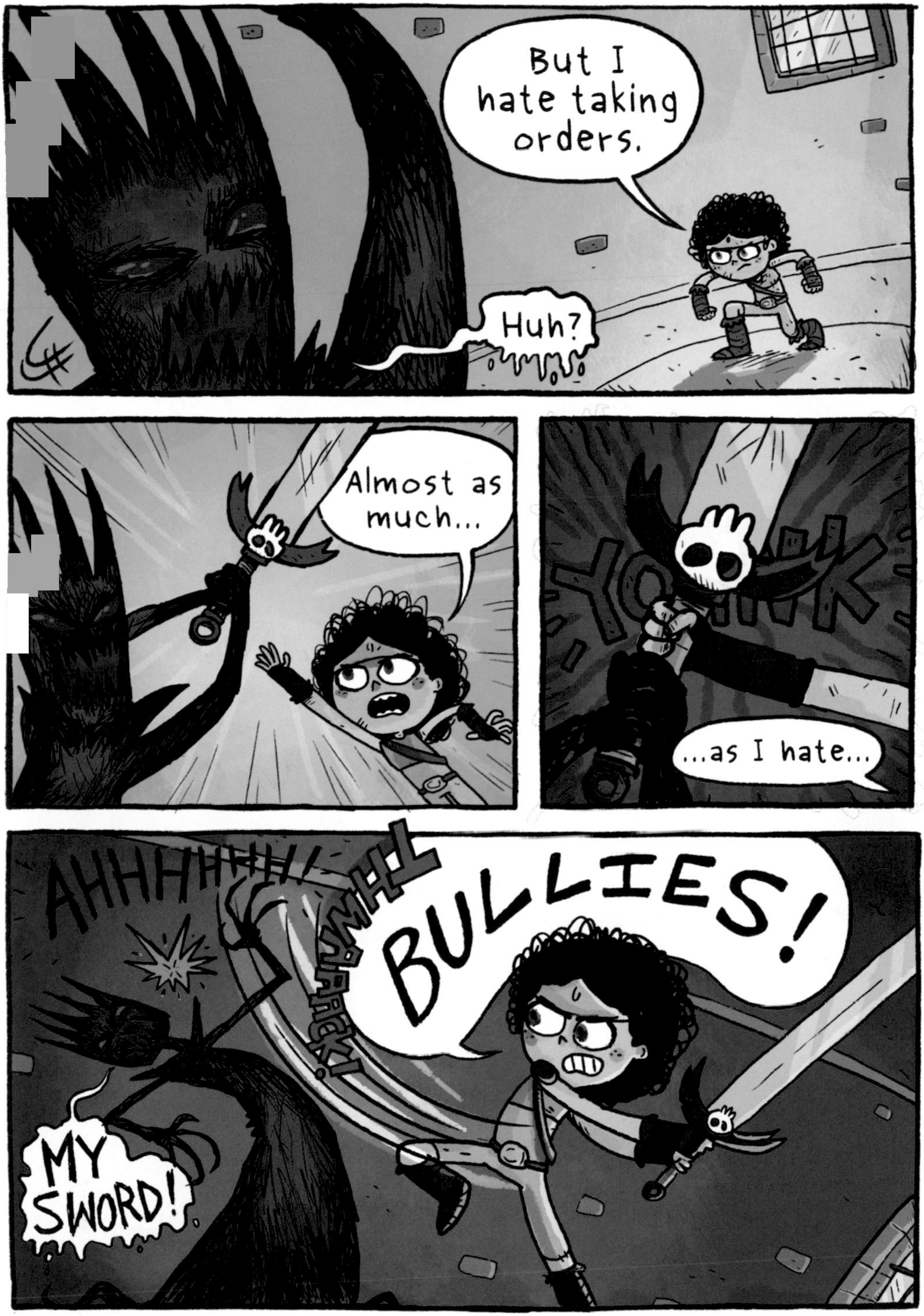
But I hate taking orders.
Huh?
Almost as much...
...as I hate...
BULLIES!
MY SWORD!

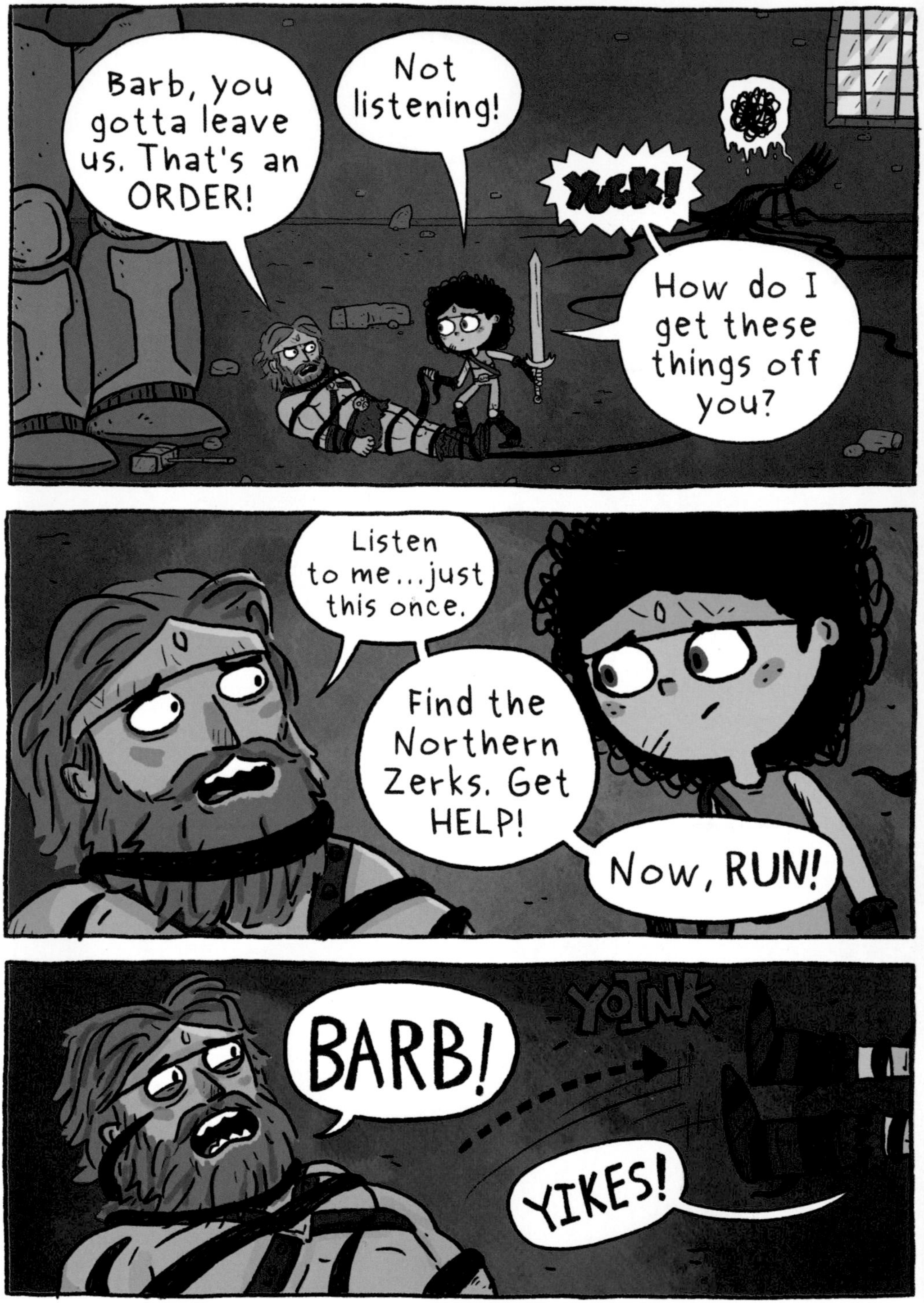

Barb, you gotta leave us. That's an ORDER!
Not listening!
YUCK!
How do I get these things off you?
Listen to me...just this once.
Find the Northern Zerks. Get HELP!
Now, RUN!
BARB!
YOINK
YIKES!

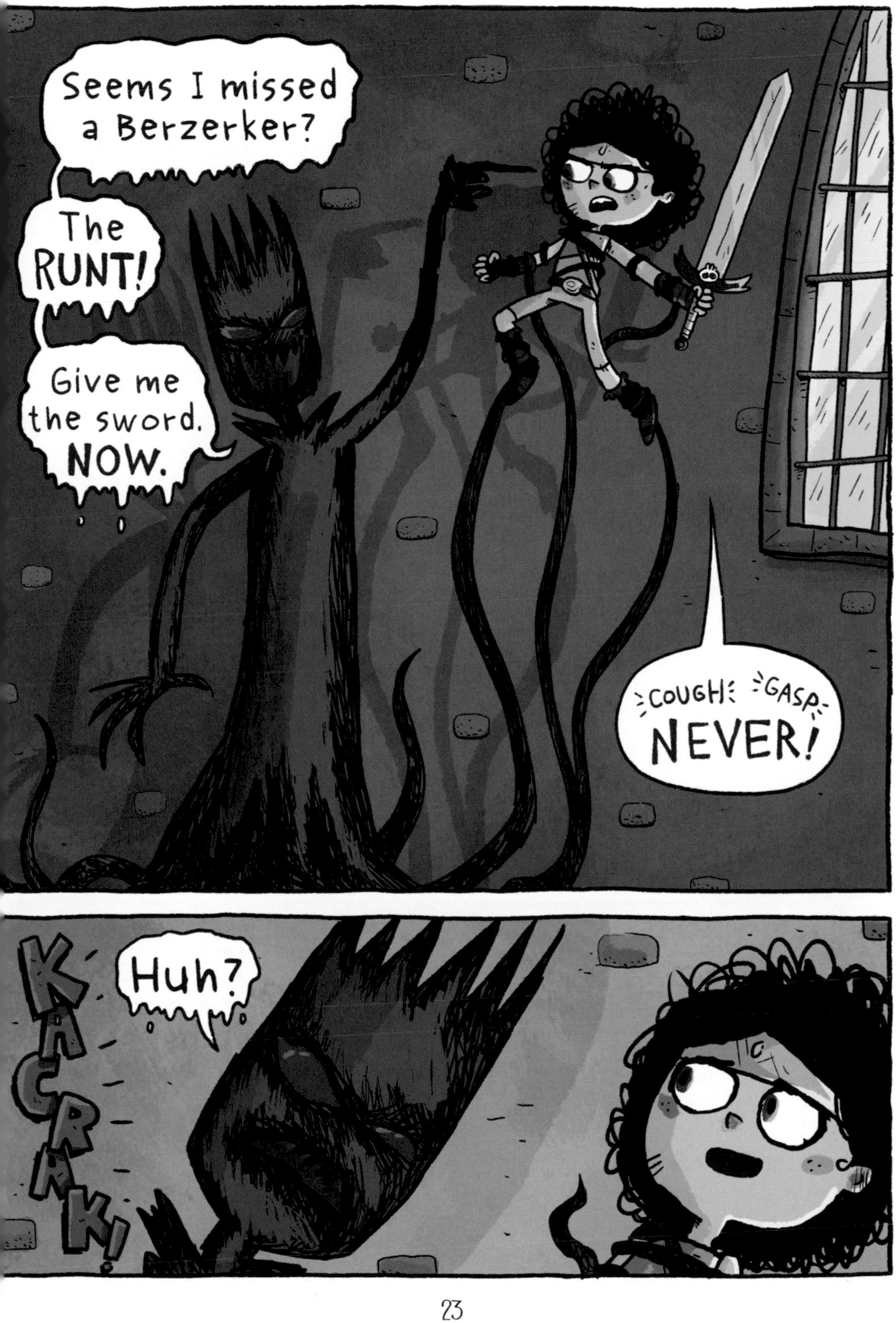
Seems I missed a Berzerker?
The RUNT!
Give me the sword. NOW.
COUGH GASP
NEVER!
KACRAK!
Huh?

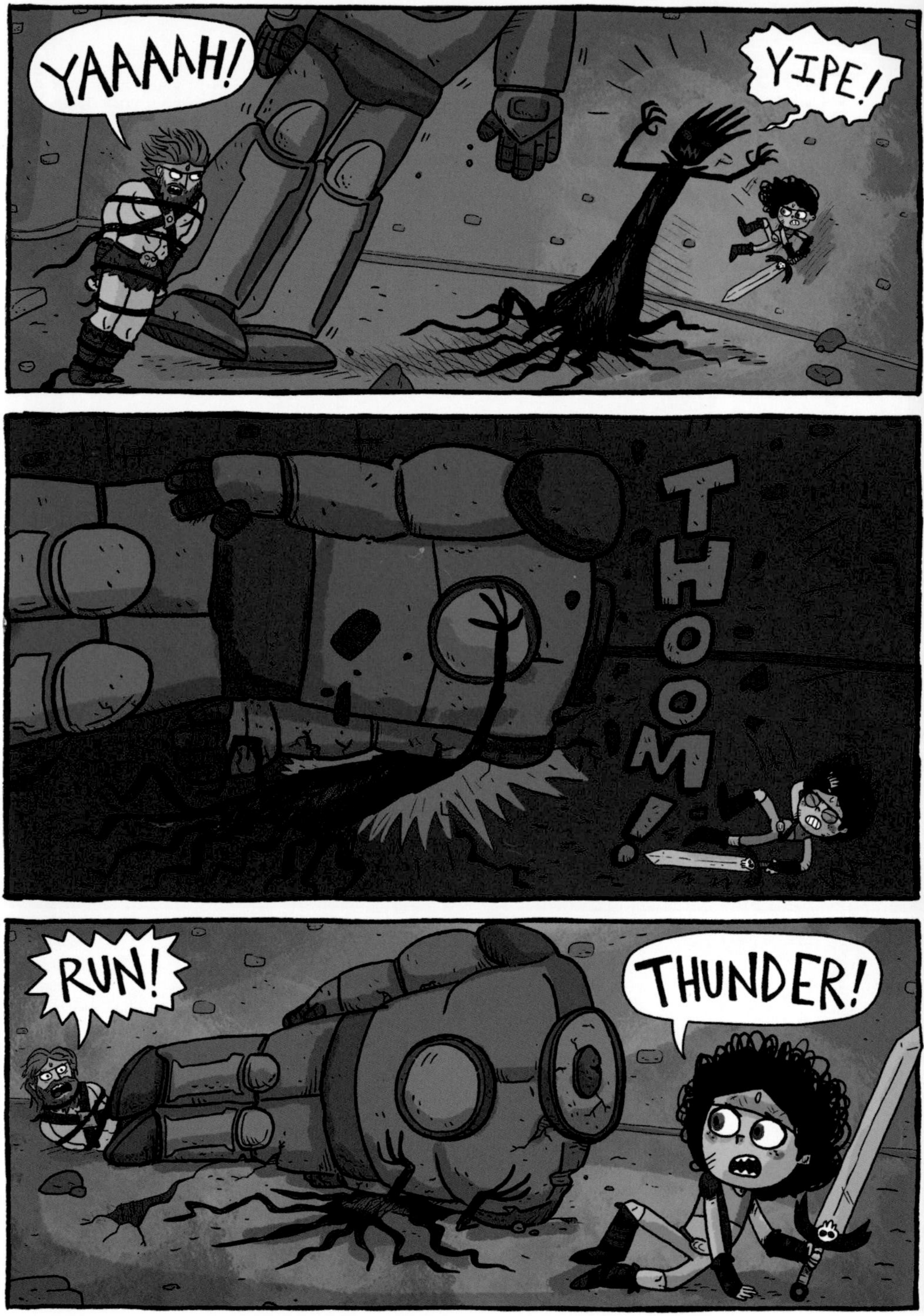
YAAAAH!
YIPE!
THOOOM!
RUN!
THUNDER!

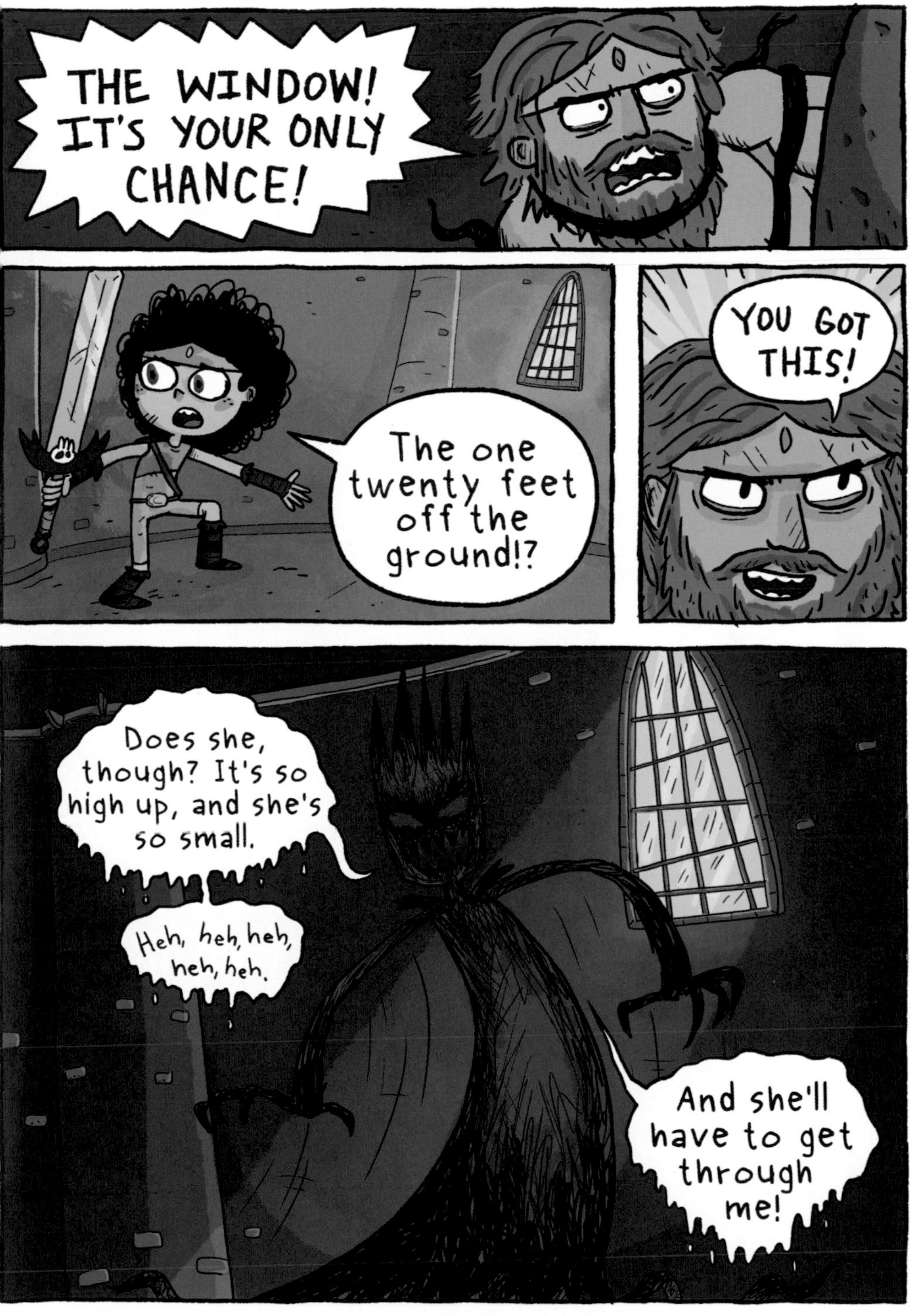
THE WINDOW! IT'S YOUR ONLY CHANCE!
The one twenty feet off the ground!?
YOU GOT THIS!
Does she, though? It's so high up, and she's so small.
Heh, heh, heh, heh, heh.
And she'll have to get through me!

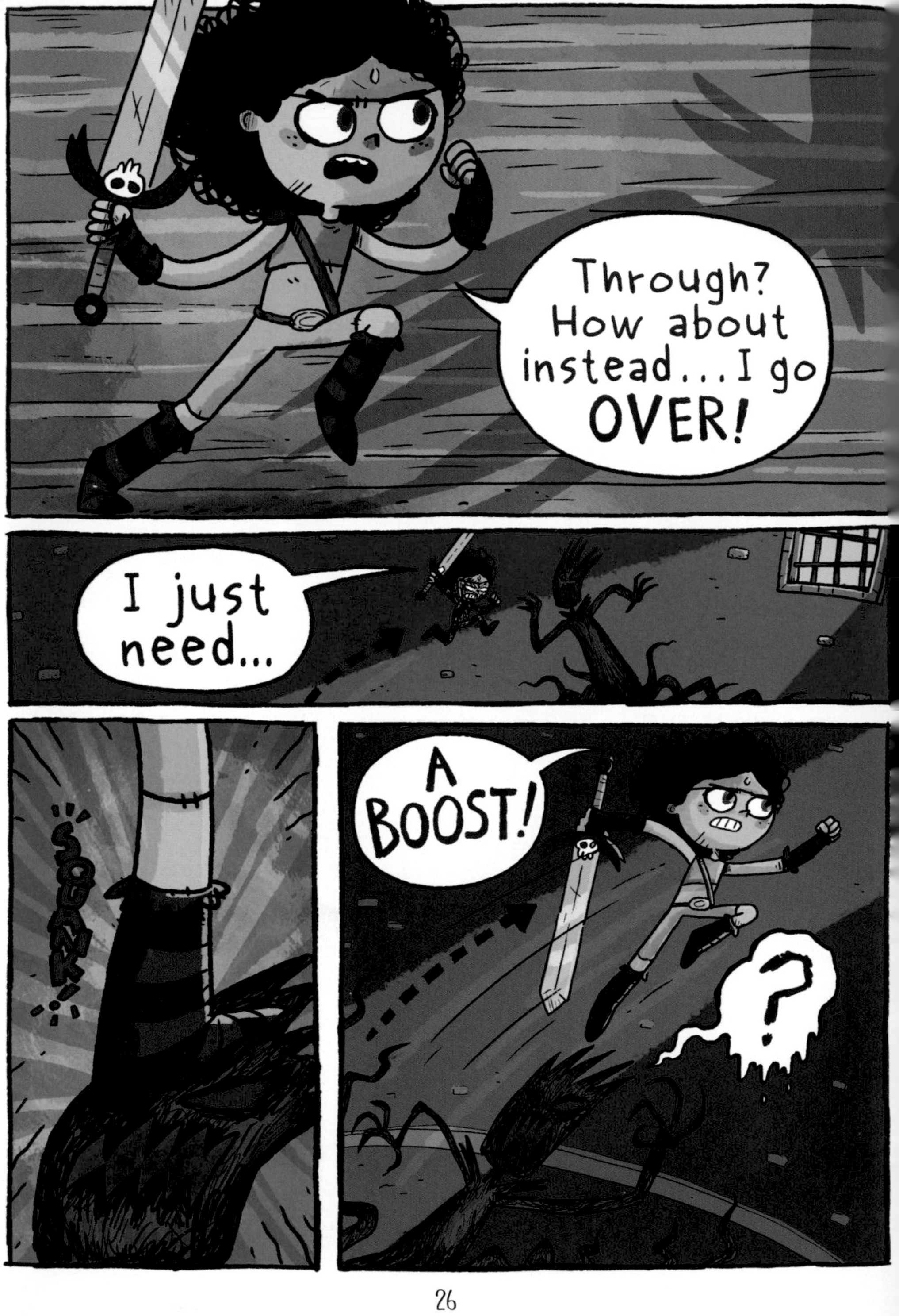
Through? How about instead...I go OVER!
I just need...
SQUAWK!
A BOOST!
?

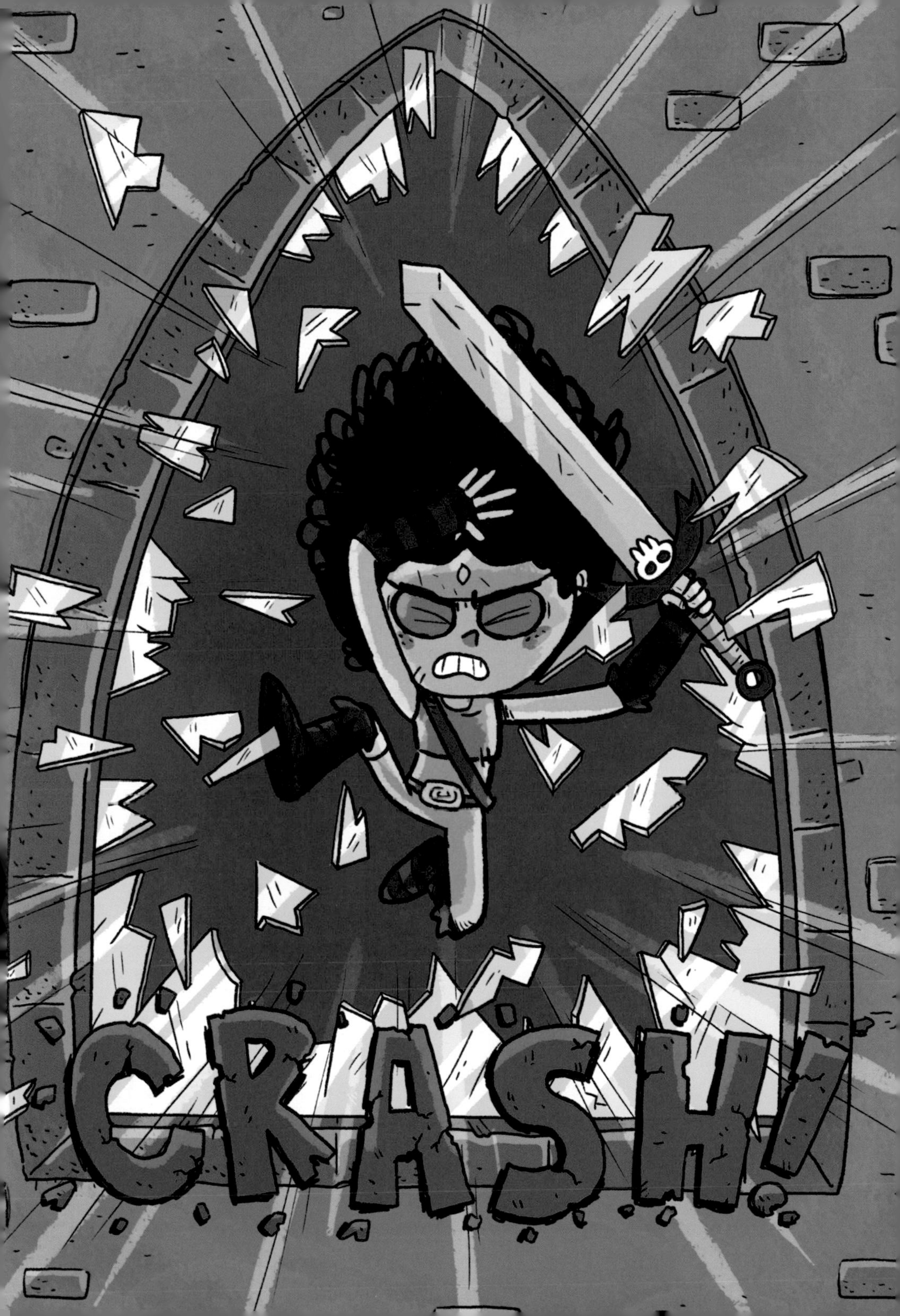
CRASH!

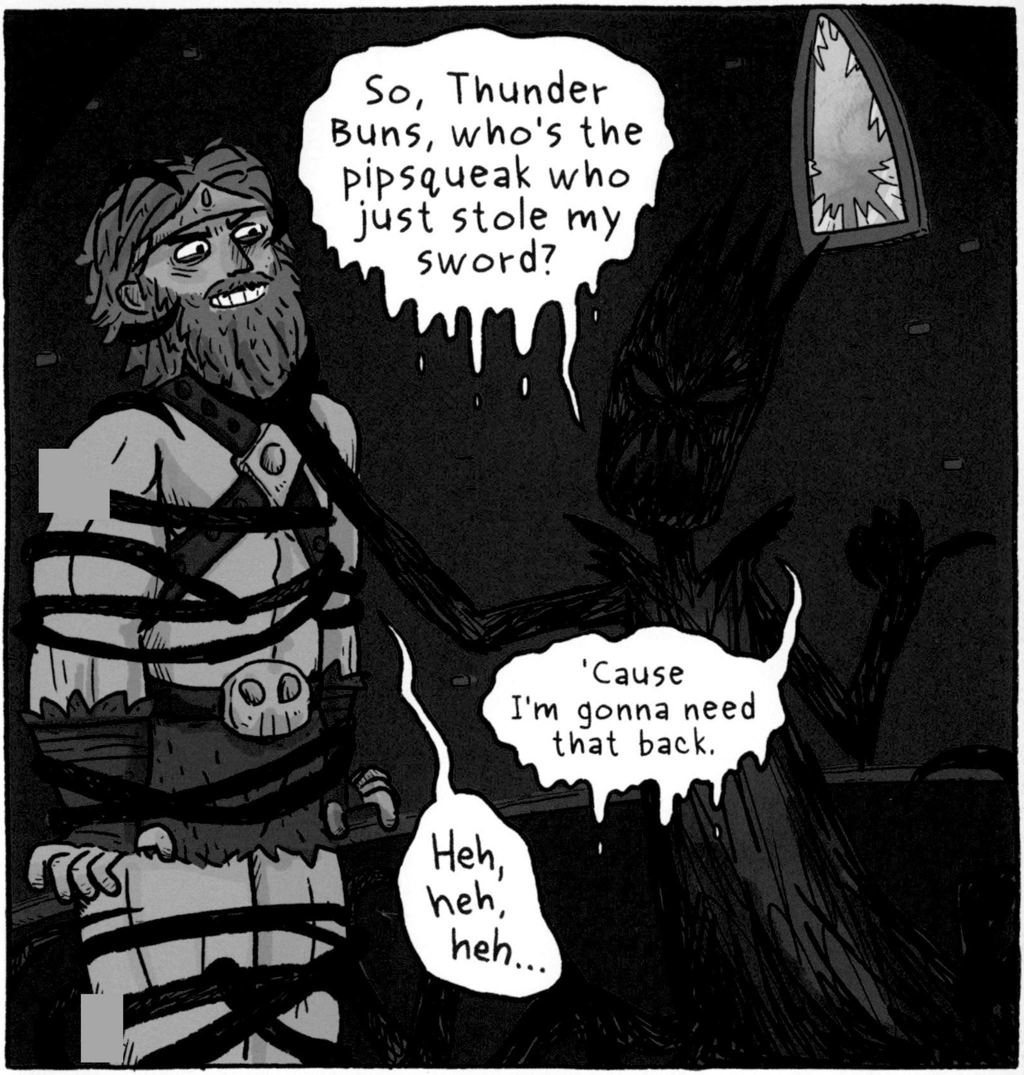
So, Thunder Buns, who's the pipsqueak who just stole my sword?
'Cause I'm gonna need that back.
Heh, heh, heh...

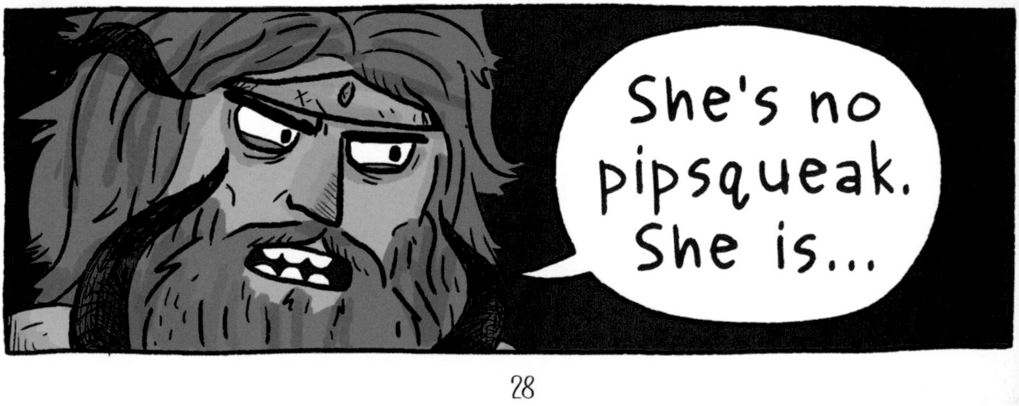
She's no pipsqueak. She is...

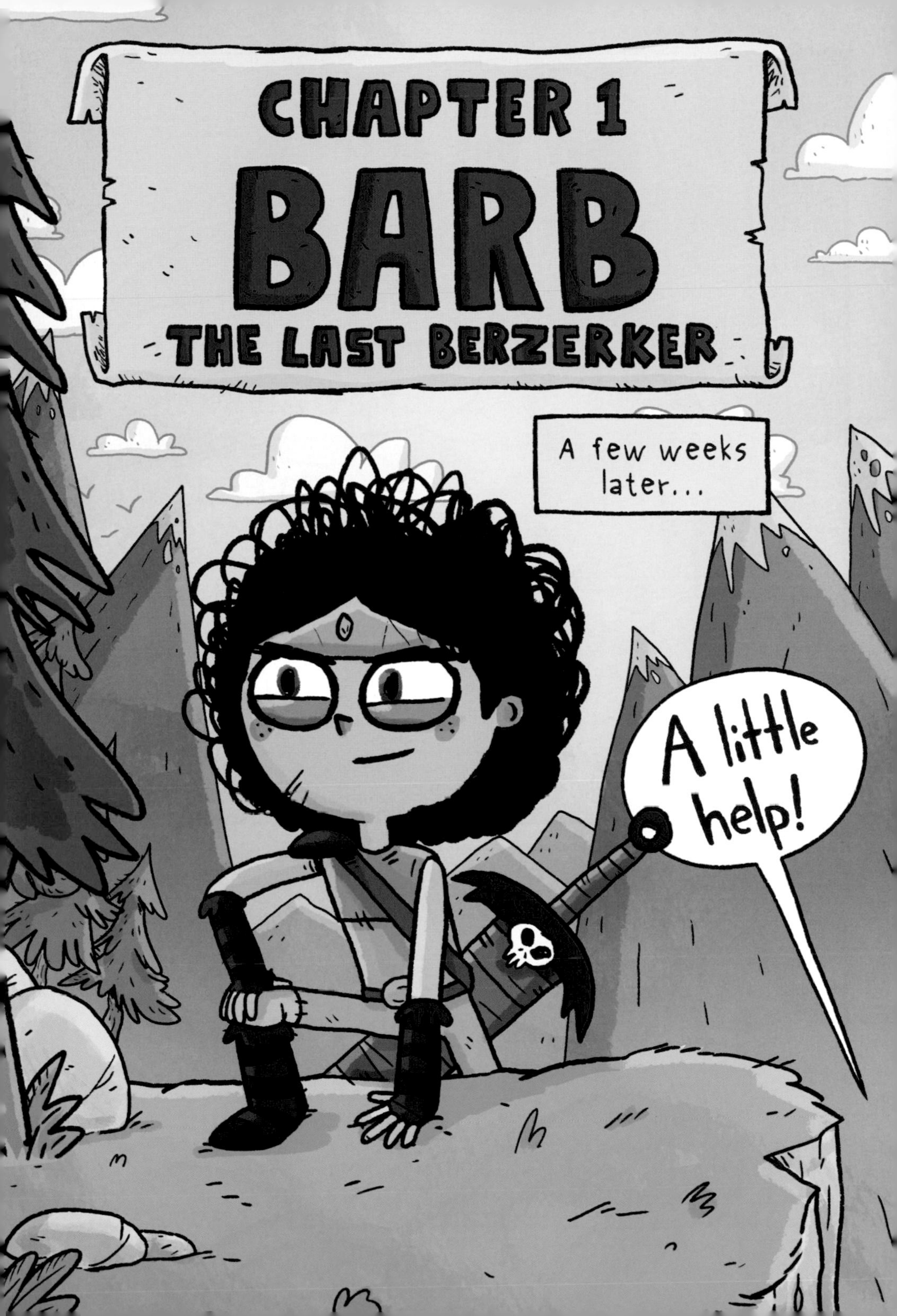
CHAPTER 1
BARB
THE LAST BERZERKER
A few weeks later...
A little help!

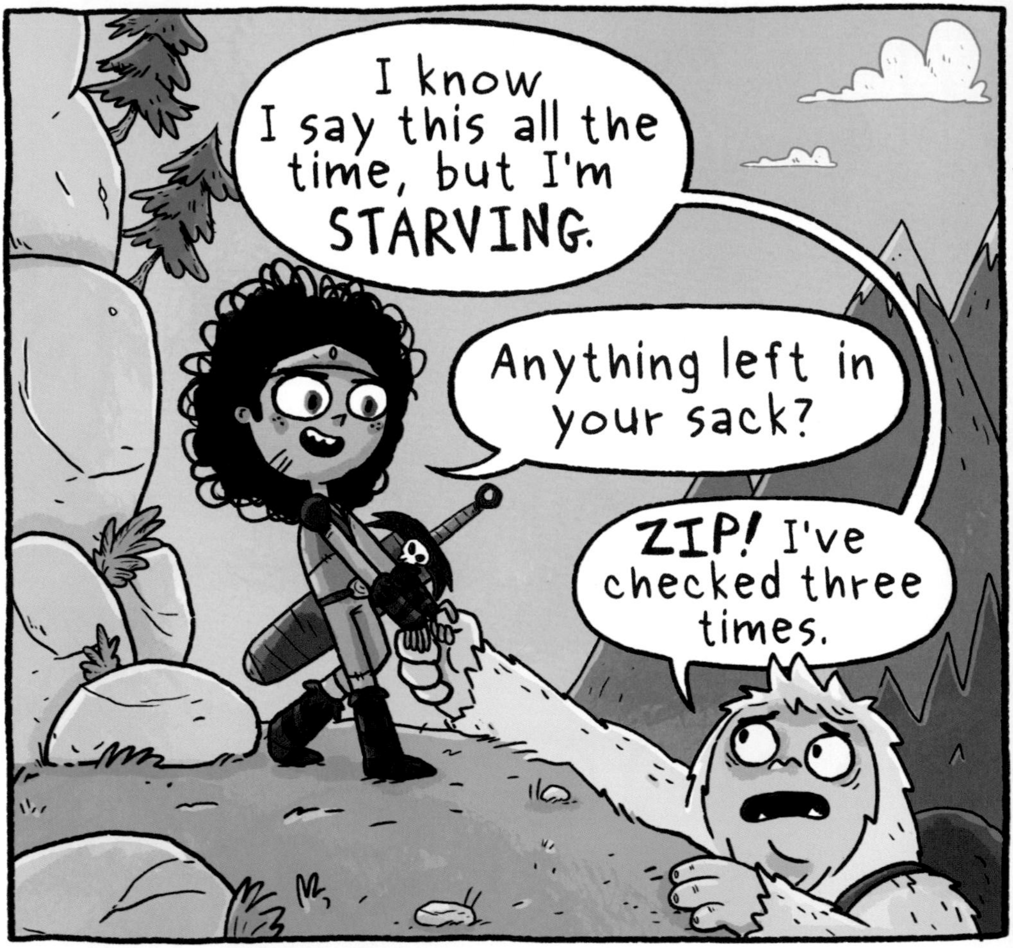
I know I say this all the time, but I'm STARVING.
Anything left in your sack?
ZIP! I've checked three times.

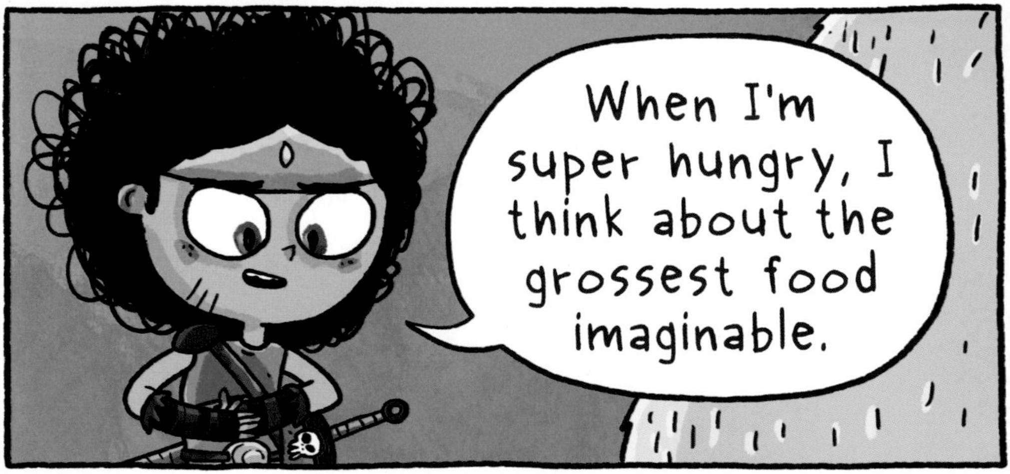
When I'm super hungry, I think about the grossest food imaginable.

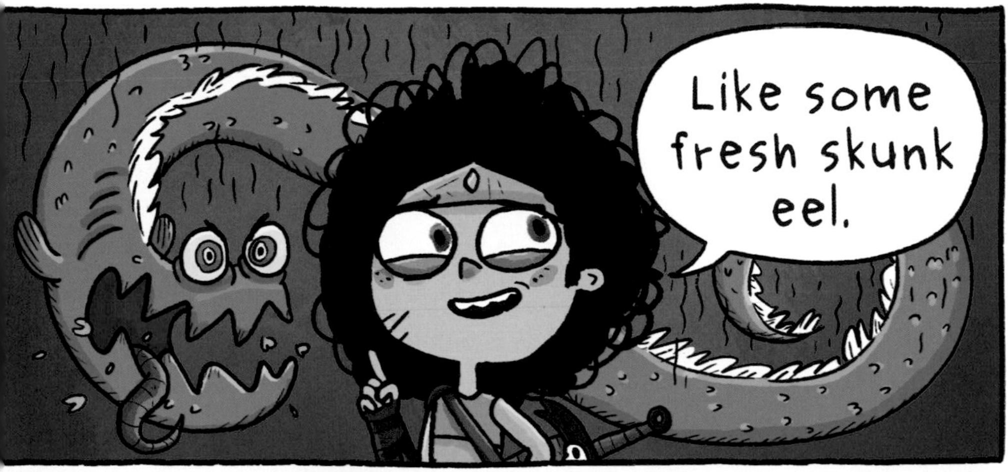
Like some fresh skunk eel.

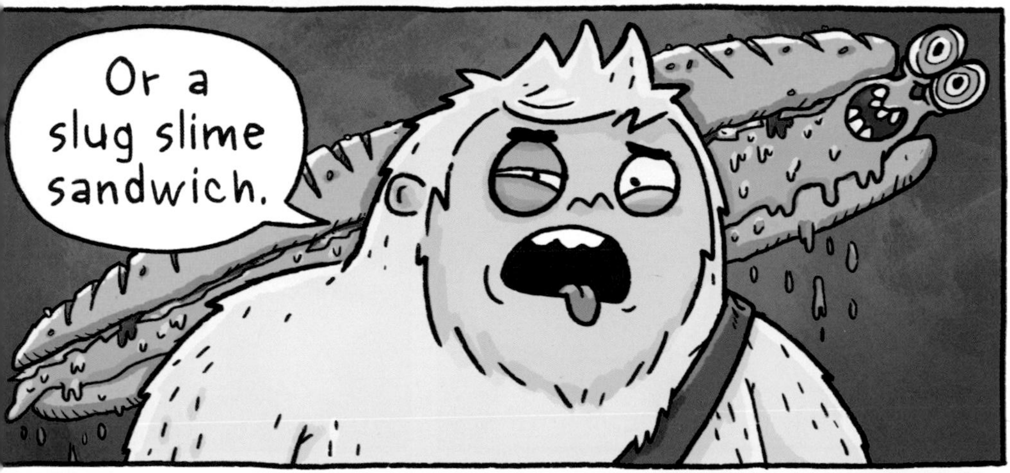
Or a slug slime sandwich.

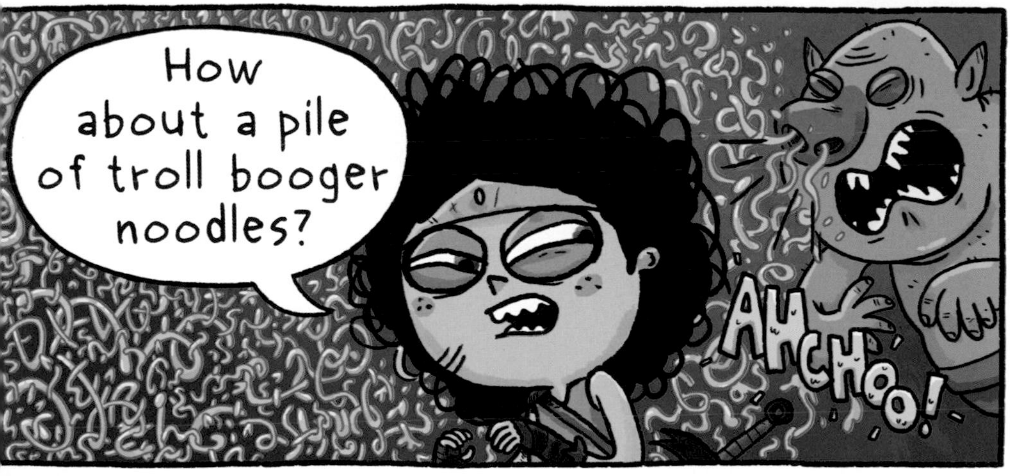
How about a pile of troll booger noodles?
AHCHOO!

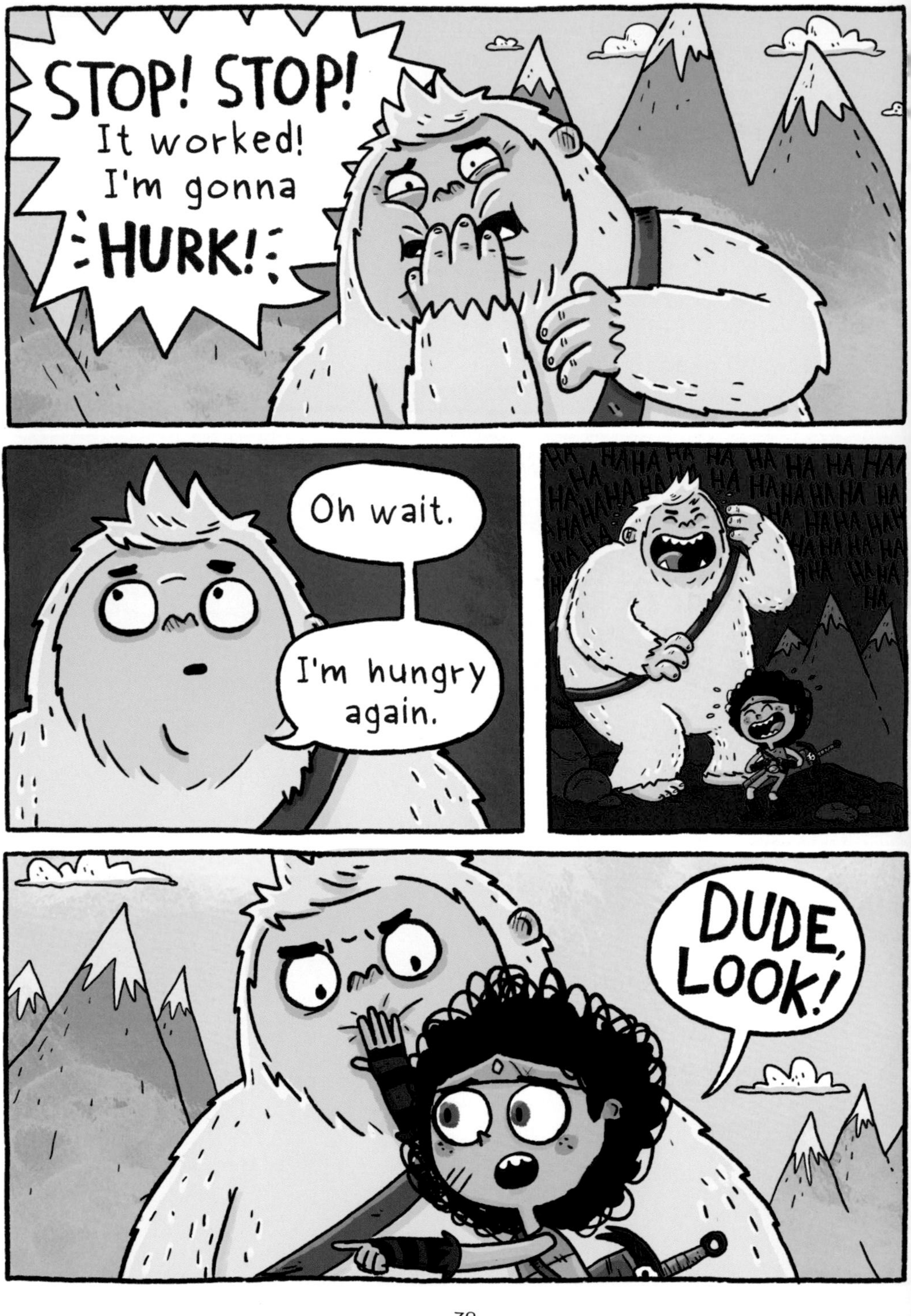
STOP! STOP! It worked! I'm gonna HURK!
Oh wait.
I'm hungry again.
HA HA HA HA HA HA HA HA HA
DUDE, LOOK!

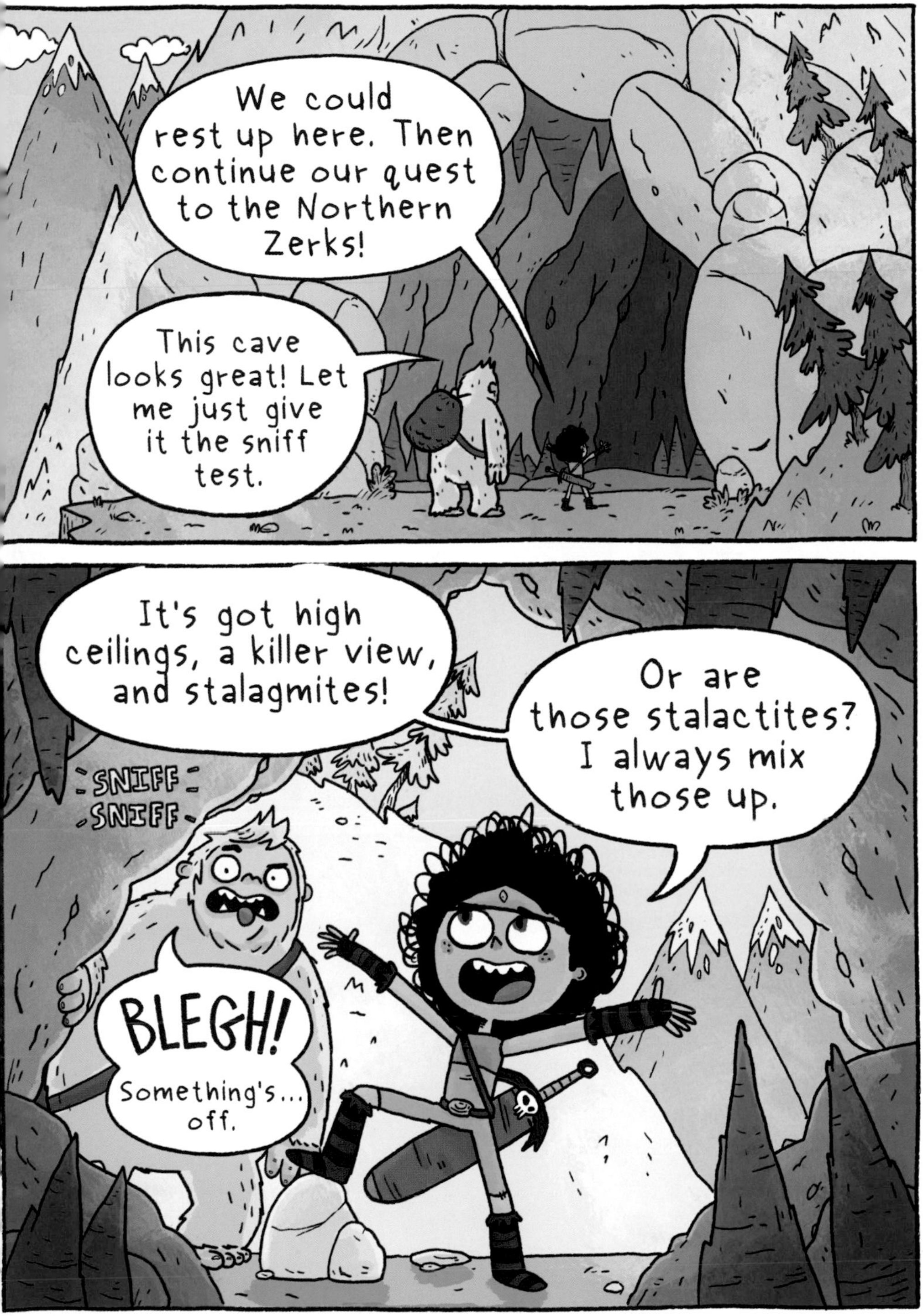
We could rest up here. Then continue our quest to the Northern Zerks!
This cave looks great! Let me just give it the sniff test.
It's got high ceilings, a killer view, and stalagmites!
Or are those stalactites? I always mix those up.
SNIFF SNIFF
BLEGH! Something's... off.

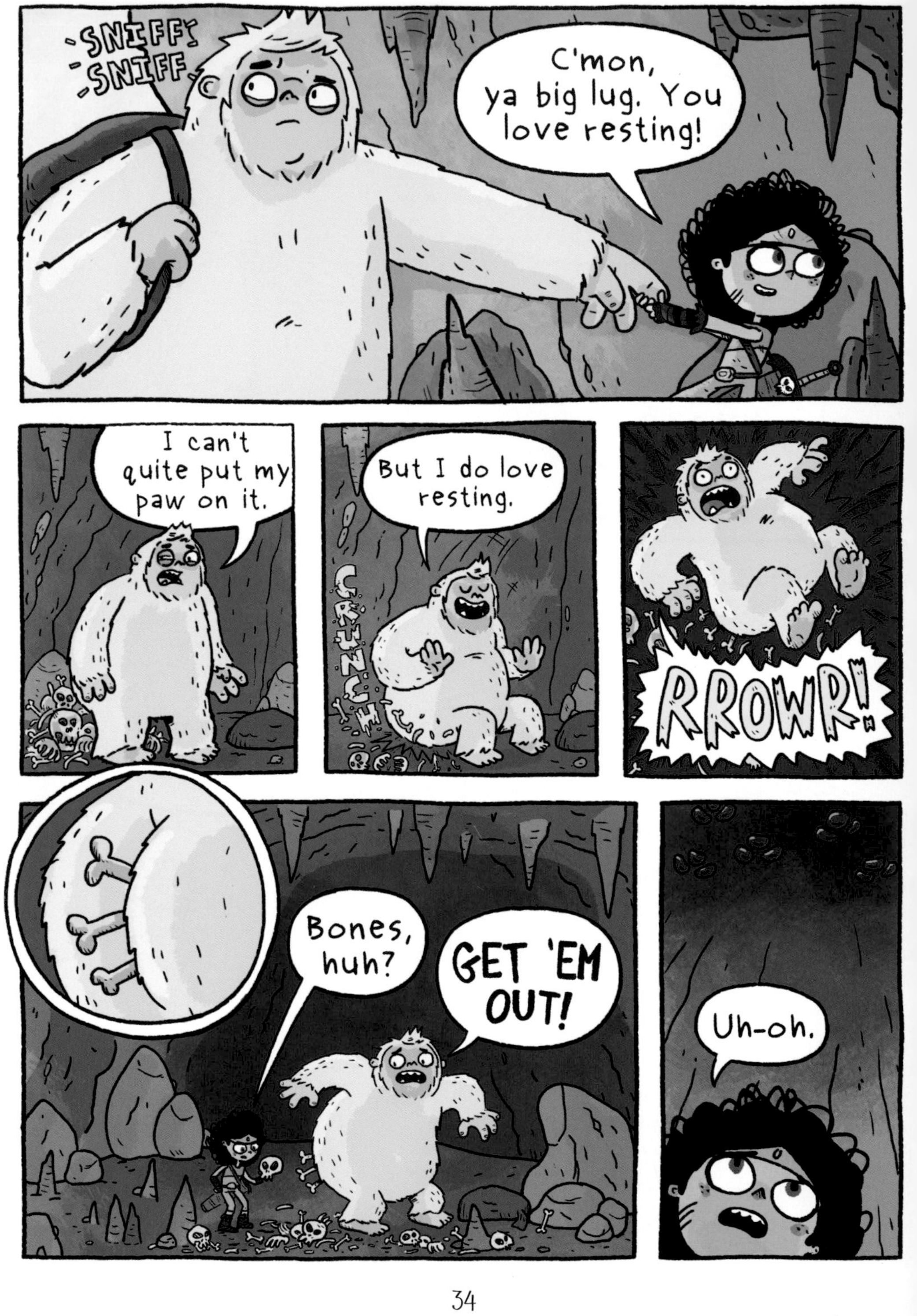
SNIFF SNIFF
C'mon, ya big lug. You love resting!
I can't quite put my paw on it.
But I do love resting.
CRUNCH
RROWR!
Bones, huh?
GET 'EM OUT!
Uh-oh.

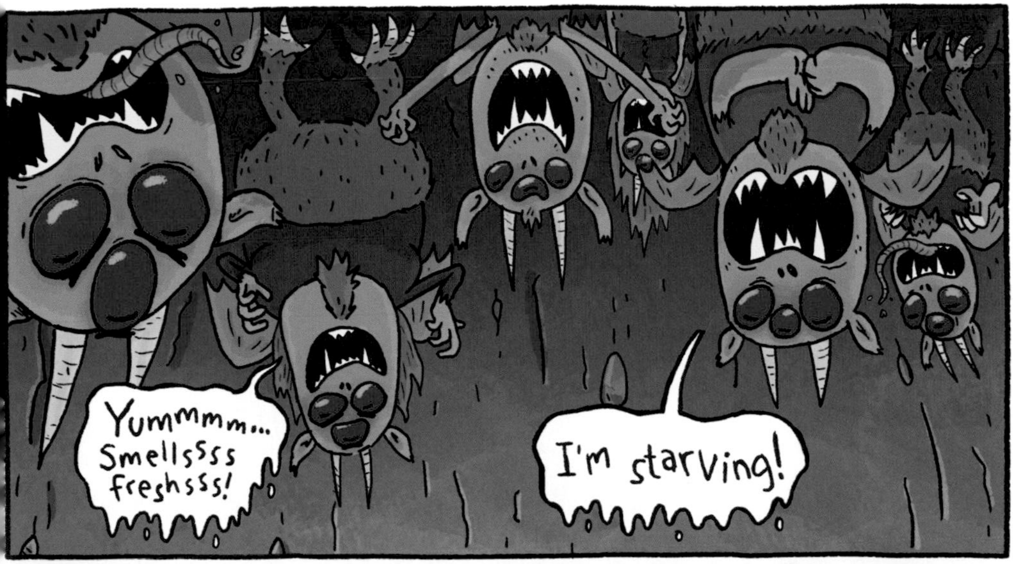
Yummmm... Smellssss freshsss!
I'm starving!

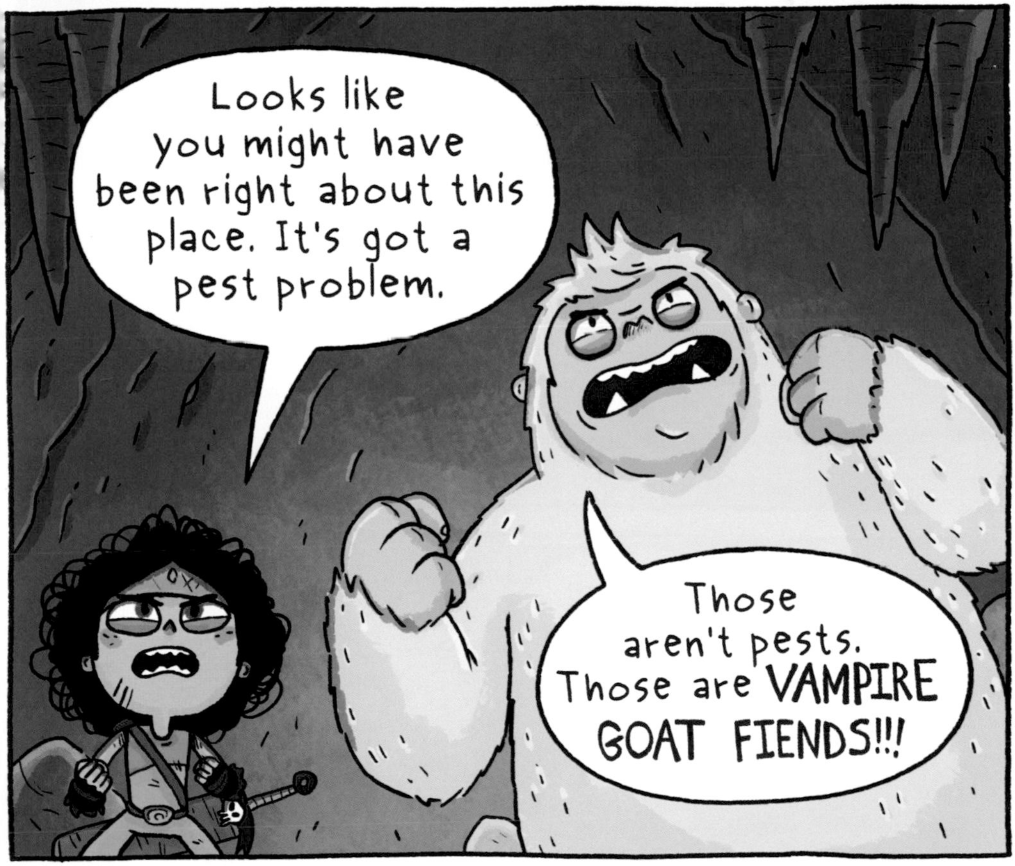
Looks like you might have been right about this place. It's got a pest problem.
Those aren't pests. Those are VAMPIRE GOAT FIENDS!!!

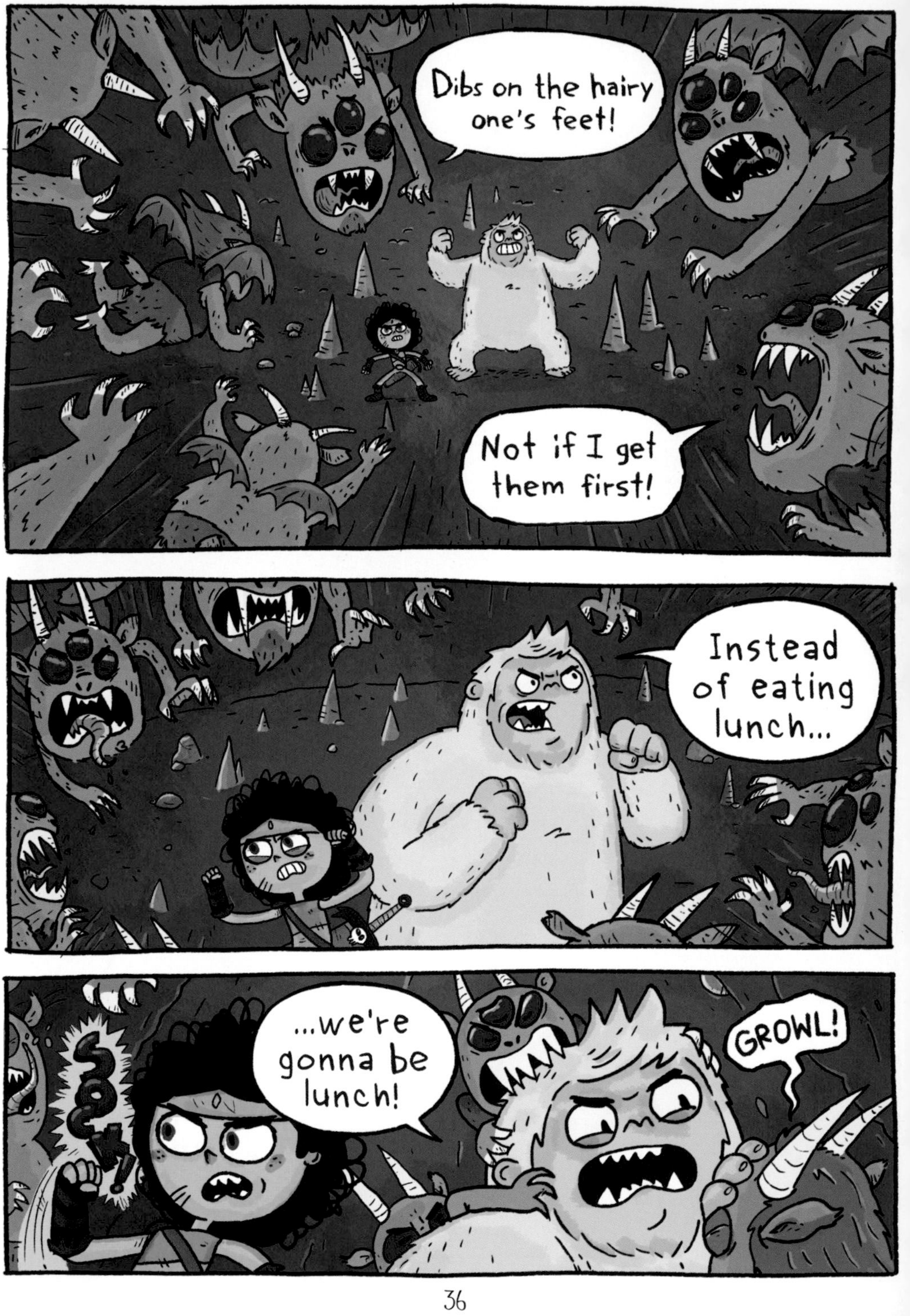
Dibs on the hairy one's feet!
Not if I get them first!
Instead of eating lunch...
SOCK!
...we're gonna be lunch!
GROWL!

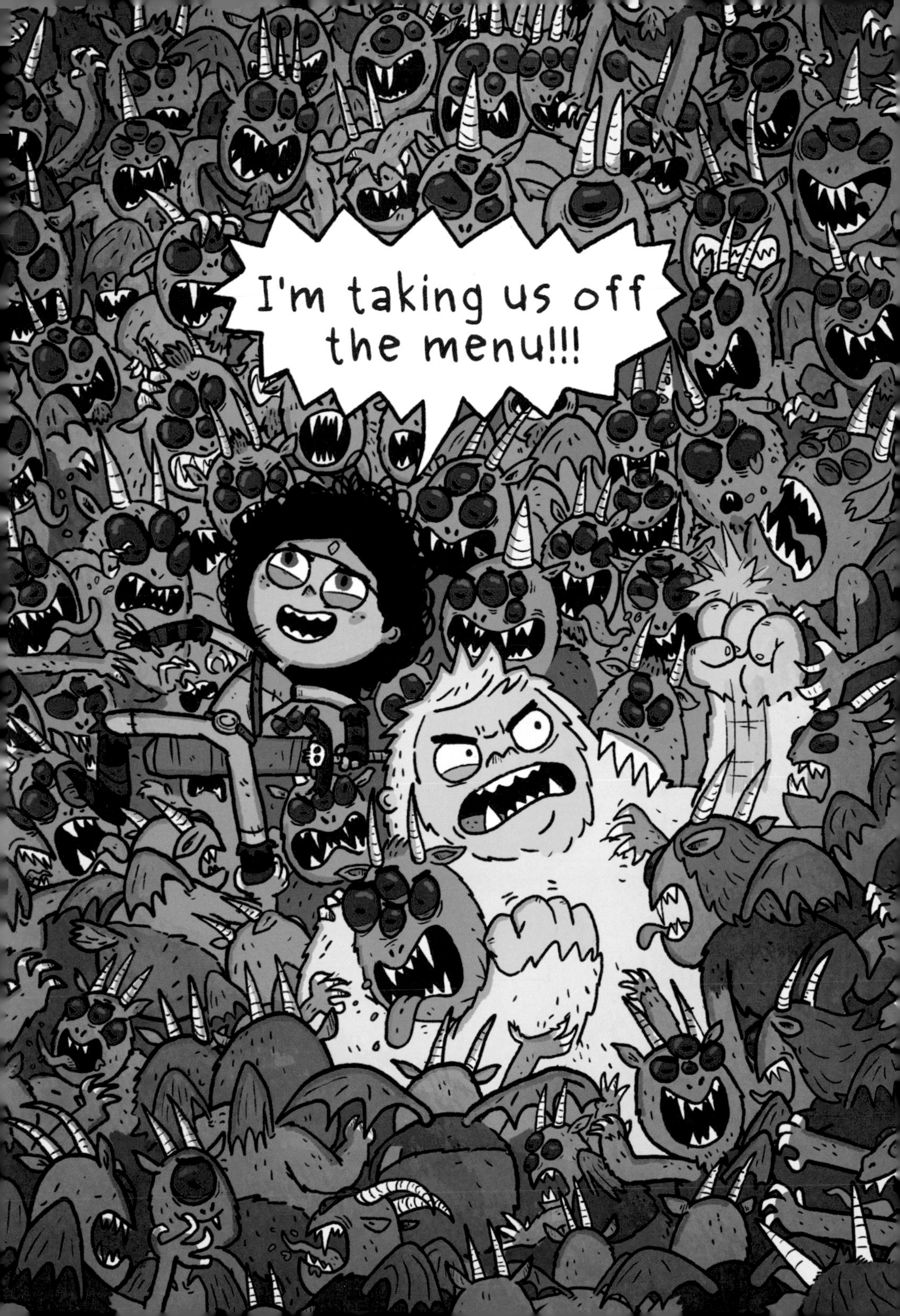
I'm taking us off the menu!!!

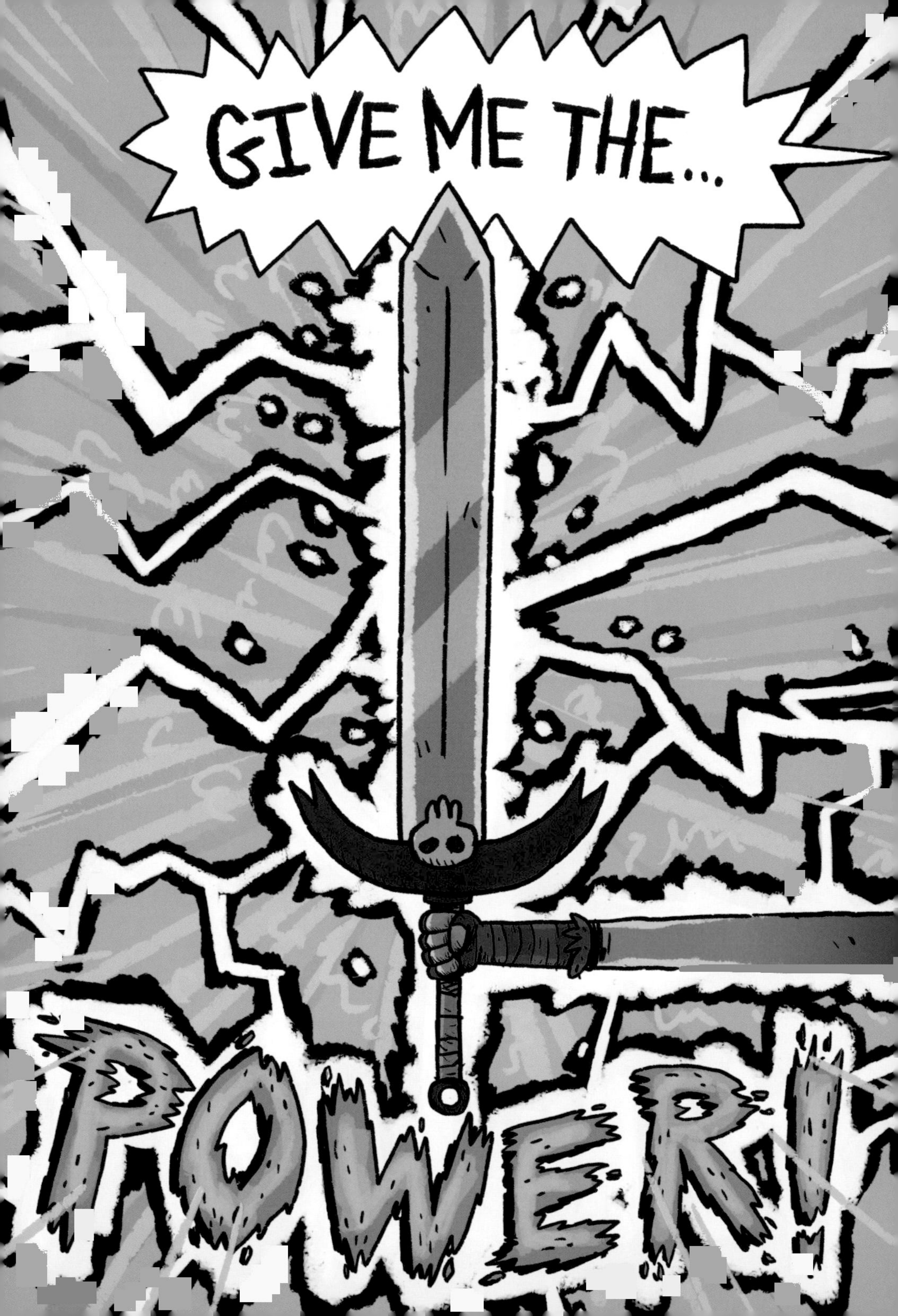
GIVE ME THE...
POWER!

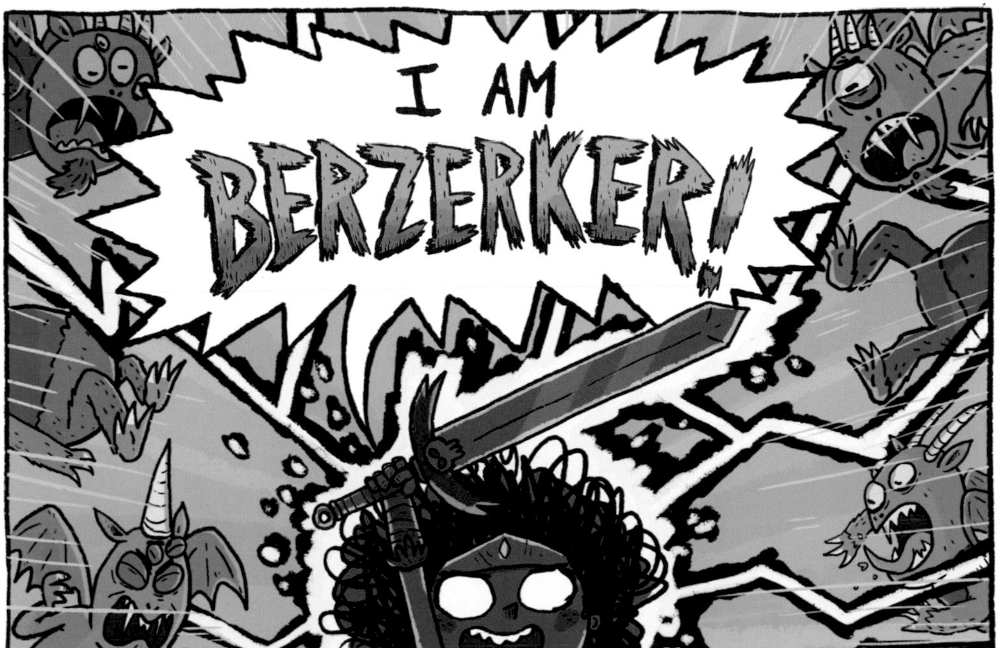
I AM
BERZERKER!
Heh heh heh,
AWESOME!
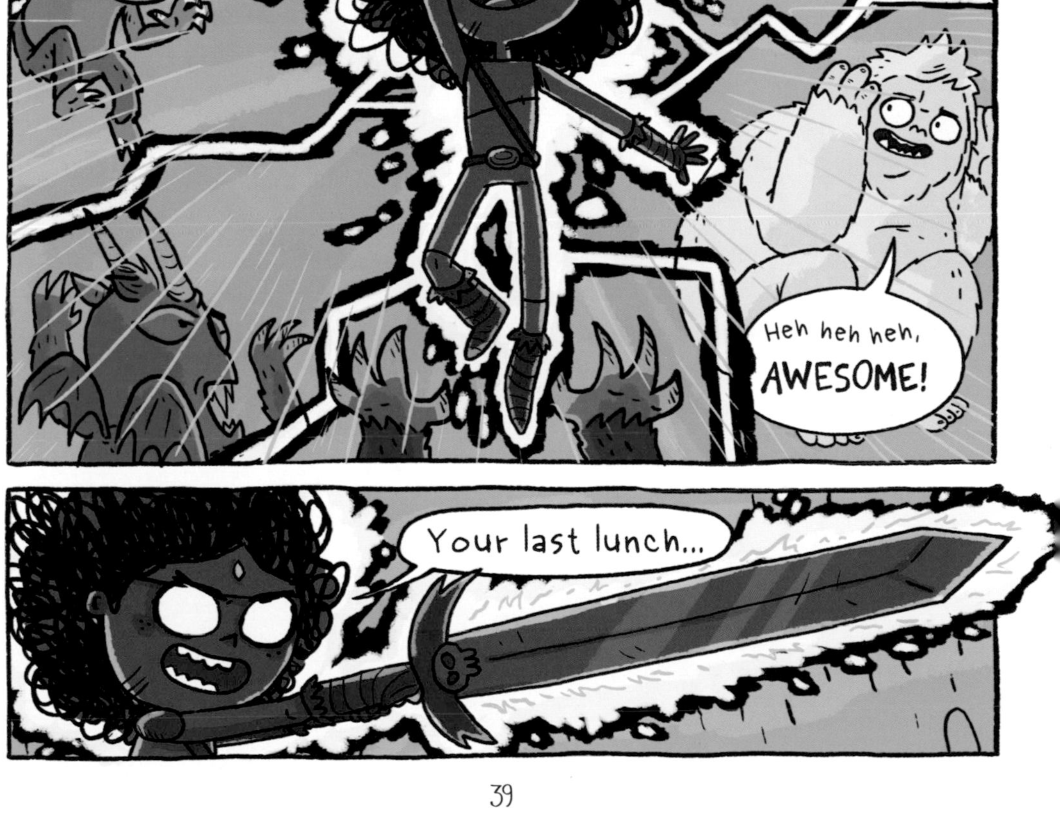
Your last lunch...

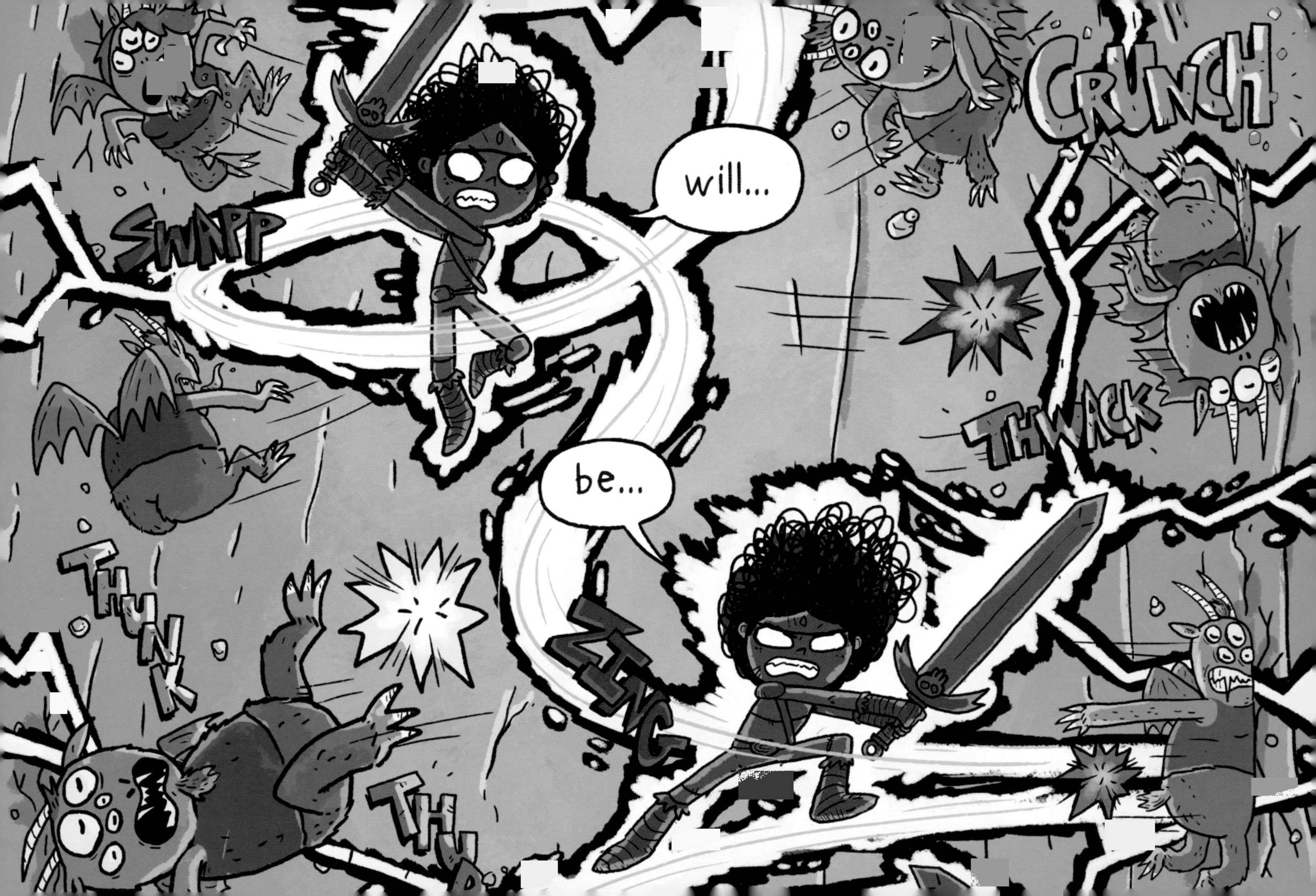
SWAPP
will...
CRUNCH
THWACK
be...
ZING
THUNK

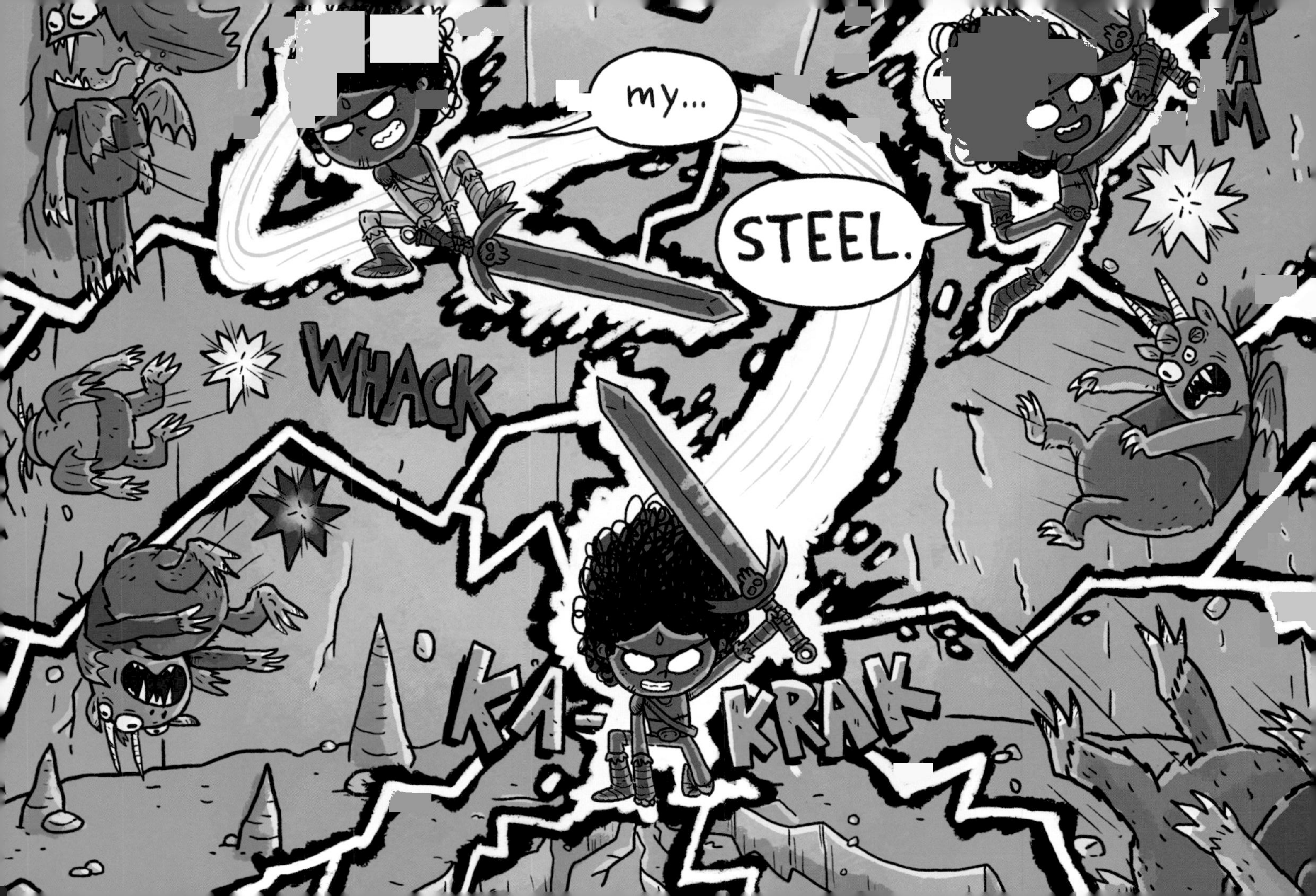
my...
STEEL.
WHACK
KA-KRAK

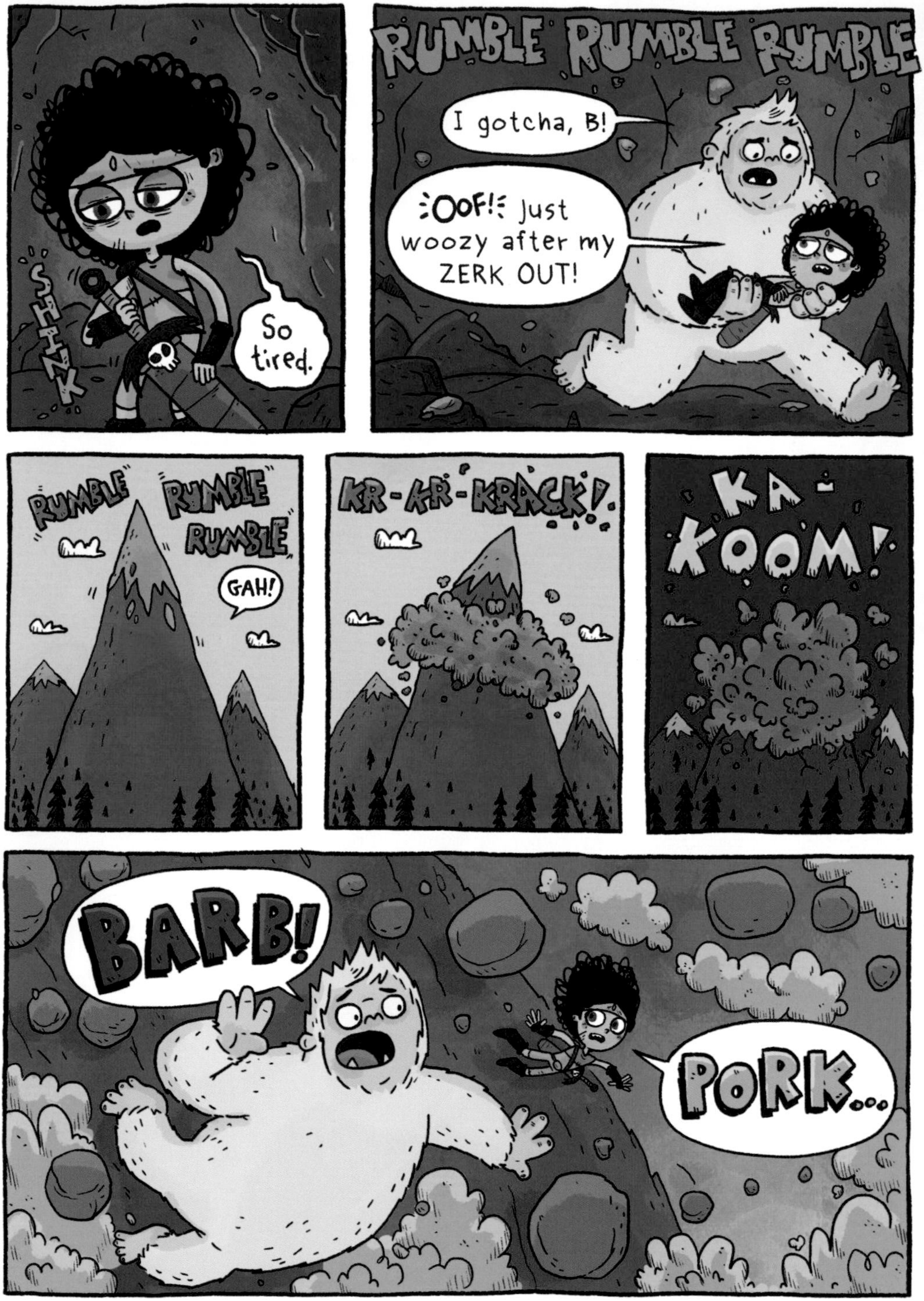
SHINK
So tired.
RUMBLE RUMBLE RUMBLE
I gotcha, B!
OOF! Just woozy after my ZERK OUT!
RUMBLE RUMBLE RUMBLE
GAH!
KR-KR-KRACK!
KA-KOOM!
BARB!
PORK...

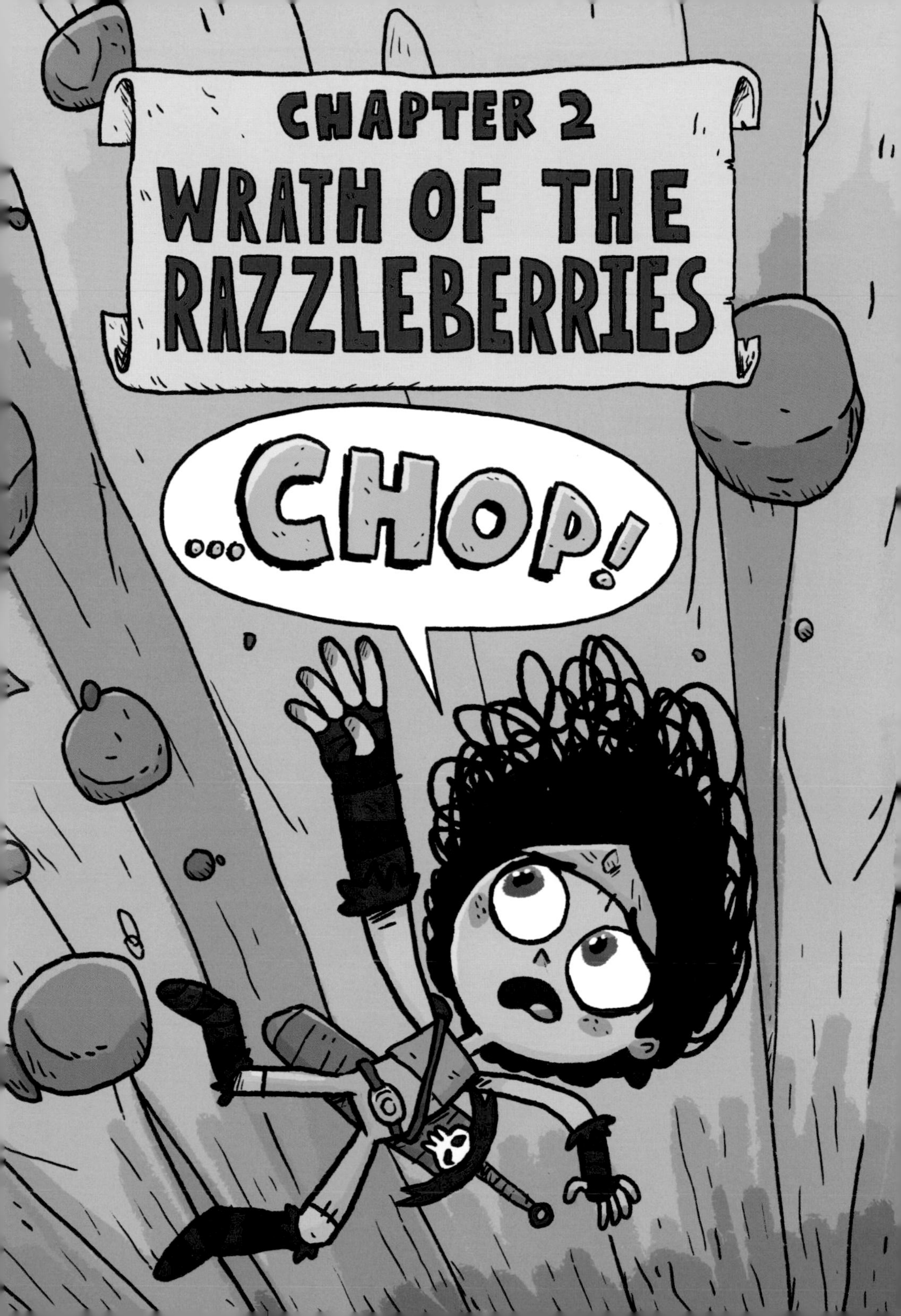
CHAPTER 2
WRATH OF THE RAZZLEBERRIES
...CHOP!

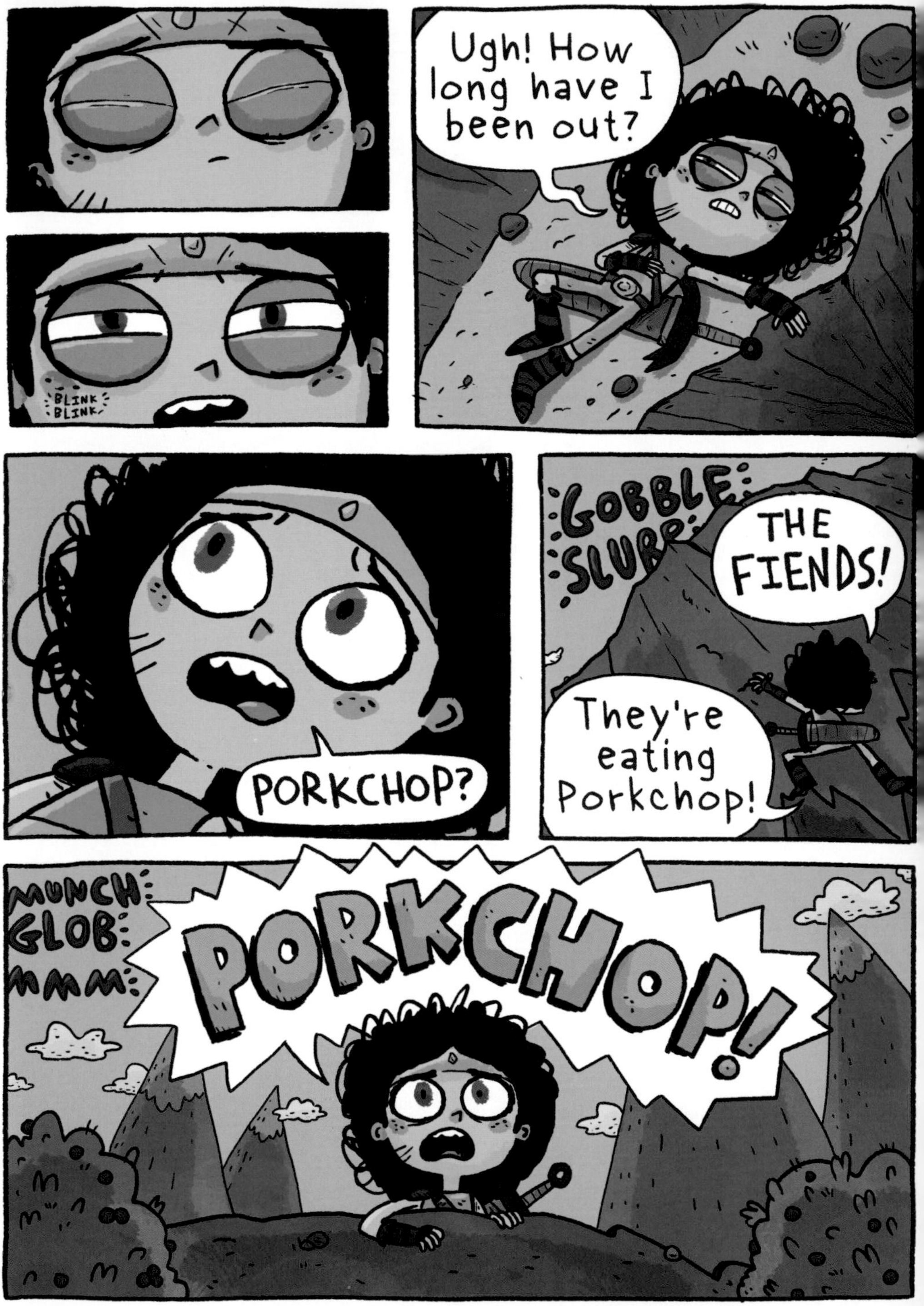
BLINK
BLINK
Ugh! How long have I been out?
PORKCHOP?
GOBBLE
SLURP
THE FIENDS!
They're eating Porkchop!
MUNCH
GLOB
MMM
PORKCHOP!

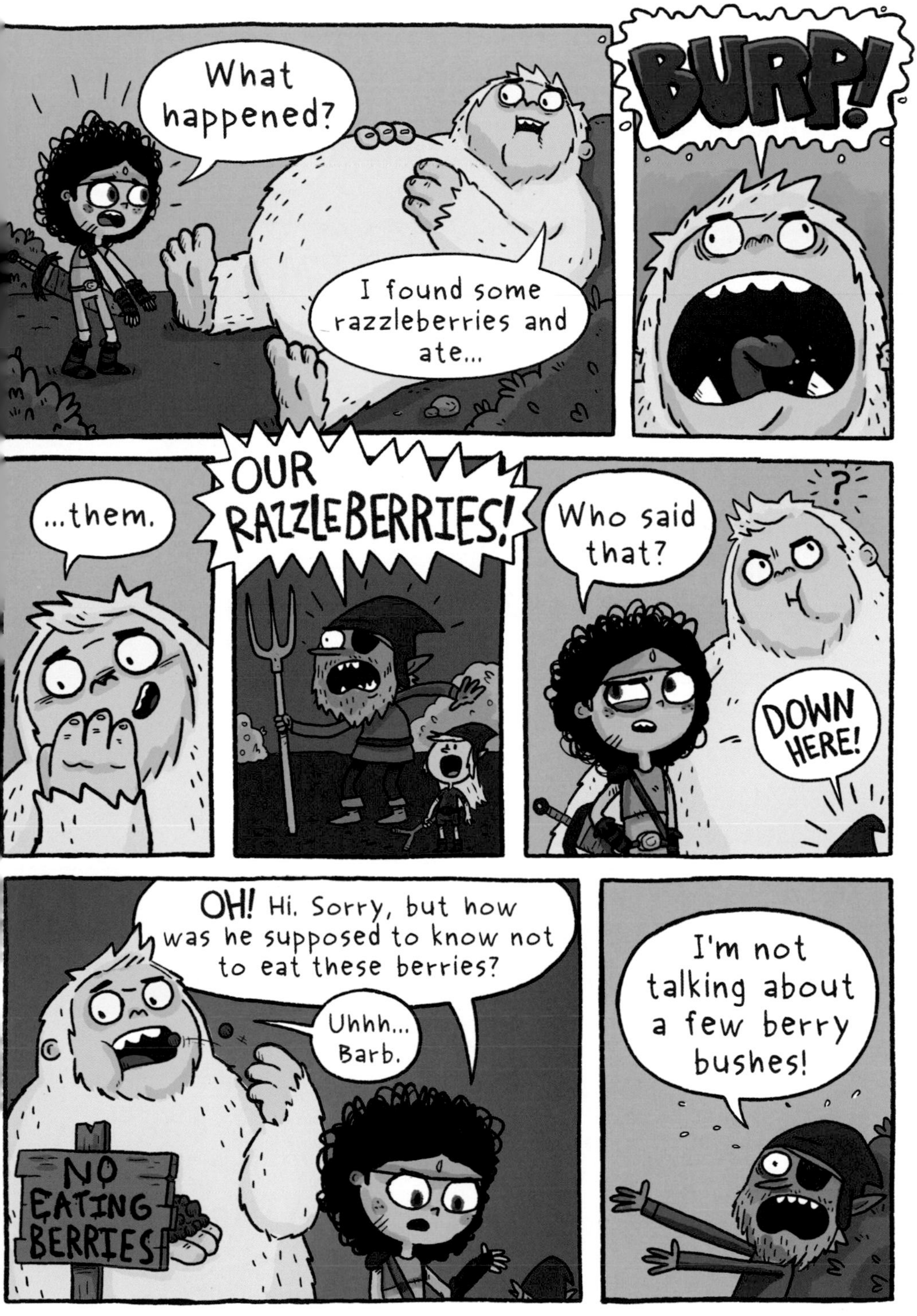

What happened?
I found some razzleberries and ate...
BURP!
...them.
OUR RAZZLEBERRIES!
Who said that?
DOWN HERE!
OH! Hi. Sorry, but how was he supposed to know not to eat these berries?
Uhhh... Barb.
NO EATING BERRIES
I'm not talking about a few berry bushes!

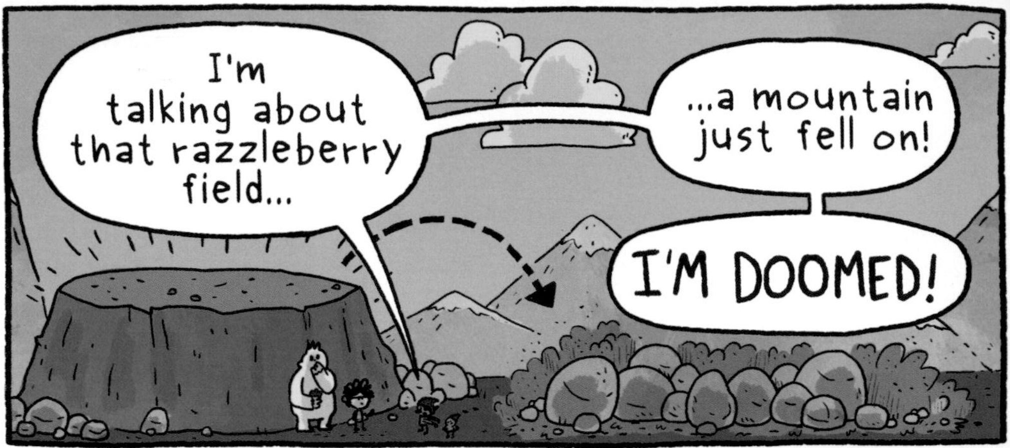
I'm talking about that razzleberry field...
...a mountain just fell on!
I'M DOOMED!

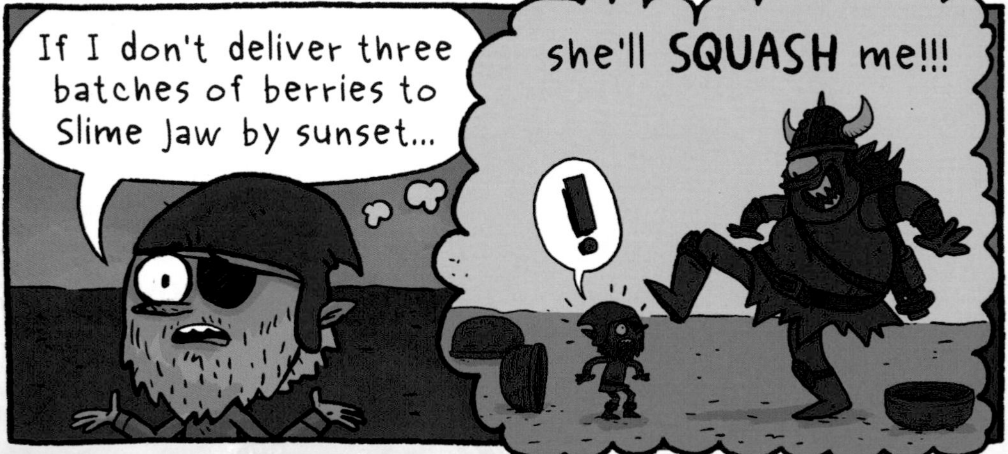
If I don't deliver three batches of berries to Slime Jaw by sunset...
she'll SQUASH me!!!
!

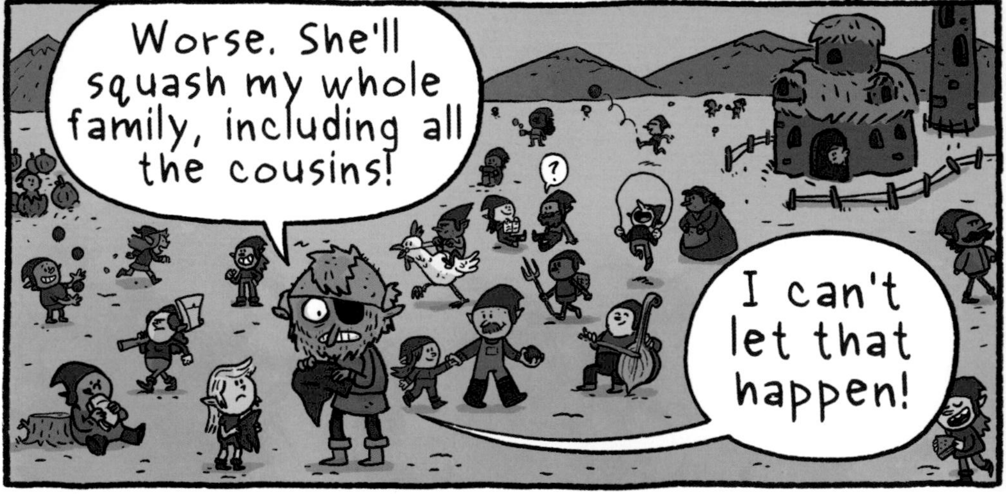
Worse. She'll squash my whole family, including all the cousins!
?
I can't let that happen!

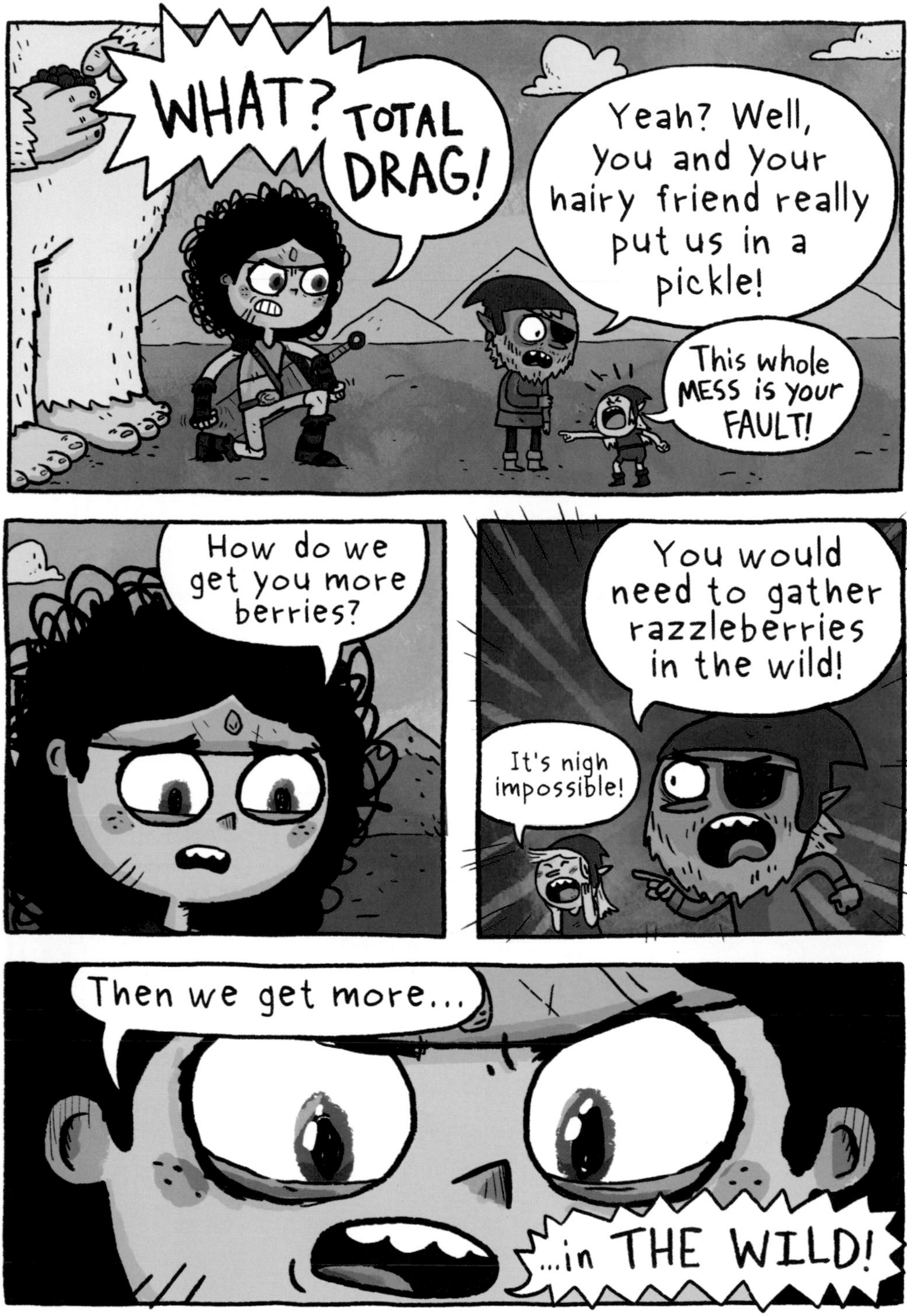
WHAT? TOTAL DRAG!
Yeah? Well, you and your hairy friend really put us in a pickle!
This whole MESS is your FAULT!
How do we get you more berries?
You would need to gather razzleberries in the wild!
It's nigh impossible!
Then we get more...
...in THE WILD!

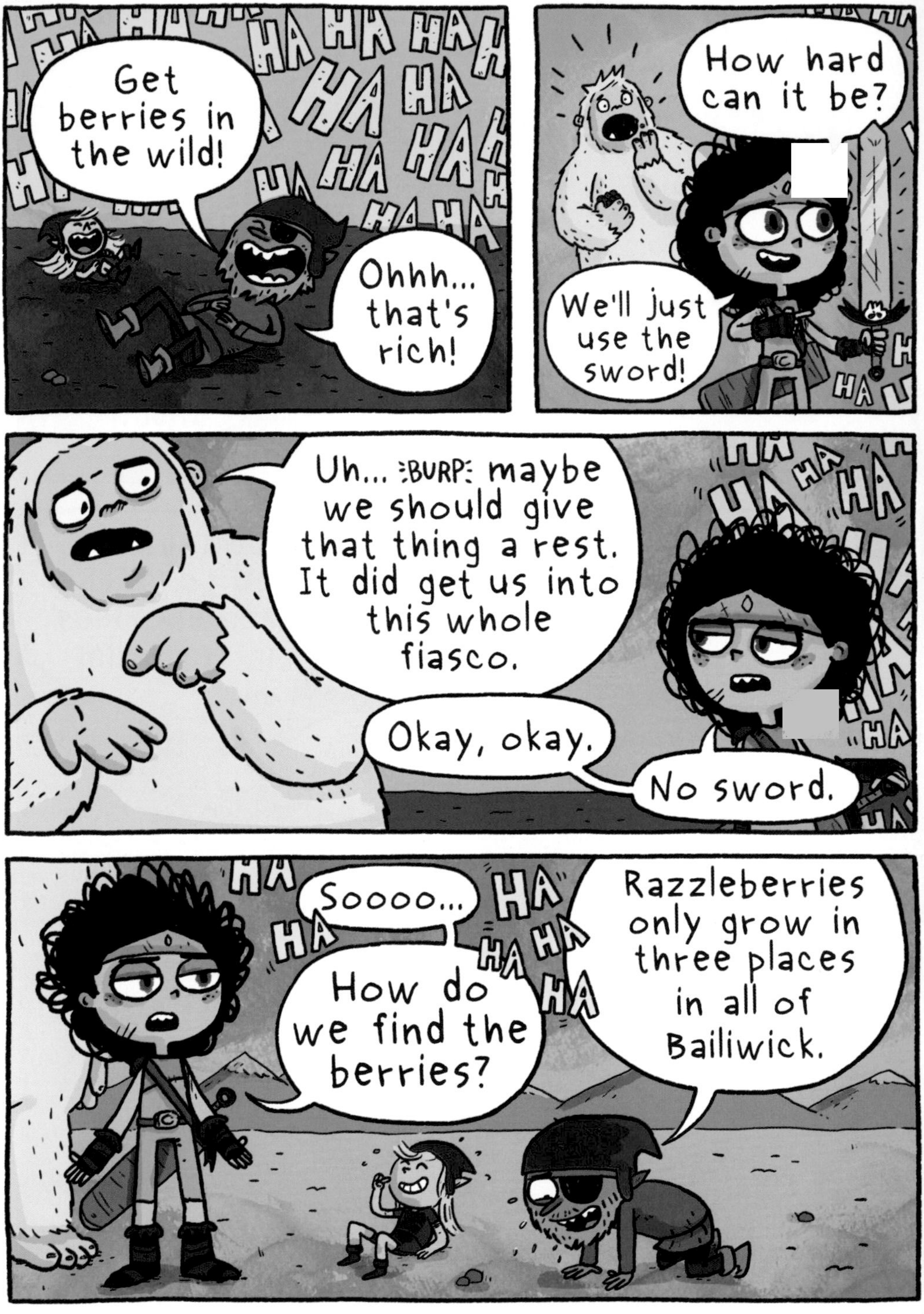
HA HA HA HA HA HA HA HA HA
Get berries in the wild!
Ohhh... that's rich!
How hard can it be?
We'll just use the sword!
HA HA
Uh... BURP maybe we should give that thing a rest. It did get us into this whole fiasco.
HA HA HA HA
Okay, okay.
No sword.
HA HA HA HA HA HA
Soooo...
How do we find the berries?
Razzleberries only grow in three places in all of Bailiwick.

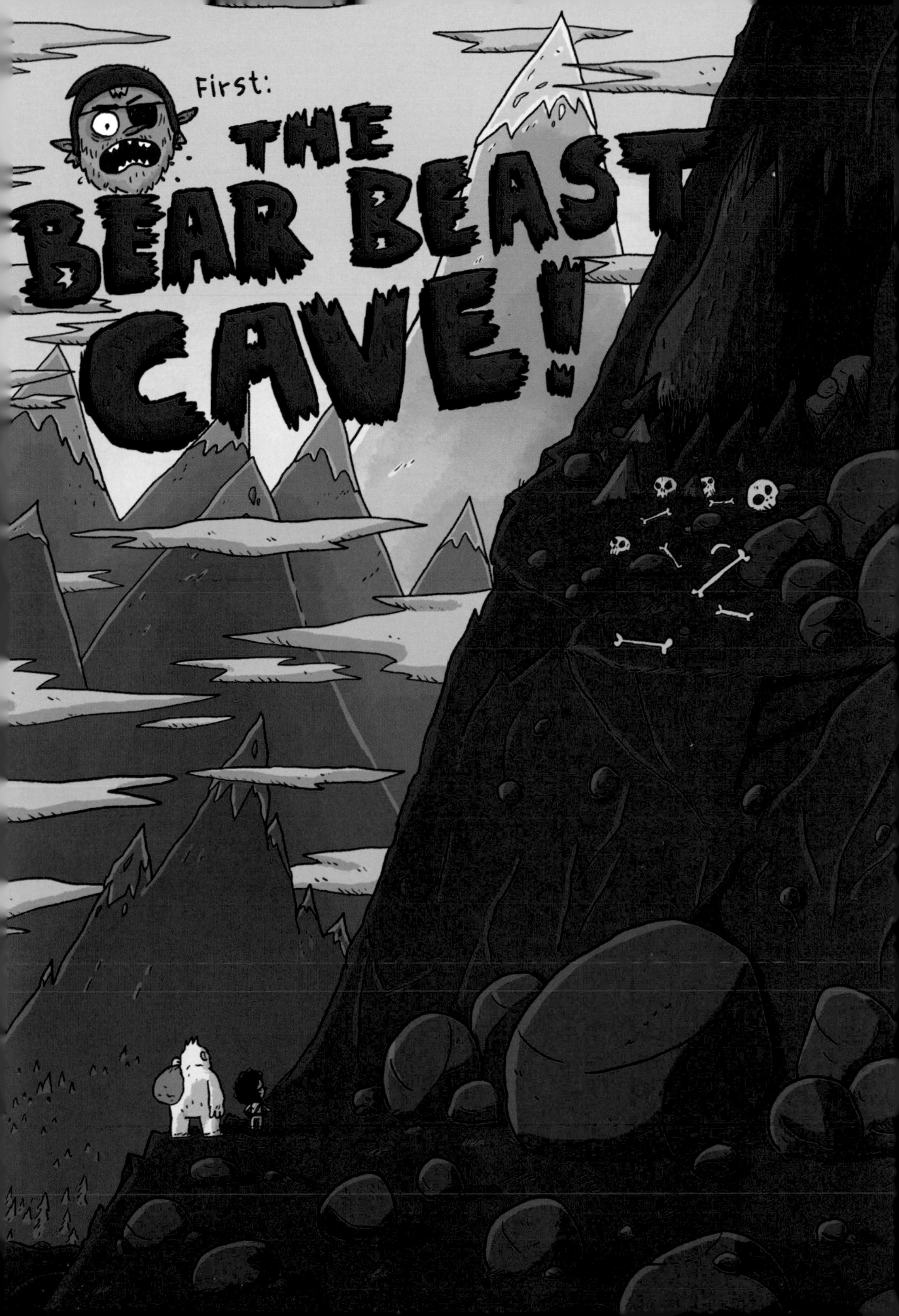
First:
THE BEAR BEAST CAVE!

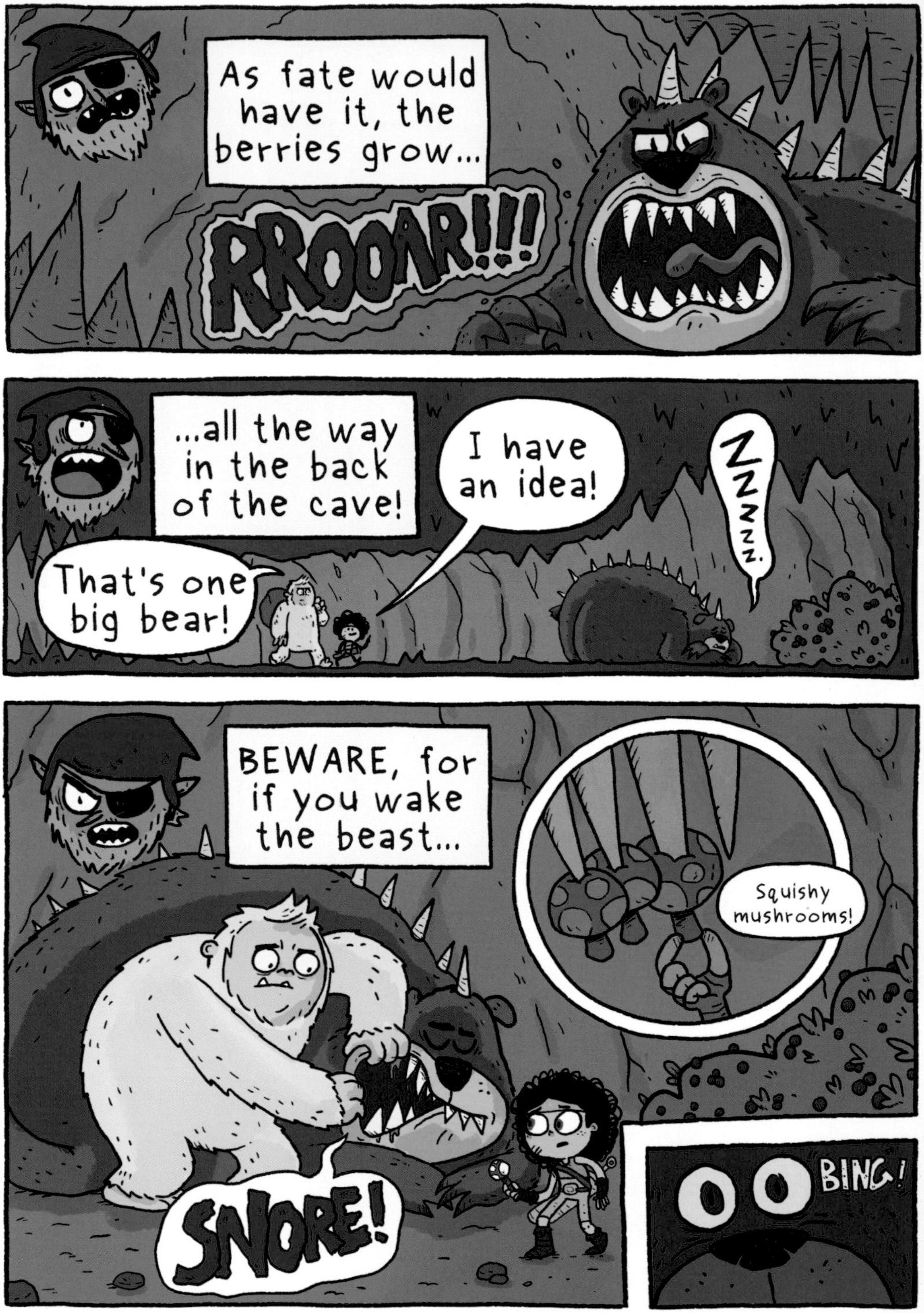

As fate would have it, the berries grow...
RROOAR!!!
...all the way in the back of the cave!
I have an idea!
ZZZZZ.
That's one big bear!
BEWARE, for if you wake the beast...
Squishy mushrooms!
SNORE!
BING!

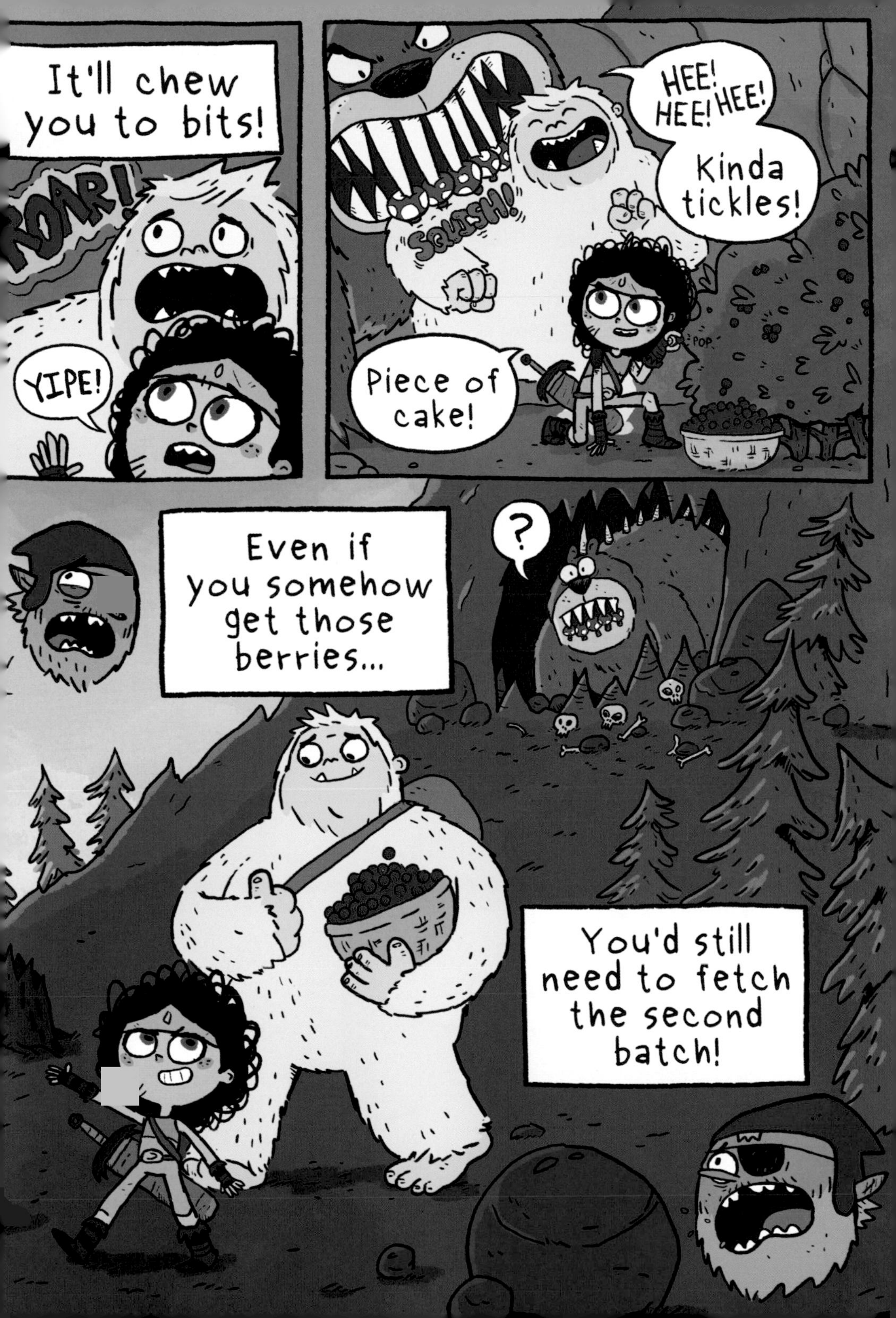
It'll chew you to bits!
ROAR!
YIPE!
SQUISH!
HEE! HEE! HEE!
Kinda tickles!
POP
Piece of cake!
Even if you somehow get those berries...
?
You'd still need to fetch the second batch!

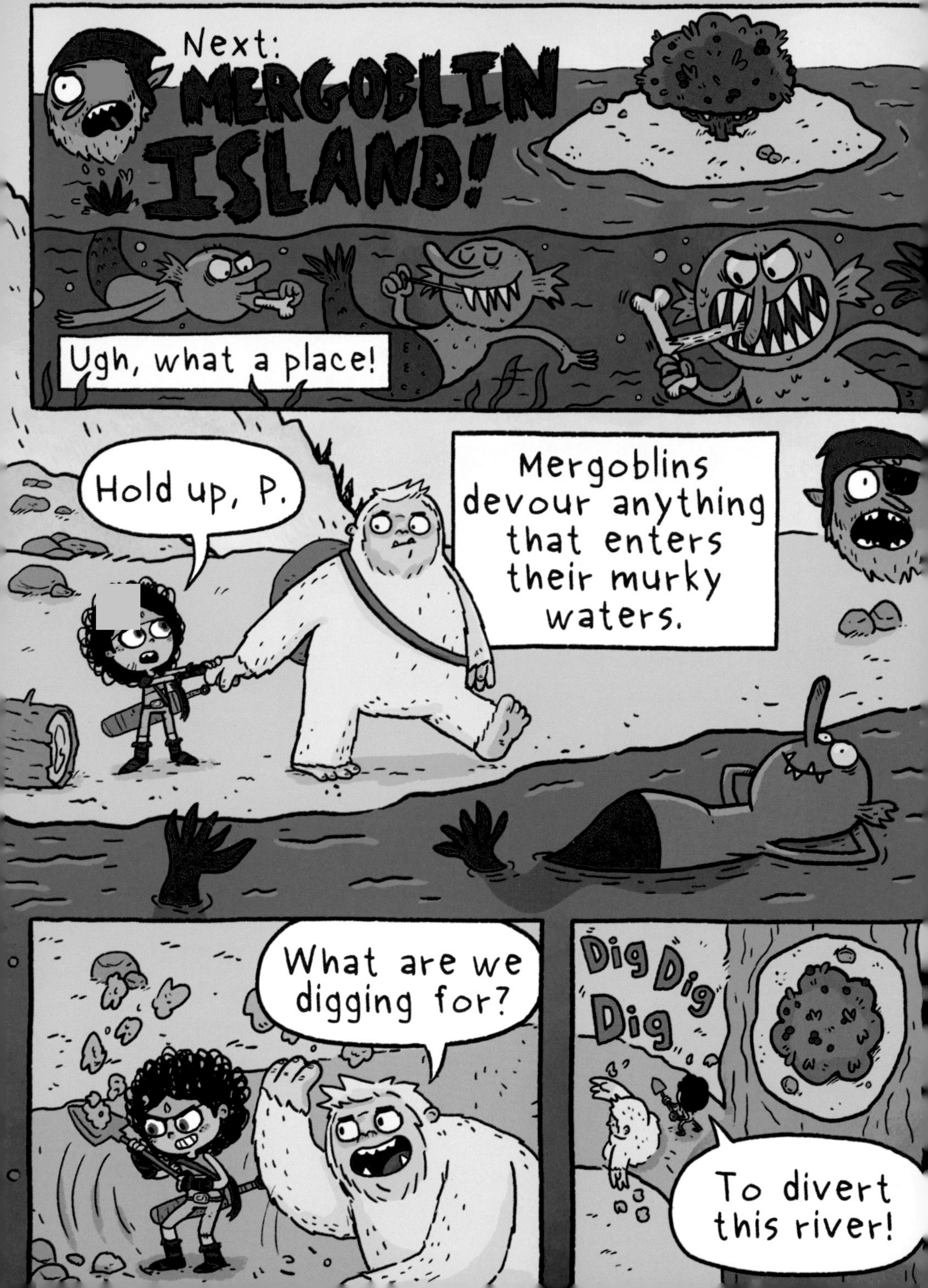
Next:
MERGOBLIN ISLAND!
Ugh, what a place!
Hold up, P.
Mergoblins devour anything that enters their murky waters.
What are we digging for?
Dig Dig Dig
To divert this river!

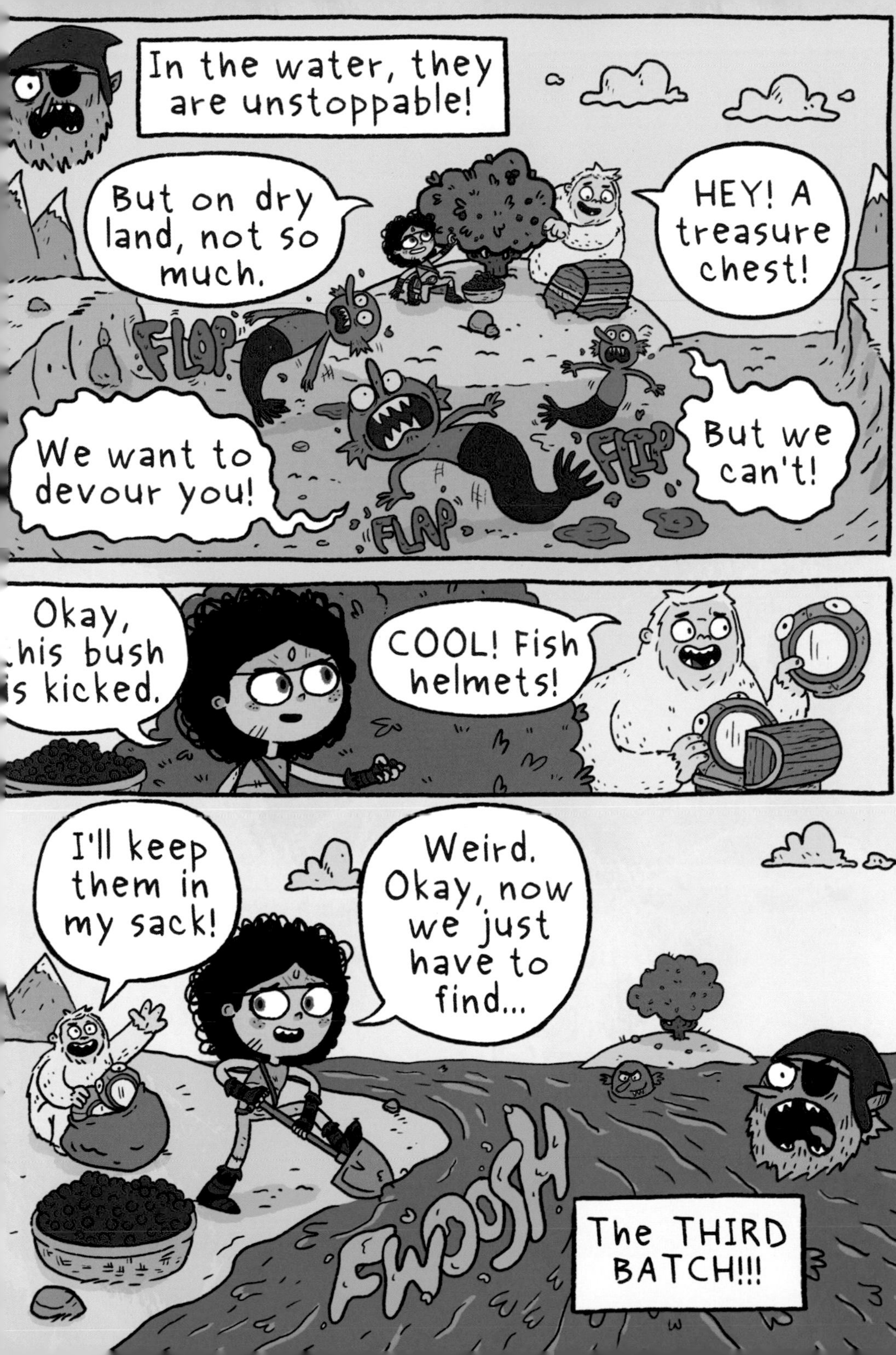
In the water, they are unstoppable!
But on dry land, not so much.
HEY! A treasure chest!
FLOP
We want to devour you!
But we can't!
FLIP
FLAP
Okay, his bush is kicked.
COOL! Fish helmets!
I'll keep them in my sack!
Weird. Okay, now we just have to find...
FWOOSH
The THIRD BATCH!!!

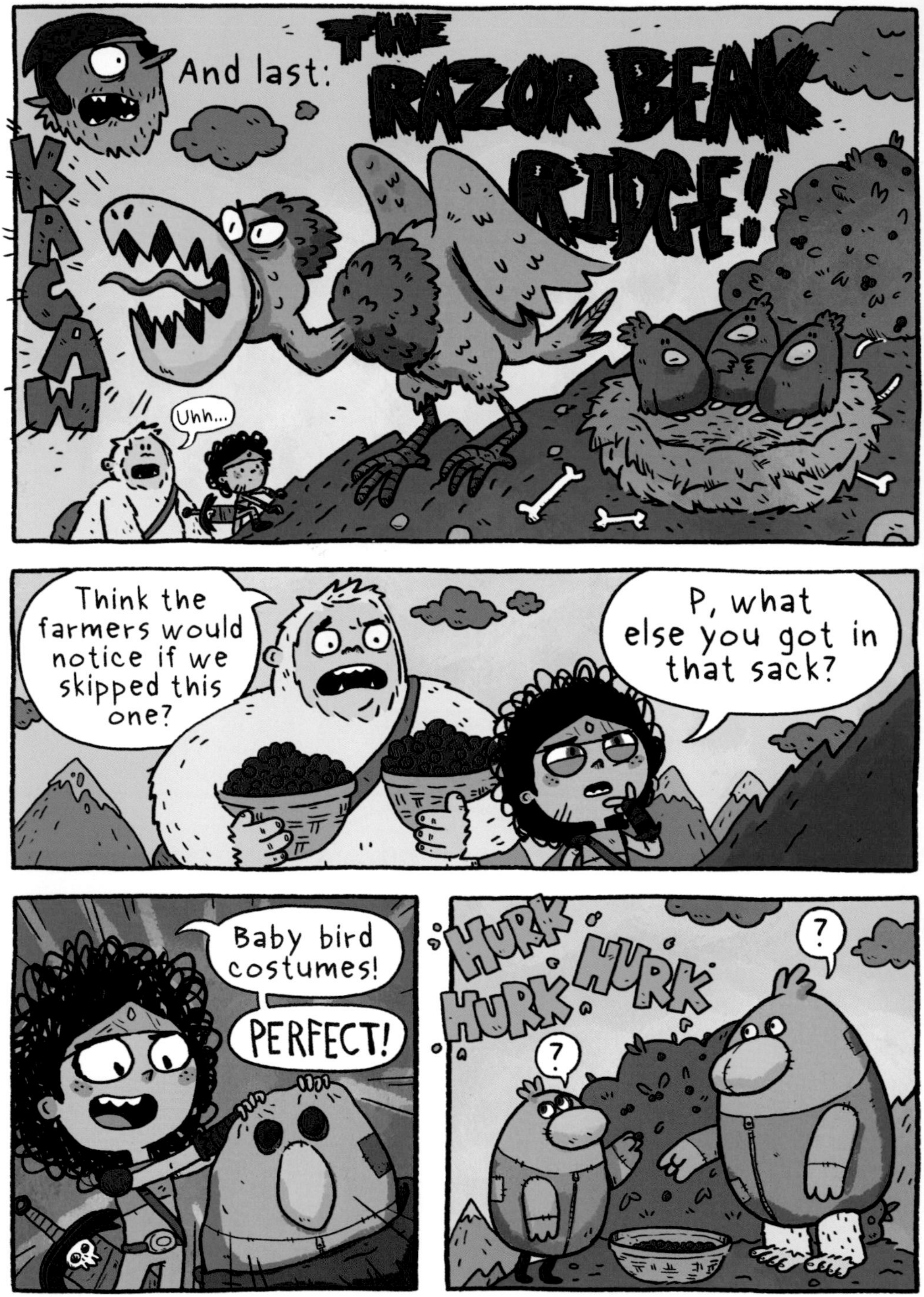
And last:
THE RAZOR BEAK RIDGE!
KACAW
Uhh...
Think the farmers would notice if we skipped this one?
P, what else you got in that sack?
Baby bird costumes!
PERFECT!
HURK
HURK
HURK
?
?

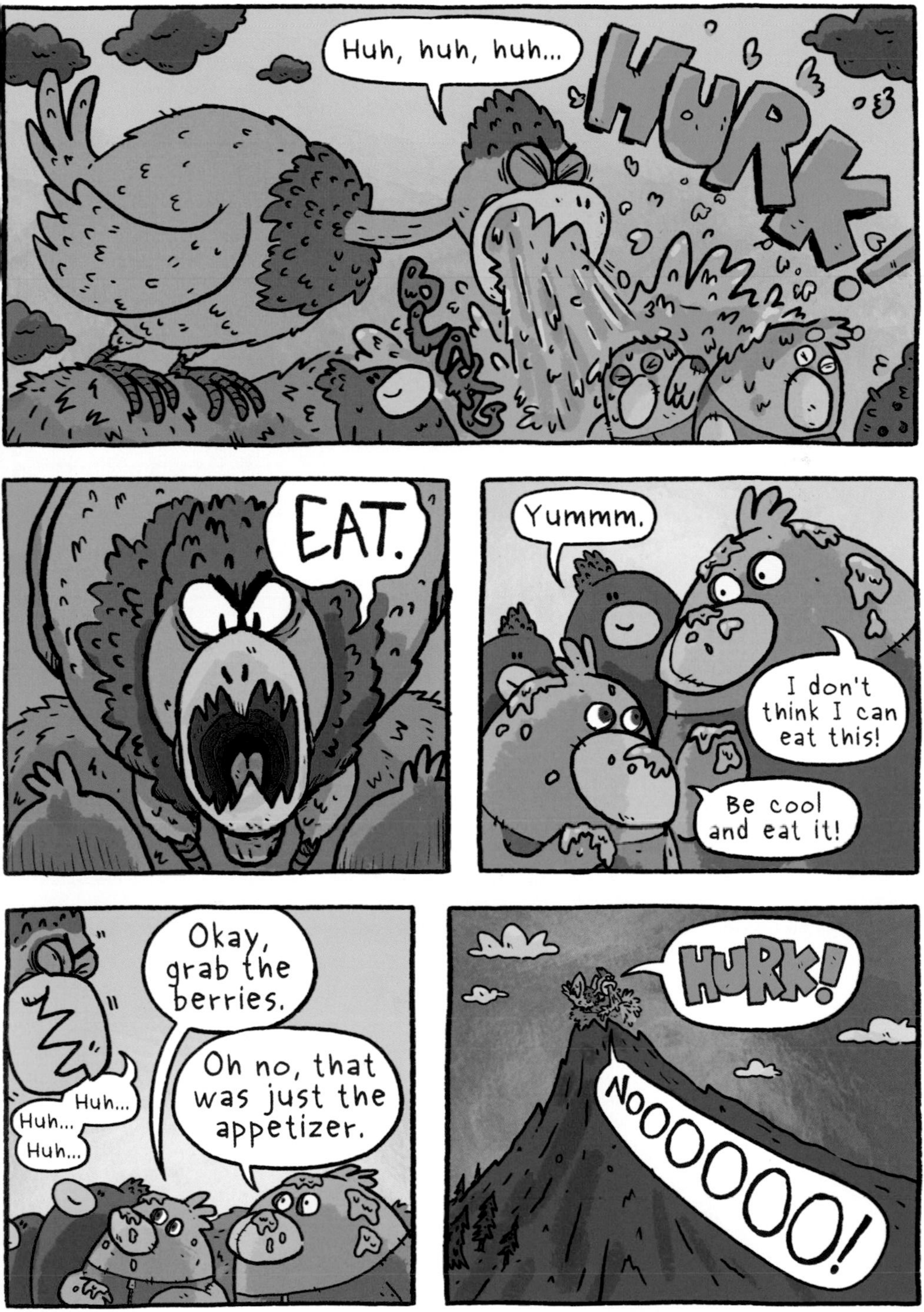
Huh, huh, huh...
HURK!
EAT.
Yummm.
I don't think I can eat this!
Be cool and eat it!
Okay, grab the berries.
Oh no, that was just the appetizer.
Huh...
Huh...
Huh...
HURK!
NOOOOOO!

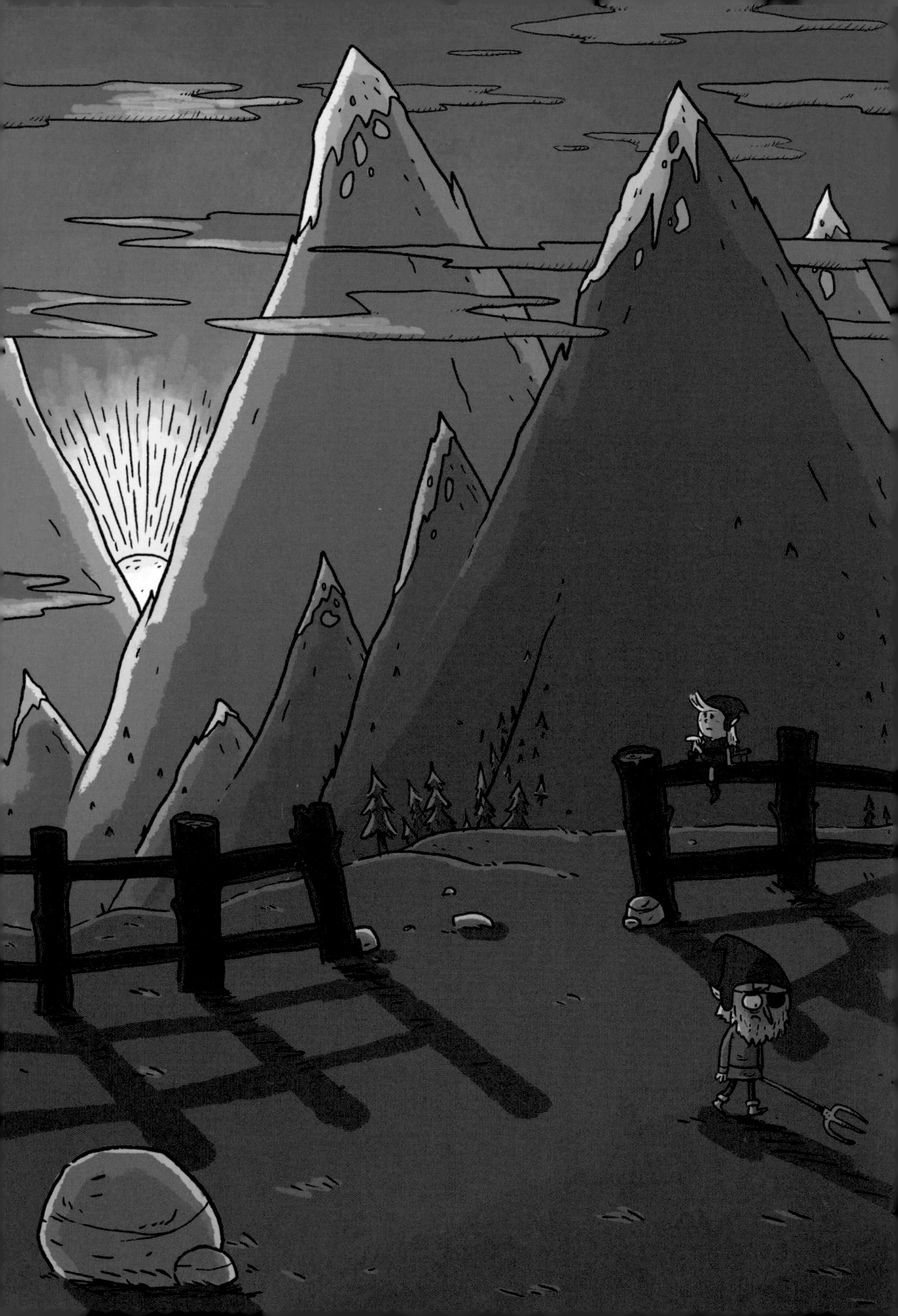

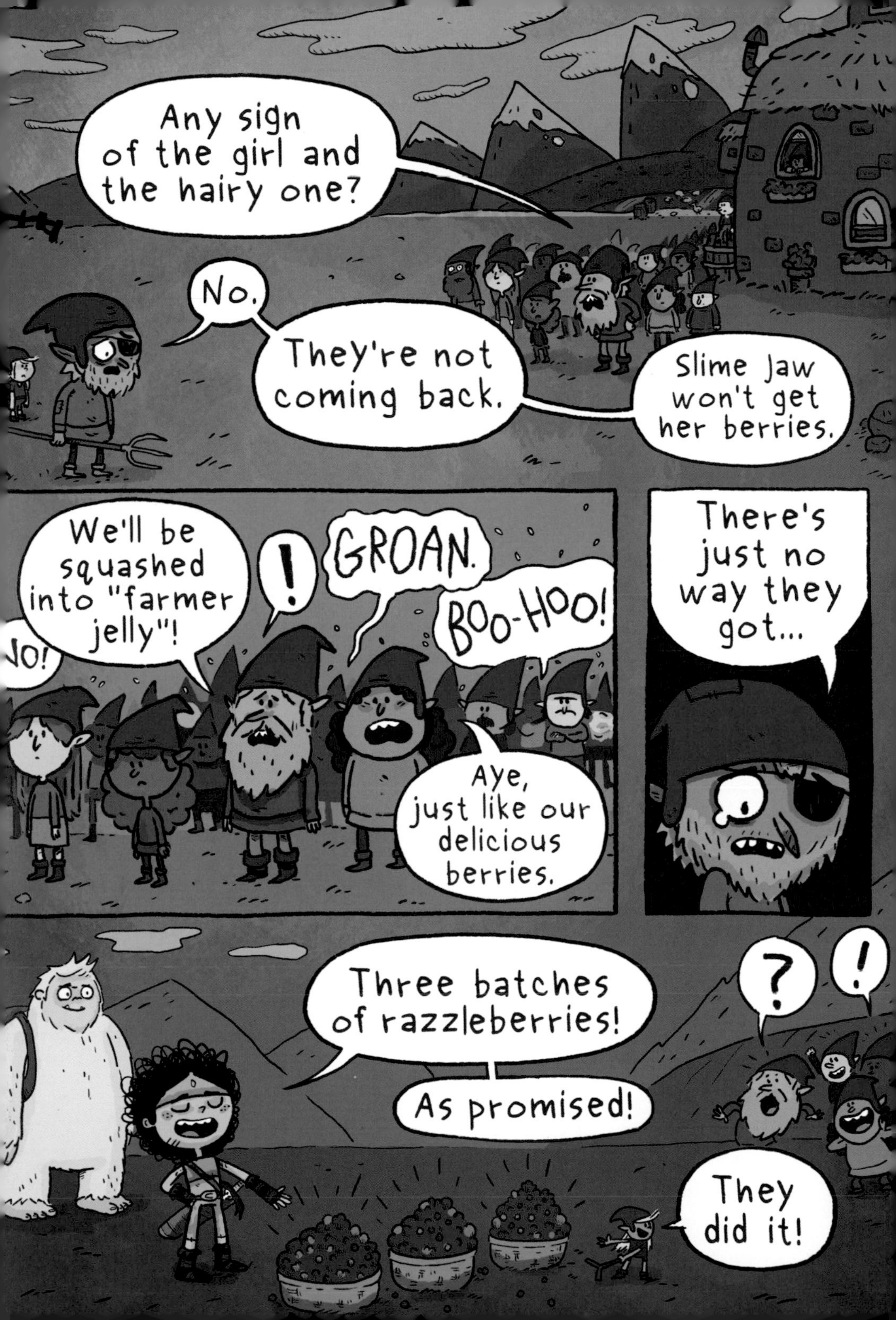

Any sign of the girl and the hairy one?
No.
They're not coming back.
Slime Jaw won't get her berries.
NO!
We'll be squashed into "farmer jelly"!
!
GROAN.
BOO-HOO!
Aye, just like our delicious berries.
There's just no way they got...
Three batches of razzleberries!
As promised!
?
!
They did it!

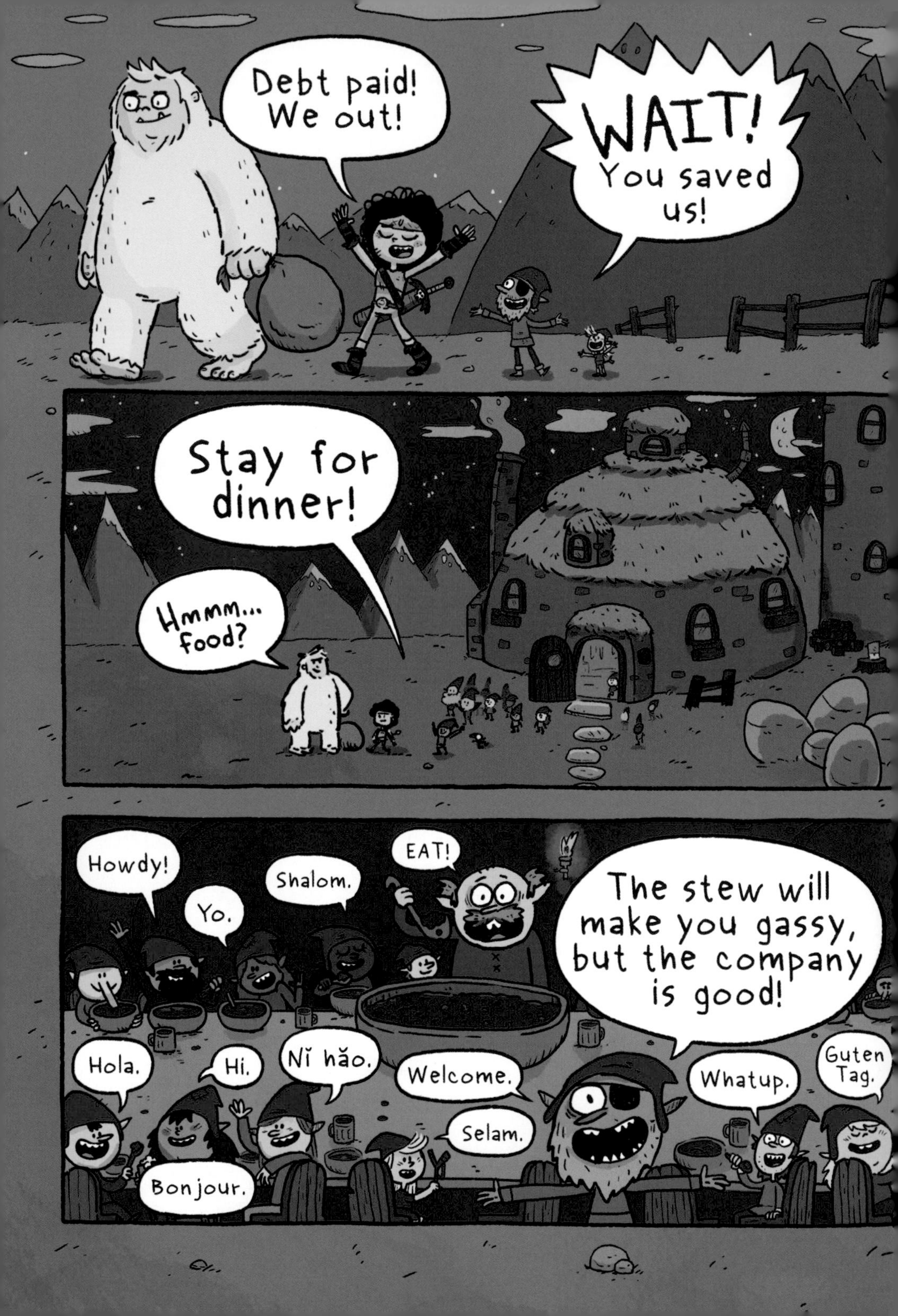

Debt paid! We out!
WAIT! You saved us!
Stay for dinner!
Hmmm... food?
Howdy!
Yo.
Shalom.
EAT!
The stew will make you gassy, but the company is good!
Hola.
Hi.
Nĭ hăo.
Welcome.
Selam.
Bonjour.
Whatup.
Guten Tag.

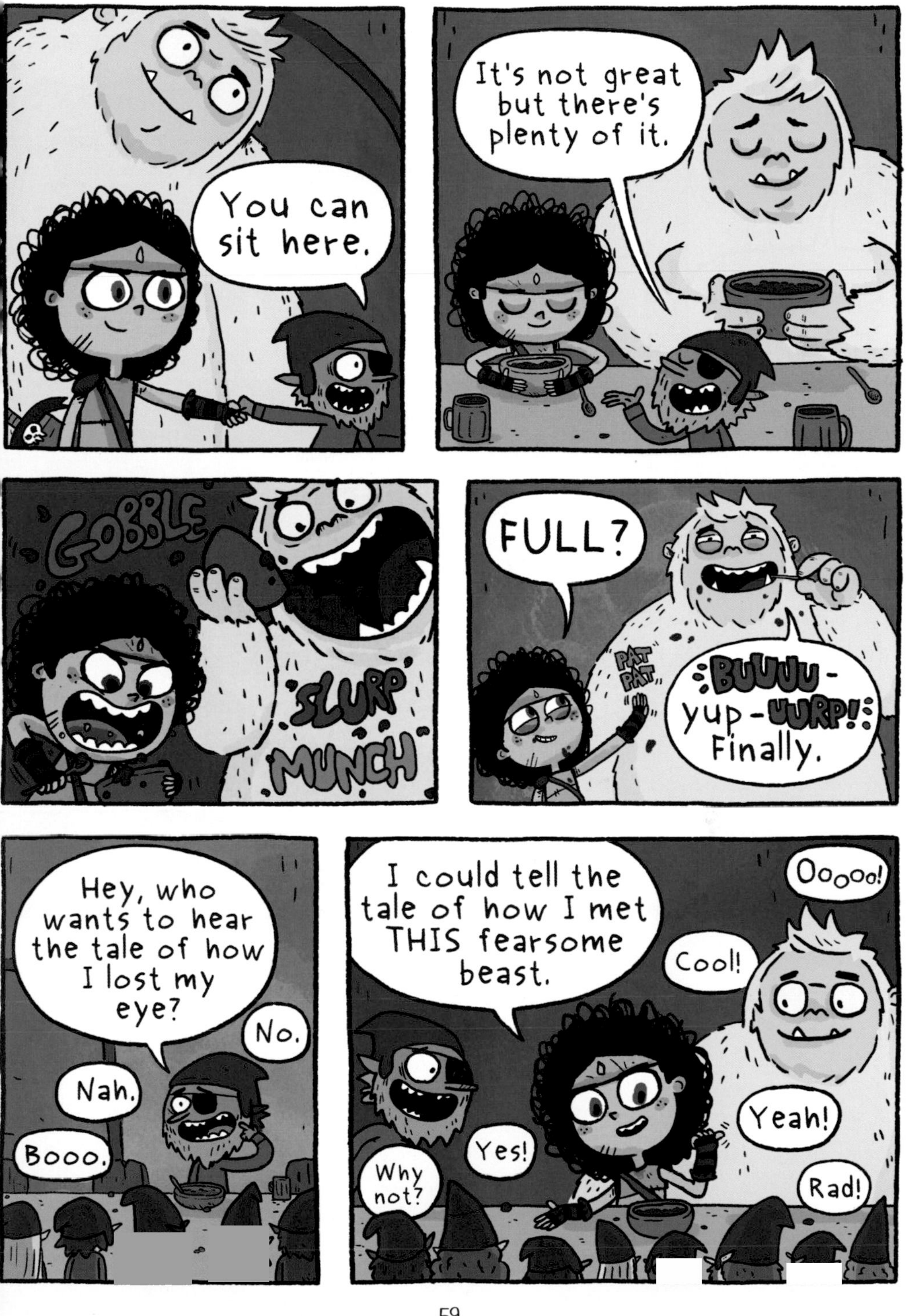
You can sit here.
It's not great but there's plenty of it.
GOBBLE
SLURP
MUNCH
FULL?
PAT PAT
BUUUU-yup-UURP! Finally.
Hey, who wants to hear the tale of how I lost my eye?
No.
Nah.
Booo.
I could tell the tale of how I met THIS fearsome beast.
Ooooo!
Cool!
Yes!
Why not?
Yeah!
Rad!

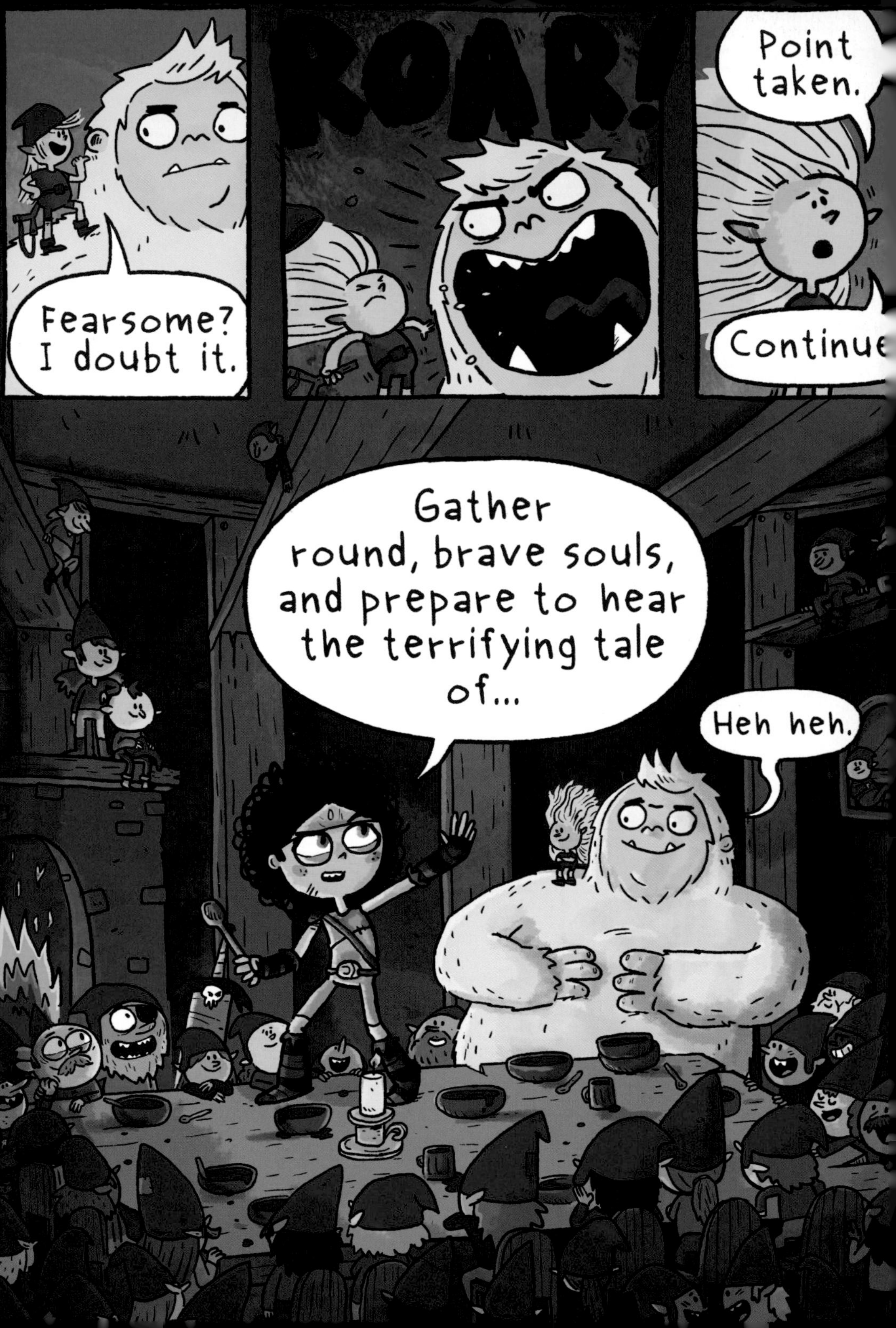
Fearsome? I doubt it.
ROAR!
Point taken.
Continue
Gather round, brave souls, and prepare to hear the terrifying tale of...
Heh heh.

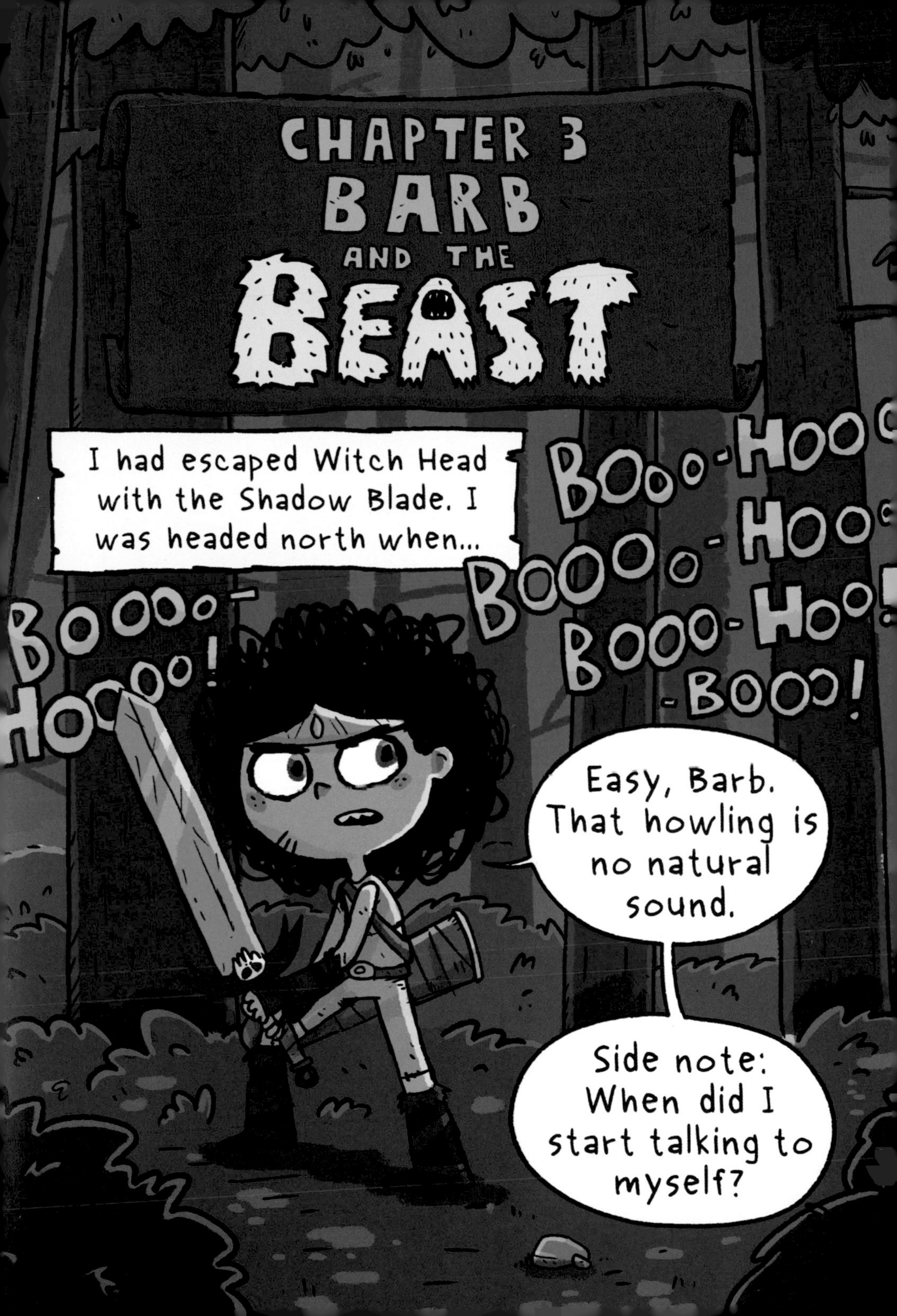
CHAPTER 3
BARB AND THE BEAST
I had escaped Witch Head with the Shadow Blade. I was headed north when...
BOOO-HOOO!
BOOO-HOOO
BOOOO-HOOO
BOOO-HOO!
BOOO-HOO
-BOOO!
Easy, Barb. That howling is no natural sound.
Side note: When did I start talking to myself?

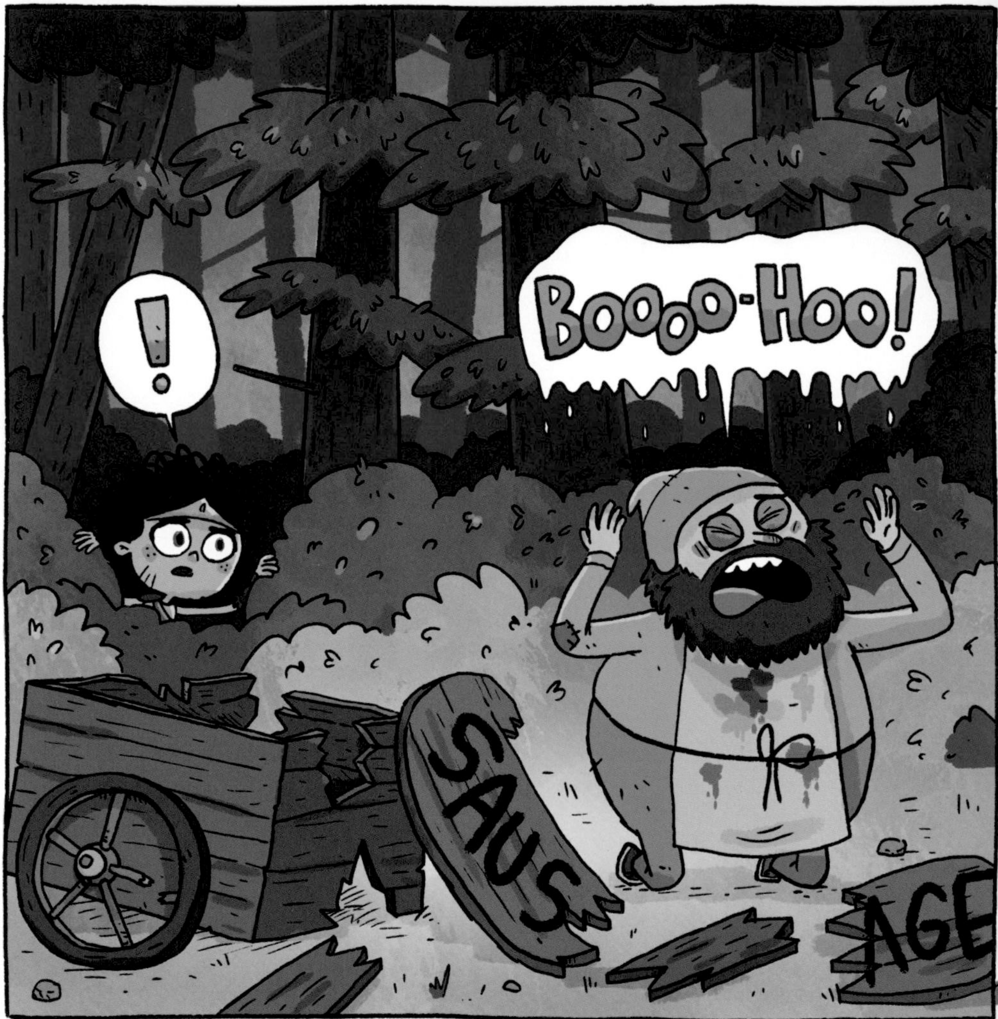
!
BOOOO-HOO!
SAUS
AGE

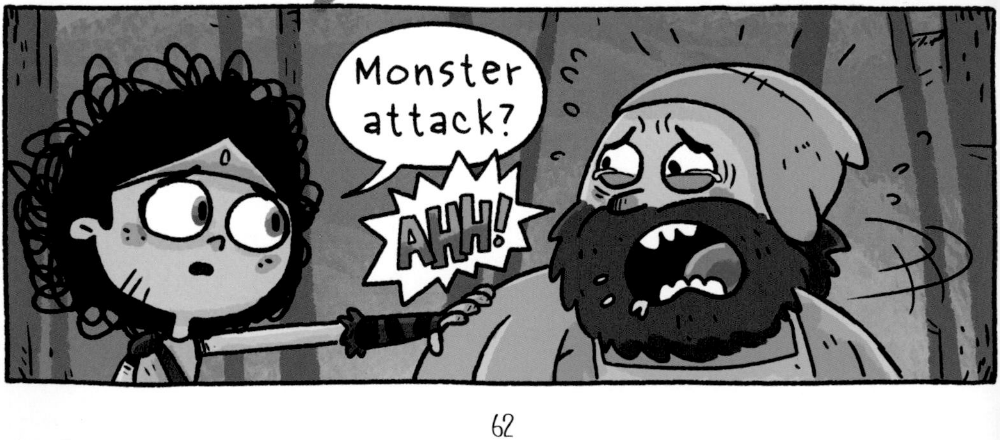
Monster attack?
AHH!

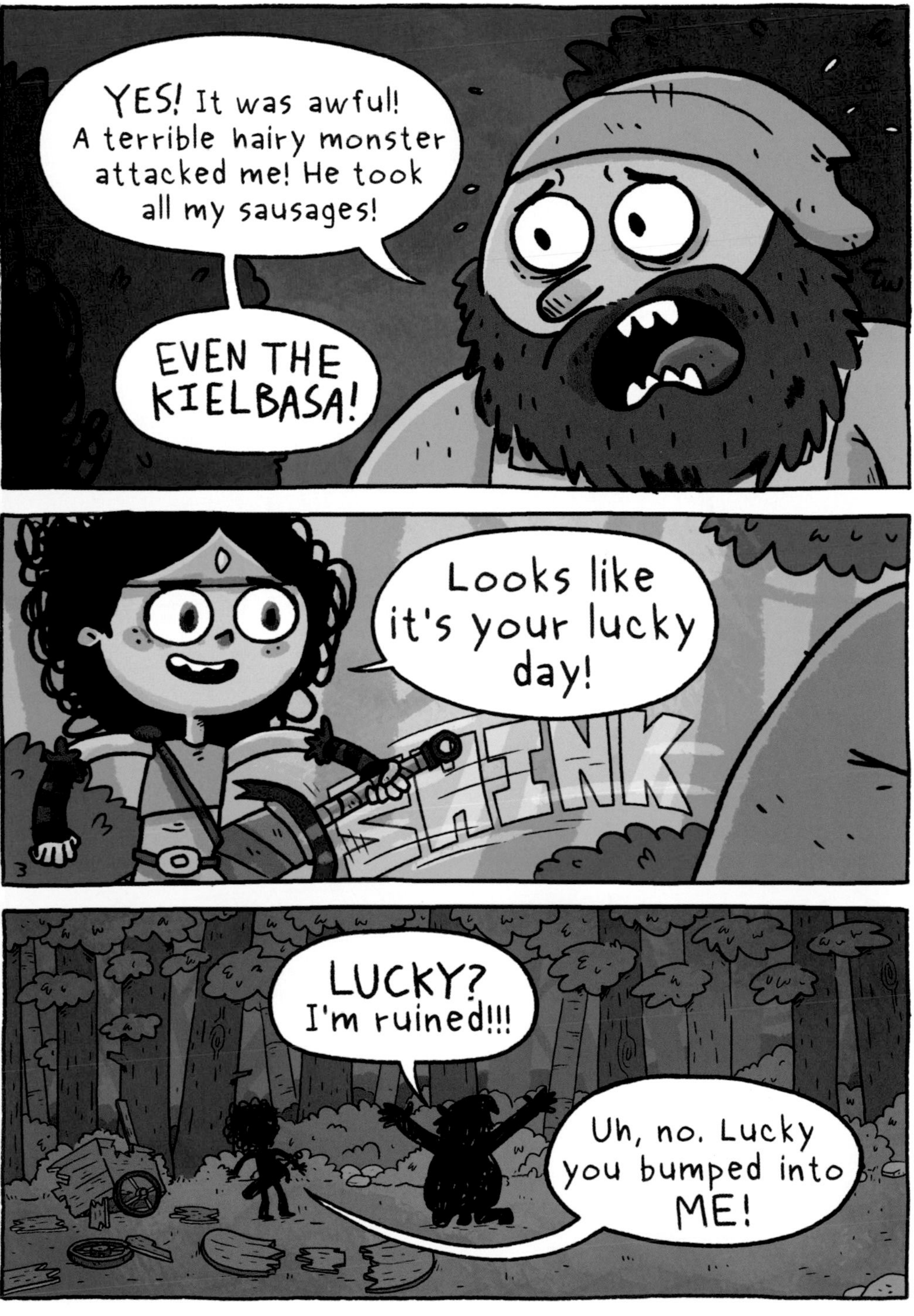
YES! It was awful! A terrible hairy monster attacked me! He took all my sausages!
EVEN THE KIELBASA!
Looks like it's your lucky day!
SHINK
LUCKY? I'm ruined!!!
Uh, no. Lucky you bumped into ME!

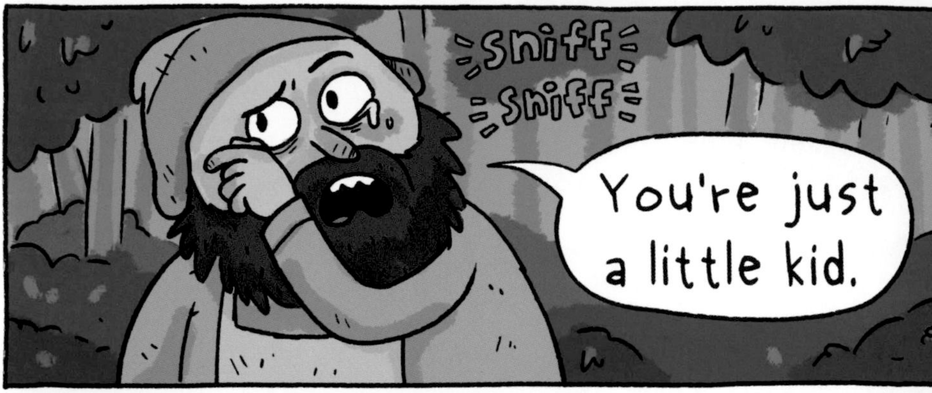
SNIFF
SNIFF
You're just a little kid.

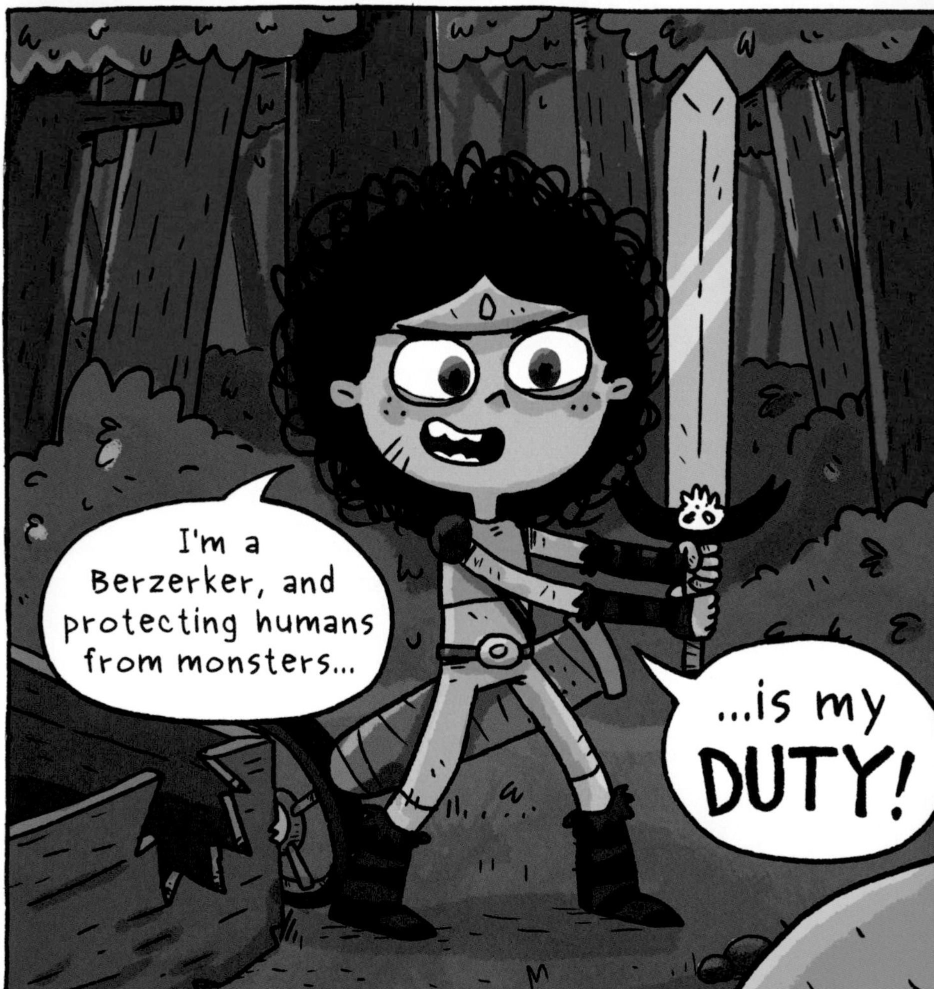
I'm a Berzerker, and protecting humans from monsters...
...is my DUTY!

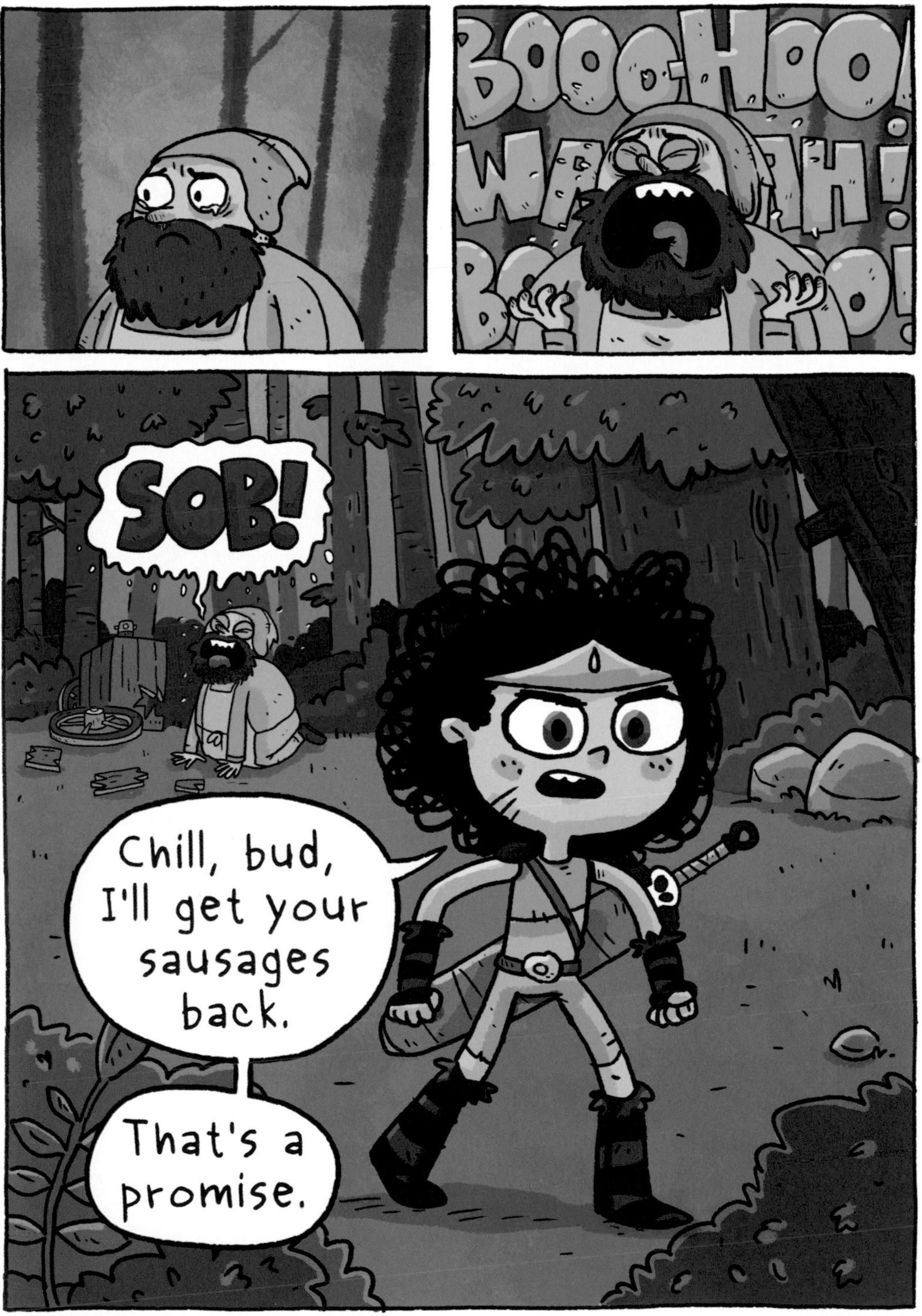
BOO-HOO!
SOB!
Chill, bud, I'll get your sausages back.
That's a promise.

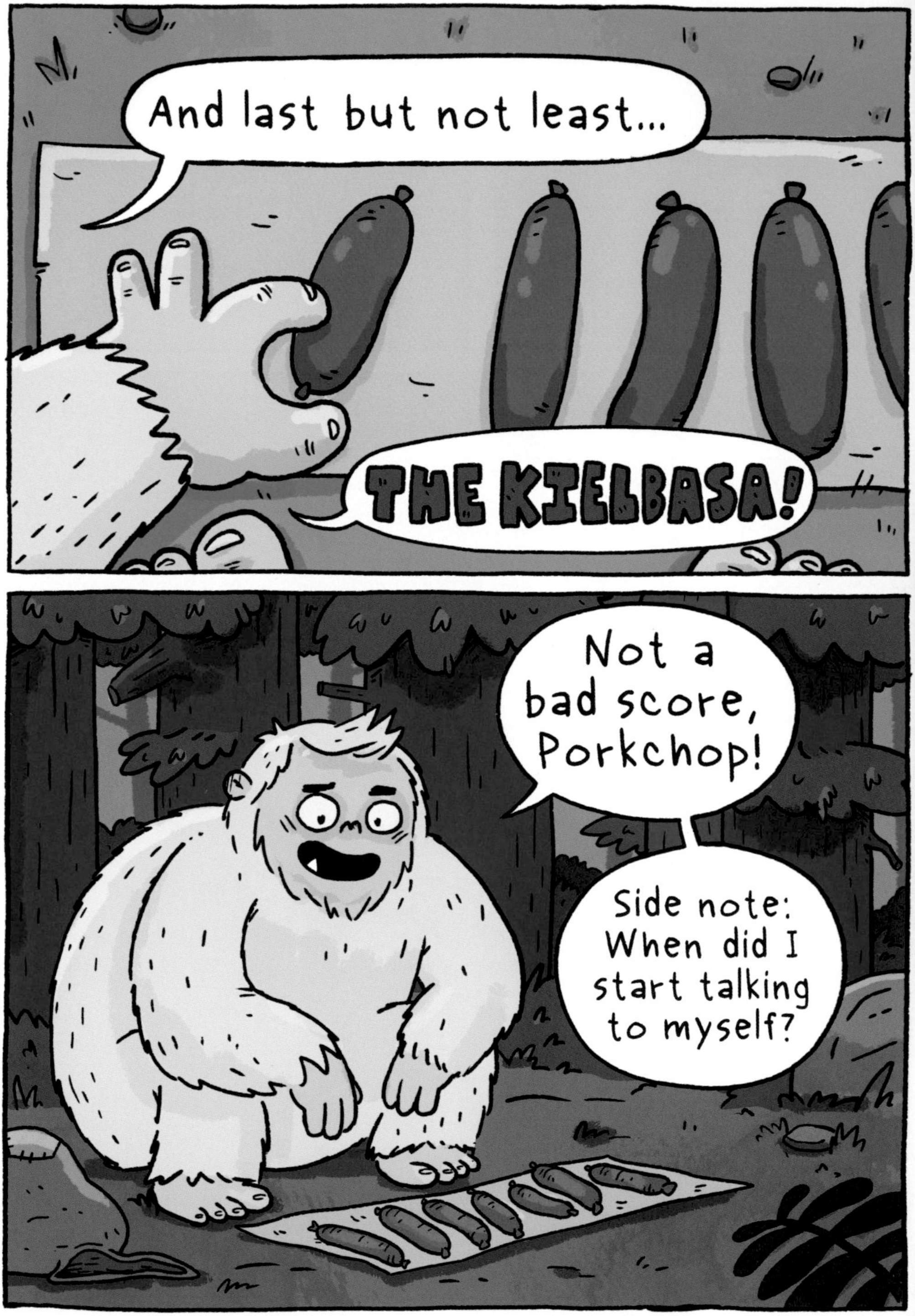

And last but not least...
THE KIELBASA!
Not a bad score, Porkchop!
Side note: When did I start talking to myself?

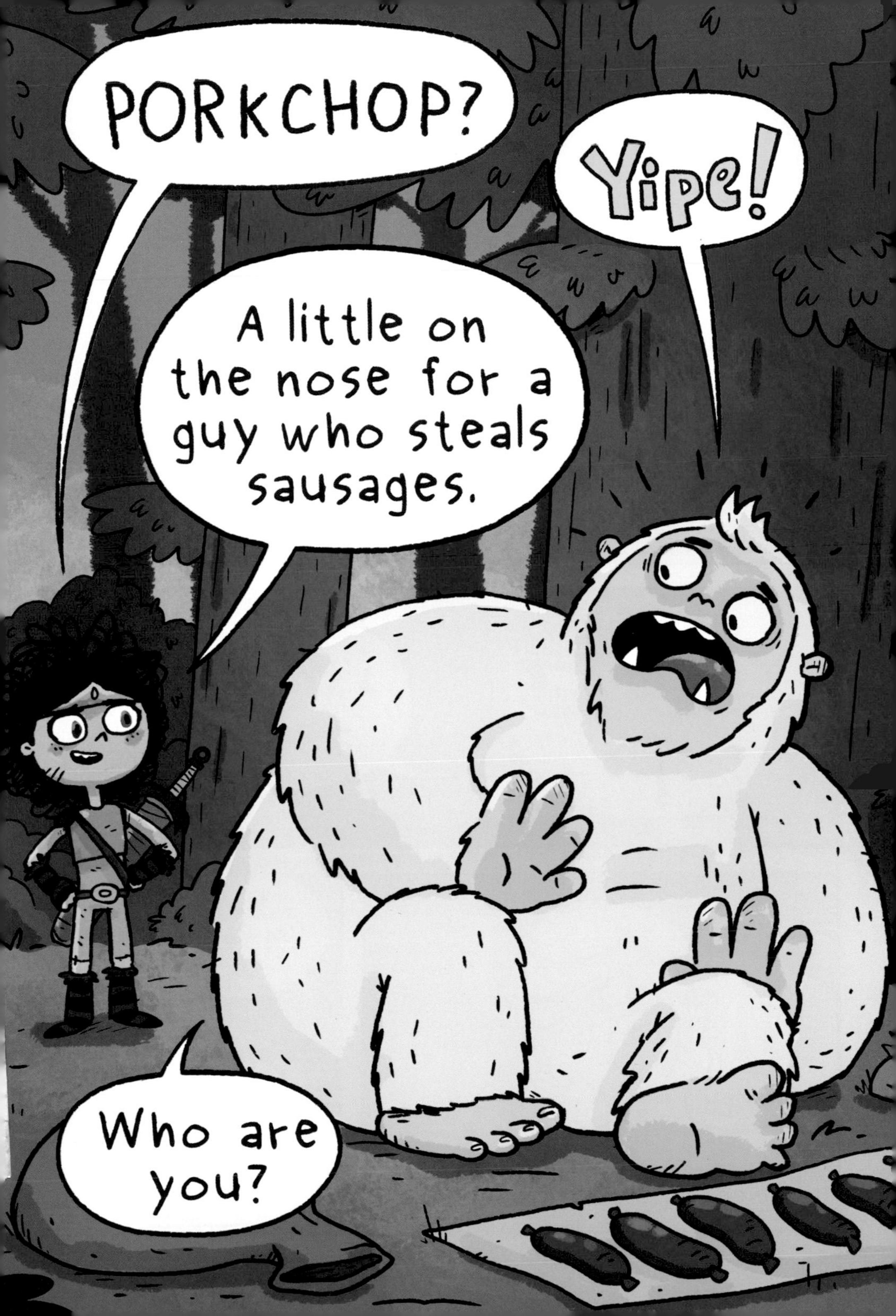
PORKCHOP?
Yipe!
A little on the nose for a guy who steals sausages.
Who are you?

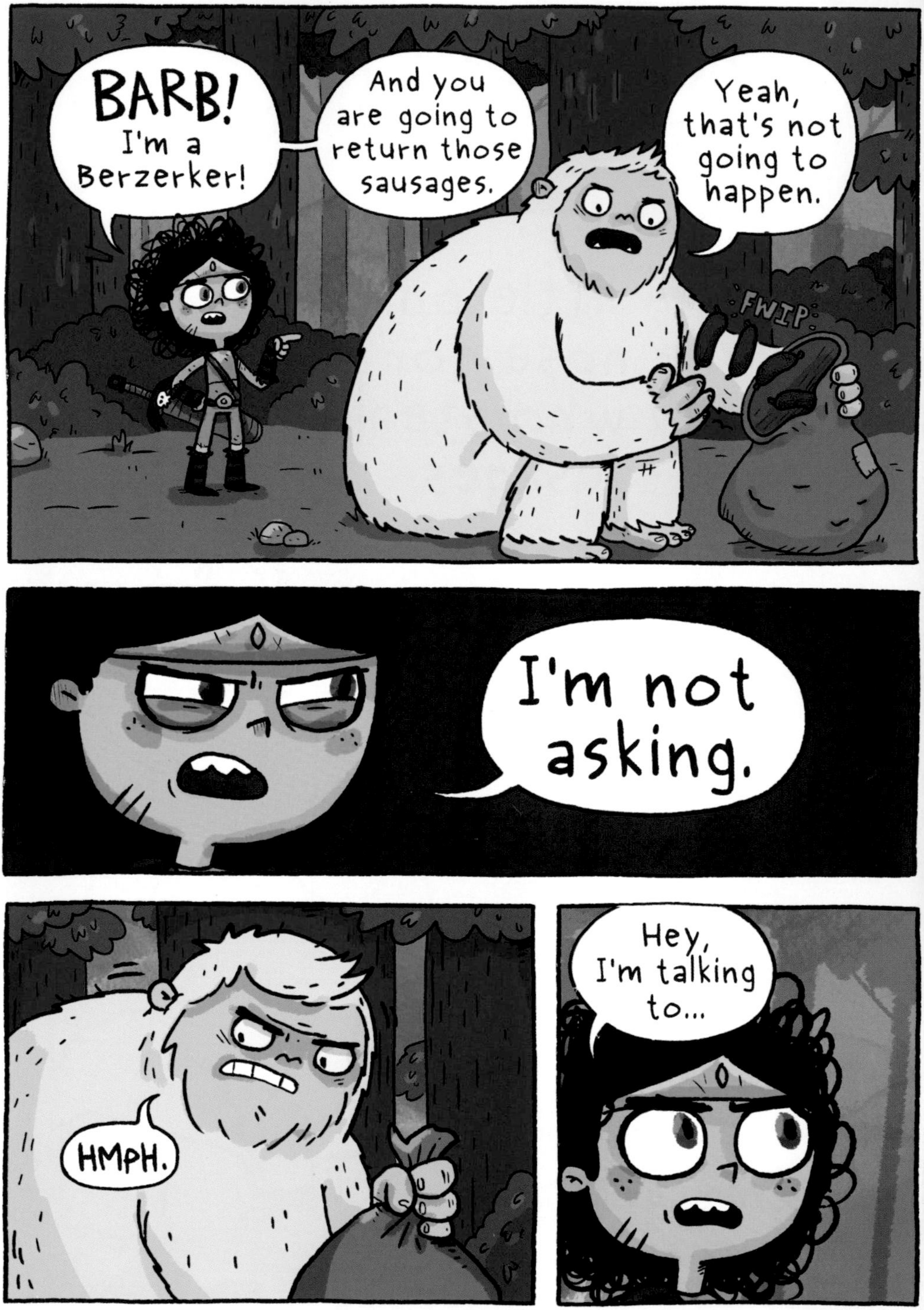
BARB! I'm a Berzerker!
And you are going to return those sausages.
Yeah, that's not going to happen.
FWIP
I'm not asking.
HMPH.
Hey, I'm talking to...

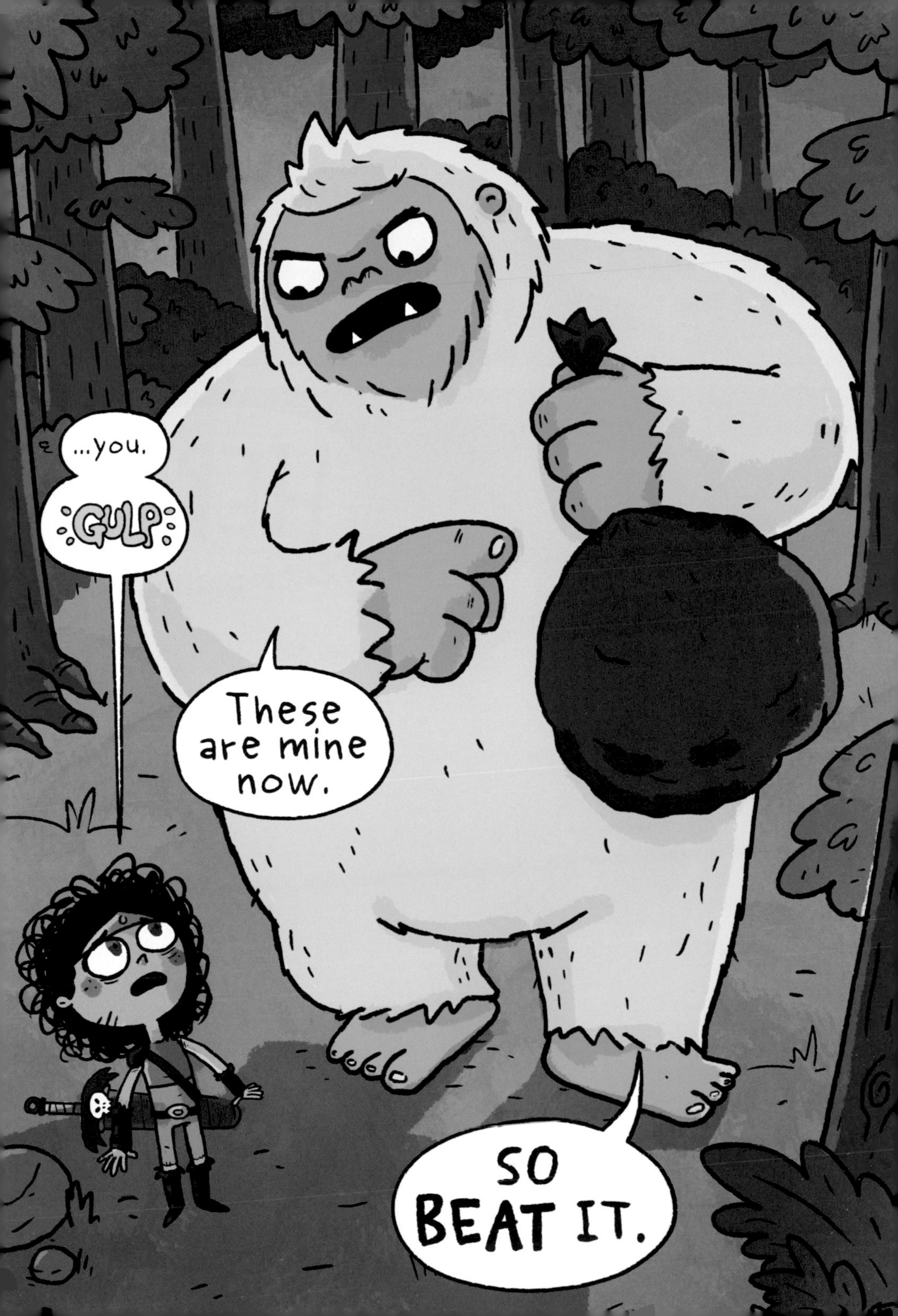
...you.
GULP
These are mine now.
SO BEAT IT.

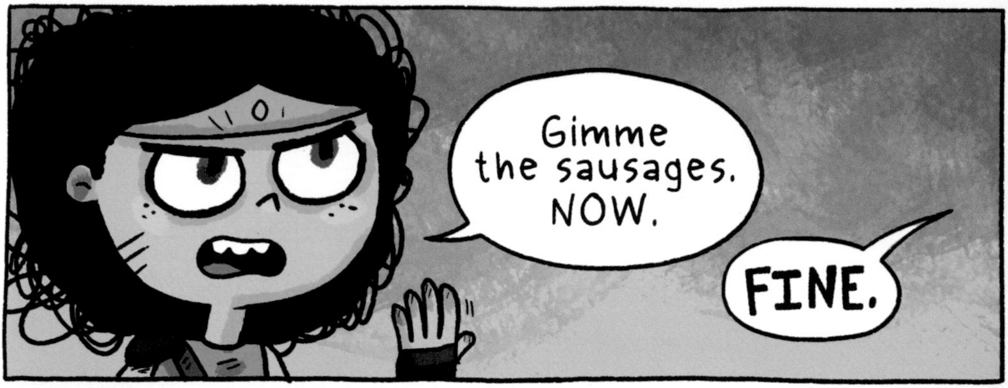
Gimme the sausages. NOW.
FINE.

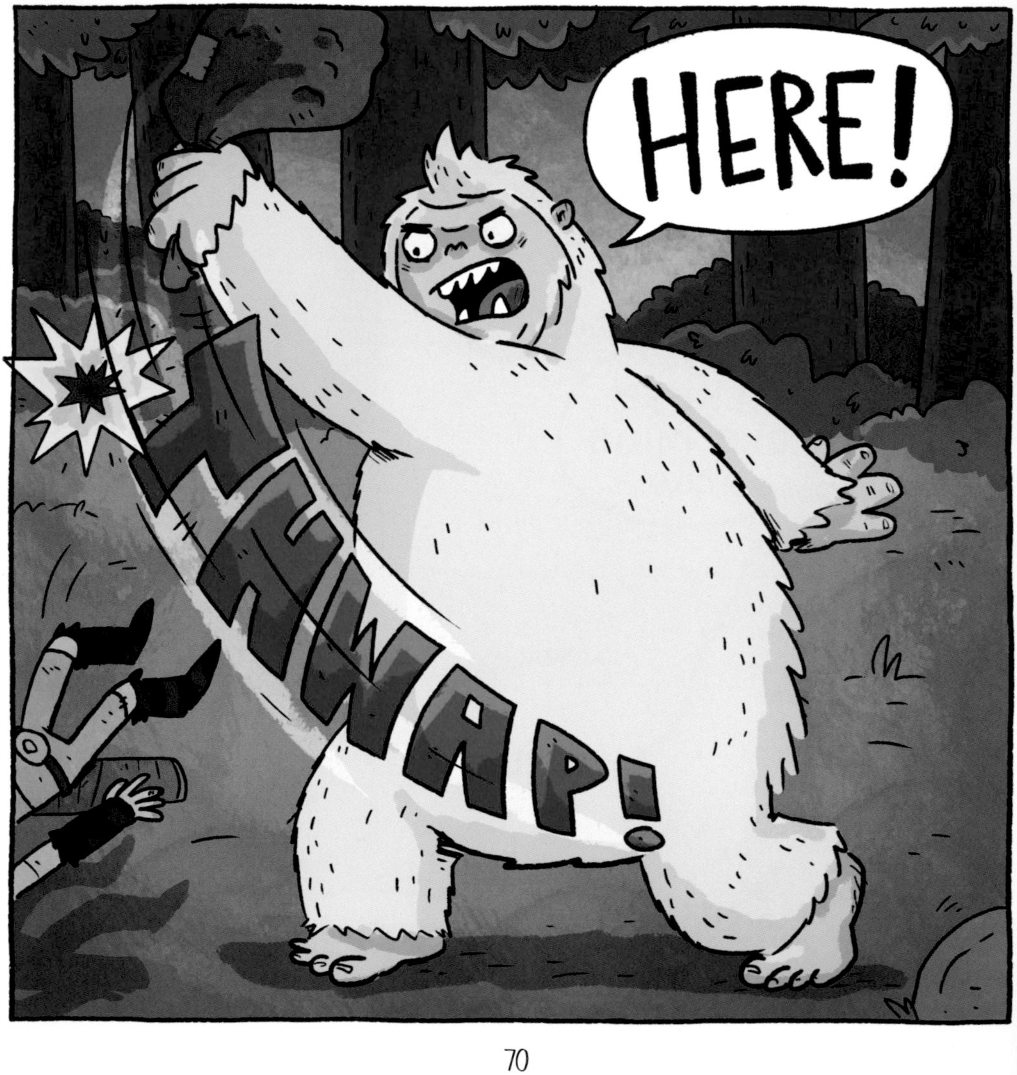
HERE!
THWAP!

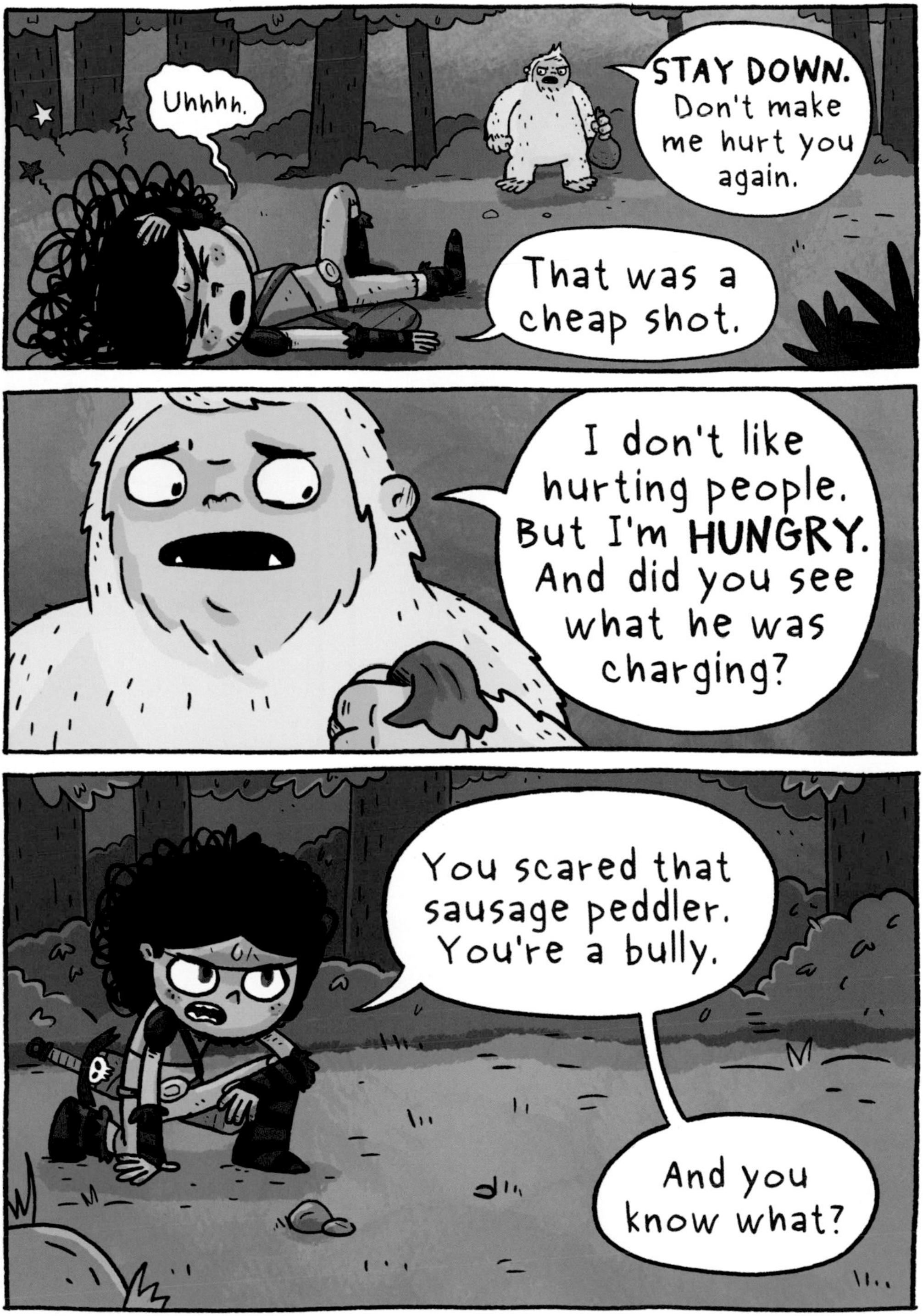
Uhhhh.
STAY DOWN. Don't make me hurt you again.
That was a cheap shot.
I don't like hurting people. But I'm HUNGRY. And did you see what he was charging?
You scared that sausage peddler. You're a bully.
And you know what?

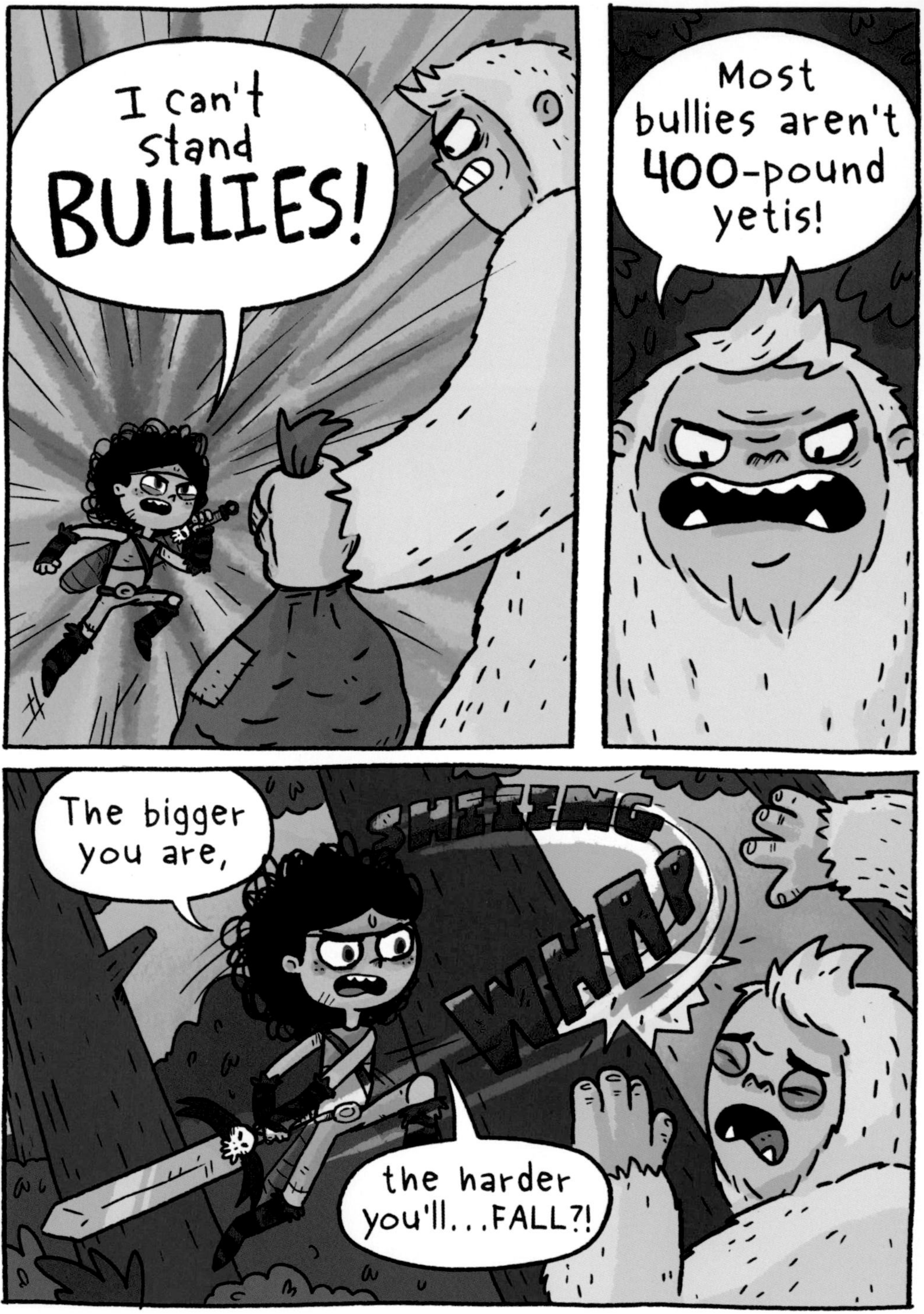
I can't stand BULLIES!
Most bullies aren't 400-pound yetis!
The bigger you are,
WHAP
the harder you'll...FALL?!

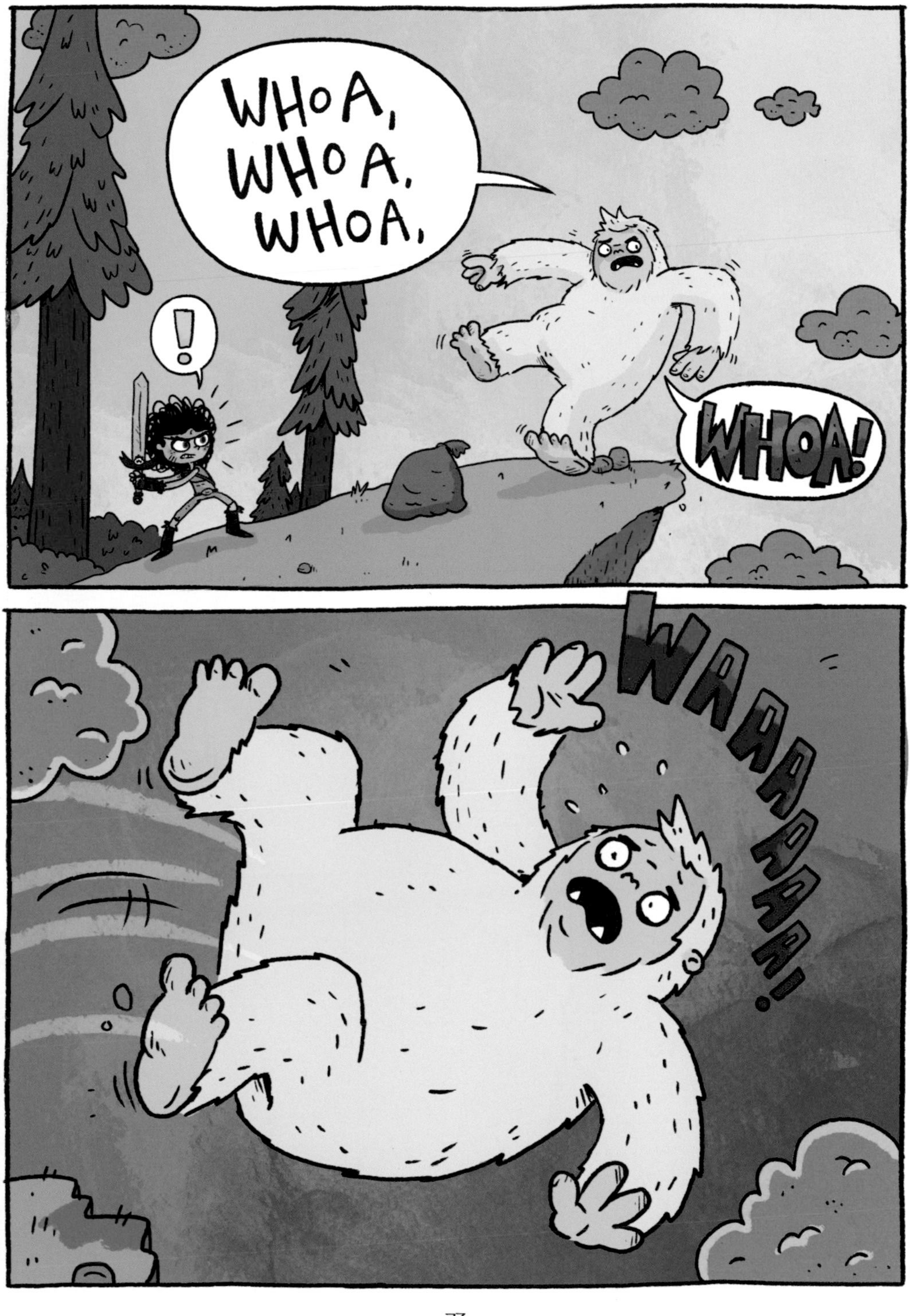
WHOA, WHOA, WHOA,
!
WHOA!
WAAAAAAAA!

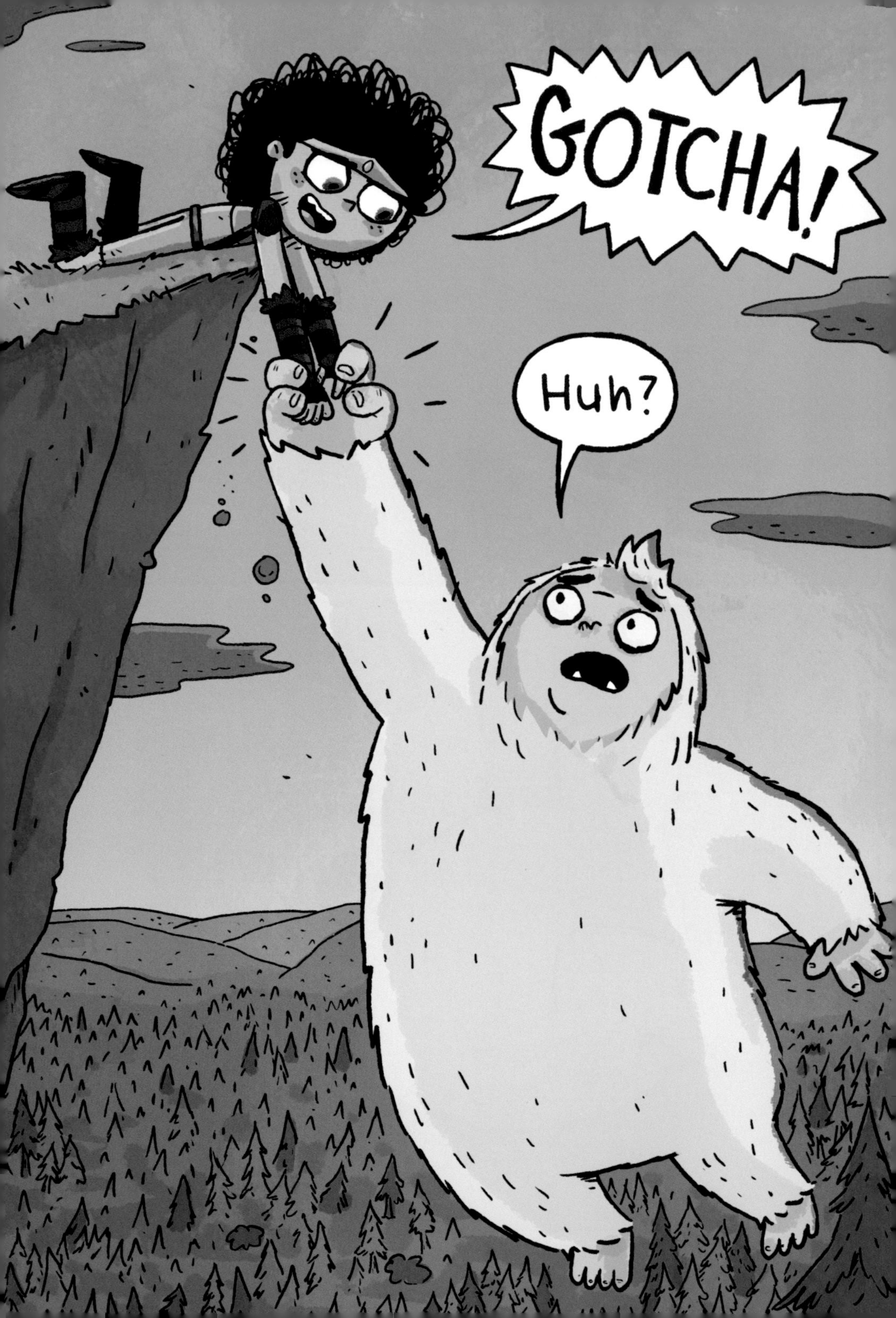
GOTCHA!
Huh?

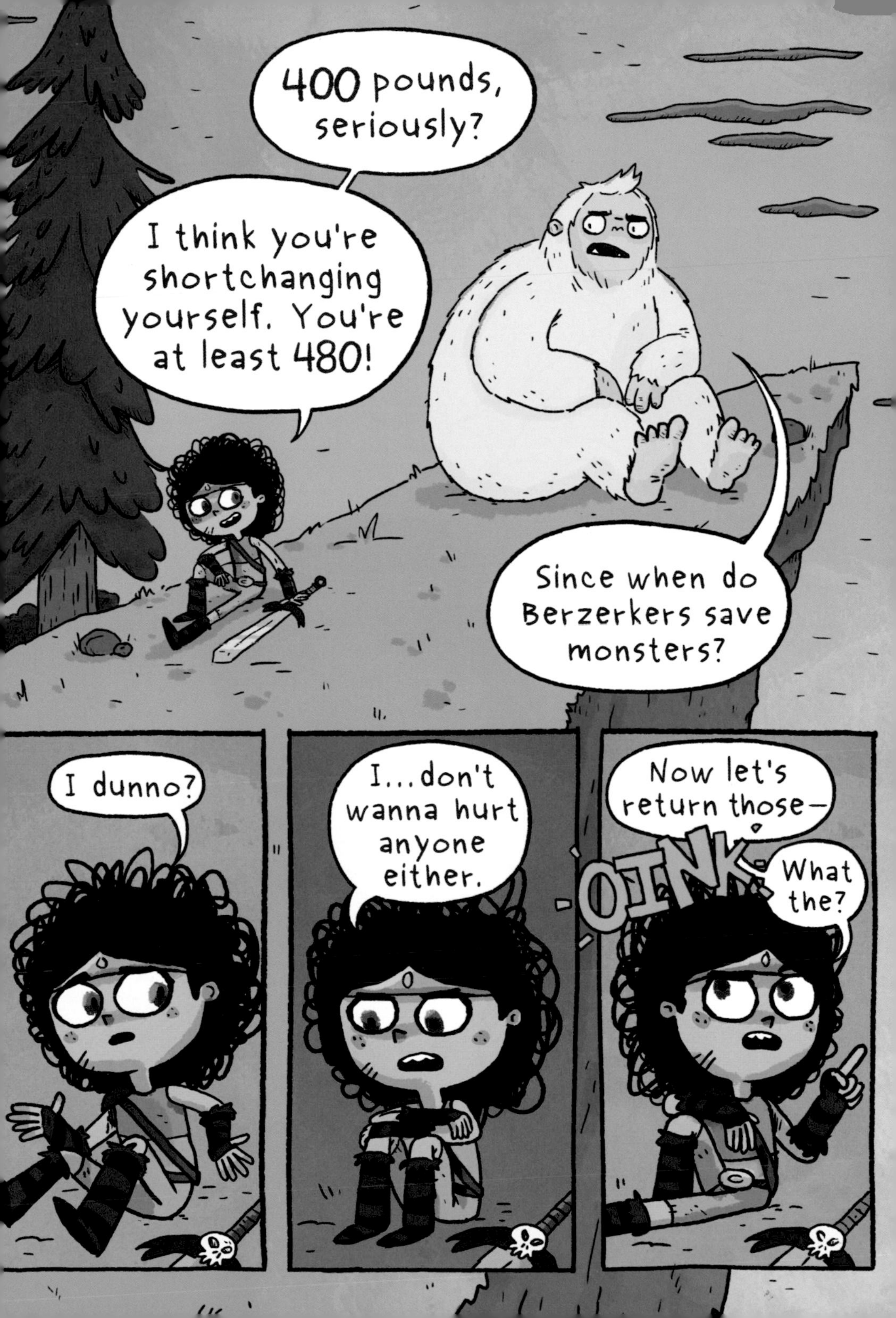

400 pounds, seriously?
I think you're shortchanging yourself. You're at least 480!
Since when do Berzerkers save monsters?
I dunno?
I...don't wanna hurt anyone either.
Now let's return those—
OINK
What the?

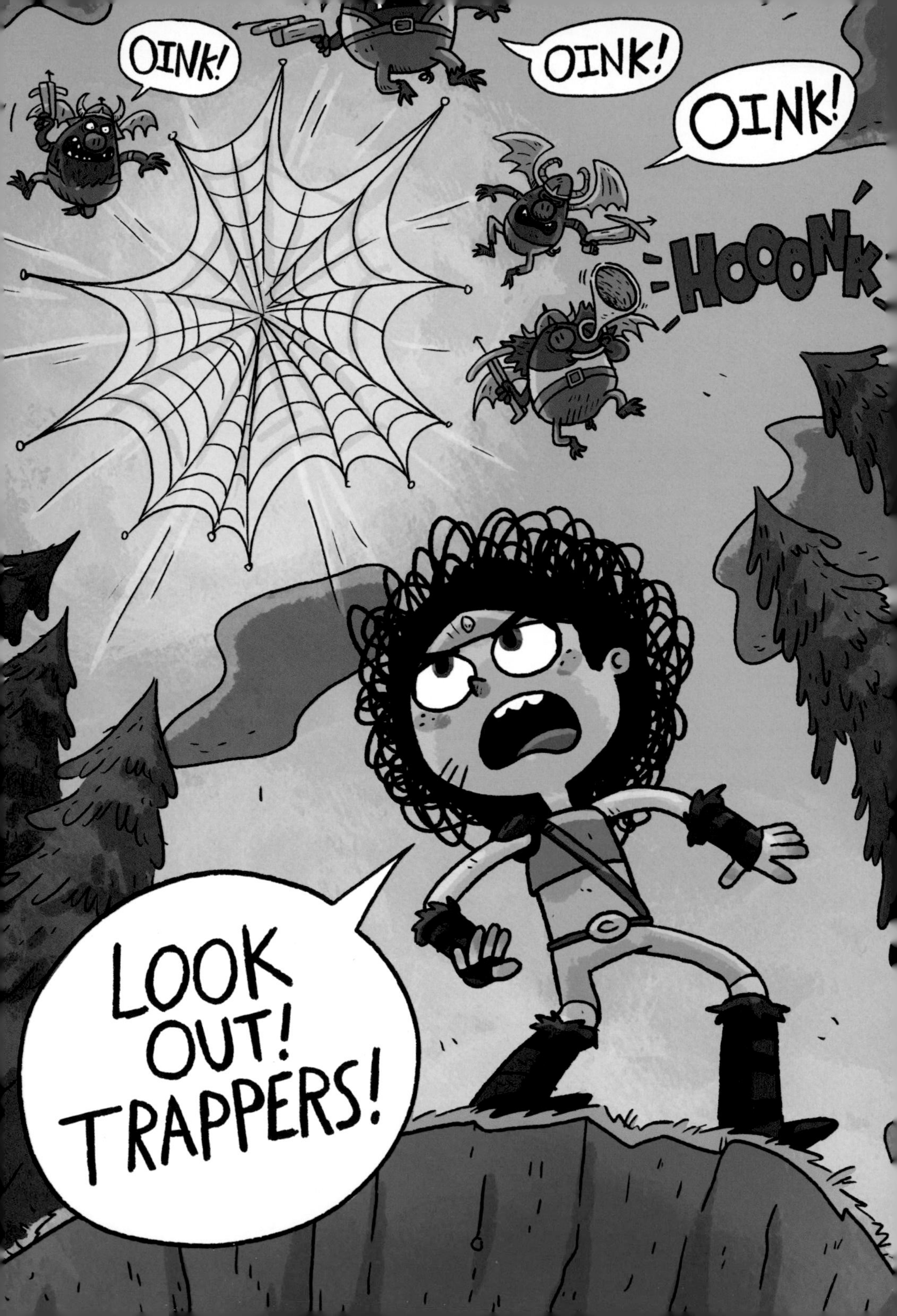
OINK!
OINK!
OINK!
HOOONK
LOOK OUT! TRAPPERS!

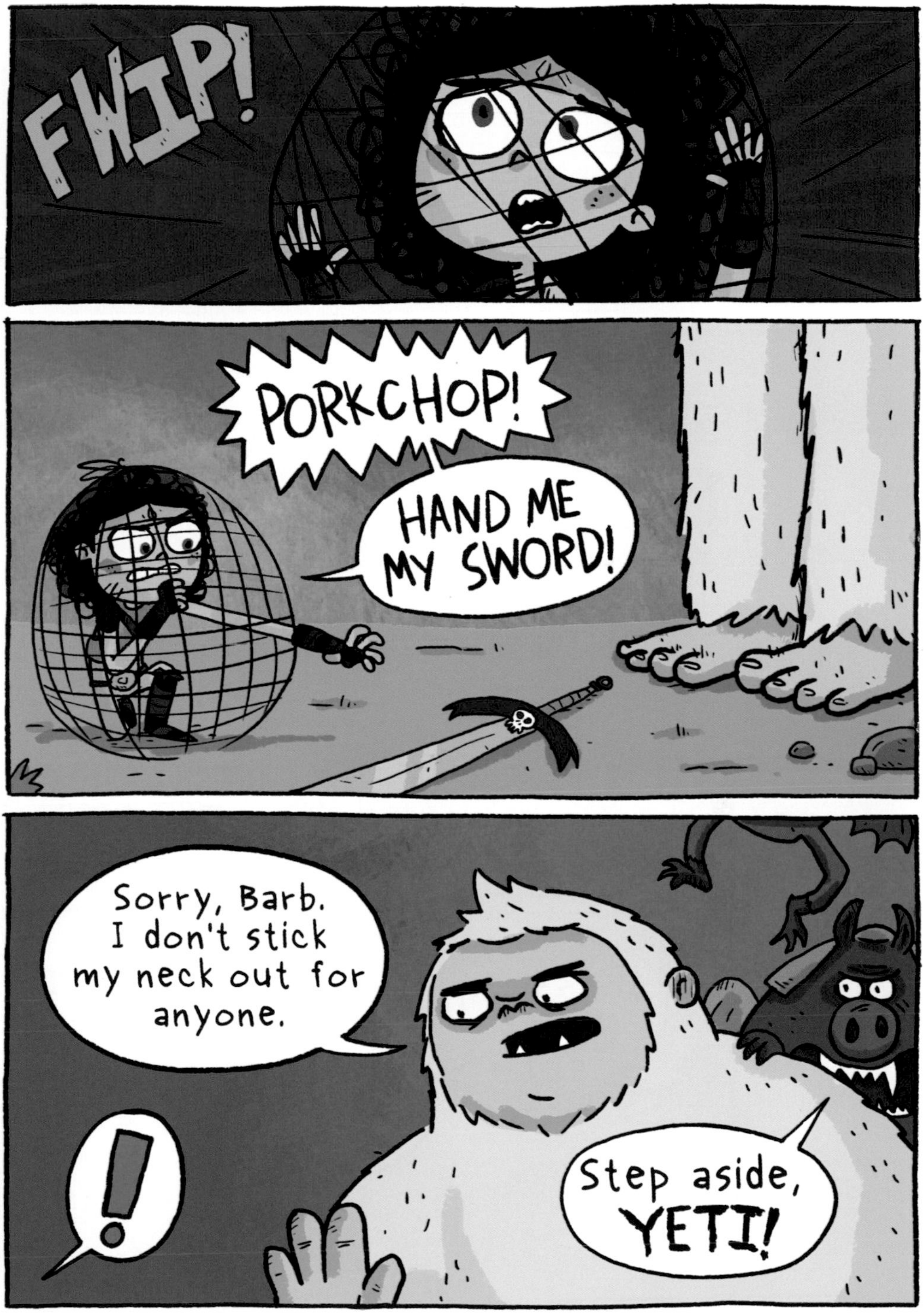
FWIP!
PORKCHOP!
HAND ME MY SWORD!
Sorry, Barb. I don't stick my neck out for anyone.
!
Step aside, YETI!

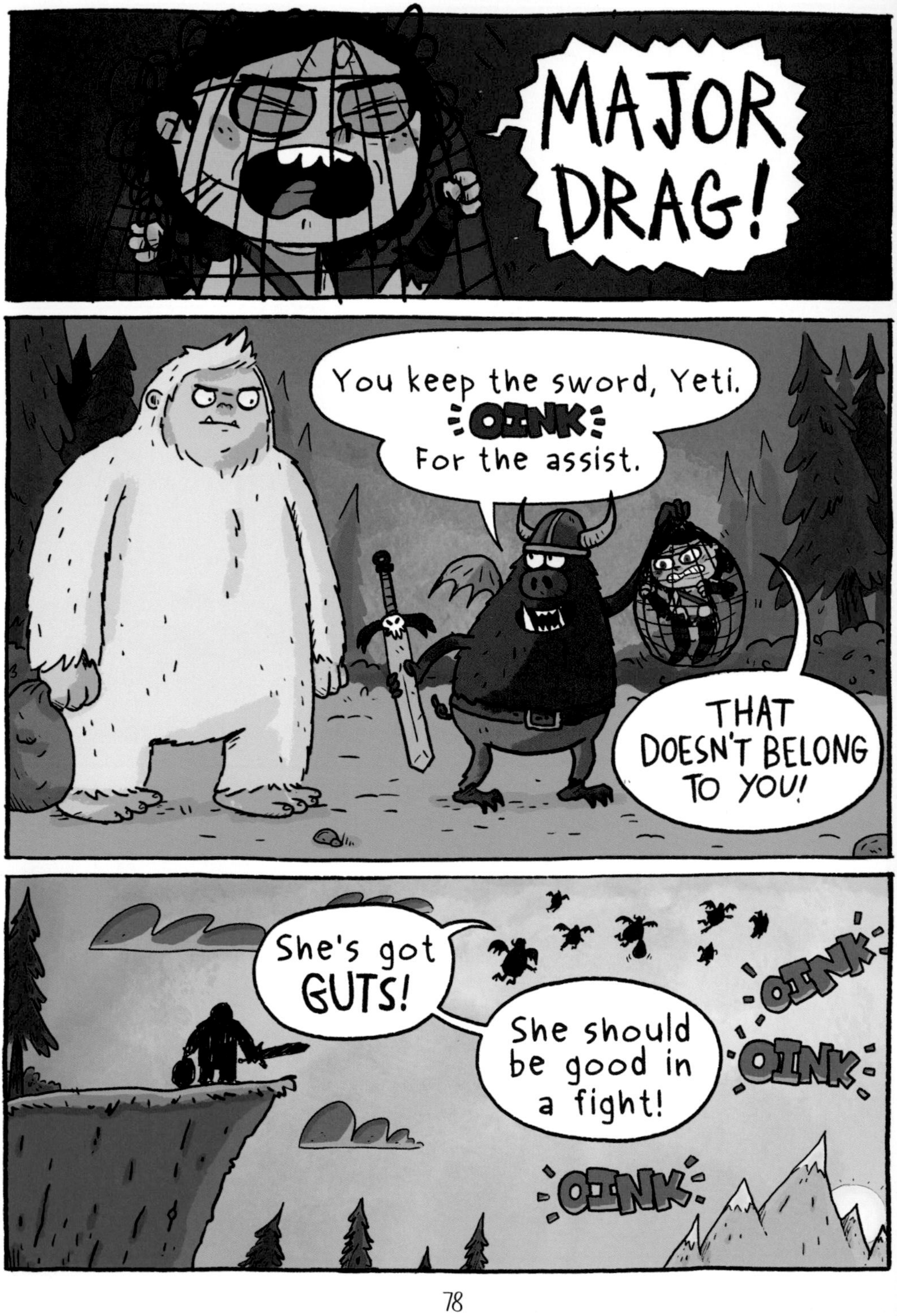
MAJOR DRAG!
You keep the sword, Yeti.
OINK
For the assist.
THAT DOESN'T BELONG TO YOU!
She's got GUTS!
She should be good in a fight!
OINK
OINK
OINK

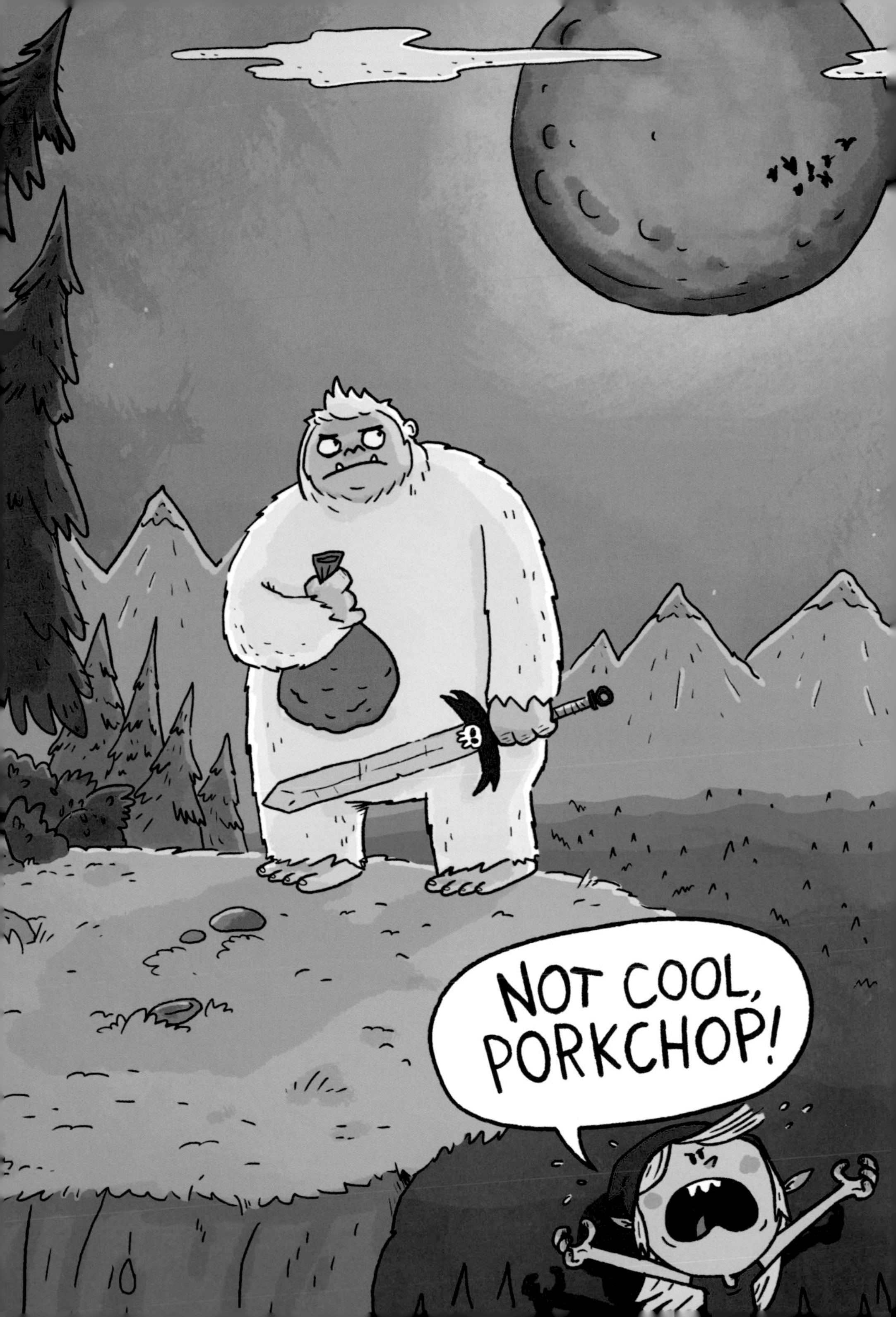
NOT COOL, PORKCHOP!

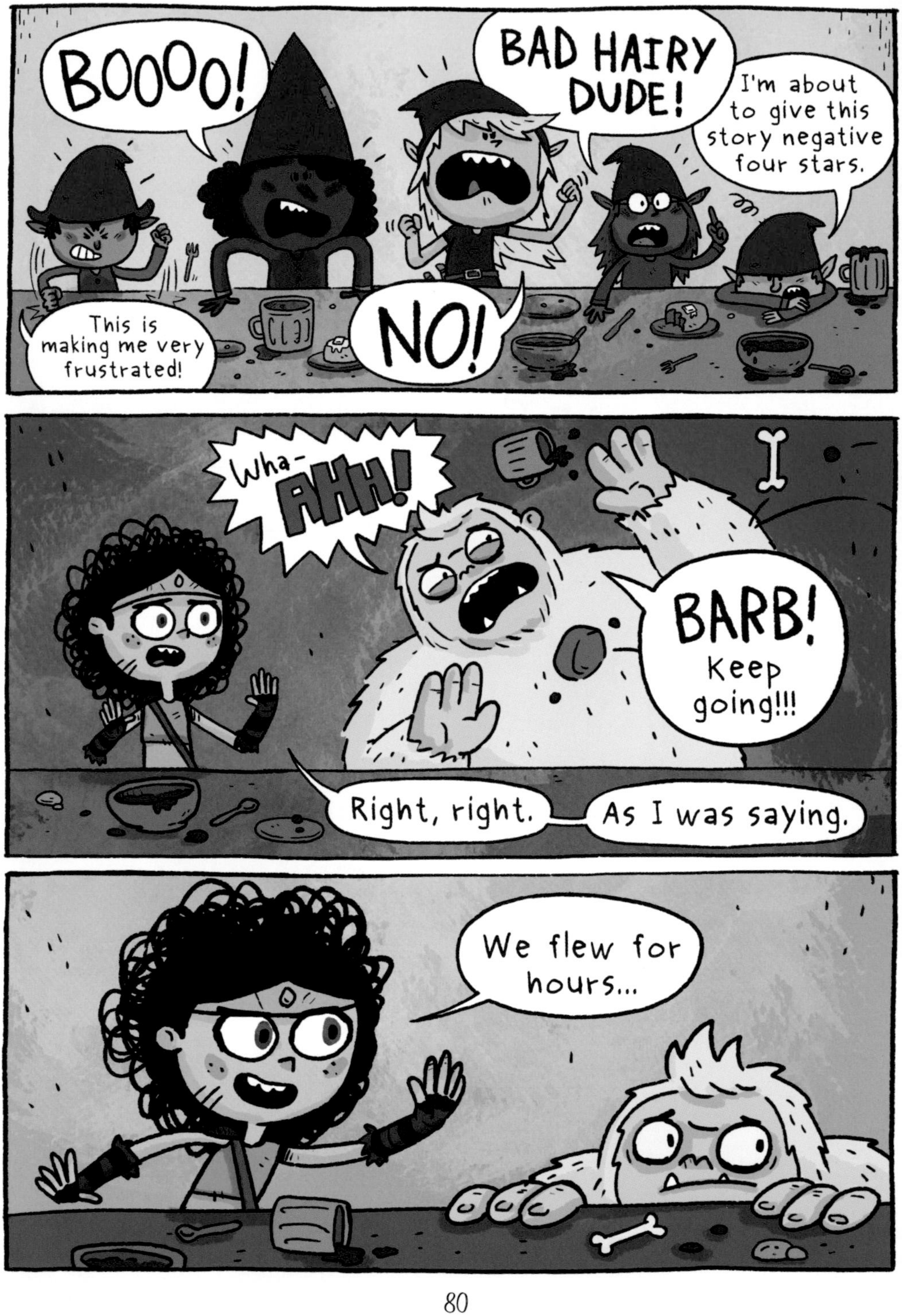
BOOOO!
BAD HAIRY DUDE!
I'm about to give this story negative four stars.
This is making me very frustrated!
NO!
Wha-AHH!
BARB! Keep going!!!
Right, right.
As I was saying.
We flew for hours...

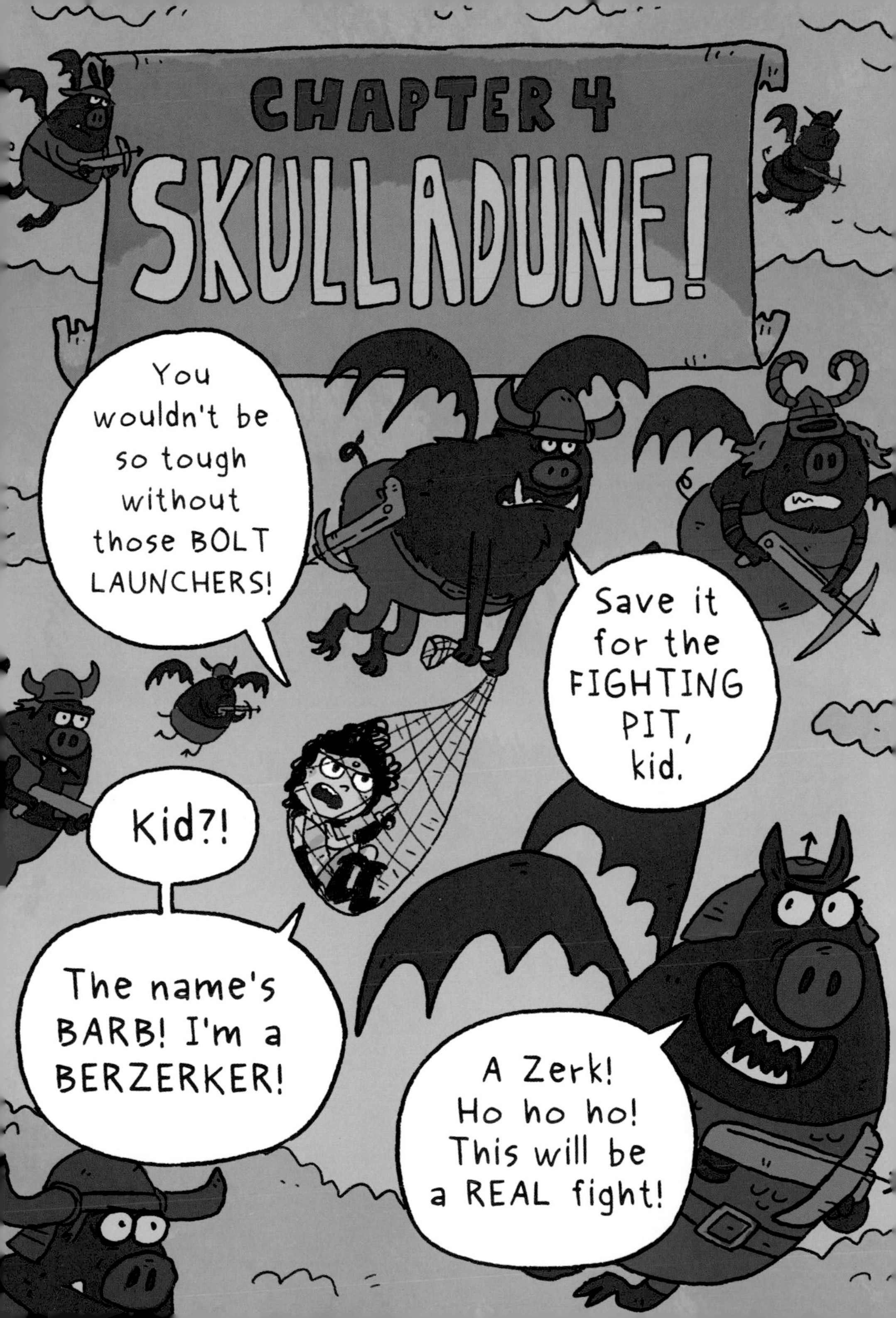
CHAPTER 4
SKULLADUNE!
You wouldn't be so tough without those BOLT LAUNCHERS!
Save it for the FIGHTING PIT, kid.
Kid?!
The name's BARB! I'm a BERZERKER!
A Zerk! Ho ho ho! This will be a REAL fight!

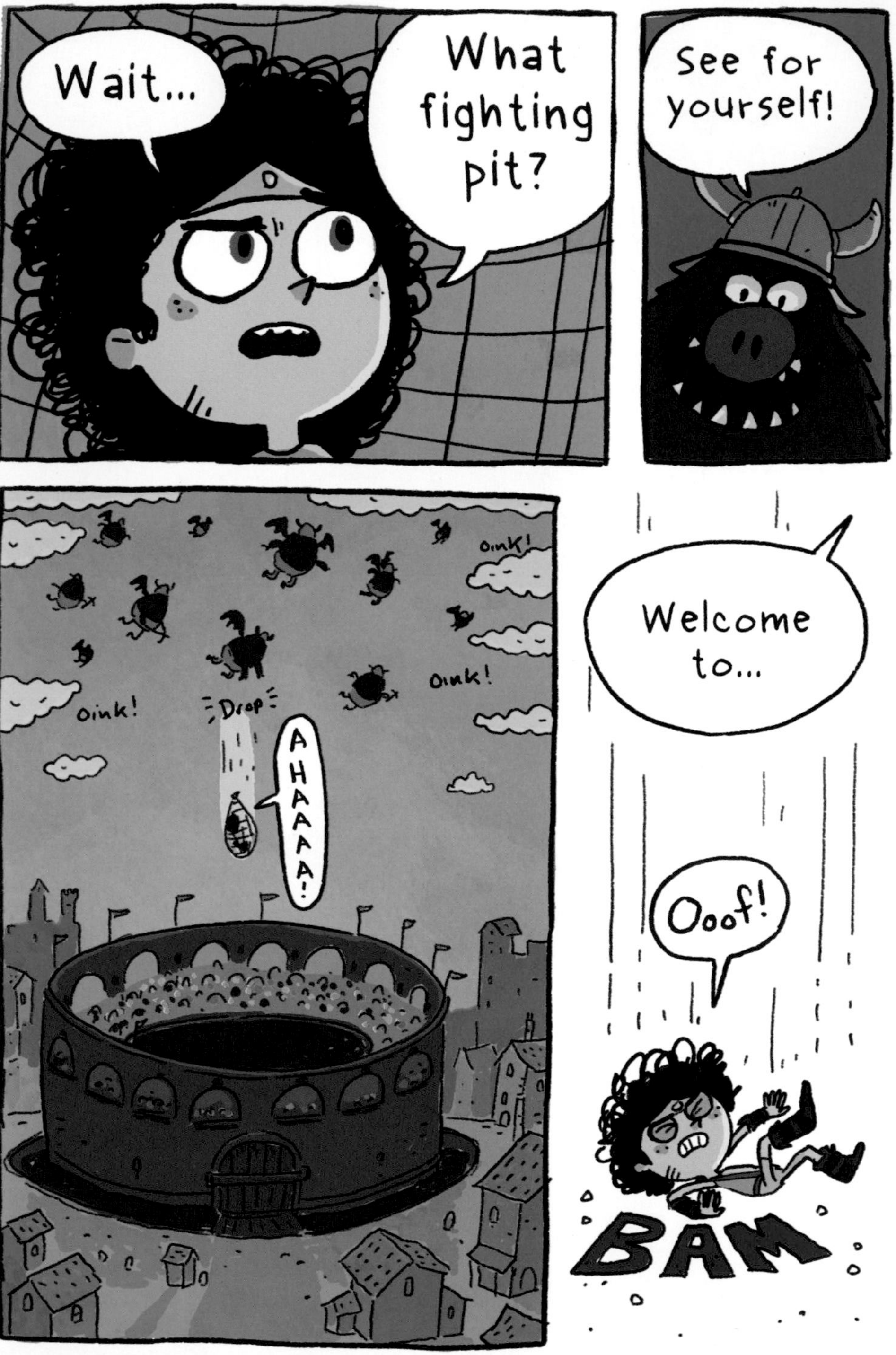
Wait...
What fighting pit?
See for yourself!
Oink!
Oink!
Oink!
Drop
AHAAAAA!
Welcome to...
Ooof!
BAM

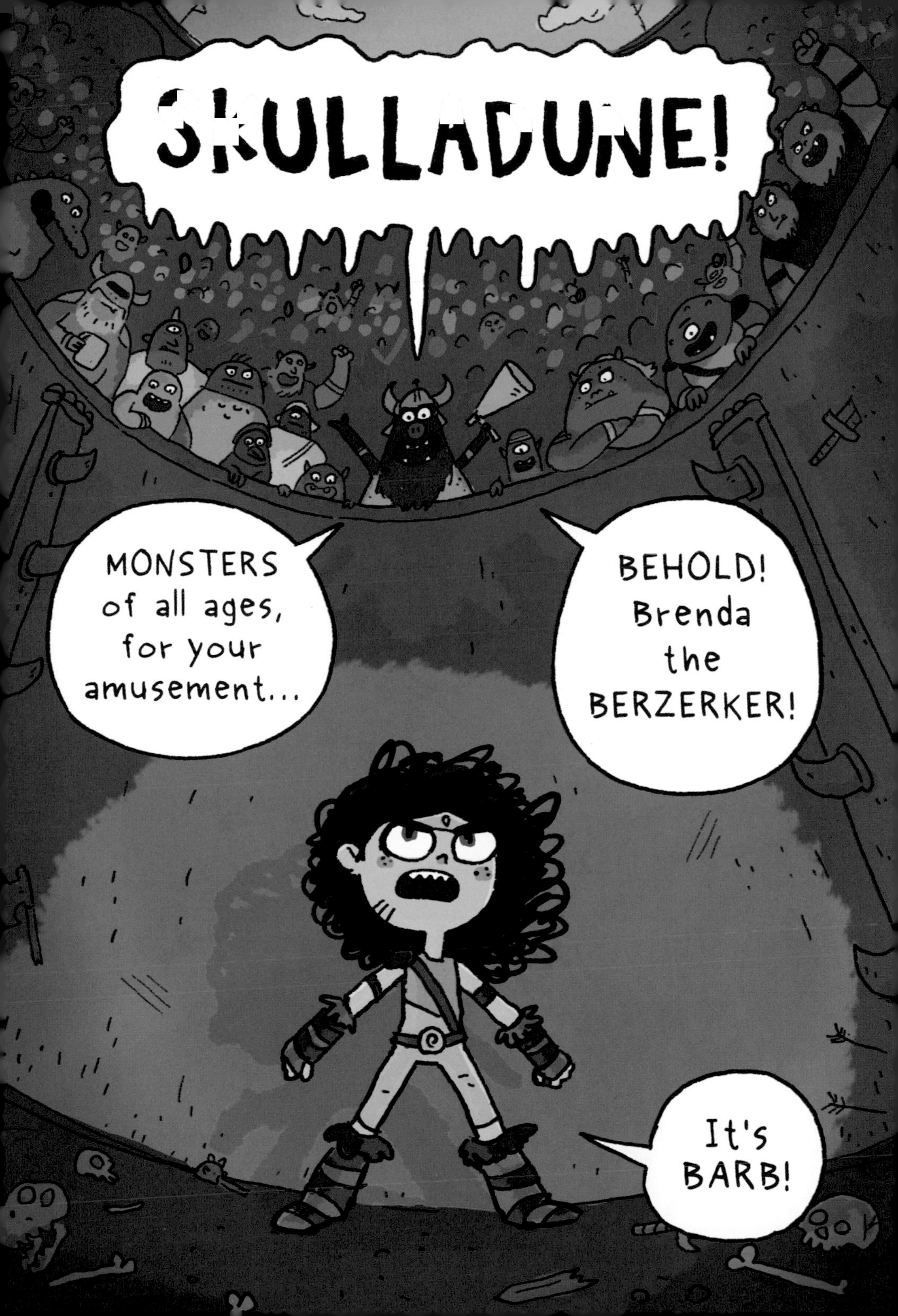
SKULLADUNE!
MONSTERS of all ages, for your amusement...
BEHOLD! Brenda the BERZERKER!
It's BARB!

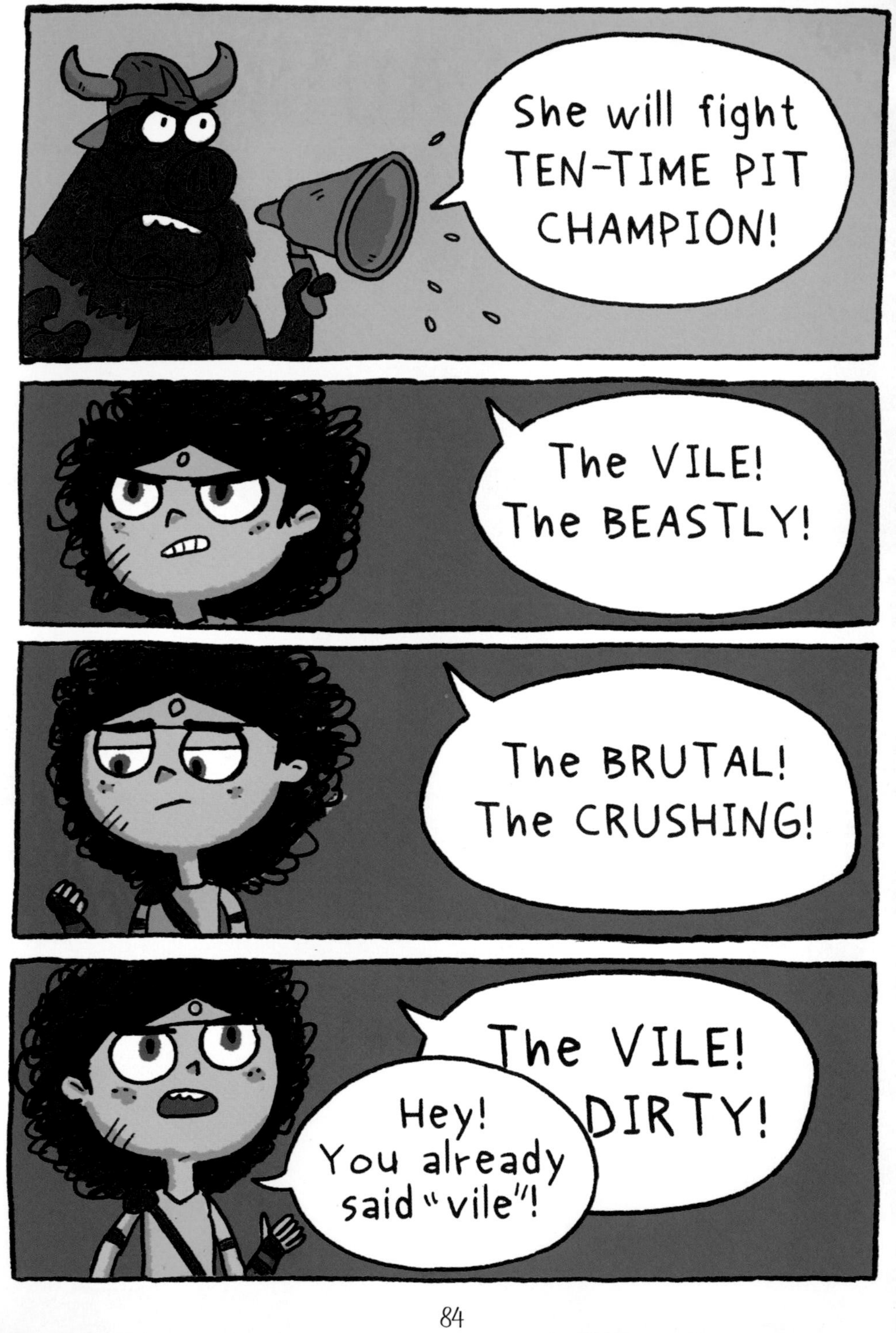
She will fight TEN-TIME PIT CHAMPION!
The VILE! The BEASTLY!
The BRUTAL! The CRUSHING!
The VILE!
DIRTY!
Hey! You already said "vile"!

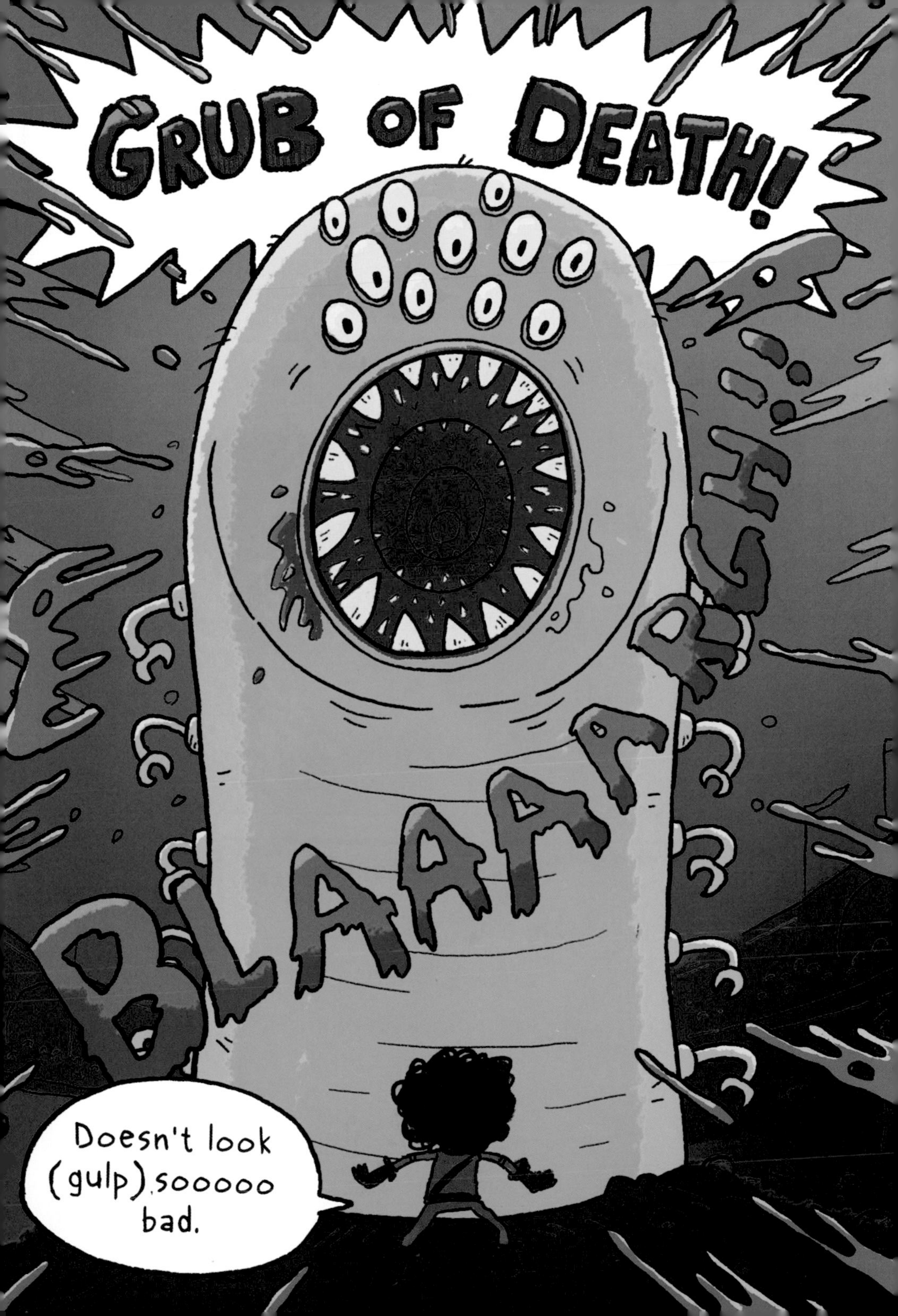
GRUB OF DEATH!
BLAAAARGH!
Doesn't look (gulp) sooooo bad.

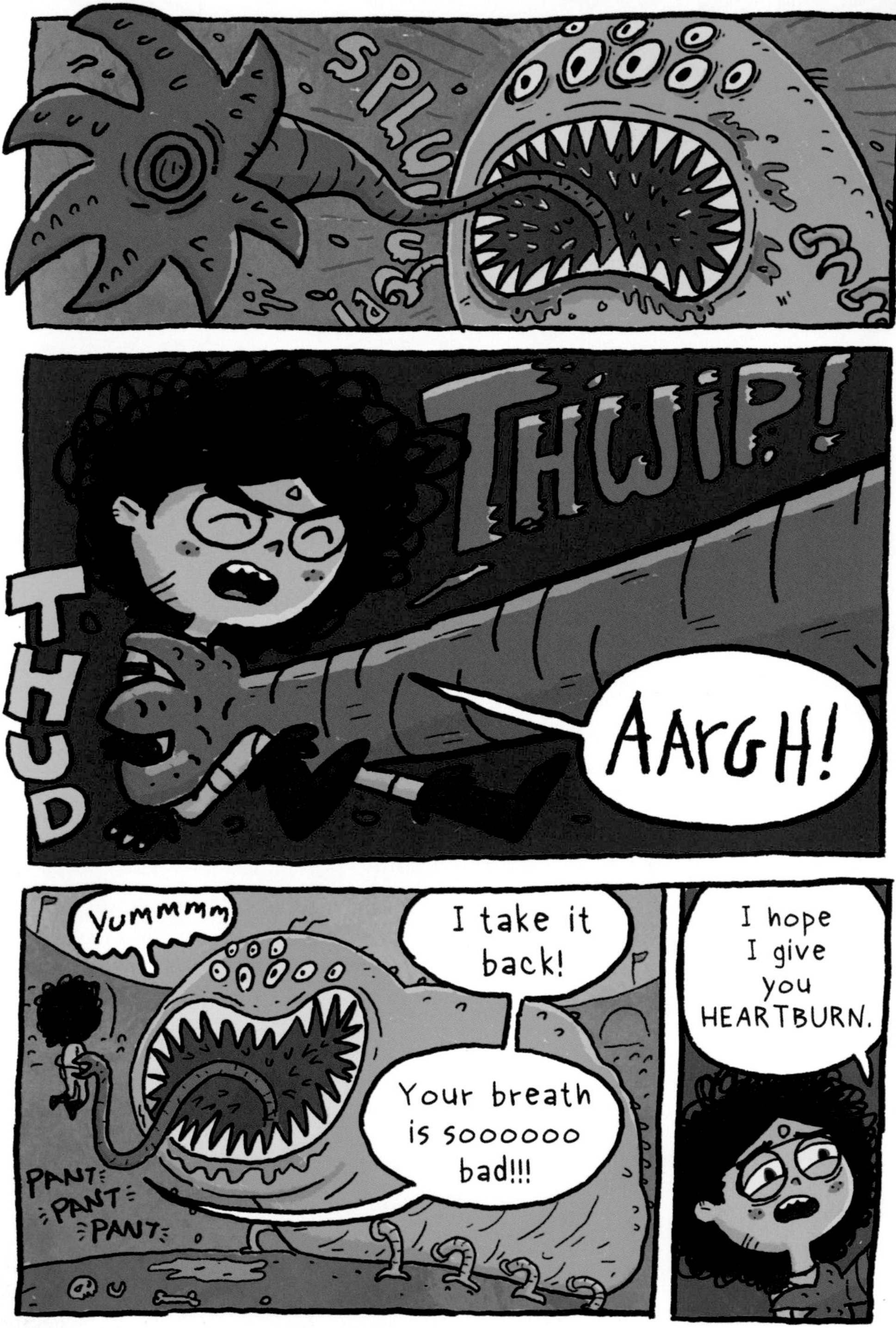
SPLUCK
THWIP!
THUD
AARGH!
yummmm
I take it back!
Your breath is soooooo bad!!!
PANT PANT PANT
I hope I give you HEARTBURN.

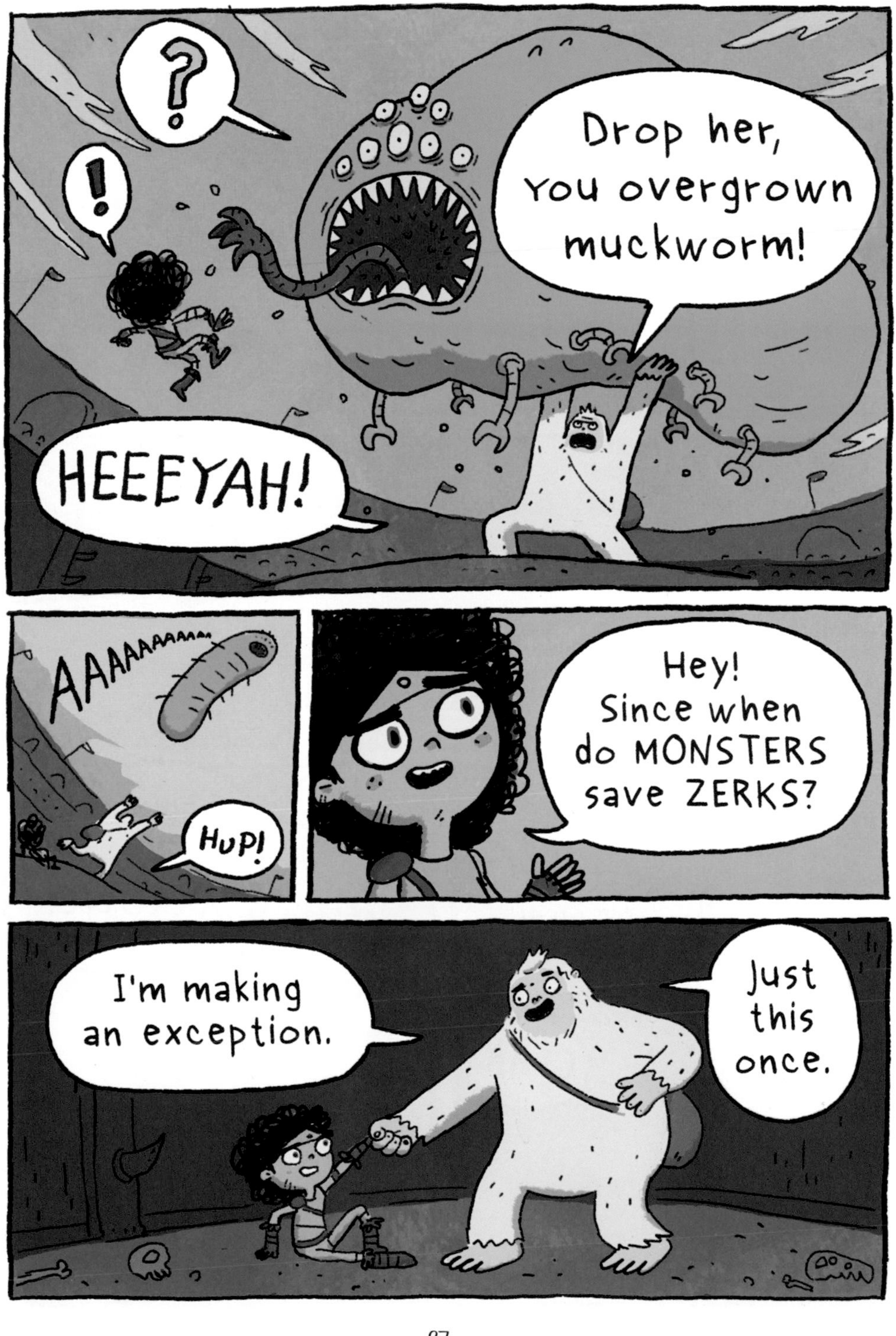
?
!
Drop her, You overgrown muckworm!
HEEEYAH!
AAAAAAAAAA
HUP!
Hey! Since when do MONSTERS save ZERKS?
I'm making an exception.
Just this once.

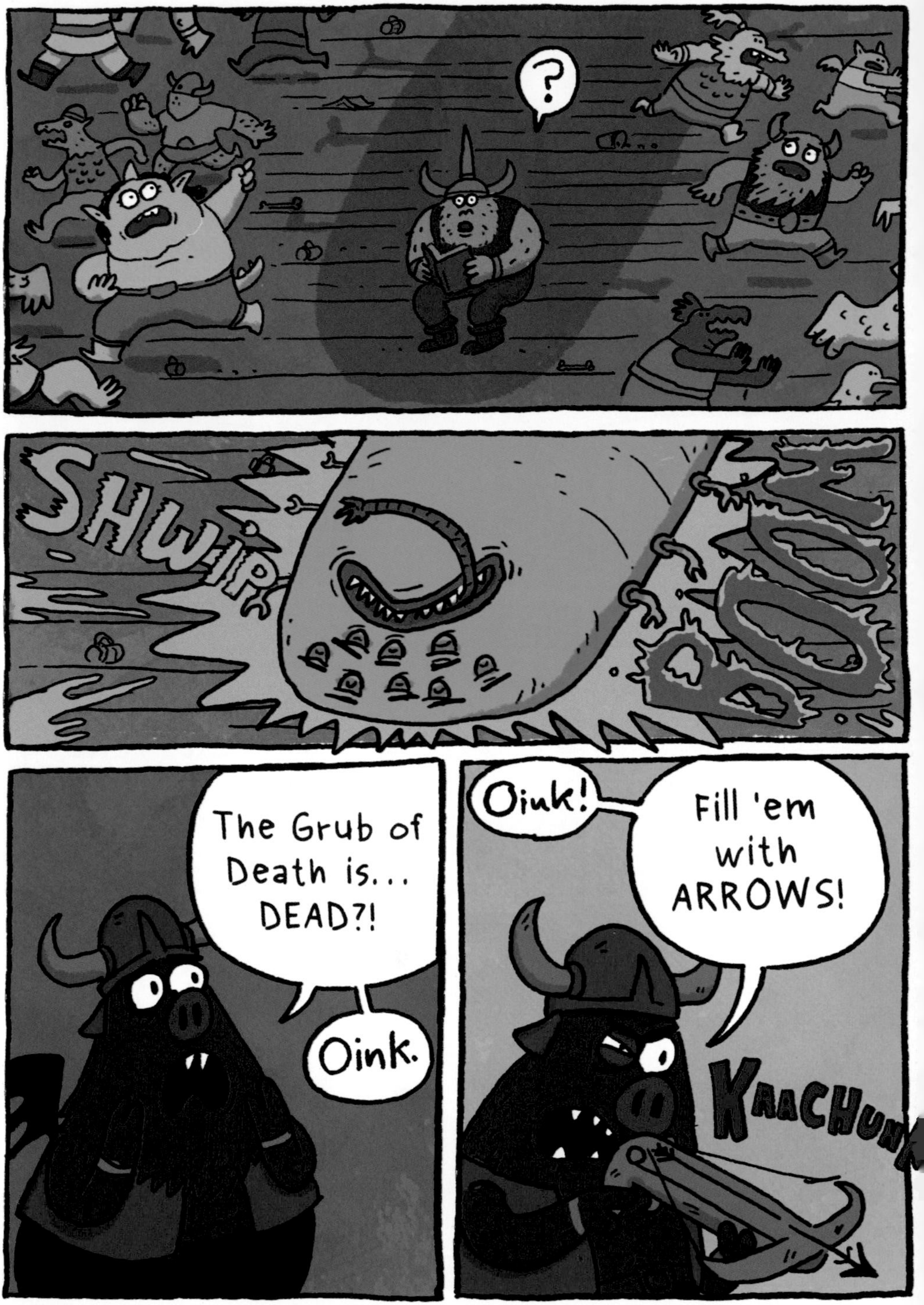
?
SHWIP
BOOM
The Grub of Death is... DEAD?!
Oink.
Oink!
Fill 'em with ARROWS!
KAACHUNK

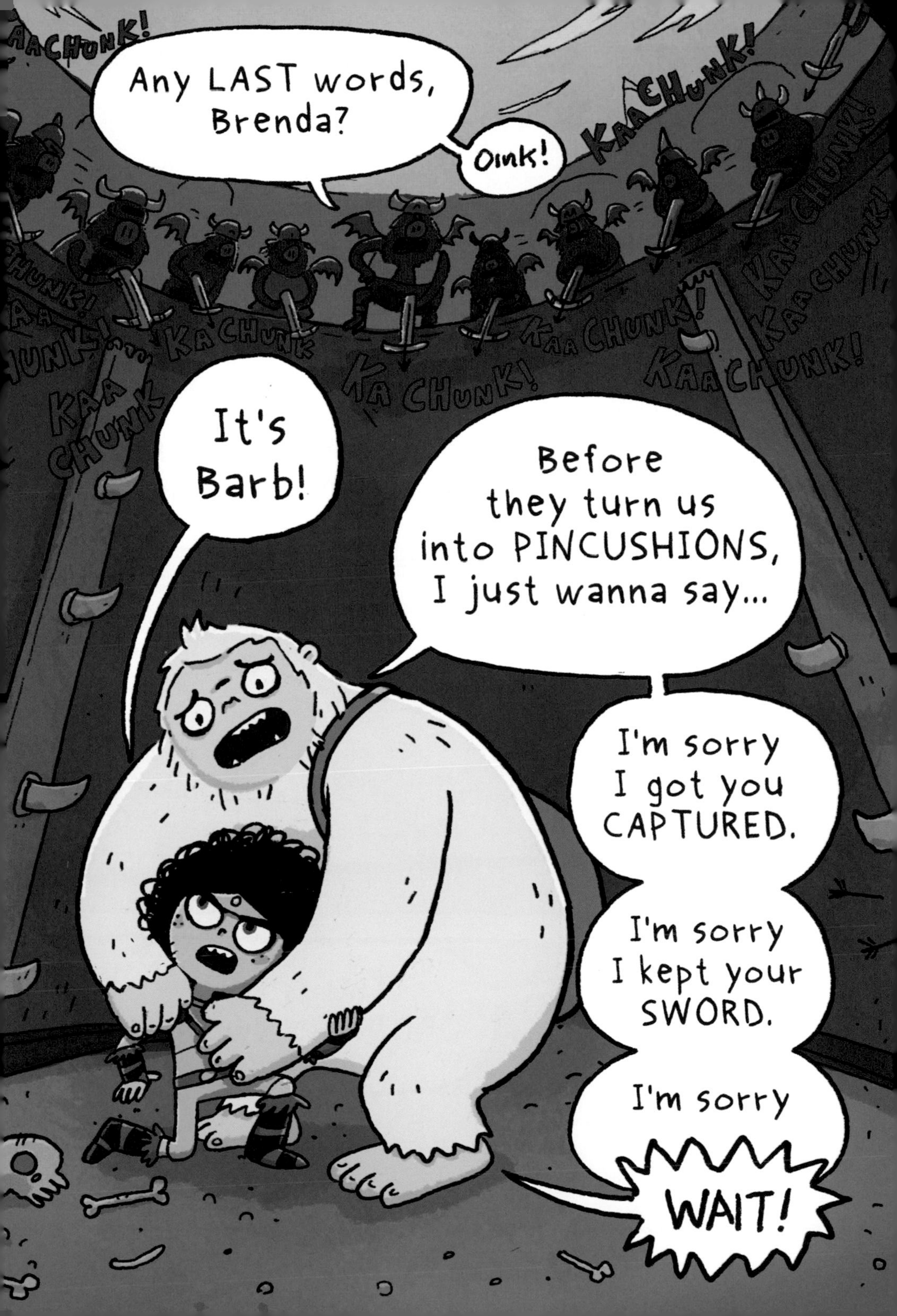
KAACHUNK!
Any LAST words, Brenda?
Oink!
KAACHUNK!
KAACHUNK!
KA CHUNK
KA CHUNK!
KAA CHUNK!
KAA CHUNK!
KAA CHUNK
KAA CHUNK!
KAA CHUNK!
It's Barb!
Before they turn us into PINCUSHIONS, I just wanna say...
I'm sorry I got you CAPTURED.
I'm sorry I kept your SWORD.
I'm sorry
WAIT!

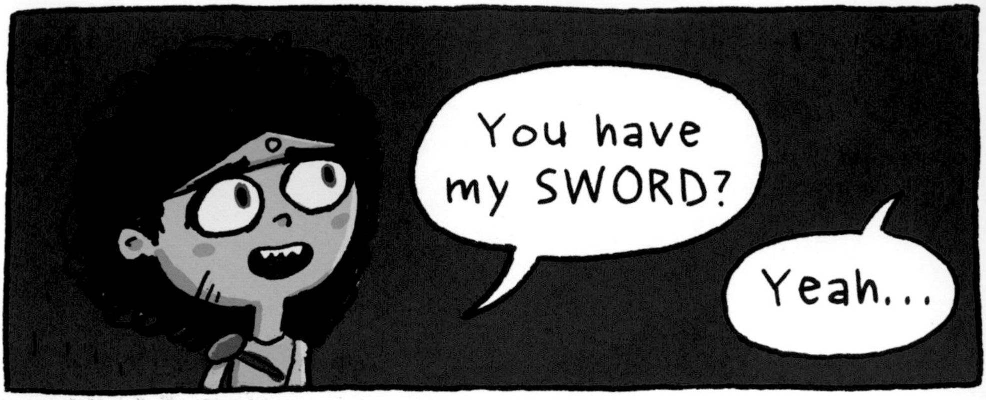
You have my SWORD?
Yeah...

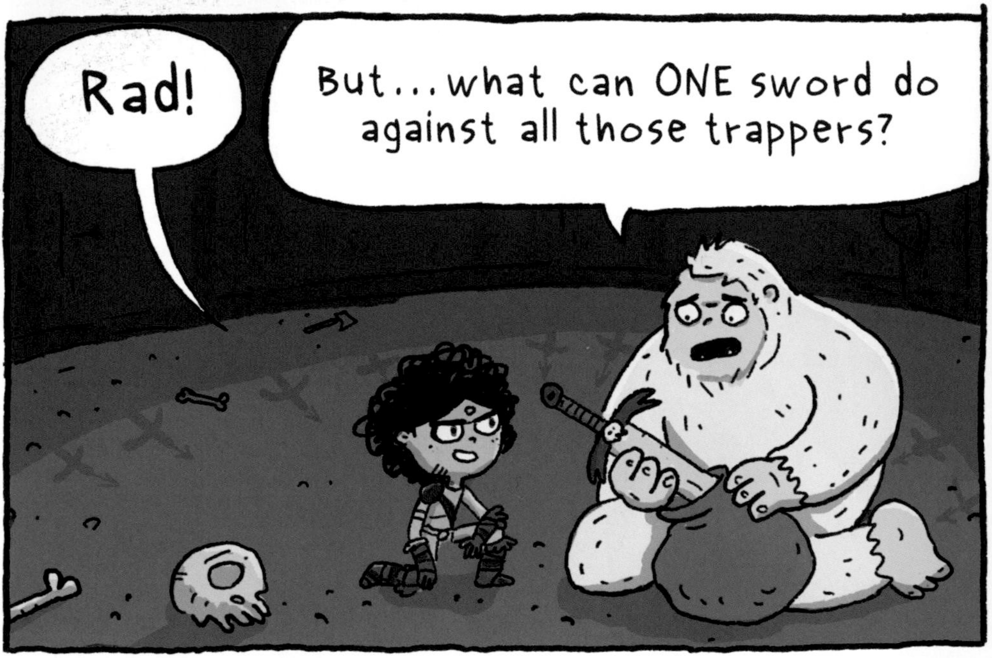
Rad!
But...what can ONE sword do against all those trappers?

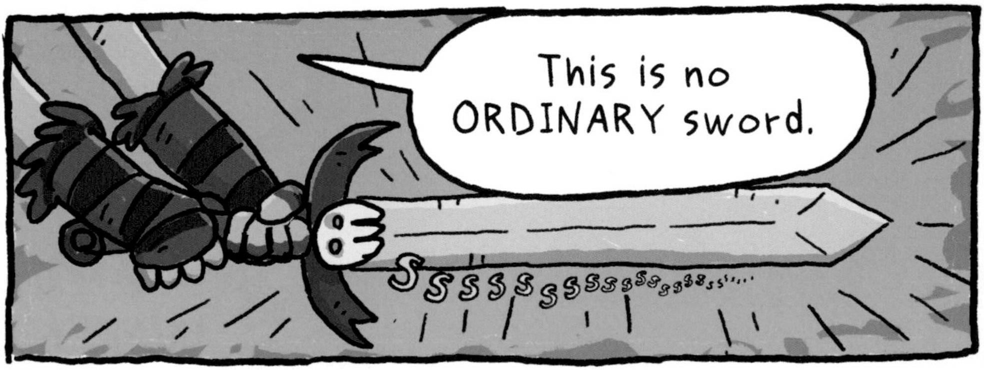
This is no ORDINARY sword.
SSSSSSSSSSSSSSSS

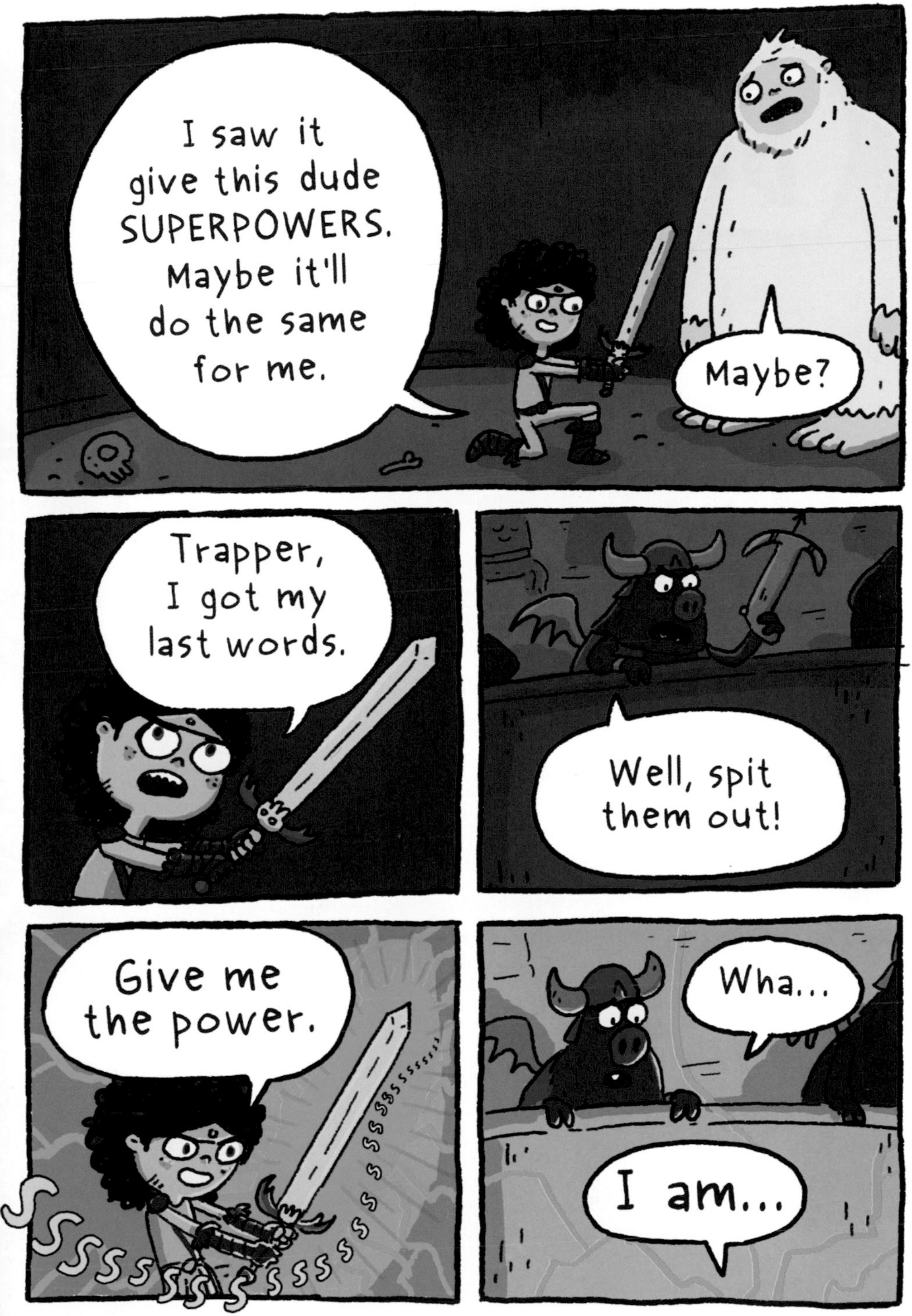
I saw it give this dude SUPERPOWERS. Maybe it'll do the same for me.
Maybe?
Trapper, I got my last words.
Well, spit them out!
Give me the power.
SSSSSSSSSSSSSSS
Wha...
I am...

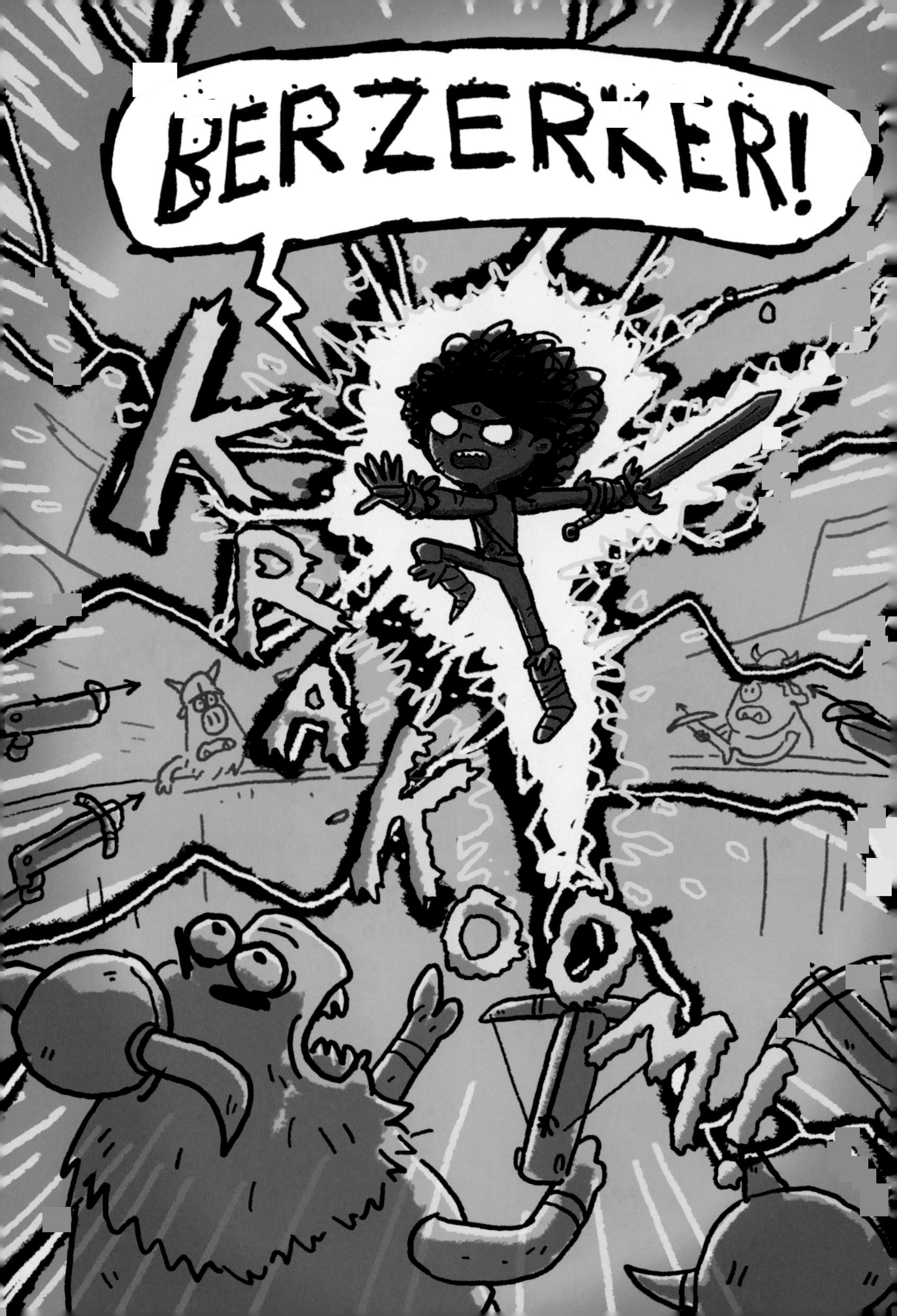
BERZERKER!
KRAKOOM

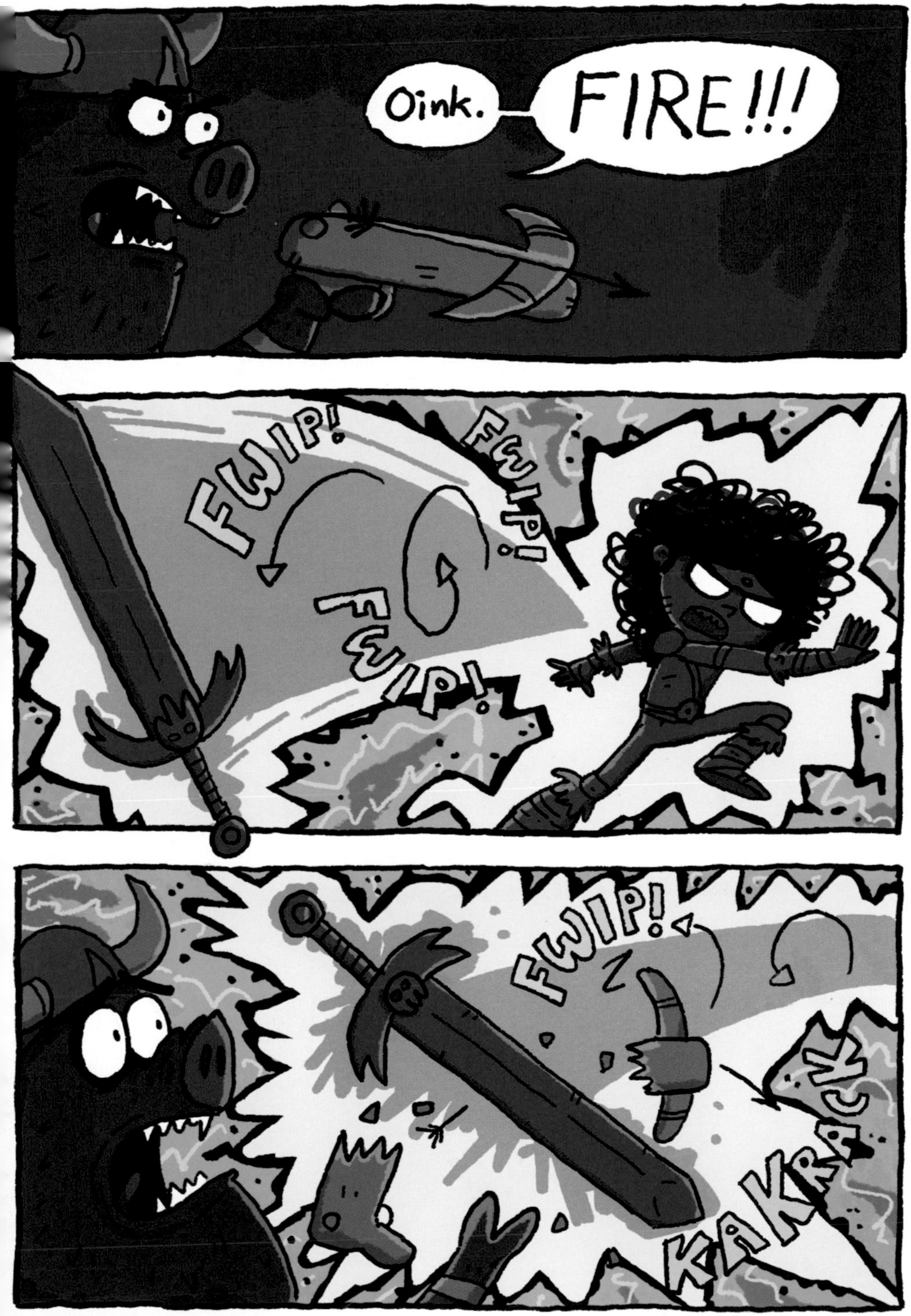
Oink.
FIRE!!!
FWIP!
FWIP!
FWIP!
FWIP!
KAKRACK

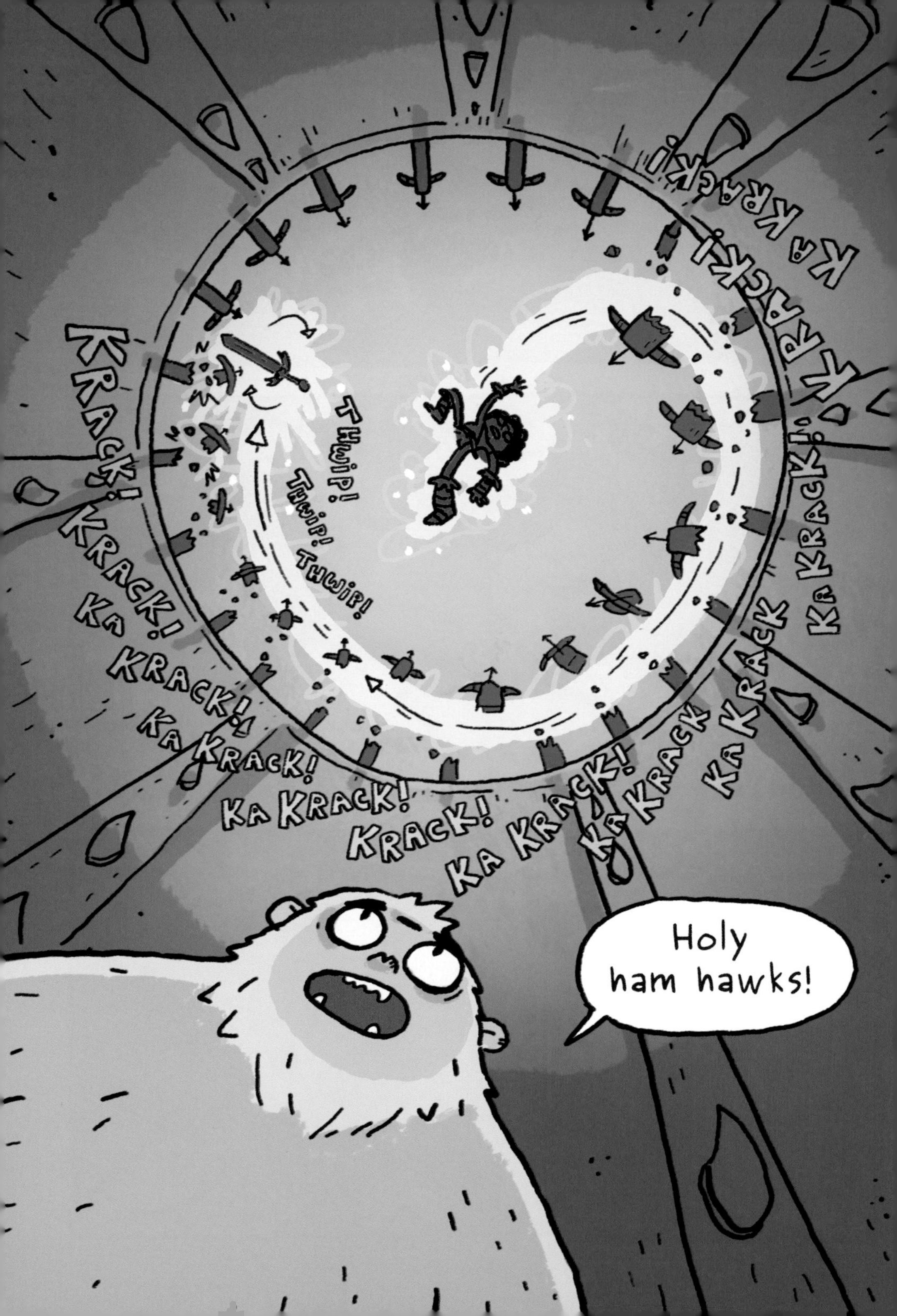
THWIP!
THWIP!
THWIP!
KRACK!
KRACK!
KRACK!
KA KRACK!
KA KRACK!
KA KRACK!
KA KRACK!
KRACK!
KA KRACK!
KA KRACK
KA KRACK
KA KRACK
KA KRACK!
KRACK!
KA KRACK!
KA KRACK!
Holy ham hawks!

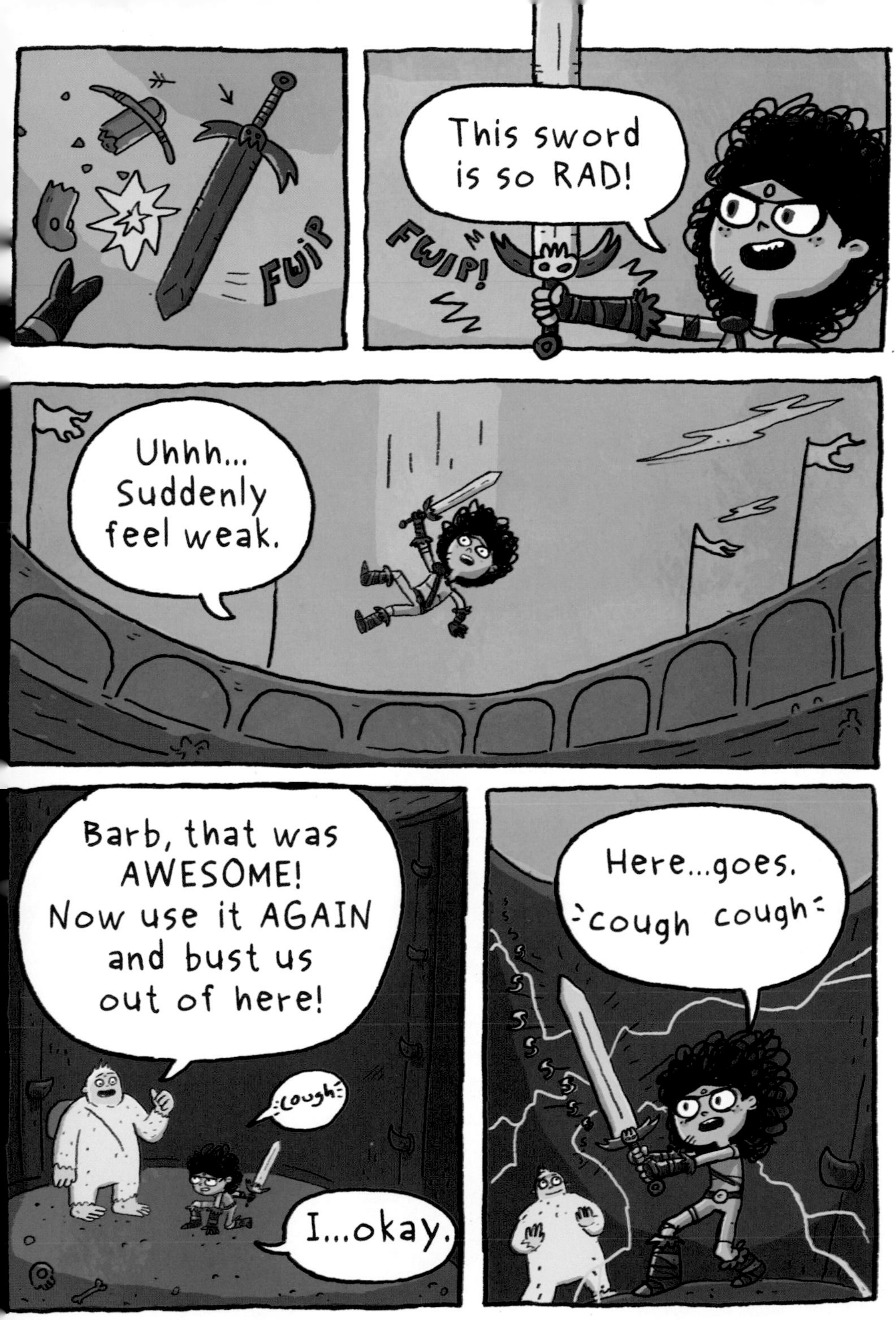
FWIP
This sword is so RAD!
FWIP!
Uhhh... Suddenly feel weak.
Barb, that was AWESOME! Now use it AGAIN and bust us out of here!
cough
I...okay.
Here...goes.
cough cough

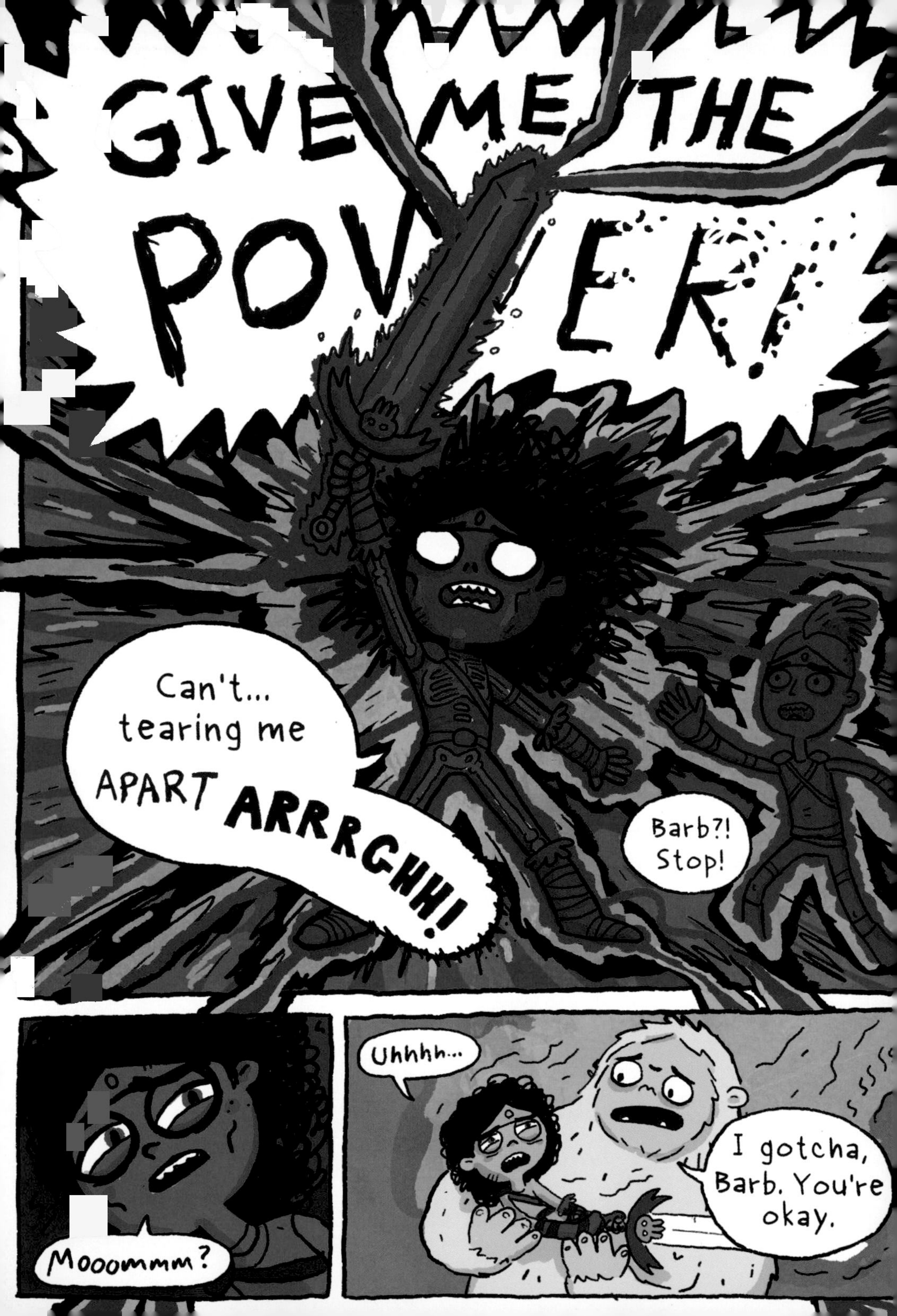
GIVE ME THE POWER!
Can't... tearing me APART ARRRGHH!
Barb?! Stop!
Mooommm?
Uhhhh...
I gotcha, Barb. You're okay.

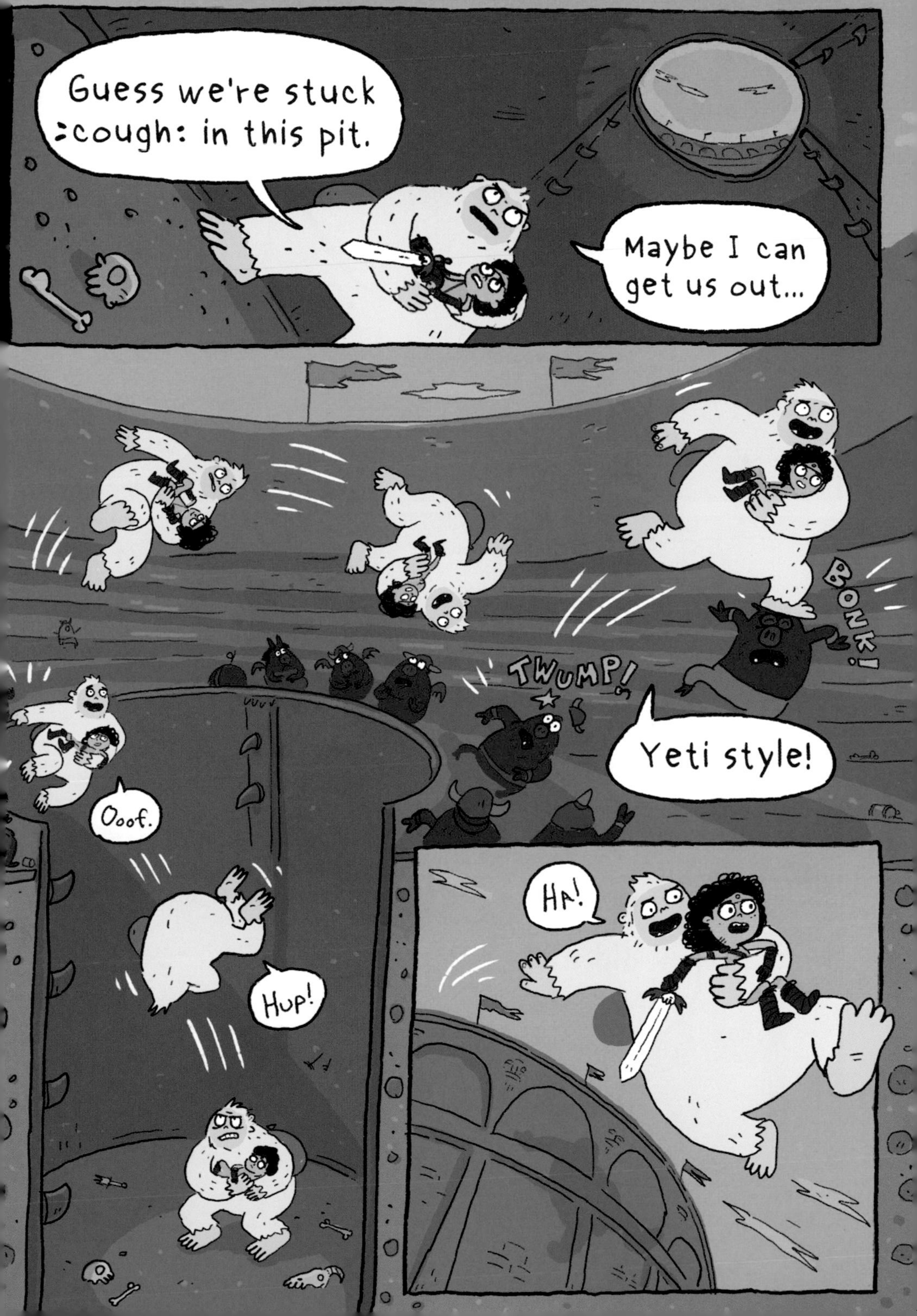
Guess we're stuck :cough: in this pit.
Maybe I can get us out...
BONK!
TWUMP!
Yeti style!
Ooof.
Hup!
HA!

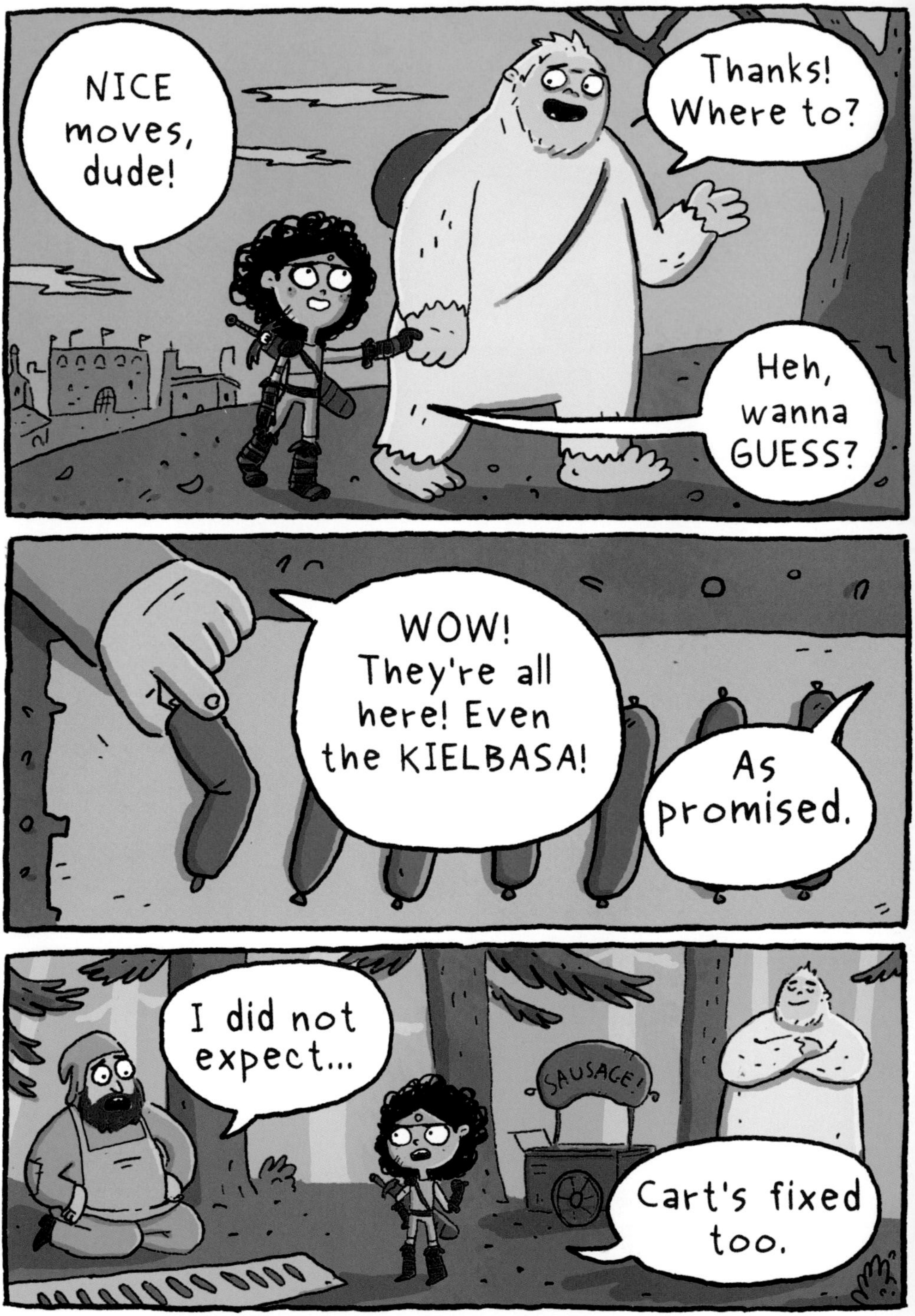

NICE moves, dude!
Thanks! Where to?
Heh, wanna GUESS?
WOW! They're all here! Even the KIELBASA!
As promised.
I did not expect...
SAUSAGE!
Cart's fixed too.

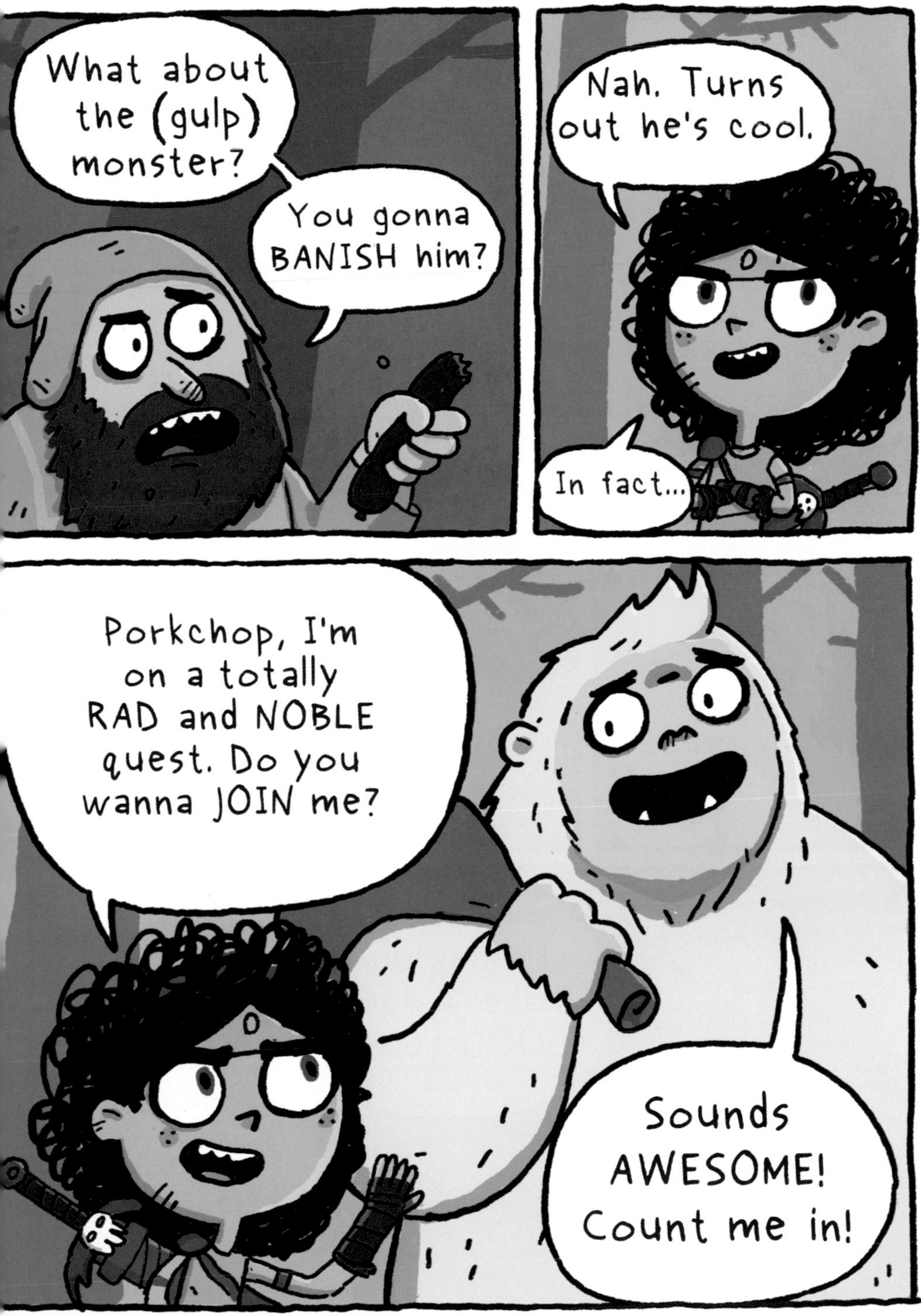
What about the (gulp) monster?
You gonna BANISH him?
Nah. Turns out he's cool.
In fact...
Porkchop, I'm on a totally RAD and NOBLE quest. Do you wanna JOIN me?
Sounds AWESOME! Count me in!

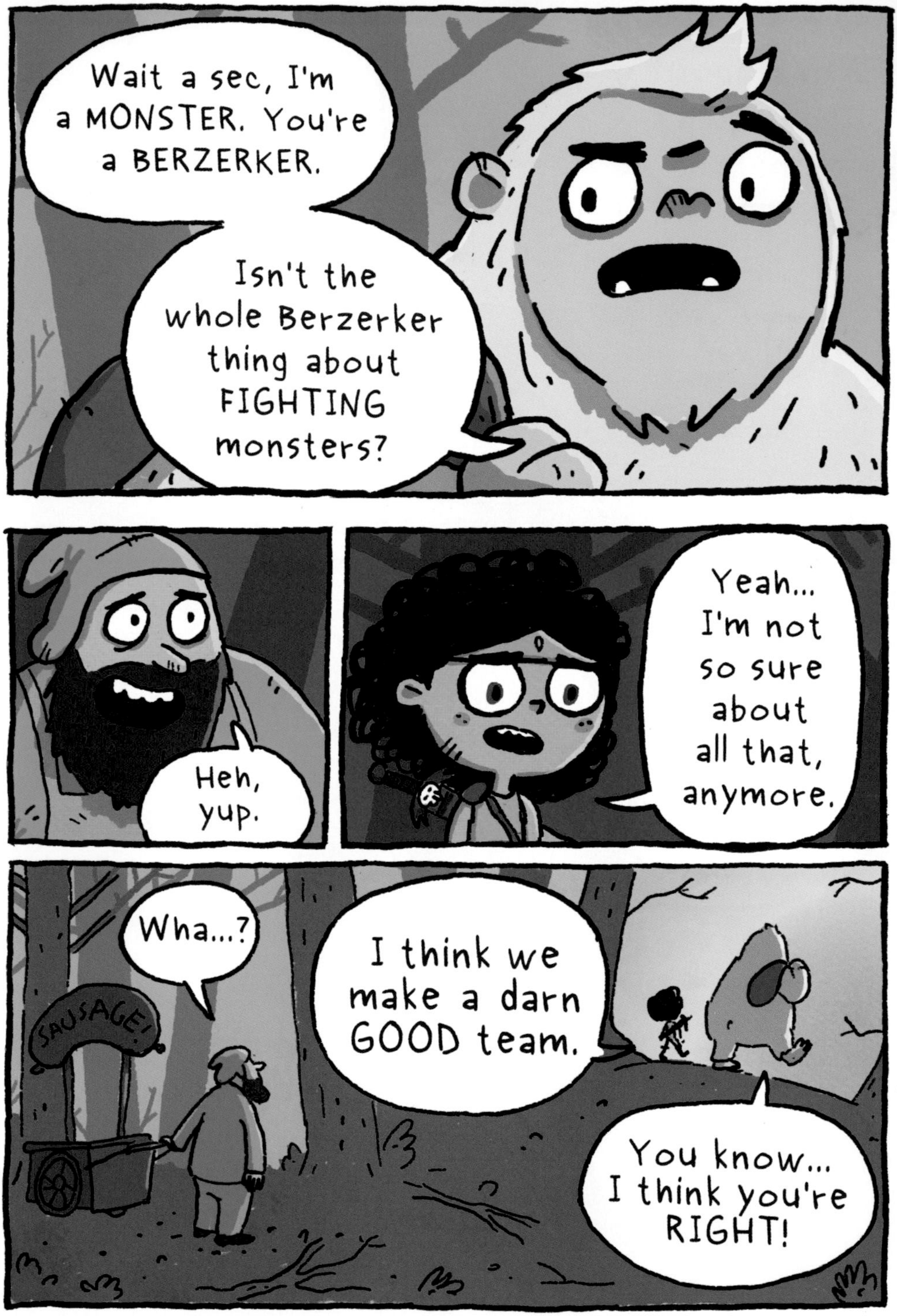
Wait a sec, I'm a MONSTER. You're a BERZERKER.
Isn't the whole Berzerker thing about FIGHTING monsters?
Heh, yup.
Yeah... I'm not so sure about all that, anymore.
Wha...?
SAUSAGE!
I think we make a darn GOOD team.
You know... I think you're RIGHT!

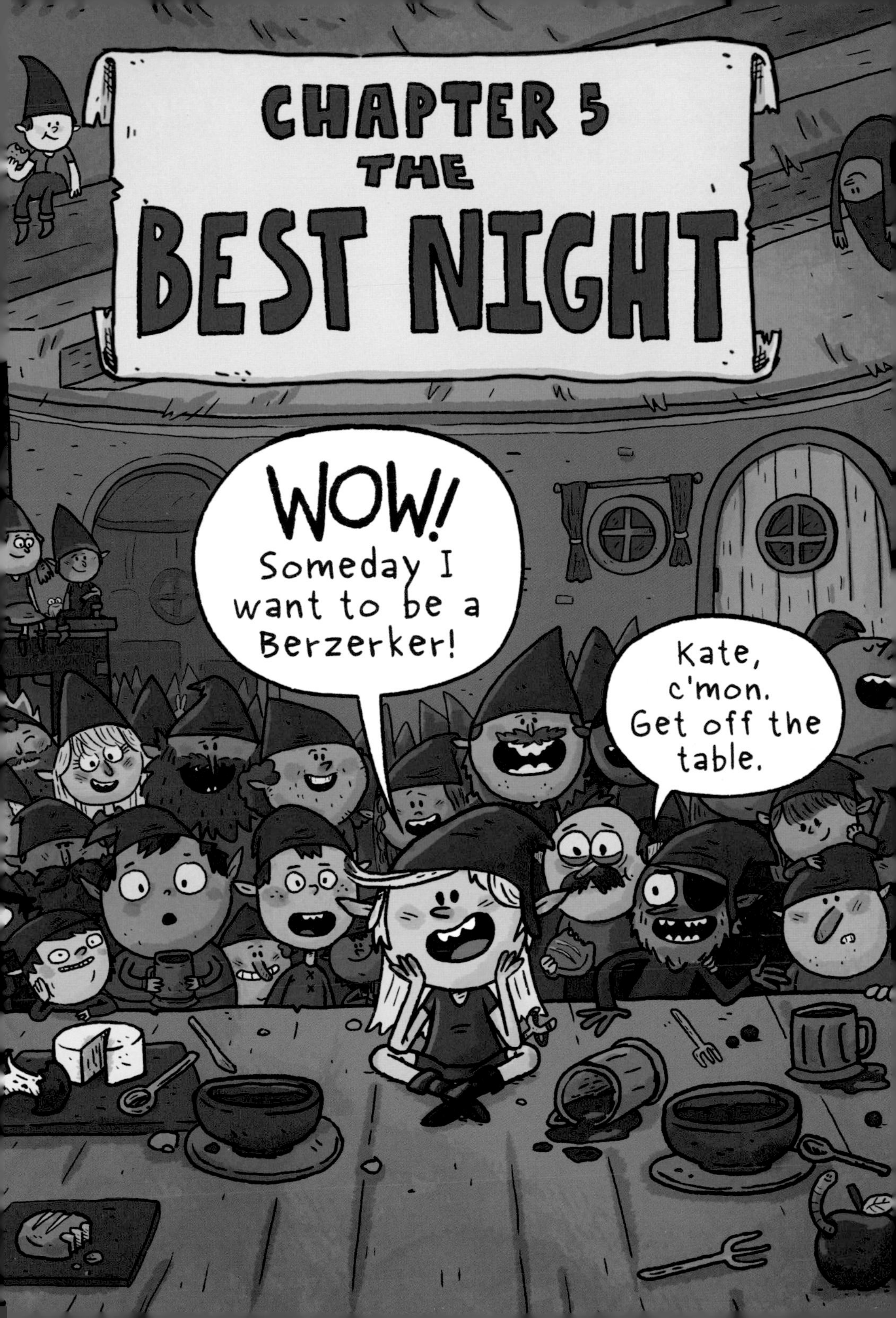
CHAPTER 5
THE
BEST NIGHT
WOW! Someday I want to be a Berzerker!
Kate, c'mon. Get off the table.

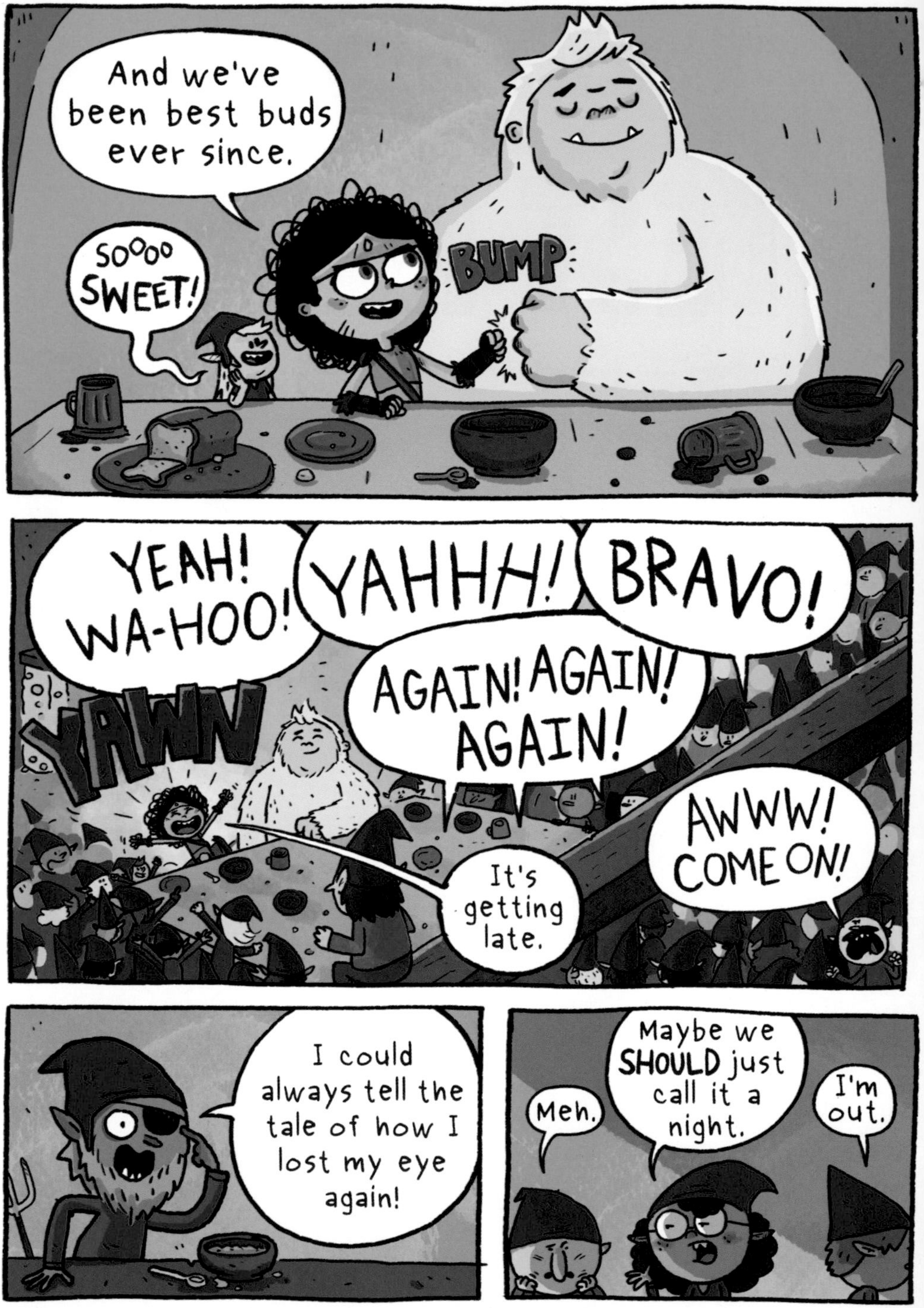
And we've been best buds ever since.
SOOOO SWEET!
BUMP
YEAH! WA-HOO!
YAHHH!
BRAVO!
AGAIN! AGAIN! AGAIN!
YAWN
It's getting late.
AWWW! COME ON!
I could always tell the tale of how I lost my eye again!
Meh.
Maybe we **SHOULD** just call it a night.
I'm out.

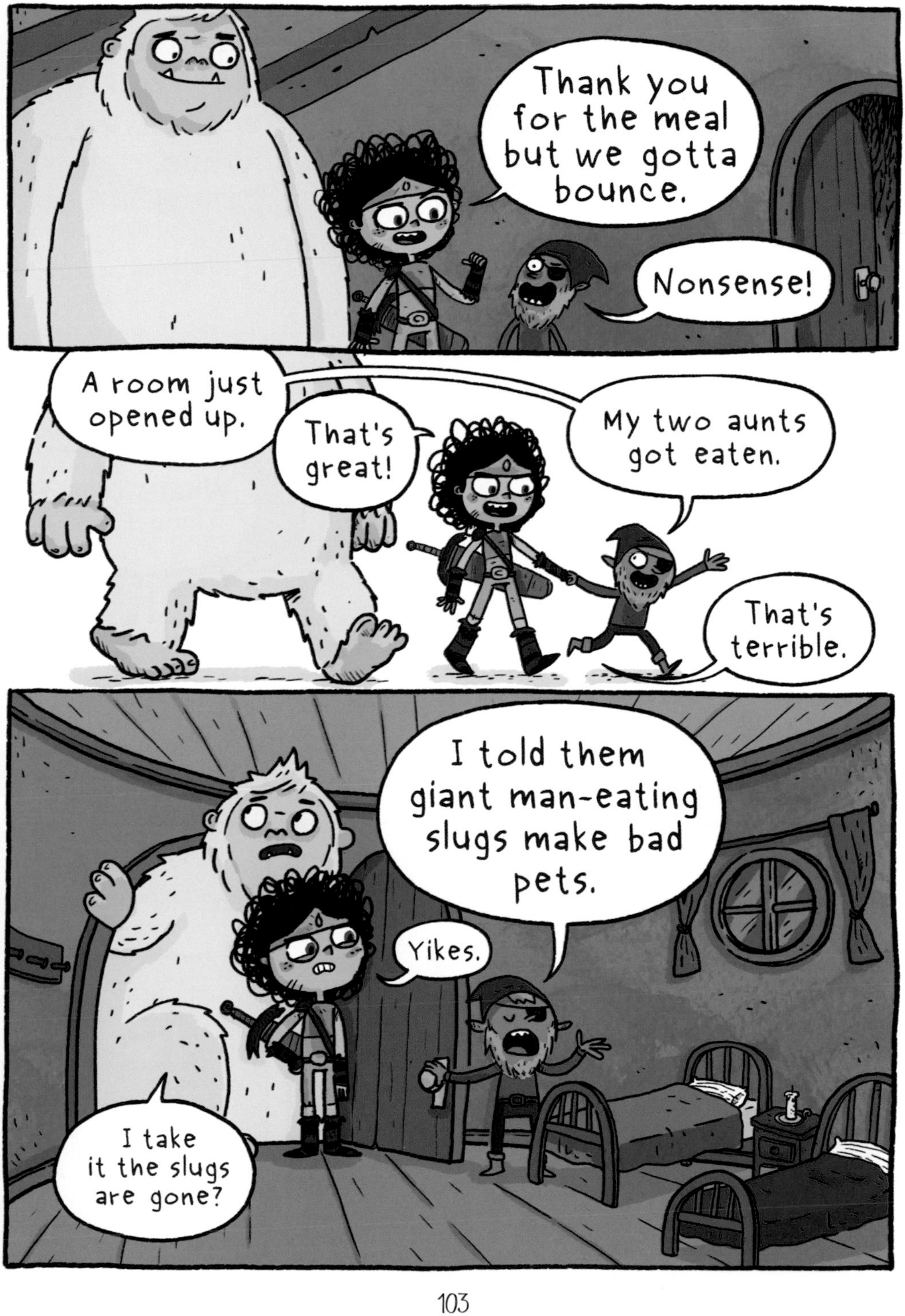
Thank you for the meal but we gotta bounce.
Nonsense!
A room just opened up.
That's great!
My two aunts got eaten.
That's terrible.
I told them giant man-eating slugs make bad pets.
Yikes.
I take it the slugs are gone?

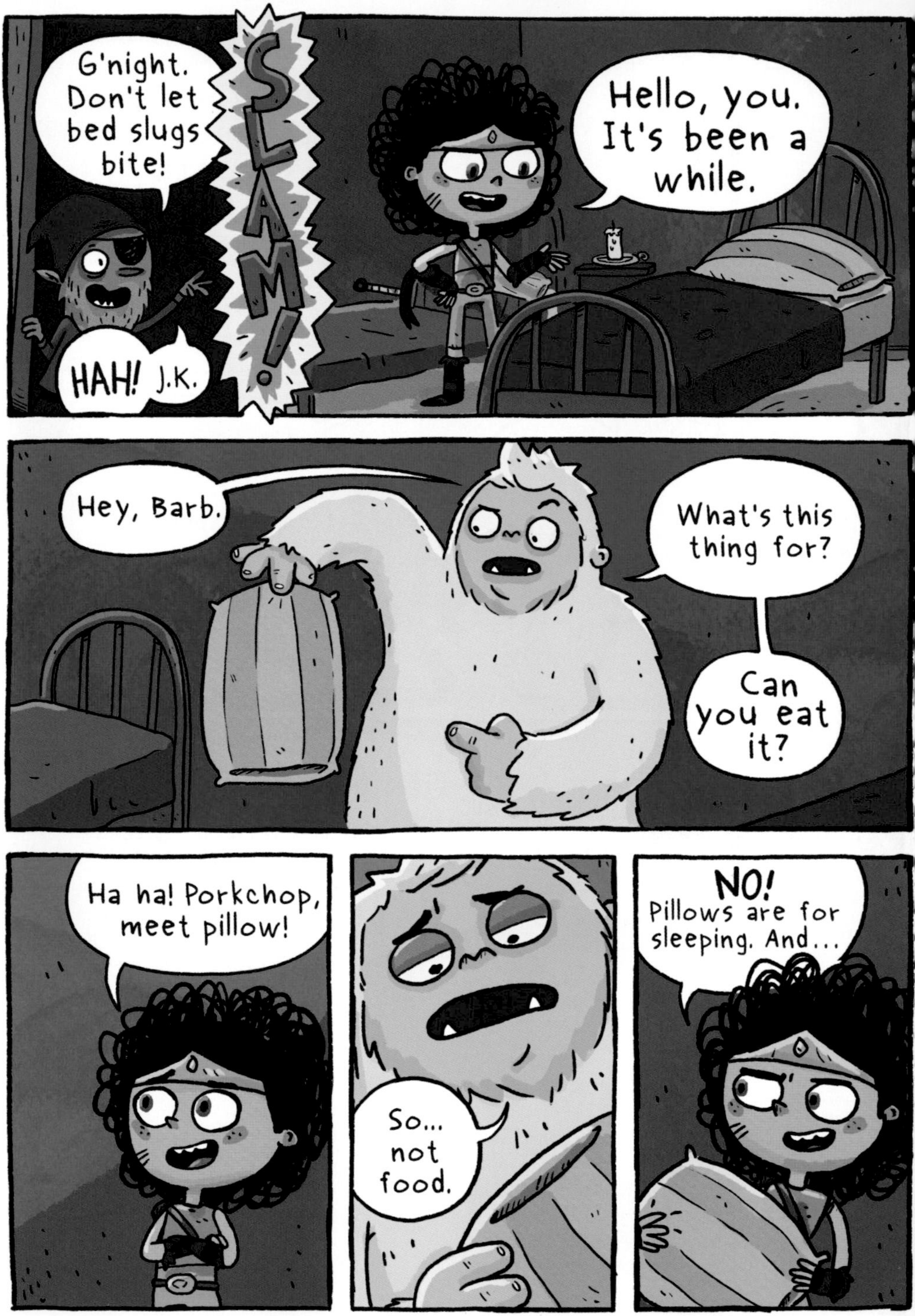
G'night. Don't let bed slugs bite!
HAH! J.K.
SLAM!
Hello, you. It's been a while.
Hey, Barb.
What's this thing for?
Can you eat it?
Ha ha! Porkchop, meet pillow!
So... not food.
NO! Pillows are for sleeping. And...

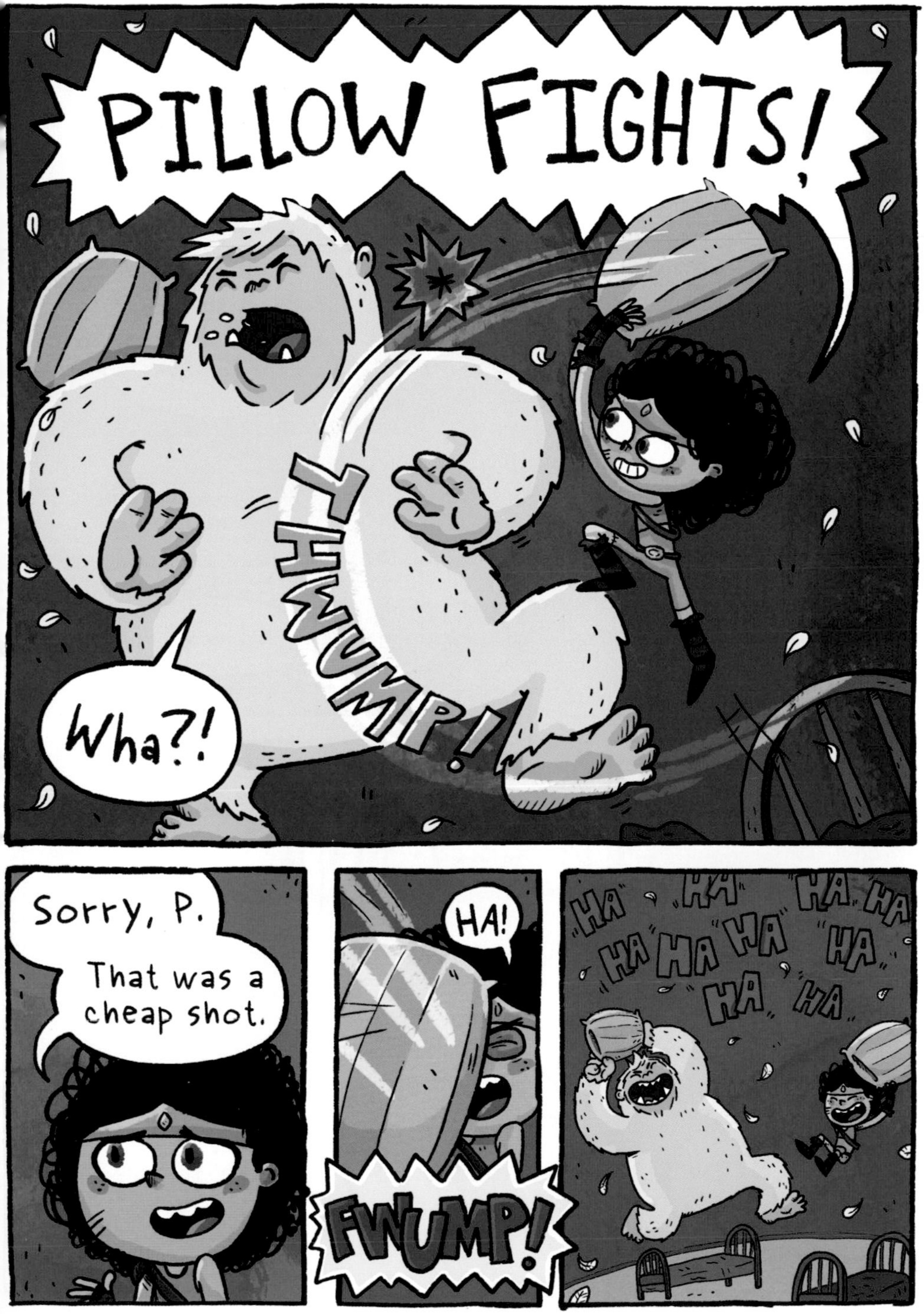
PILLOW FIGHTS!
THWUMP!
Wha?!
Sorry, P.
That was a cheap shot.
HA!
FWUMP!
HA HA HA HA HA HA HA HA HA HA HA HA HA

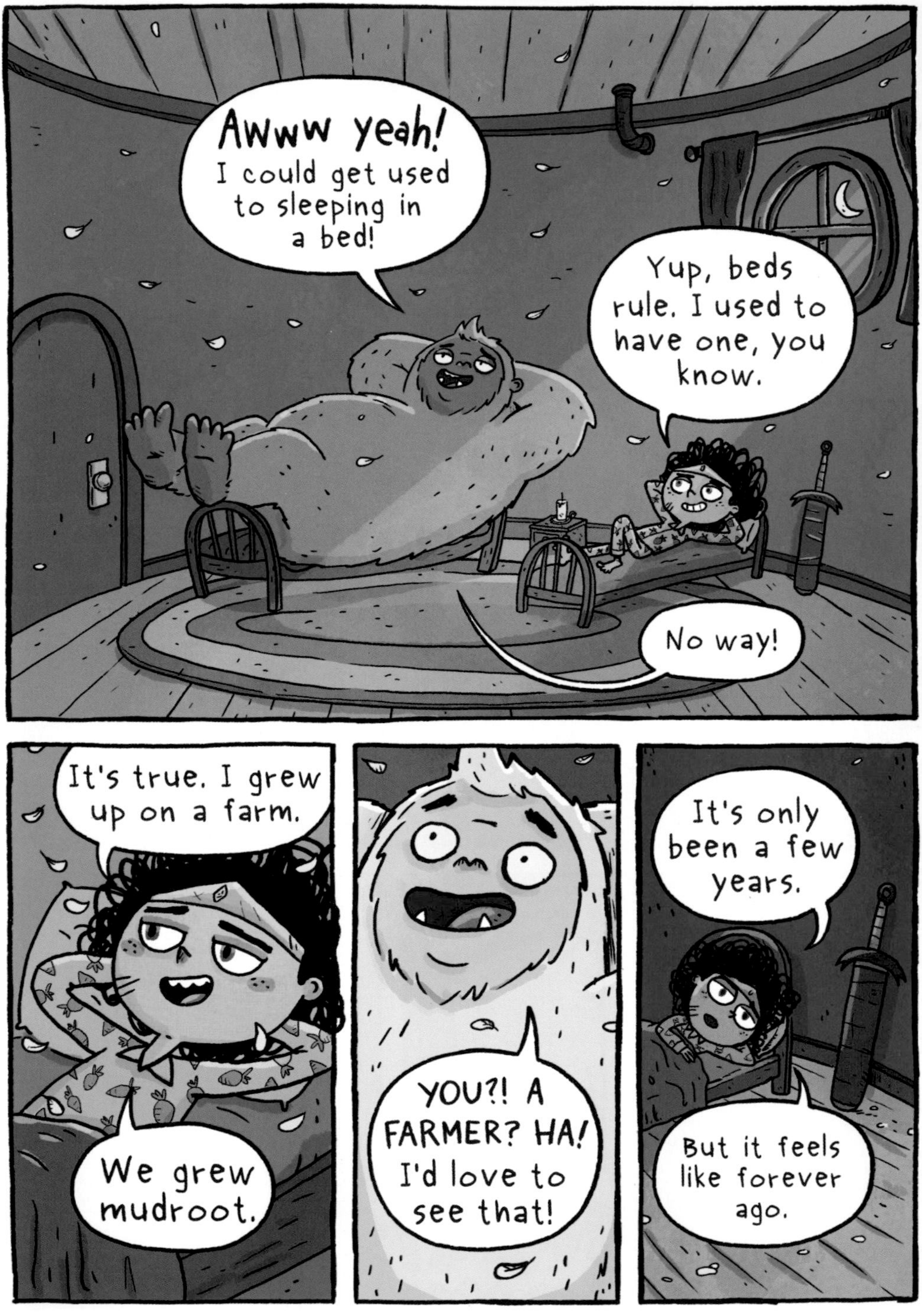
Awww yeah! I could get used to sleeping in a bed!
Yup, beds rule. I used to have one, you know.
No way!
It's true. I grew up on a farm.
We grew mudroot.
YOU?! A FARMER? HA! I'd love to see that!
It's only been a few years.
But it feels like forever ago.

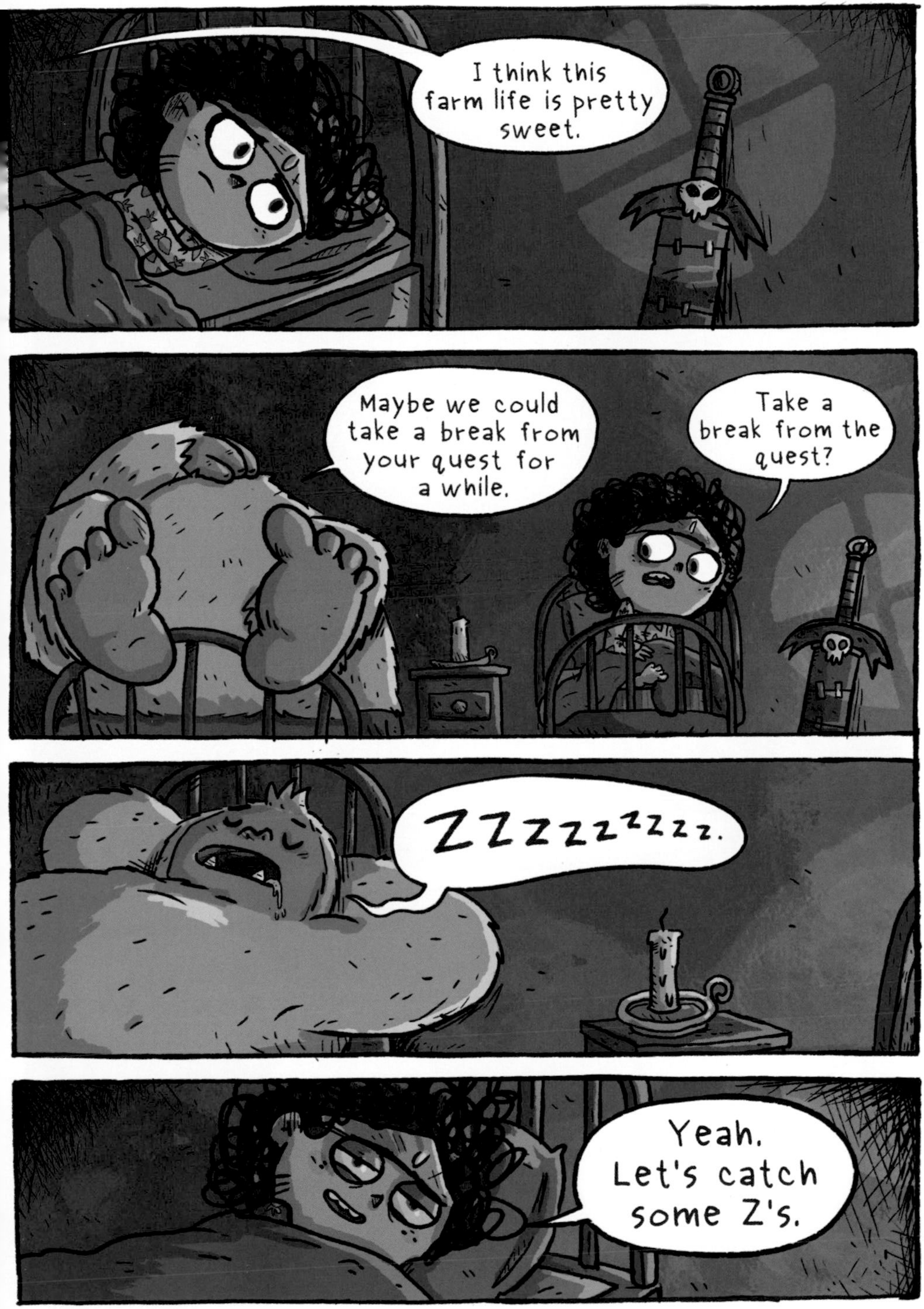
I think this farm life is pretty sweet.
Maybe we could take a break from your quest for a while.
Take a break from the quest?
ZZzzzzzzz.
Yeah. Let's catch some Z's.

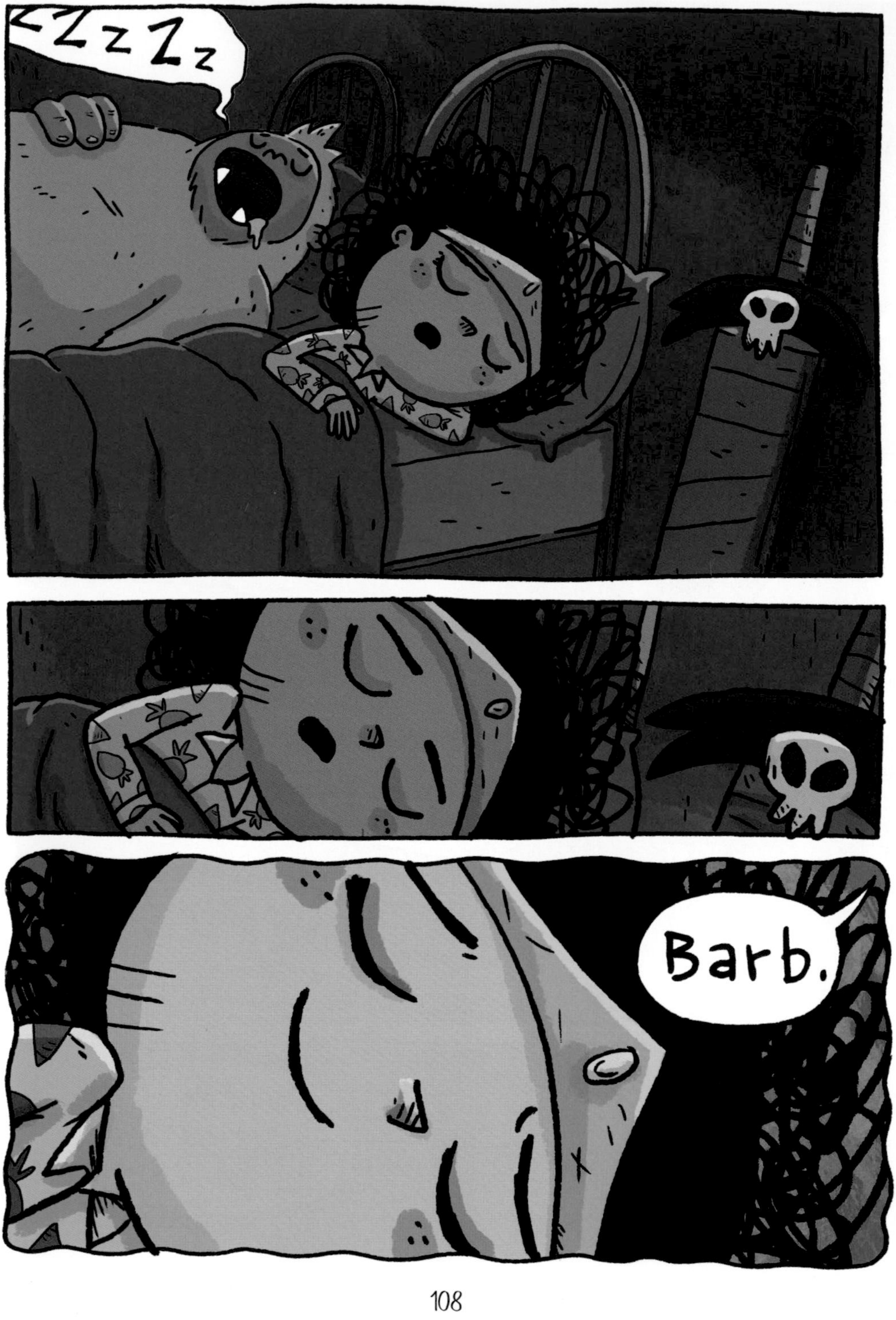
ZZzZz
Barb.

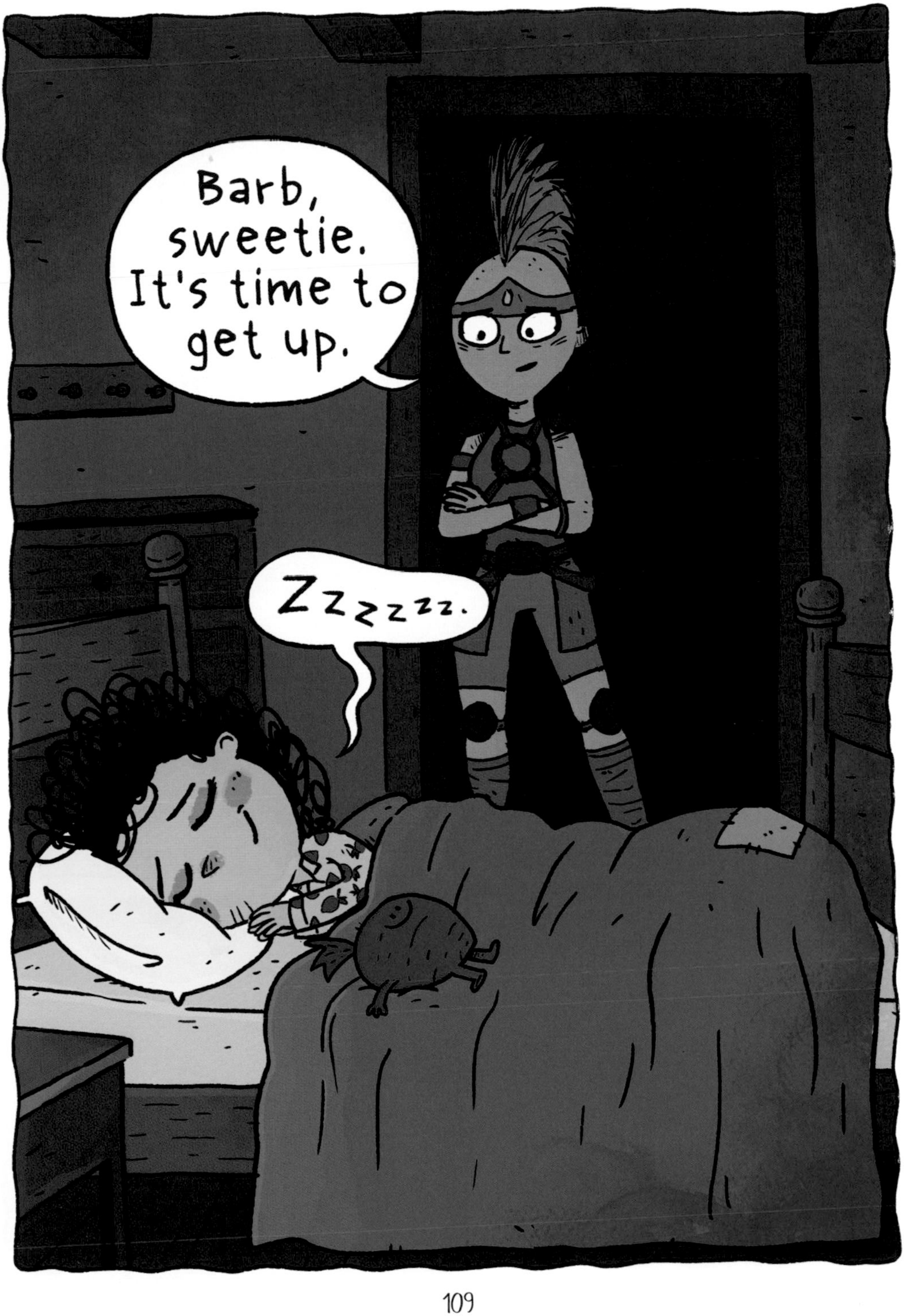
Barb, sweetie. It's time to get up.
Zzzzzz.

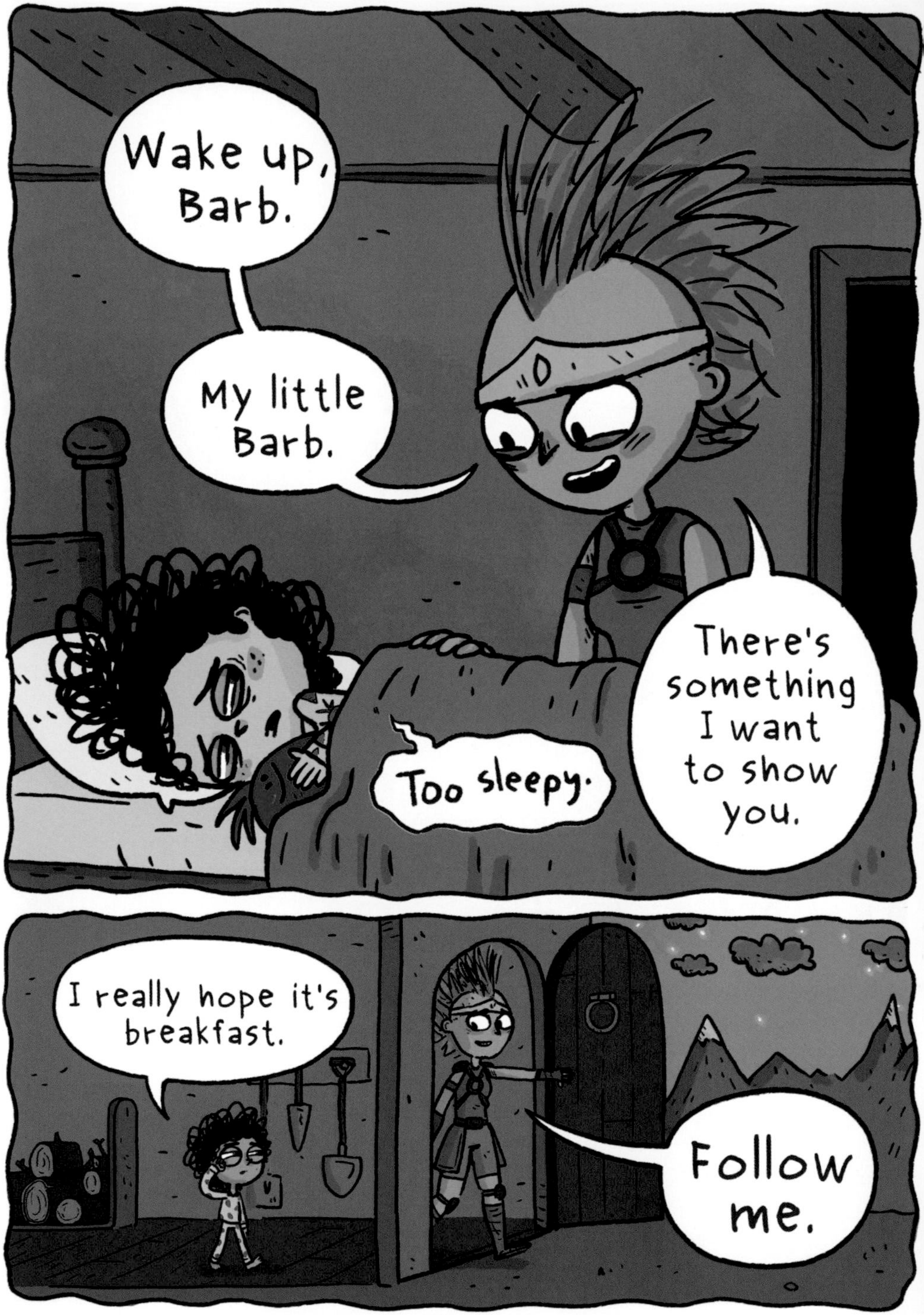
Wake up, Barb.
My little Barb.
There's something I want to show you.
Too sleepy.
I really hope it's breakfast.
Follow me.

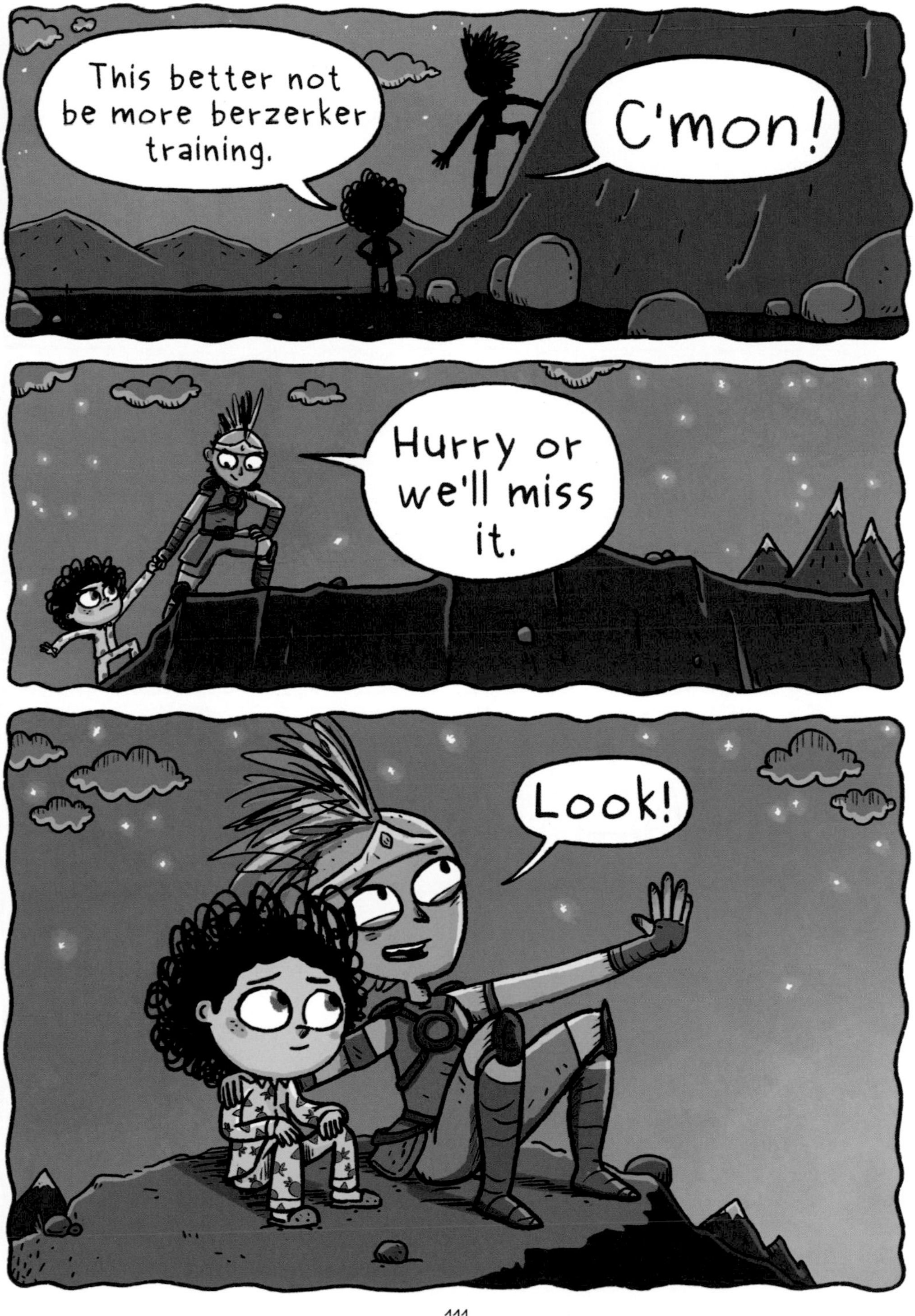
This better not be more berzerker training.
C'mon!
Hurry or we'll miss it.
Look!

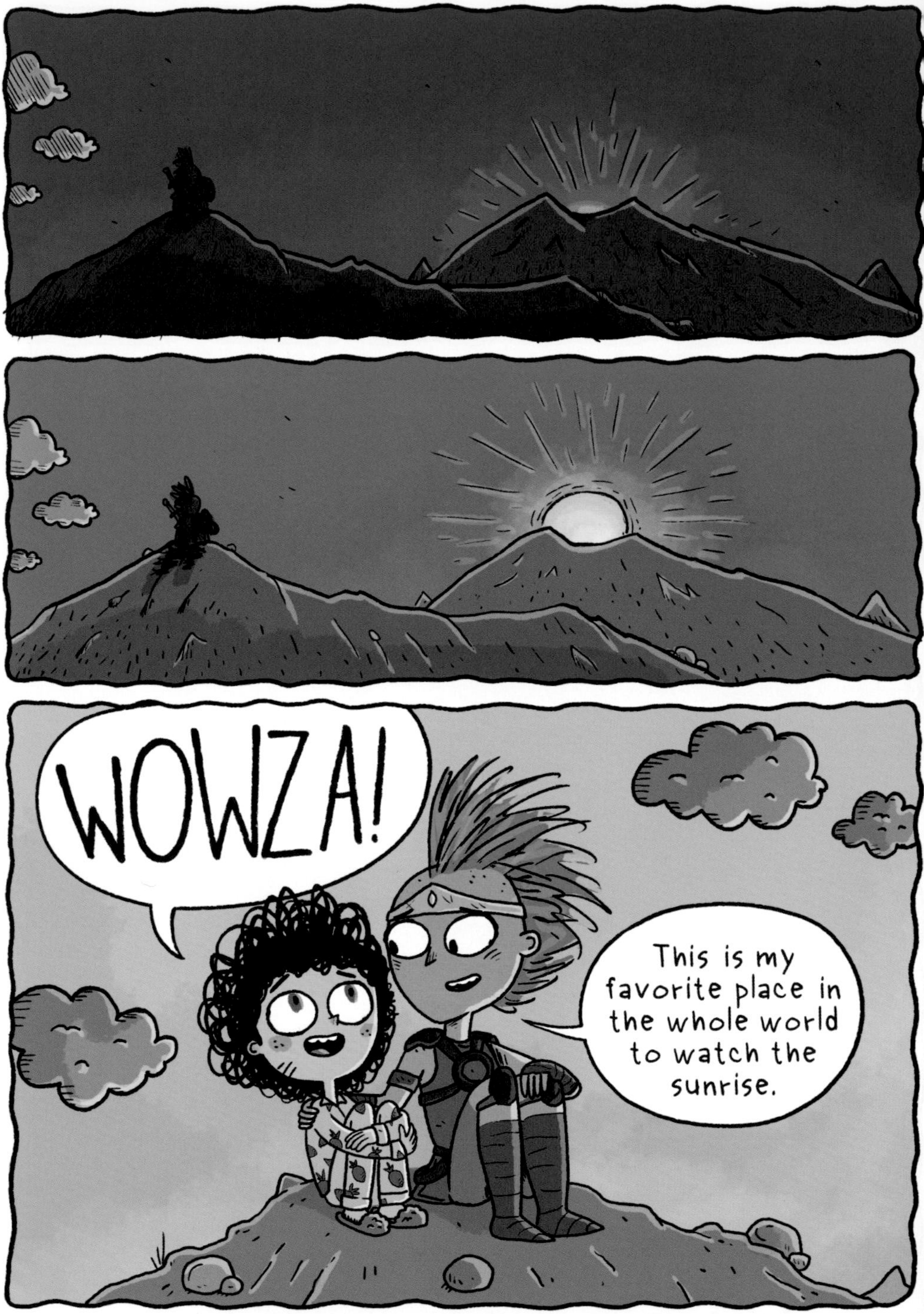
WOWZA!
This is my favorite place in the whole world to watch the sunrise.

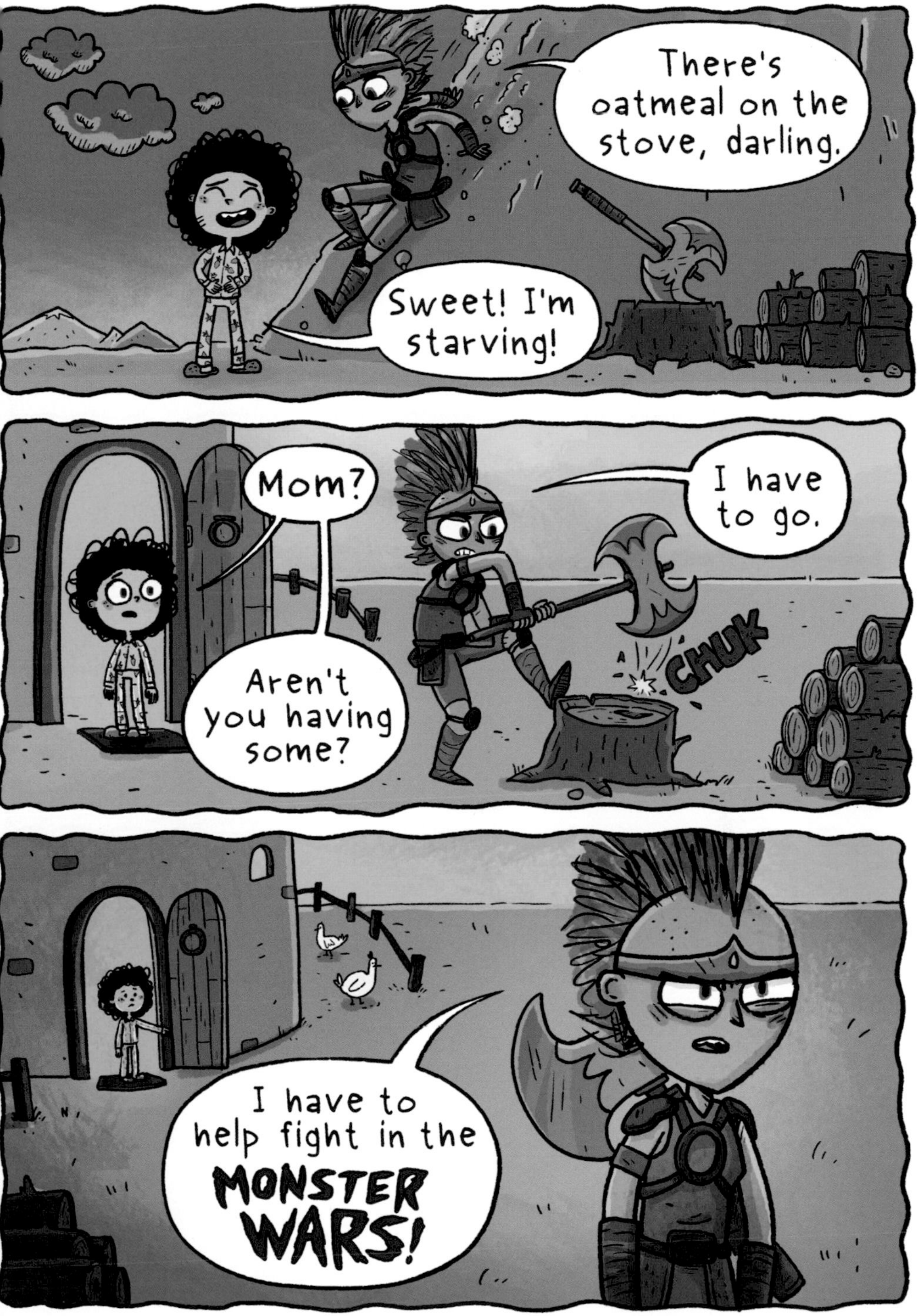
There's oatmeal on the stove, darling.
Sweet! I'm starving!
Mom?
Aren't you having some?
I have to go.
CHUK
I have to help fight in the MONSTER WARS!

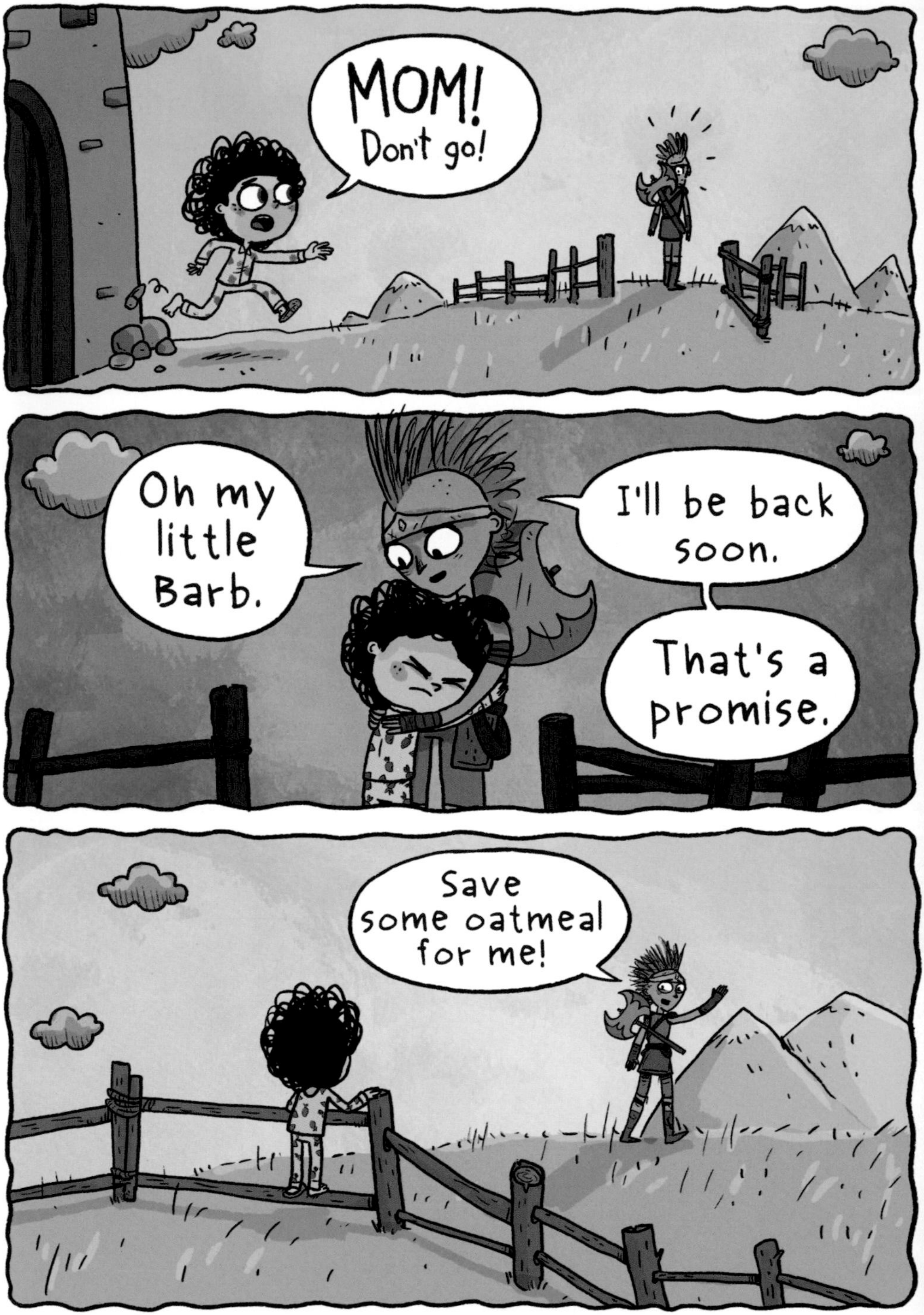
MOM! Don't go!
Oh my little Barb.
I'll be back soon.
That's a promise.
Save some oatmeal for me!

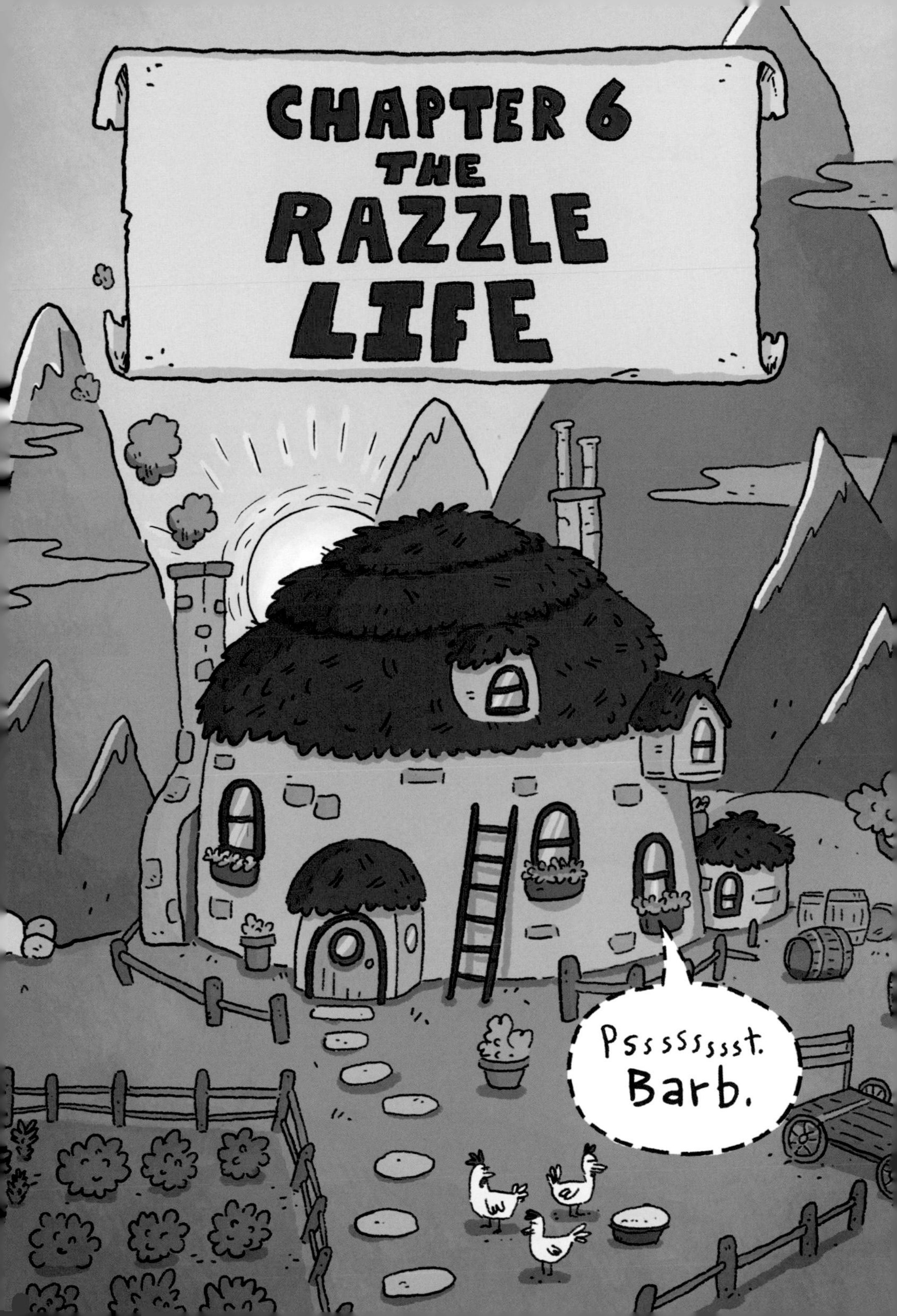
CHAPTER 6
THE
RAZZLE
LIFE
Psssssssst.
Barb.

Barb.

PSSSSSST...
BARB!

GAAHH!!!!

SHHH...IIING

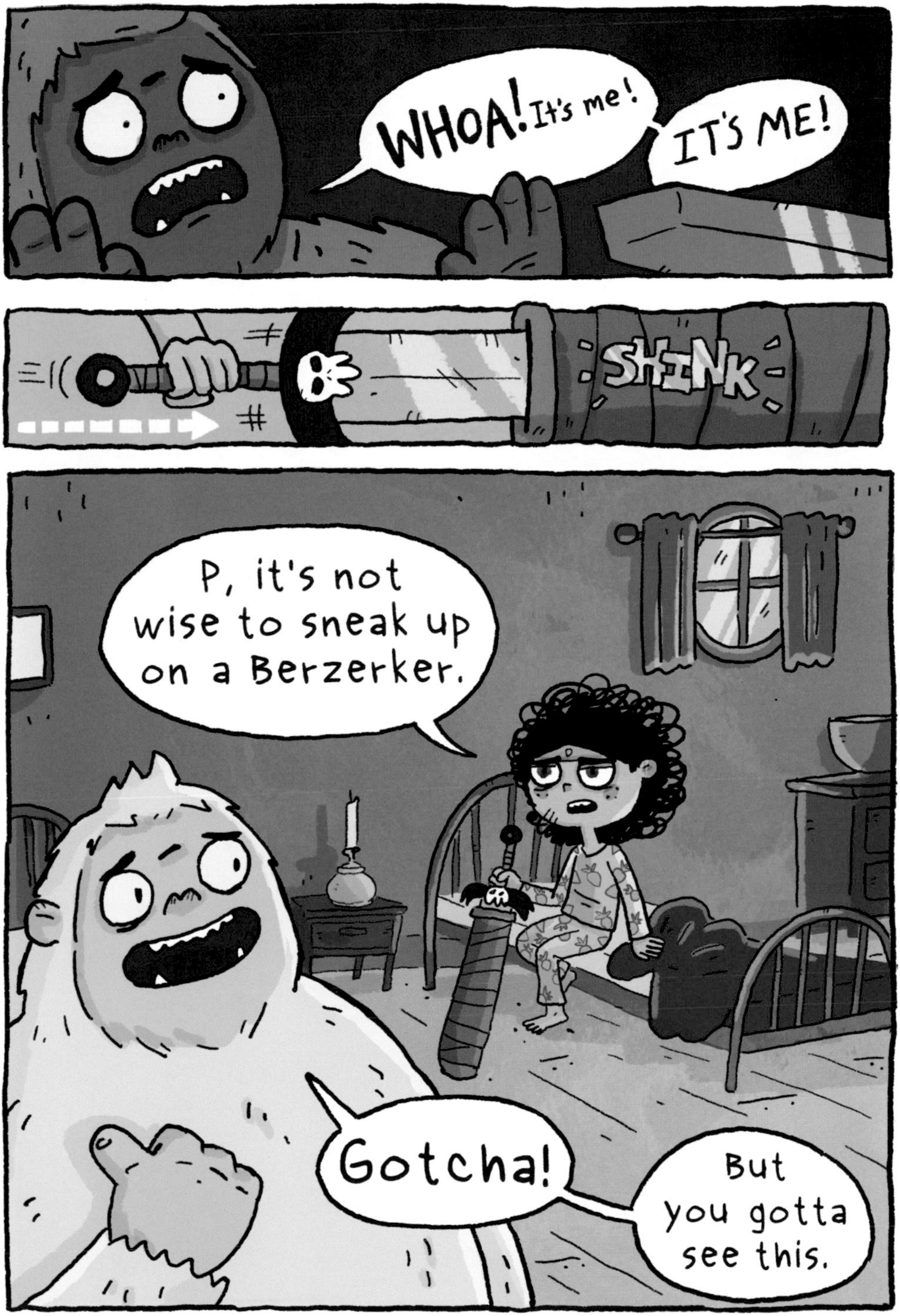
WHOA! It's me!
IT'S ME!
SHINK
P, it's not wise to sneak up on a Berzerker.
Gotcha!
But you gotta see this.

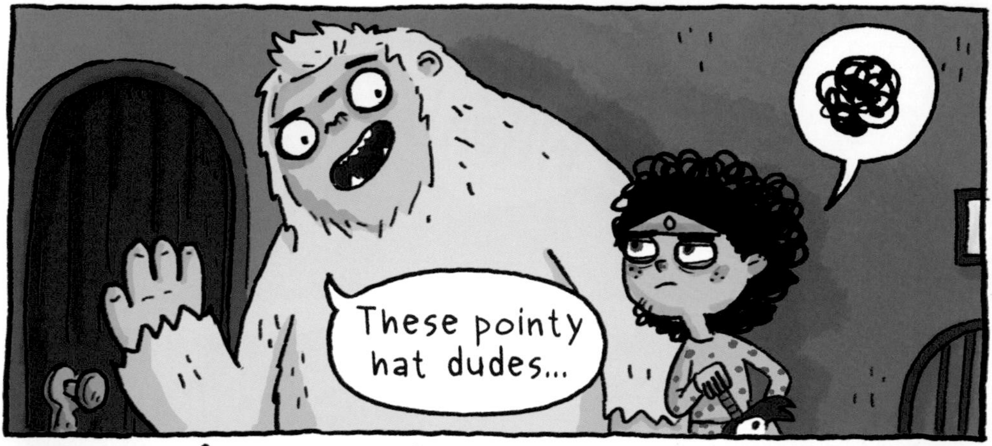
These pointy hat dudes...

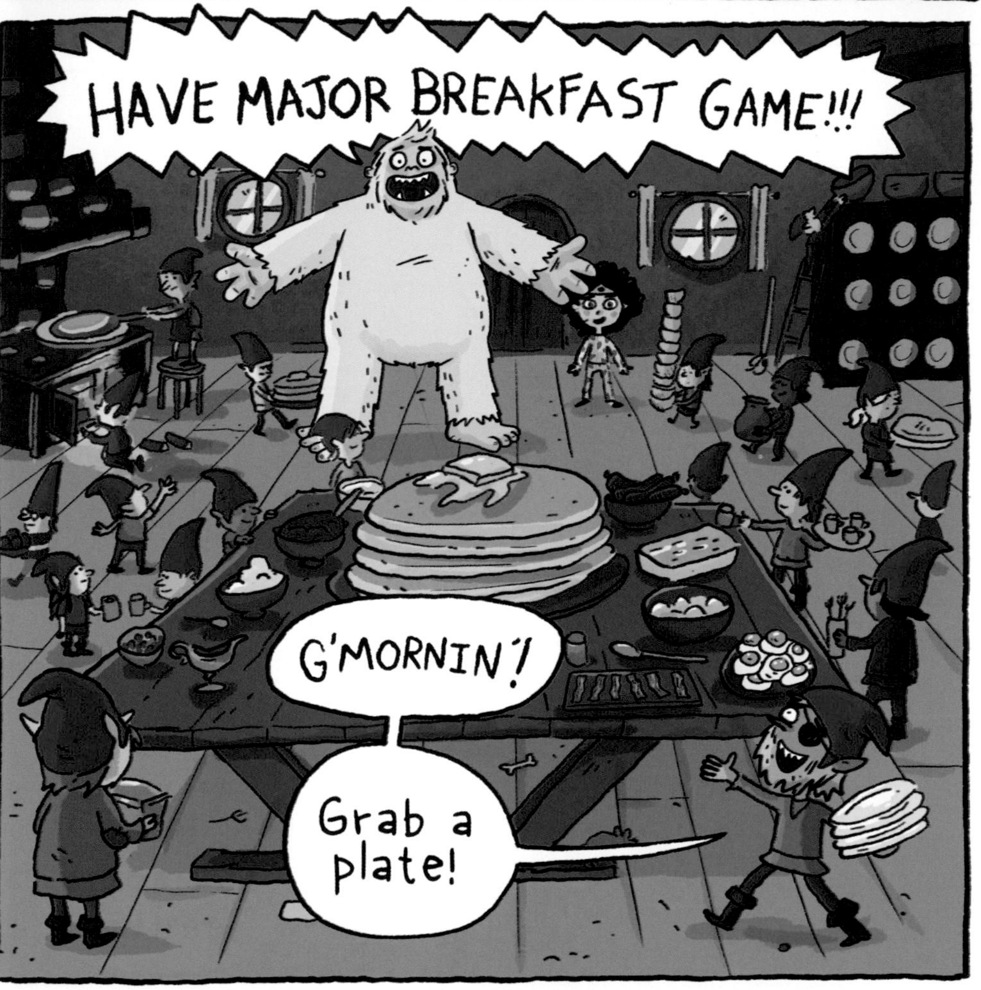
HAVE MAJOR BREAKFAST GAME!!!
G'MORNIN'!
Grab a plate!

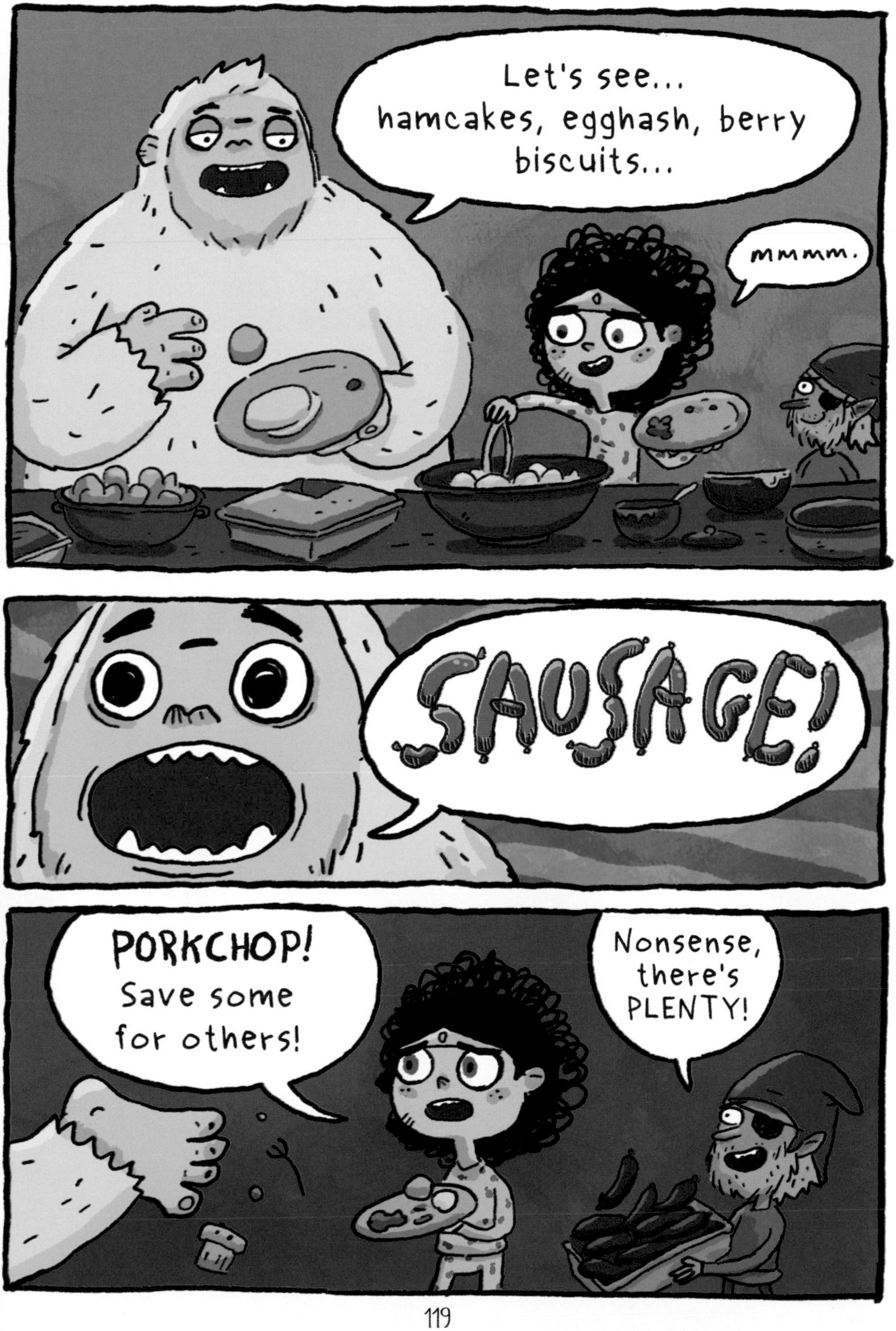
Let's see... hamcakes, egghash, berry biscuits...
mmmm.
SAUSAGE!
PORKCHOP! Save some for others!
Nonsense, there's PLENTY!

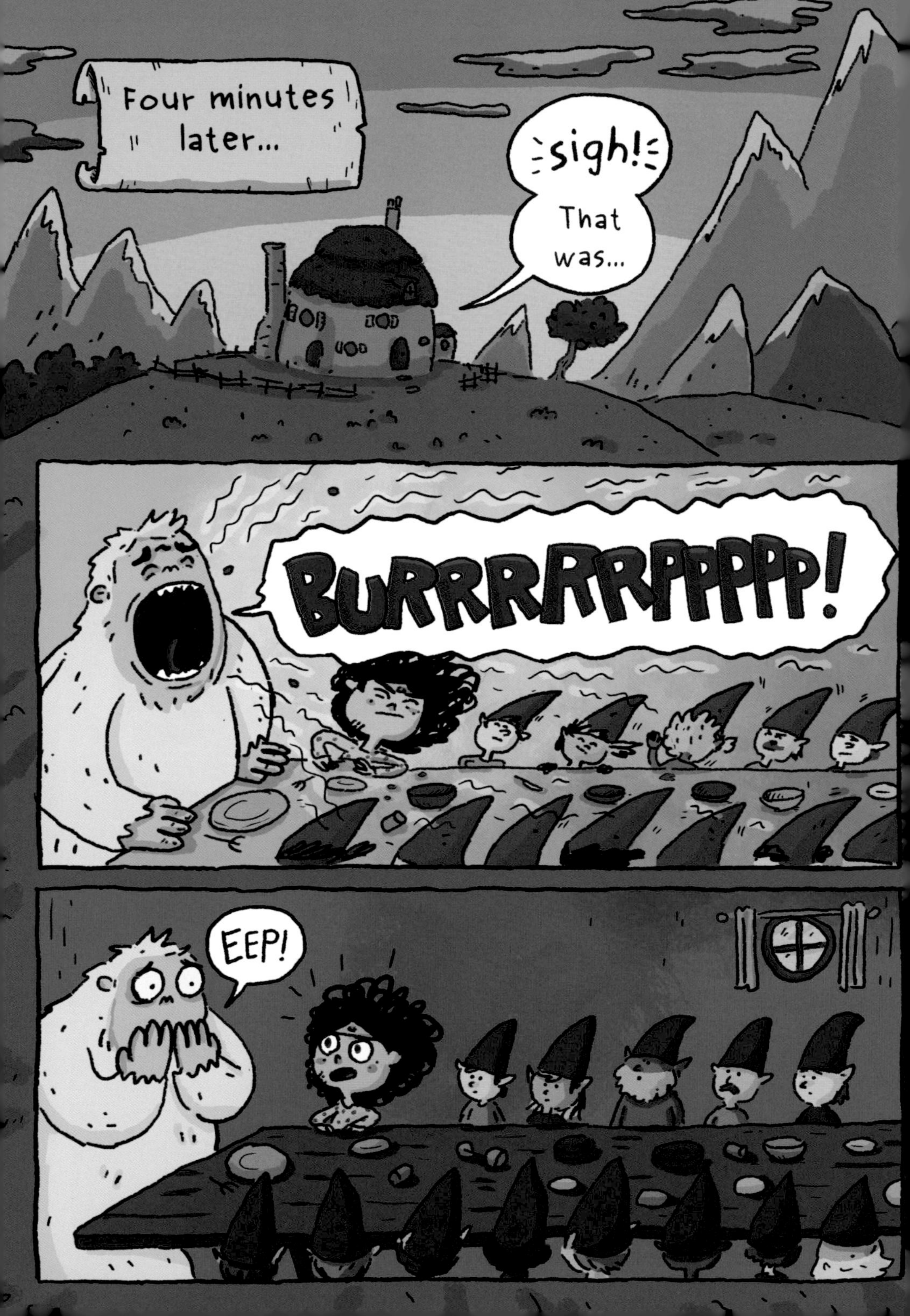

Four minutes later...
sigh!
That was...
BURRRRRRPPPPP!
EEP!

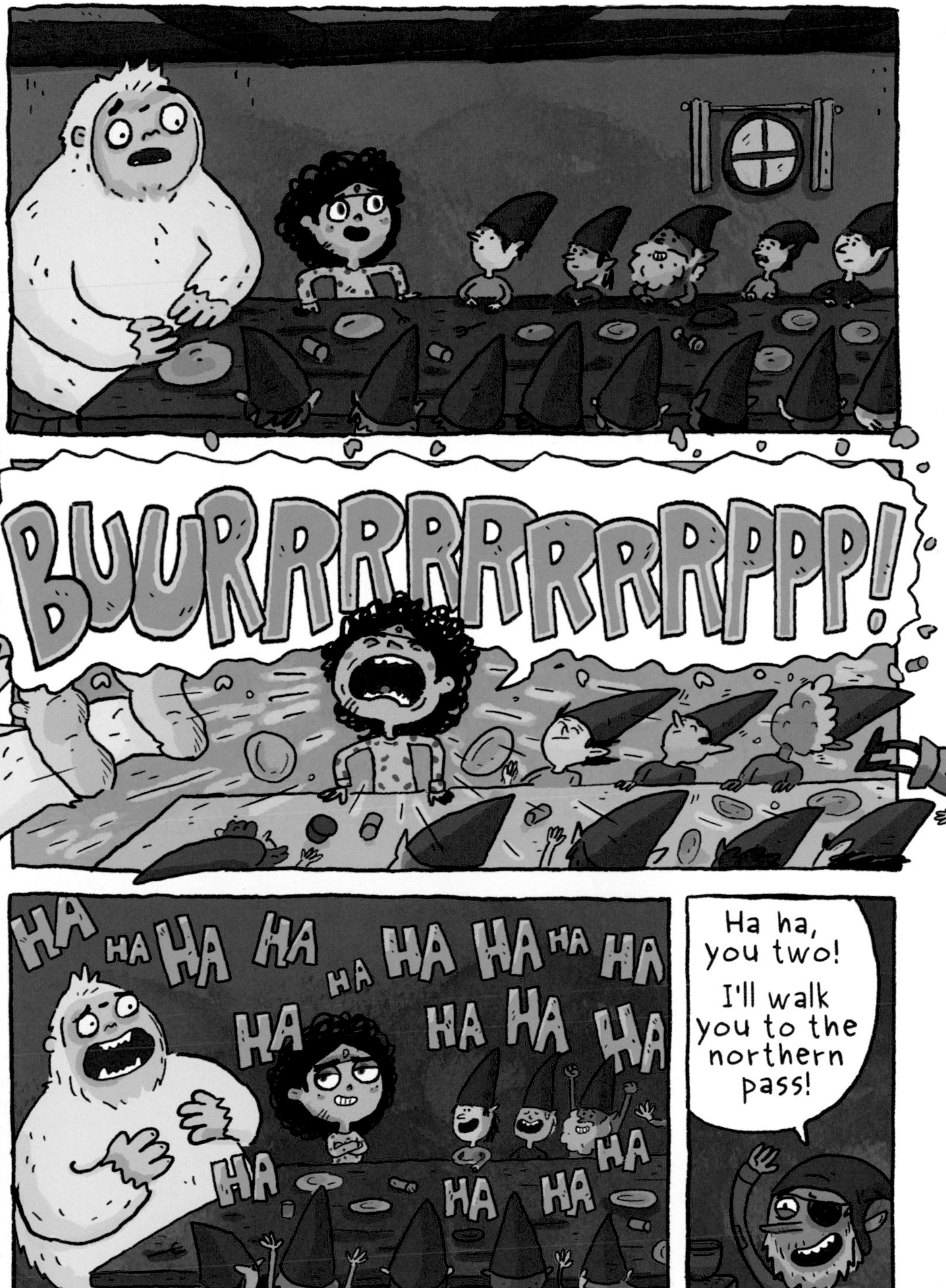
BUURRRRRRRRPPP!
HA HA HA HA HA HA HA HA HA HA HA
HA HA HA HA
HA HA HA HA
Ha ha, you two!
I'll walk you to the northern pass!

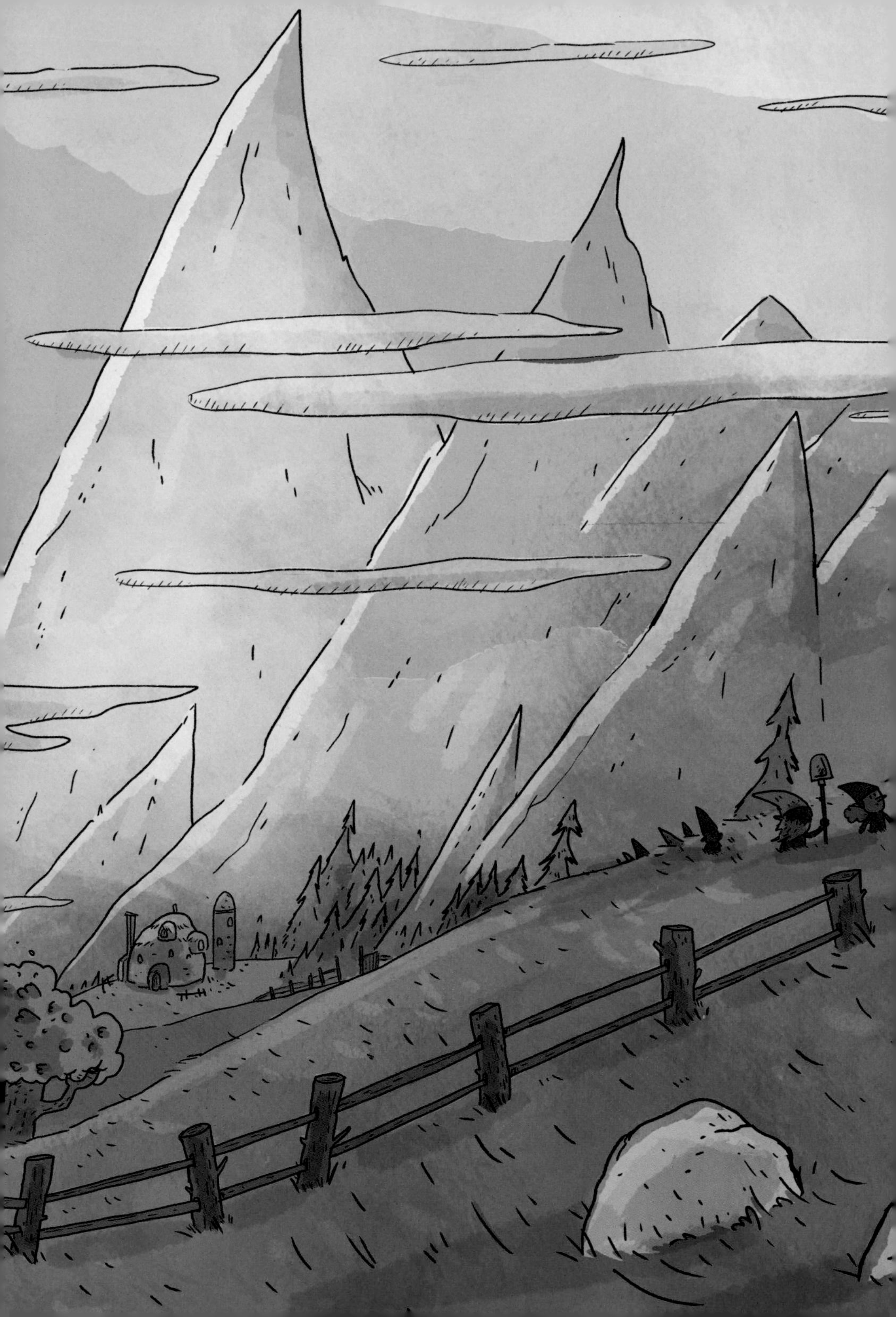

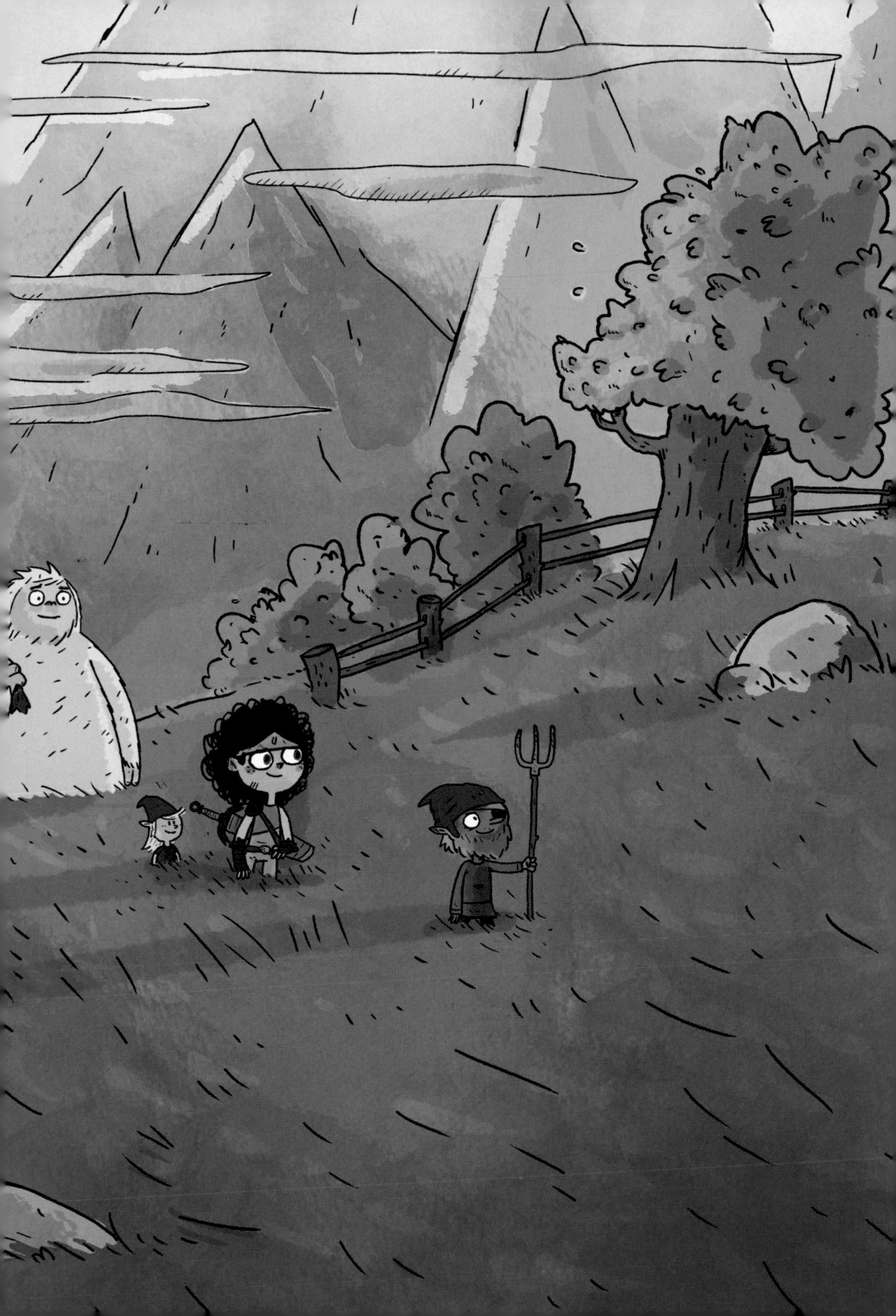

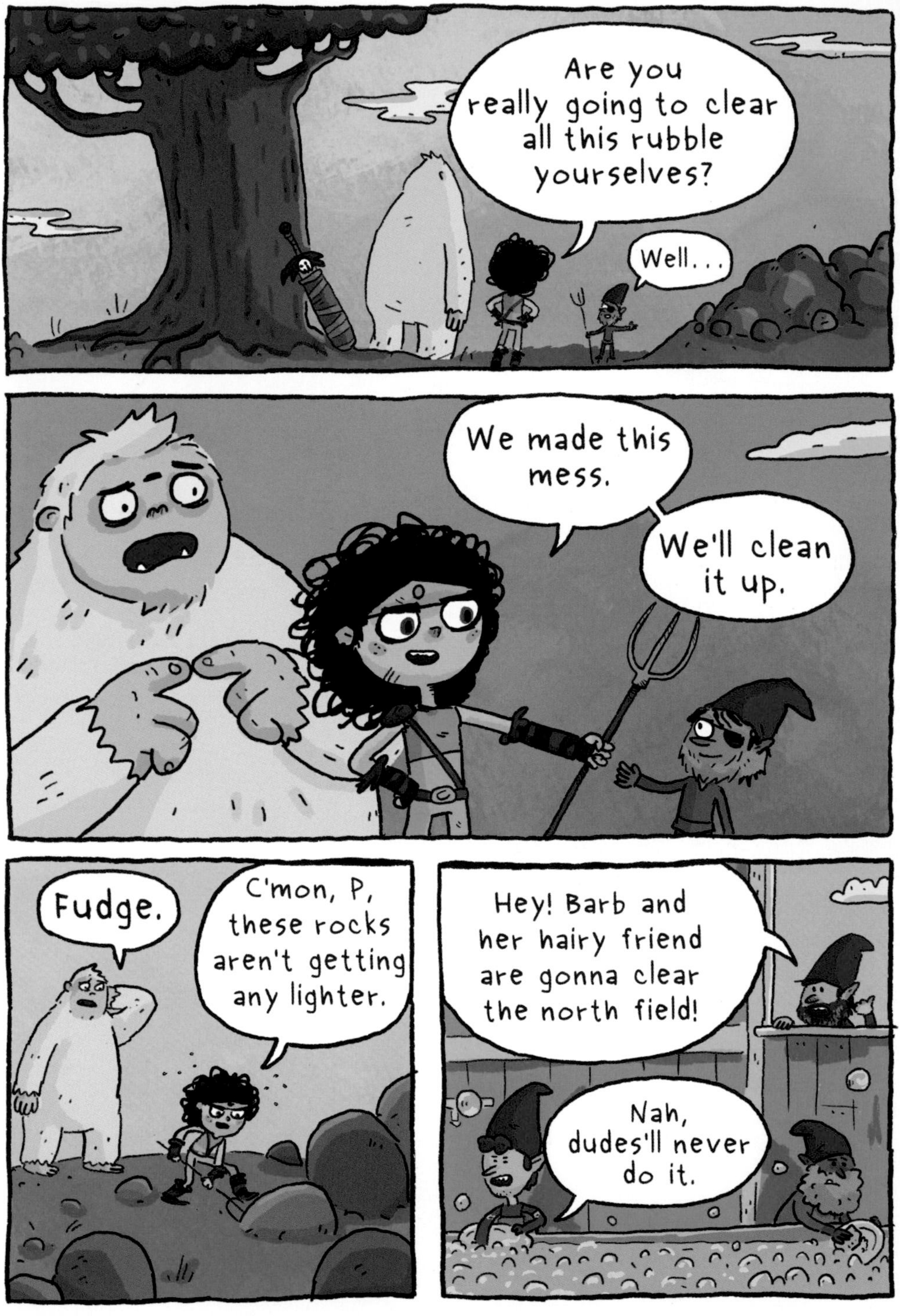
Are you really going to clear all this rubble yourselves?
Well...
We made this mess.
We'll clean it up.
Fudge.
C'mon, P, these rocks aren't getting any lighter.
Hey! Barb and her hairy friend are gonna clear the north field!
Nah, dudes'll never do it.

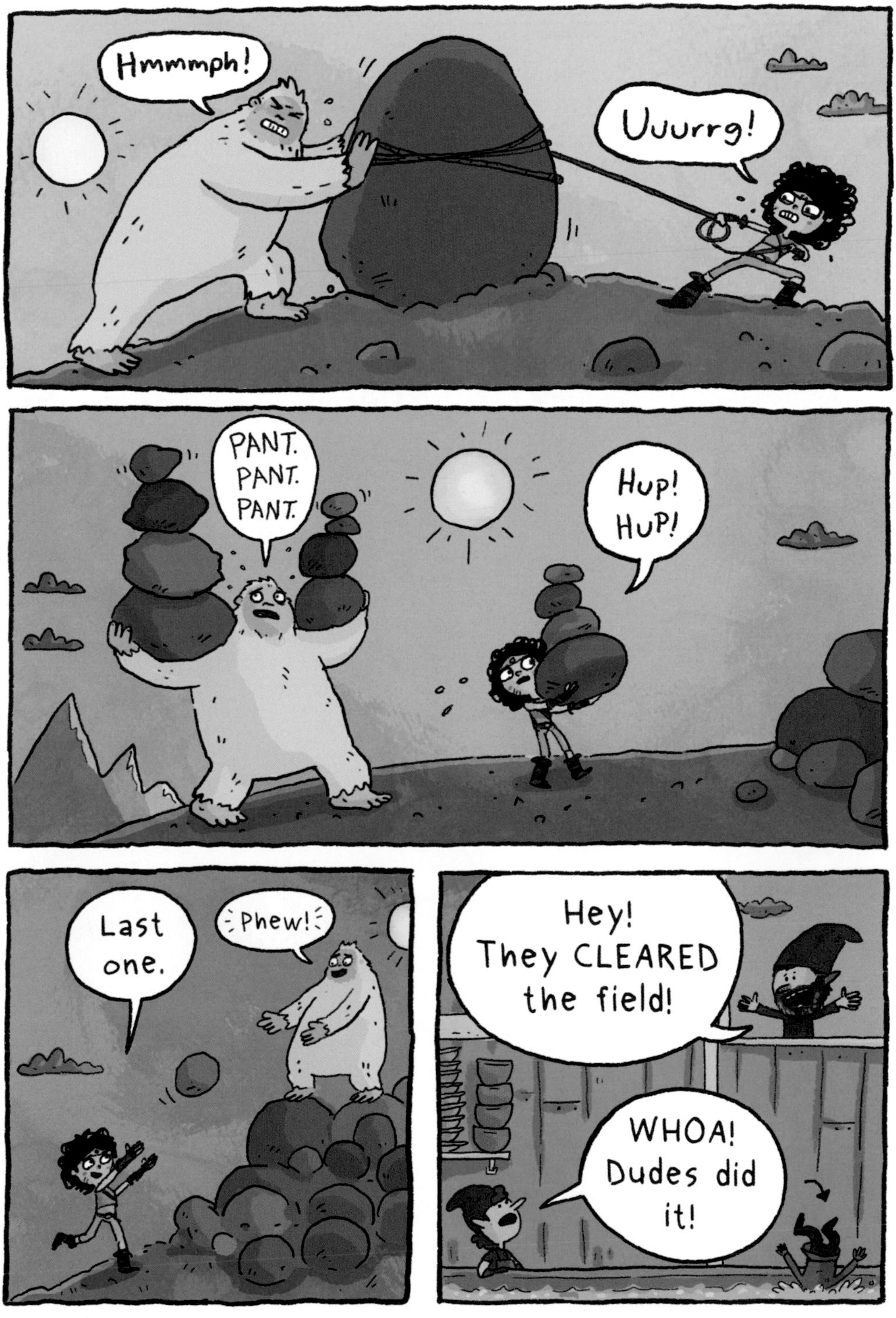

Hmmmph!
Uuurrg!
PANT. PANT. PANT.
Hup! Hup!
Last one.
Phew!
Hey! They CLEARED the field!
WHOA! Dudes did it!

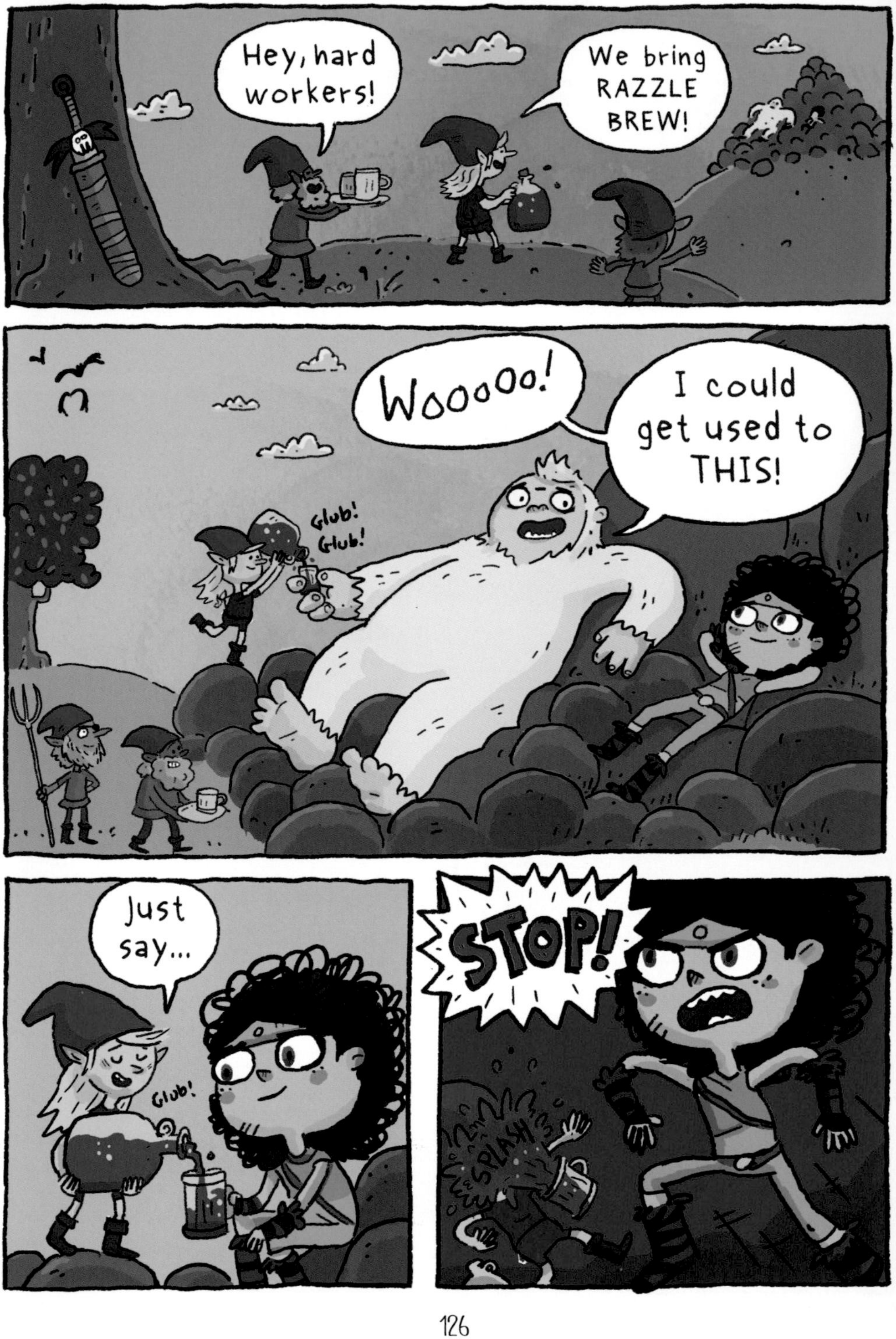
Hey, hard workers!
We bring RAZZLE BREW!
WoooOo!
I could get used to THIS!
Glub! Glub!
Just say...
Glub!
STOP!
SPLASH

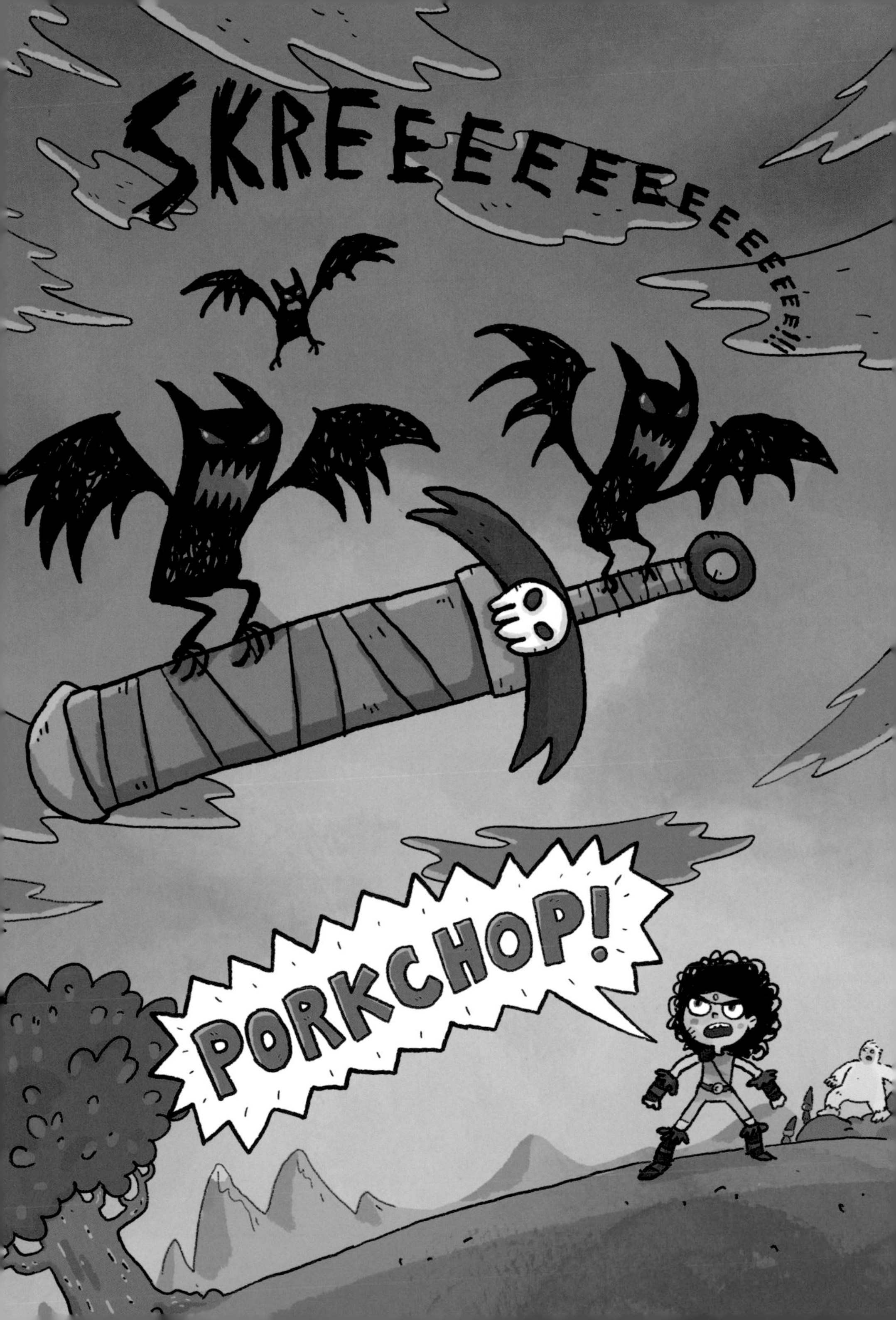
SKREEEEEEEEEEEEEEE!!!
PORKCHOP!

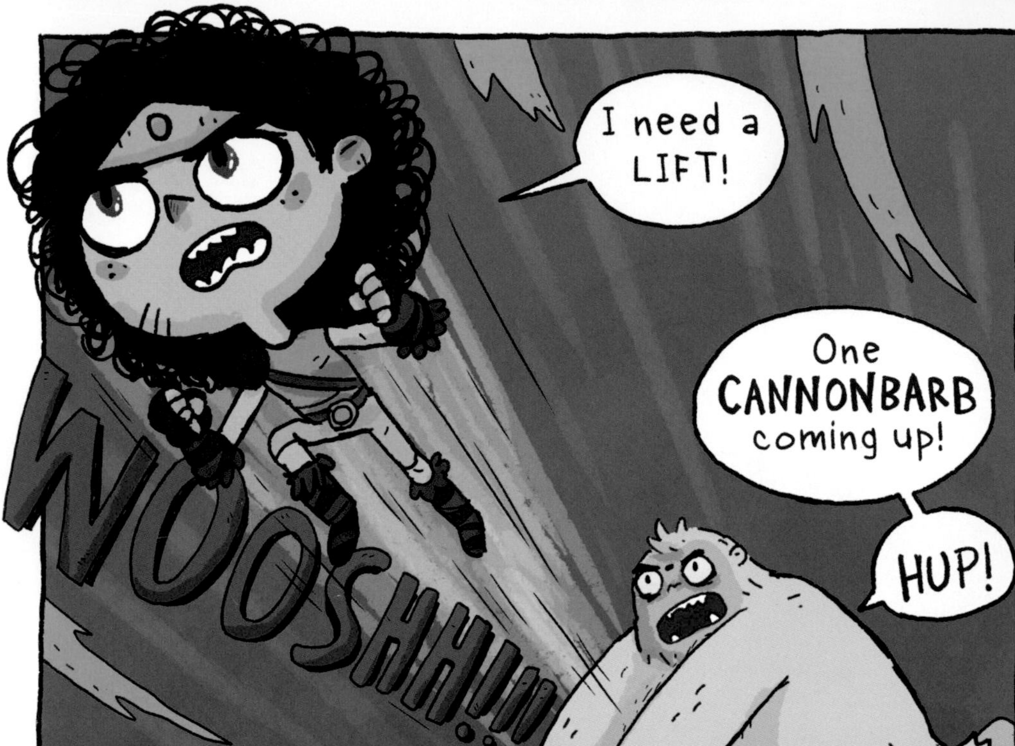
I need a LIFT!
One CANNONBARB coming up!
HUP!
WOOSHH!!!

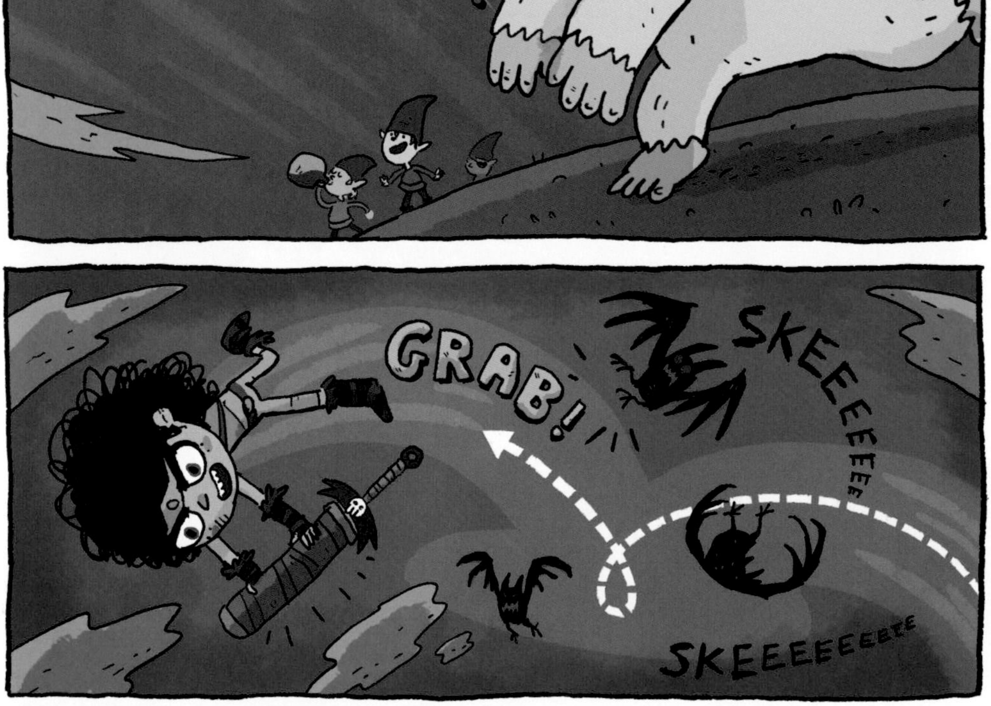
GRAB!
SKEEEEEEEE
SKEEEEEEEEE

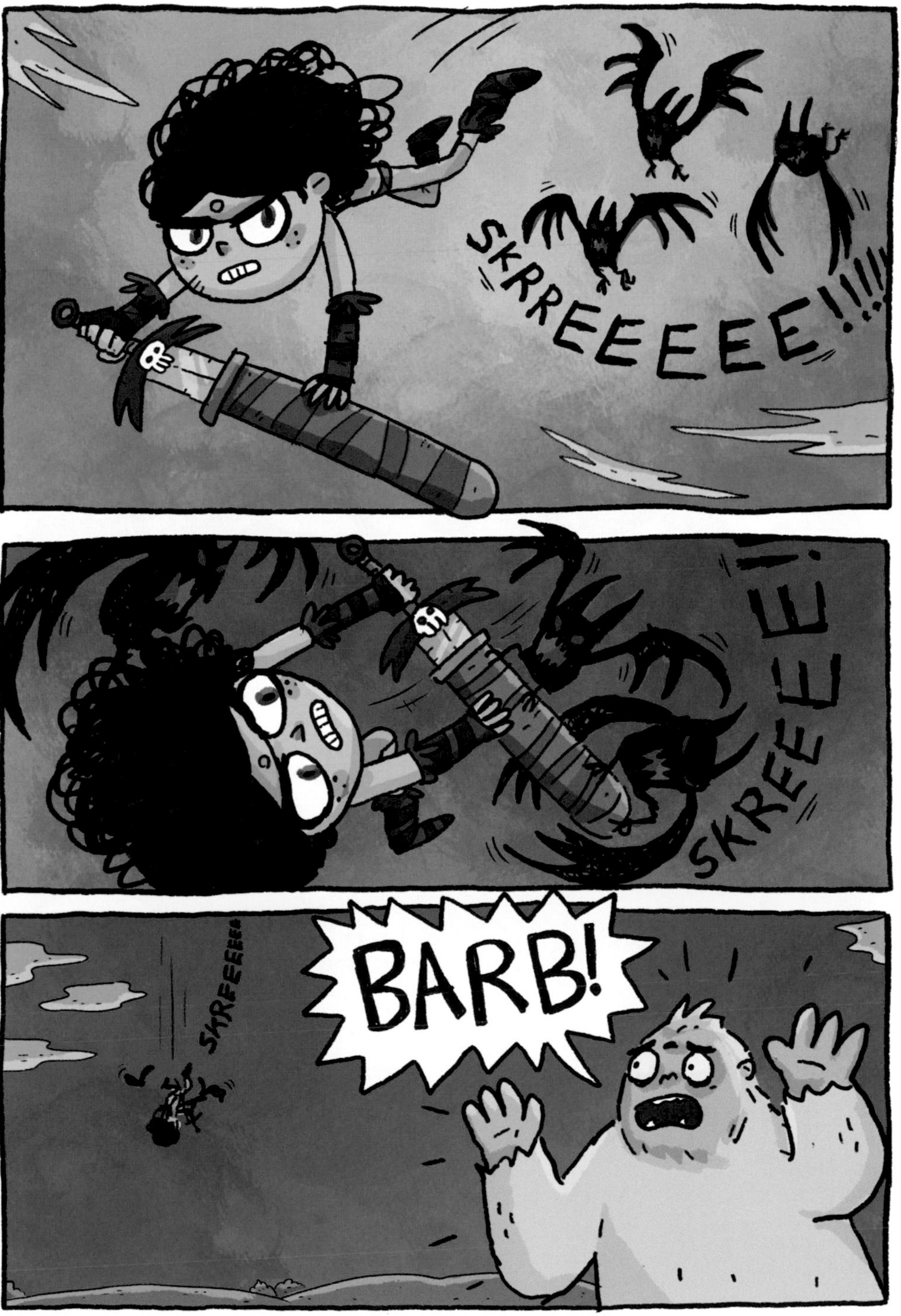
SKRREEEEEE!!!!!
SKREEEEE!
SKREEEEEE
BARB!

SSSSSSSS
OWsss
THWAK!
SSH
NG!
THUMP!
THAP!
OUCHsss!
BARB! I GOTCHA!
SPLASH
I...
...don't gotcha.
DANGER DEEP MUD

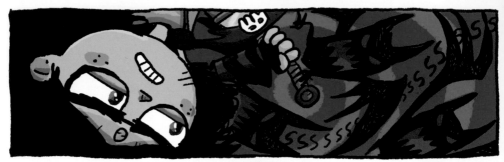

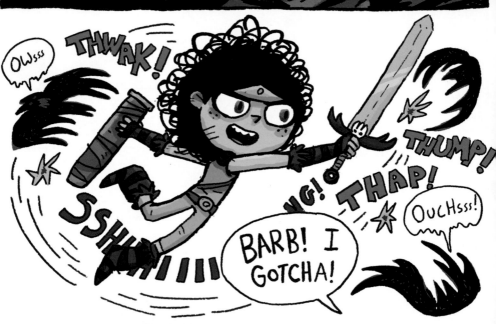

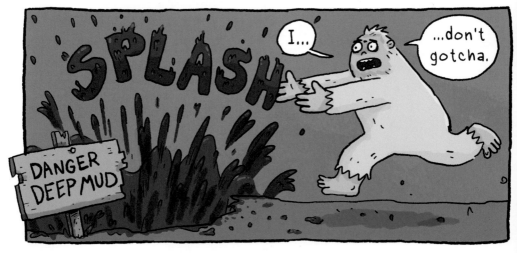

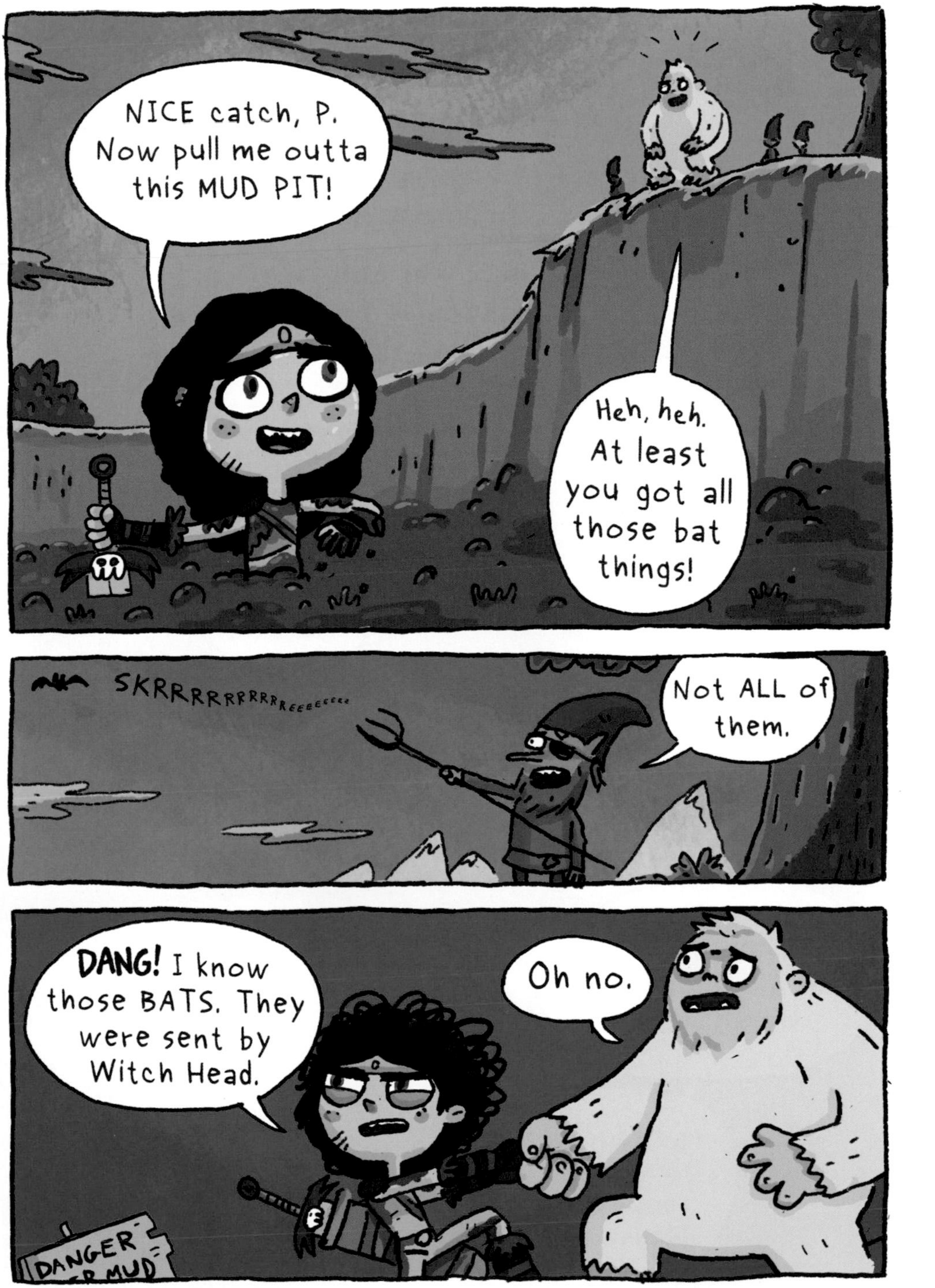
NICE catch, P. Now pull me outta this MUD PIT!
Heh, heh. At least you got all those bat things!
SKRRRRRRRRRReeeeeee
Not ALL of them.
DANG! I know those BATS. They were sent by Witch Head.
Oh no.
DANGER

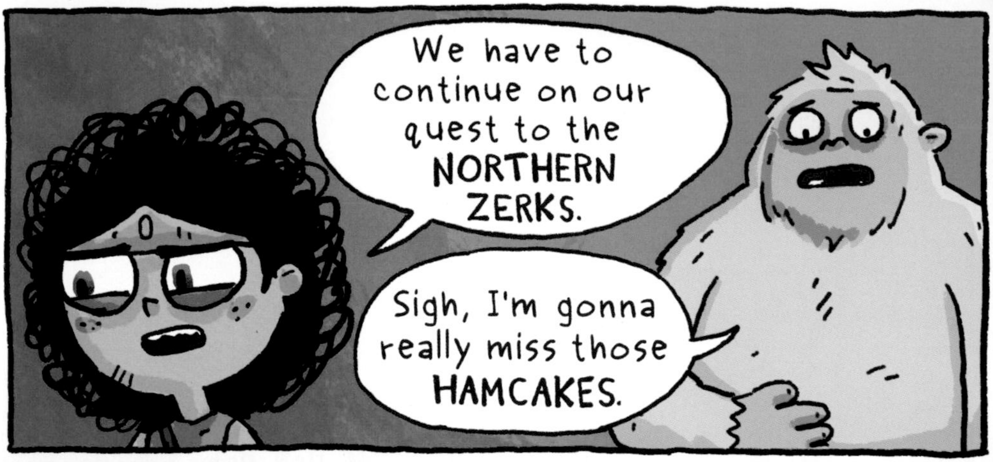
We have to continue on our quest to the NORTHERN ZERKS.
Sigh, I'm gonna really miss those HAMCAKES.

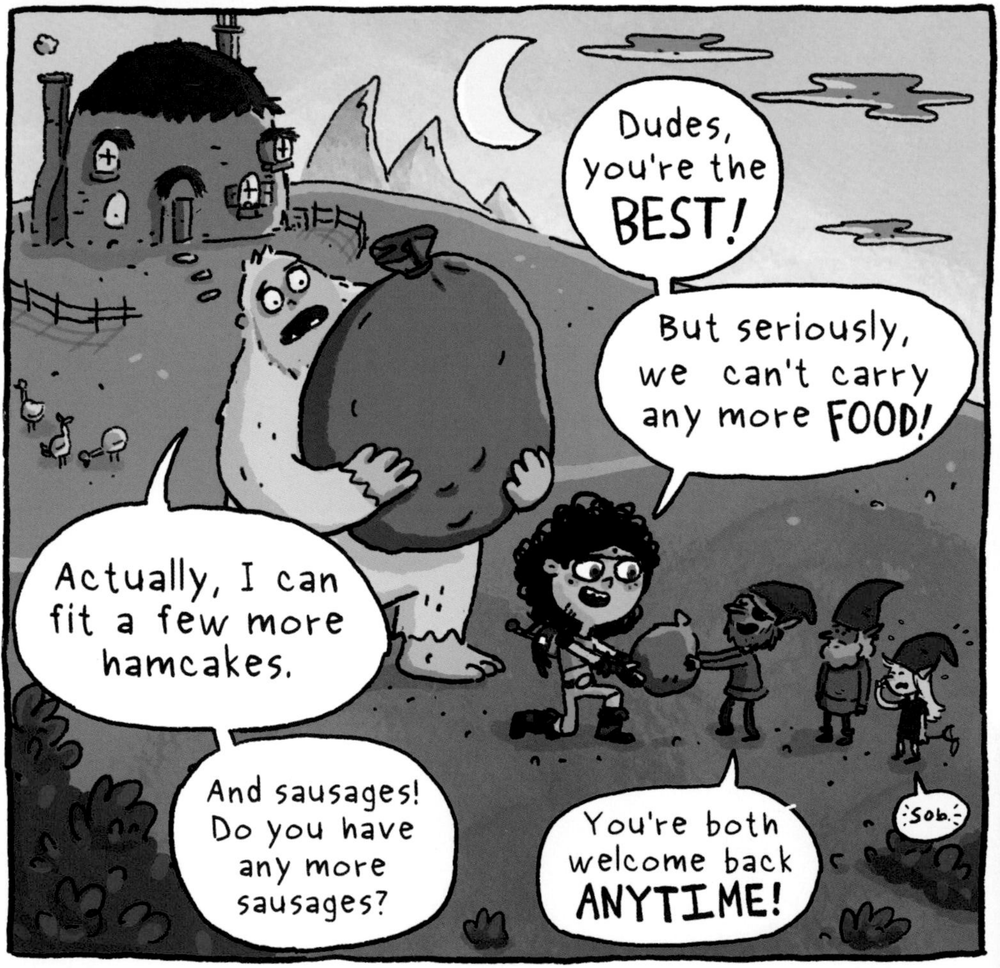
Dudes, you're the BEST!
But seriously, we can't carry any more FOOD!
Actually, I can fit a few more hamcakes.
And sausages! Do you have any more sausages?
You're both welcome back ANYTIME!
Sob.

CHAPTER 7
MENACE OF THE MIND

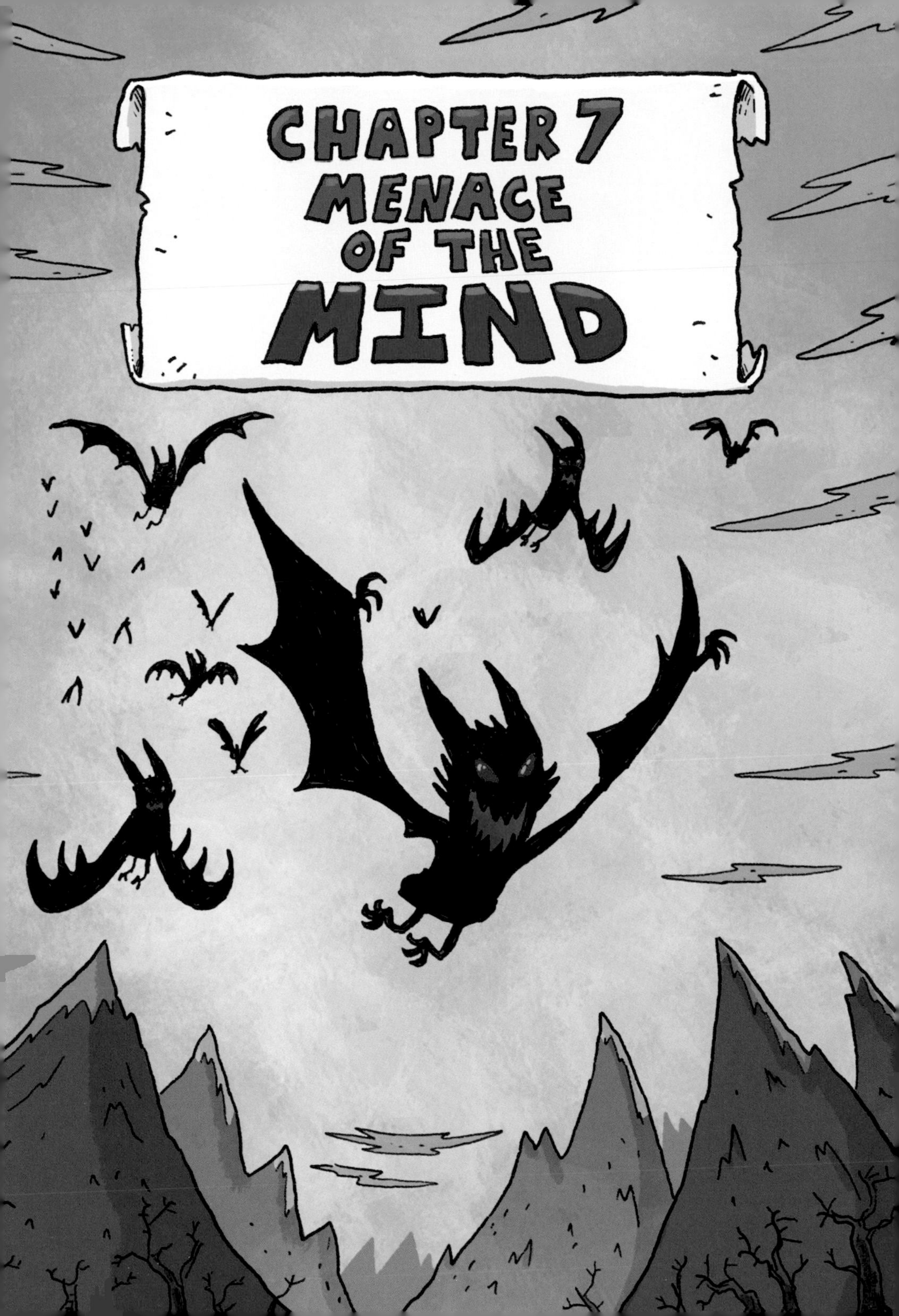

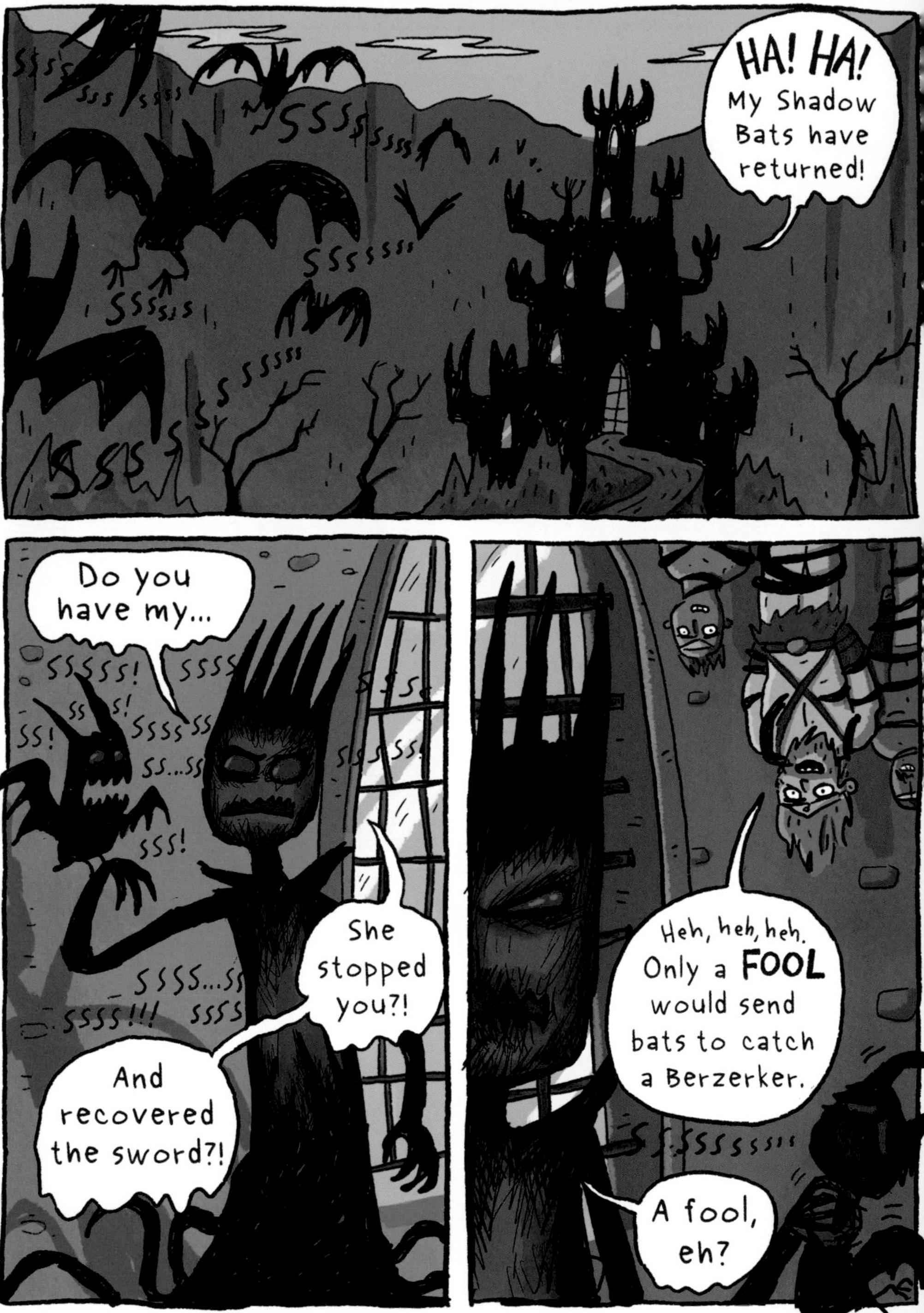

HA! HA! My Shadow Bats have returned!
Do you have my...
She stopped you?!
And recovered the sword?!
Heh, heh, heh. Only a FOOL would send bats to catch a Berzerker.
A fool, eh?

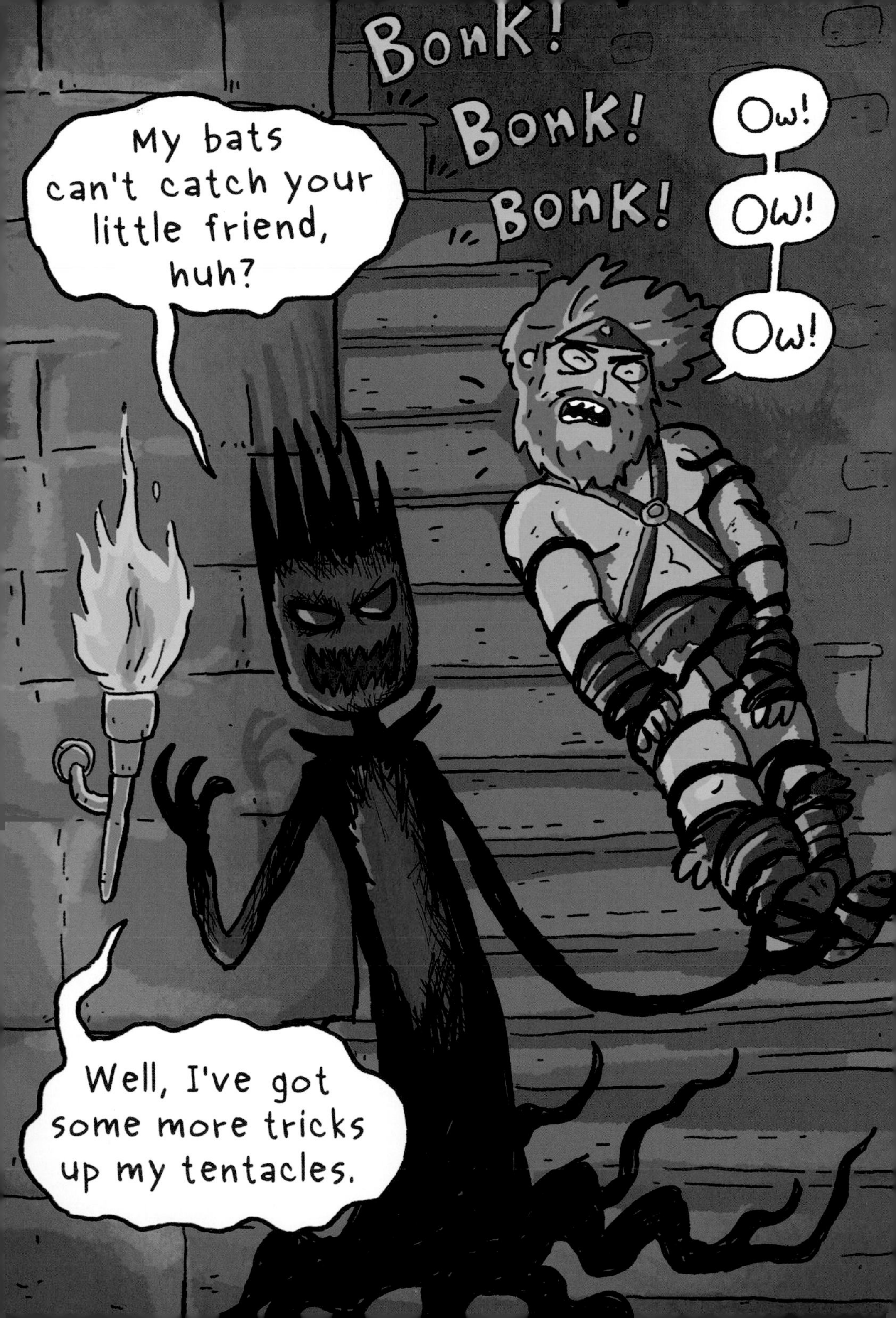
BONK!
BONK!
BONK!
Ow!
Ow!
Ow!
My bats can't catch your little friend, huh?
Well, I've got some more tricks up my tentacles.

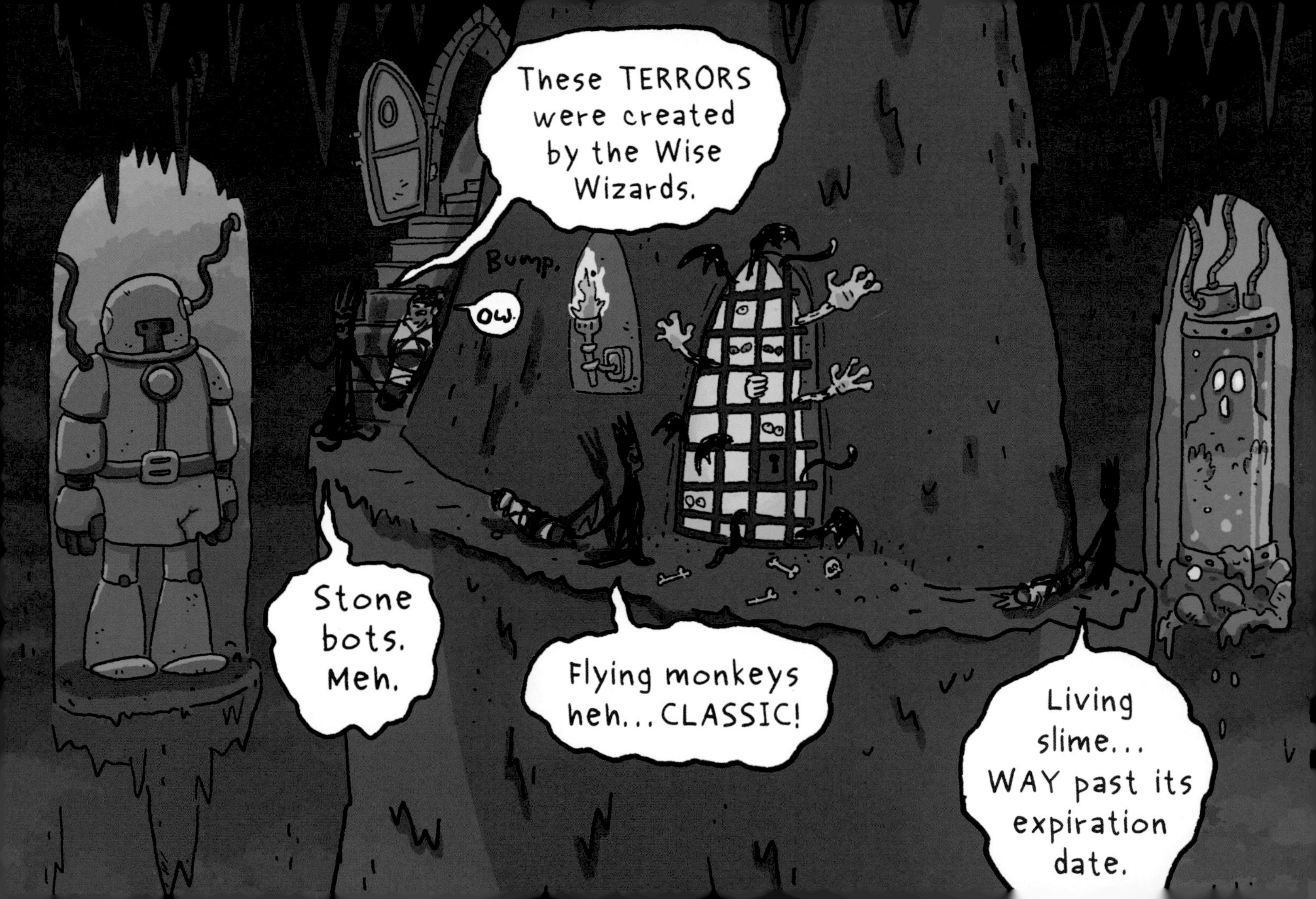
These TERRORS were created by the Wise Wizards.
Bump.
Ow.
Stone bots. Meh.
Flying monkeys heh...CLASSIC!
Living slime... WAY past its expiration date.

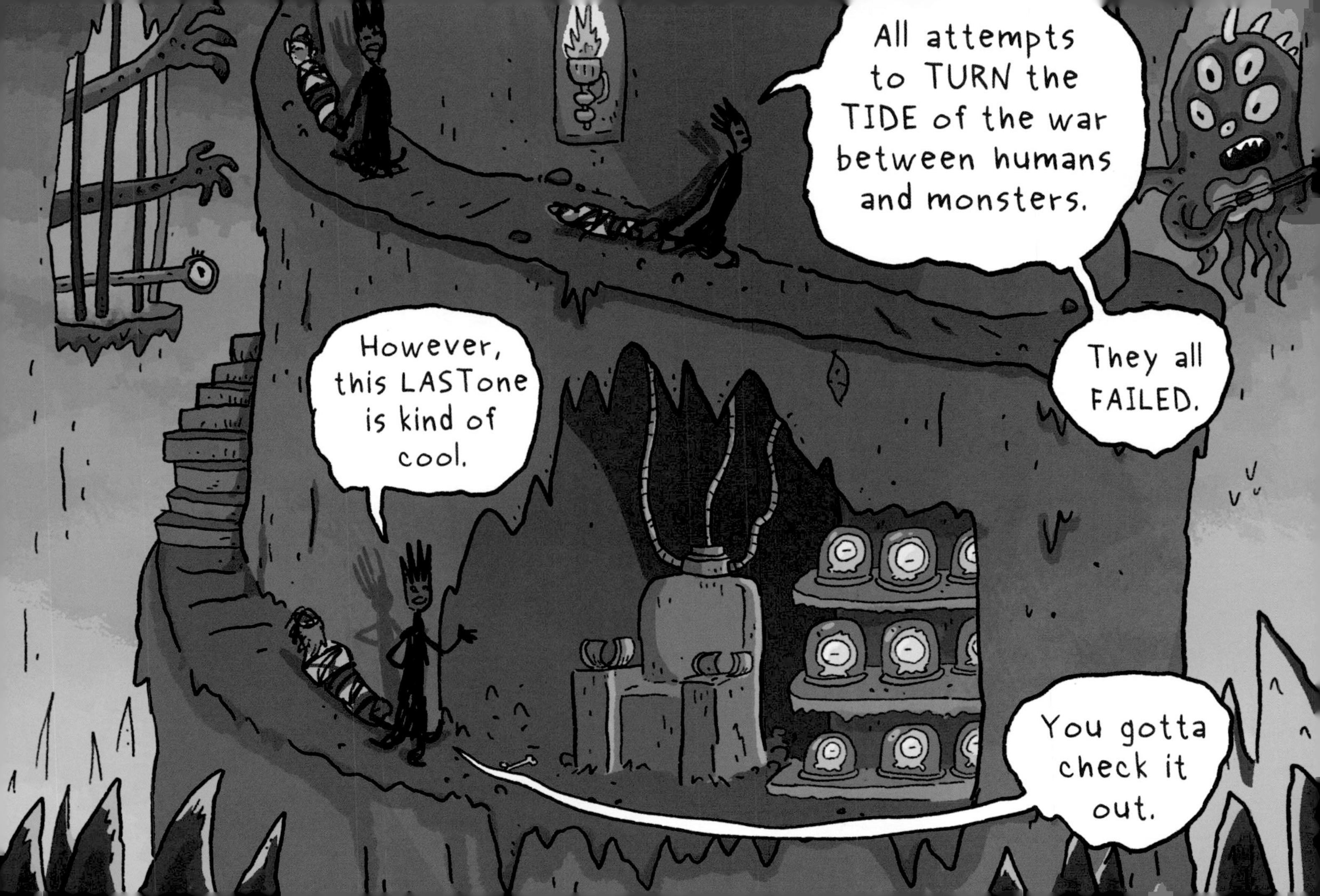
All attempts to TURN the TIDE of the war between humans and monsters.
They all FAILED.
However, this LASTone is kind of cool.
You gotta check it out.

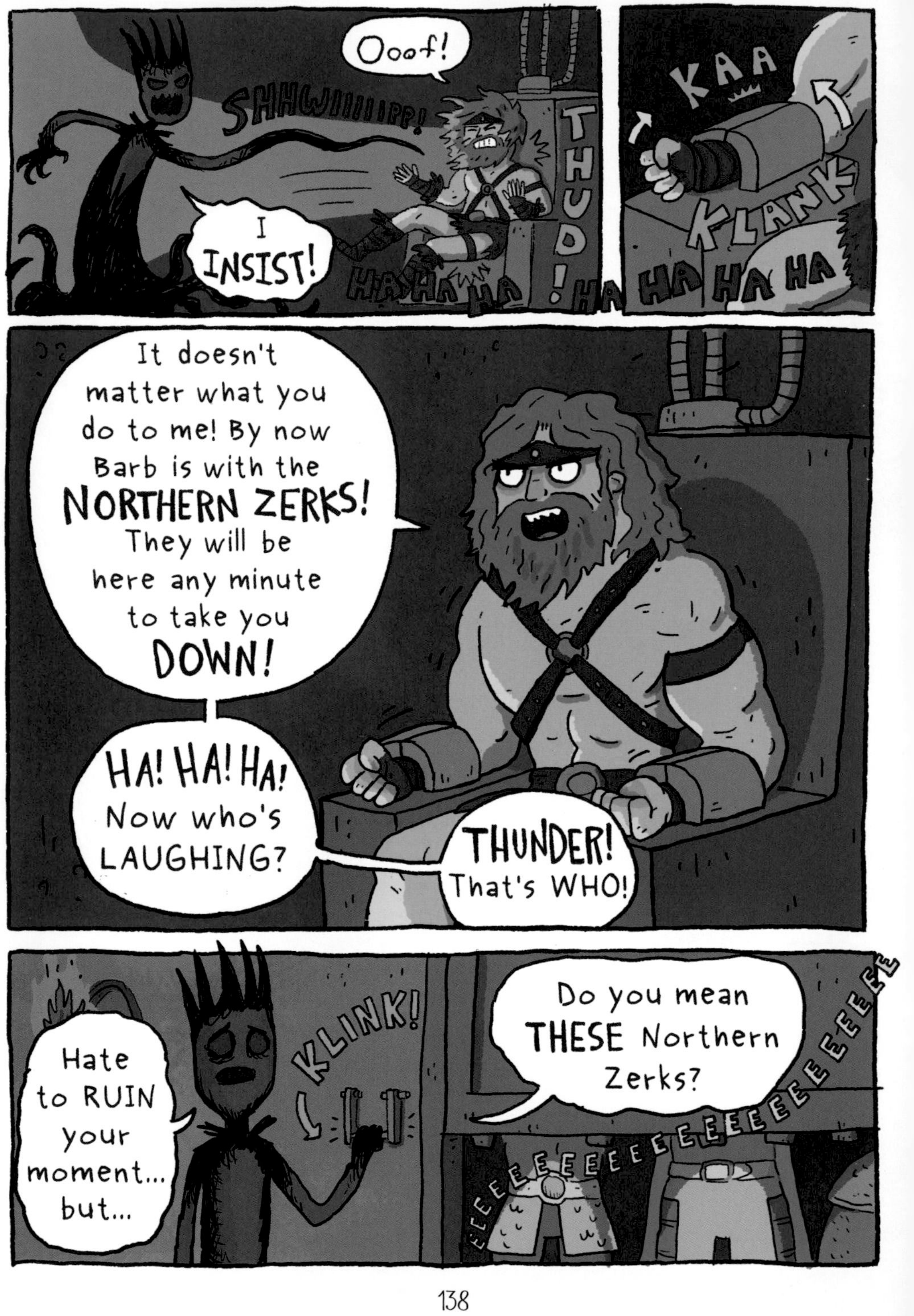
Ooof!
SHHWIIIIIIPP!
I INSIST!
THUD!
HA HA HA HA HA
KAA
KLANK
HA HA HA HA
It doesn't matter what you do to me! By now Barb is with the NORTHERN ZERKS! They will be here any minute to take you DOWN!
HA! HA! HA! Now who's LAUGHING?
THUNDER! That's WHO!
Hate to RUIN your moment... but...
KLINK!
Do you mean THESE Northern Zerks?
EEEEEEEEEEEEEEEEEEEEEEEEEEEE

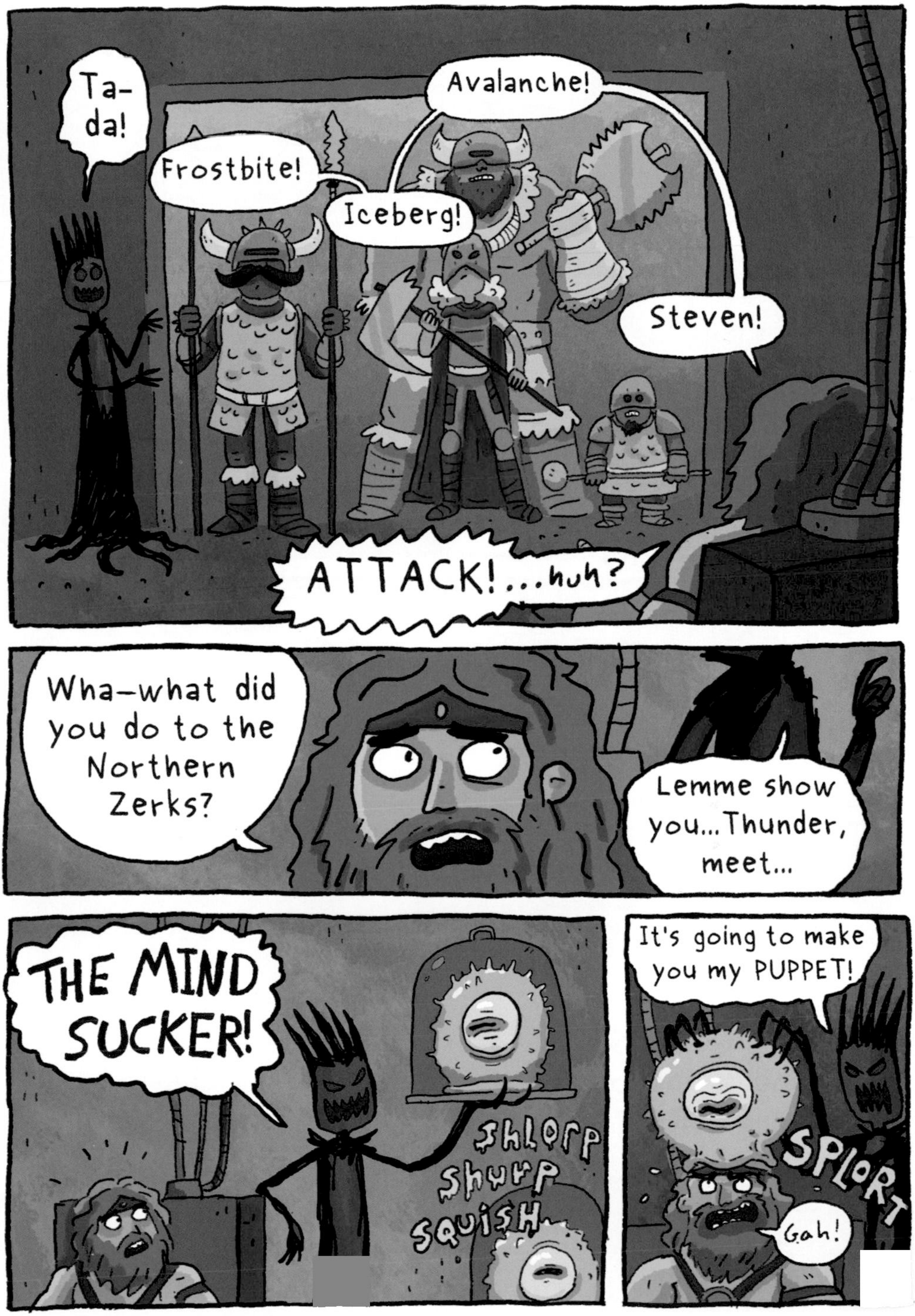
Ta-da!
Frostbite!
Iceberg!
Avalanche!
Steven!
ATTACK! ...huh?
Wha-what did you do to the Northern Zerks?
Lemme show you... Thunder, meet...
THE MIND SUCKER!
SHLORP
SHURP
SQUISH
It's going to make you my PUPPET!
SPLORT
Gah!

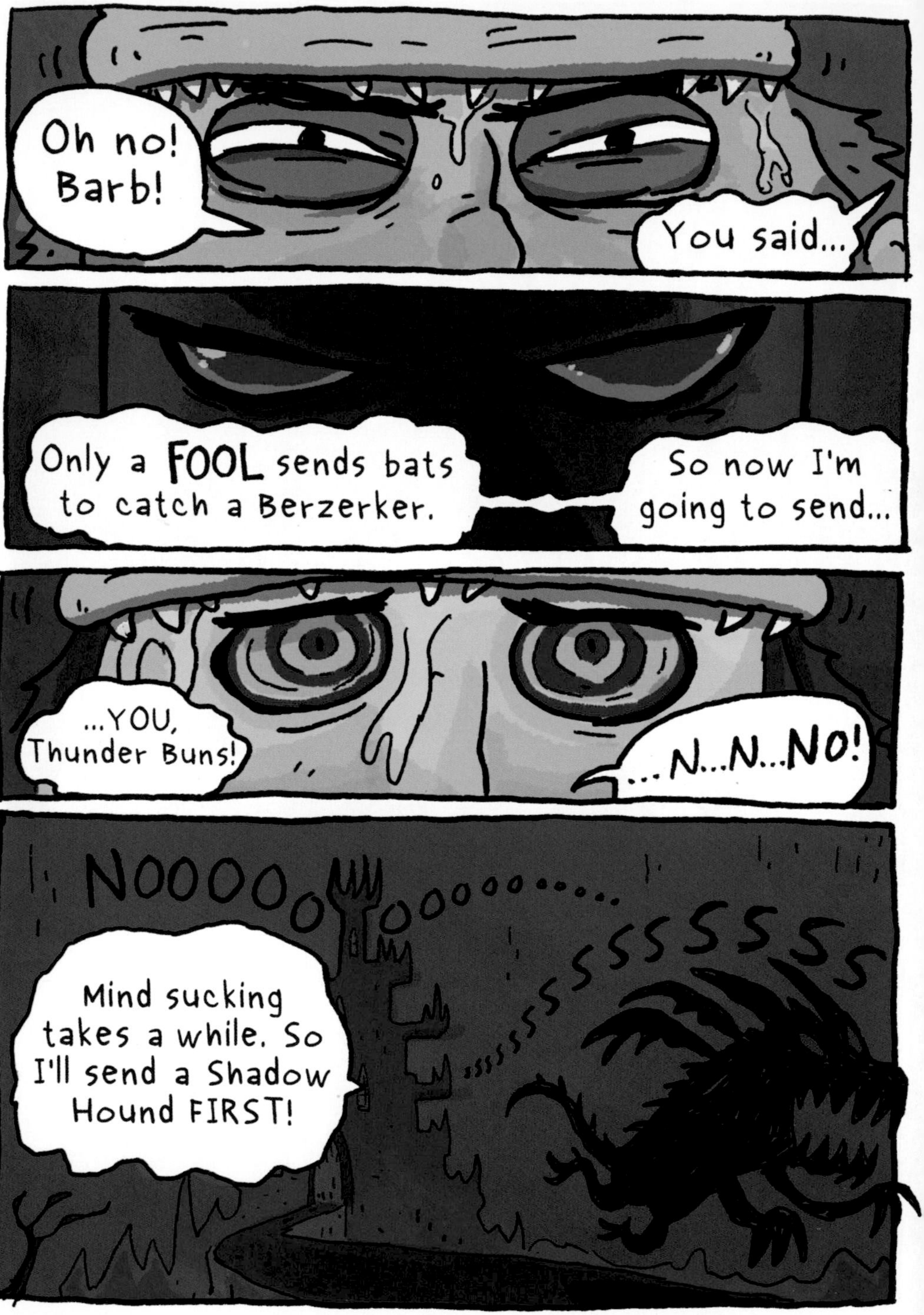
Oh no! Barb!
You said...
Only a FOOL sends bats to catch a Berzerker.
So now I'm going to send...
...YOU, Thunder Buns!
...N...N...NO!
NOOOOOoooooo.....
Mind sucking takes a while. So I'll send a Shadow Hound FIRST!
SSSSSSSSSS

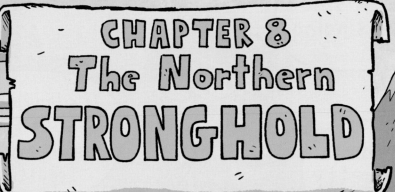

CHAPTER 8
The Northern
STRONGHOLD

We'll make our way north, along the Spire Path.

North it is!

I need some frost on my fur!

We gotta make up for lost time.

Hey, that reminds me of a song...

♪Frosty toes! ♪ I got frosty...

Barb... er...what's wrong?

Is it my singing?

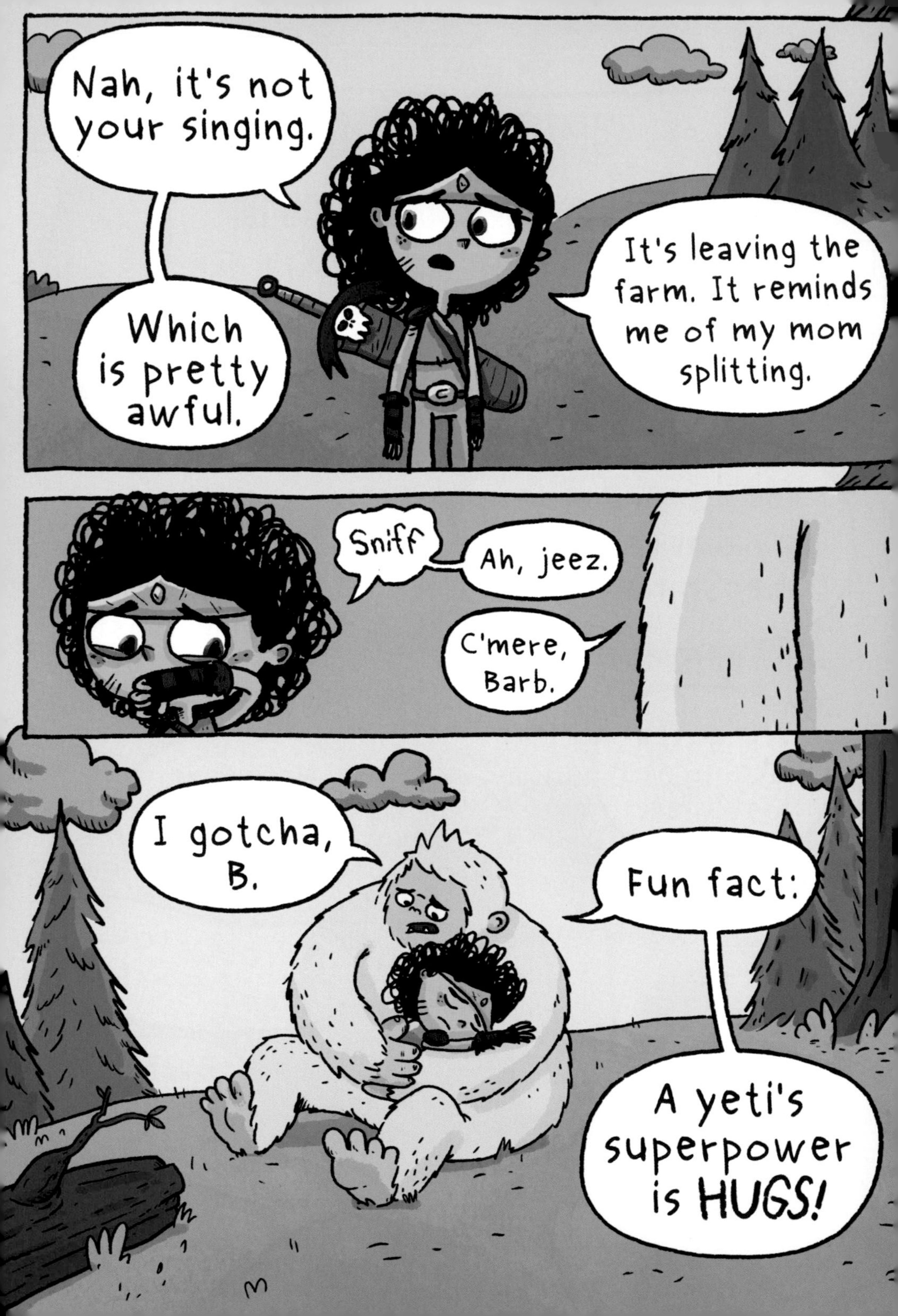
Nah, it's not your singing.
Which is pretty awful.
It's leaving the farm. It reminds me of my mom splitting.
Sniff
Ah, jeez.
C'mere, Barb.
I gotcha, B.
Fun fact:
A yeti's superpower is HUGS!

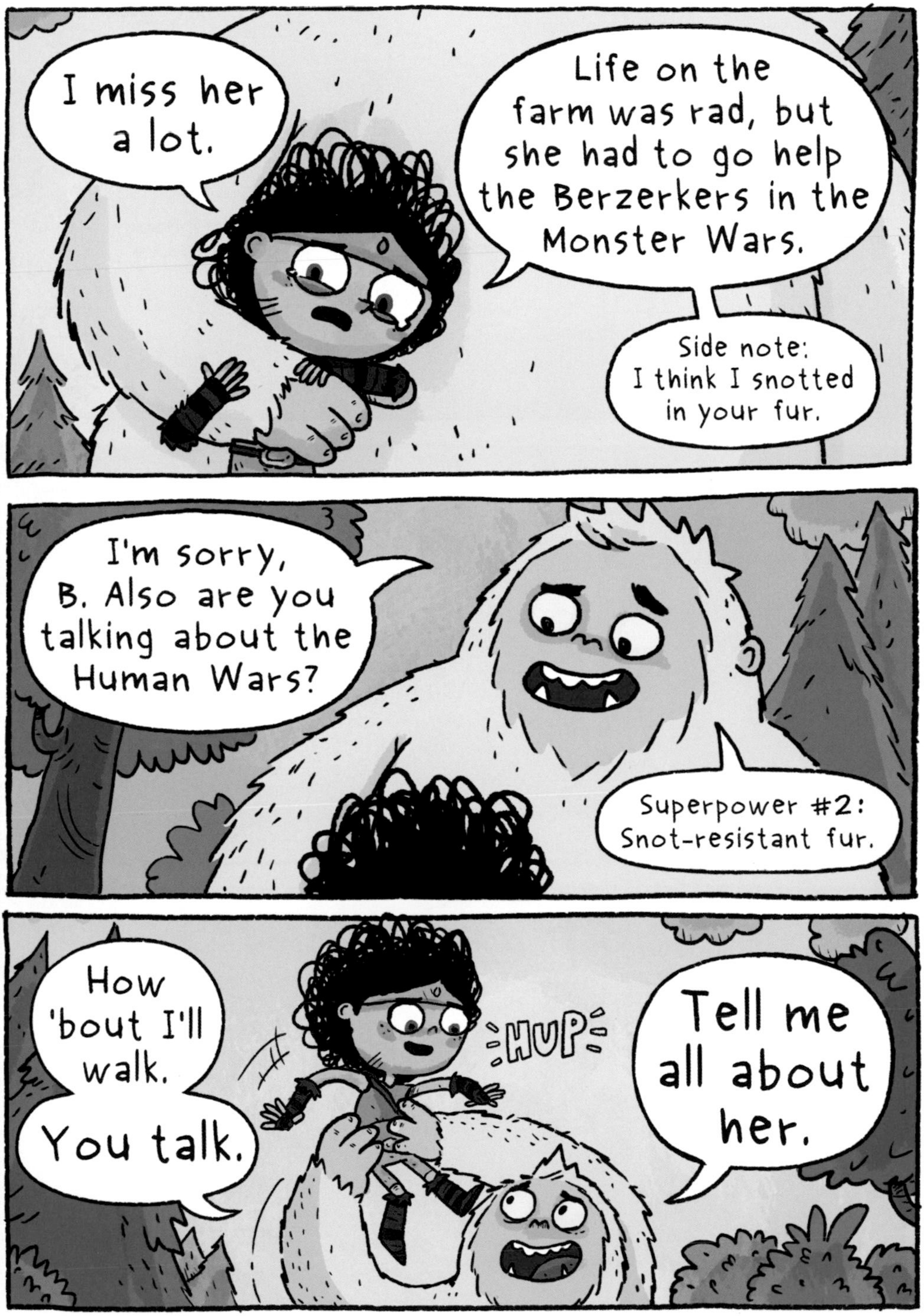
I miss her a lot.
Life on the farm was rad, but she had to go help the Berzerkers in the Monster Wars.
Side note: I think I snotted in your fur.
I'm sorry, B. Also are you talking about the Human Wars?
Superpower #2: Snot-resistant fur.
How 'bout I'll walk.
You talk.
HUP
Tell me all about her.

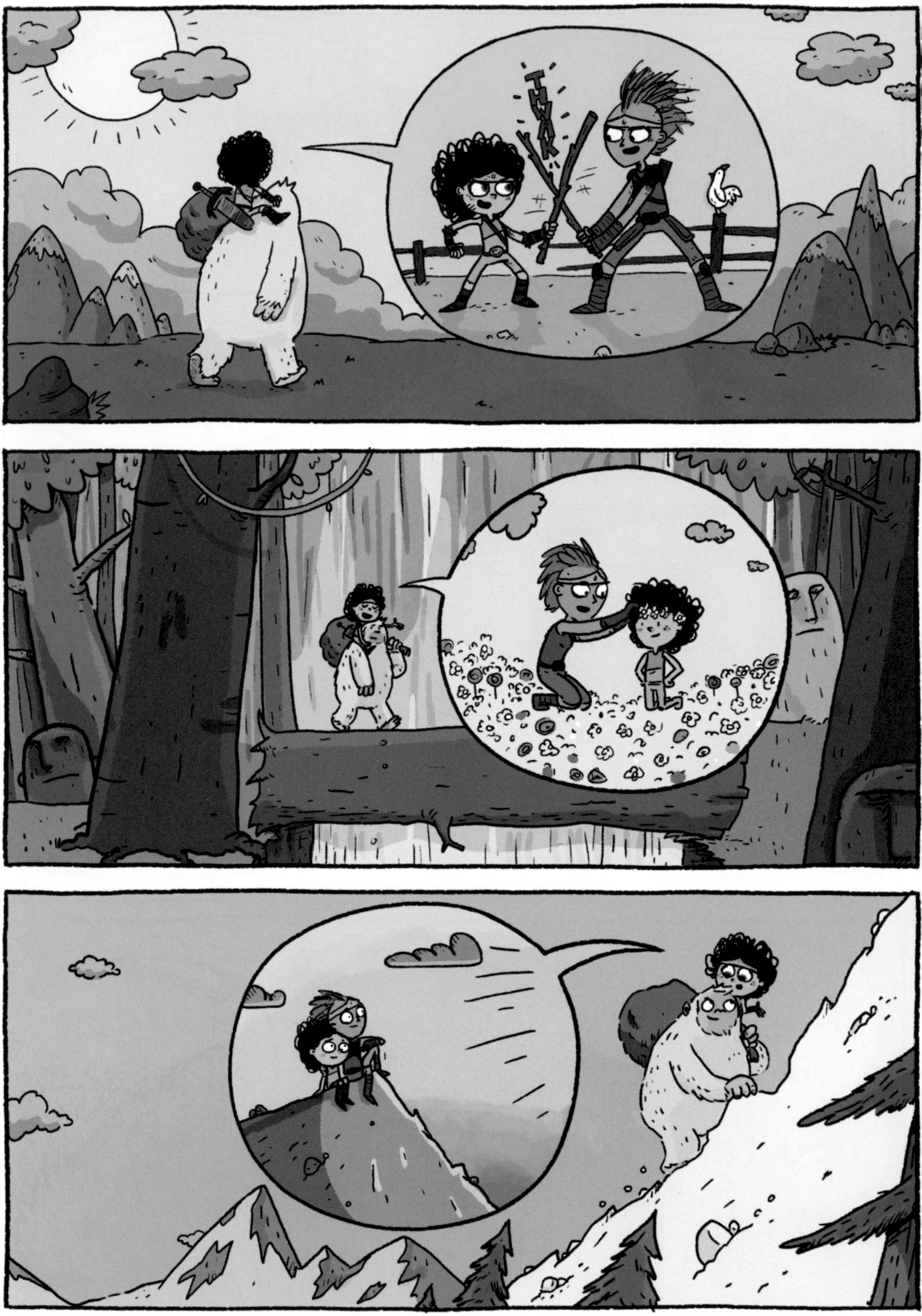
THWAK

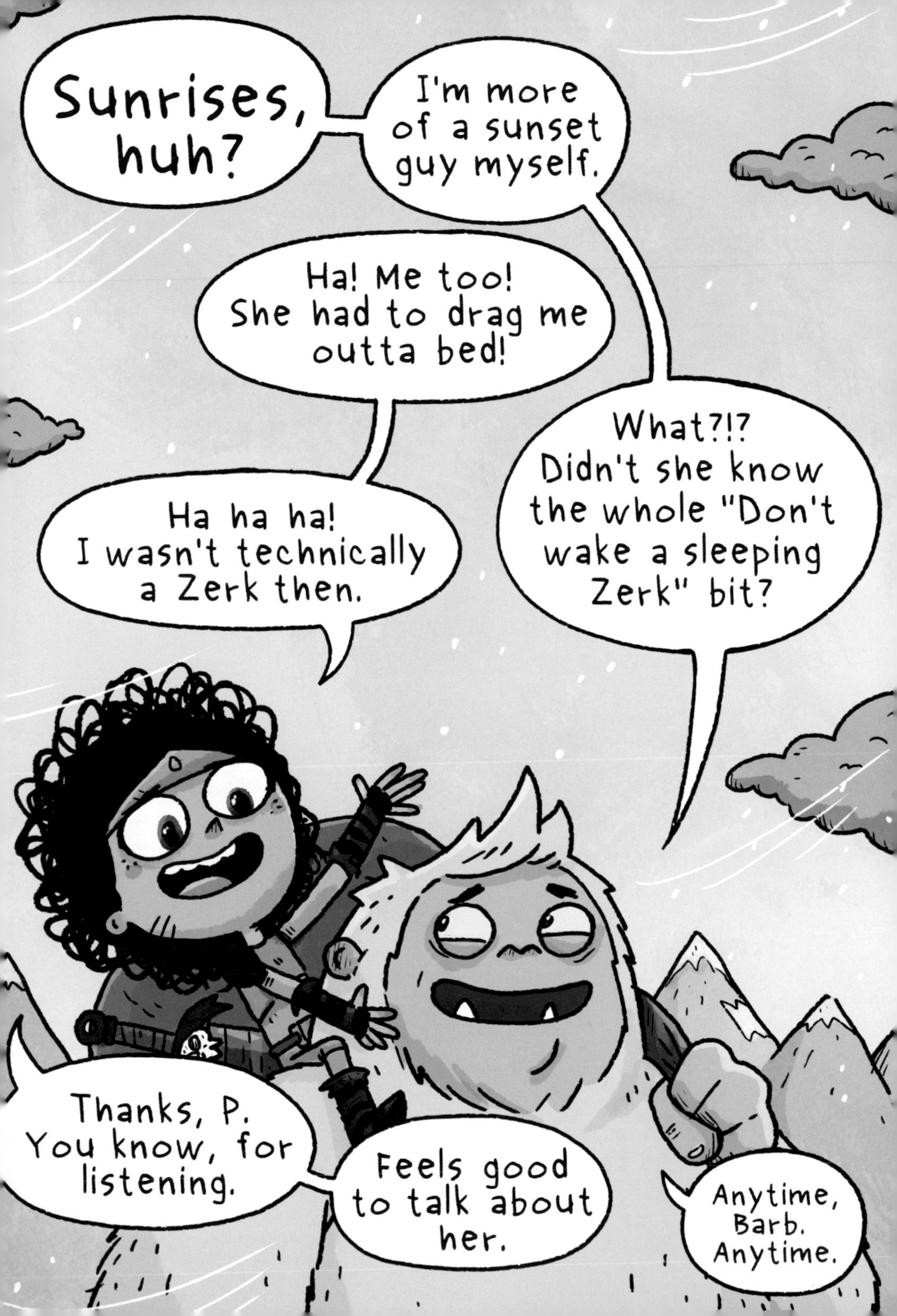
Sunrises, huh?
I'm more of a sunset guy myself.
Ha! Me too! She had to drag me outta bed!
What?!? Didn't she know the whole "Don't wake a sleeping Zerk" bit?
Ha ha ha! I wasn't technically a Zerk then.
Thanks, P. You know, for listening.
Feels good to talk about her.
Anytime, Barb. Anytime.

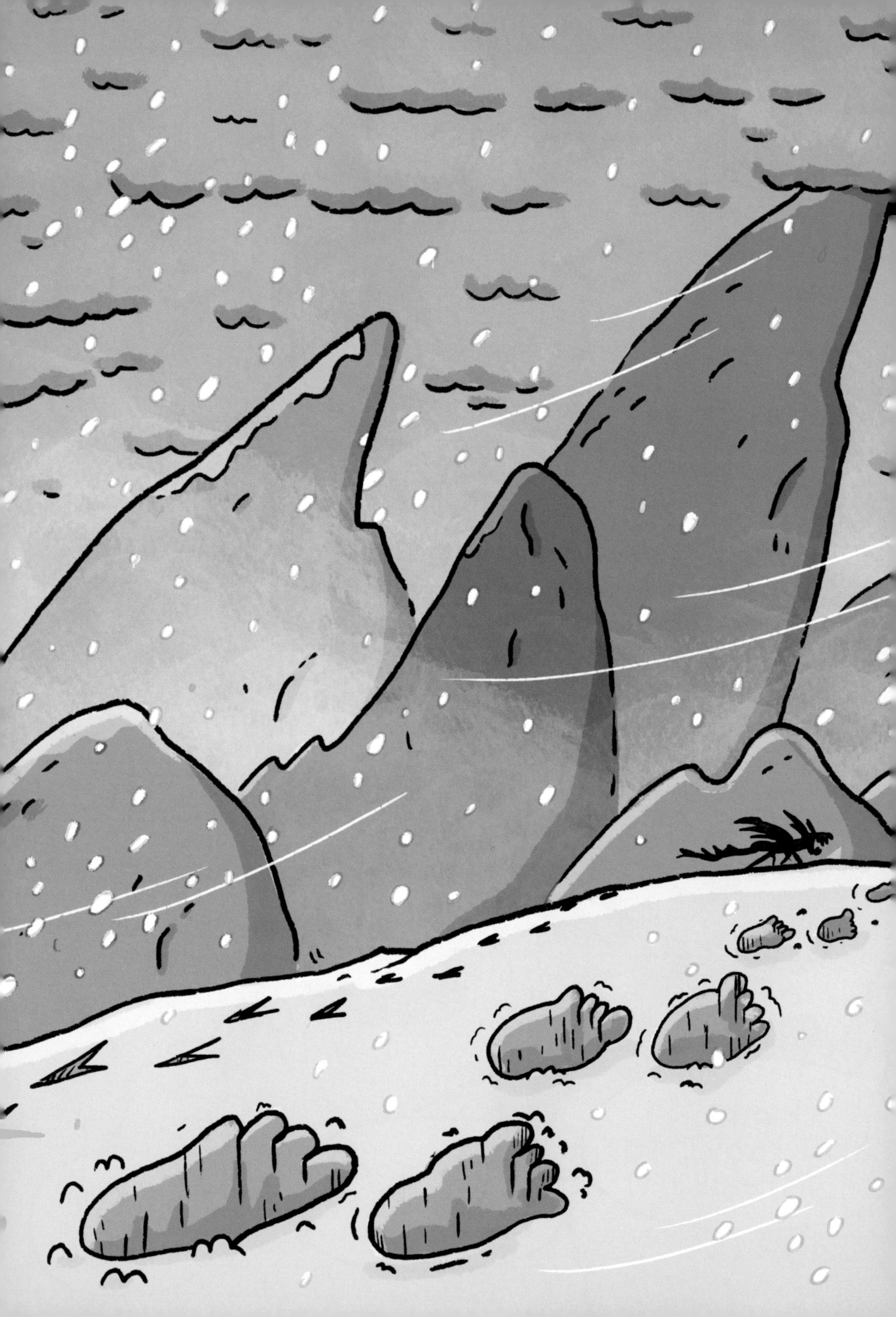

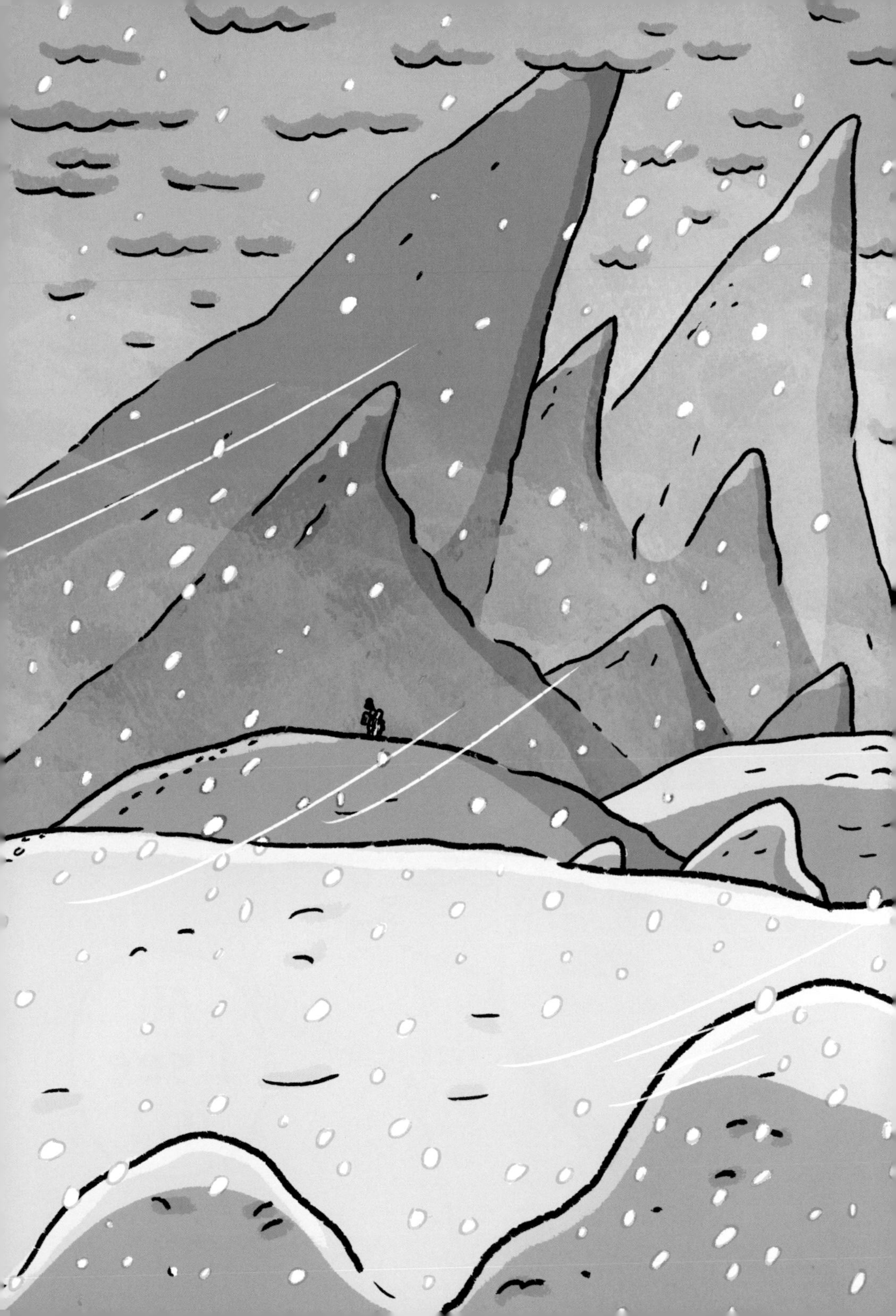

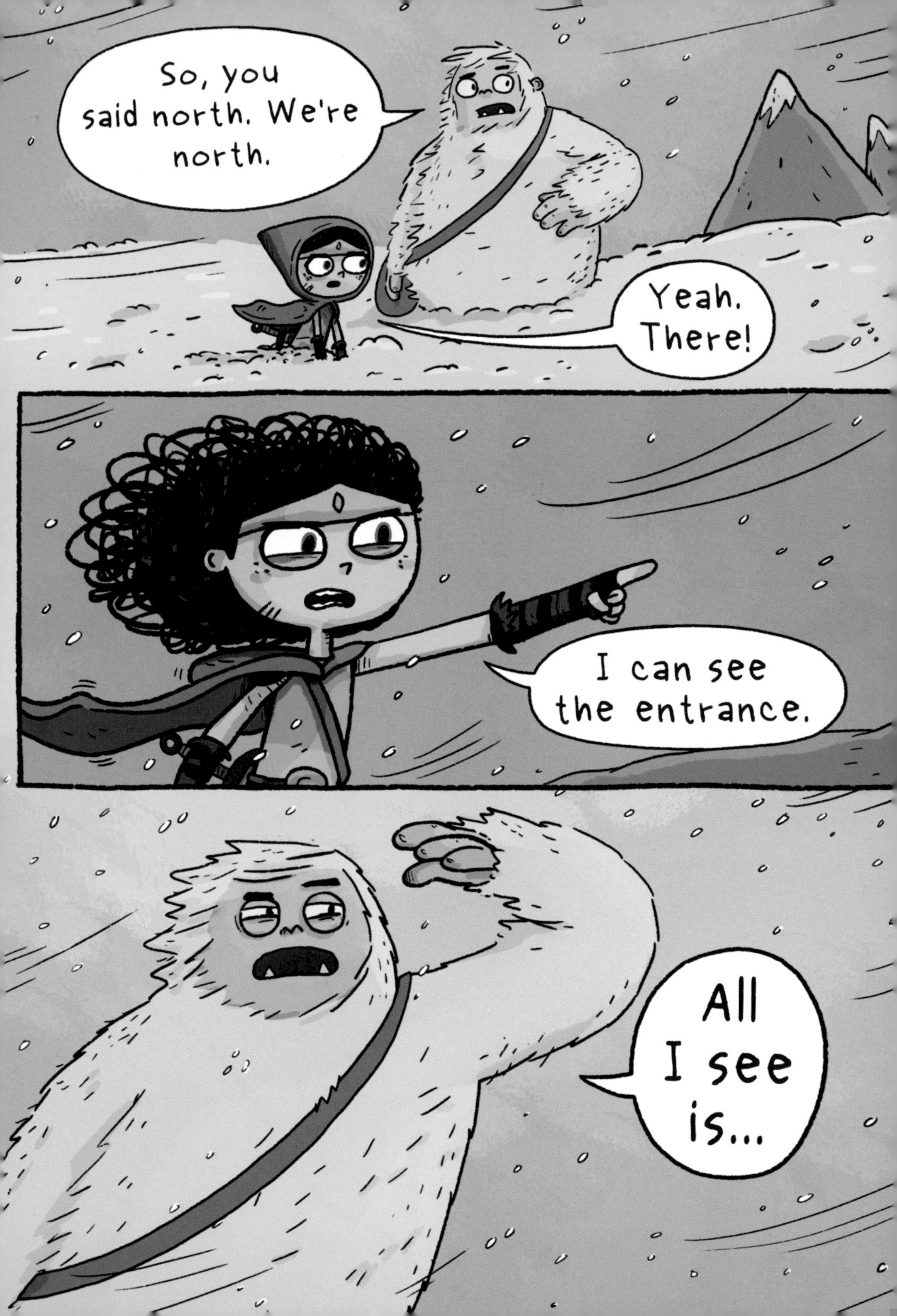
So, you said north. We're north.
Yeah. There!
I can see the entrance.
All I see is...

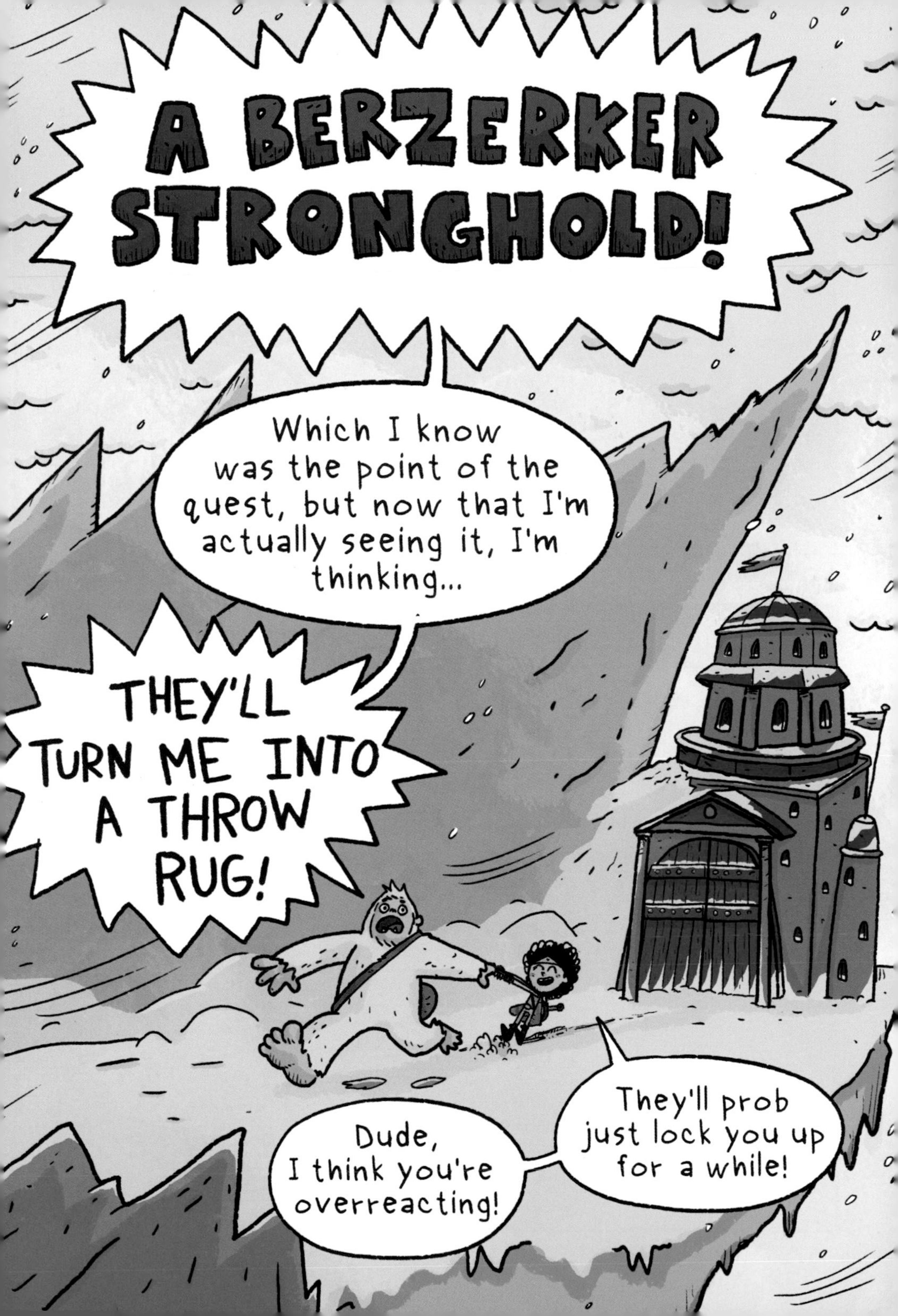
A BERZERKER STRONGHOLD!
Which I know was the point of the quest, but now that I'm actually seeing it, I'm thinking...
THEY'LL TURN ME INTO A THROW RUG!
Dude, I think you're overreacting!
They'll prob just lock you up for a while!

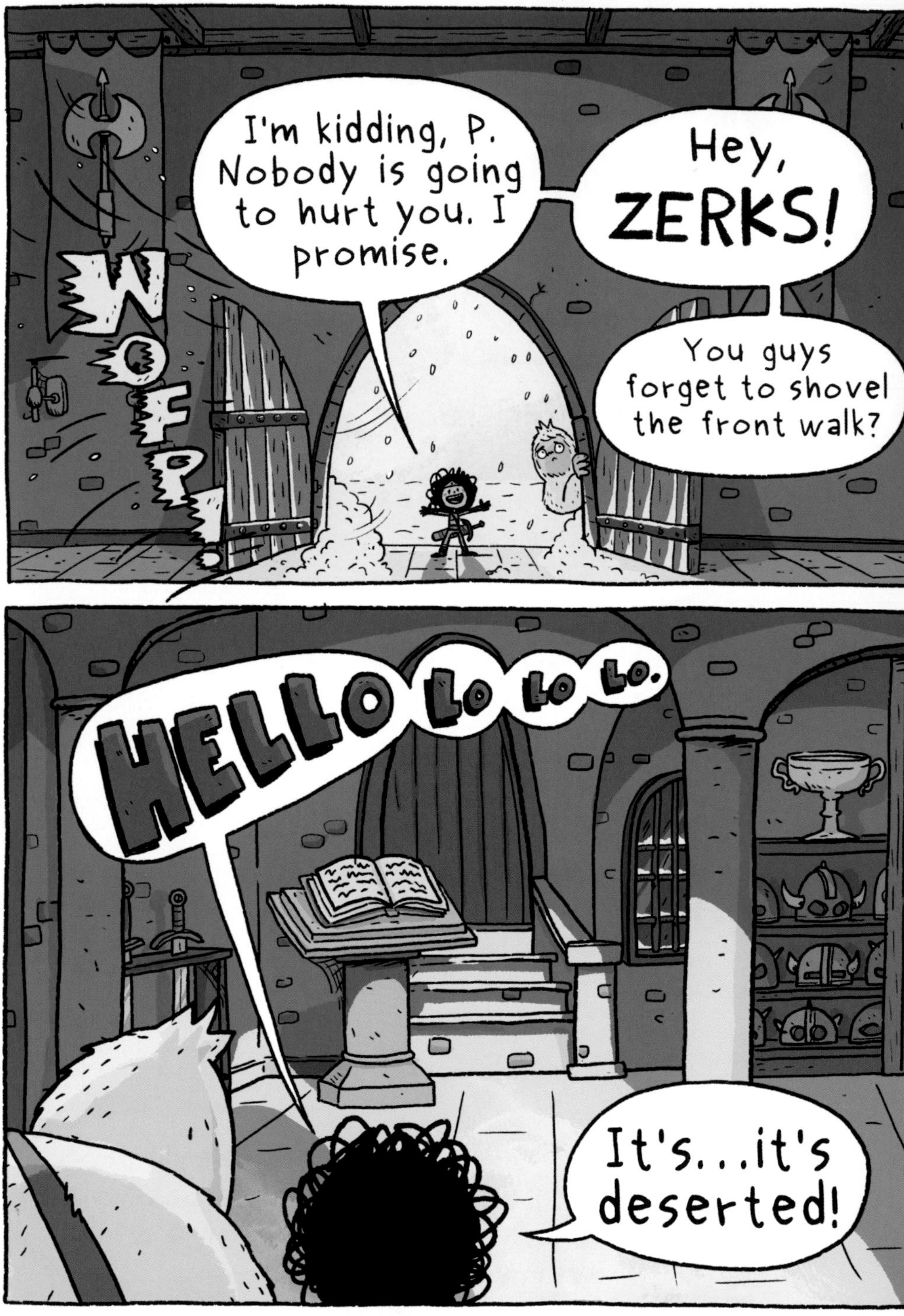
WOOFP!
I'm kidding, P. Nobody is going to hurt you. I promise.
Hey, ZERKS!
You guys forget to shovel the front walk?
HELLO LO LO LO.
It's...it's deserted!

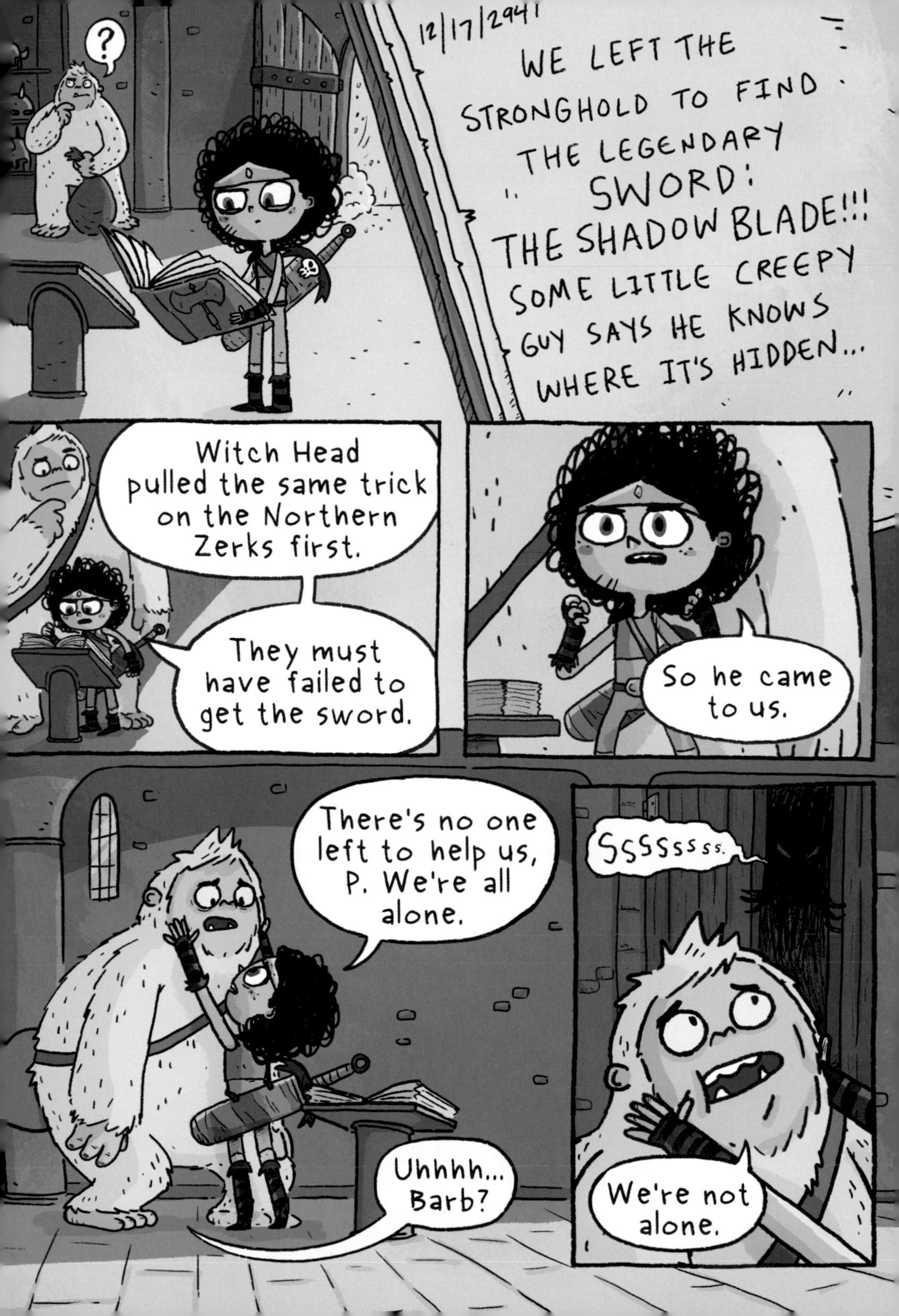
?
12/17/2941
WE LEFT THE STRONGHOLD TO FIND THE LEGENDARY SWORD: THE SHADOW BLADE!!! SOME LITTLE CREEPY GUY SAYS HE KNOWS WHERE IT'S HIDDEN...
Witch Head pulled the same trick on the Northern Zerks first.
They must have failed to get the sword.
So he came to us.
There's no one left to help us, P. We're all alone.
Uhhhh... Barb?
Sssssss.
We're not alone.

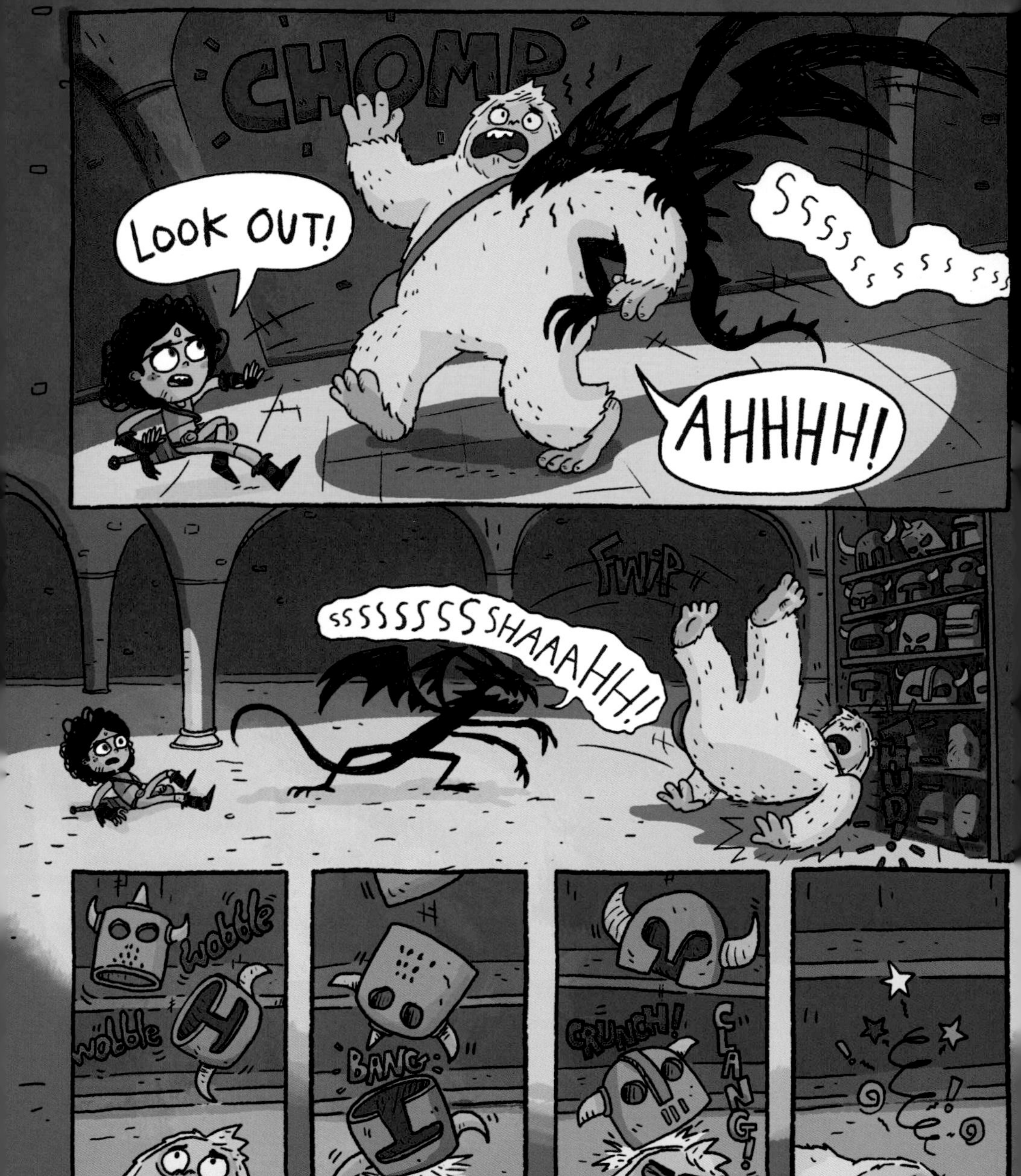

CHOMP
LOOK OUT!
SSSSSSSSSSSS
AHHHH!
FWIP
SSSSSSSSSHAAAHH!
THUD
wobble
wobble
BANG
BONK
CRUNCH!
CLANG!
THUNK!
BANG!

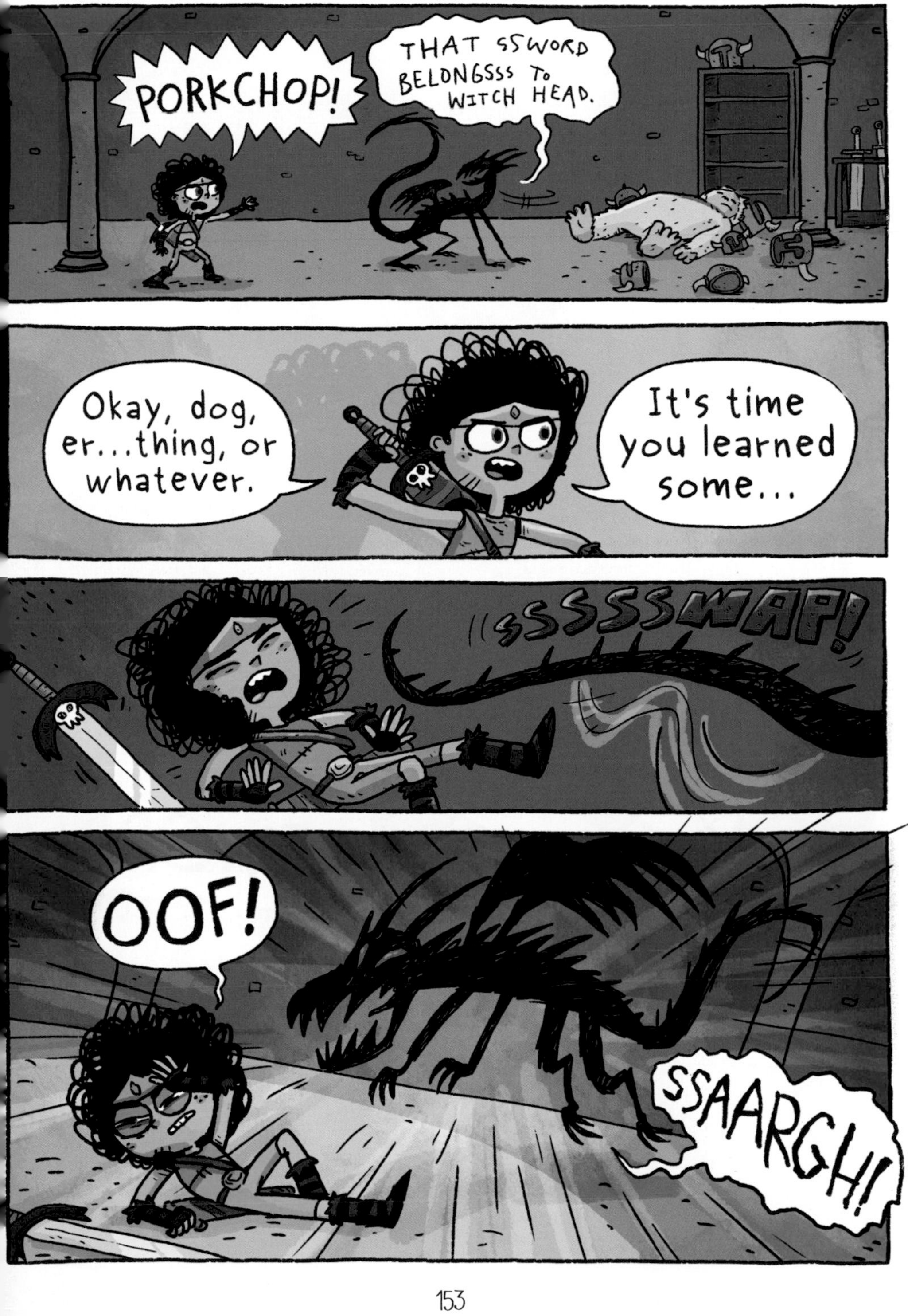
PORKCHOP!
THAT SSWORD BELONGSSS TO WITCH HEAD.
Okay, dog, er...thing, or whatever.
It's time you learned some...
SSSSSWAP!
OOF!
SSAARGH!

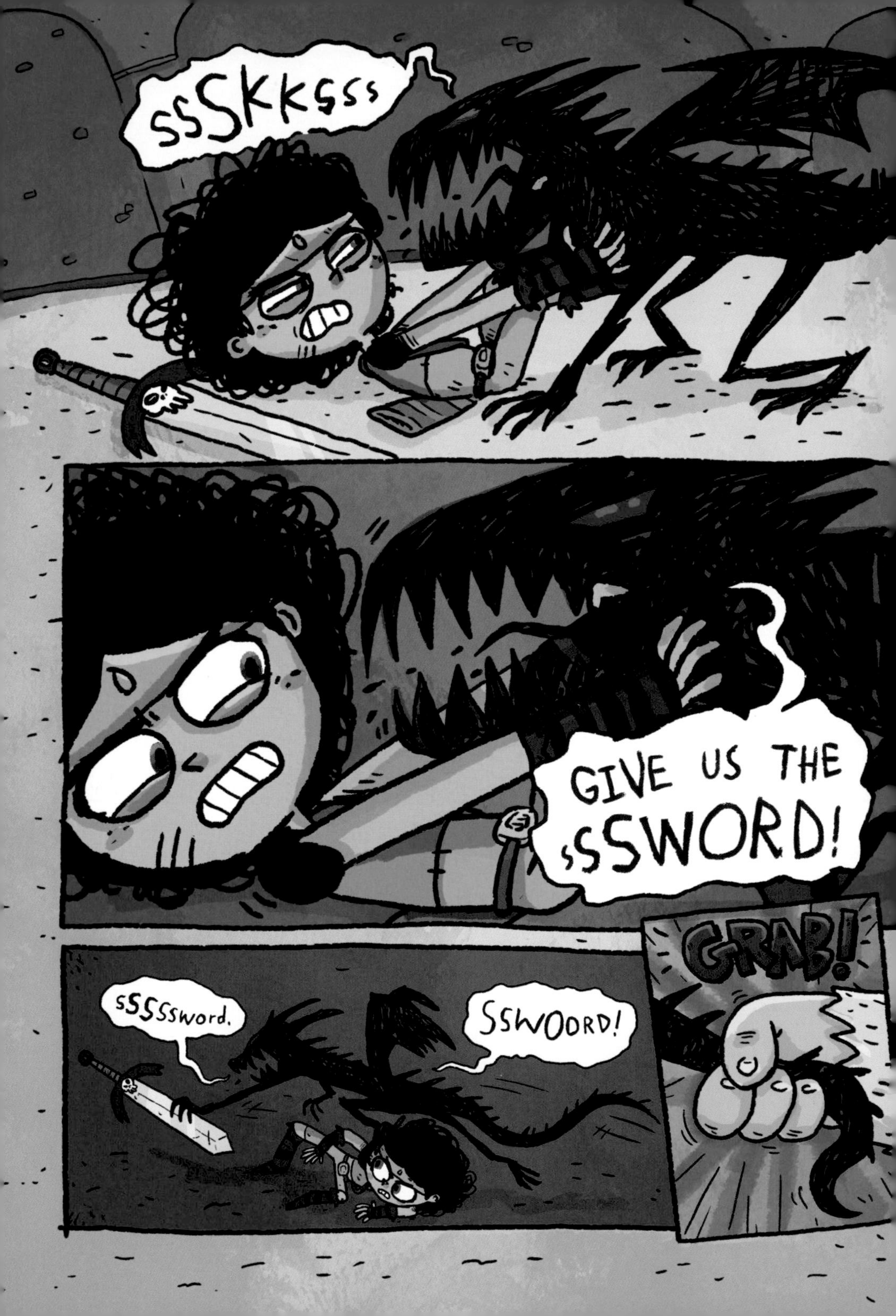

sSSKKsss
GIVE US THE sSSWORD!
sSSSsword.
SSWOORD!
GRAB!

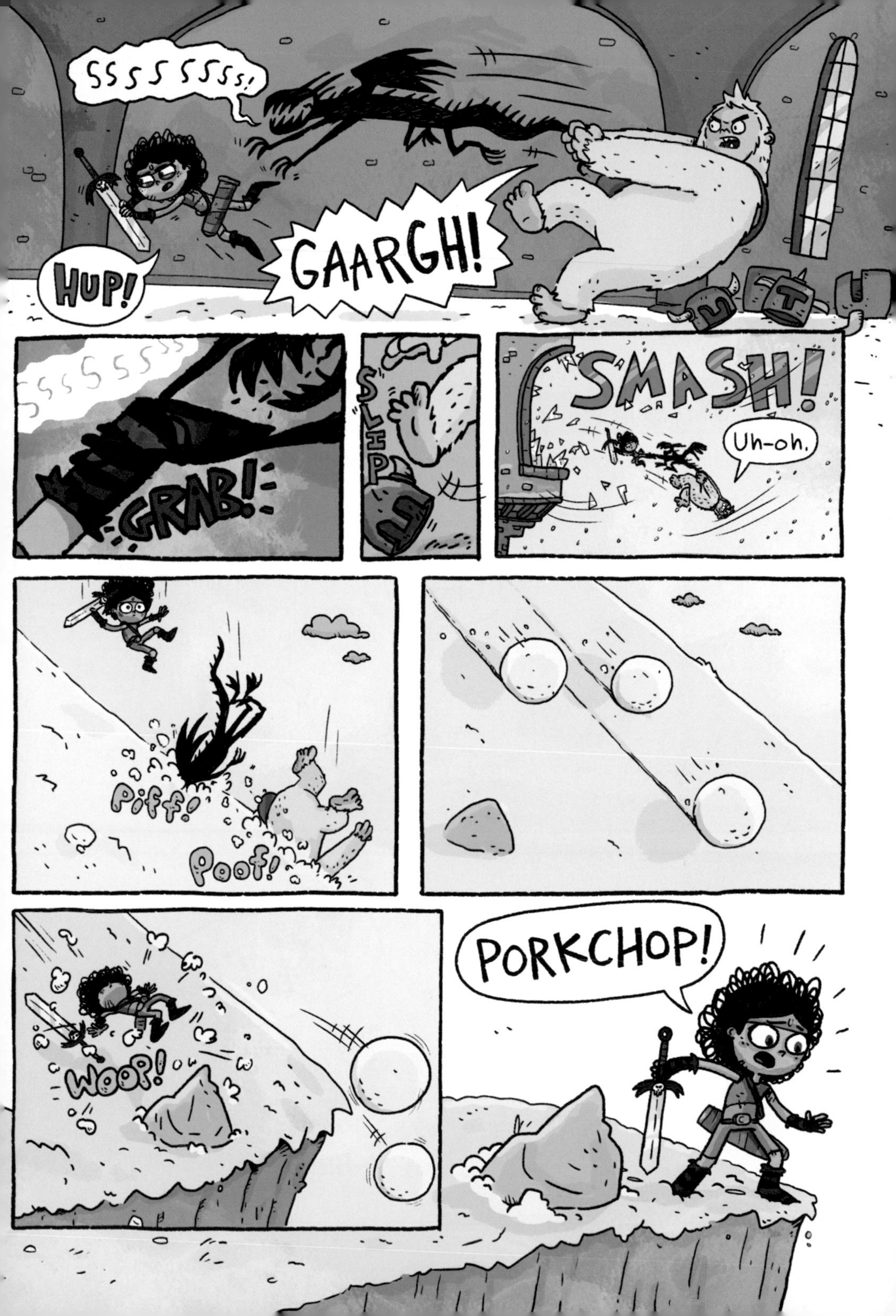

SSSSSSSs!
HUP!
GAARGH!
SSSSSSS
GRAB!
SLIP
SMASH!
Uh-oh.
Piff!
Poof!
WOOP!
PORKCHOP!

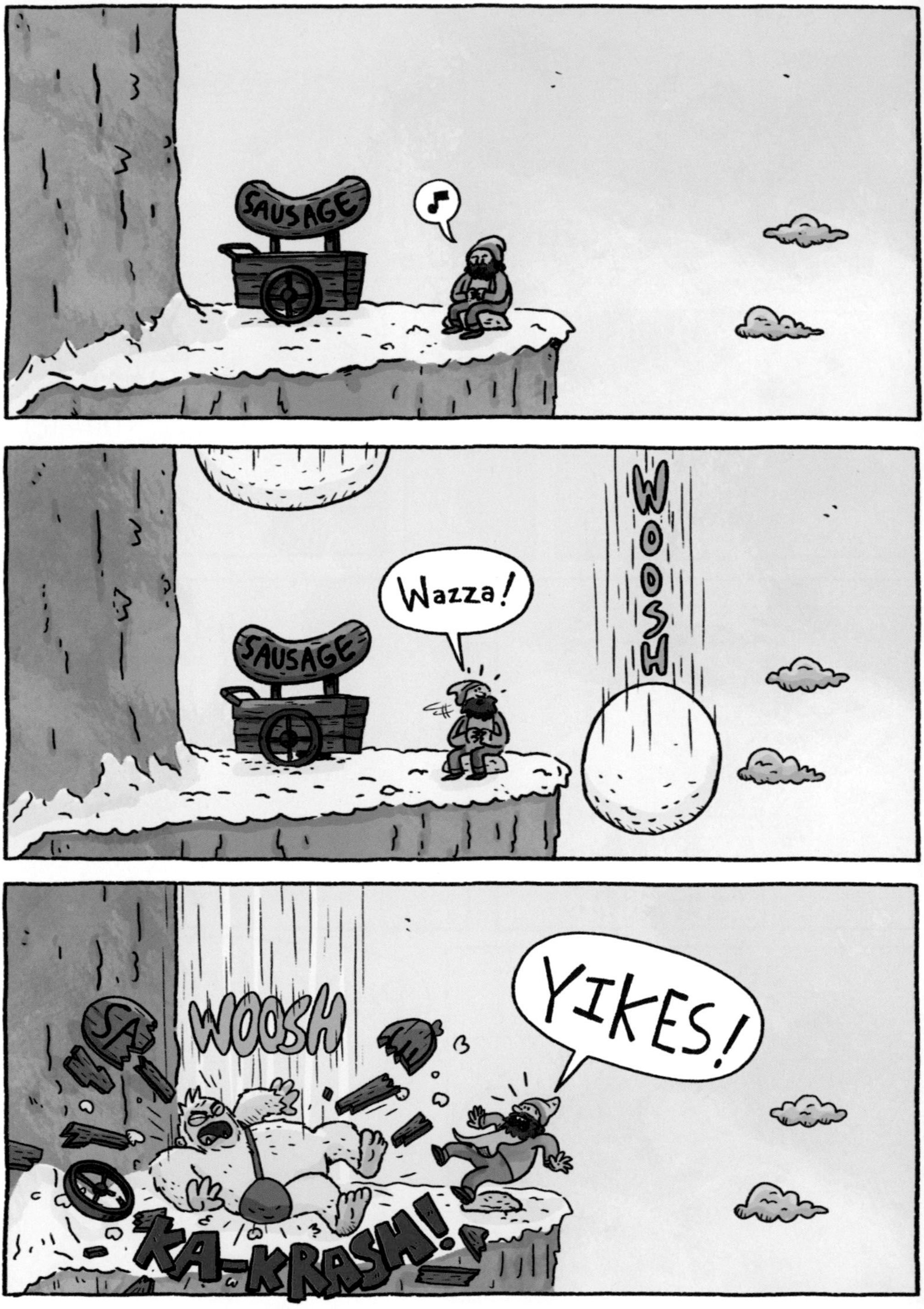
SAUSAGE
SAUSAGE
Wazza!
WOOSH
SA
WOOSH
YIKES!
KA-KRASH!

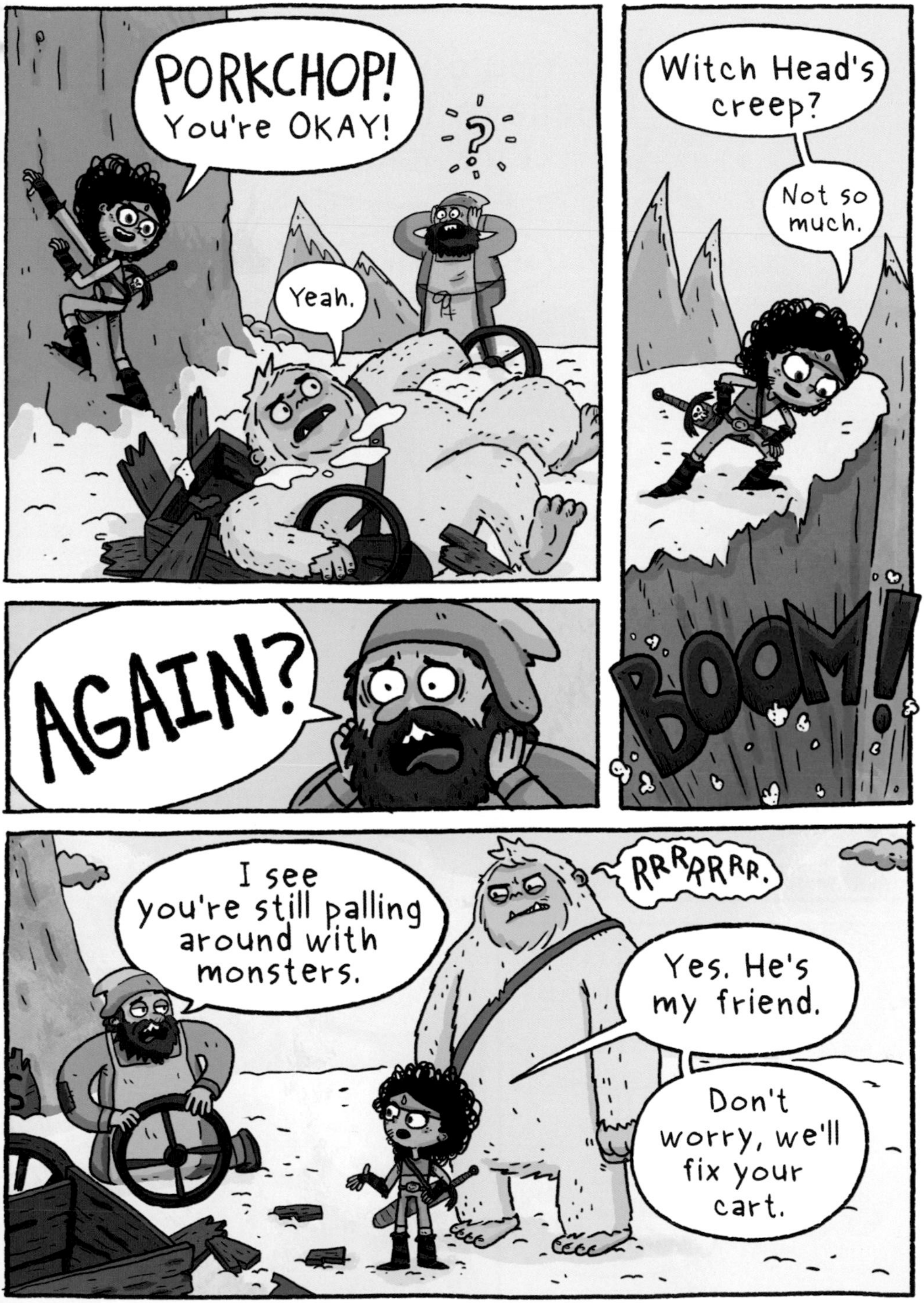
PORKCHOP! You're OKAY!
?
Yeah.
Witch Head's creep?
Not so much.
AGAIN?
BOOM!
I see you're still palling around with monsters.
RRRRRRR.
Yes. He's my friend.
Don't worry, we'll fix your cart.

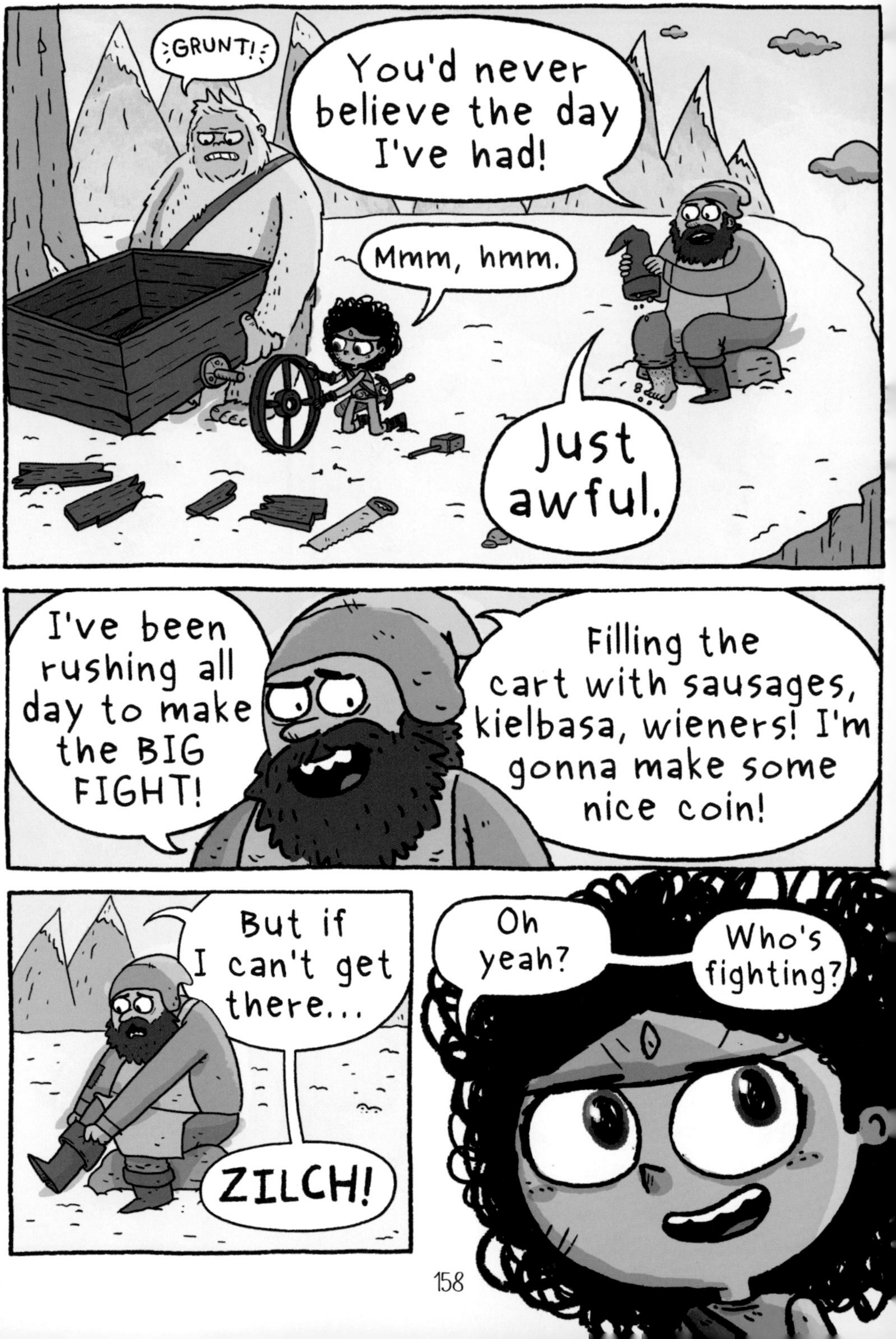
GRUNT!
You'd never believe the day I've had!
Mmm, hmm.
Just awful.
I've been rushing all day to make the BIG FIGHT!
Filling the cart with sausages, kielbasa, wieners! I'm gonna make some nice coin!
But if I can't get there...
ZILCH!
Oh yeah?
Who's fighting?

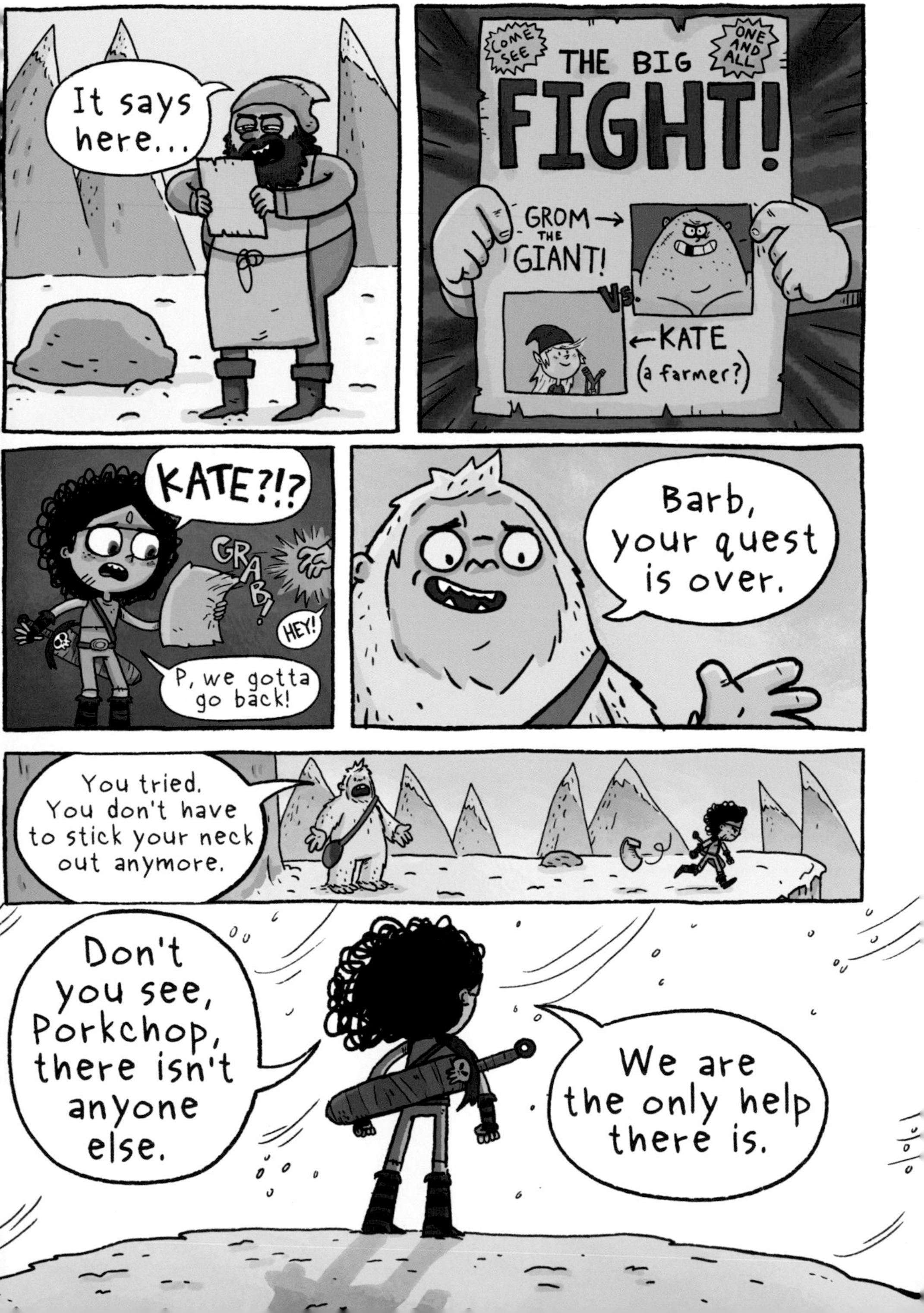
It says here...
COME SEE
THE BIG
ONE AND ALL
FIGHT!
GROM THE GIANT!
VS.
KATE
(a farmer?)
KATE?!?
GRAB!
HEY!
P, we gotta go back!
Barb, your quest is over.
You tried. You don't have to stick your neck out anymore.
Don't you see, Porkchop, there isn't anyone else.
We are the only help there is.

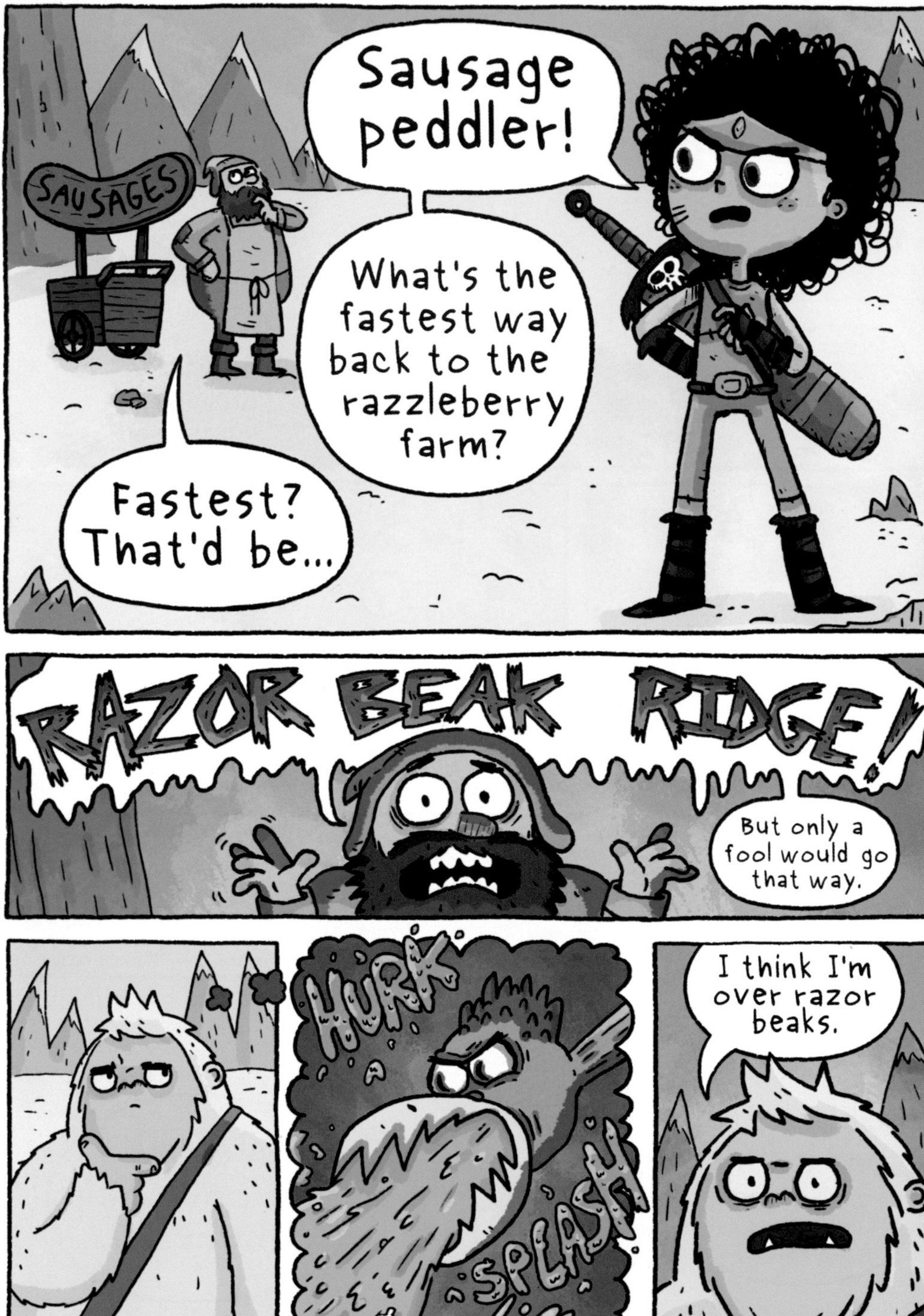

SAUSAGES
Sausage peddler!
What's the fastest way back to the razzleberry farm?
Fastest? That'd be...
RAZOR BEAK RIDGE!
But only a fool would go that way.
HURK
SPLASH
I think I'm over razor beaks.

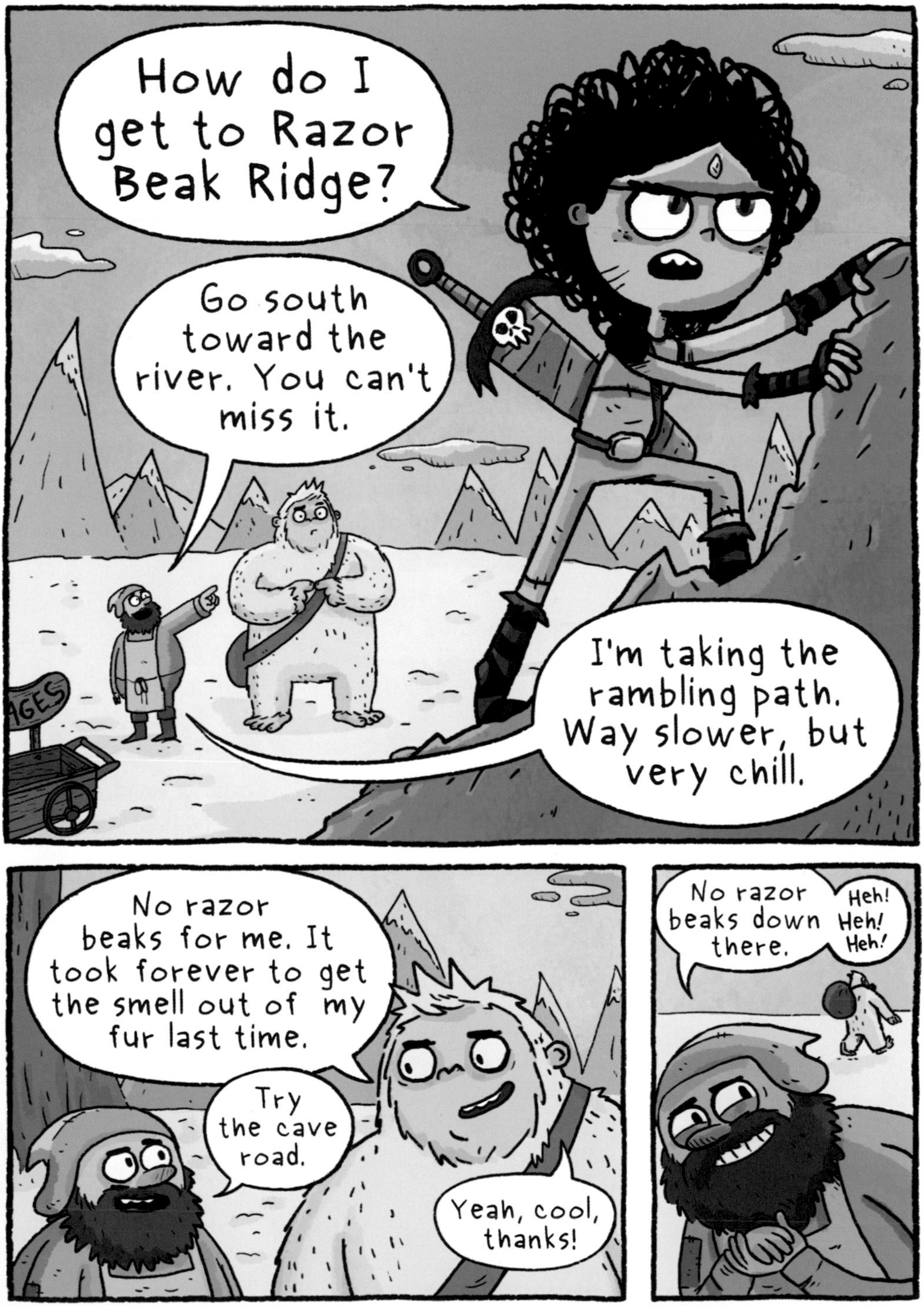
How do I get to Razor Beak Ridge?
Go south toward the river. You can't miss it.
I'm taking the rambling path. Way slower, but very chill.
No razor beaks for me. It took forever to get the smell out of my fur last time.
Try the cave road.
Yeah, cool, thanks!
No razor beaks down there.
Heh! Heh! Heh!

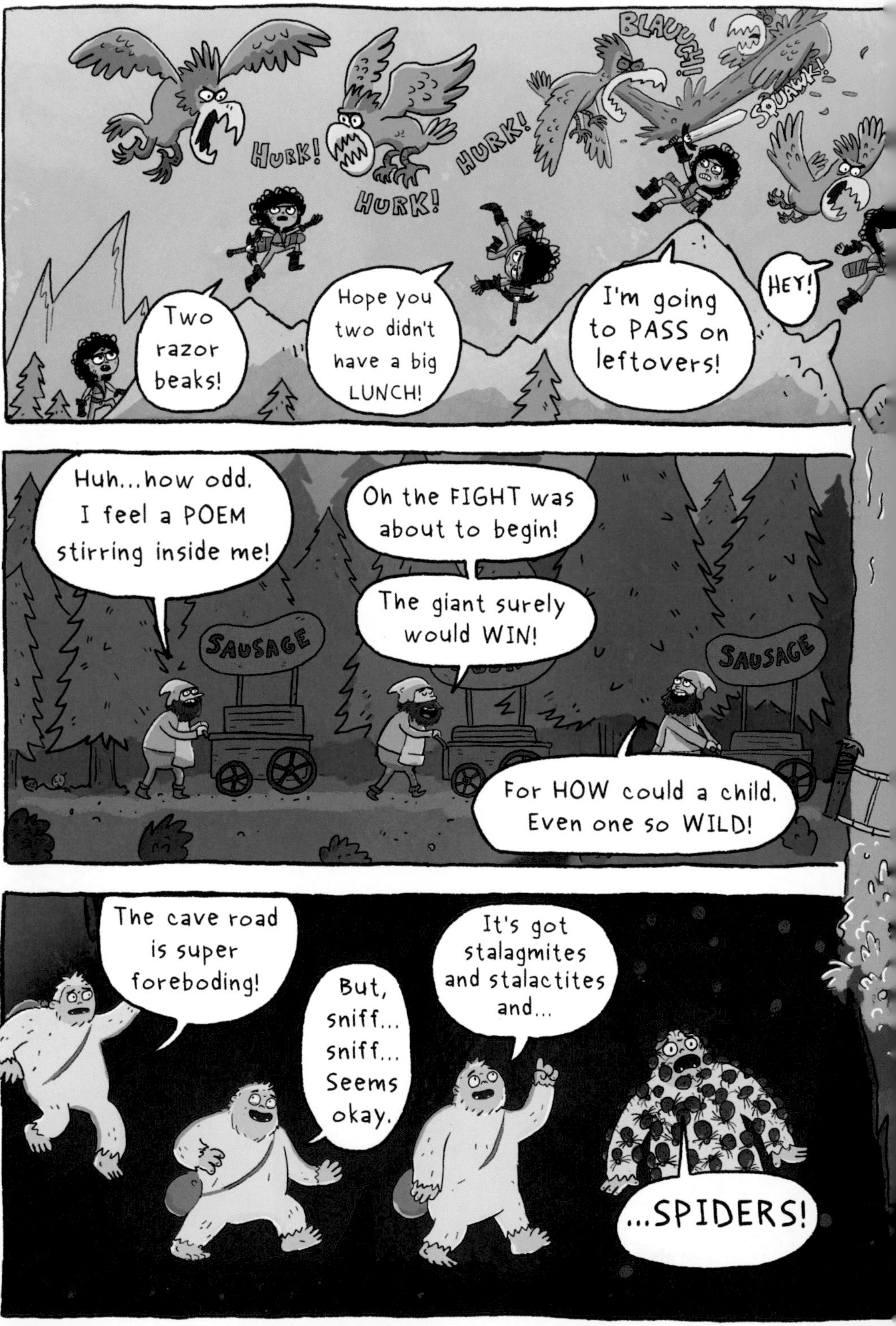
BLAUGH!
SQUAWK!
HURK!
HURK!
HURK!
Two razor beaks!
Hope you two didn't have a big LUNCH!
I'm going to PASS on leftovers!
HEY!
Huh...how odd. I feel a POEM stirring inside me!
SAUSAGE
Oh the FIGHT was about to begin!
The giant surely would WIN!
SAUSAGE
For HOW could a child. Even one so WILD!
The cave road is super foreboding!
But, sniff... sniff... Seems okay.
It's got stalagmites and stalactites and...
...SPIDERS!

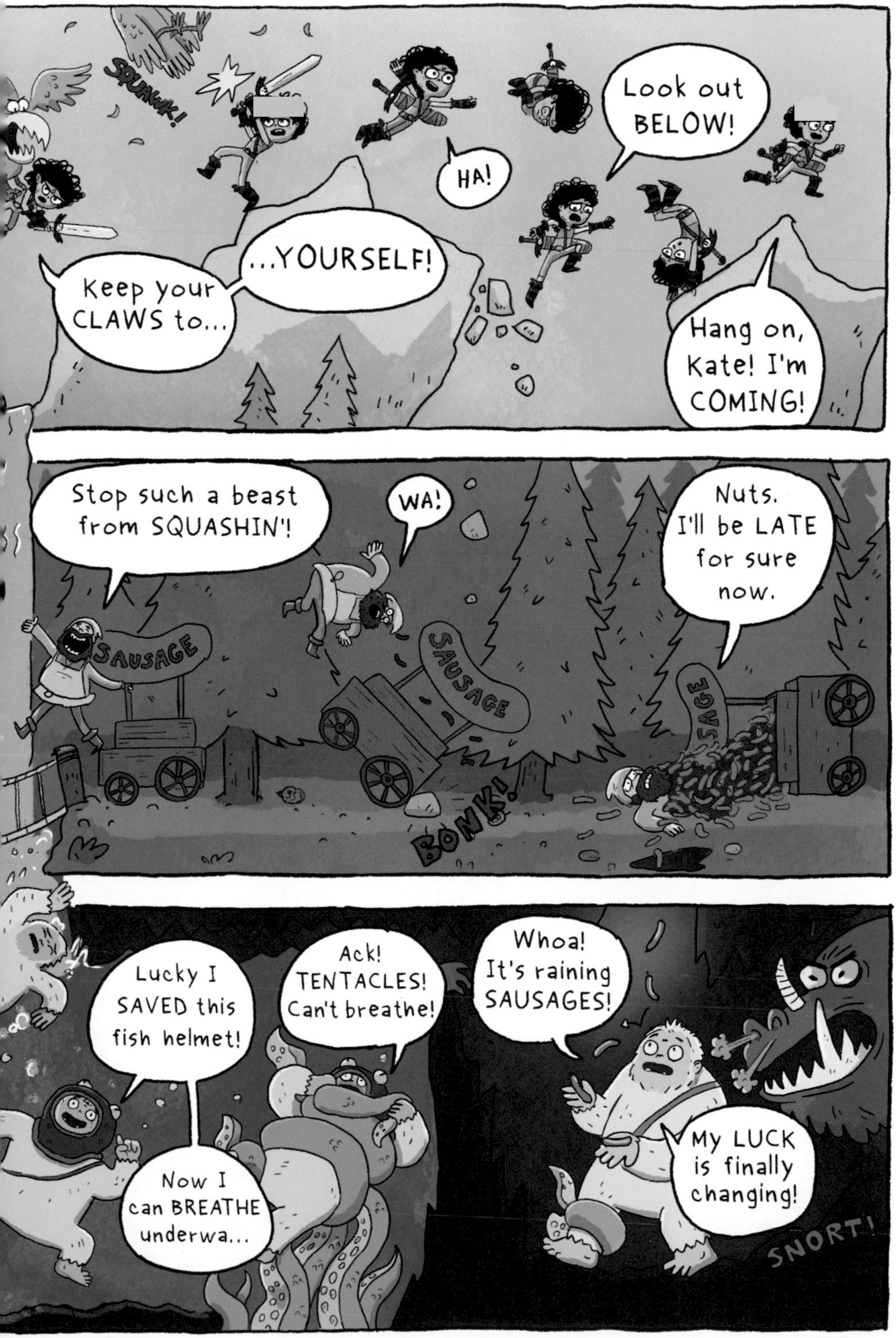
SQUAWK!
Keep your CLAWS to...
...YOURSELF!
HA!
Look out BELOW!
Hang on, Kate! I'm COMING!
Stop such a beast from SQUASHIN'!
SAUSAGE
WA!
SAUSAGE
BONK!
Nuts. I'll be LATE for sure now.
Lucky I SAVED this fish helmet!
Now I can BREATHE underwa...
Ack! TENTACLES! Can't breathe!
Whoa! It's raining SAUSAGES!
My LUCK is finally changing!
SNORT!

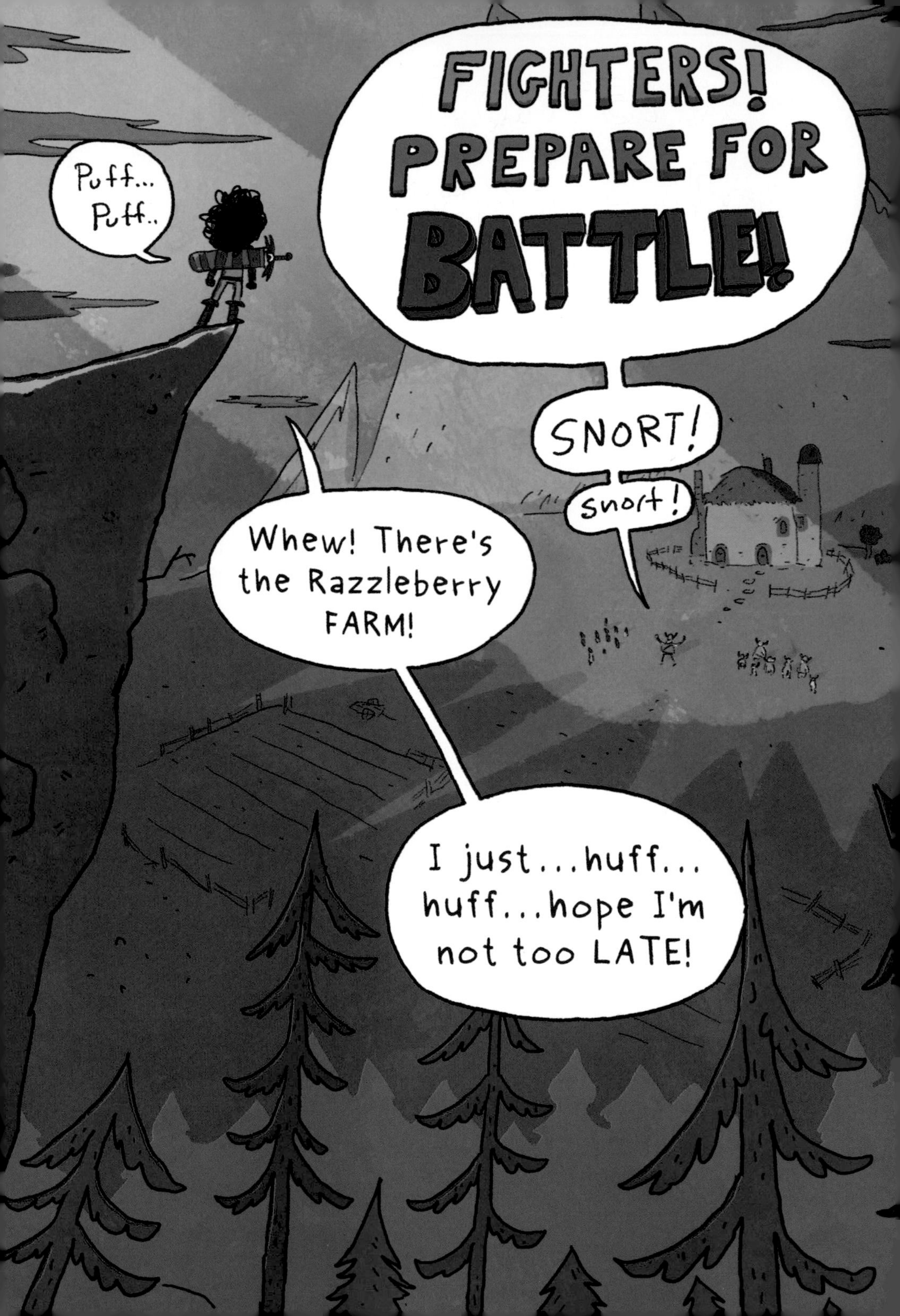
Puff... Puff..
FIGHTERS! PREPARE FOR BATTLE!
SNORT!
snort!
Whew! There's the Razzleberry FARM!
I just...huff... huff...hope I'm not too LATE!

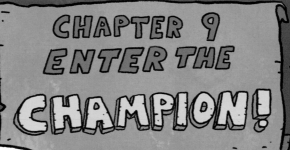

CHAPTER 9
ENTER THE
CHAMPION!

Kate, why did you challenge the SNOT GOBLINS to a FIGHT?

I'm sick of those dudes bullying us!

It's a total DRAG!

But now you gotta face their champion. He's a BEAST!

He will EAT you in one BITE!

He will STOMP you into JELLY!

He will TEAR you...

Thanks, Keith, I think I get it.

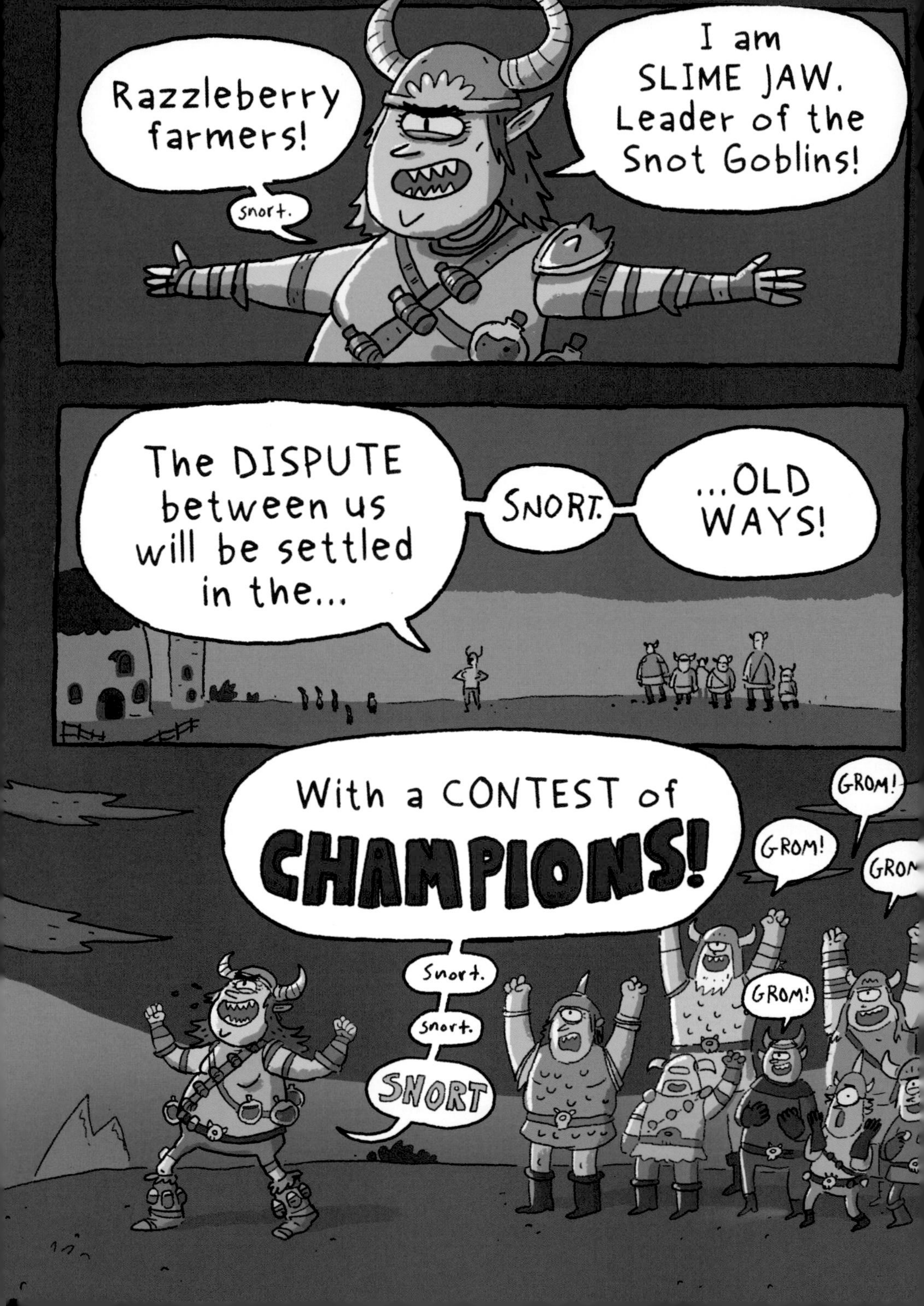
Razzleberry farmers!
snort.
I am SLIME JAW. Leader of the Snot Goblins!
The DISPUTE between us will be settled in the...
SNORT.
...OLD WAYS!
With a CONTEST of CHAMPIONS!
GROM!
GROM!
Snort.
snort.
SNORT
GROM!

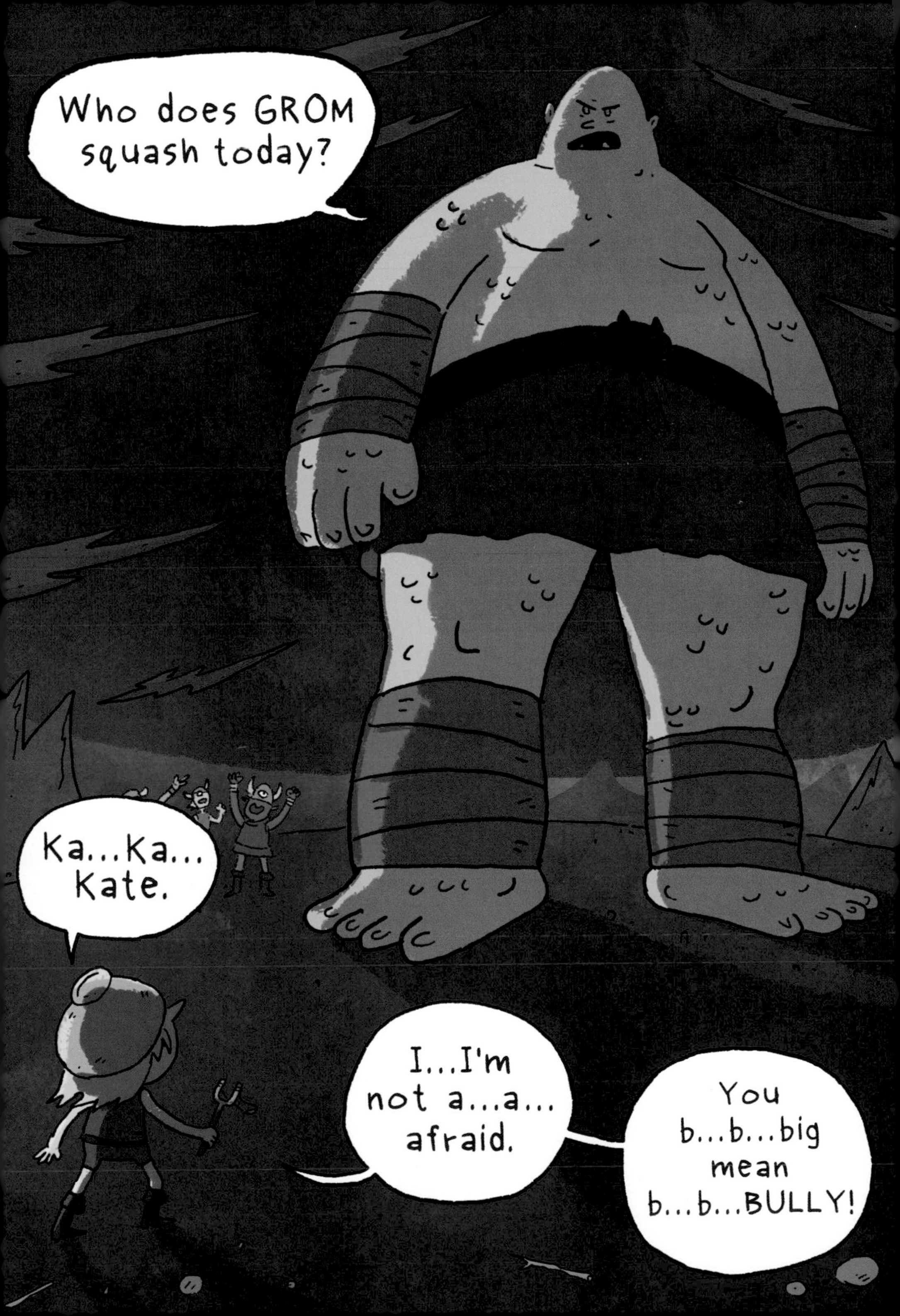
Who does GROM squash today?
Ka...Ka... Kate.
I...I'm not a...a... afraid.
You b...b...big mean b...b...BULLY!

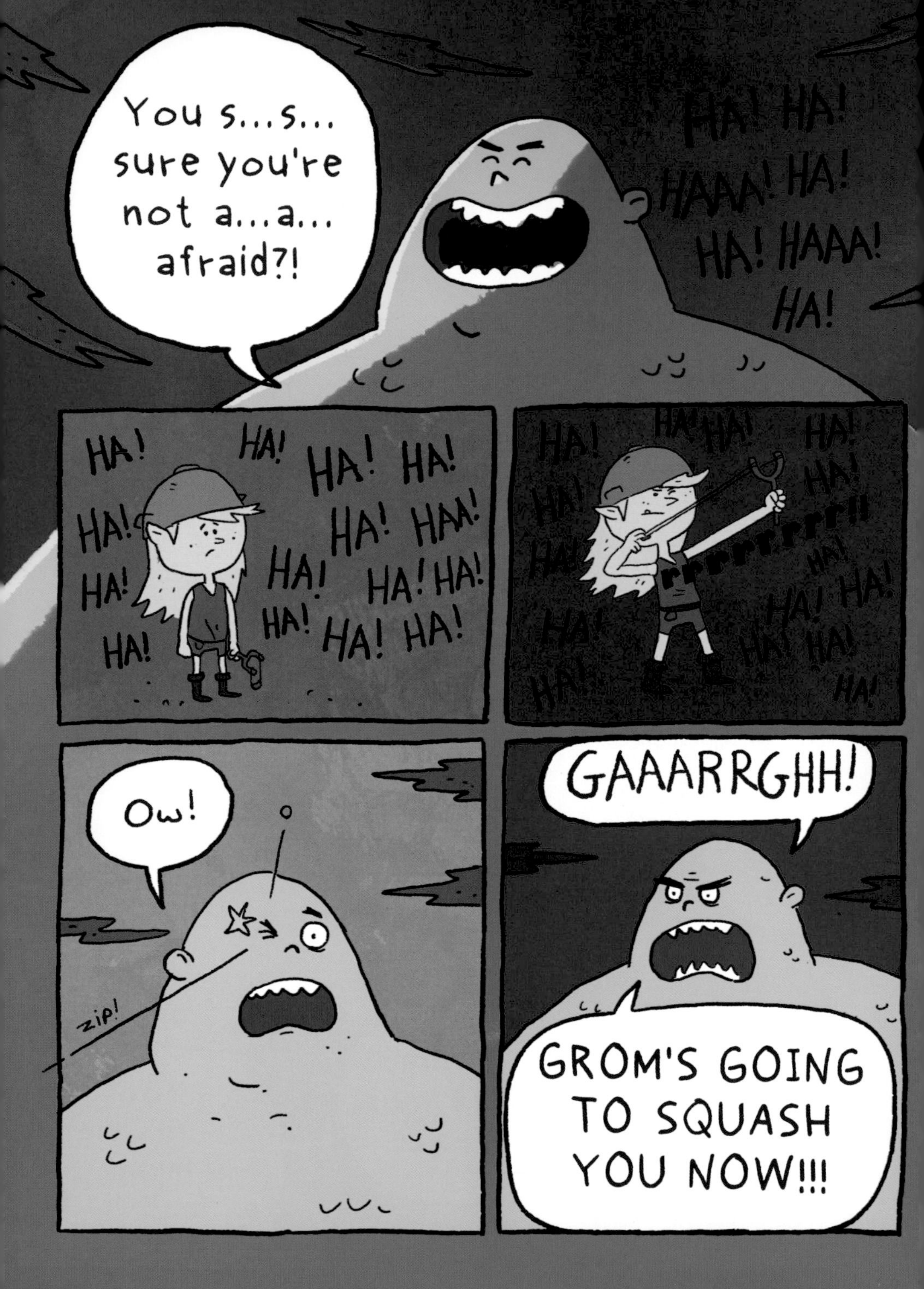

You s...s... sure you're not a...a... afraid?!
HA! HA! HAAA! HA! HA! HAAA! HA!
HA! HA! HA! HA! HA! HA! HA! HA! HAA! HA! HA! HA! HA! HA! HA! HA!
Grrrrrrrrrrr!!
Ow!
zip!
GAAARRGHH!
GROM'S GOING TO SQUASH YOU NOW!!!

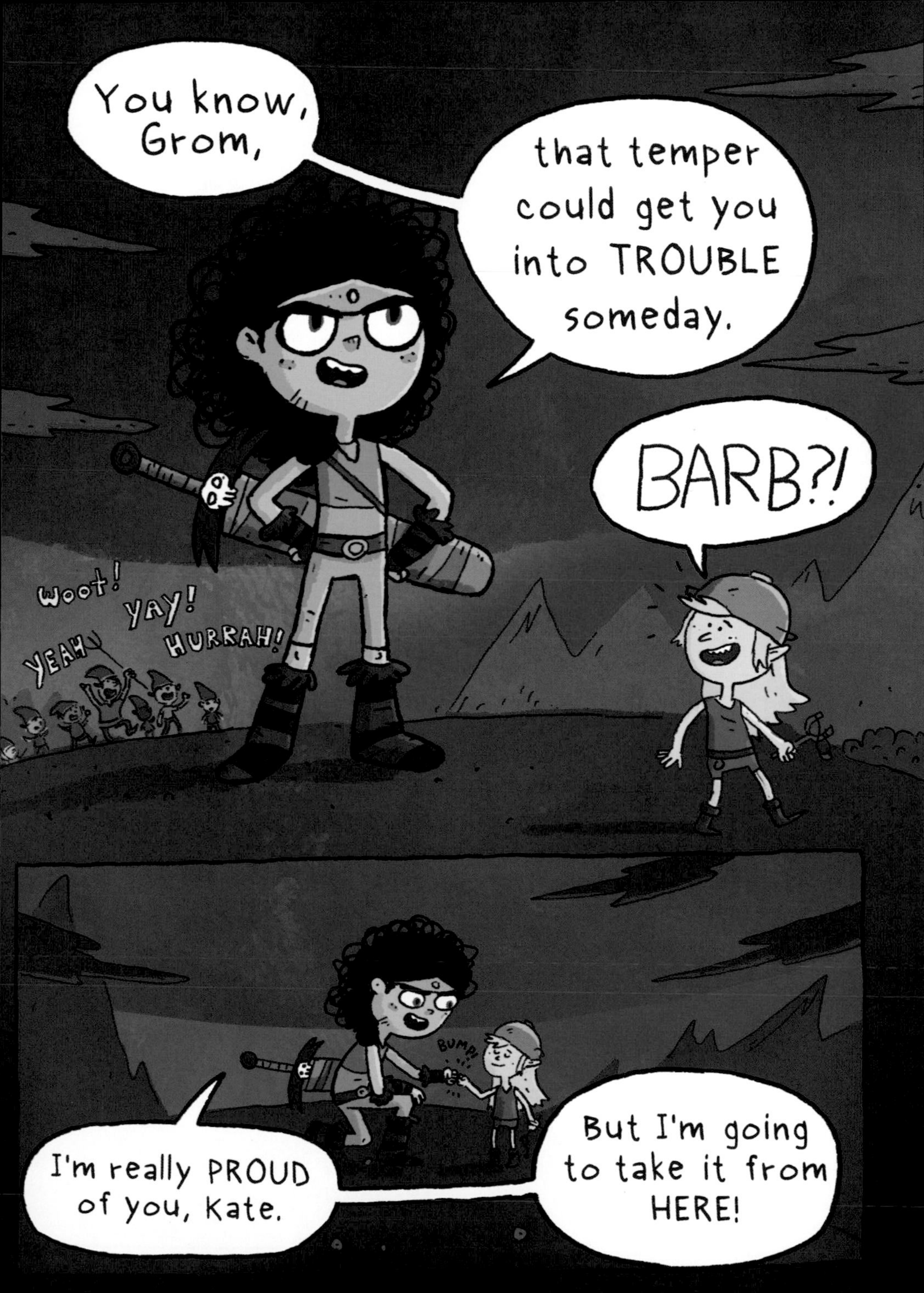
You know, Grom,
that temper could get you into TROUBLE someday.
BARB?!
Woot!
YAY!
HURRAH!
YEAH
BUMP!
I'm really PROUD of you, Kate.
But I'm going to take it from HERE!

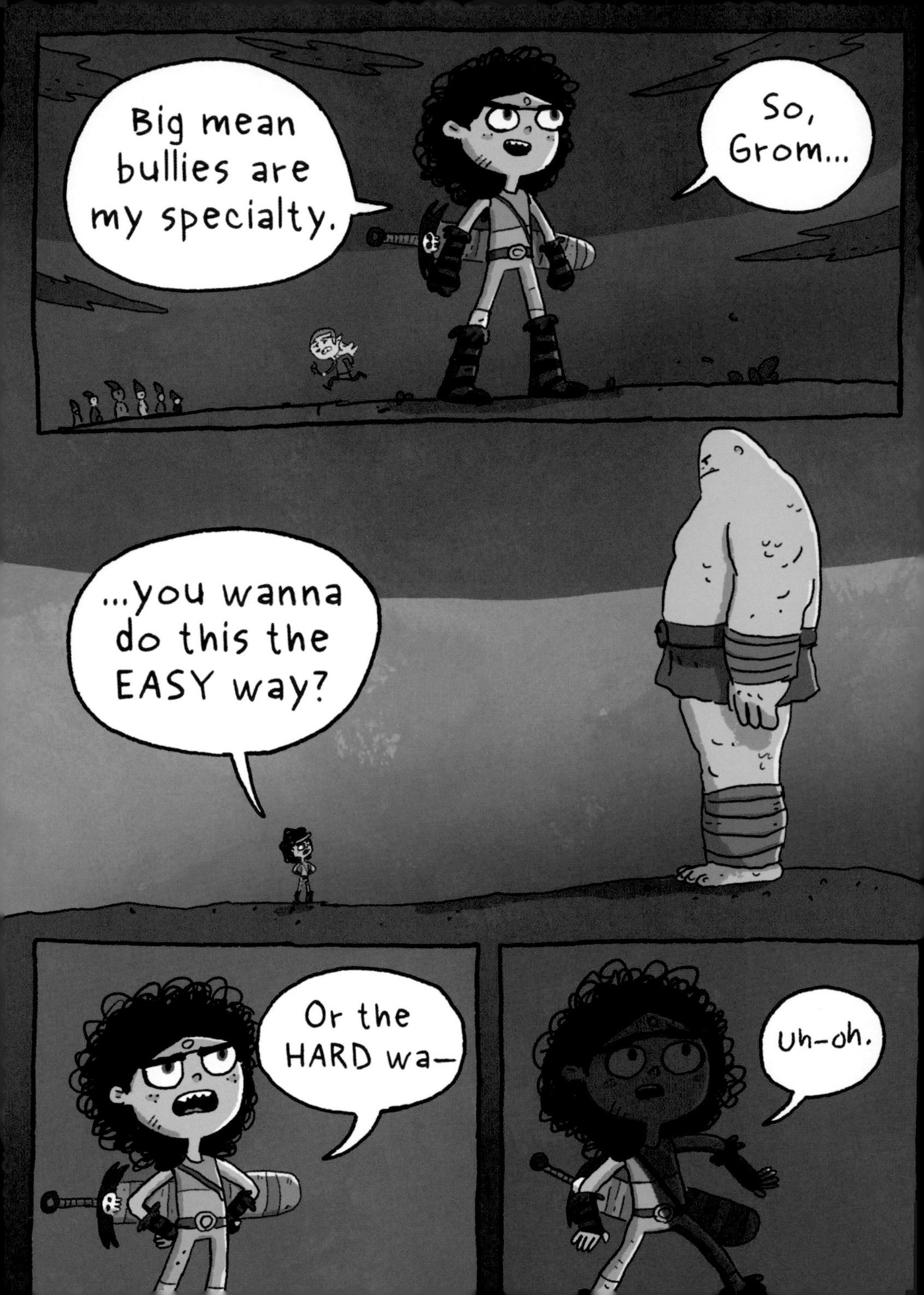
Big mean bullies are my specialty.
So, Grom...
...you wanna do this the EASY way?
Or the HARD wa—
Uh-oh.

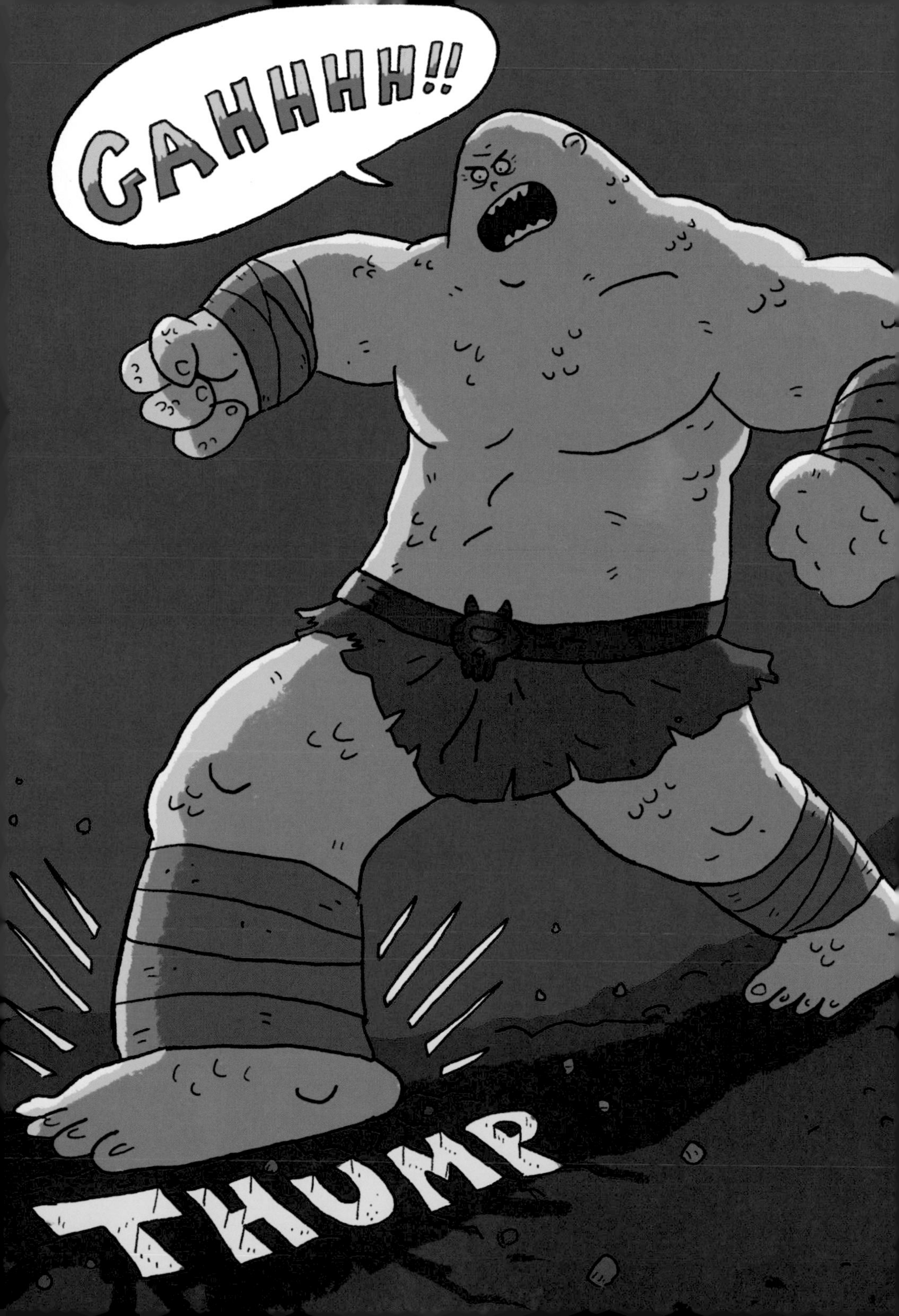
GAHHHH!!
THUMP

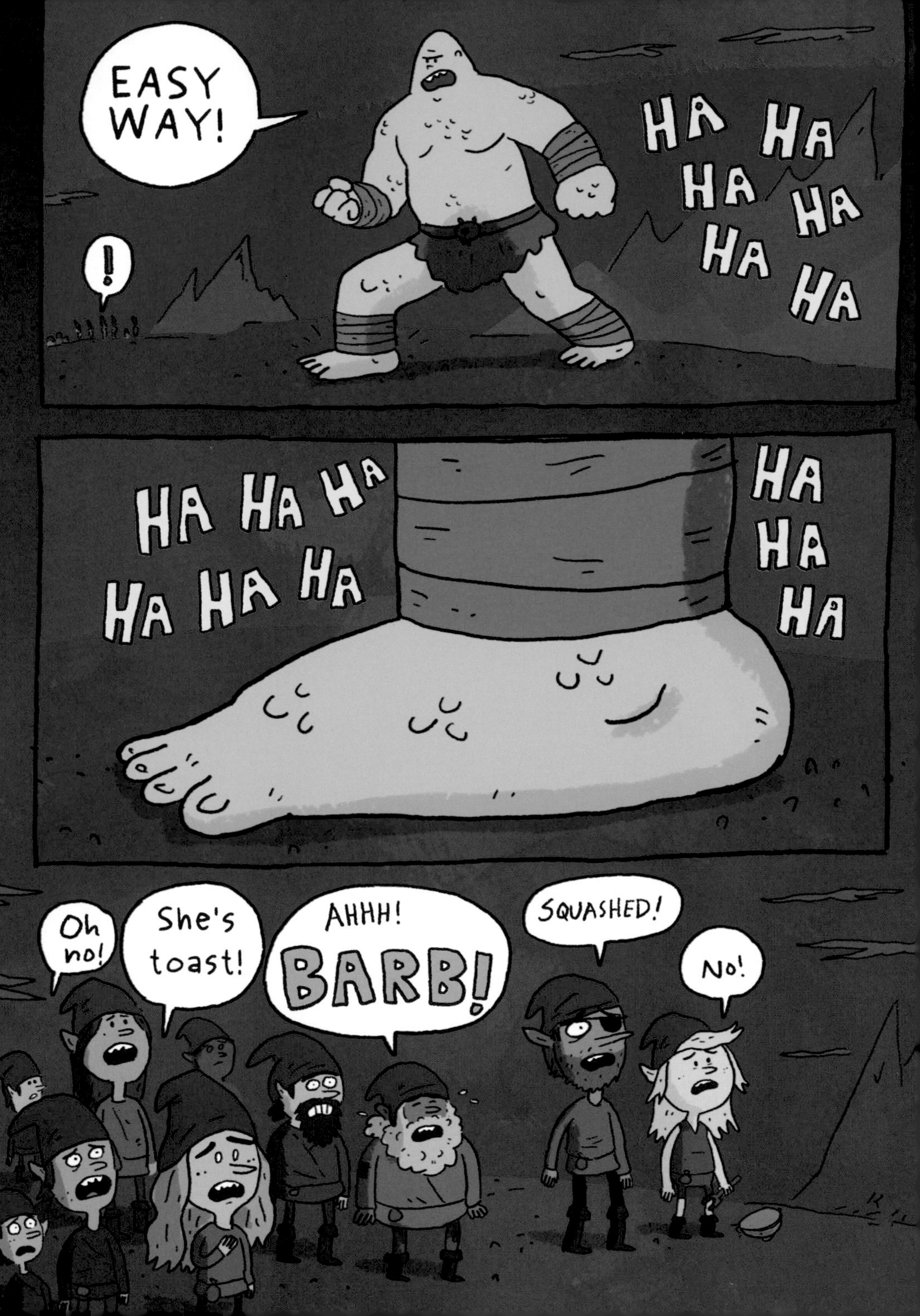
EASY WAY!
HA HA HA HA HA HA HA
!
HA HA HA HA HA HA
HA HA HA HA
Oh no!
She's toast!
AHHH! BARB!
SQUASHED!
No!

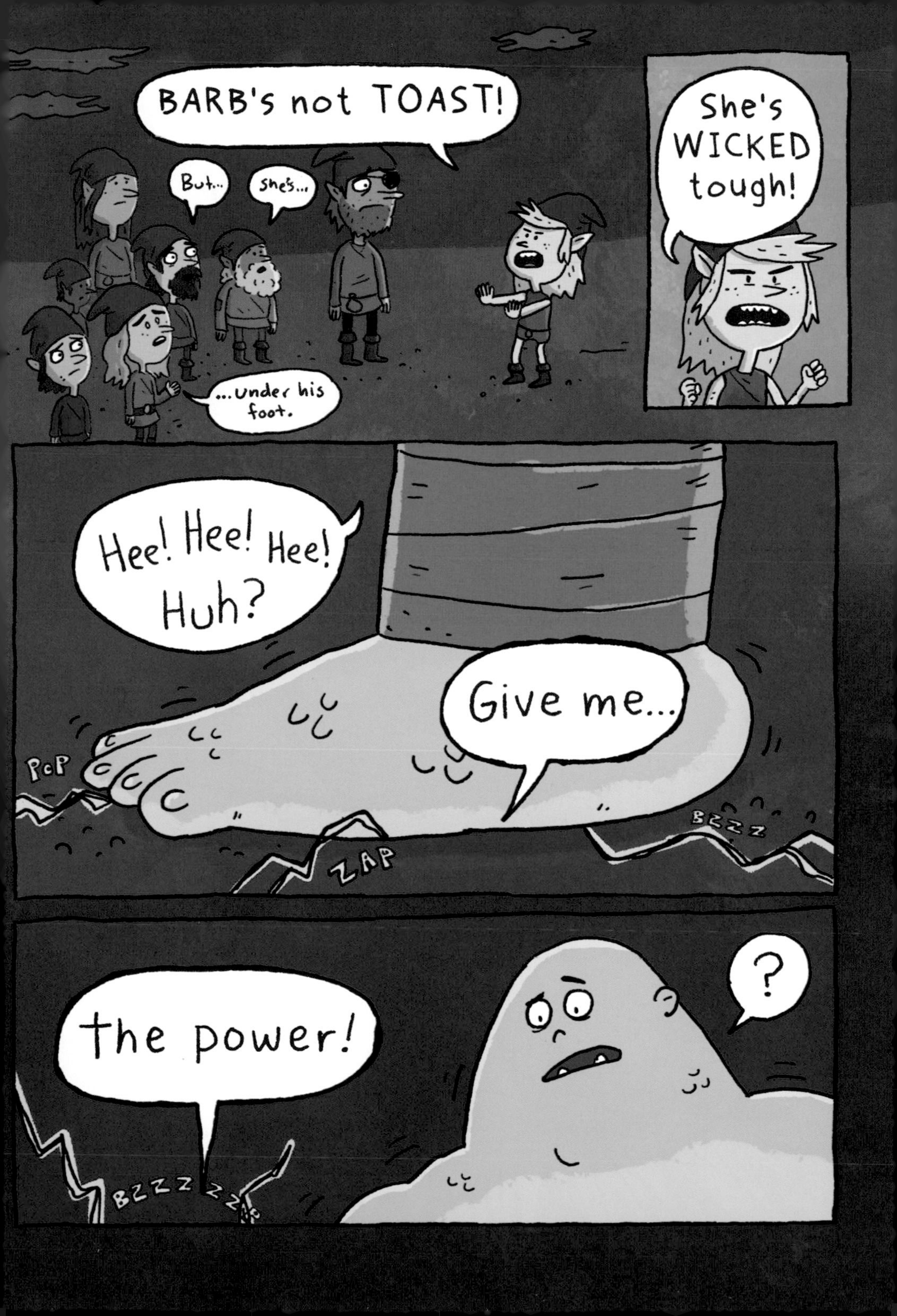
BARB's not TOAST!
But...
she's...
...under his foot.
She's WICKED tough!
Hee! Hee! Hee!
Huh?
Give me...
POP
ZAP
BZZZ
the power!
?
BZZZZZ

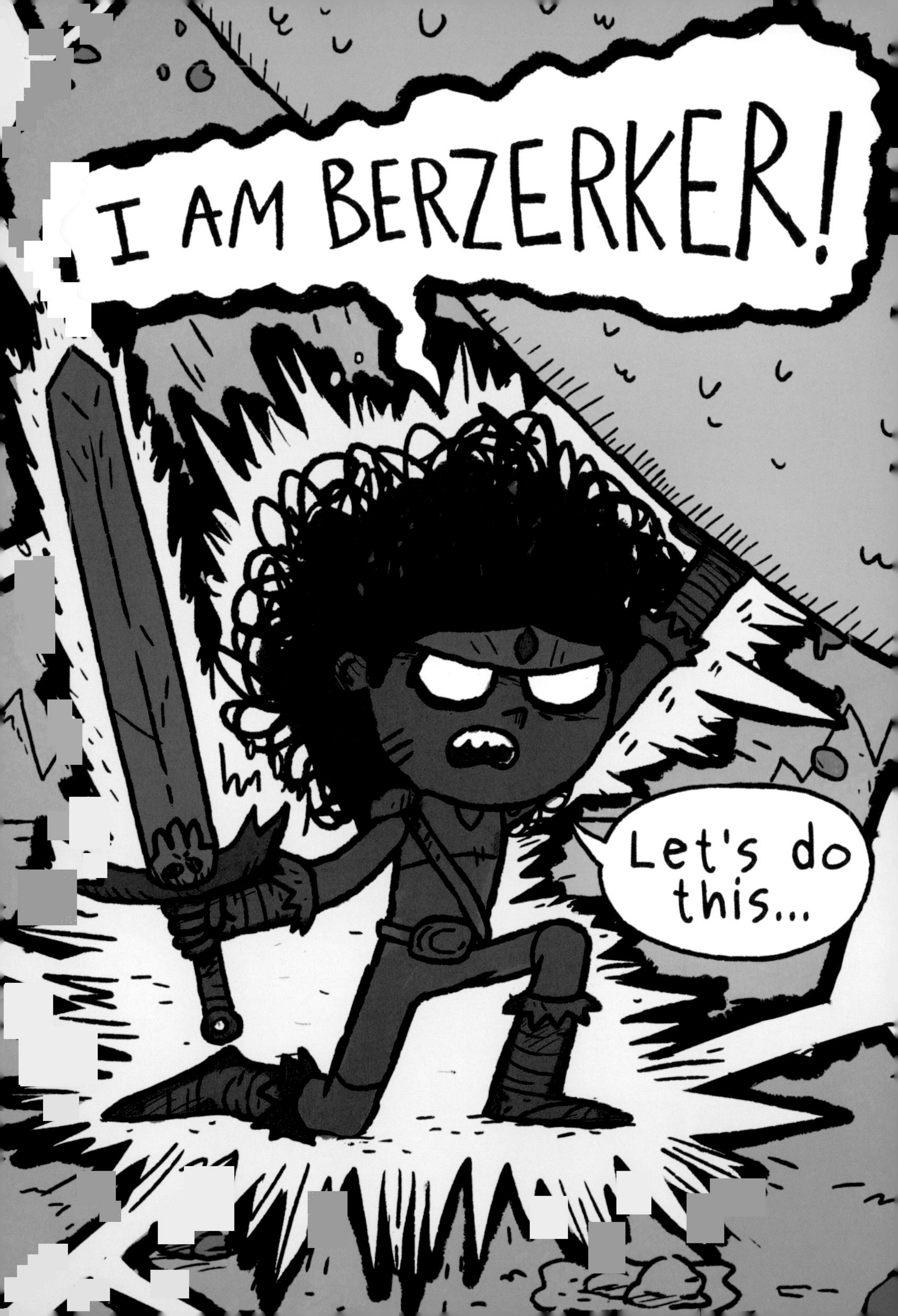
I AM BERZERKER!
Let's do this...

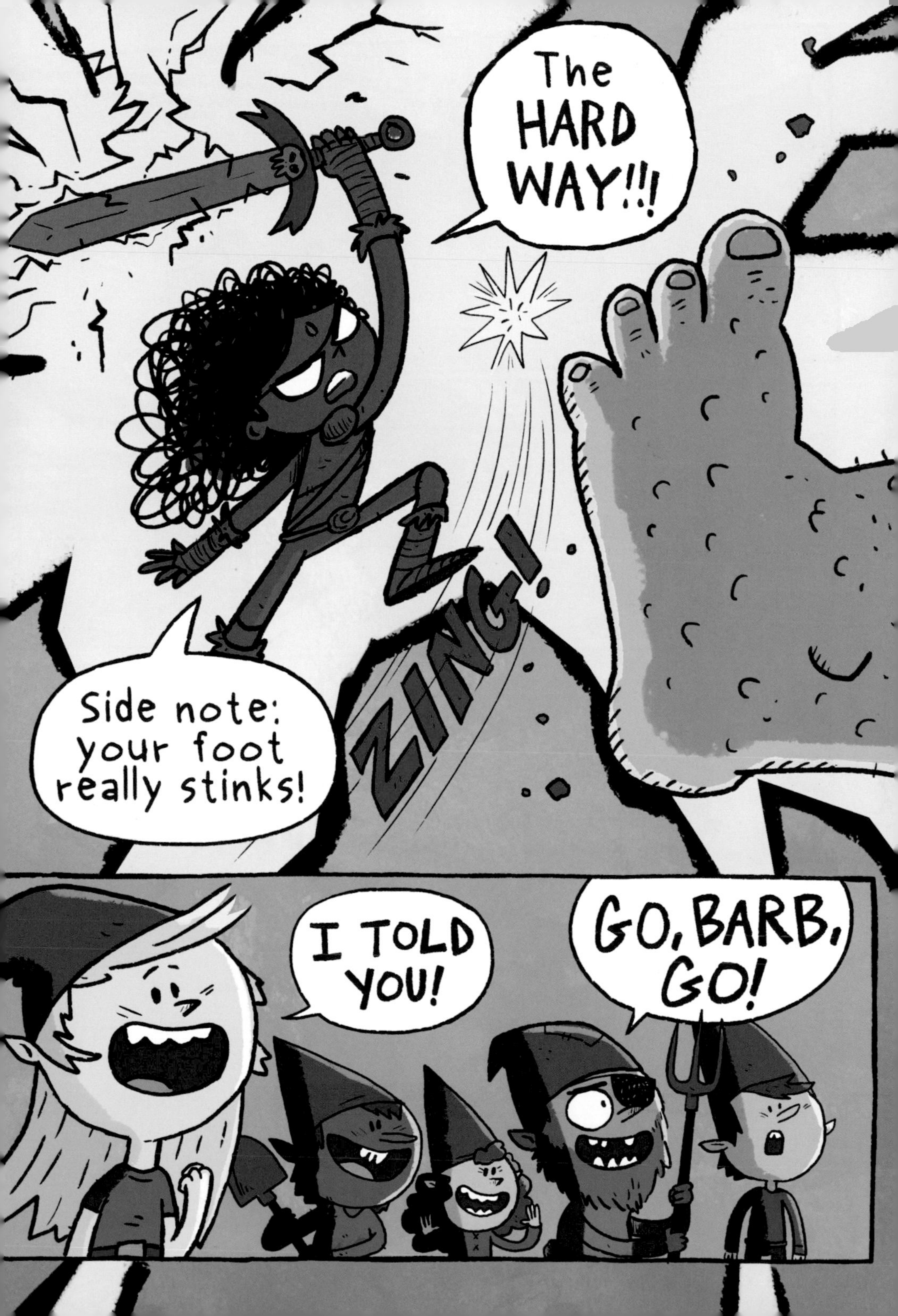
The HARD WAY!!!
Side note: your foot really stinks!
ZING!
I TOLD YOU!
GO, BARB, GO!

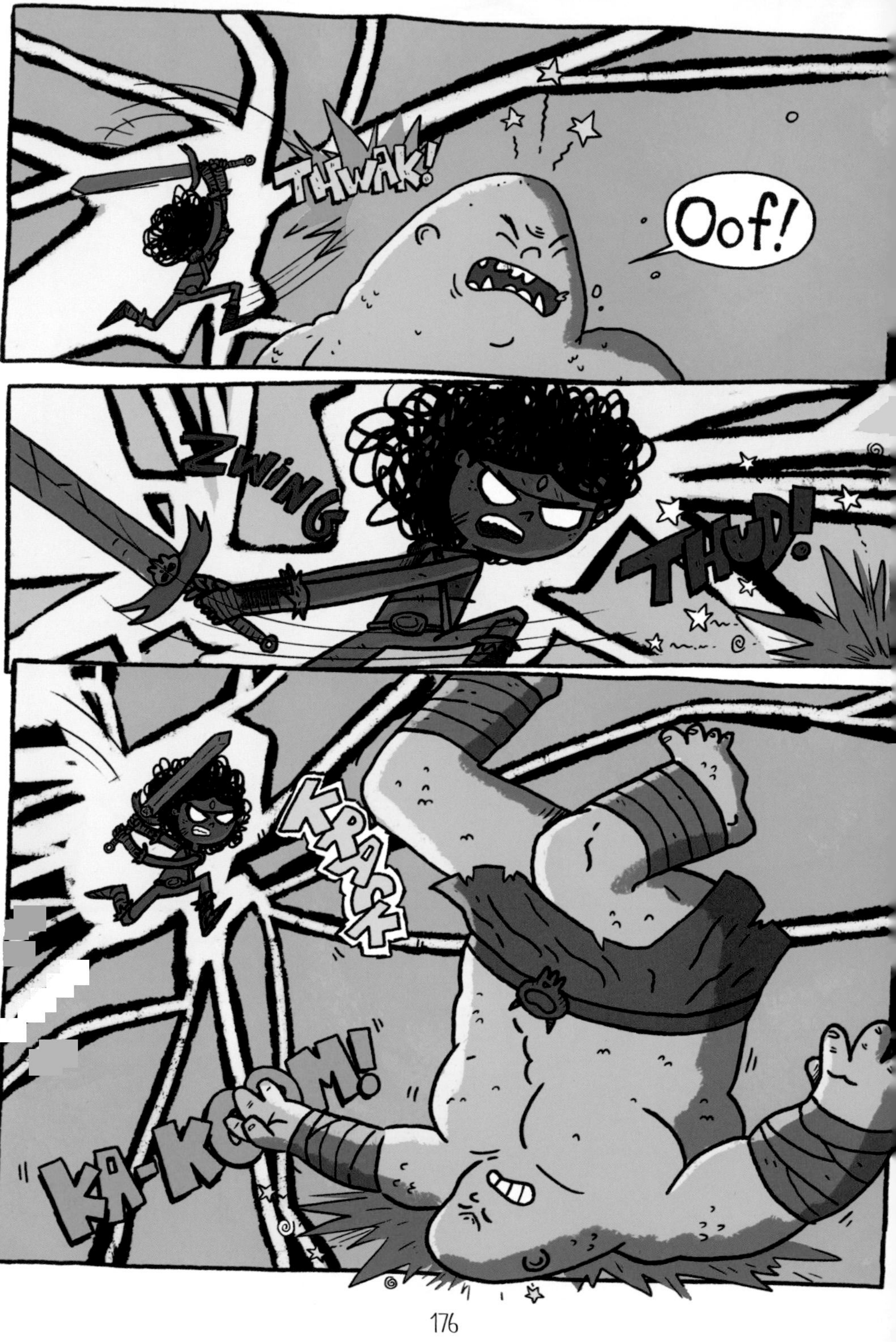
THWAK!
Oof!
ZWING
THUD!
KRACK
KA-KOOOM!

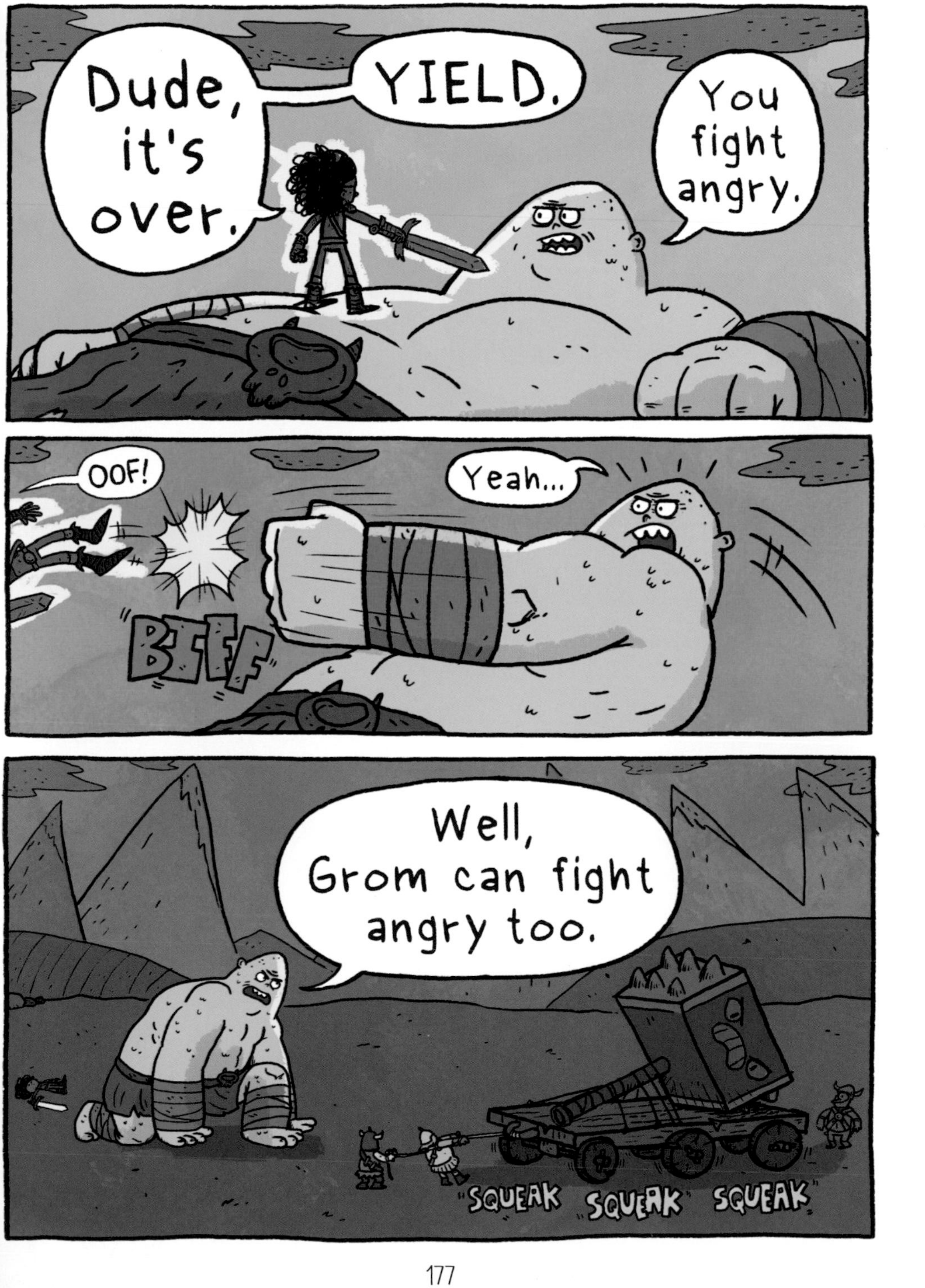
Dude, it's over.
YIELD.
You fight angry.
OOF!
Yeah...
BIFF
Well, Grom can fight angry too.
SQUEAK SQUEAK SQUEAK

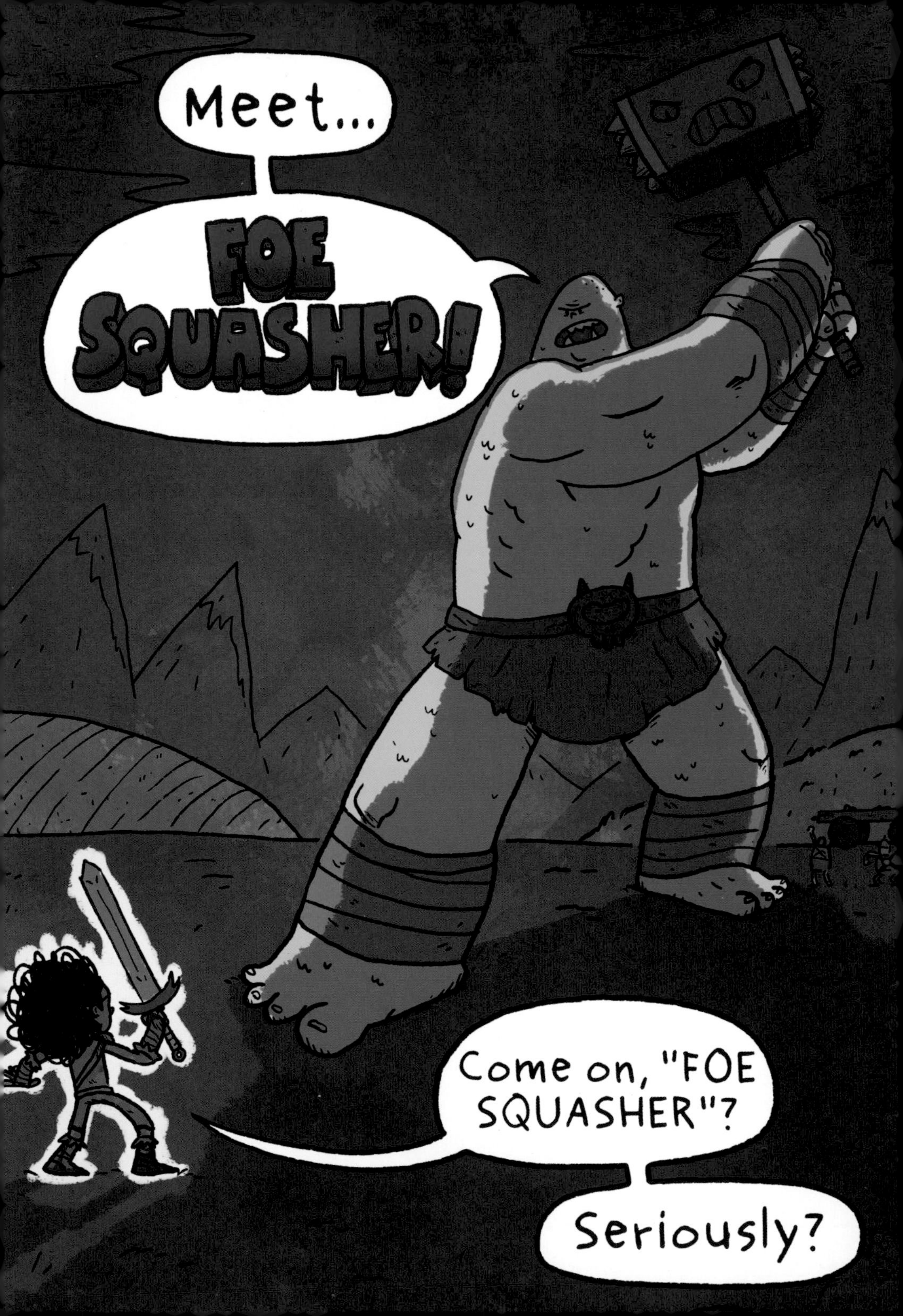
Meet...
FOE SQUASHER!
Come on, "FOE SQUASHER"?
Seriously?

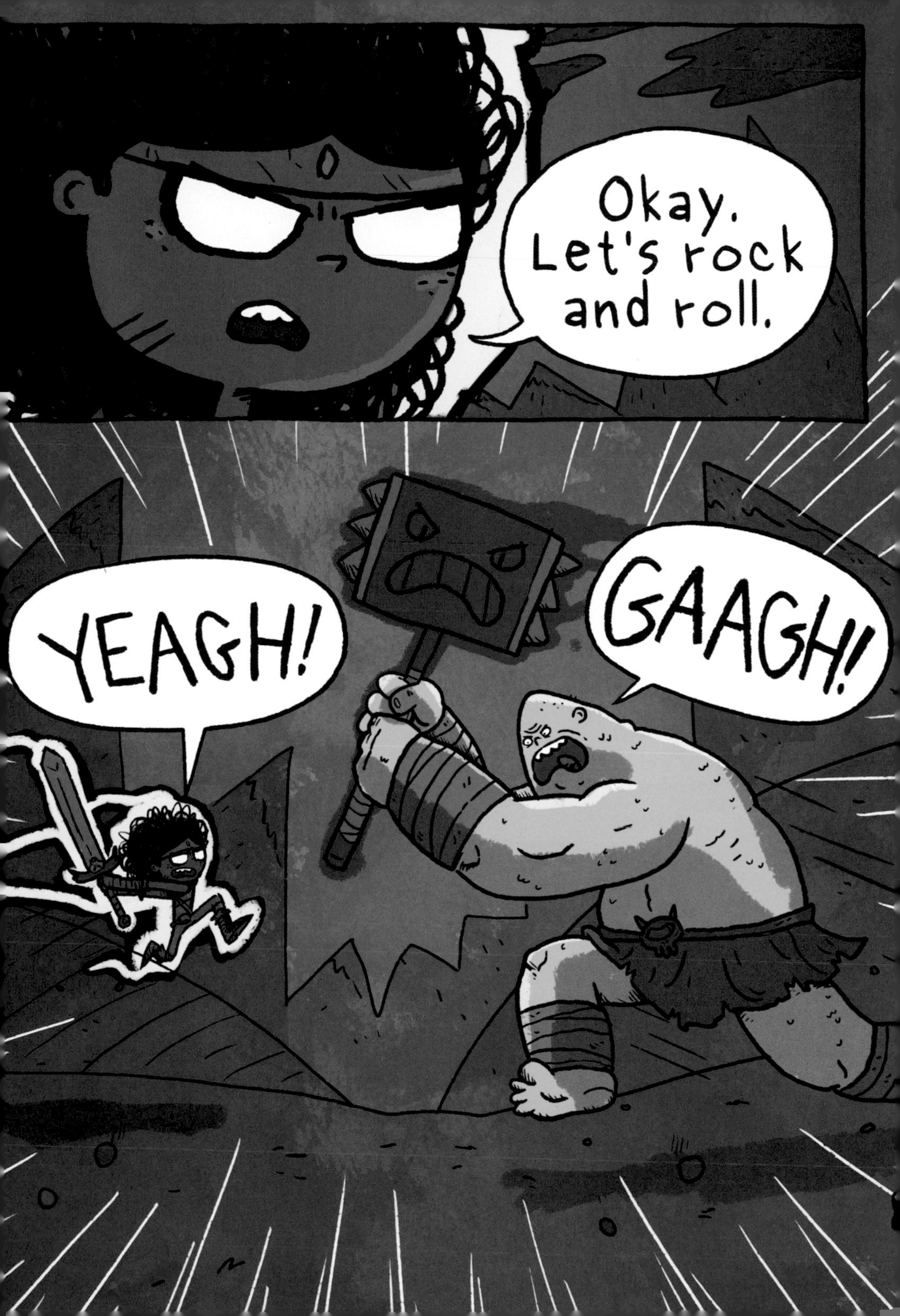
Okay. Let's rock and roll.
YEAGH!
GAAGH!

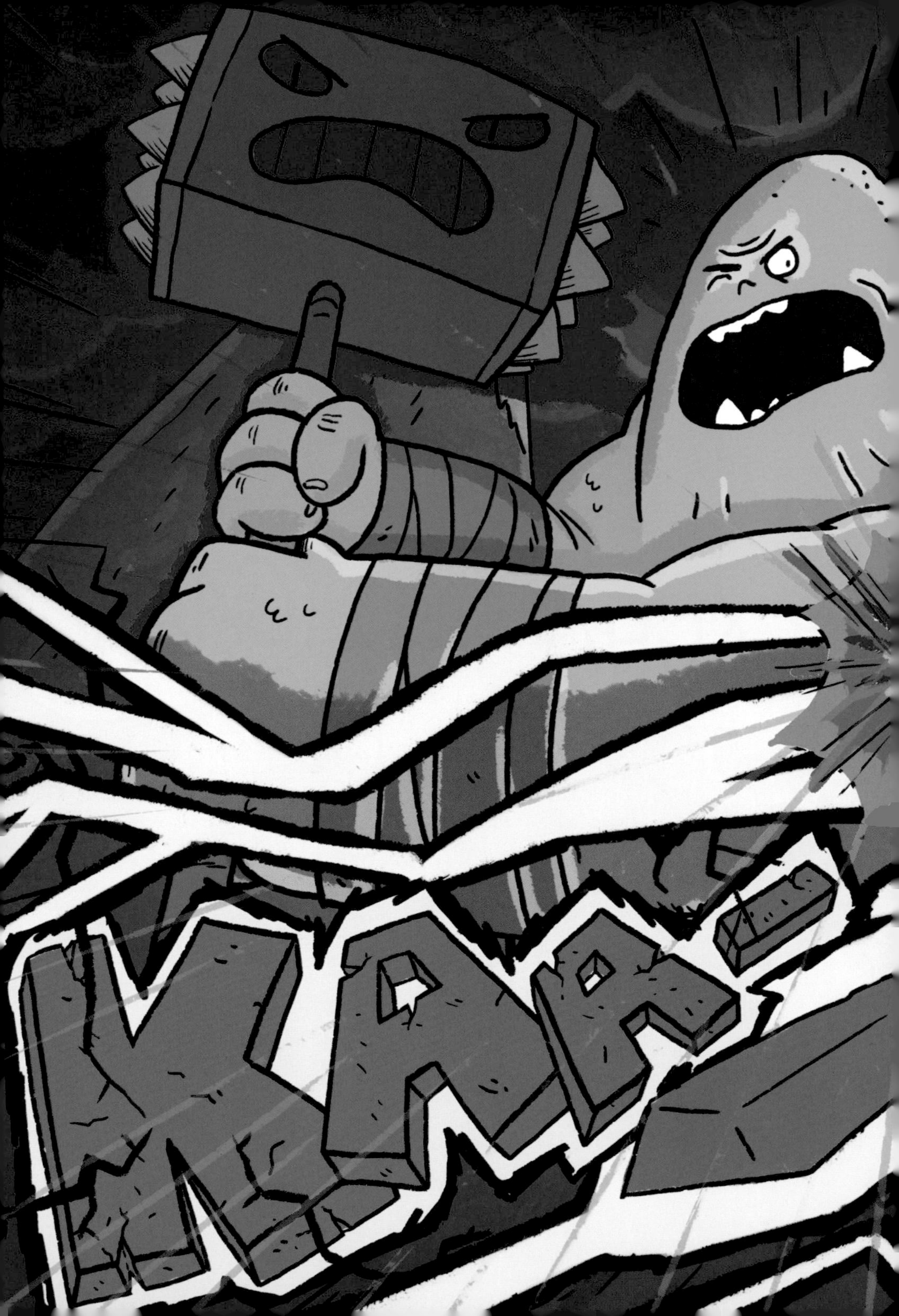
WAR-

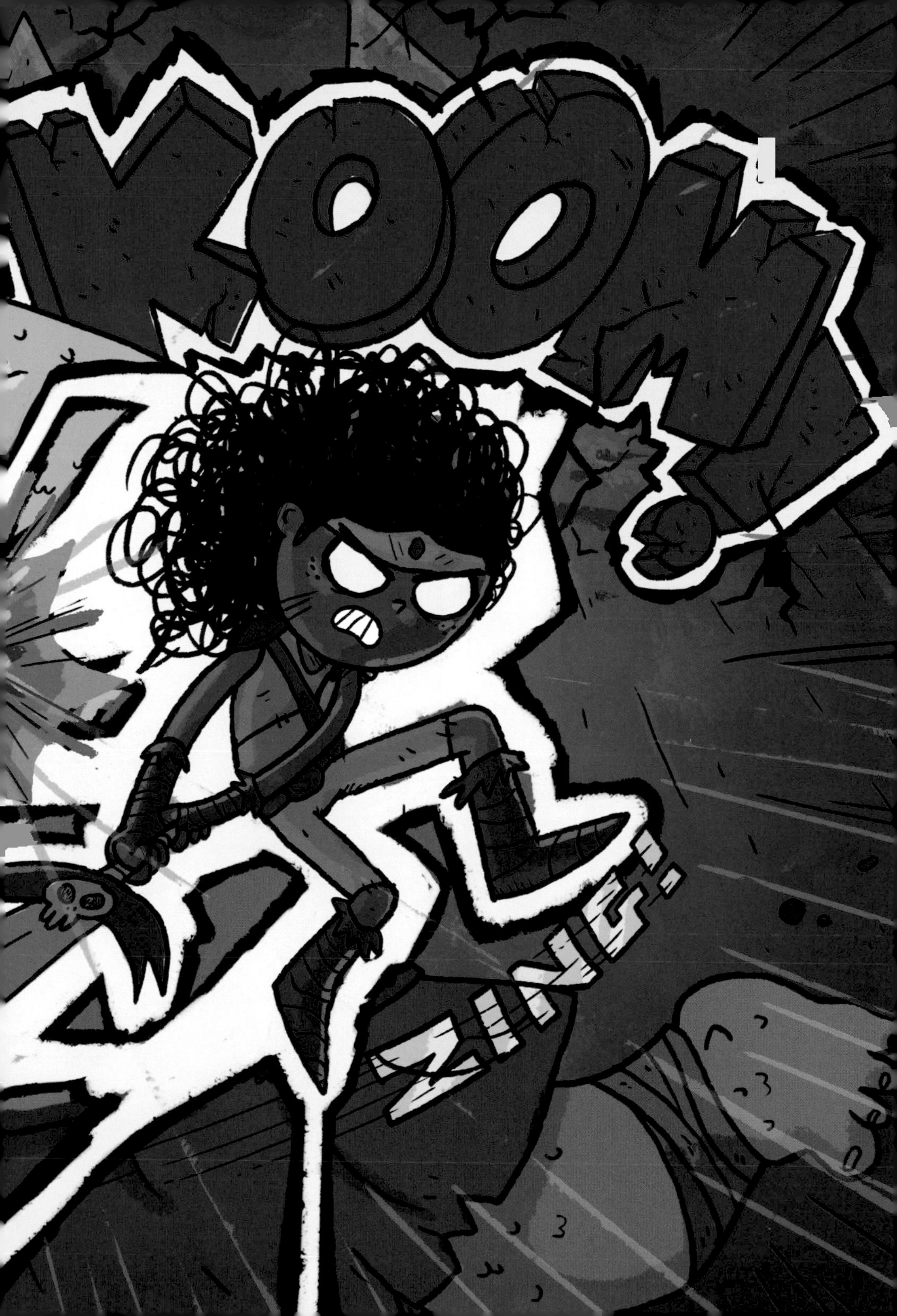

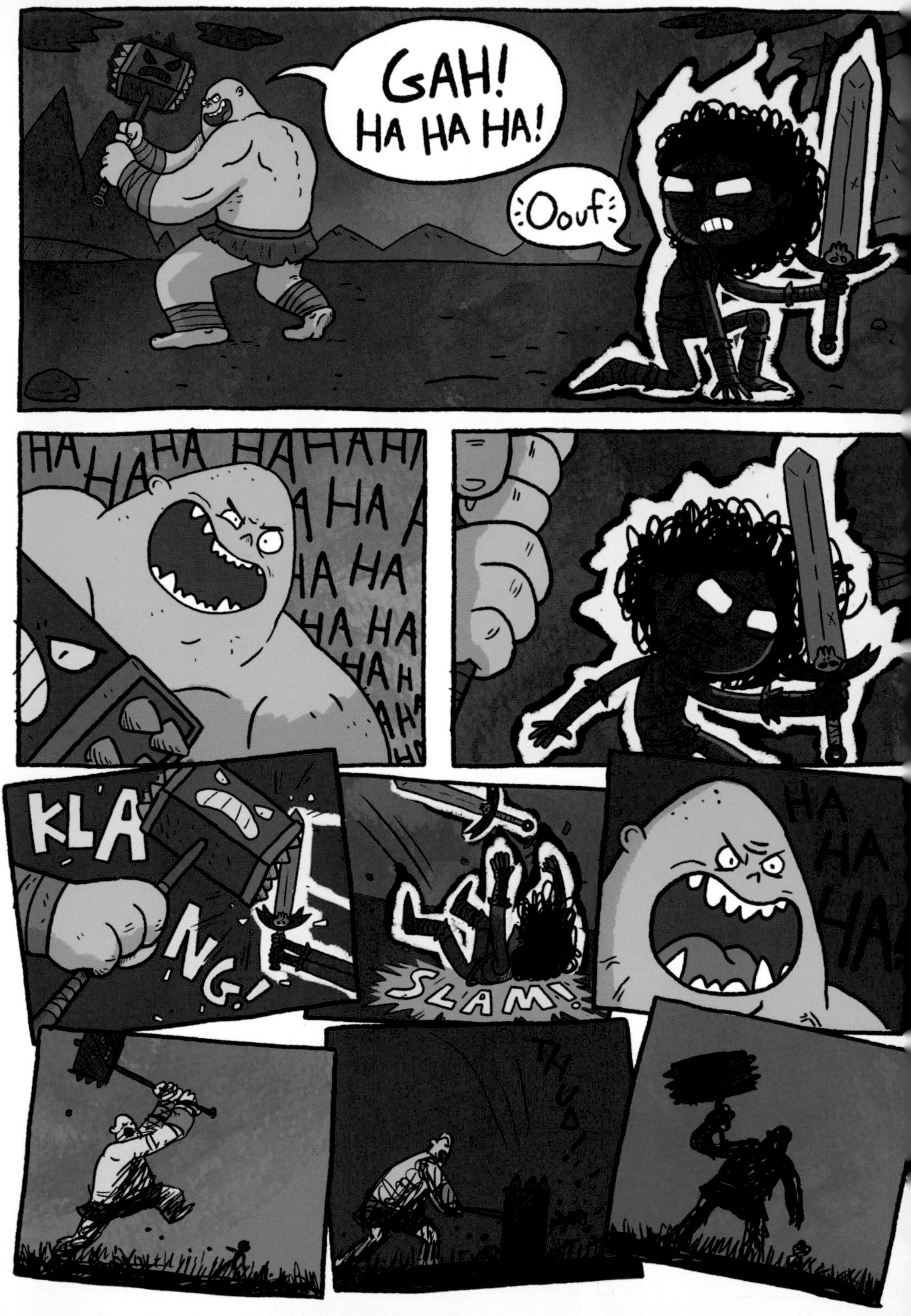
GAH! HA HA HA!
Oouf
HA HA HA HA HA HA HA HA HA HA HA HA HA HA
KLANG!
SLAM!
HA HA HA
THUD!

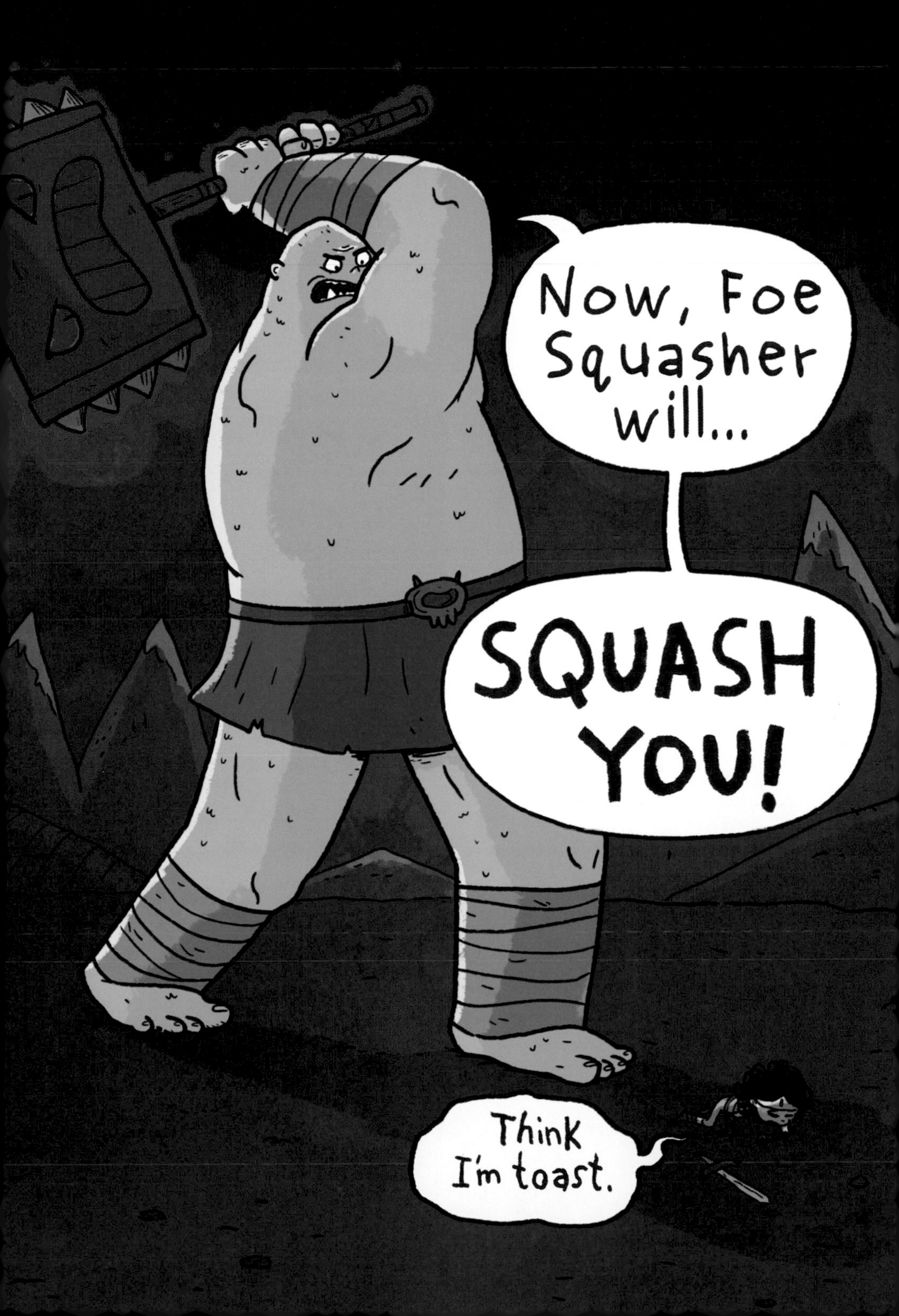
Now, Foe Squasher will...
SQUASH YOU!
Think I'm toast.

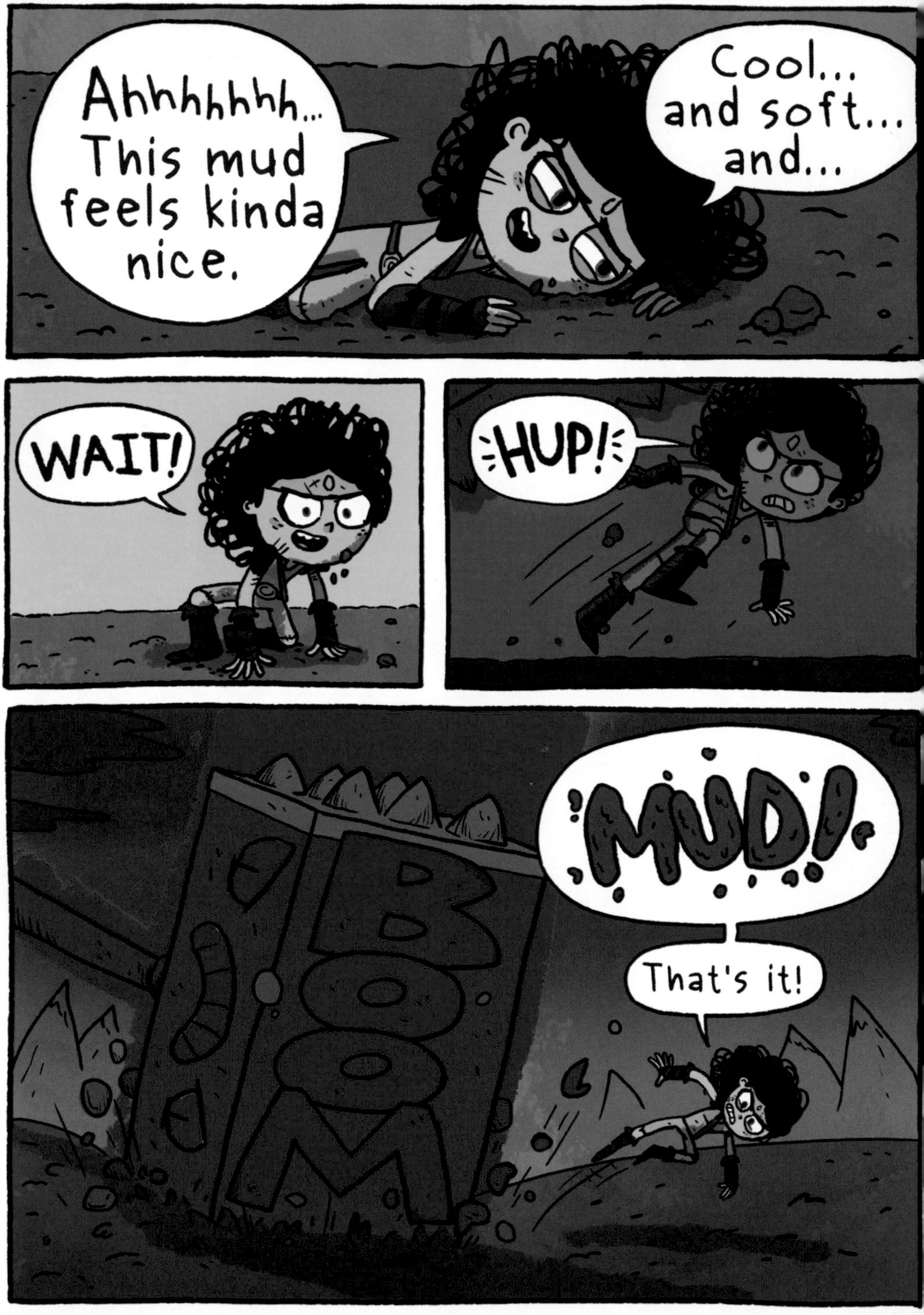
Ahhhhhhh... This mud feels kinda nice.
Cool... and soft... and...
WAIT!
HUP!
BOOM
MUD!
That's it!

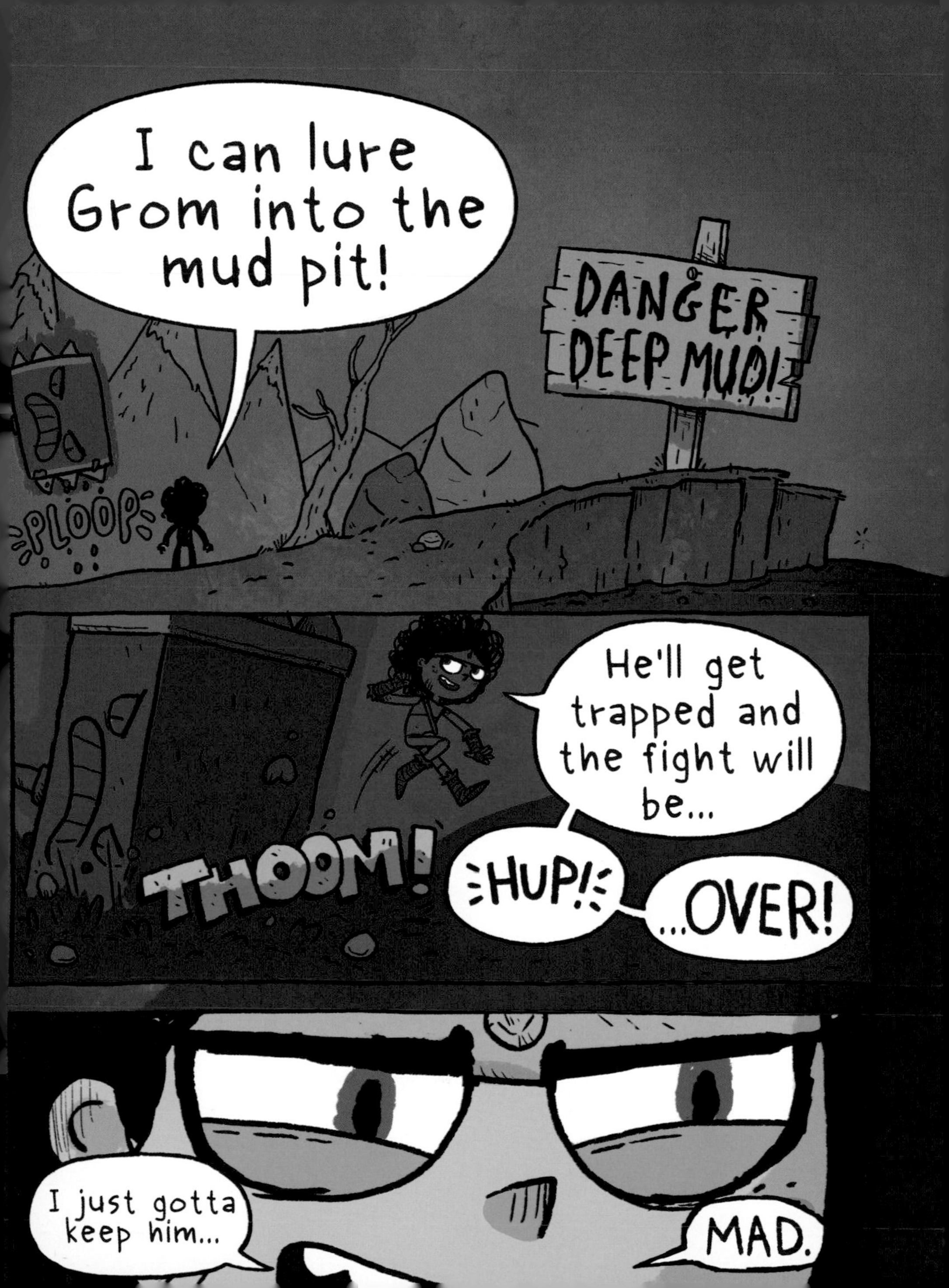
I can lure Grom into the mud pit!
DANGER DEEP MUD!
PLOOP
He'll get trapped and the fight will be...
THOOM!
HUP!
...OVER!
I just gotta keep him...
MAD.

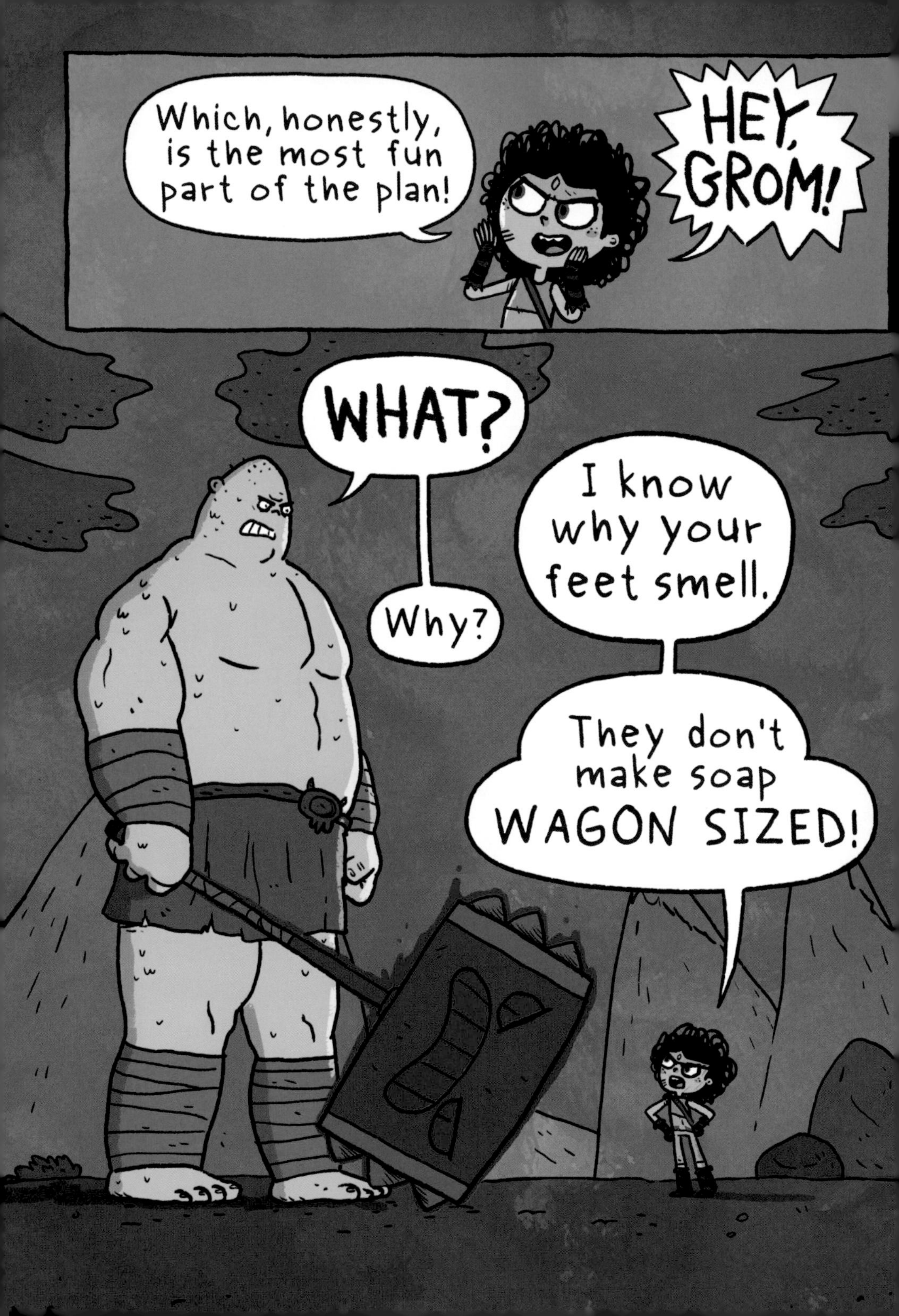
Which, honestly, is the most fun part of the plan!
HEY, GROM!
WHAT?
Why?
I know why your feet smell.
They don't make soap WAGON SIZED!

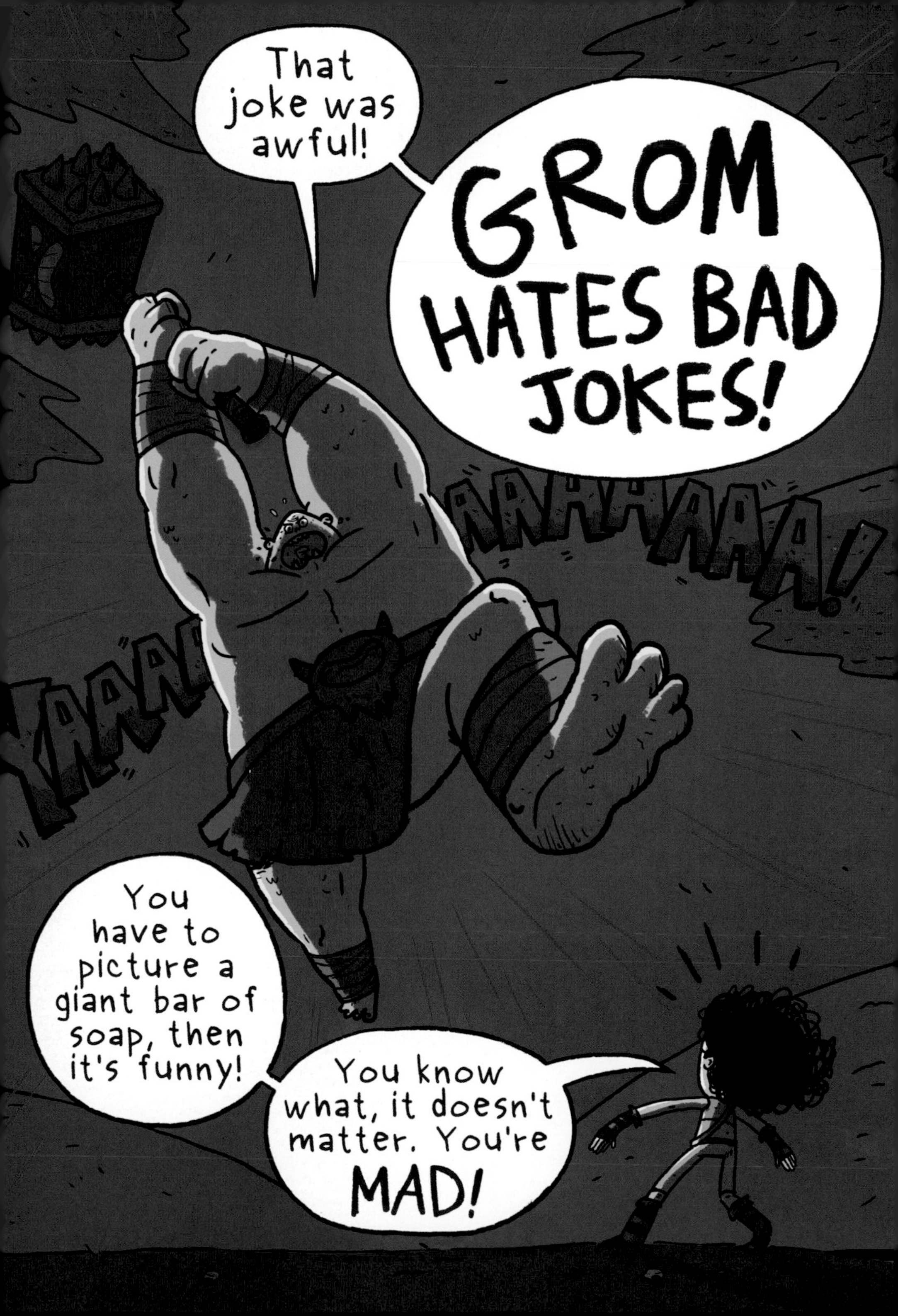

That joke was awful!
GROM HATES BAD JOKES!
YAAAAAAAAAAAA!
You have to picture a giant bar of soap, then it's funny!
You know what, it doesn't matter. You're MAD!

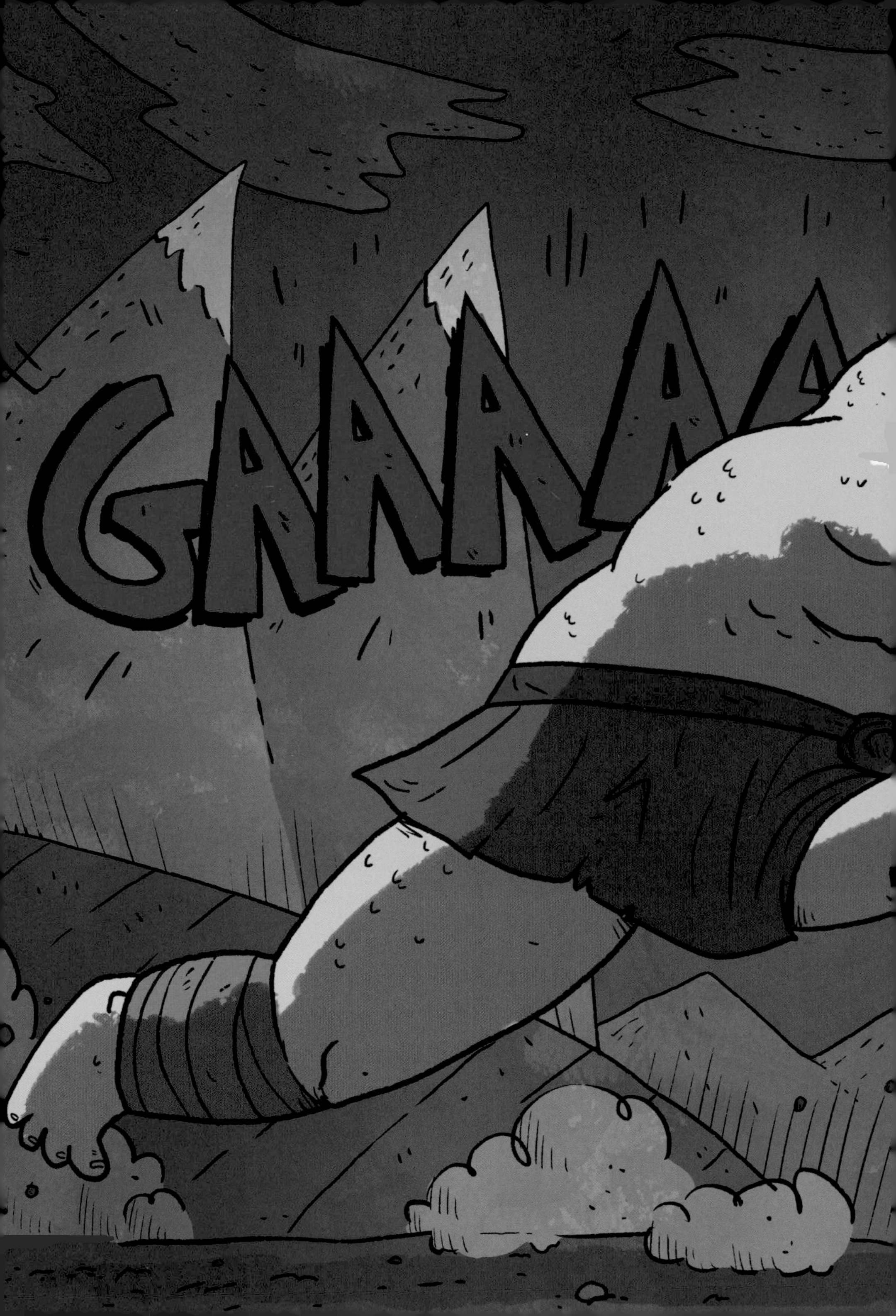
GARRAA

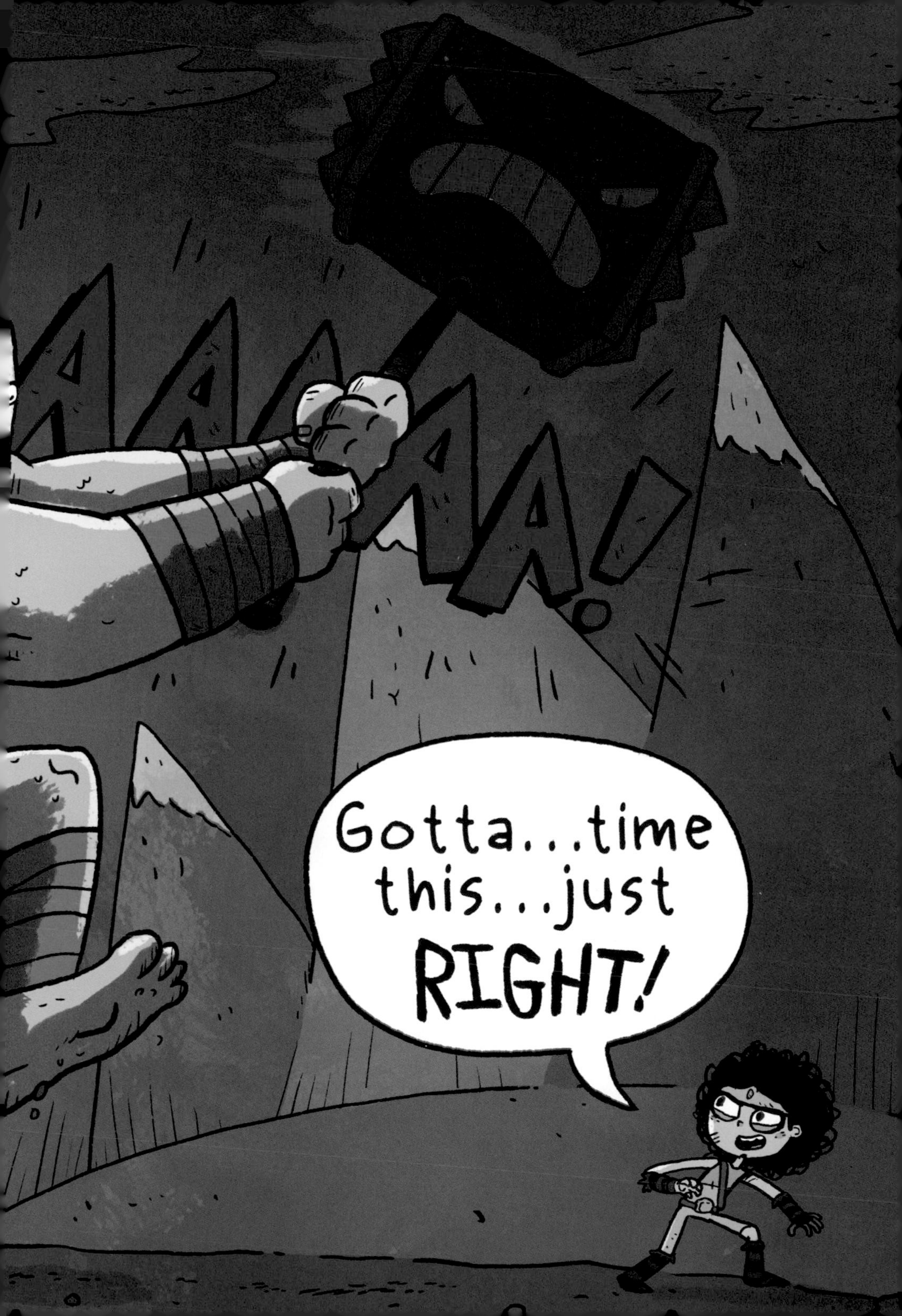
AAAAAA!
Gotta...time this...just RIGHT!

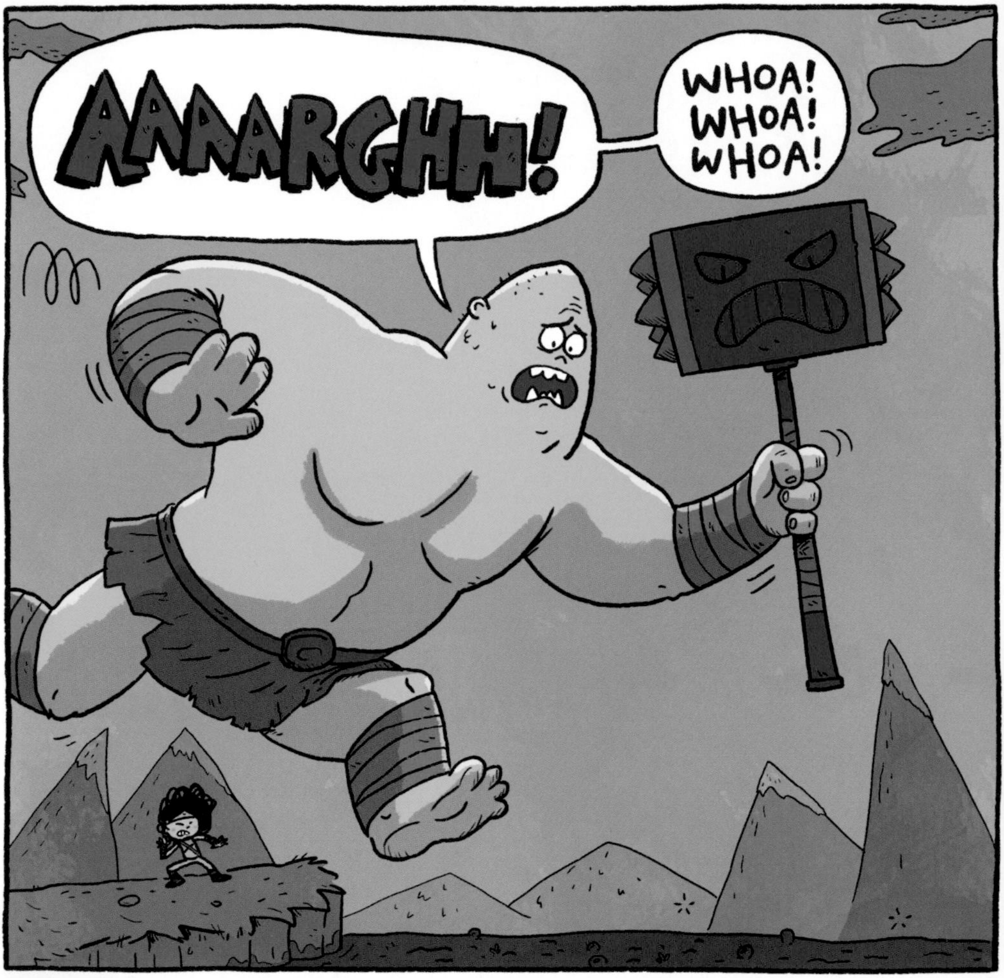
AAARARGHH!
WHOA! WHOA! WHOA!

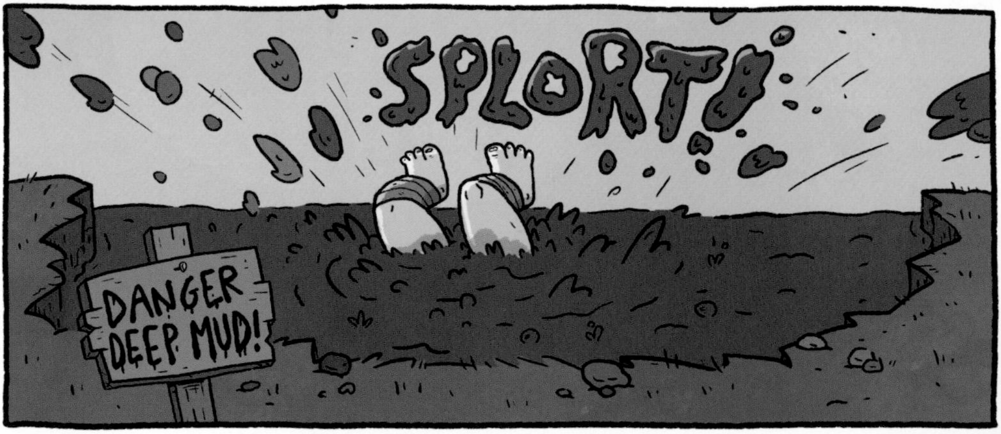
SPLORT!
DANGER DEEP MUD!

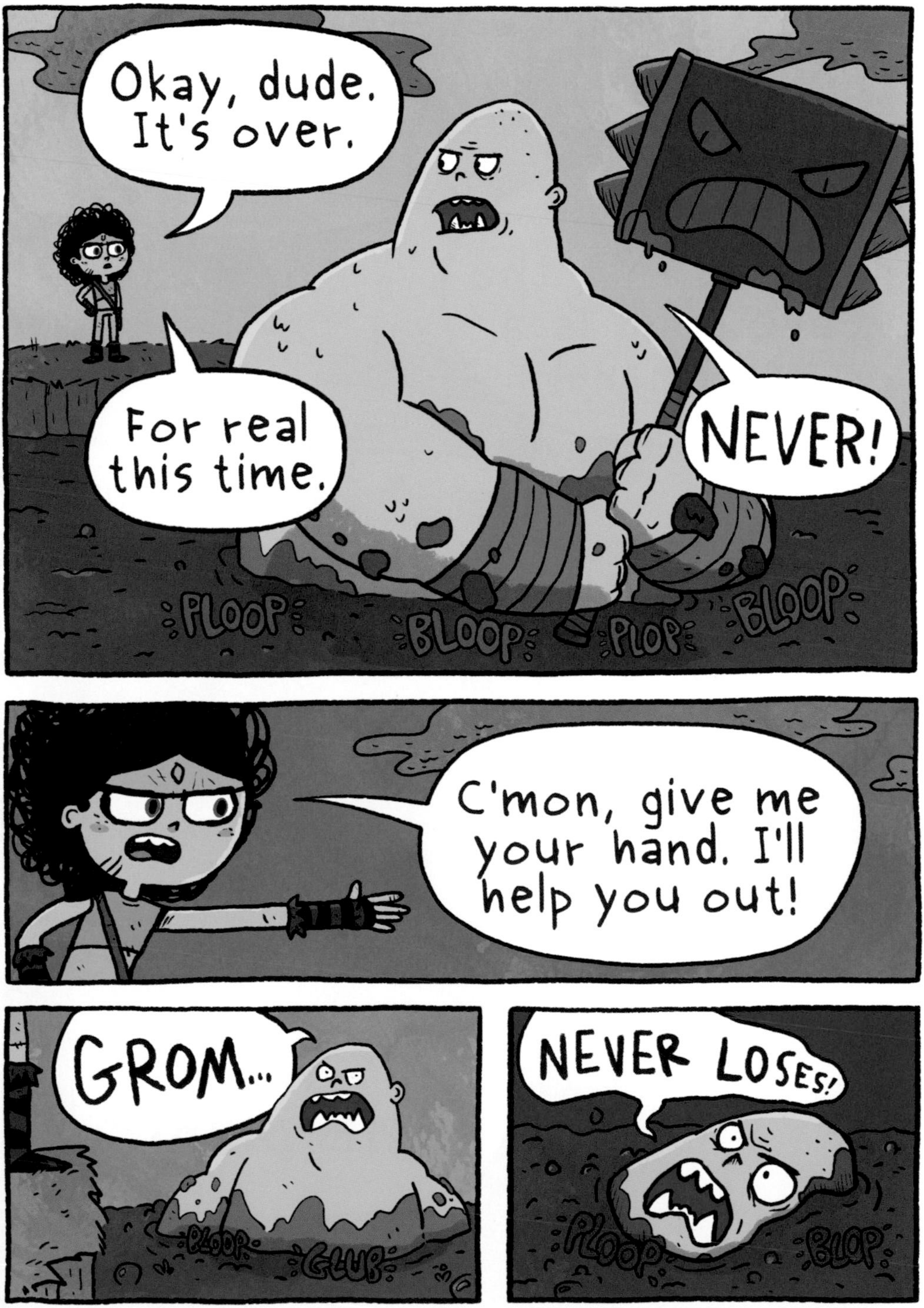
Okay, dude. It's over.
For real this time.
NEVER!
PLOOP
BLOOP
PLOP
BLOOP
C'mon, give me your hand. I'll help you out!
GROM...
BLOOP
GLUB
NEVER LOSES!
PLOOP
BLOP

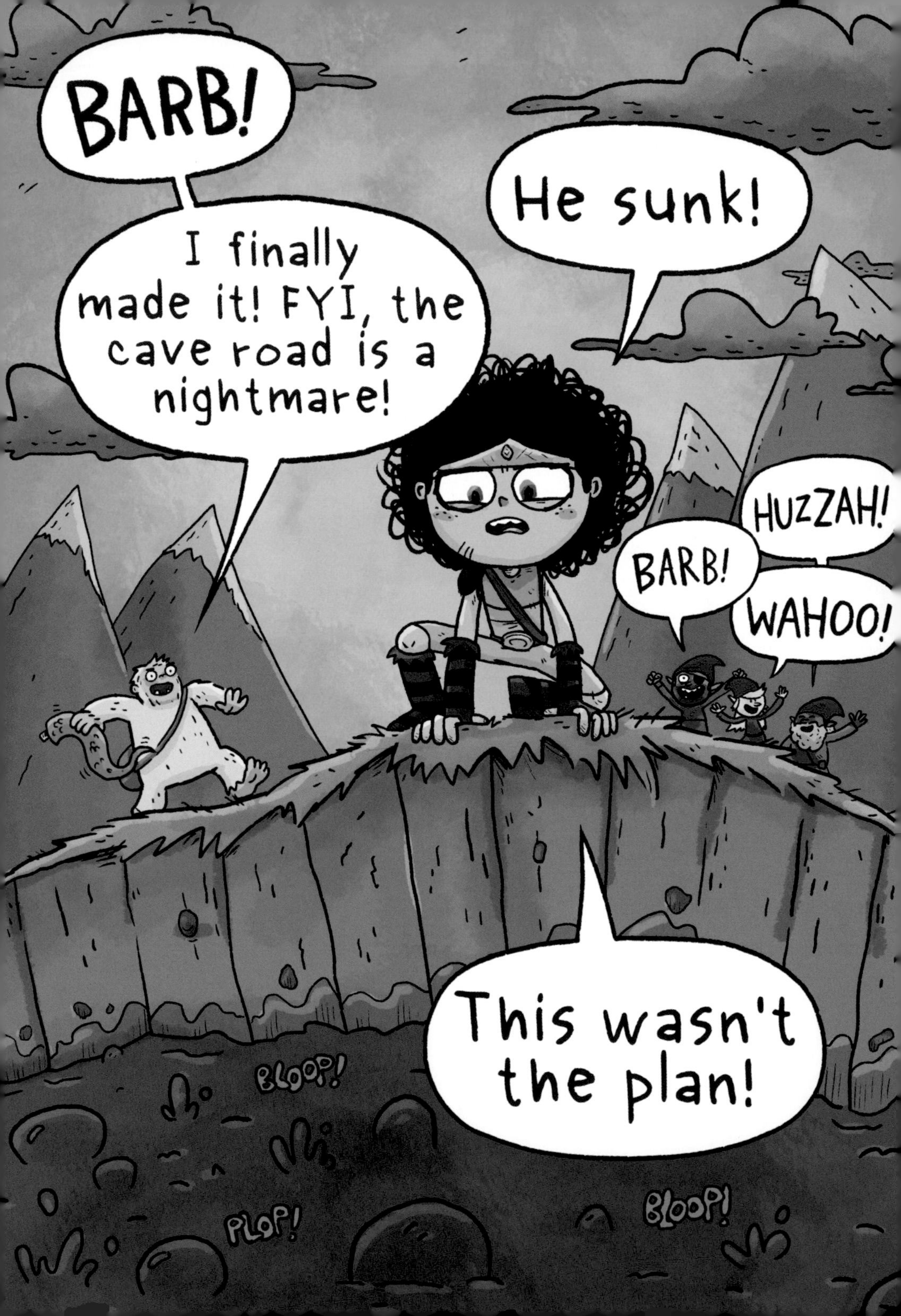
BARB!
I finally made it! FYI, the cave road is a nightmare!
He sunk!
HUZZAH!
BARB!
WAHOO!
This wasn't the plan!
BLOOP!
PLOP!
BLOOP!

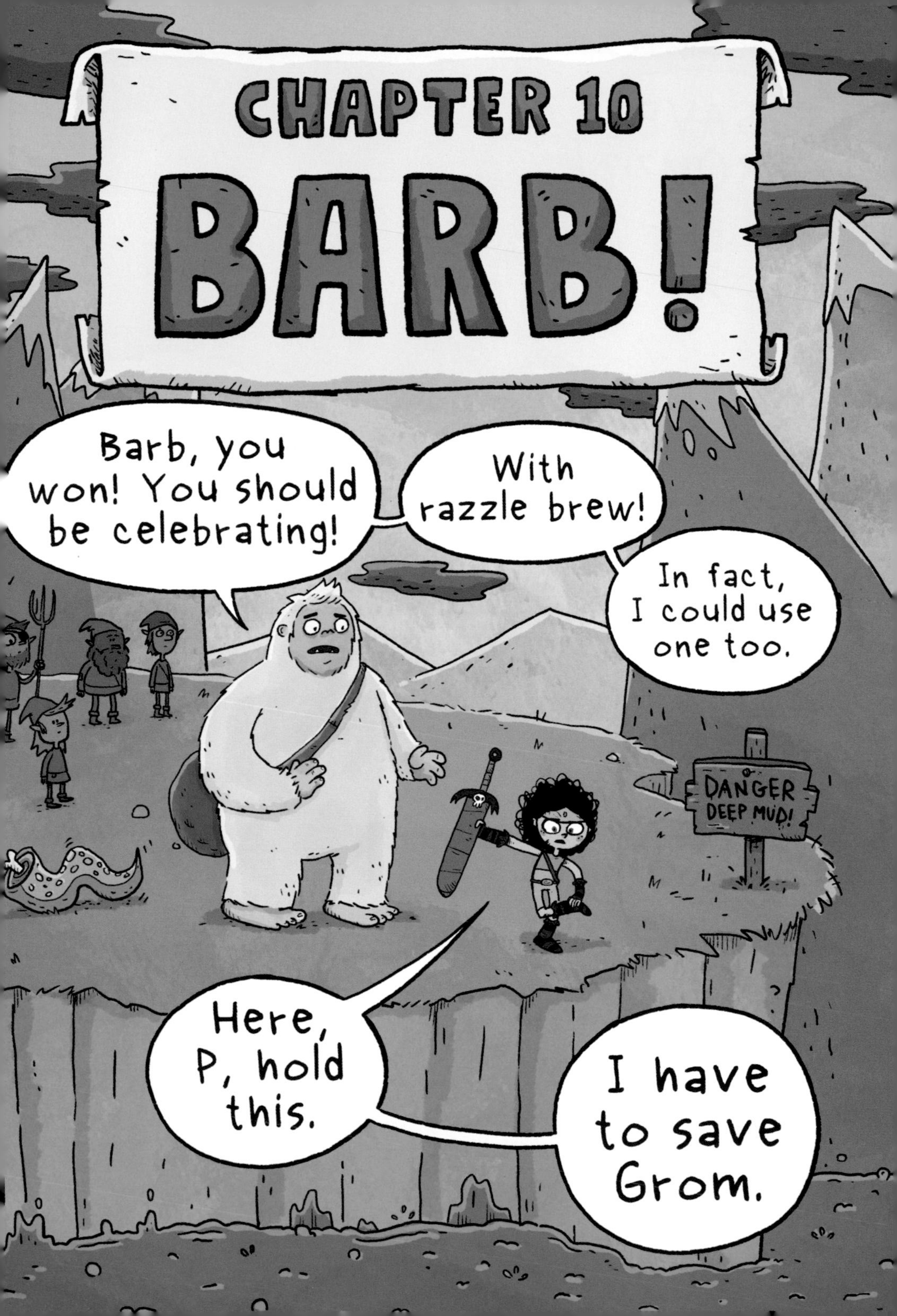
CHAPTER 10
BARB!
Barb, you won! You should be celebrating!
With razzle brew!
In fact, I could use one too.
DANGER DEEP MUD!
Here, P, hold this.
I have to save Grom.

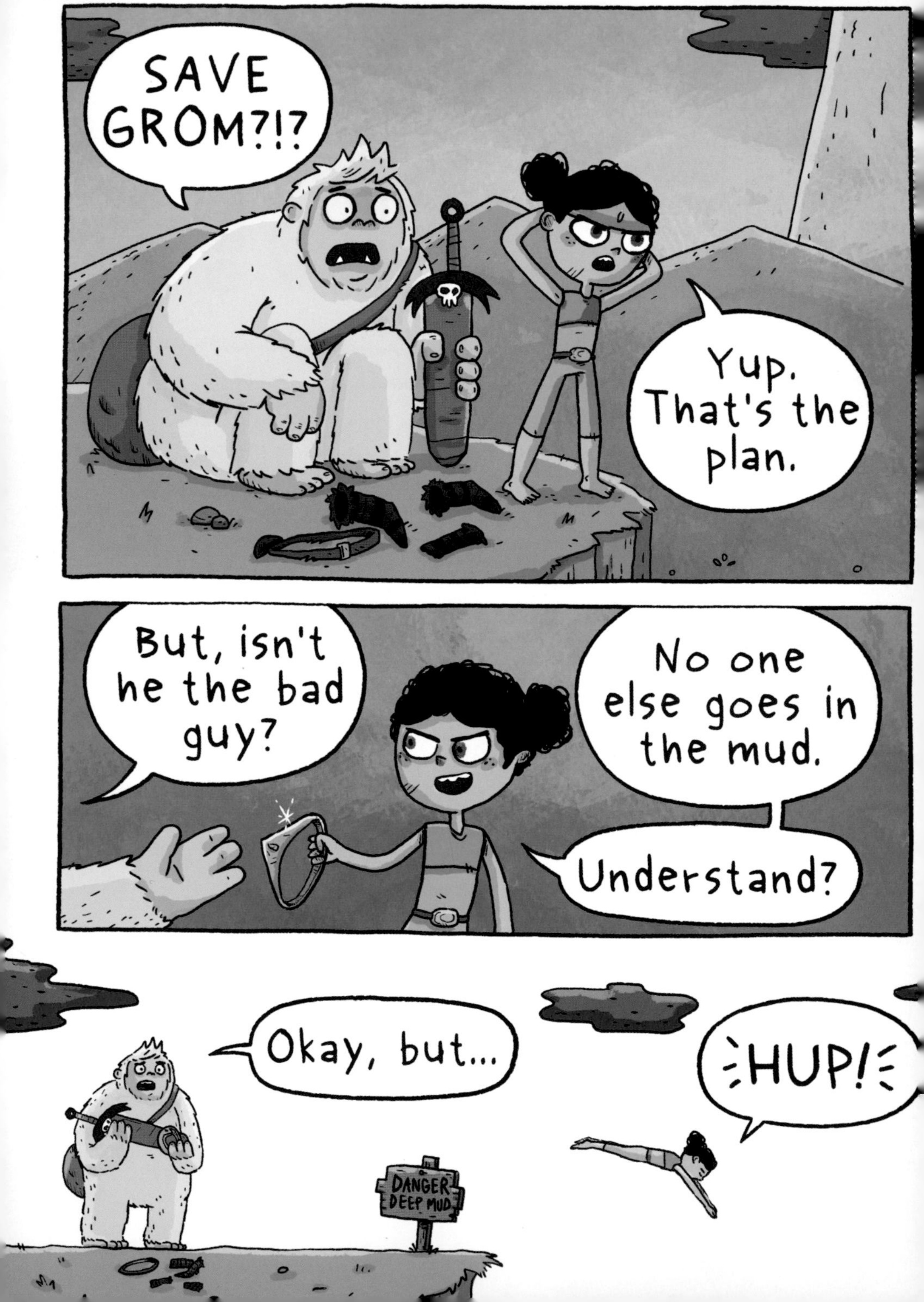
SAVE GROM?!?
Yup. That's the plan.
But, isn't he the bad guy?
No one else goes in the mud.
Understand?
Okay, but...
HUP!
DANGER DEEP MUD

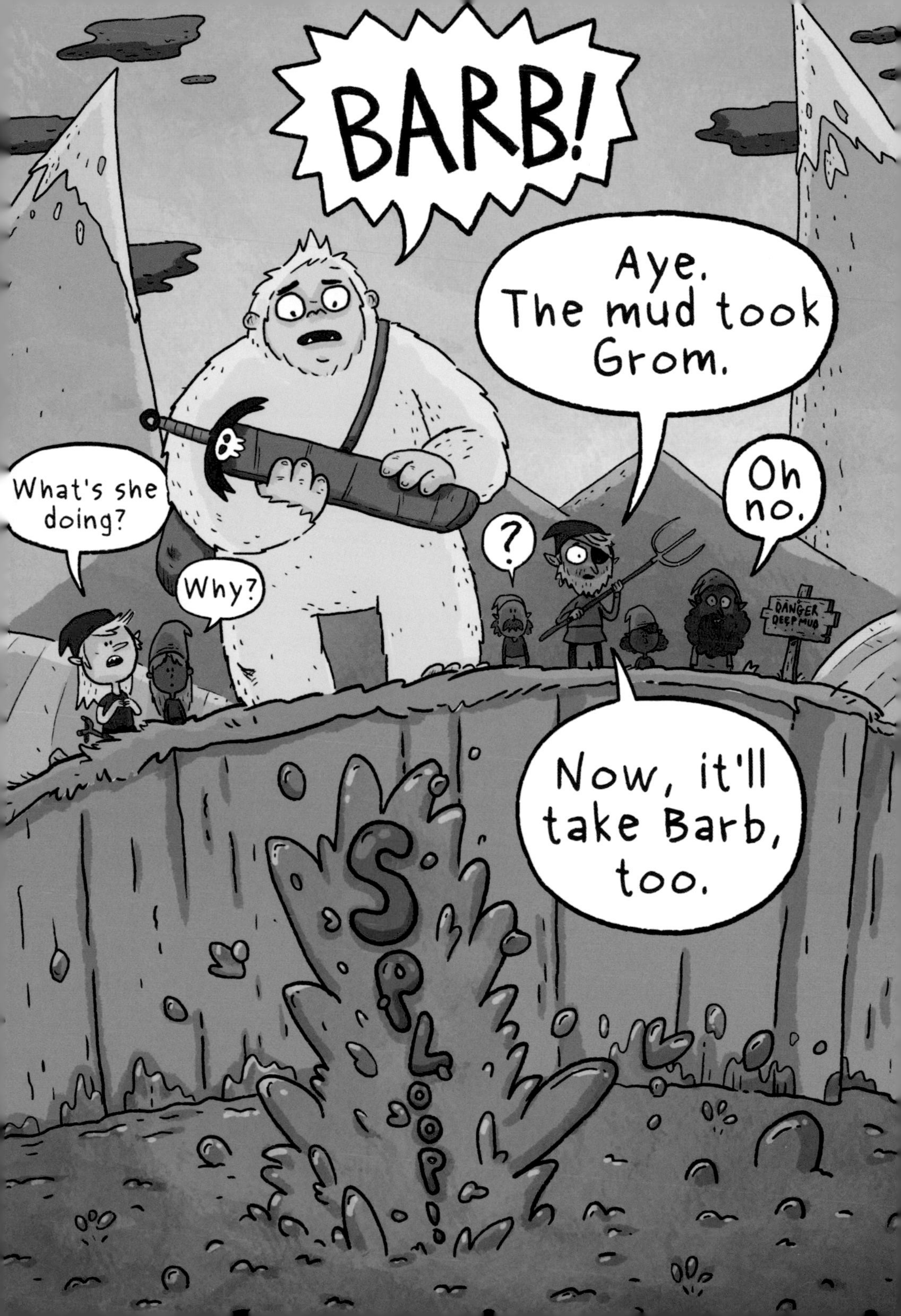
BARB!
Aye. The mud took Grom.
What's she doing?
Why?
?
Oh no.
DANGER DEEP MUD
Now, it'll take Barb, too.
SPLOOOP!

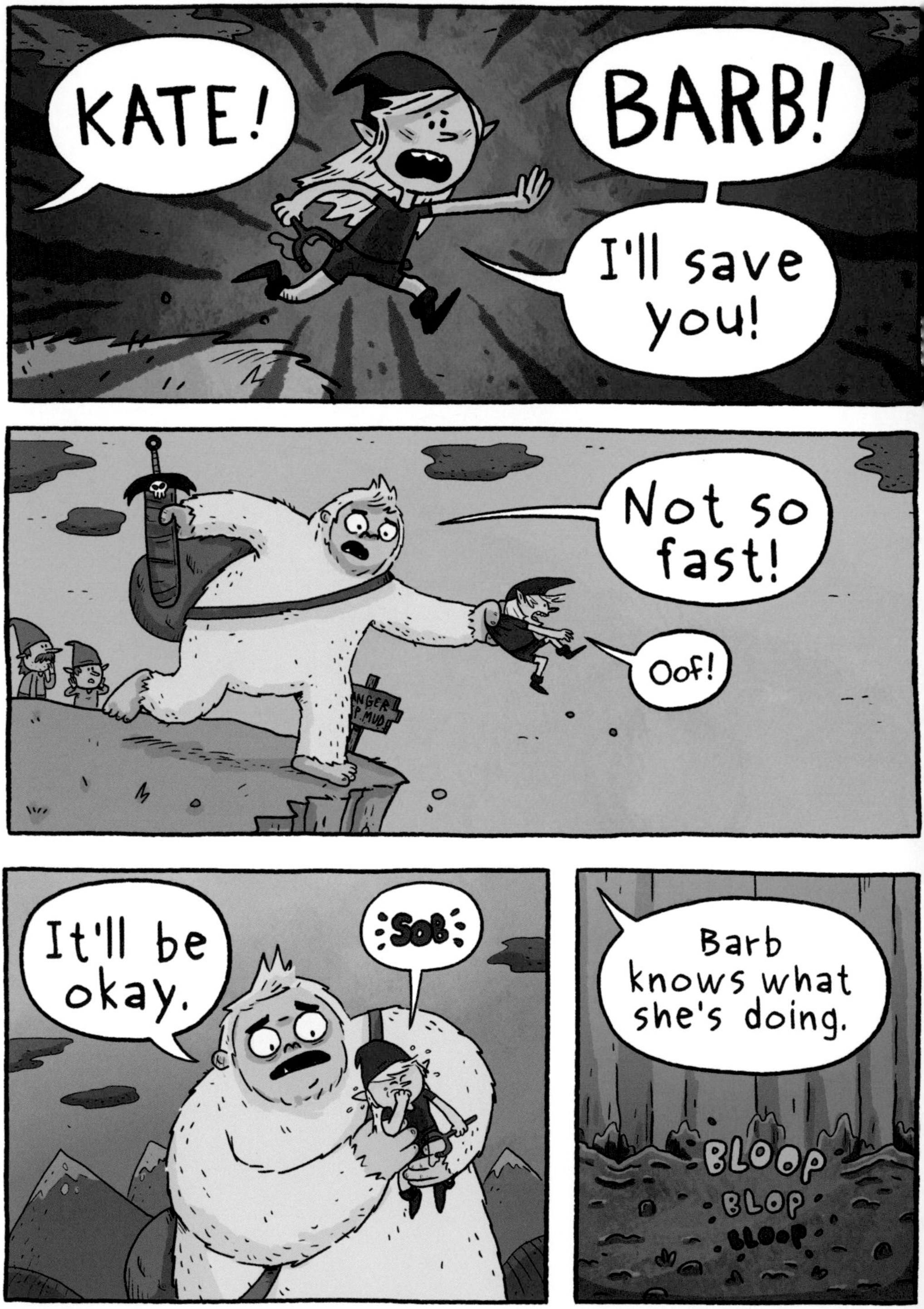
KATE!
BARB!
I'll save you!
Not so fast!
Oof!
It'll be okay.
SOB
Barb knows what she's doing.
BLOOP
BLOP
BLOOP

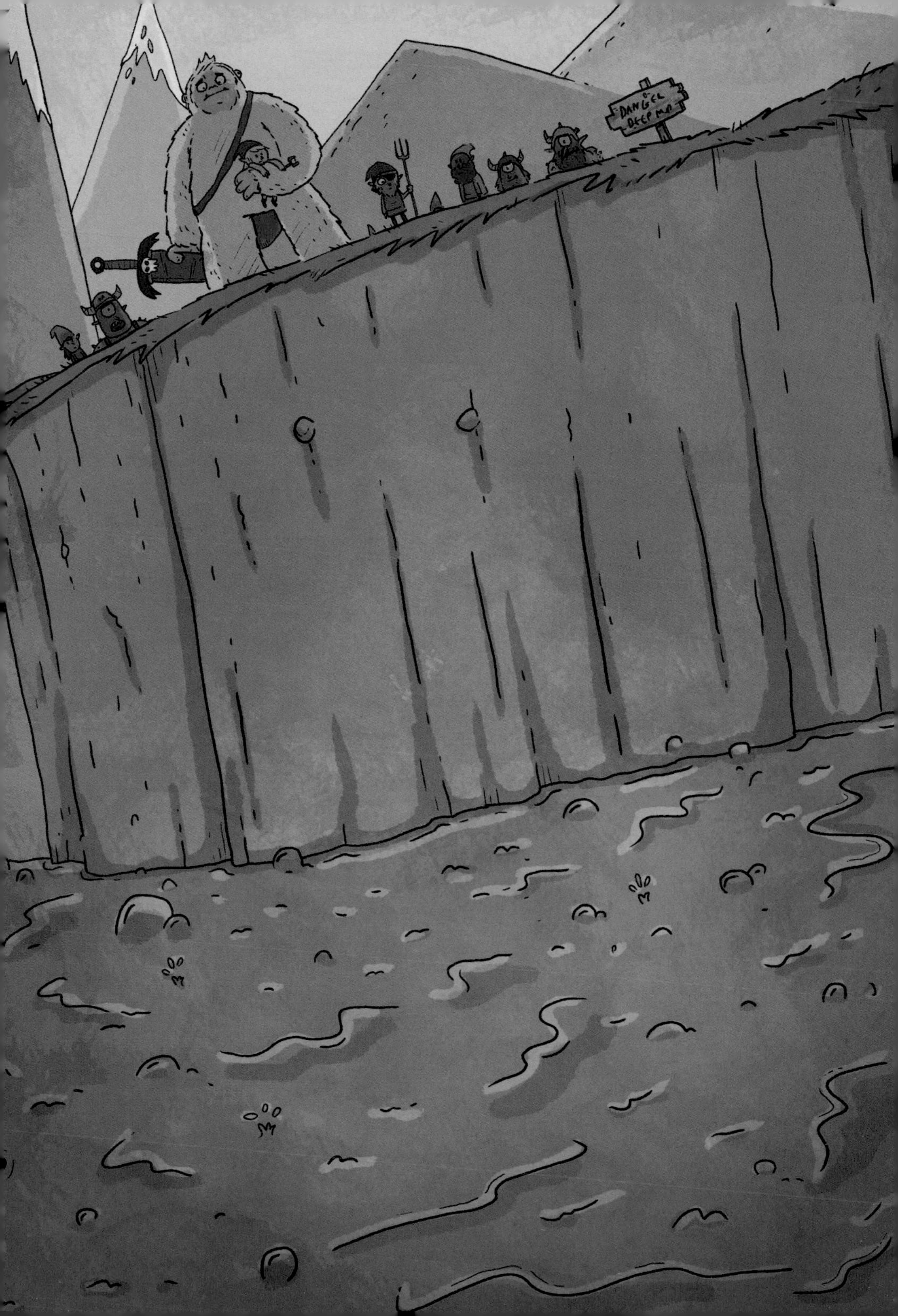
DANGER
DEEP

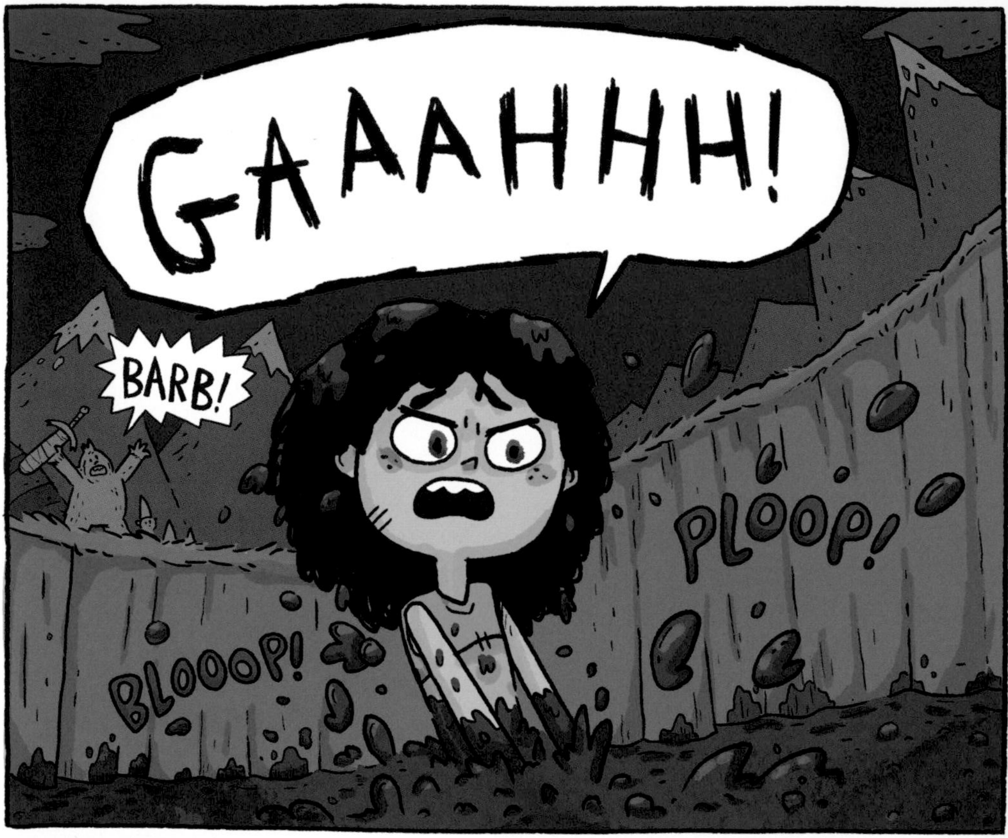
GAAHHH!
BARB!
PLOOP!
BLOOOP!

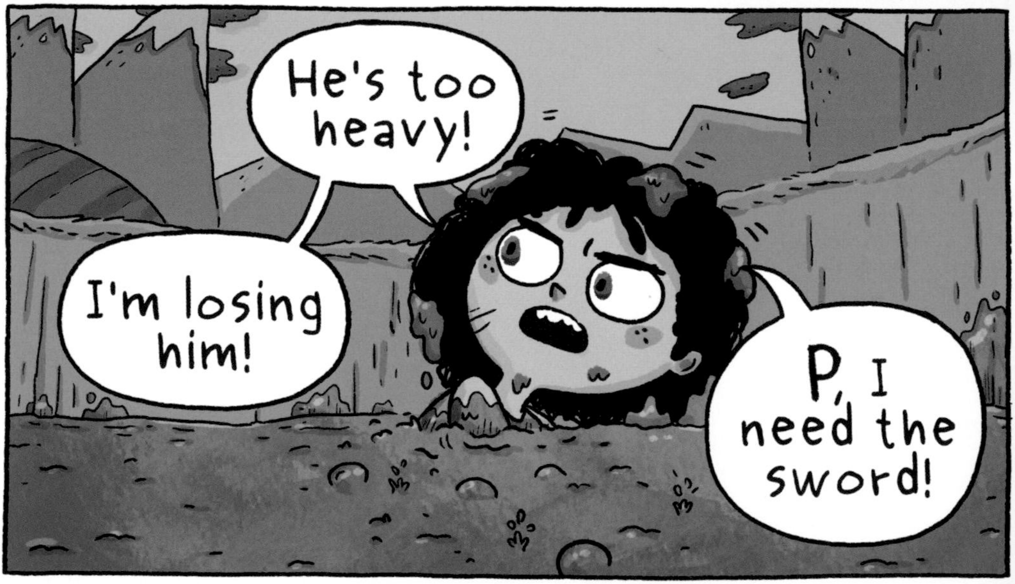
He's too heavy!
I'm losing him!
P, I need the sword!

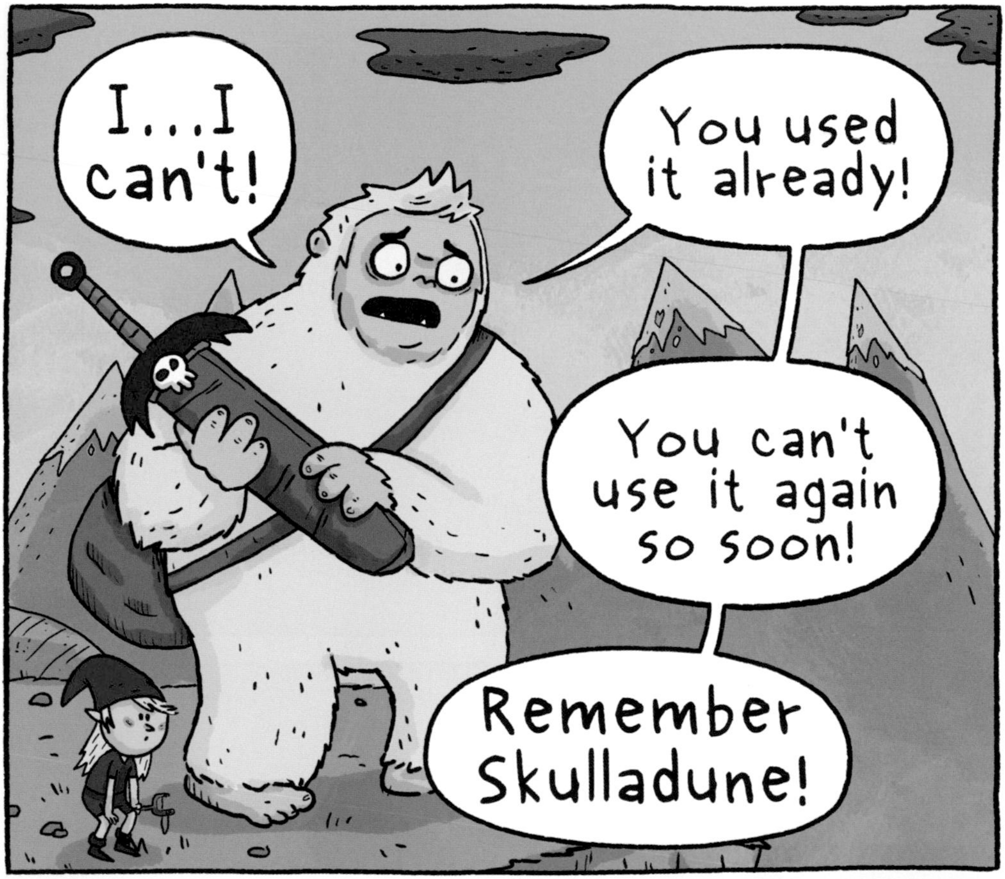
I...I can't!
You used it already!
You can't use it again so soon!
Remember Skulladune!

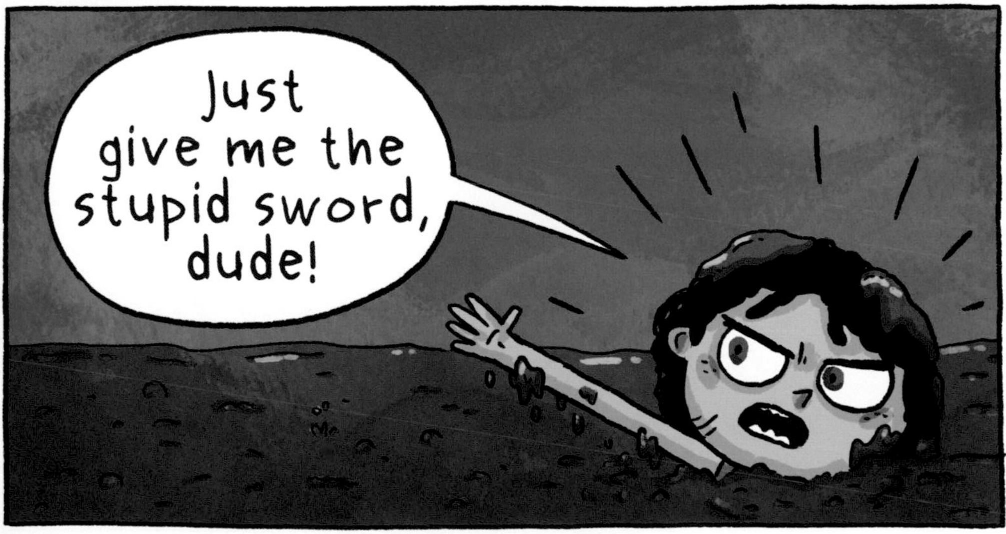
Just give me the stupid sword, dude!

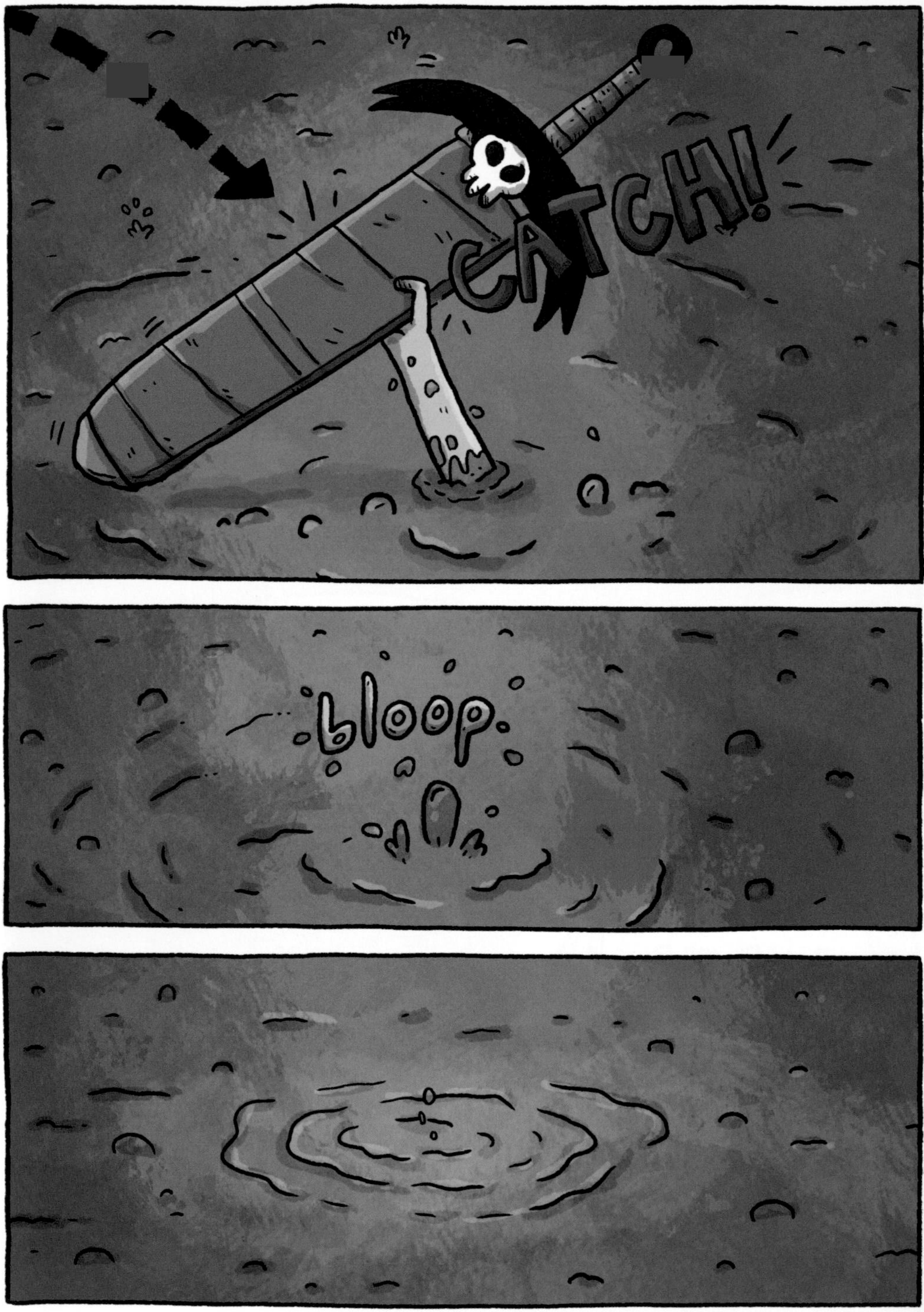
CATCH!
bloop

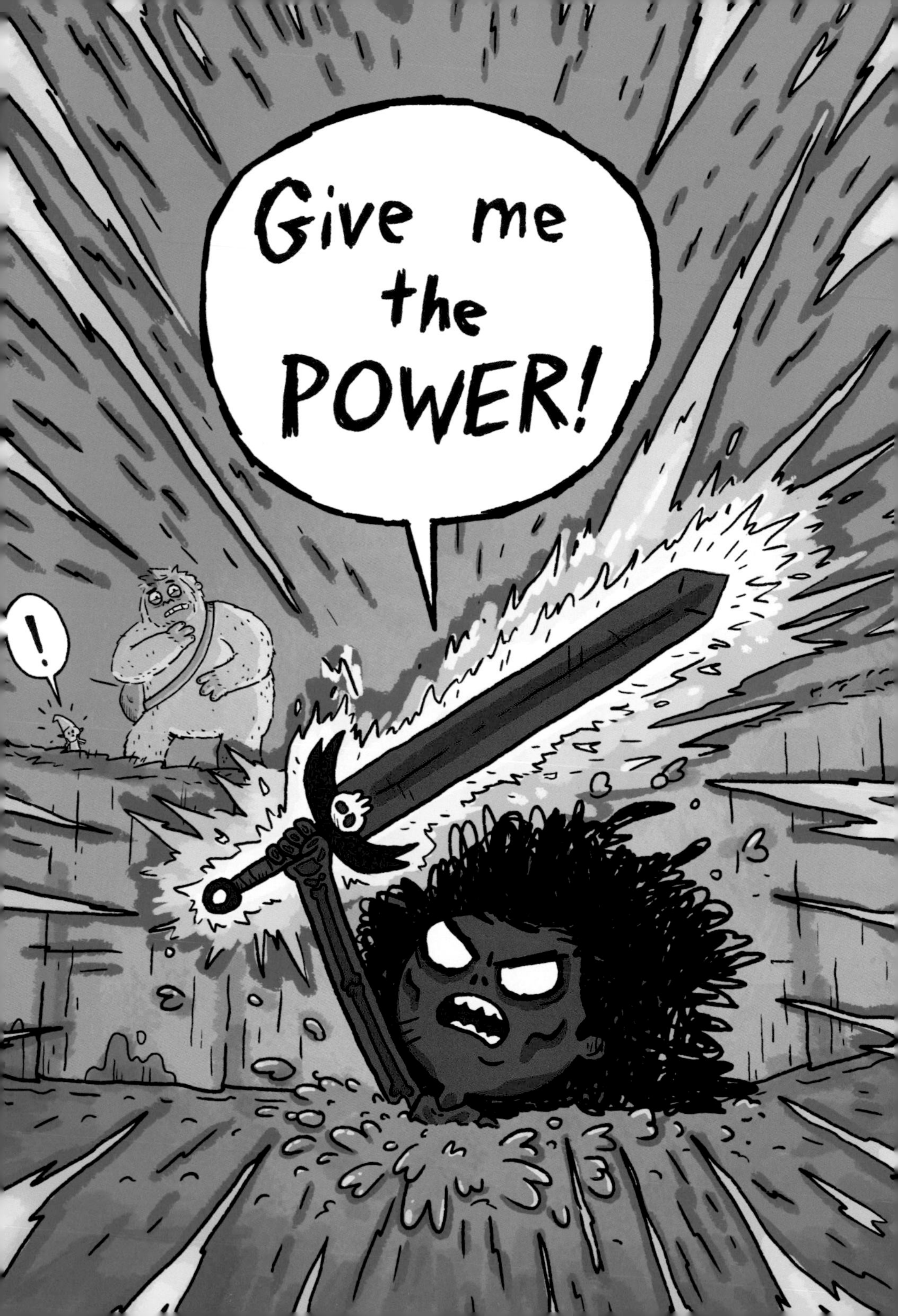
!
Give me the POWER!

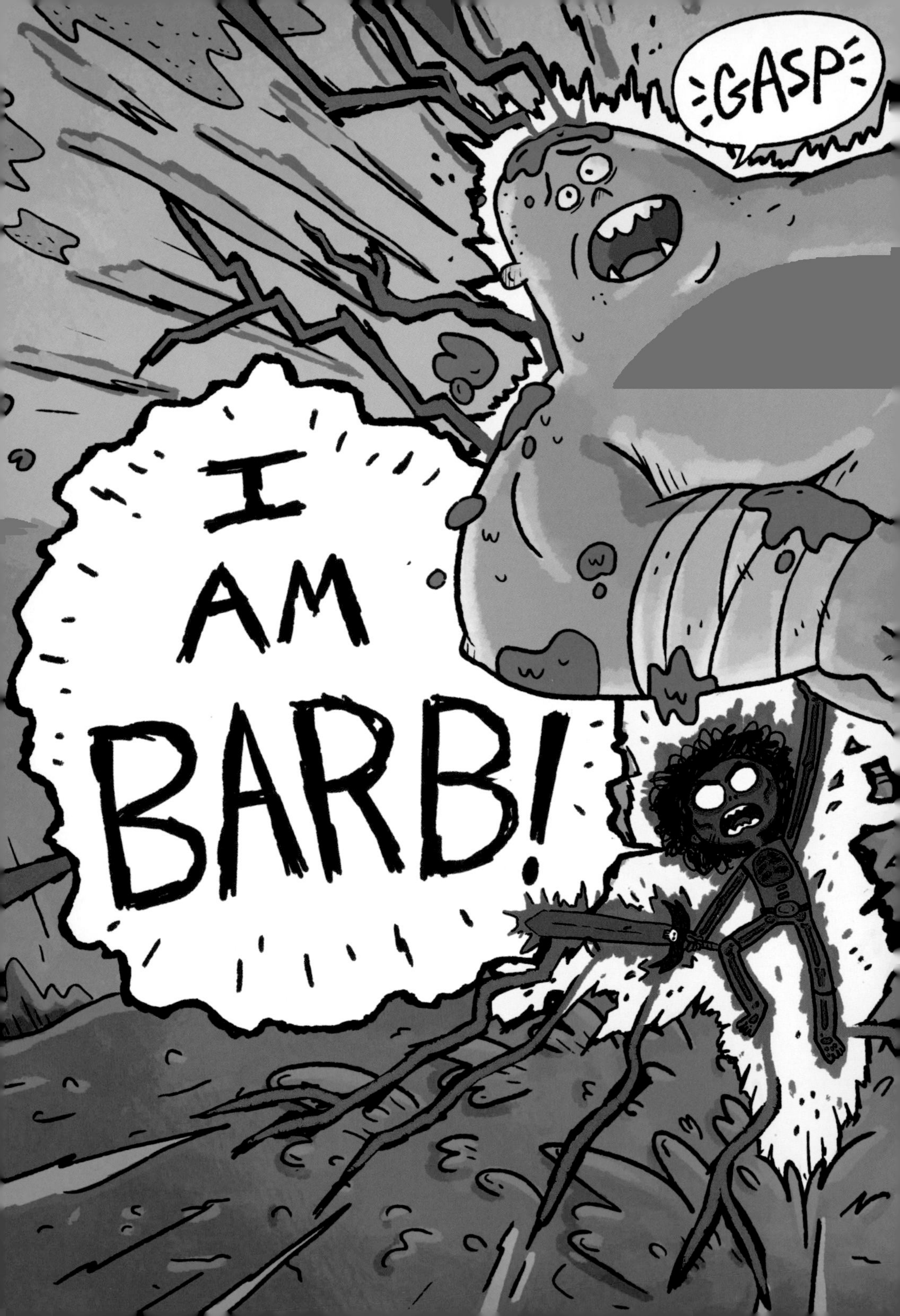
GASP
I AM BARB!

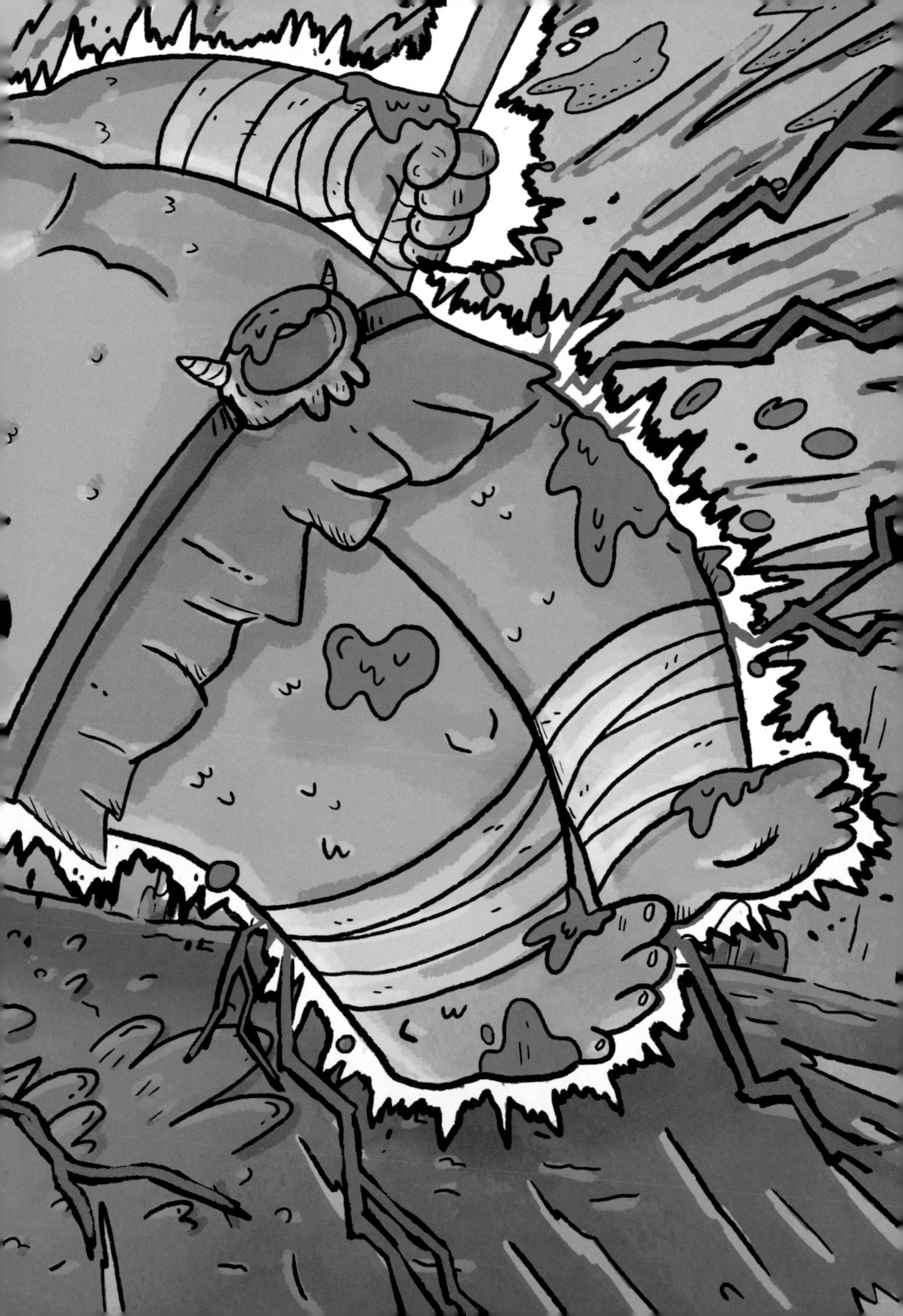

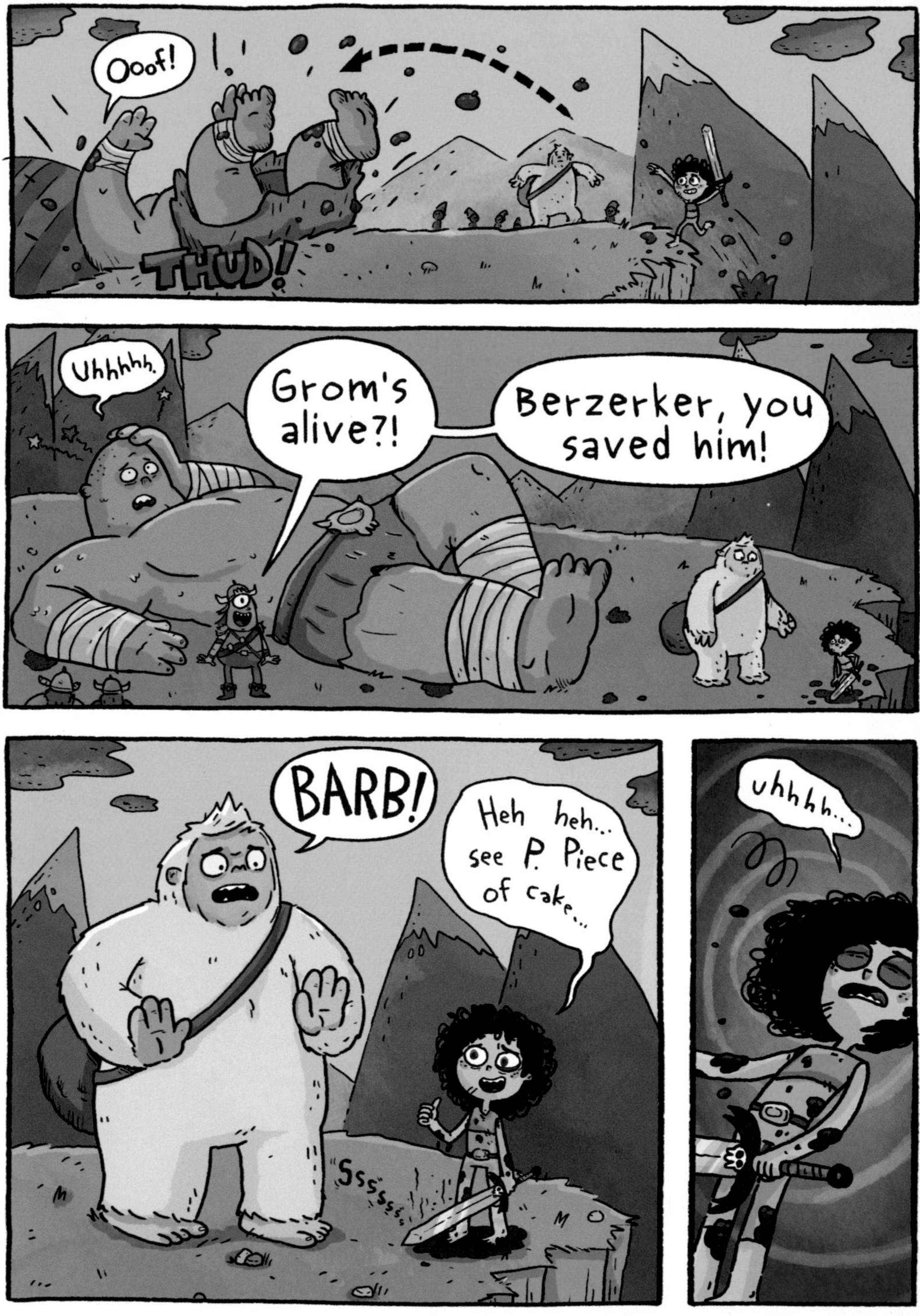
Ooof!
THUD!
Uhhhhh.
Grom's alive?!
Berzerker, you saved him!
BARB!
Heh heh... see P. Piece of cake...
Ssssssss
uhhhh...

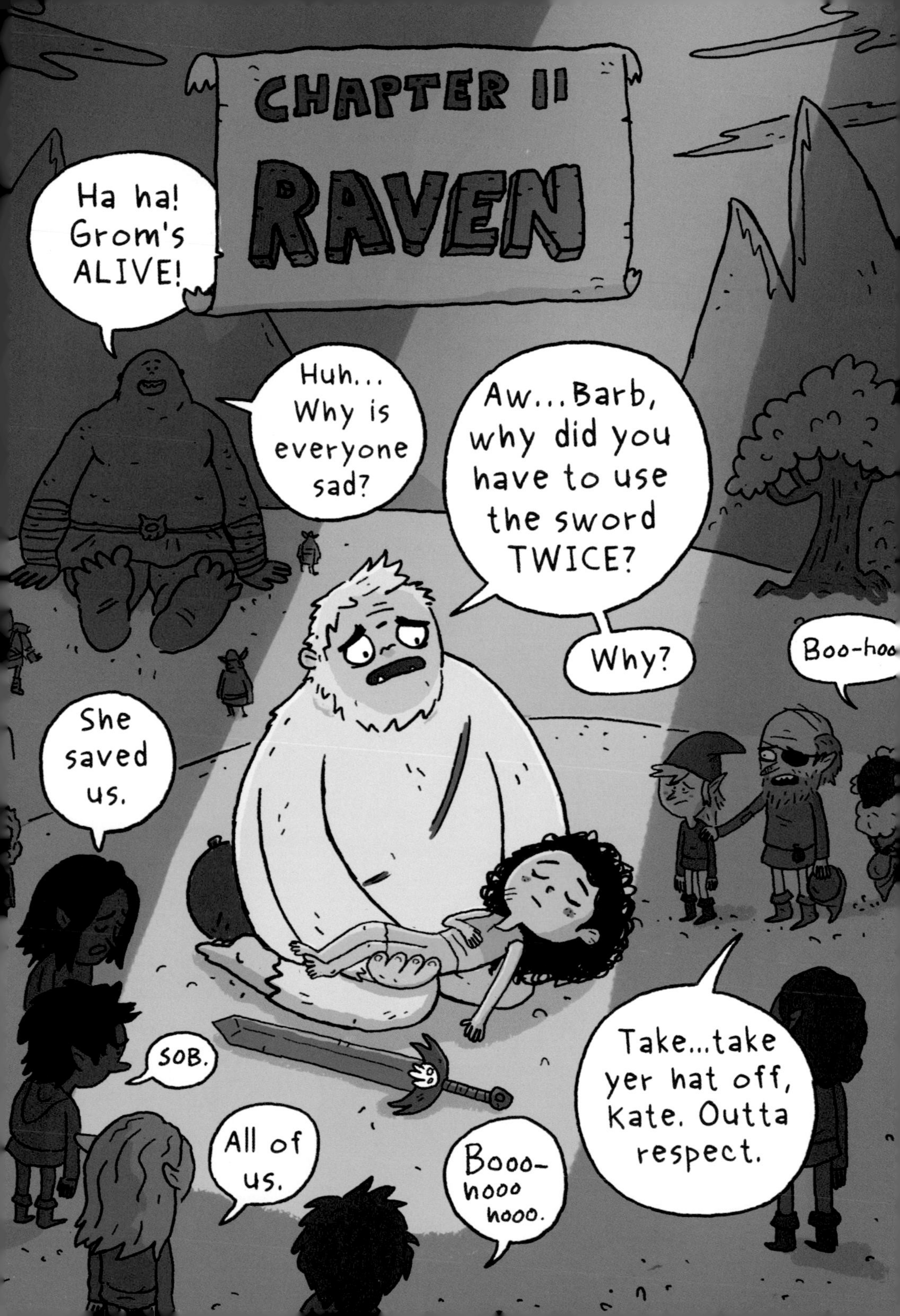
CHAPTER 11
RAVEN
Ha ha! Grom's ALIVE!
Huh... Why is everyone sad?
Aw...Barb, why did you have to use the sword TWICE?
Why?
Boo-hoo
She saved us.
SOB.
All of us.
Booo-hooo hooo.
Take...take yer hat off, Kate. Outta respect.

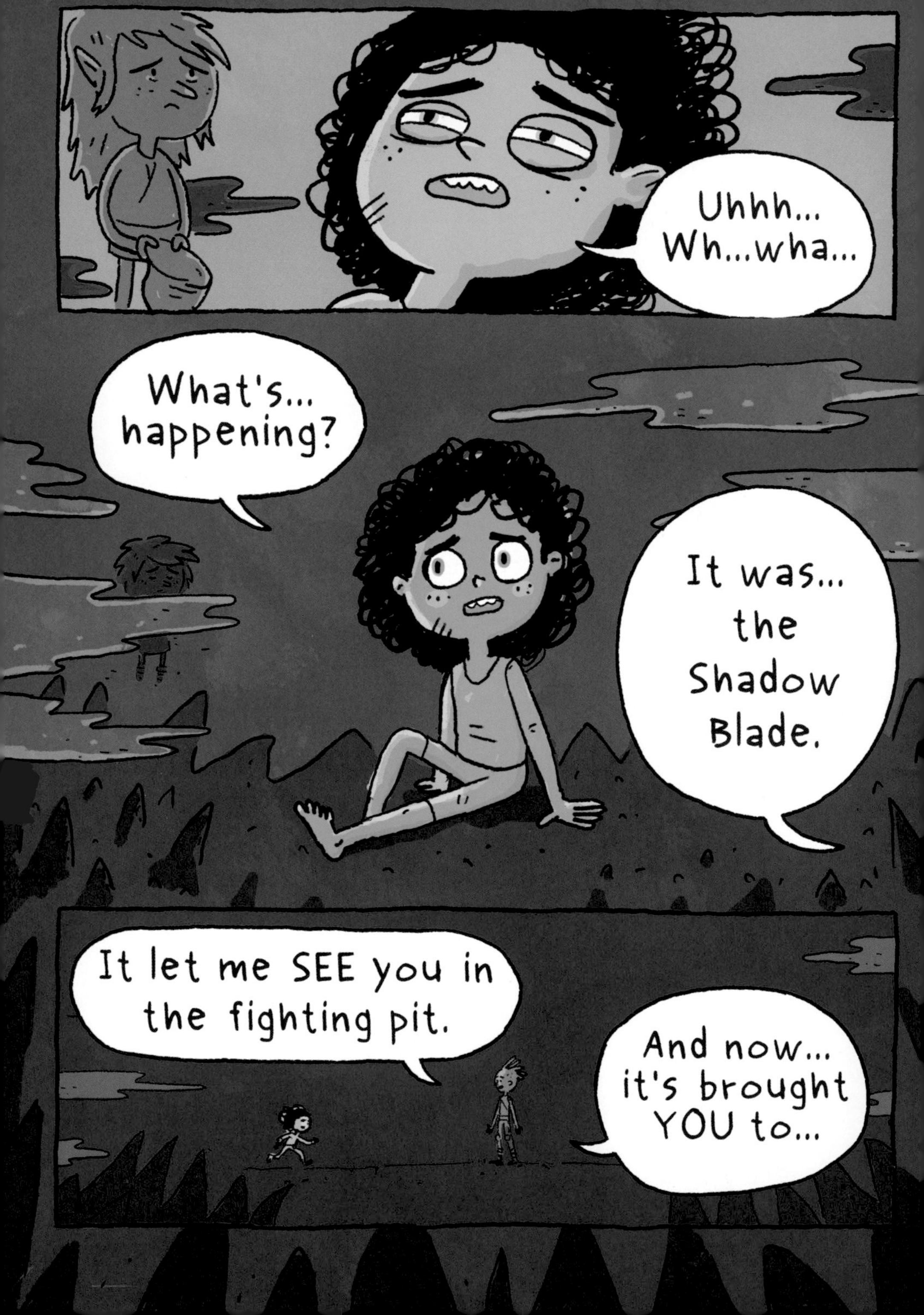
Uhhh... Wh...wha...
What's... happening?
It was... the Shadow Blade.
It let me SEE you in the fighting pit.
And now... it's brought YOU to...

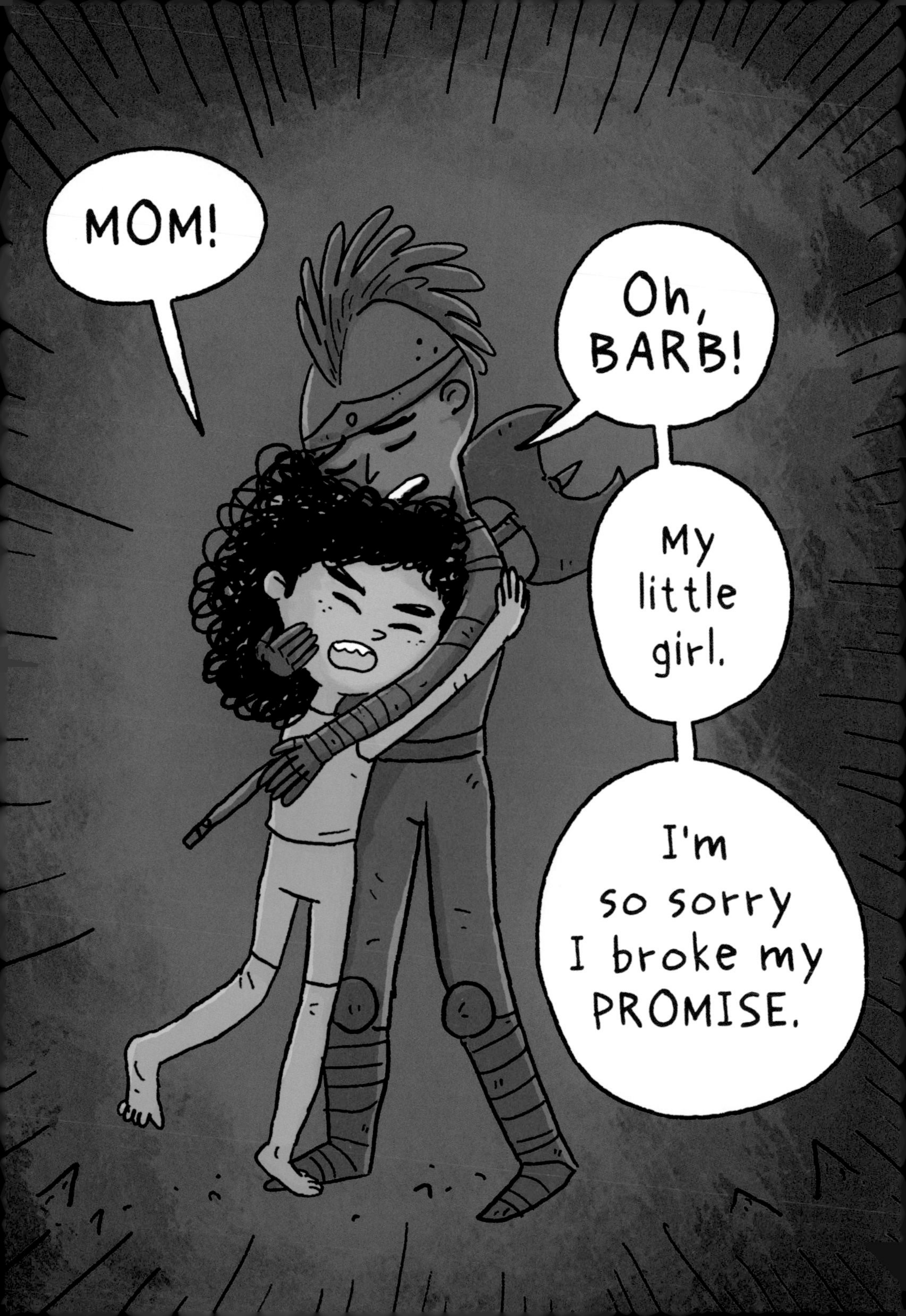
MOM!
Oh, BARB!
My little girl.
I'm so sorry I broke my PROMISE.

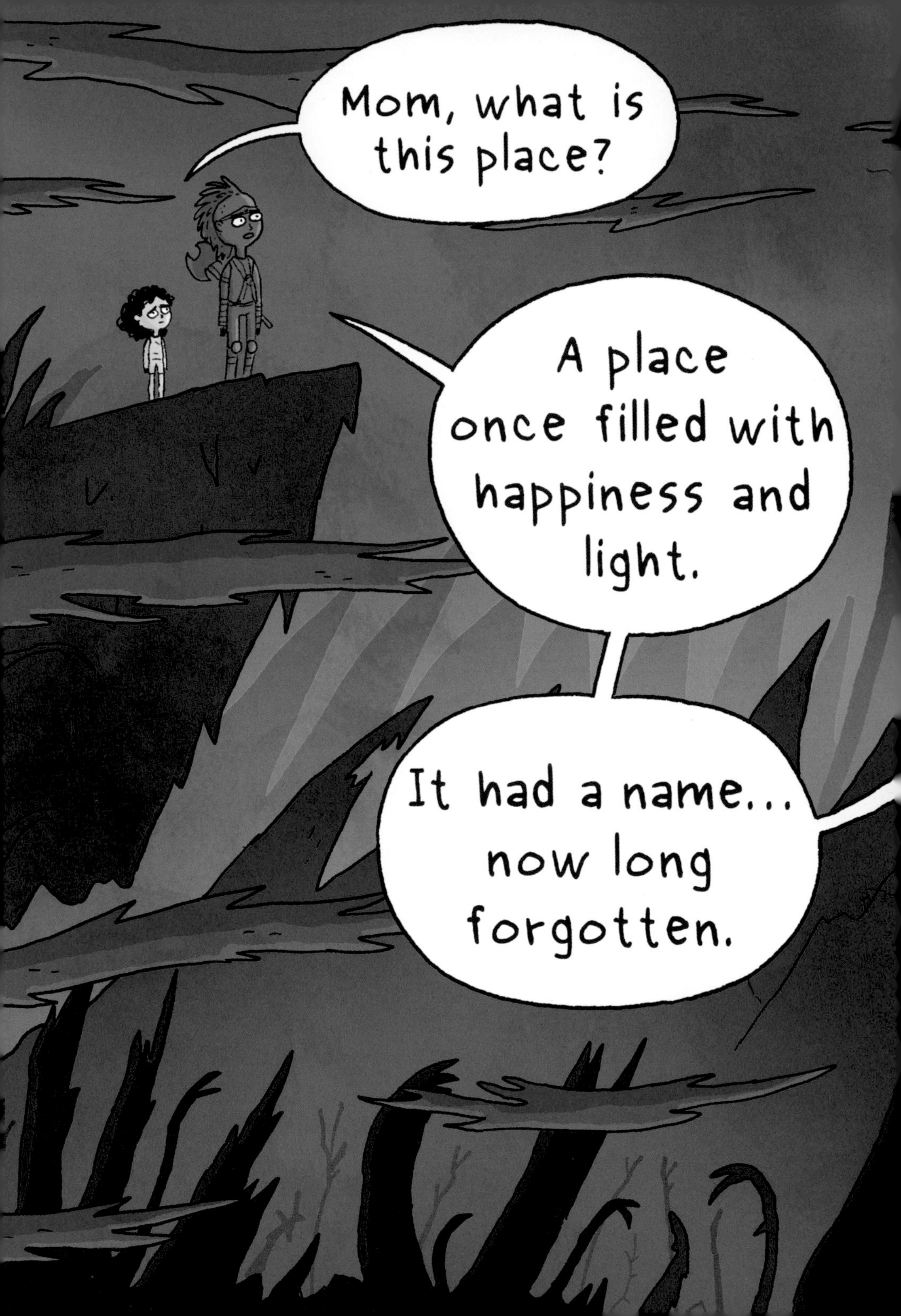
Mom, what is this place?
A place once filled with happiness and light.
It had a name... now long forgotten.

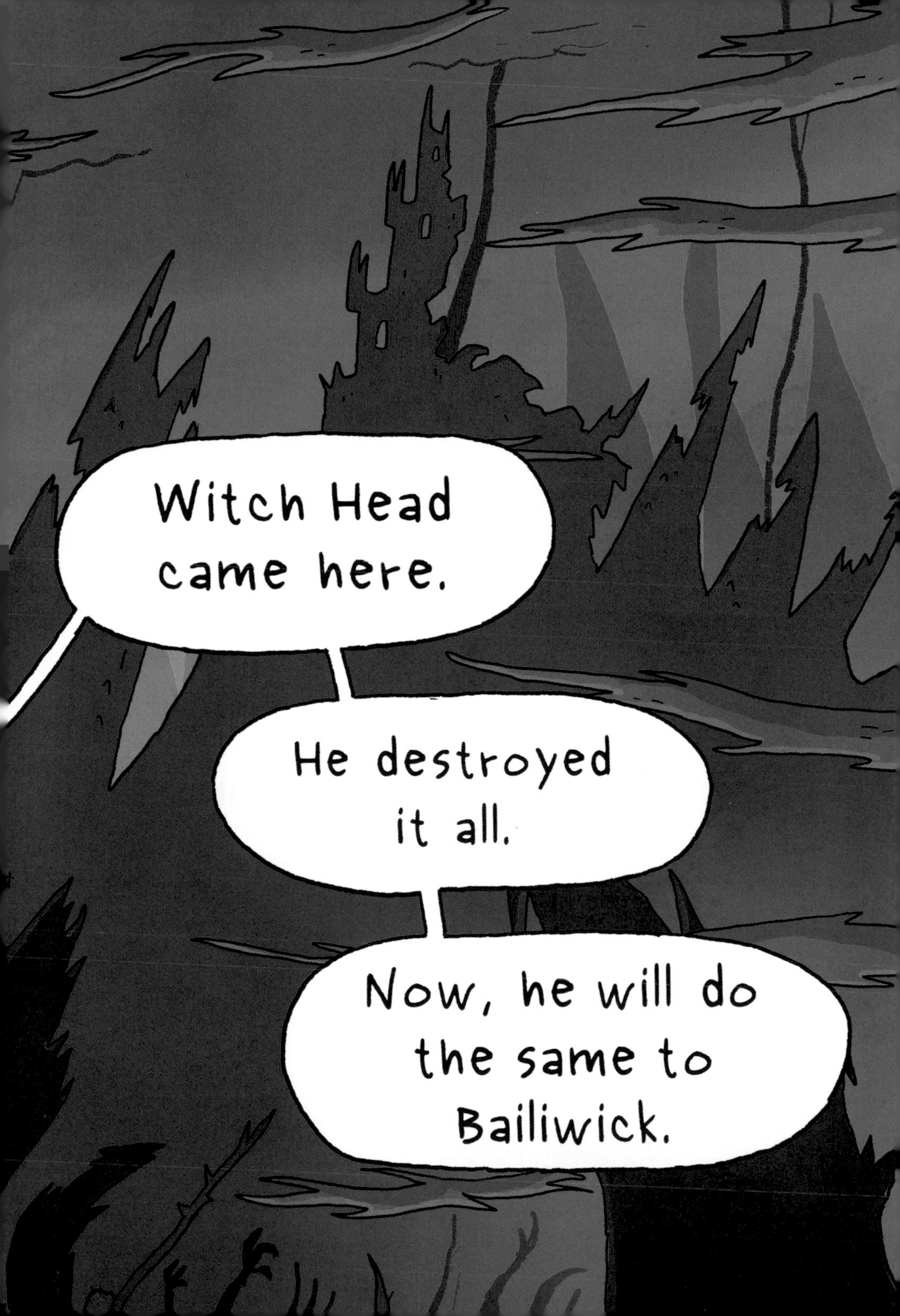
Witch Head came here.
He destroyed it all.
Now, he will do the same to Bailiwick.

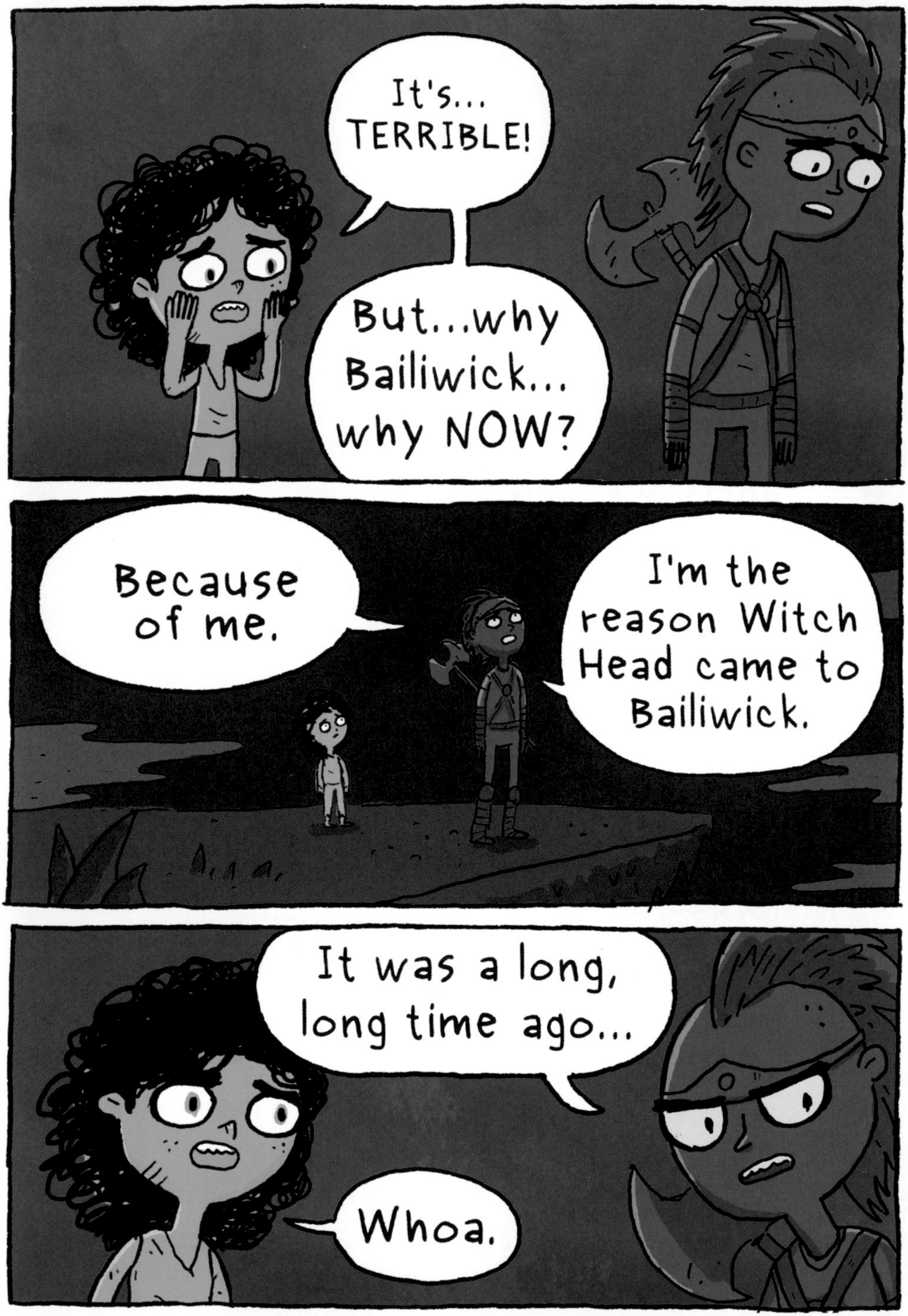
It's...
TERRIBLE!
But...why
Bailiwick...
why NOW?
Because
of me.
I'm the
reason Witch
Head came to
Bailiwick.
It was a long,
long time ago...
Whoa.

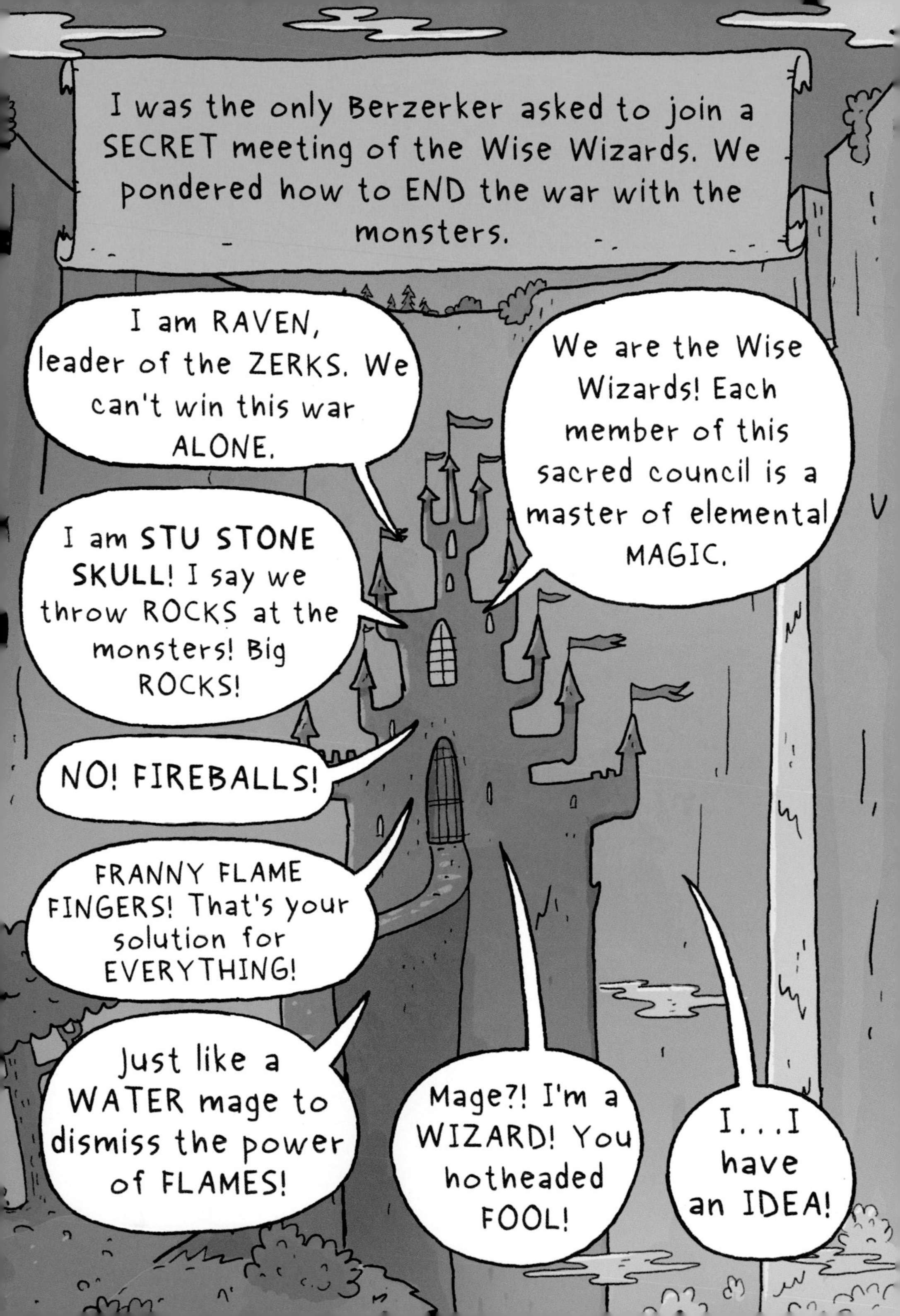
I was the only Berzerker asked to join a SECRET meeting of the Wise Wizards. We pondered how to END the war with the monsters.
I am RAVEN, leader of the ZERKS. We can't win this war ALONE.
We are the Wise Wizards! Each member of this sacred council is a master of elemental MAGIC.
I am STU STONE SKULL! I say we throw ROCKS at the monsters! Big ROCKS!
NO! FIREBALLS!
FRANNY FLAME FINGERS! That's your solution for EVERYTHING!
Just like a WATER mage to dismiss the power of FLAMES!
Mage?! I'm a WIZARD! You hotheaded FOOL!
I. . .I have an IDEA!

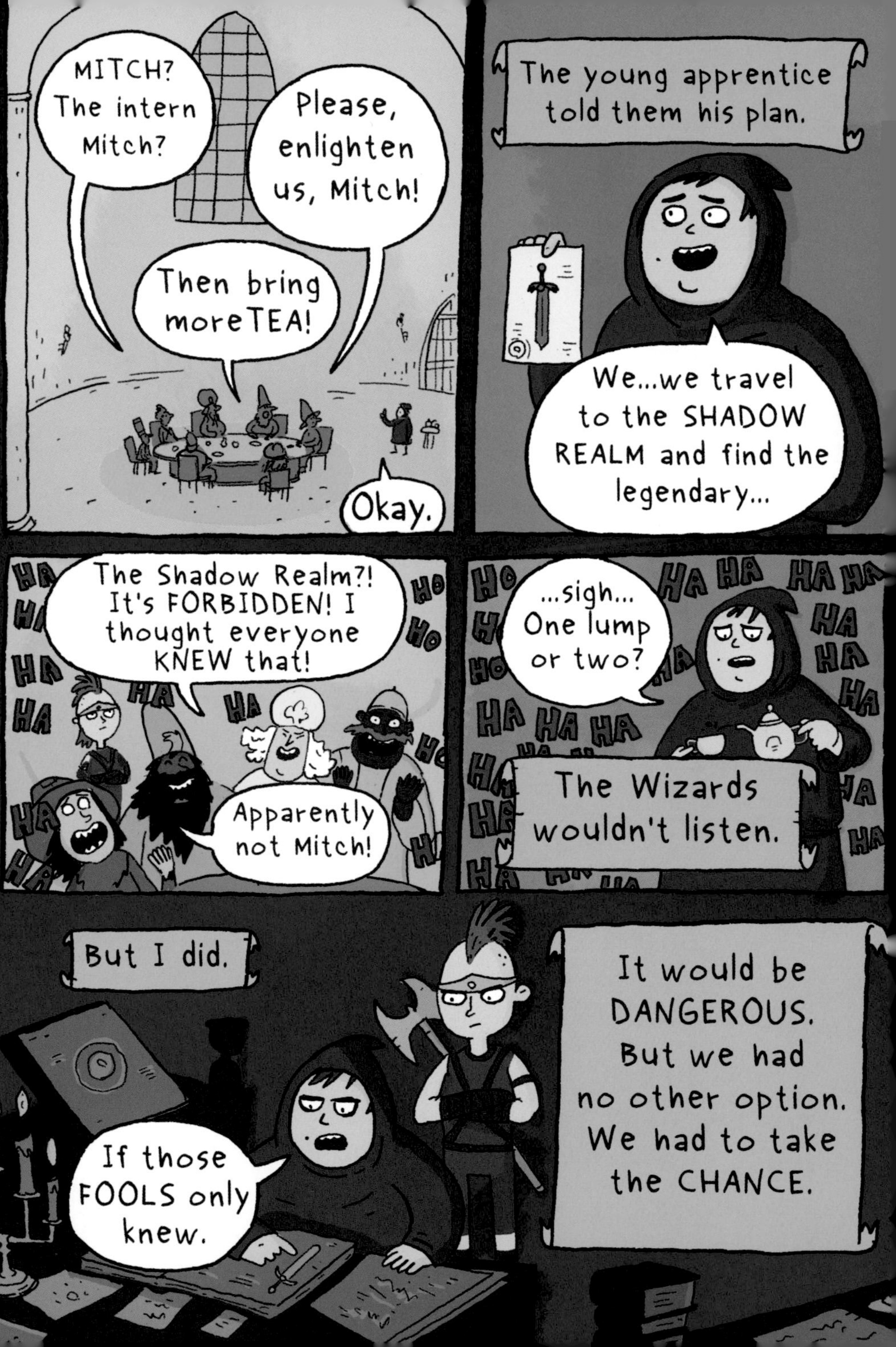
MITCH? The intern Mitch?
Please, enlighten us, Mitch!
Then bring moreTEA!
Okay.
The young apprentice told them his plan.
We...we travel to the SHADOW REALM and find the legendary...
The Shadow Realm?! It's FORBIDDEN! I thought everyone KNEW that!
Apparently not Mitch!
...sigh... One lump or two?
The Wizards wouldn't listen.
But I did.
It would be DANGEROUS. But we had no other option. We had to take the CHANCE.
If those FOOLS only knew.

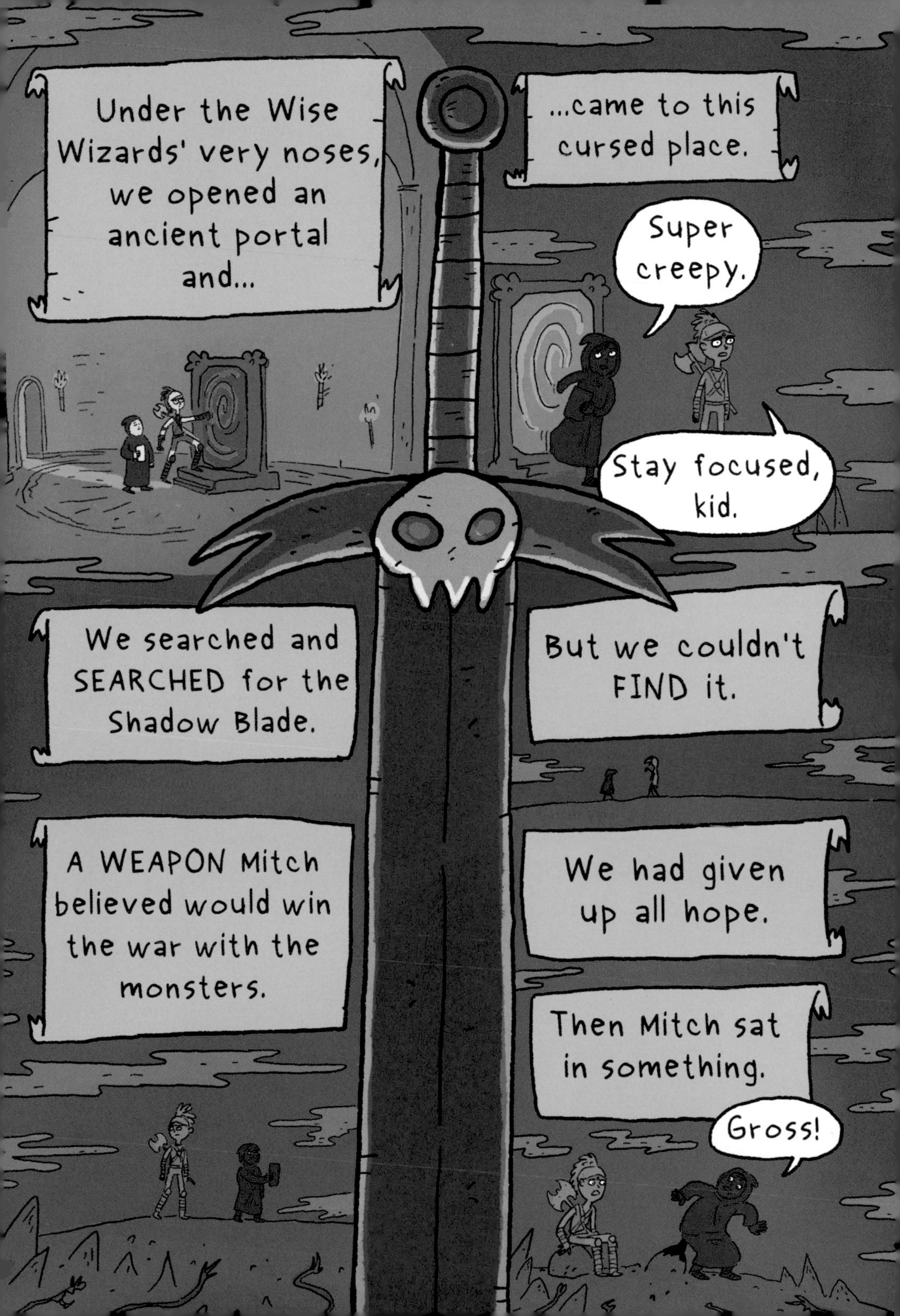
Under the Wise Wizards' very noses, we opened an ancient portal and...
...came to this cursed place.
Super creepy.
Stay focused, kid.
We searched and SEARCHED for the Shadow Blade.
But we couldn't FIND it.
A WEAPON Mitch believed would win the war with the monsters.
We had given up all hope.
Then Mitch sat in something.
Gross!

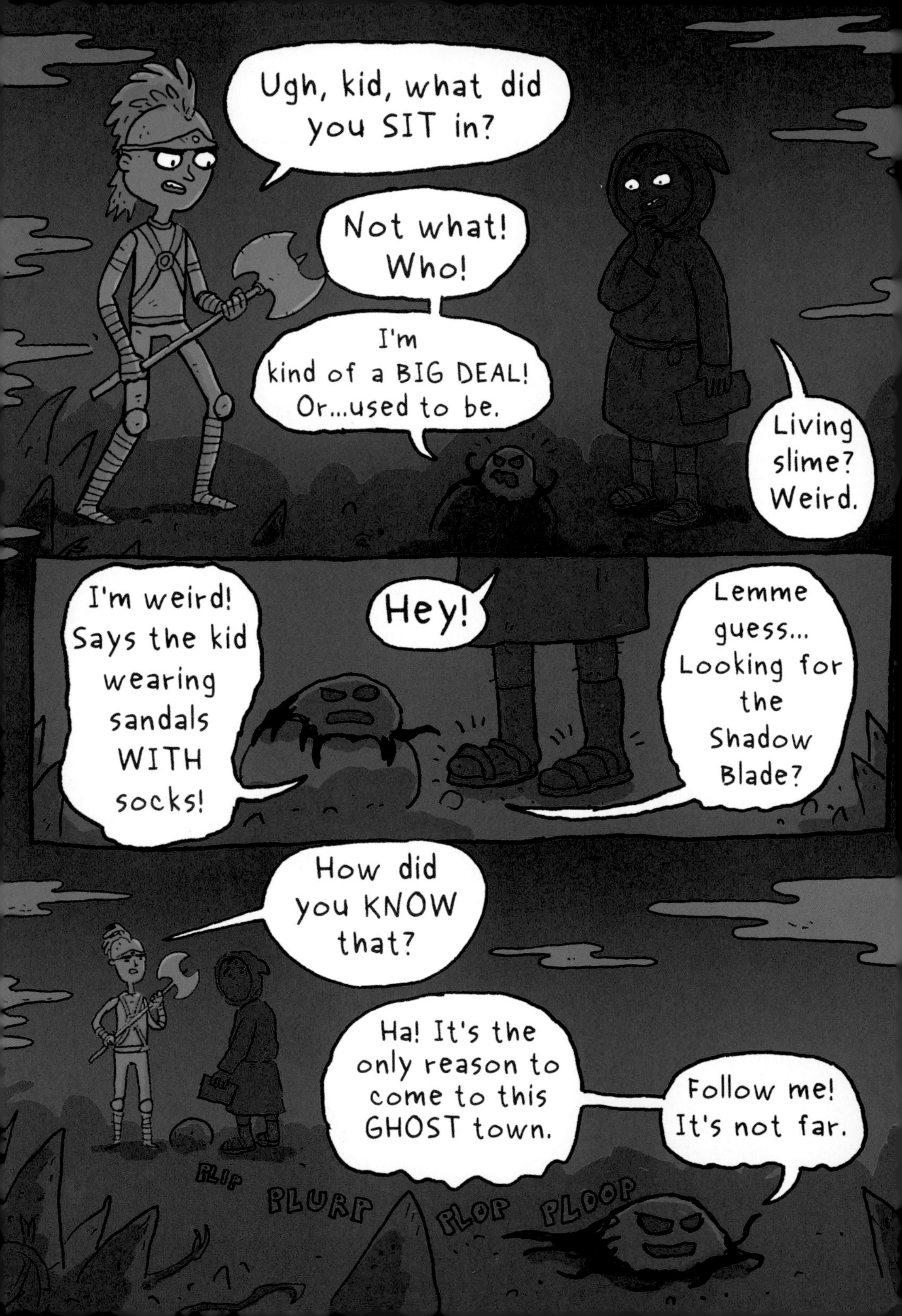

Ugh, kid, what did you SIT in?
Not what! Who!
I'm kind of a BIG DEAL! Or...used to be.
Living slime? Weird.
I'm weird! Says the kid wearing sandals WITH socks!
Hey!
Lemme guess... Looking for the Shadow Blade?
How did you KNOW that?
Ha! It's the only reason to come to this GHOST town.
Follow me! It's not far.
PLIP
PLURP
PLOP
PLOOP

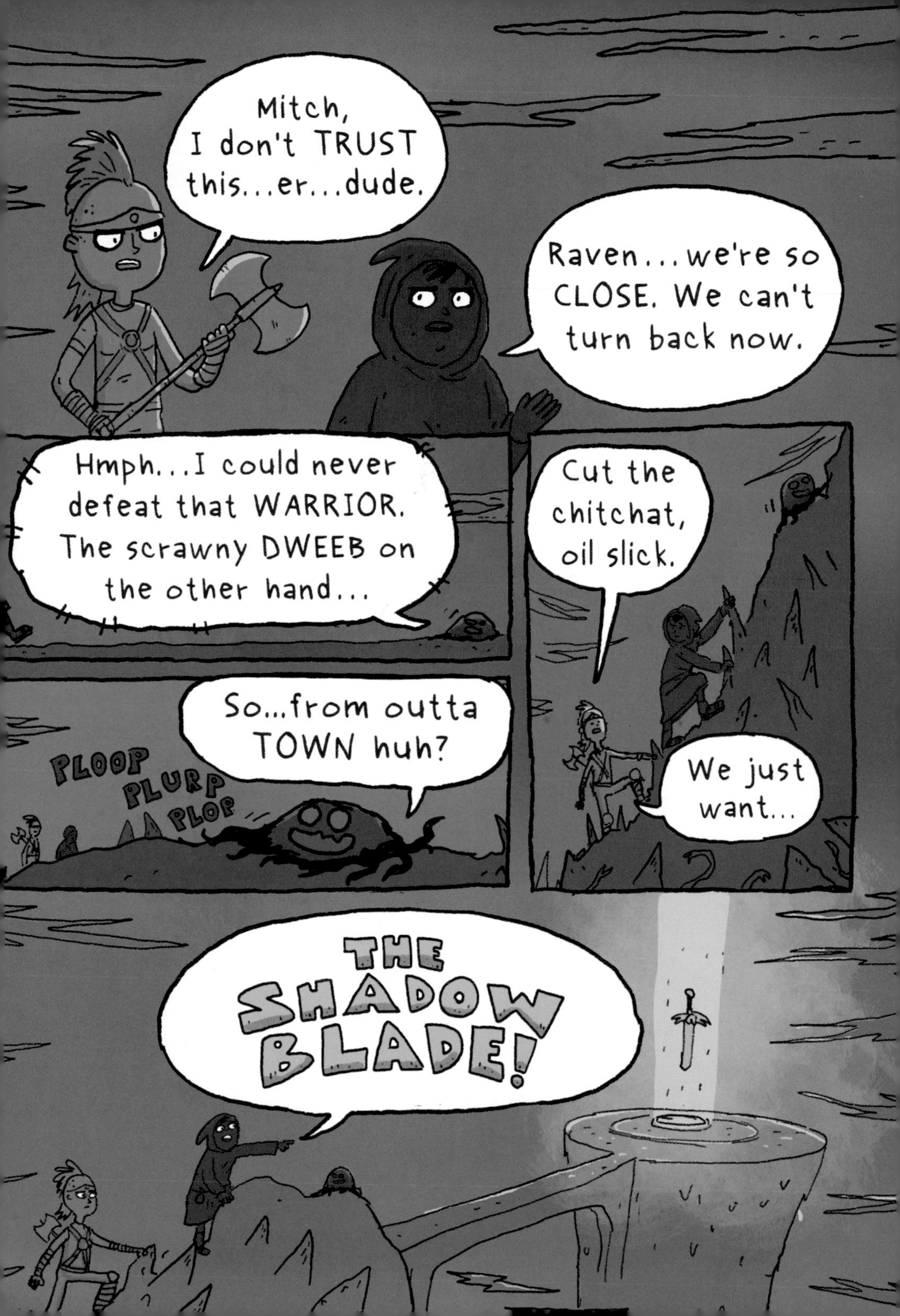
Mitch, I don't TRUST this...er...dude.
Raven...we're so CLOSE. We can't turn back now.
Hmph...I could never defeat that WARRIOR. The scrawny DWEEB on the other hand...
Cut the chitchat, oil slick.
So...from outta TOWN huh?
PLOOP
PLURP
PLOP
We just want...
THE SHADOW BLADE!

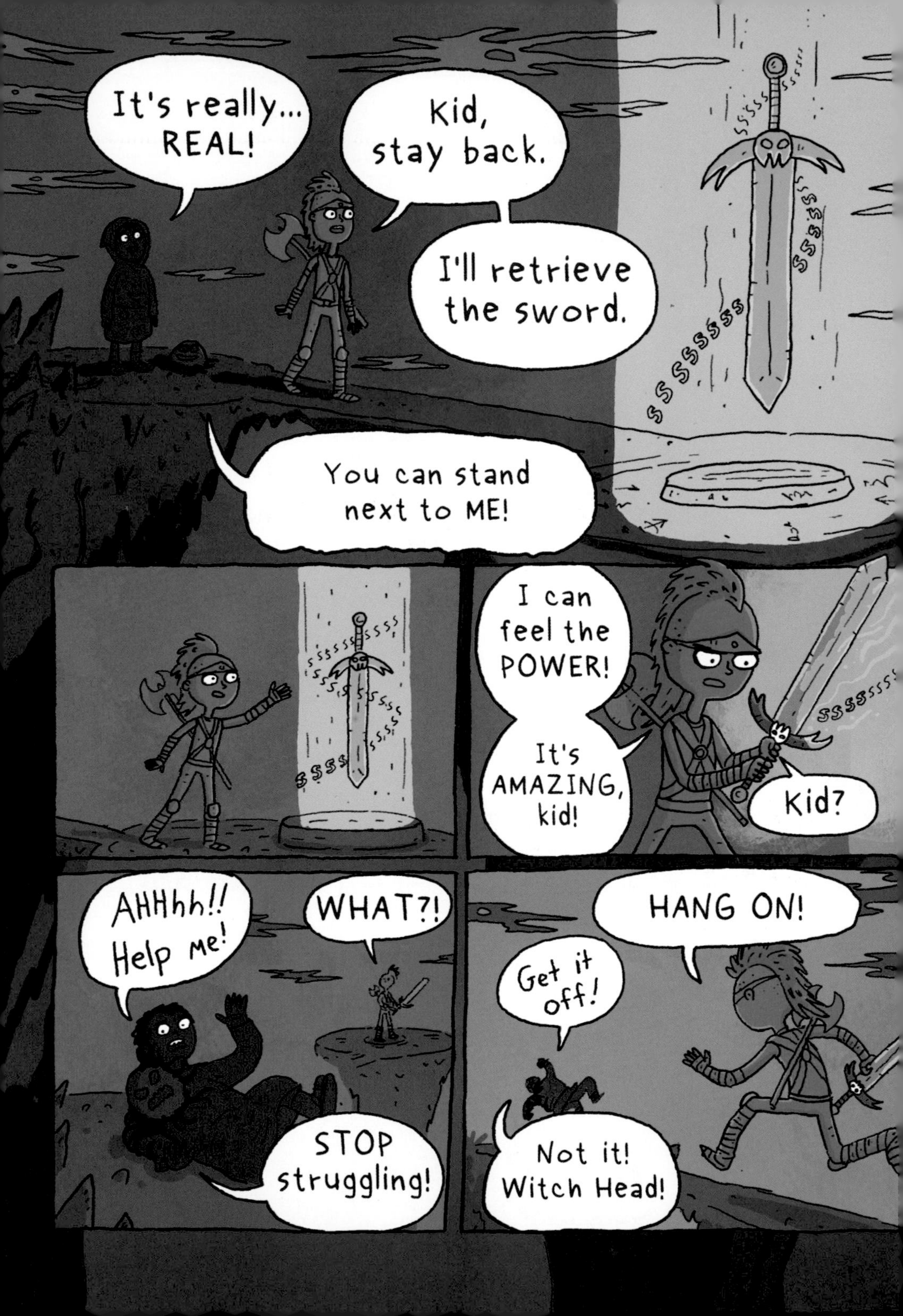

It's really... REAL!
Kid, stay back.
I'll retrieve the sword.
You can stand next to ME!
I can feel the POWER!
It's AMAZING, kid!
Kid?
AHHhh!! Help me!
WHAT?!
STOP struggling!
HANG ON!
Get it off!
Not it! Witch Head!

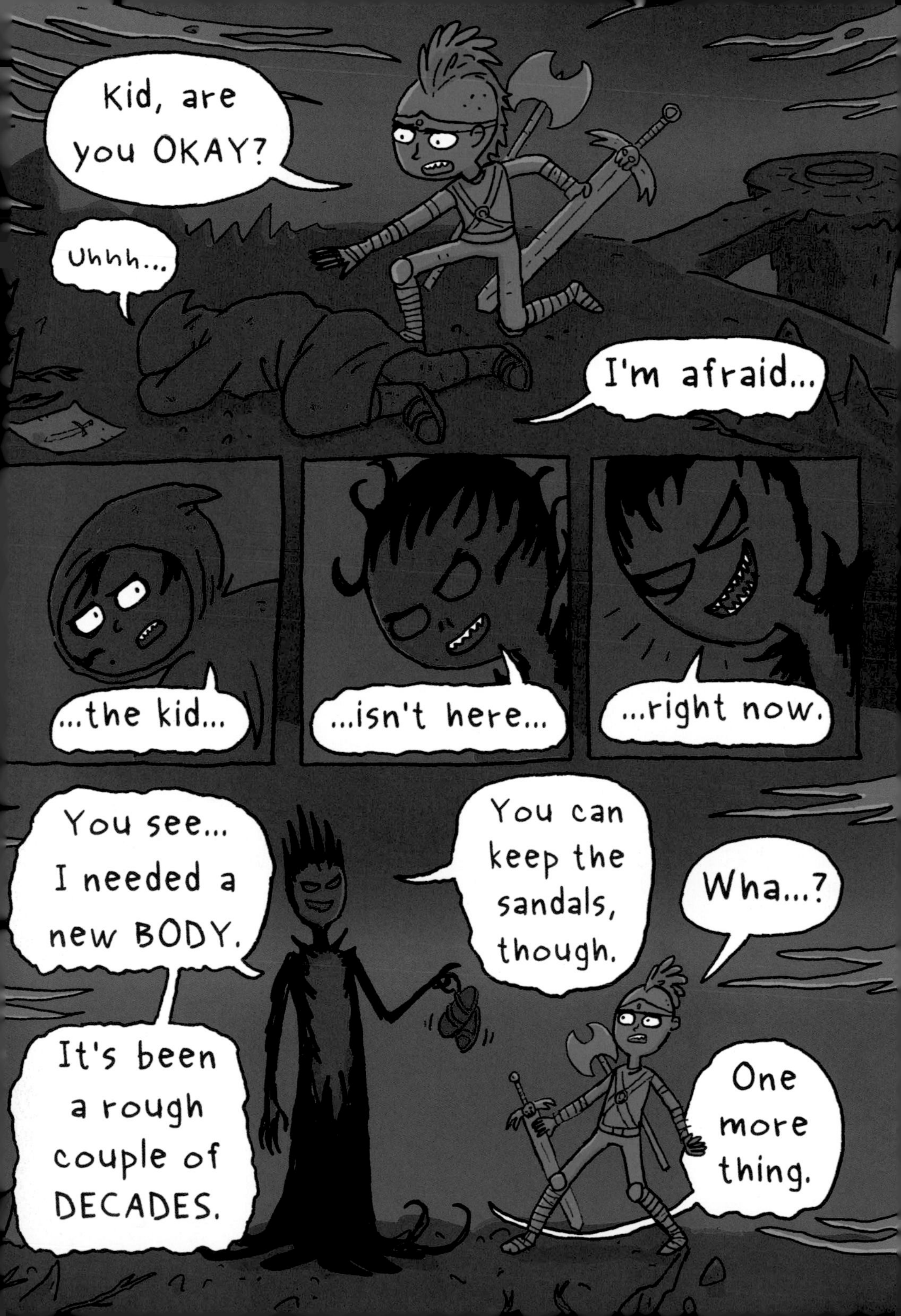
Kid, are you OKAY?
Uhhh...
I'm afraid...
...the kid...
...isn't here...
...right now.
You see... I needed a new BODY.
It's been a rough couple of DECADES.
You can keep the sandals, though.
Wha...?
One more thing.

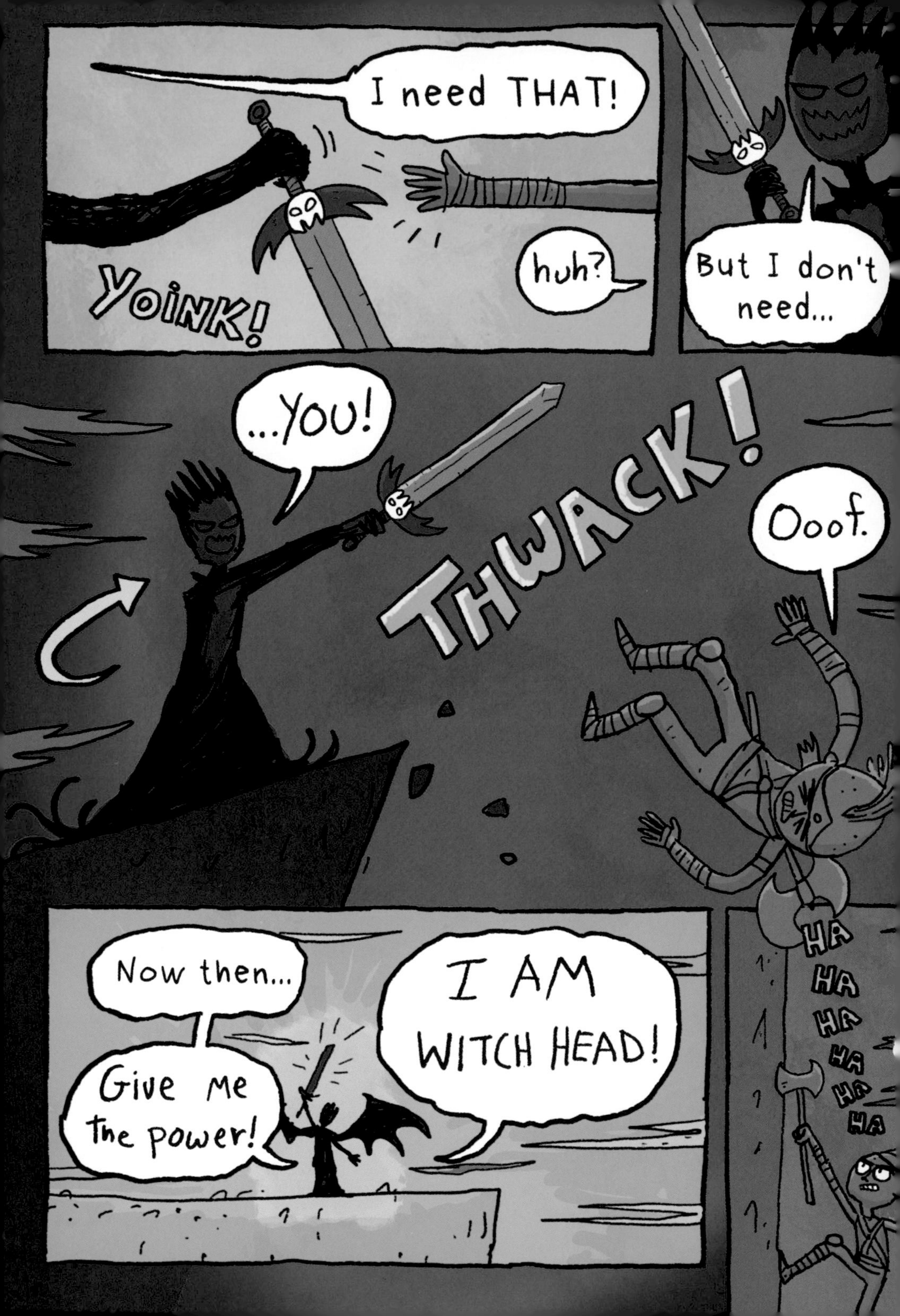
I need THAT!
YOINK!
huh?
But I don't need...
...YOU!
THWACK!
Ooof.
Now then...
Give me the power!
I AM WITCH HEAD!
HA HA HA HA HA HA

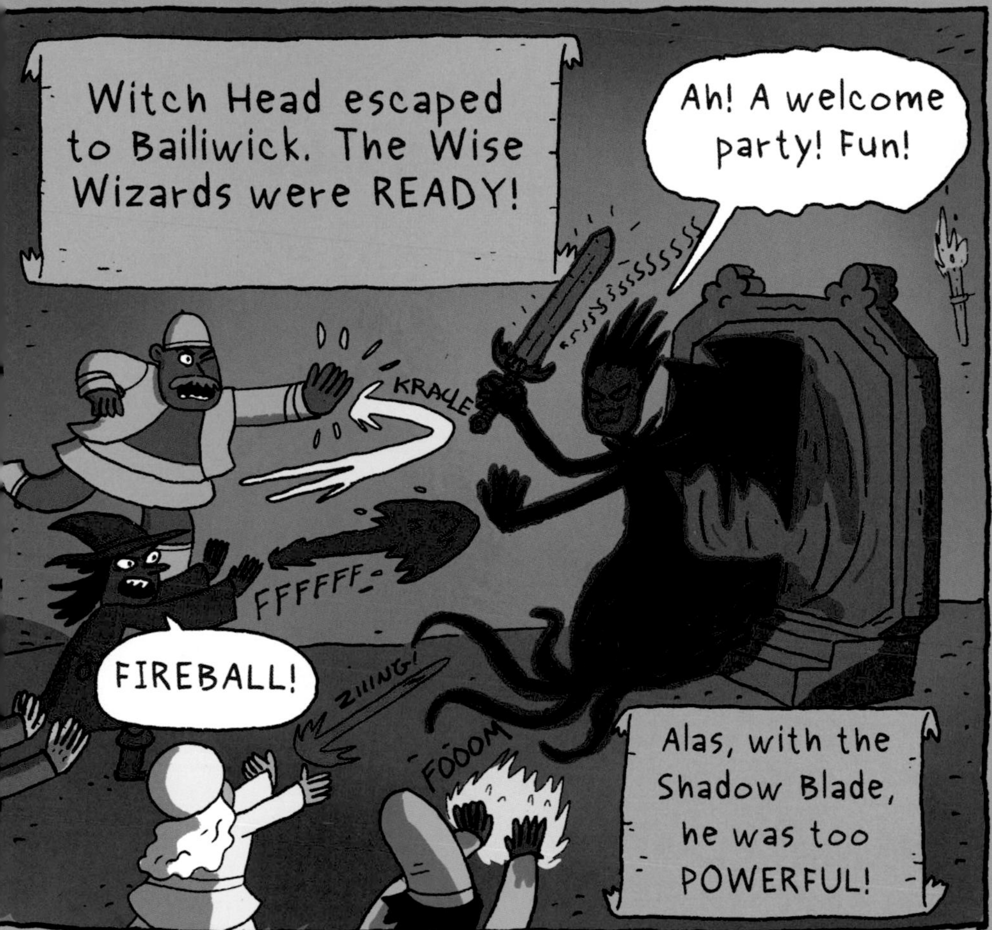
Witch Head escaped to Bailiwick. The Wise Wizards were READY!
Ah! A welcome party! Fun!
KRACLE
FFFFFF
FIREBALL!
ZIIING!
FOOOM
Alas, with the Shadow Blade, he was too POWERFUL!
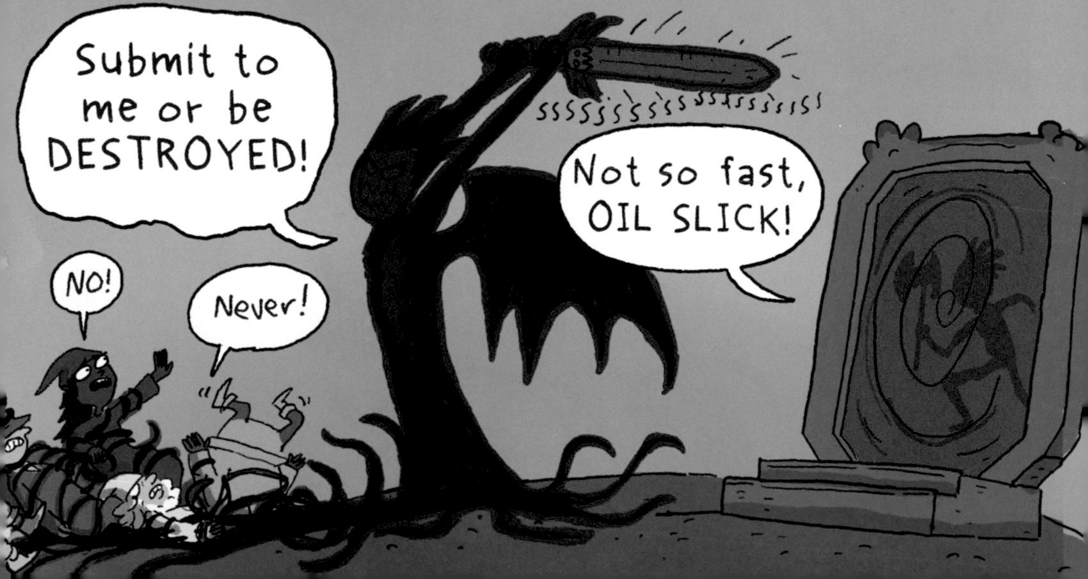
Submit to me or be DESTROYED!
Not so fast, OIL SLICK!
NO!
Never!

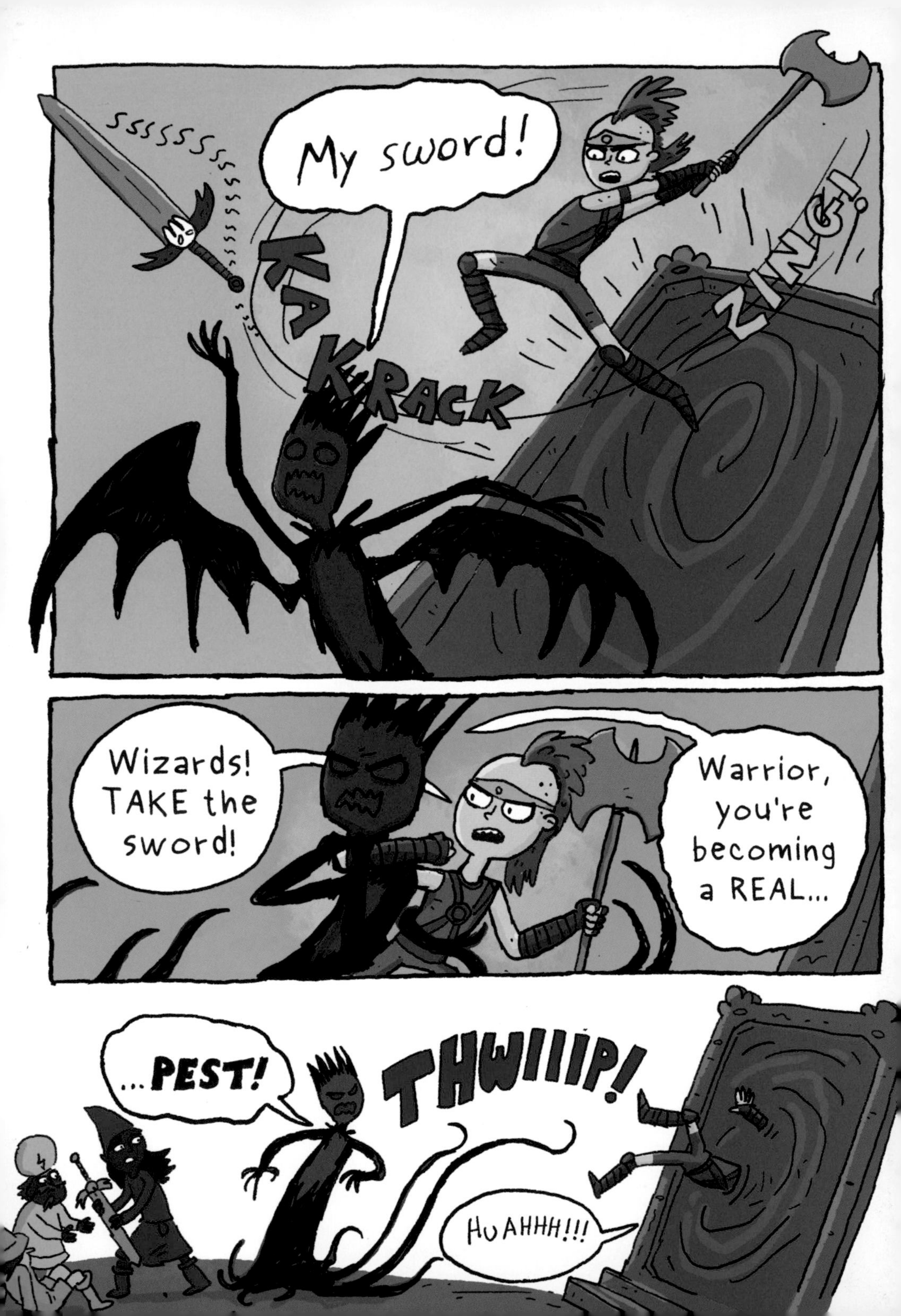
SSSSSSSSSSSSSSSS
My sword!
KA KRACK
ZING!
Wizards! TAKE the sword!
Warrior, you're becoming a REAL...
...PEST!
THWIIIP!
HUAHHH!!!

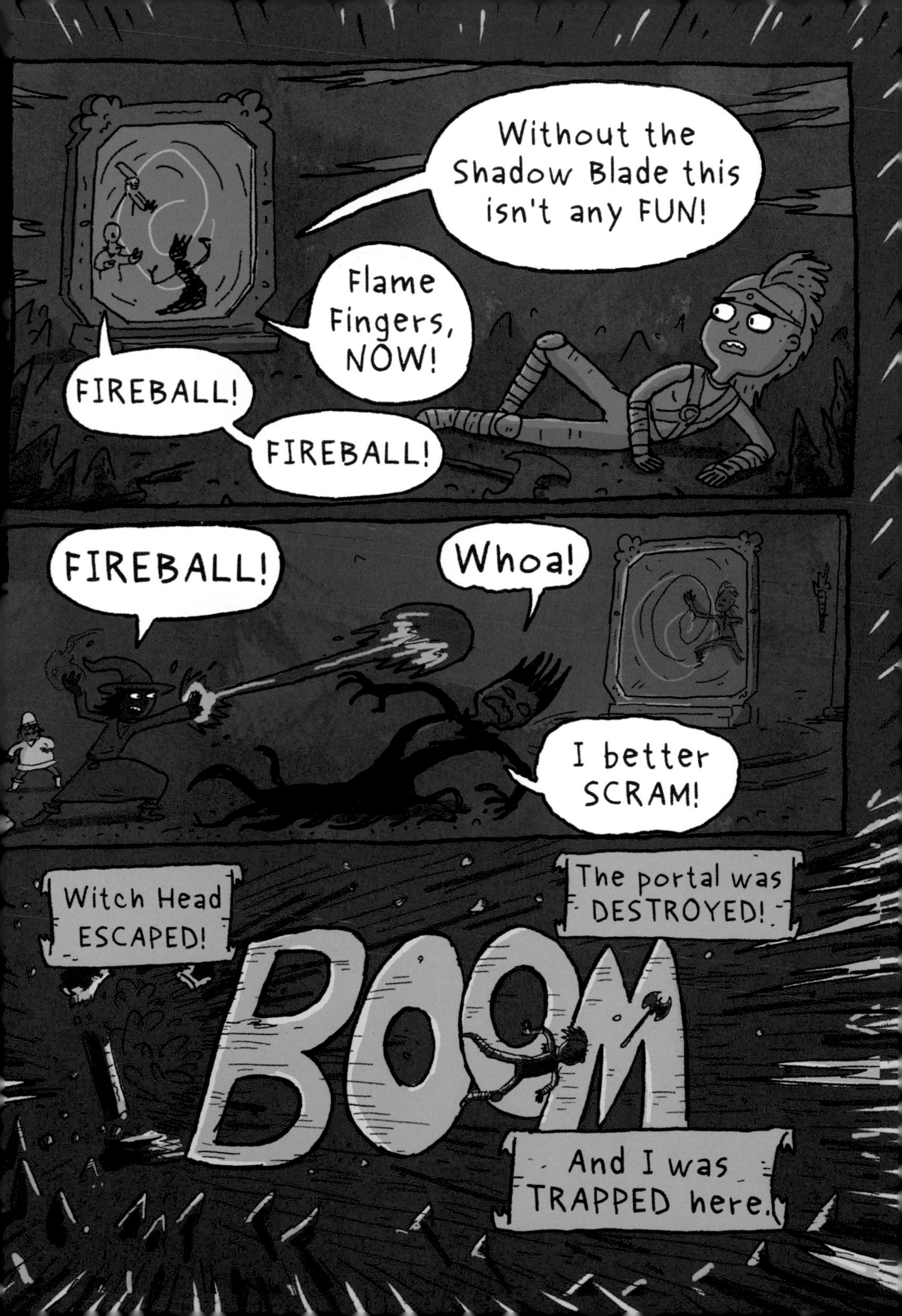

Without the Shadow Blade this isn't any FUN!
Flame Fingers, NOW!
FIREBALL!
FIREBALL!
FIREBALL!
Whoa!
I better SCRAM!
Witch Head ESCAPED!
The portal was DESTROYED!
BOOM
And I was TRAPPED here.

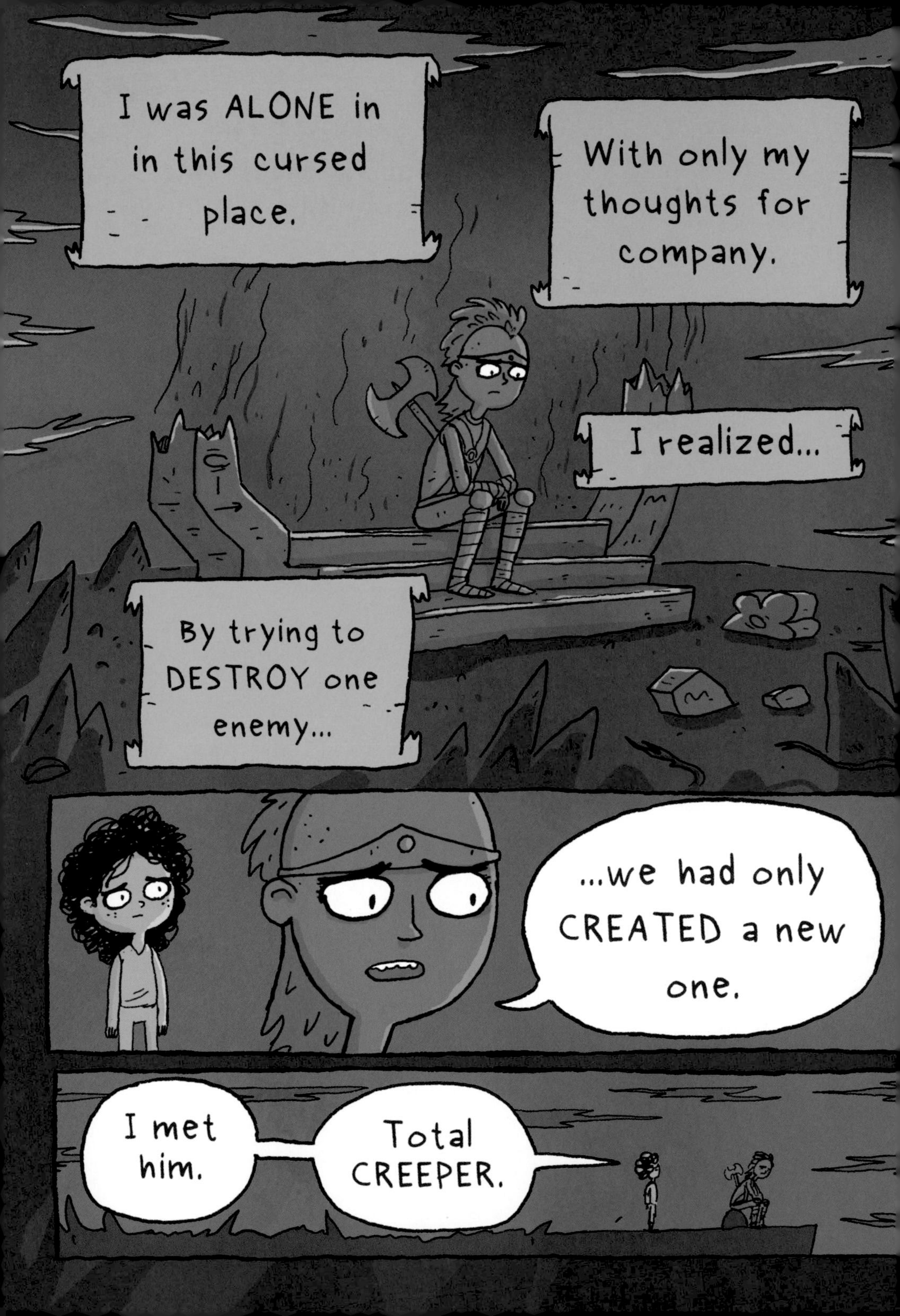

I was ALONE in in this cursed place.
With only my thoughts for company.
I realized...
By trying to DESTROY one enemy...
...we had only CREATED a new one.
I met him.
Total CREEPER.

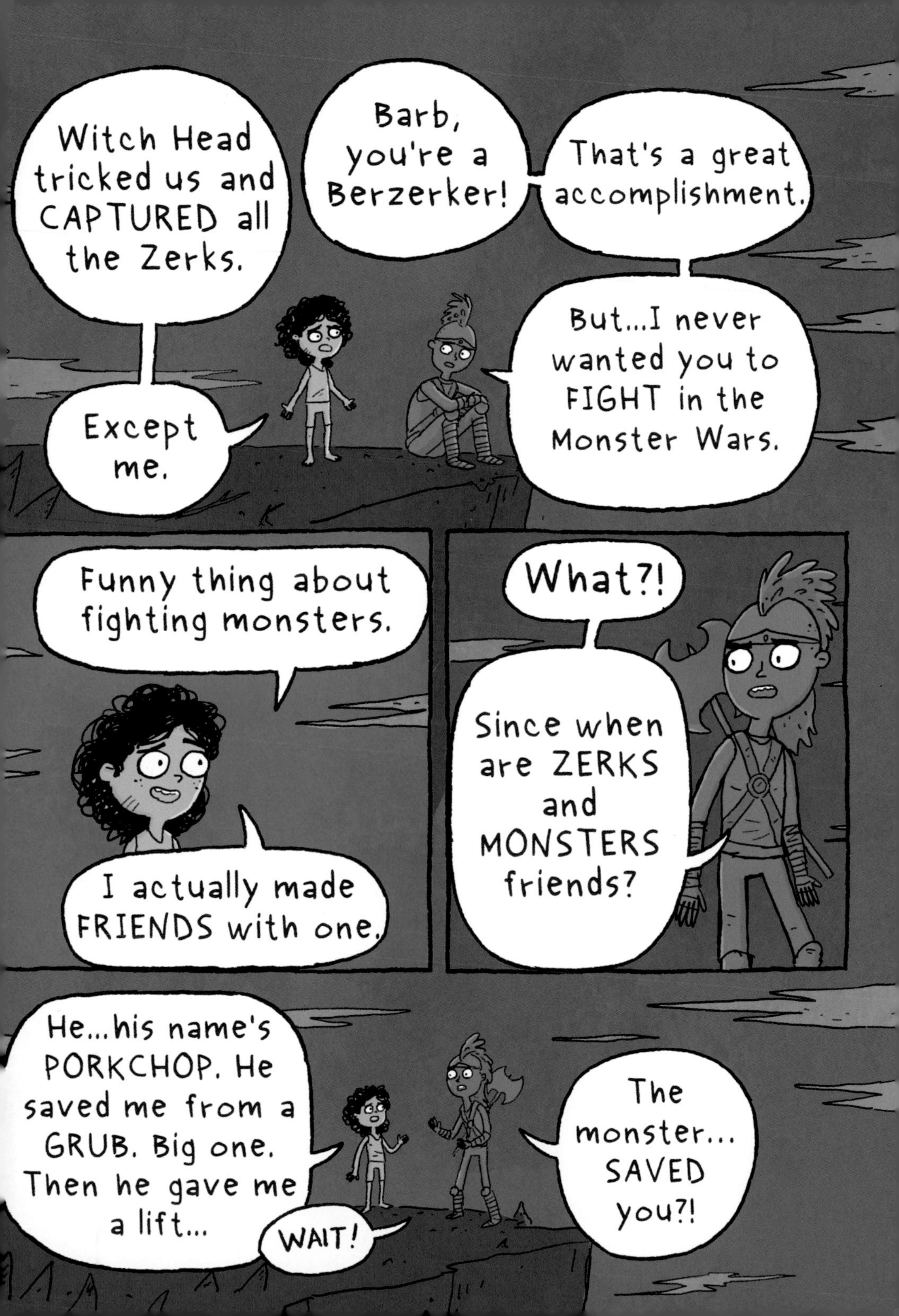
Witch Head tricked us and CAPTURED all the Zerks.
Except me.
Barb, you're a Berzerker!
That's a great accomplishment.
But...I never wanted you to FIGHT in the Monster Wars.
Funny thing about fighting monsters.
I actually made FRIENDS with one.
What?!
Since when are ZERKS and MONSTERS friends?
He...his name's PORKCHOP. He saved me from a GRUB. Big one. Then he gave me a lift...
WAIT!
The monster... SAVED you?!

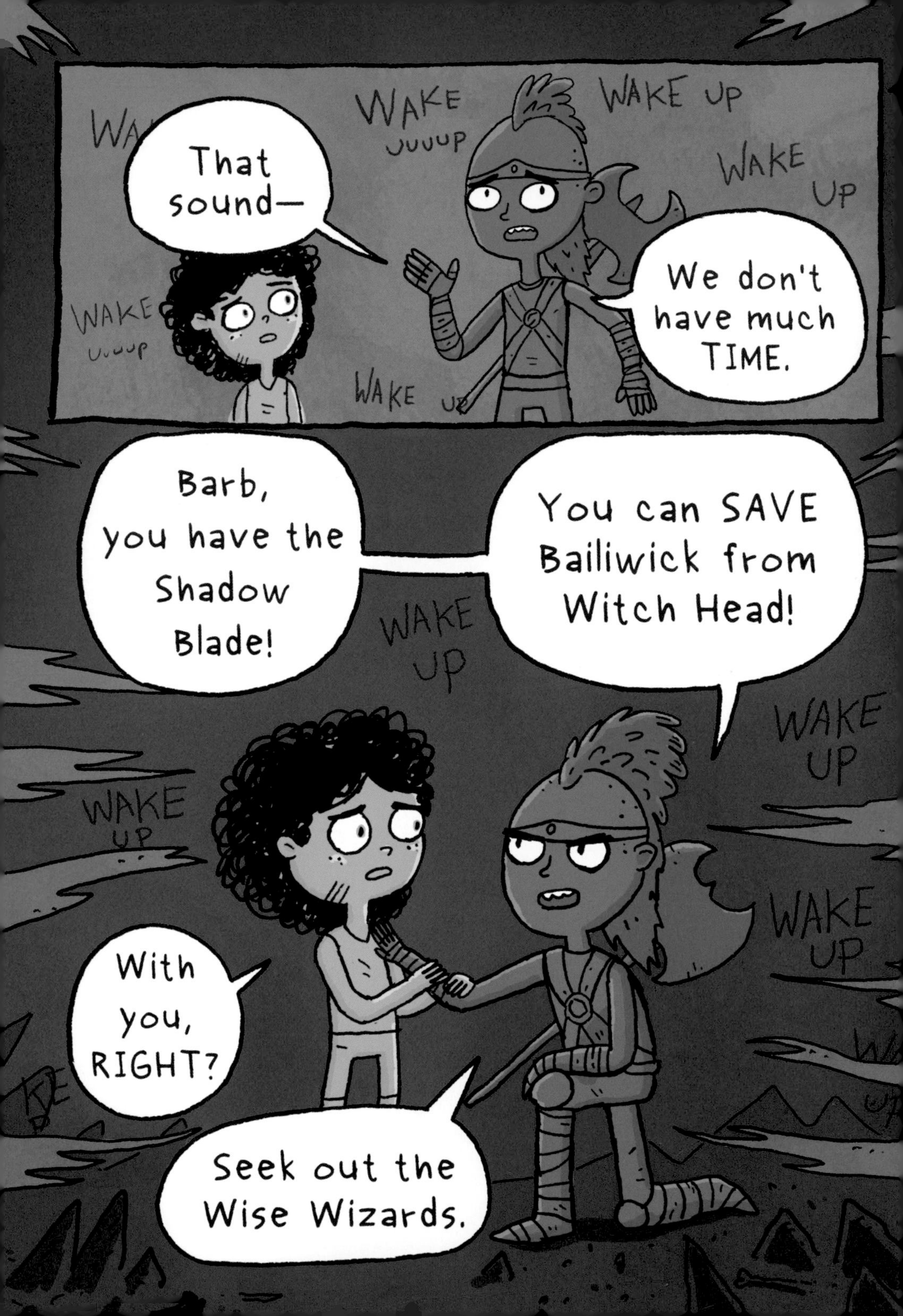
WAKE UP
WAKE UP
WAKE UUUUP
That sound—
We don't have much TIME.
WAKE UUUUP
WAKE UP
Barb, you have the Shadow Blade!
You can SAVE Bailiwick from Witch Head!
WAKE UP
WAKE UP
WAKE UP
WAKE UP
With you, RIGHT?
Seek out the Wise Wizards.

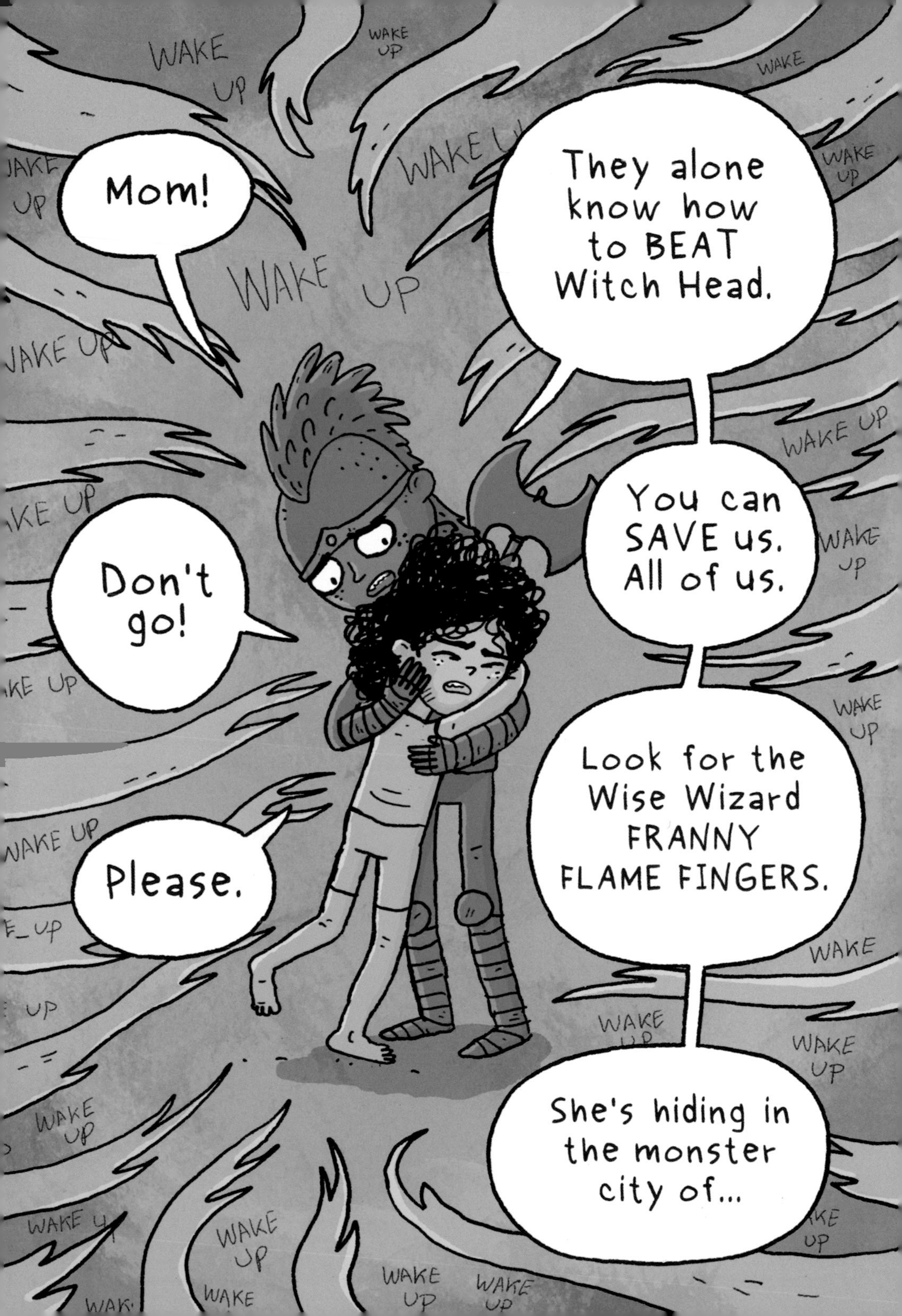
Mom!
They alone know how to BEAT Witch Head.
Don't go!
You can SAVE us. All of us.
Please.
Look for the Wise Wizard FRANNY FLAME FINGERS.
She's hiding in the monster city of...

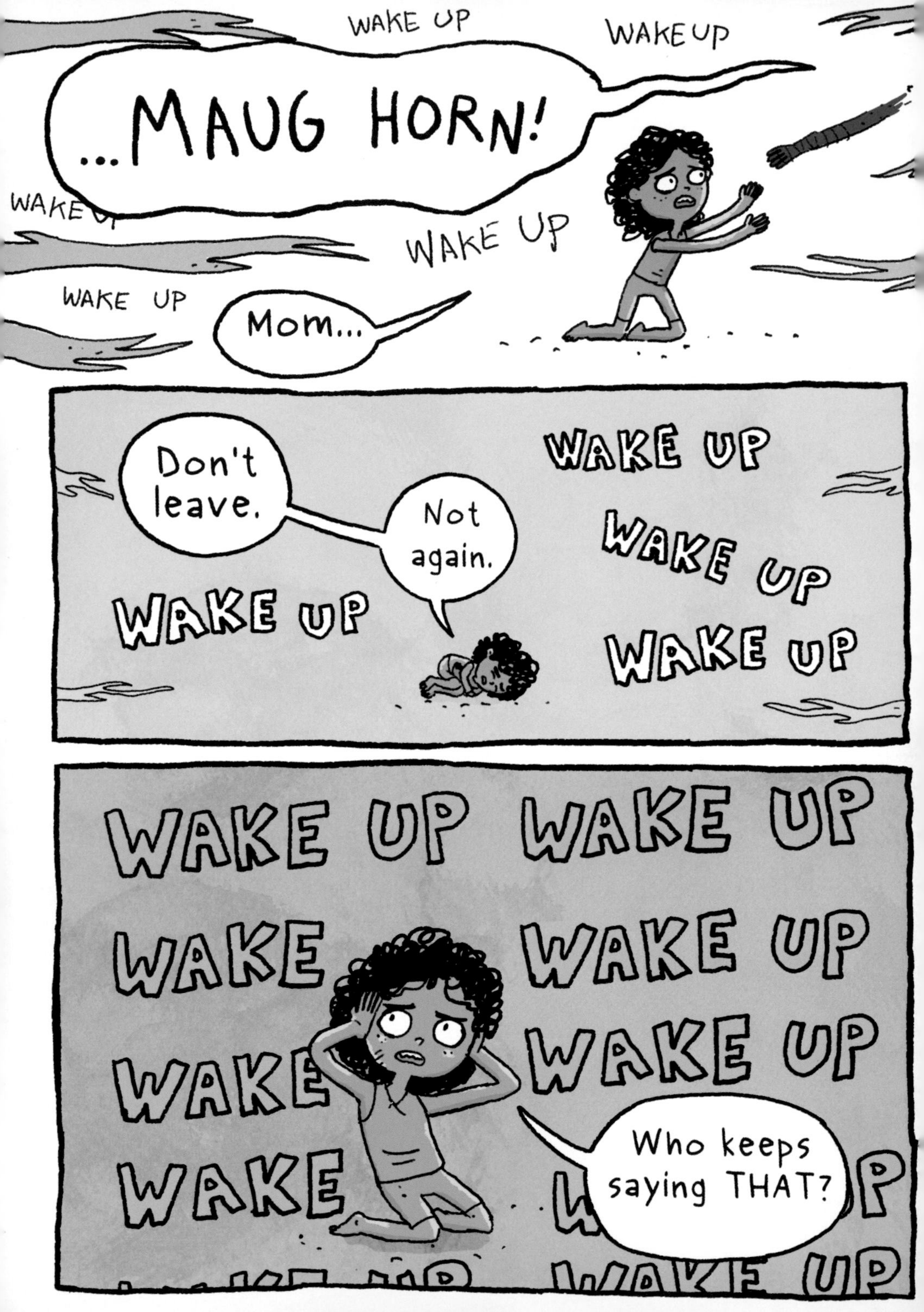
WAKE UP
WAKE UP
...MAUG HORN!
WAKE UP
WAKE UP
Mom...
Don't leave.
Not again.
WAKE UP
WAKE UP
WAKE UP
WAKE UP
WAKE UP WAKE UP
WAKE
WAKE UP
WAKE
WAKE UP
WAKE
Who keeps saying THAT?

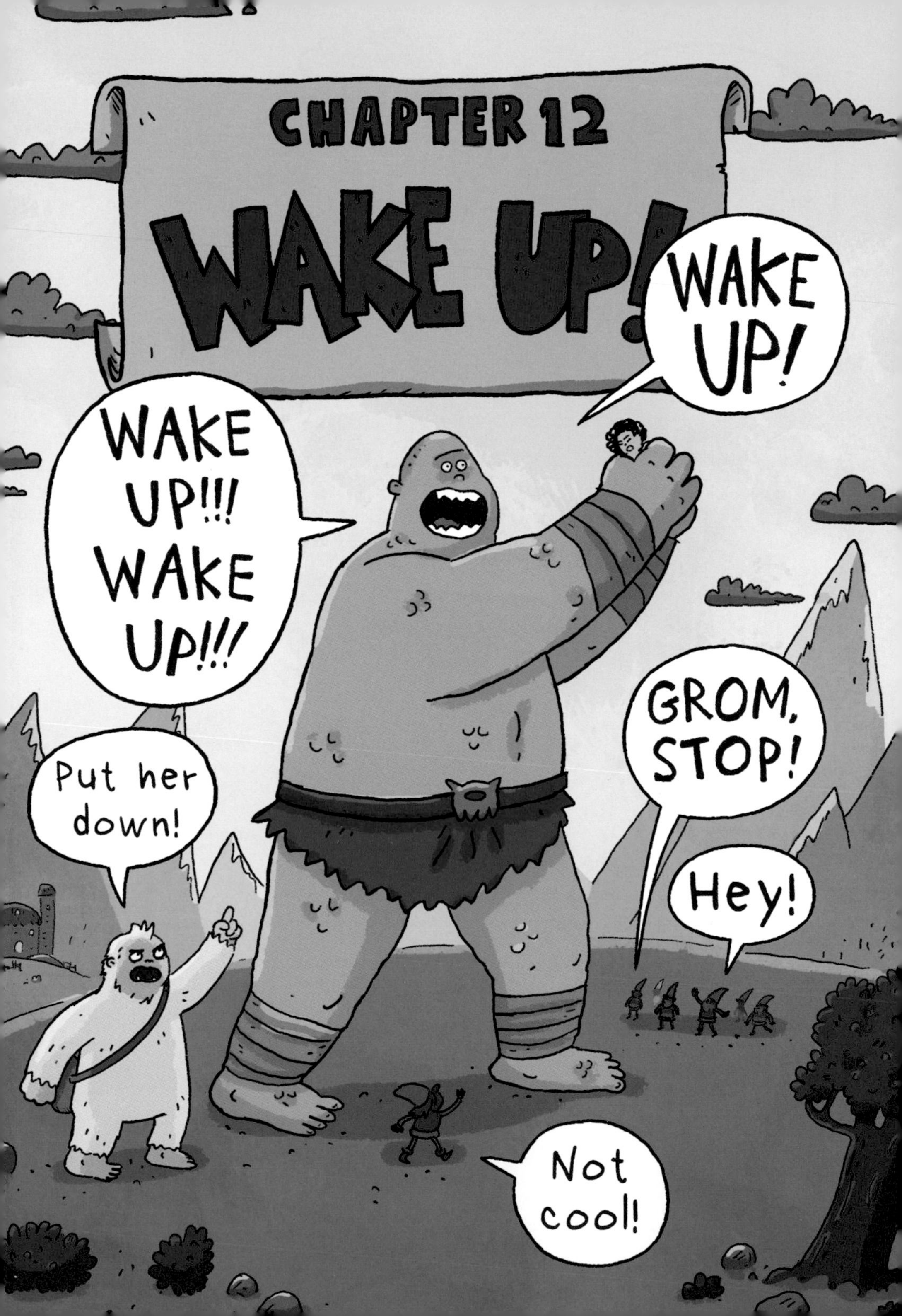
CHAPTER 12
WAKE UP!
WAKE UP!
WAKE UP!!! WAKE UP!!!
Put her down!
GROM, STOP!
Hey!
Not cool!

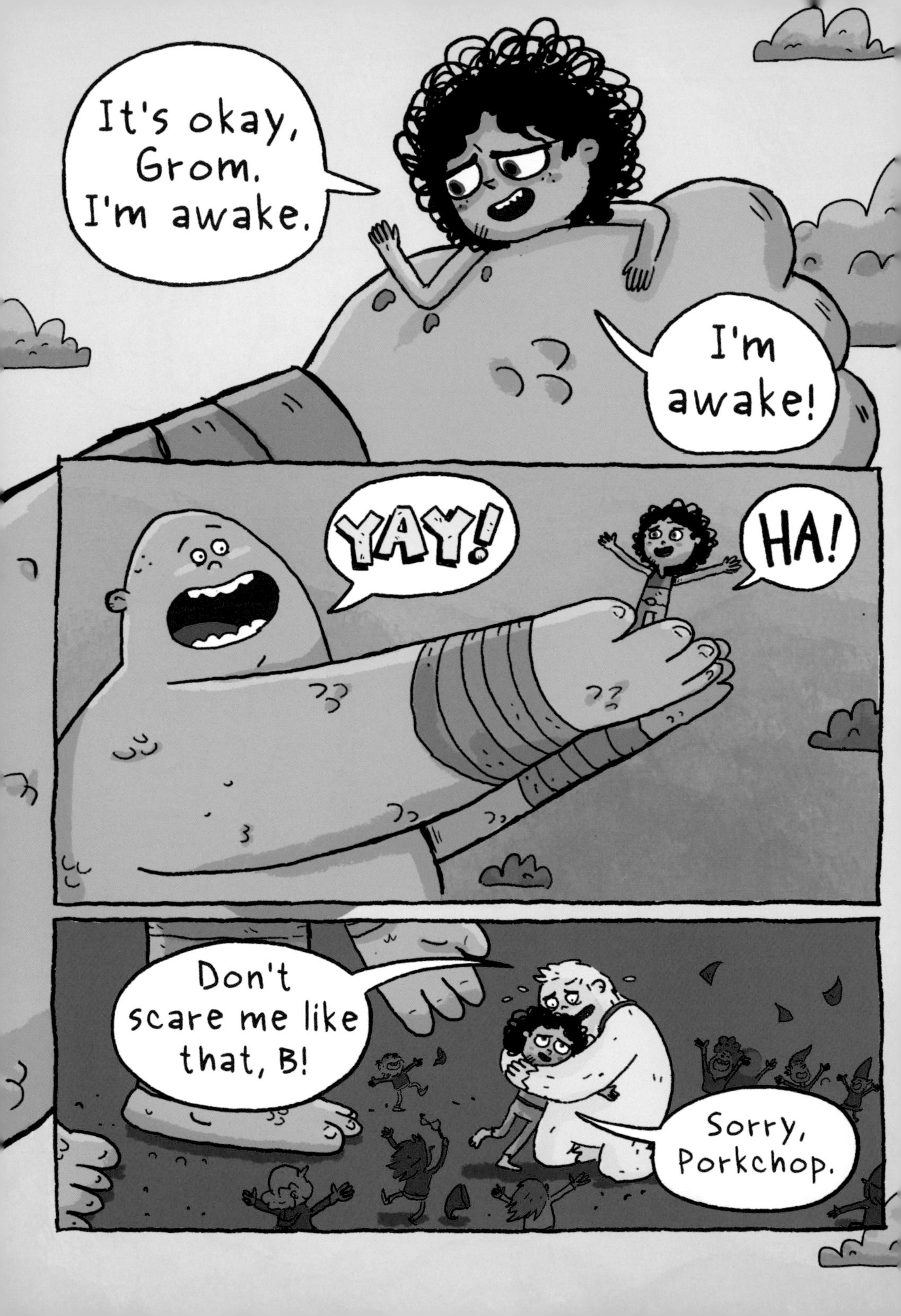
It's okay, Grom. I'm awake.
I'm awake!
YAY!
HA!
Don't scare me like that, B!
Sorry, Porkchop.

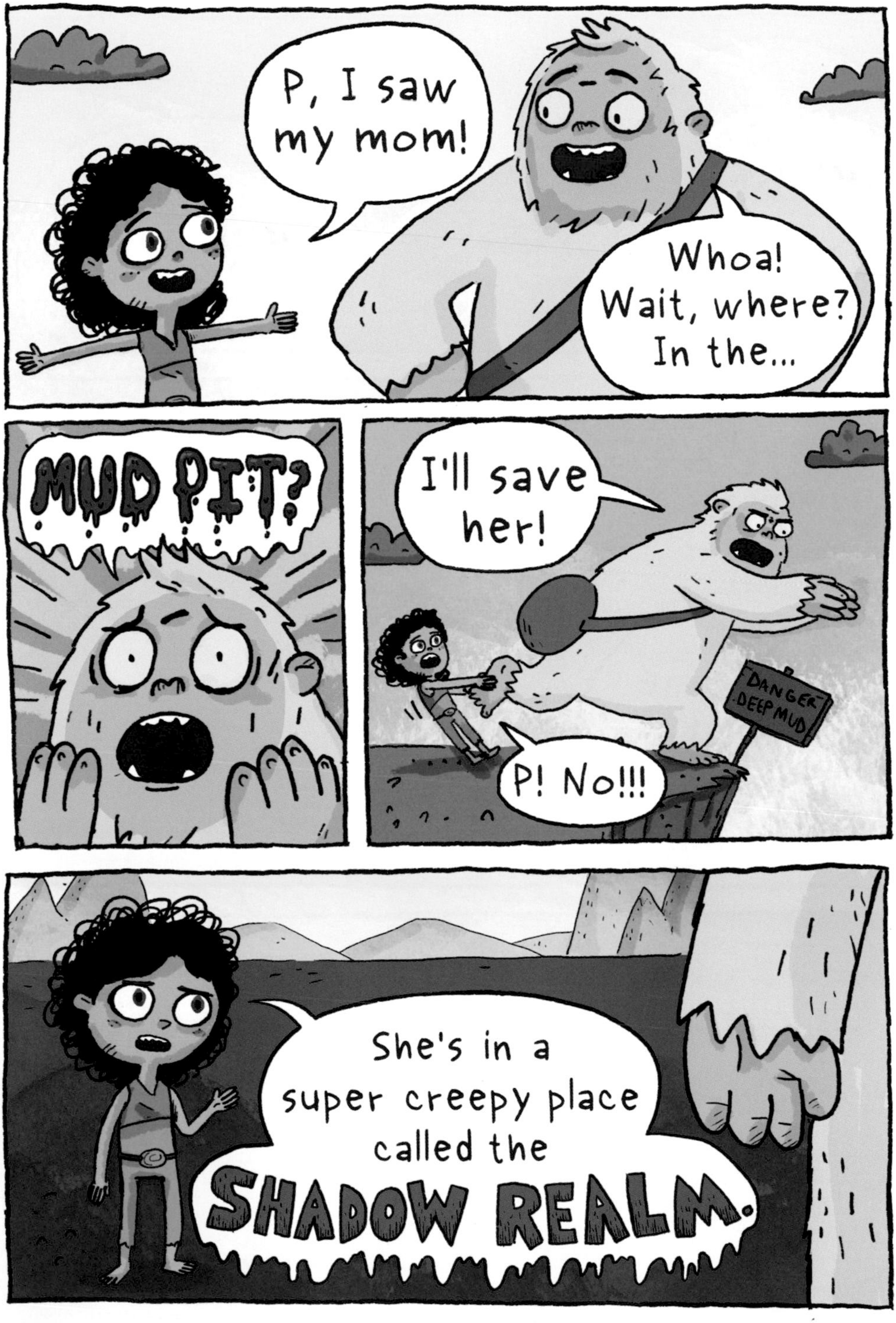
P, I saw my mom!
Whoa! Wait, where? In the...
MUD PIT?
I'll save her!
DANGER DEEP MUD
P! No!!!
She's in a super creepy place called the SHADOW REALM.

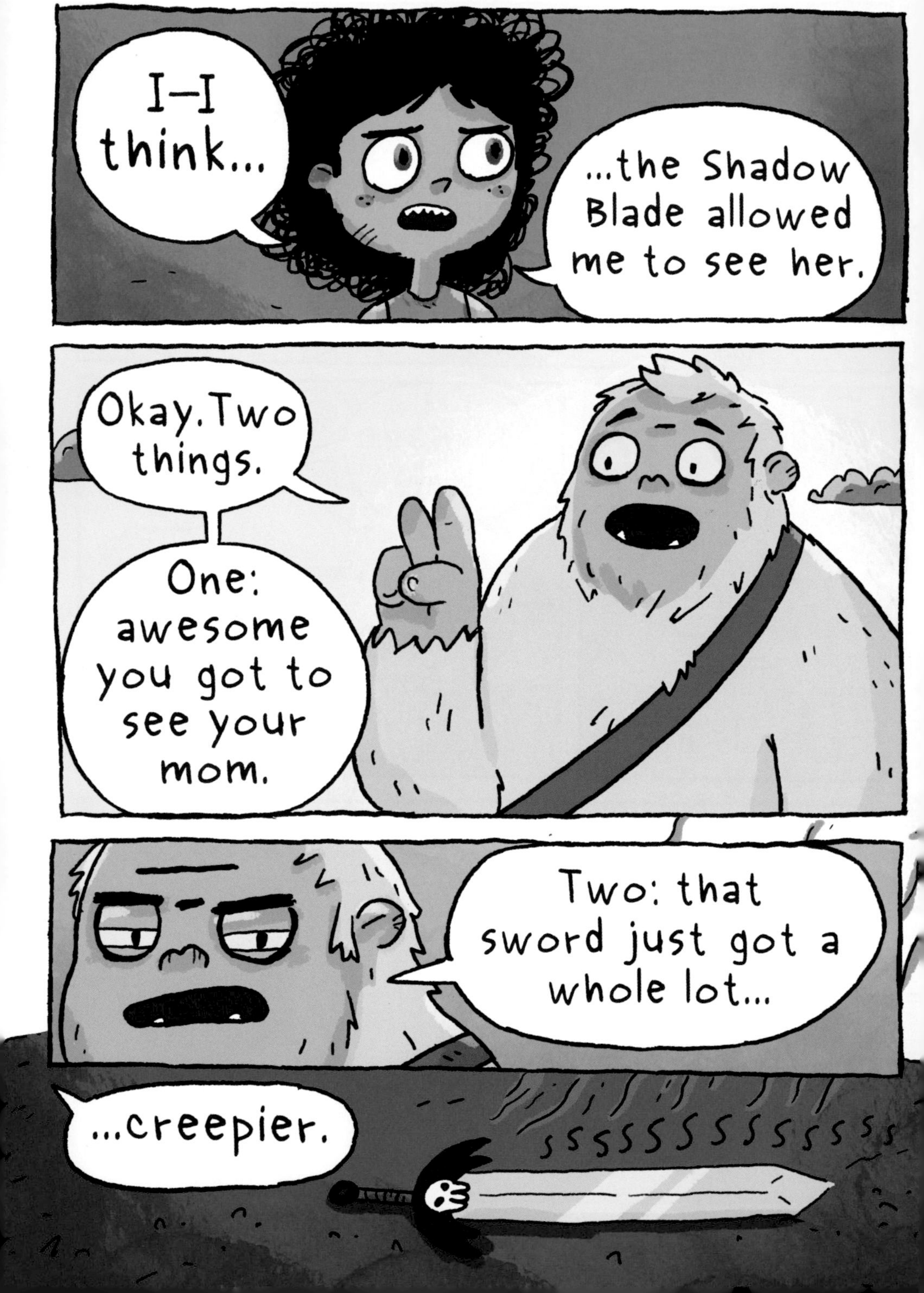
I—I think...
...the Shadow Blade allowed me to see her.
Okay. Two things.
One: awesome you got to see your mom.
Two: that sword just got a whole lot...
...creepier.
SSSSSSSSSSSSSSSS

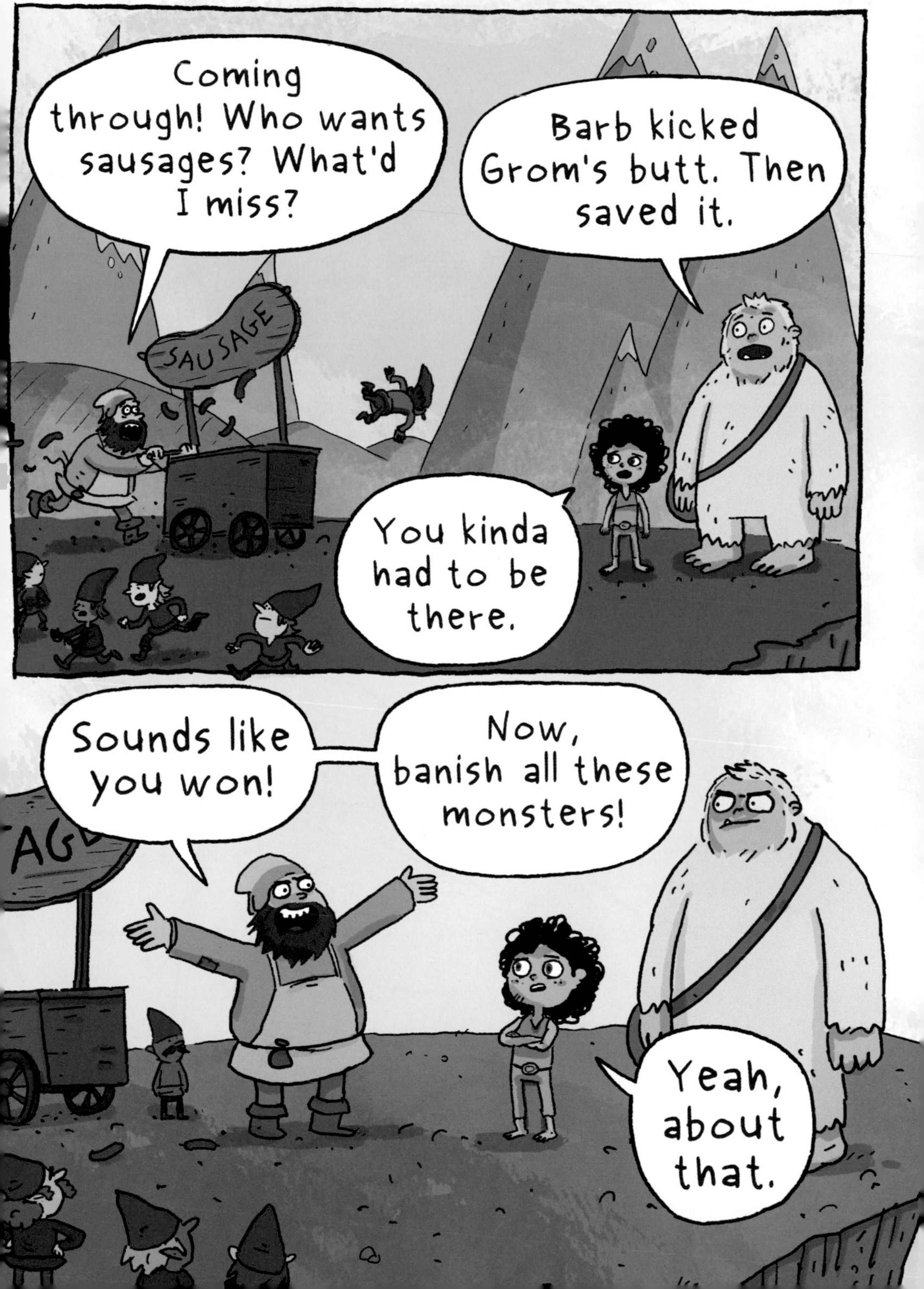
Coming through! Who wants sausages? What'd I miss?
Barb kicked Grom's butt. Then saved it.
SAUSAGE
You kinda had to be there.
Sounds like you won!
Now, banish all these monsters!
Yeah, about that.

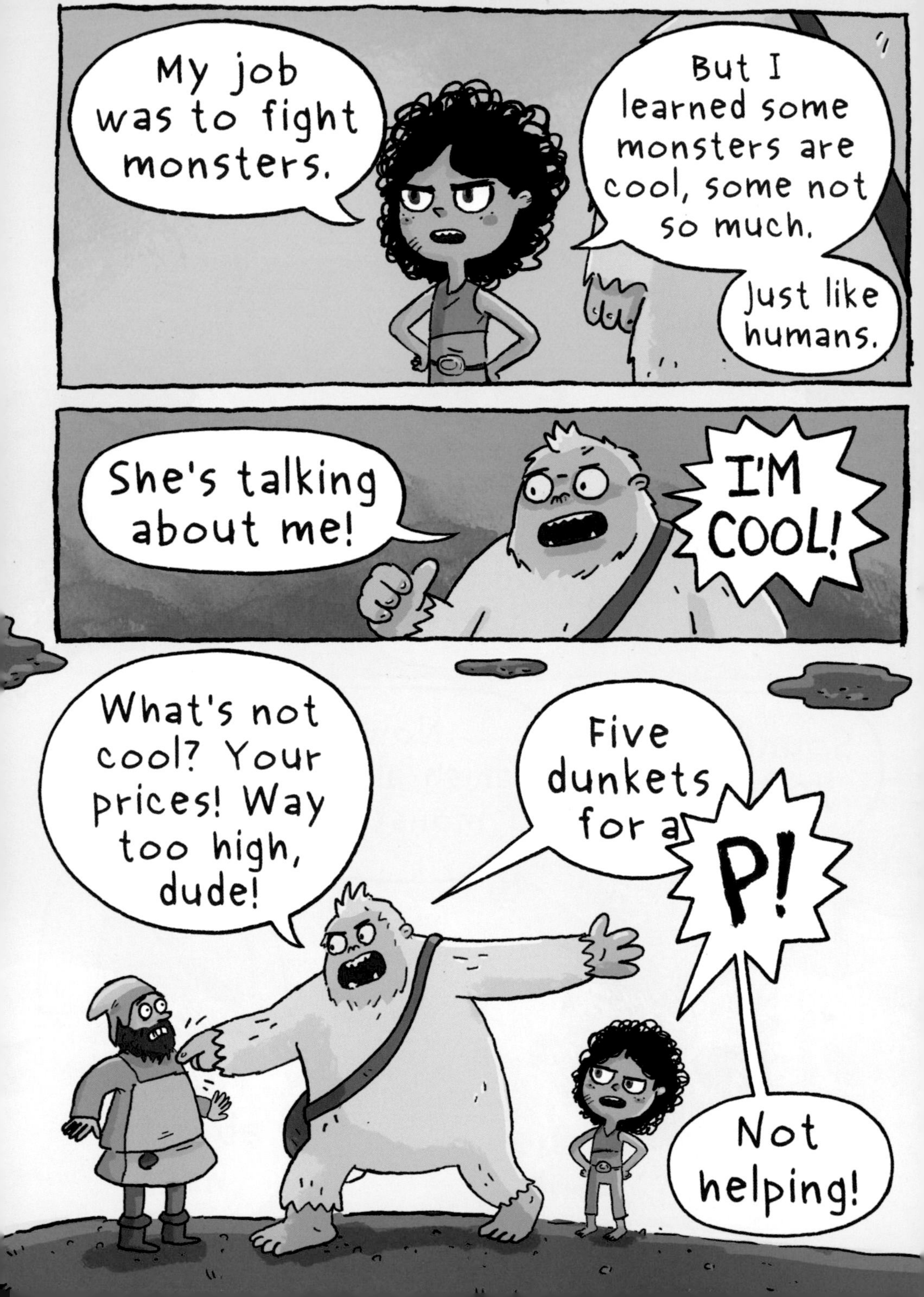
My job was to fight monsters.
But I learned some monsters are cool, some not so much.
Just like humans.
She's talking about me!
I'M COOL!
What's not cool? Your prices! Way too high, dude!
Five dunkets for a
P!
Not helping!

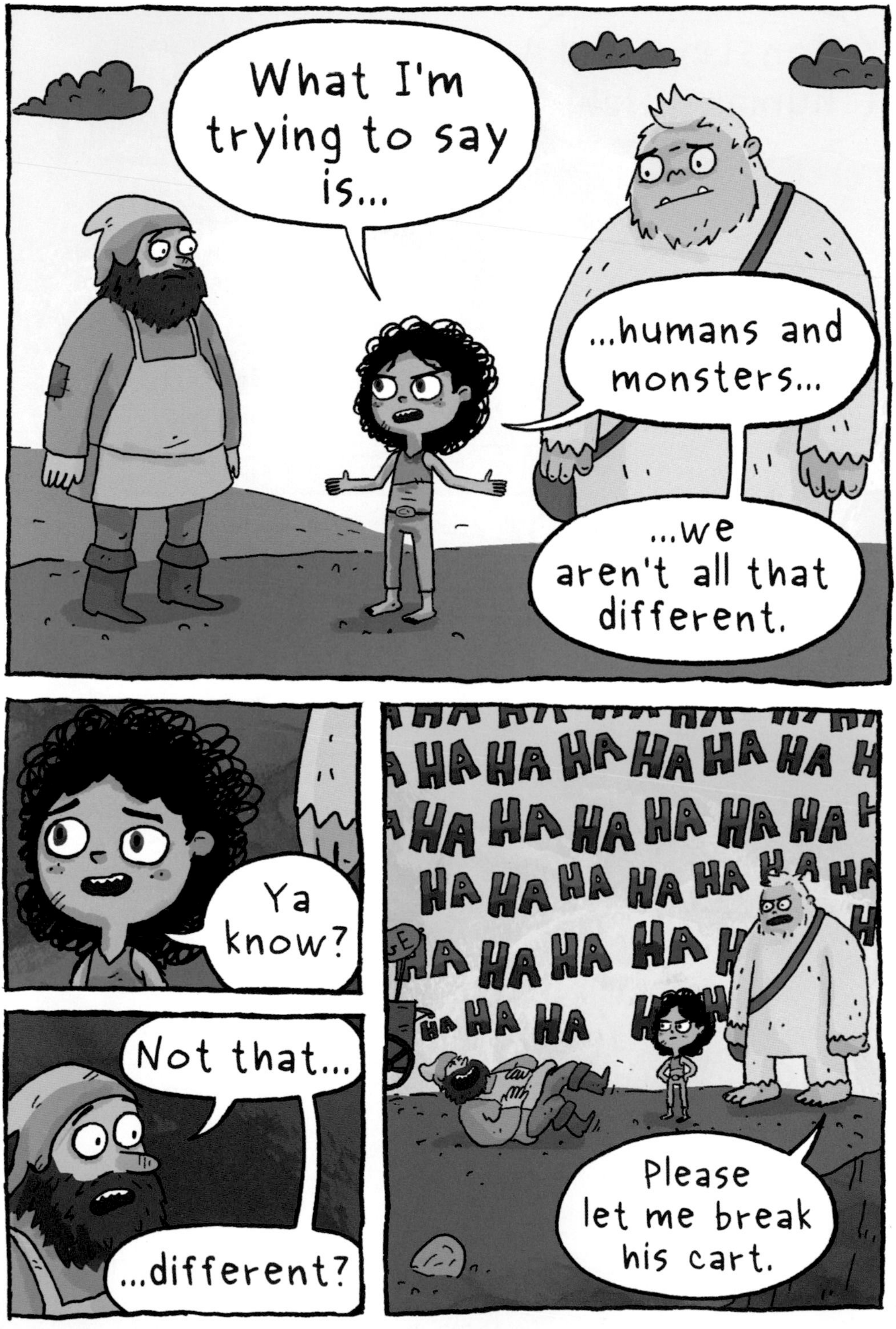
What I'm trying to say is...
...humans and monsters...
...we aren't all that different.
Ya know?
Not that...
...different?
HA HA HA HA HA HA HA HA HA HA HA HA HA HA HA HA HA HA HA HA HA HA HA HA HA HA HA HA HA HA HA HA
Please let me break his cart.

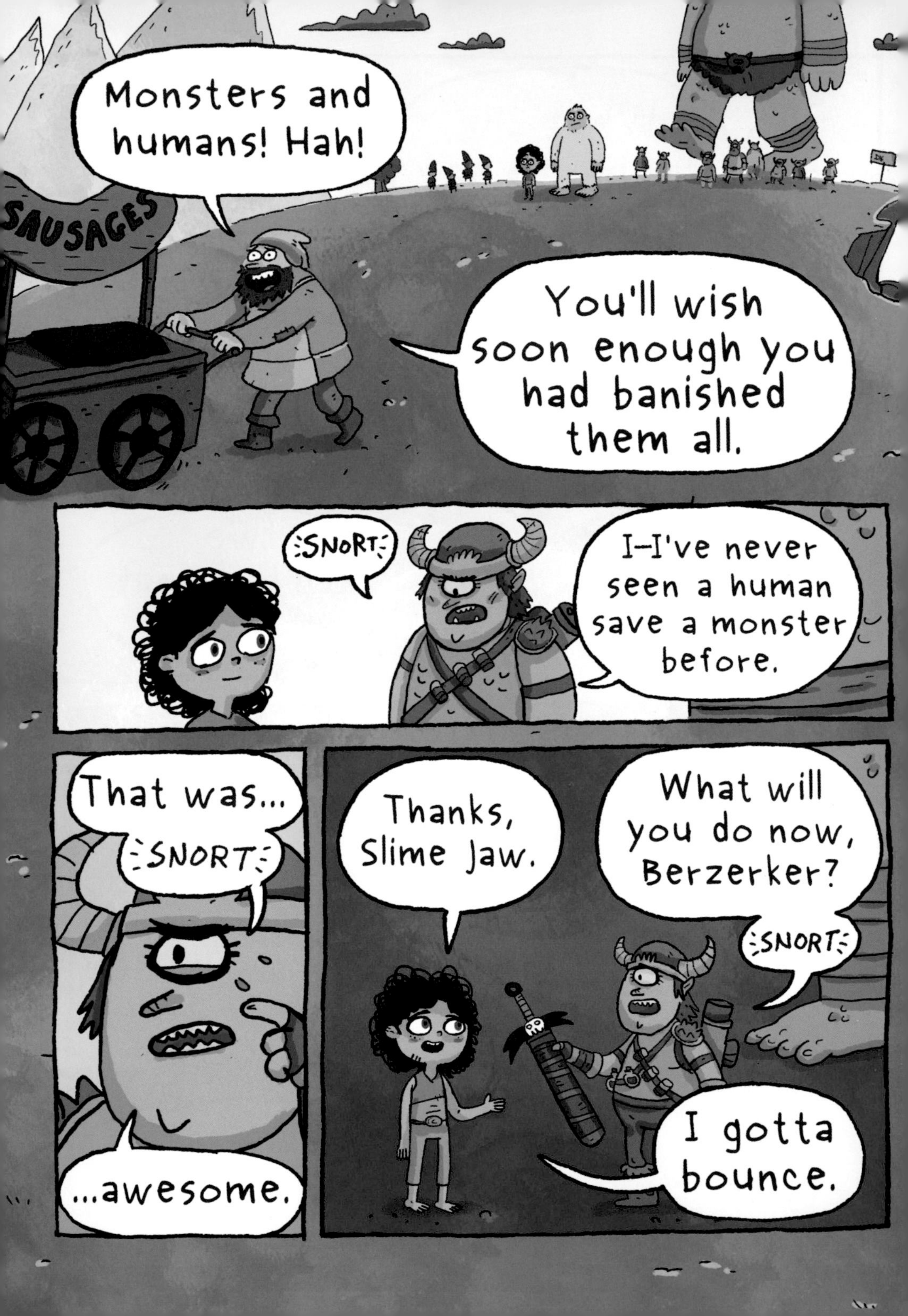
SAUSAGES
Monsters and humans! Hah!
You'll wish soon enough you had banished them all.
SNORT
I—I've never seen a human save a monster before.
That was...
SNORT
...awesome.
Thanks, Slime Jaw.
What will you do now, Berzerker?
SNORT
I gotta bounce.

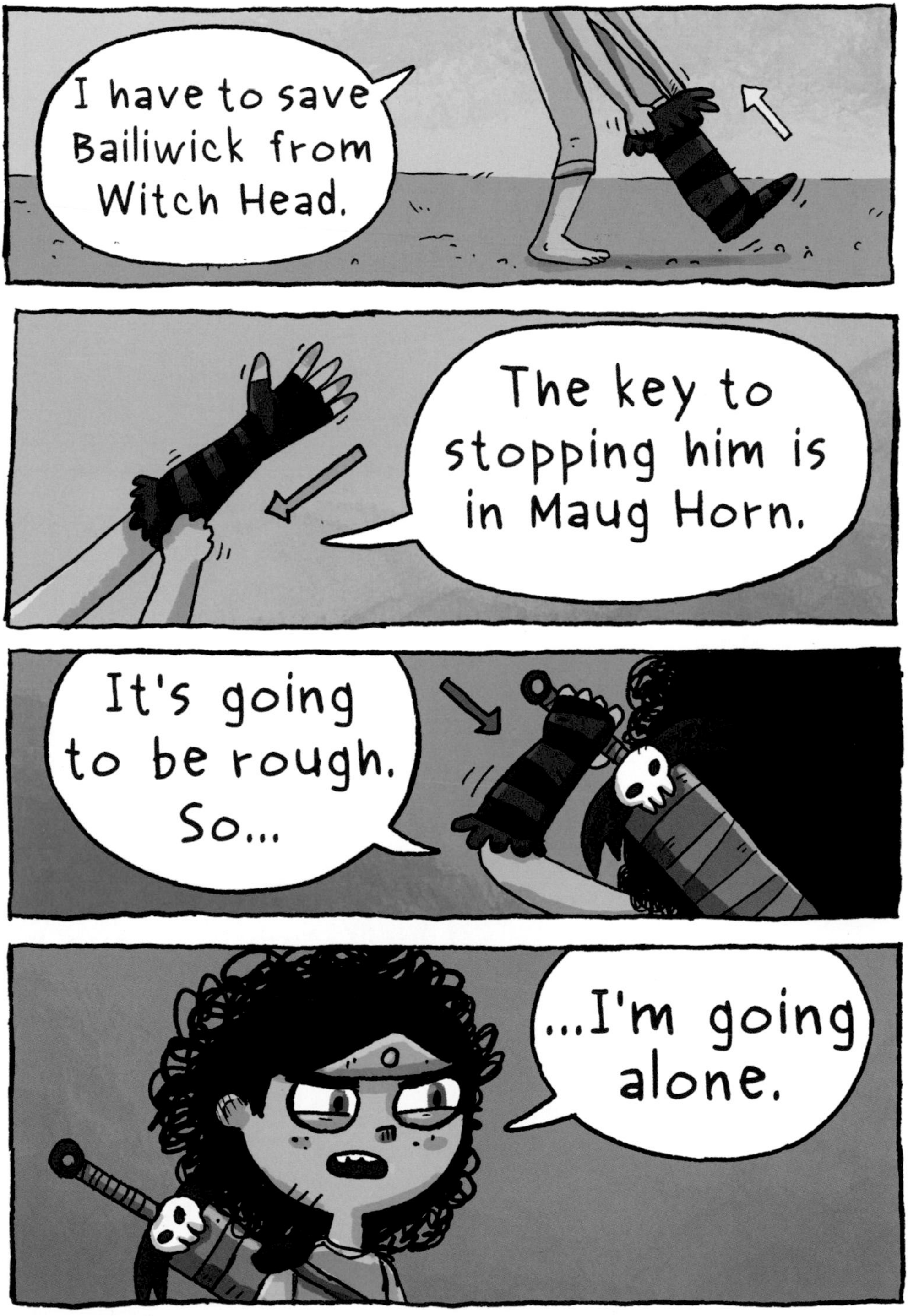
I have to save Bailiwick from Witch Head.
The key to stopping him is in Maug Horn.
It's going to be rough. So...
...I'm going alone.

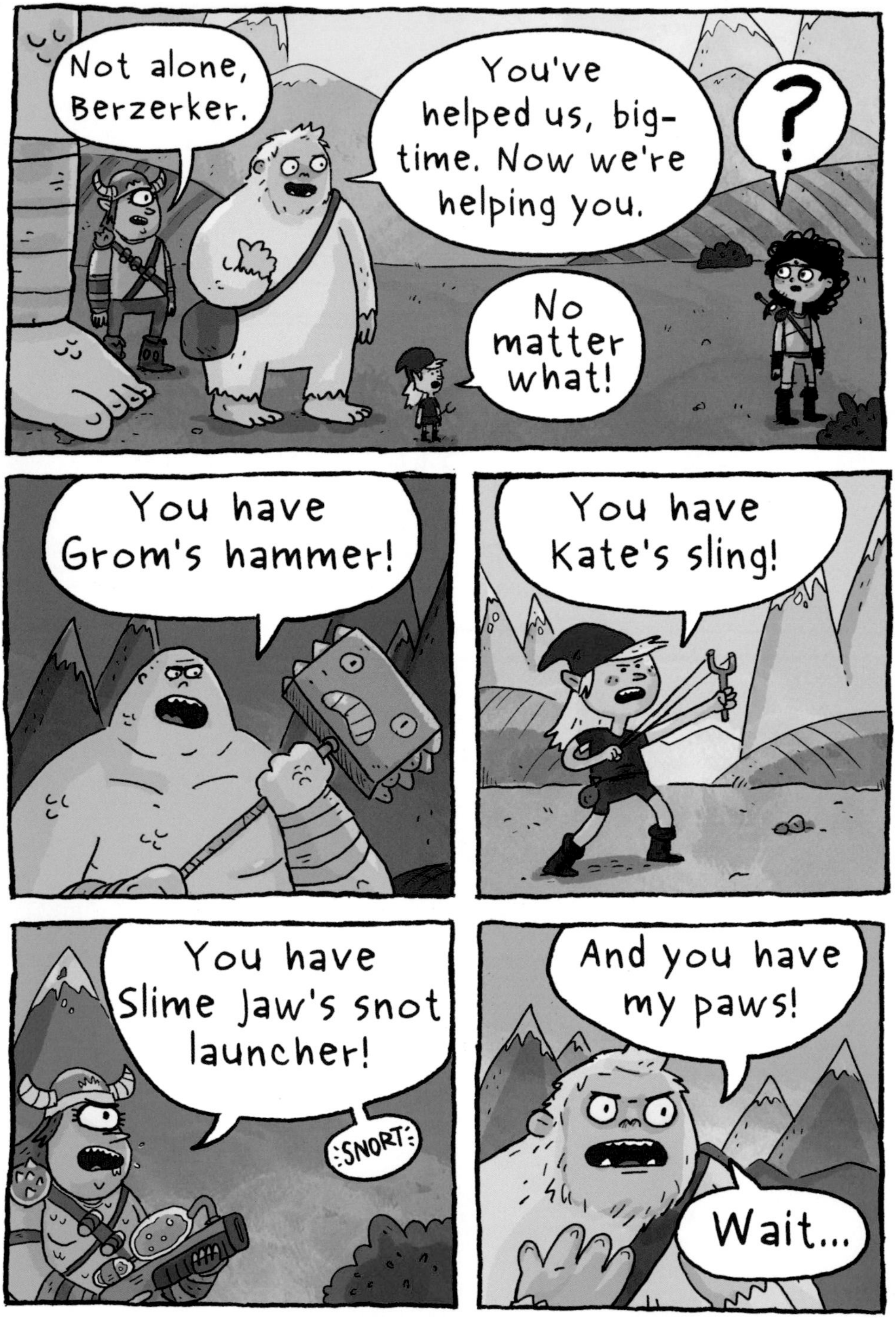
Not alone, Berzerker.
You've helped us, big-time. Now we're helping you.
?
No matter what!
You have Grom's hammer!
You have Kate's sling!
You have Slime Jaw's snot launcher!
SNORT
And you have my paws!
Wait...

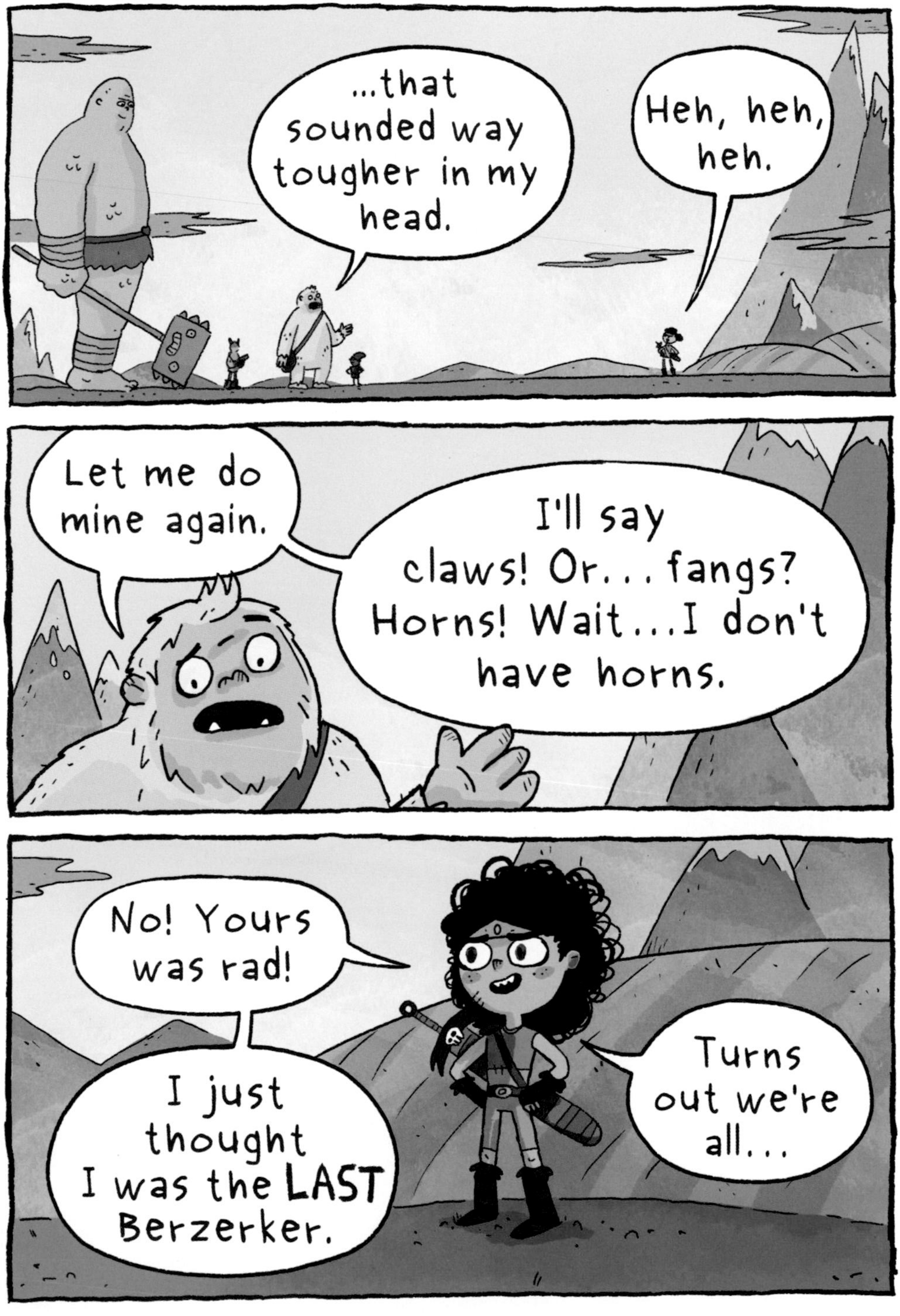
...that sounded way tougher in my head.
Heh, heh, heh.
Let me do mine again.
I'll say claws! Or... fangs? Horns! Wait...I don't have horns.
No! Yours was rad!
I just thought I was the **LAST** Berzerker.
Turns out we're all...

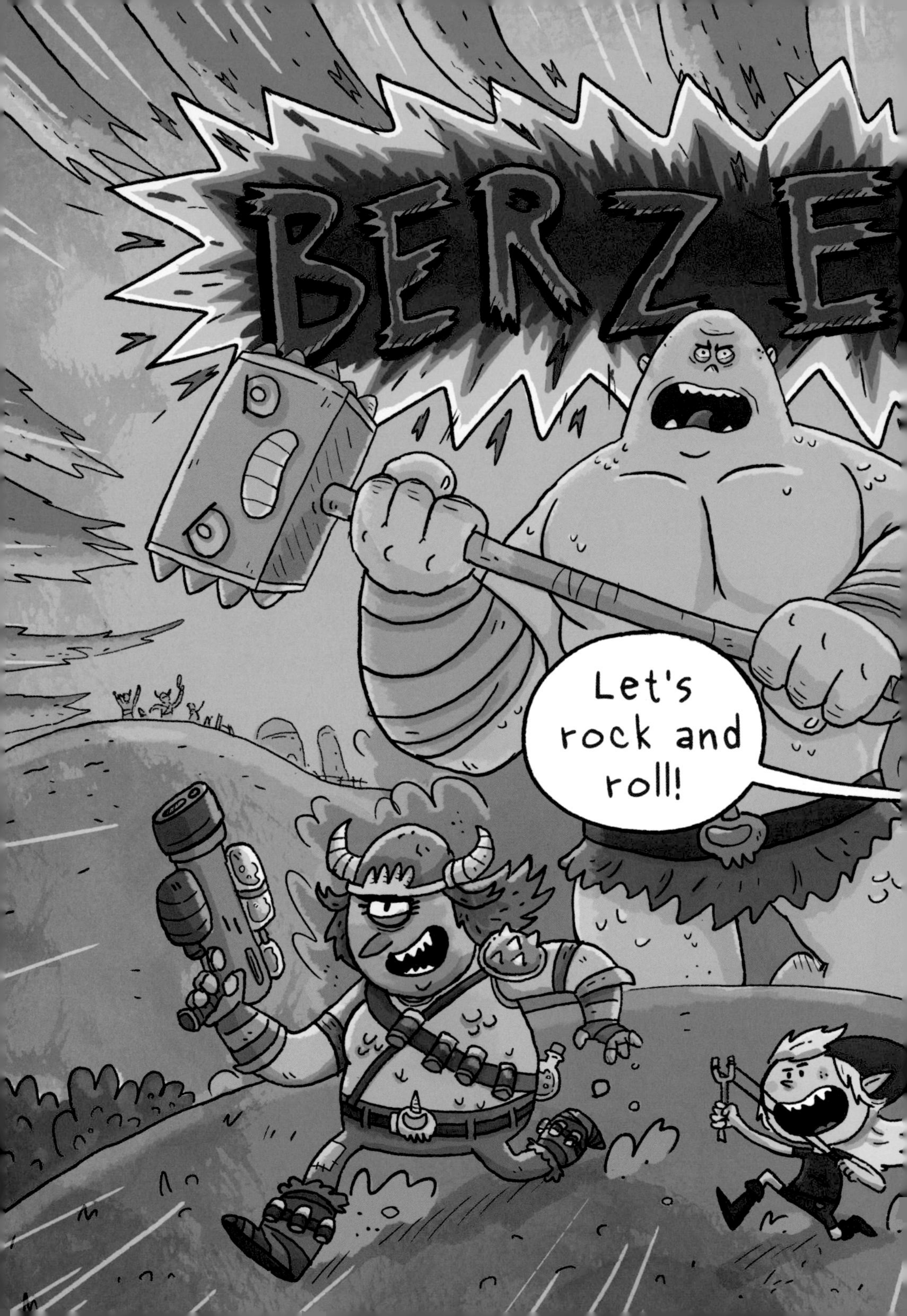
BERZE
Let's rock and roll!

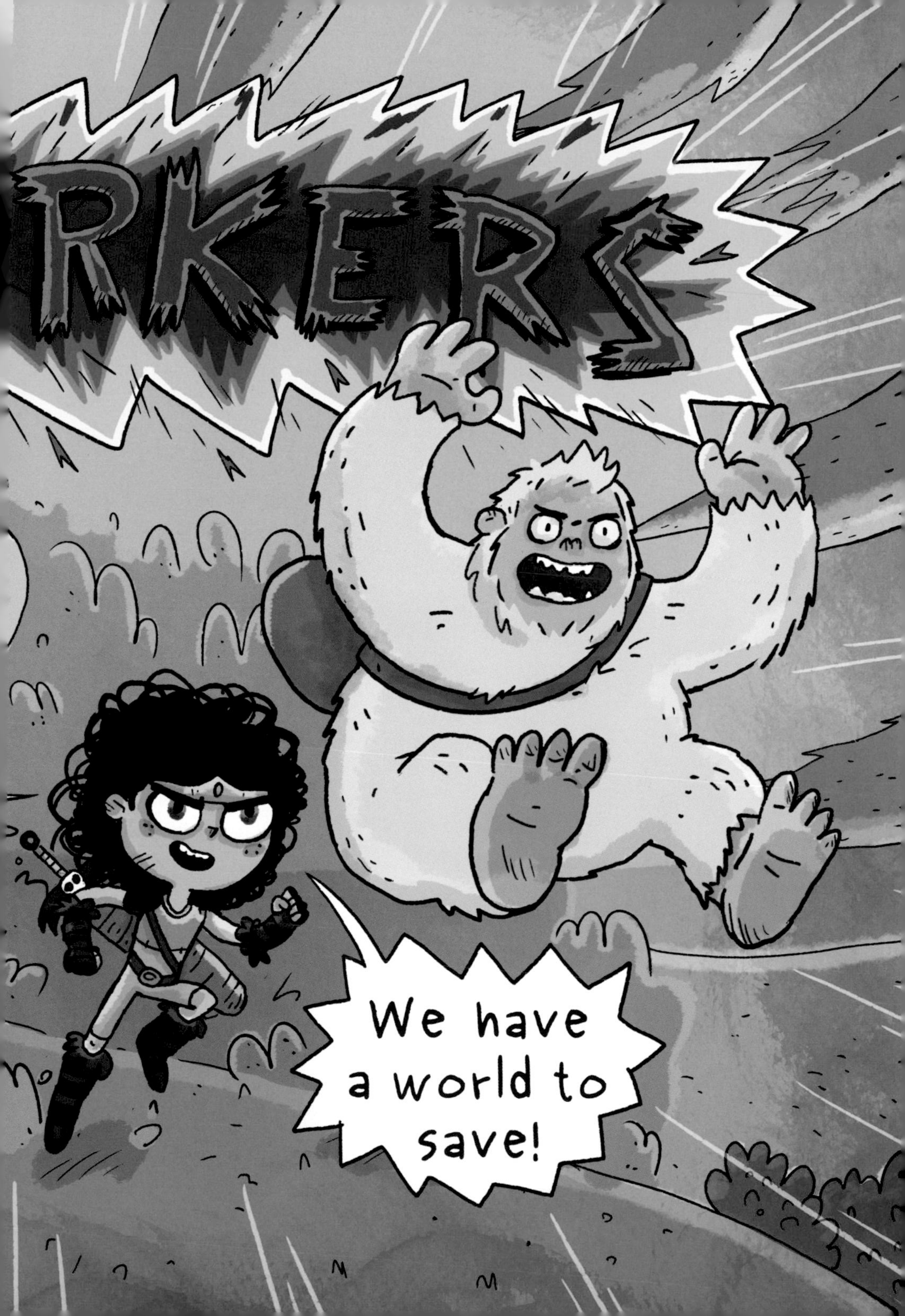
RKERS
We have a world to save!

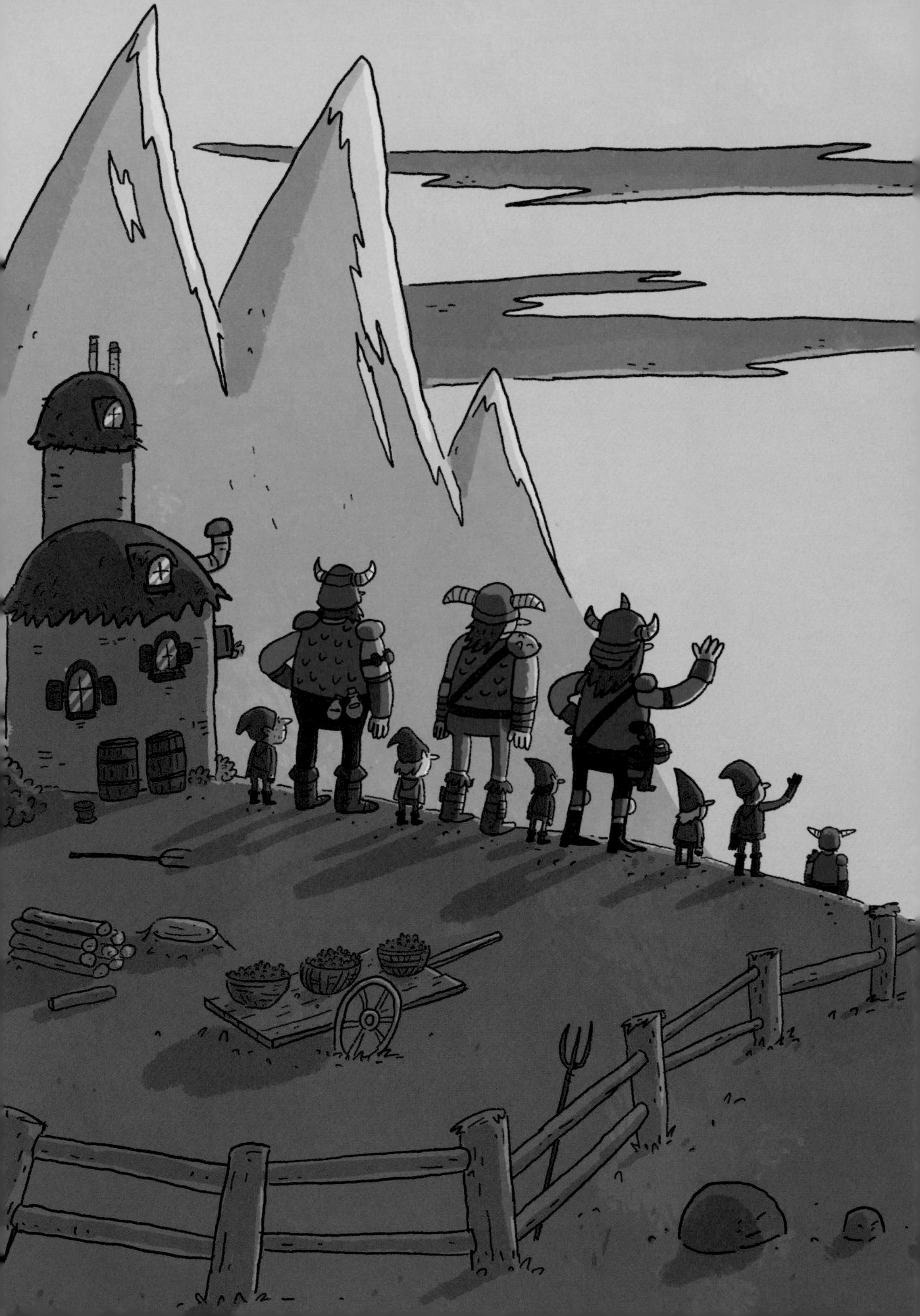

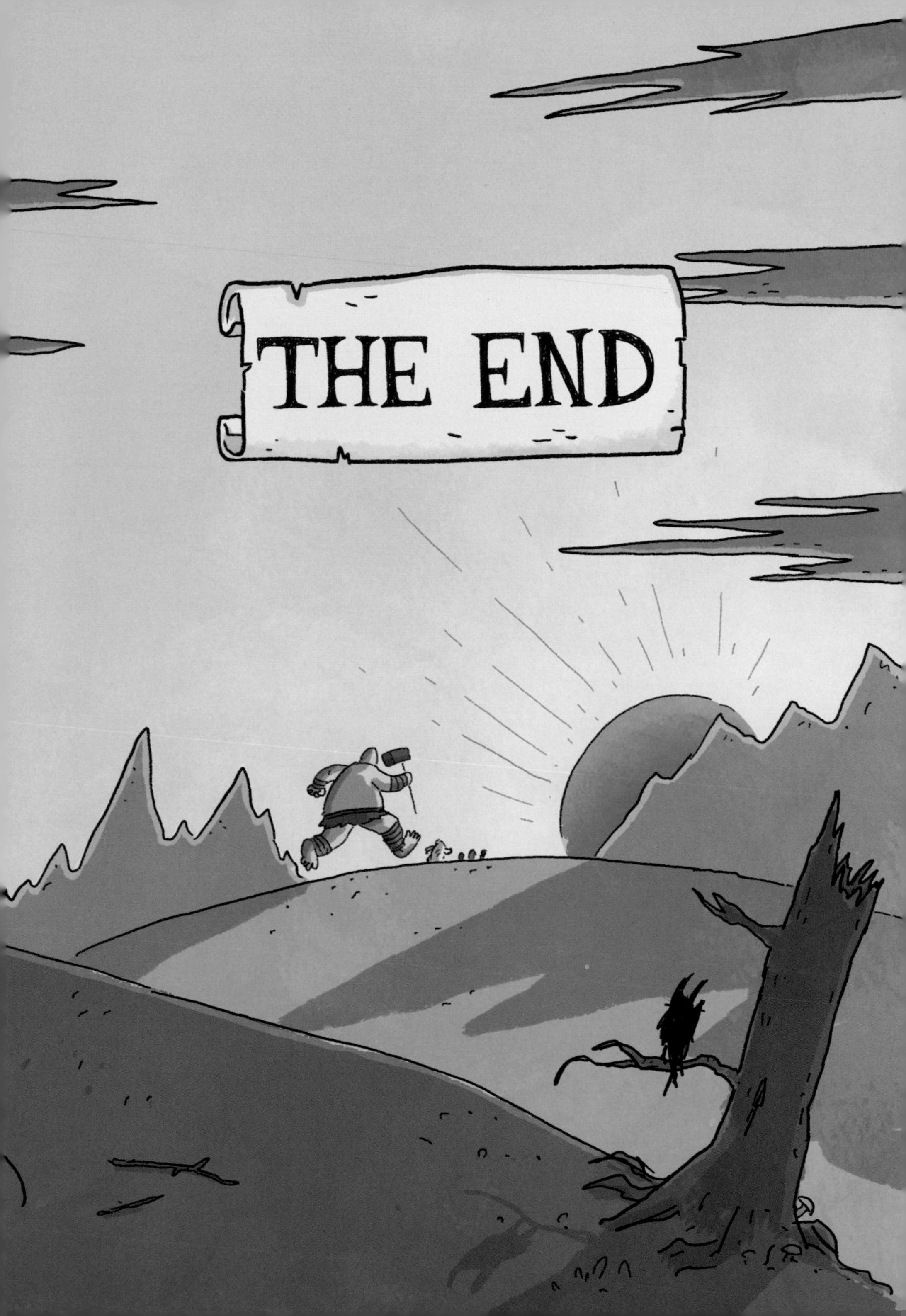
THE END

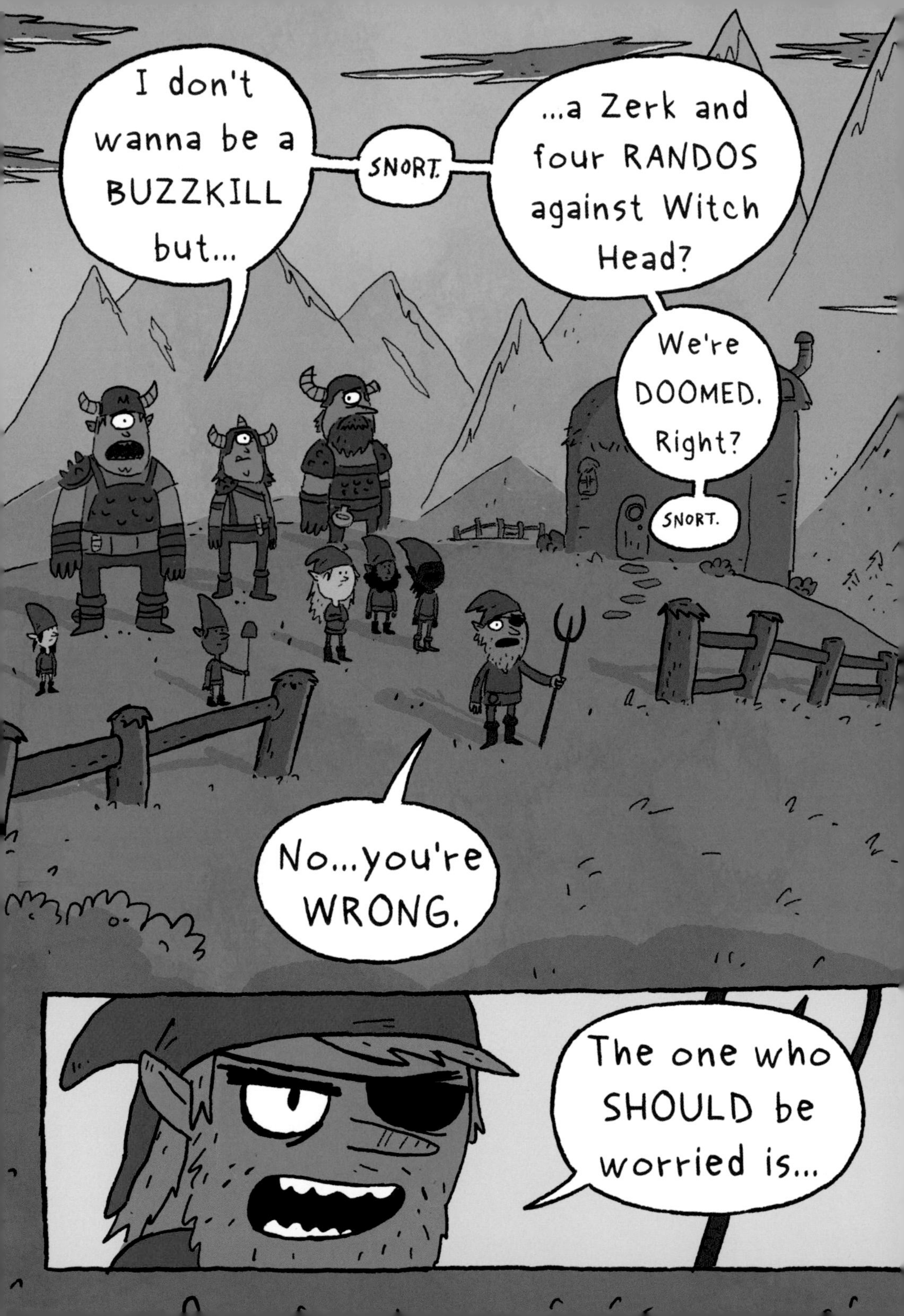
I don't wanna be a BUZZKILL but...
SNORT.
...a Zerk and four RANDOS against Witch Head?
We're DOOMED. Right?
SNORT.
No...you're WRONG.
The one who SHOULD be worried is...

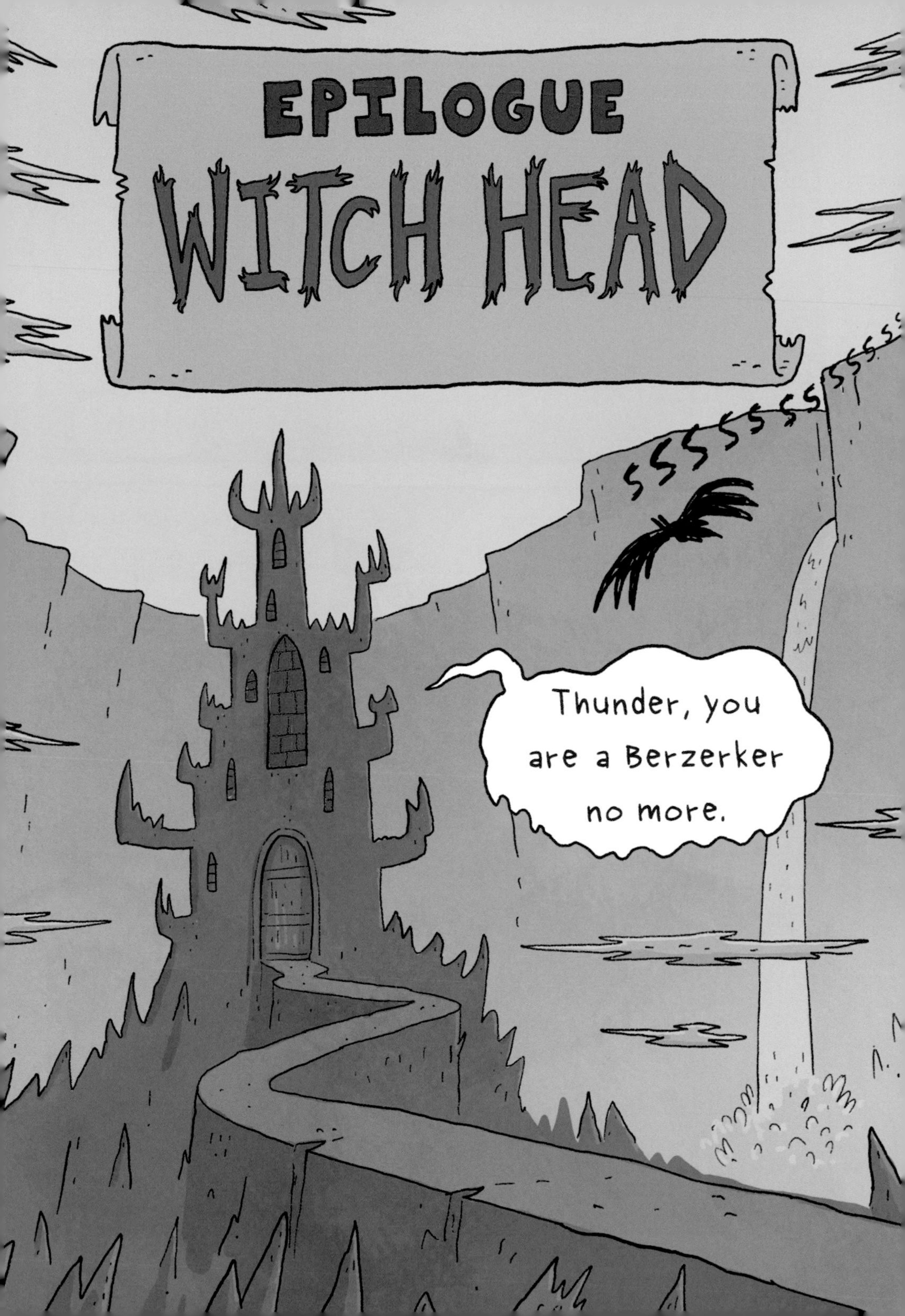
EPILOGUE
WITCH HEAD
SSSSSSSSSSSSS
Thunder, you are a Berzerker no more.

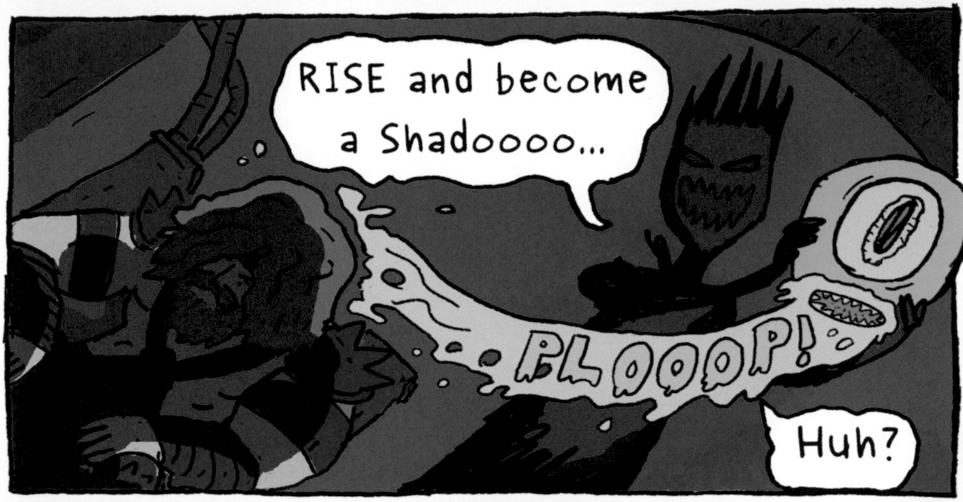
RISE and become a Shadoooo...
PLOOOP!
Huh?

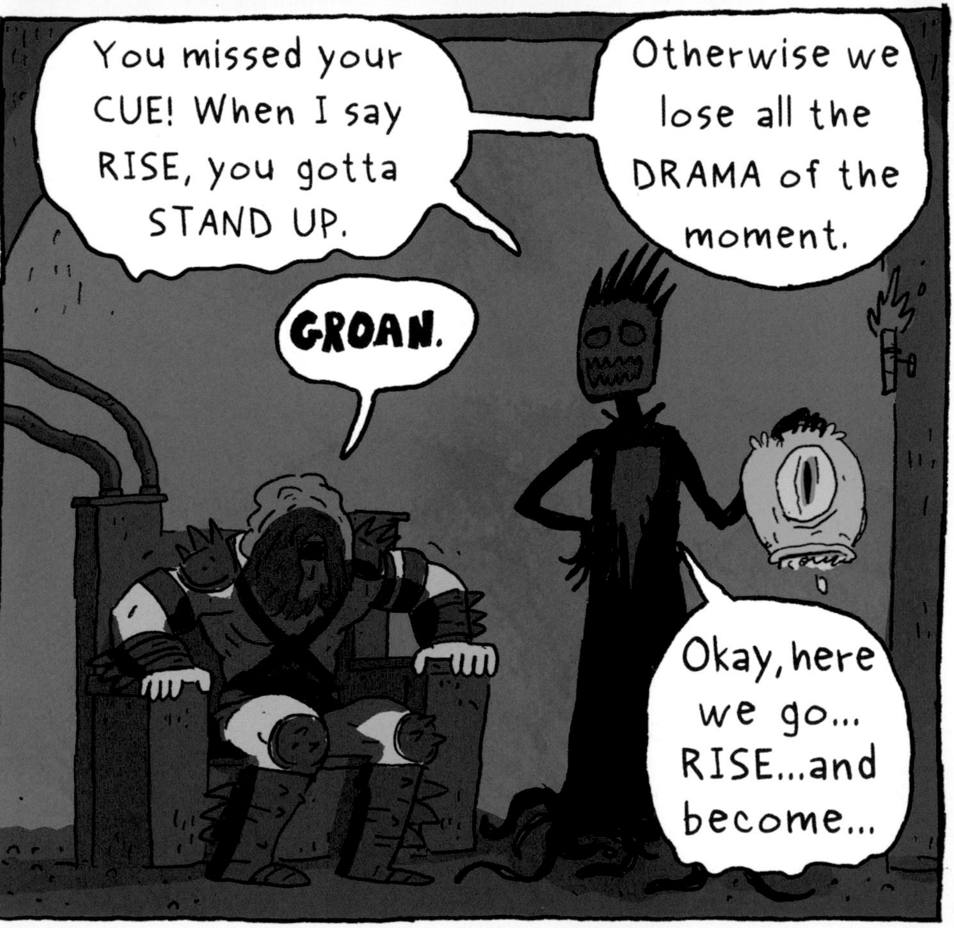
You missed your CUE! When I say RISE, you gotta STAND UP.
Otherwise we lose all the DRAMA of the moment.
GROAN.
Okay, here we go... RISE...and become...

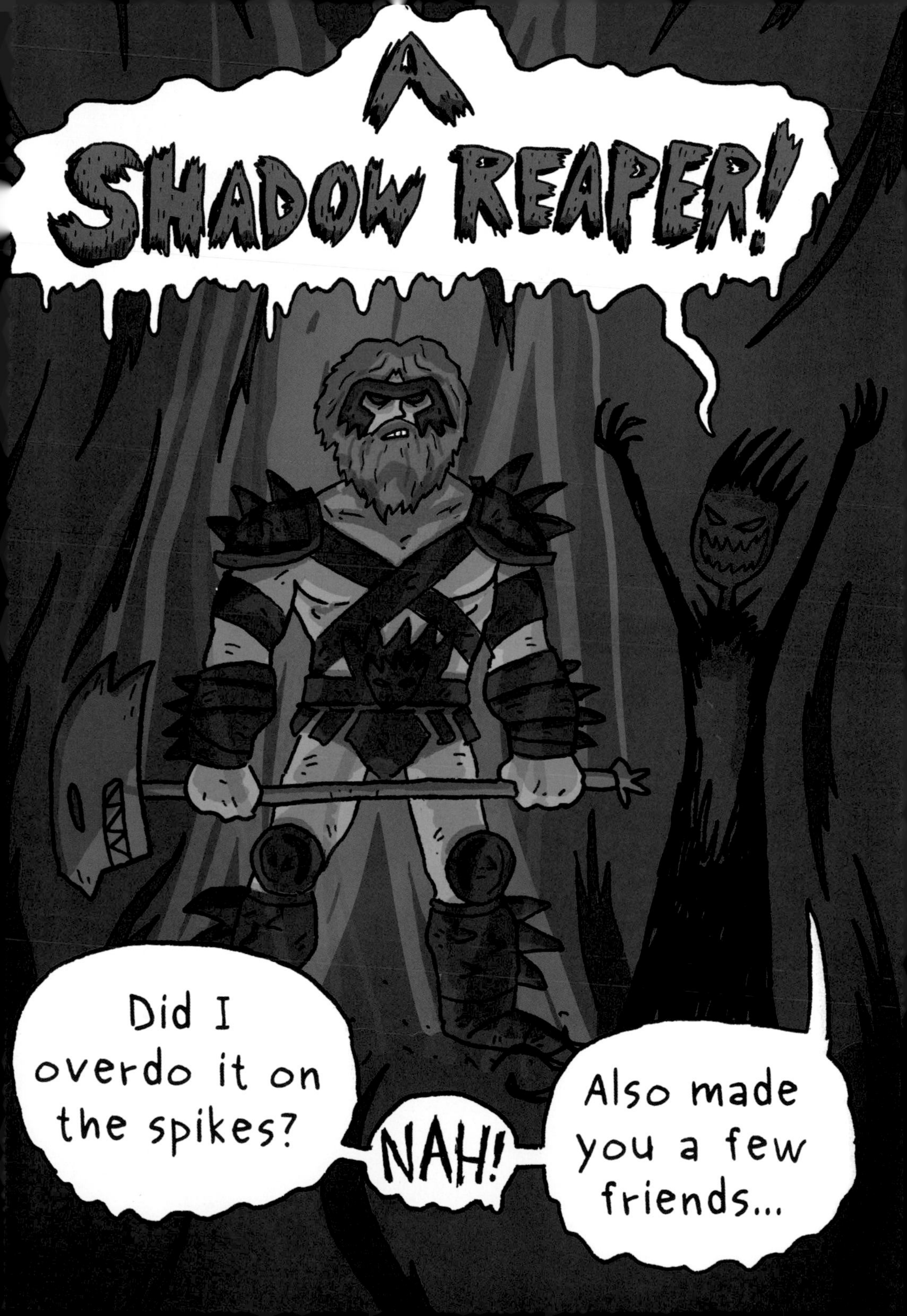
A SHADOW REAPER!
Did I overdo it on the spikes?
NAH!
Also made you a few friends...

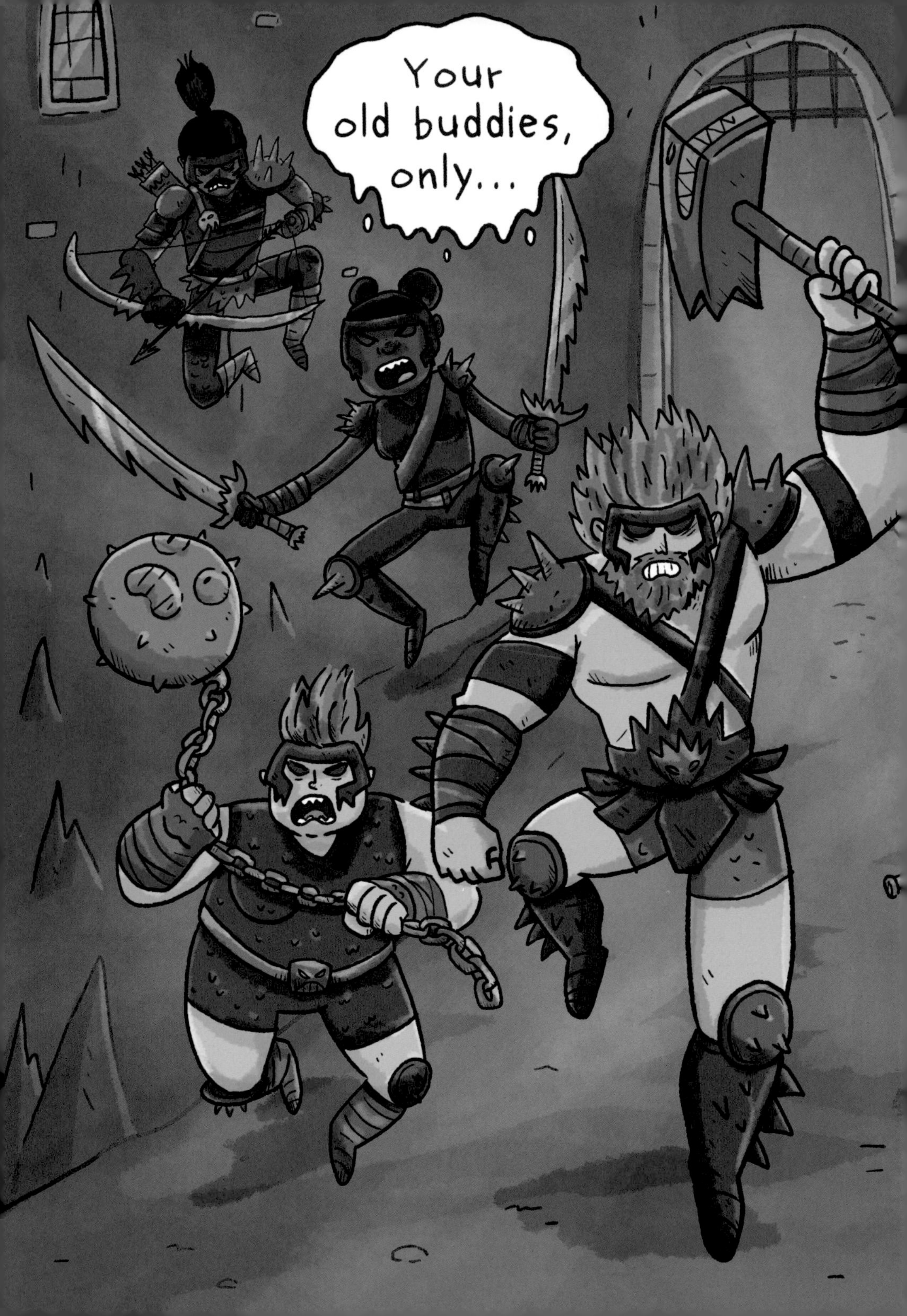
Your old buddies, only...

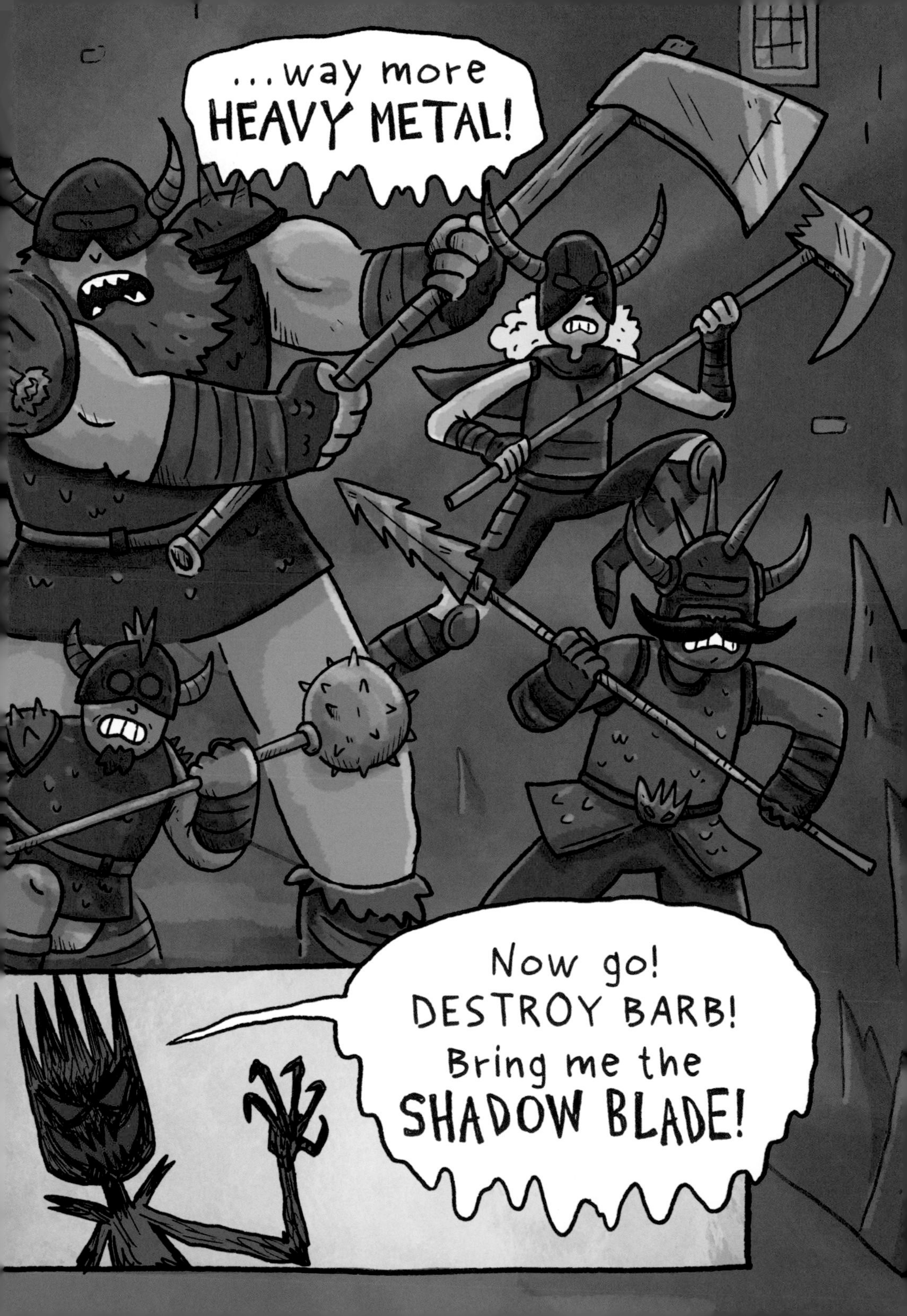
...way more HEAVY METAL!
Now go! DESTROY BARB! Bring me the SHADOW BLADE!

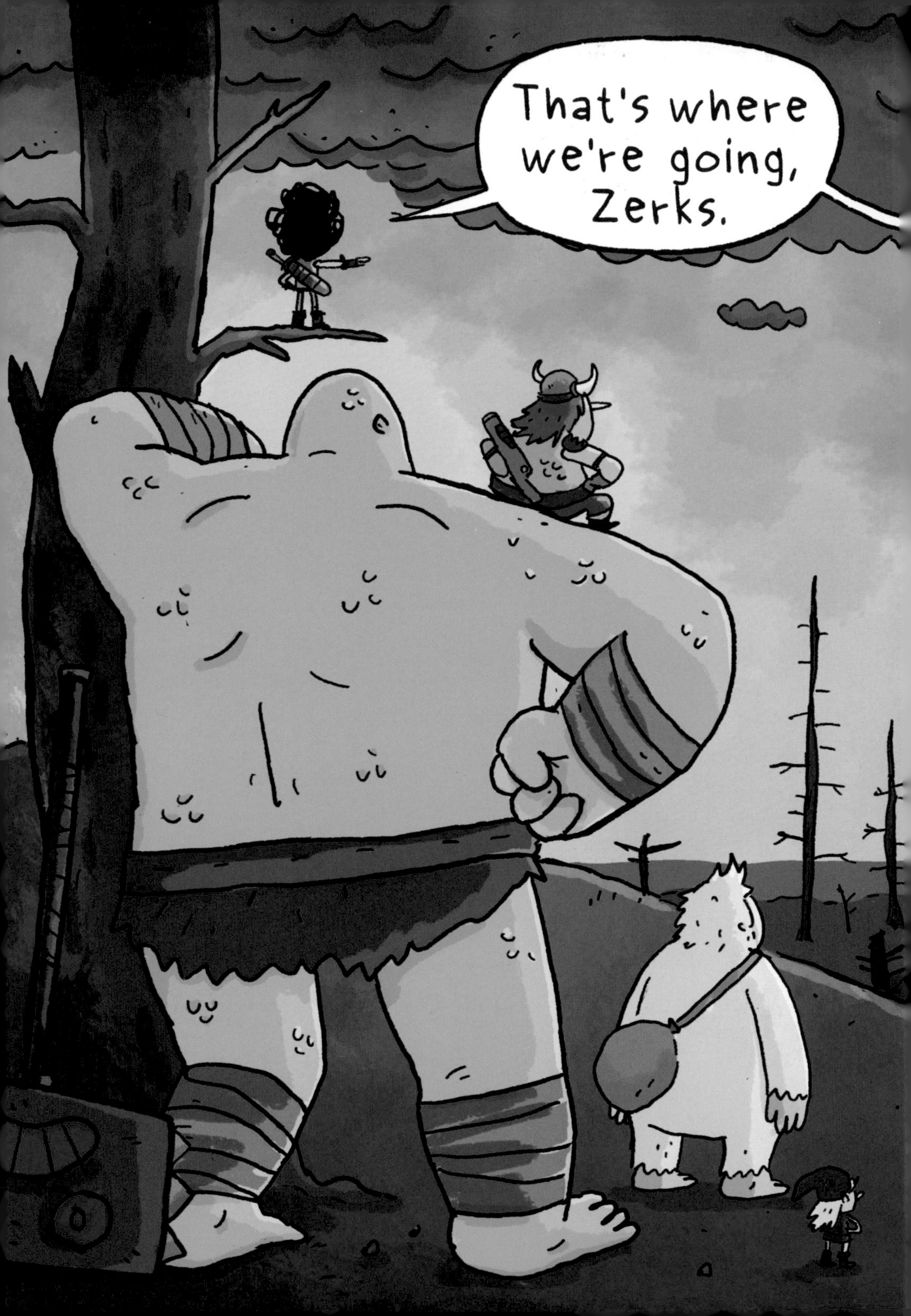
That's where we're going, Zerks.

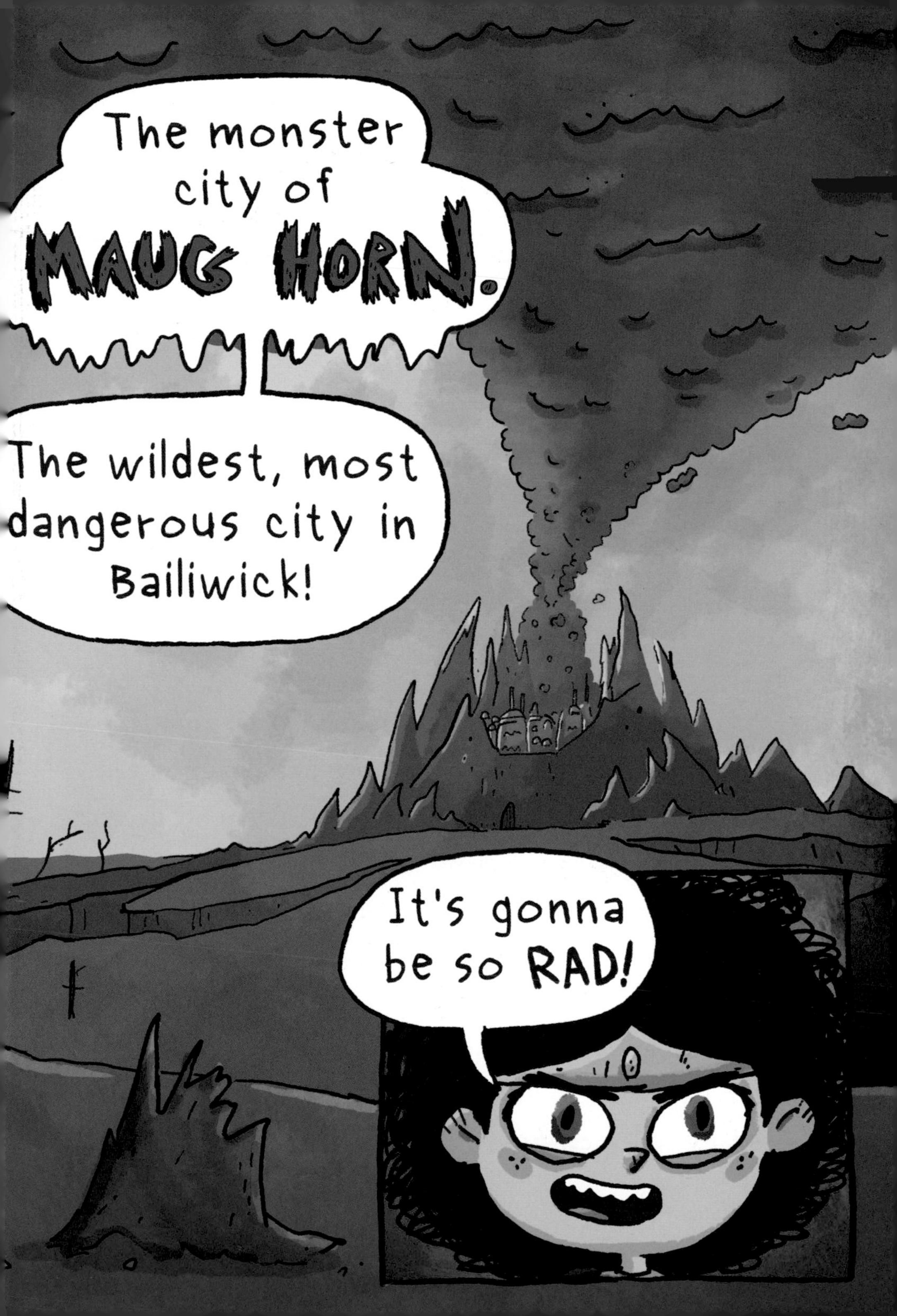

The monster city of MAUG HORN.
The wildest, most dangerous city in Bailiwick!
It's gonna be so RAD!

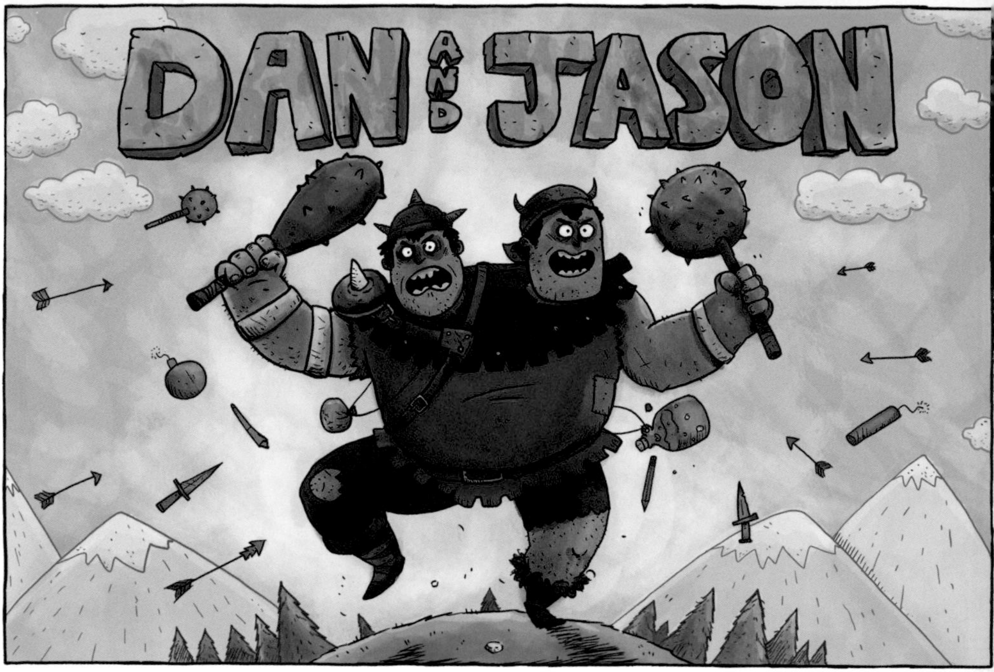
DAN AND JASON

Dan and Jason are a two-headed troll that grew up in Vermont. As a little two-headed troll they enjoyed smashing toys together, drawing comics, and joking around about stories and stuff. They were best pals back then and they are best pals today. Now fully grown, they still enjoy drawing comics and joking around, although they don't smash their toys together. . . as much. Check out their early reader graphic novel series Blue, Barry & Pancakes at all fine booksellers.

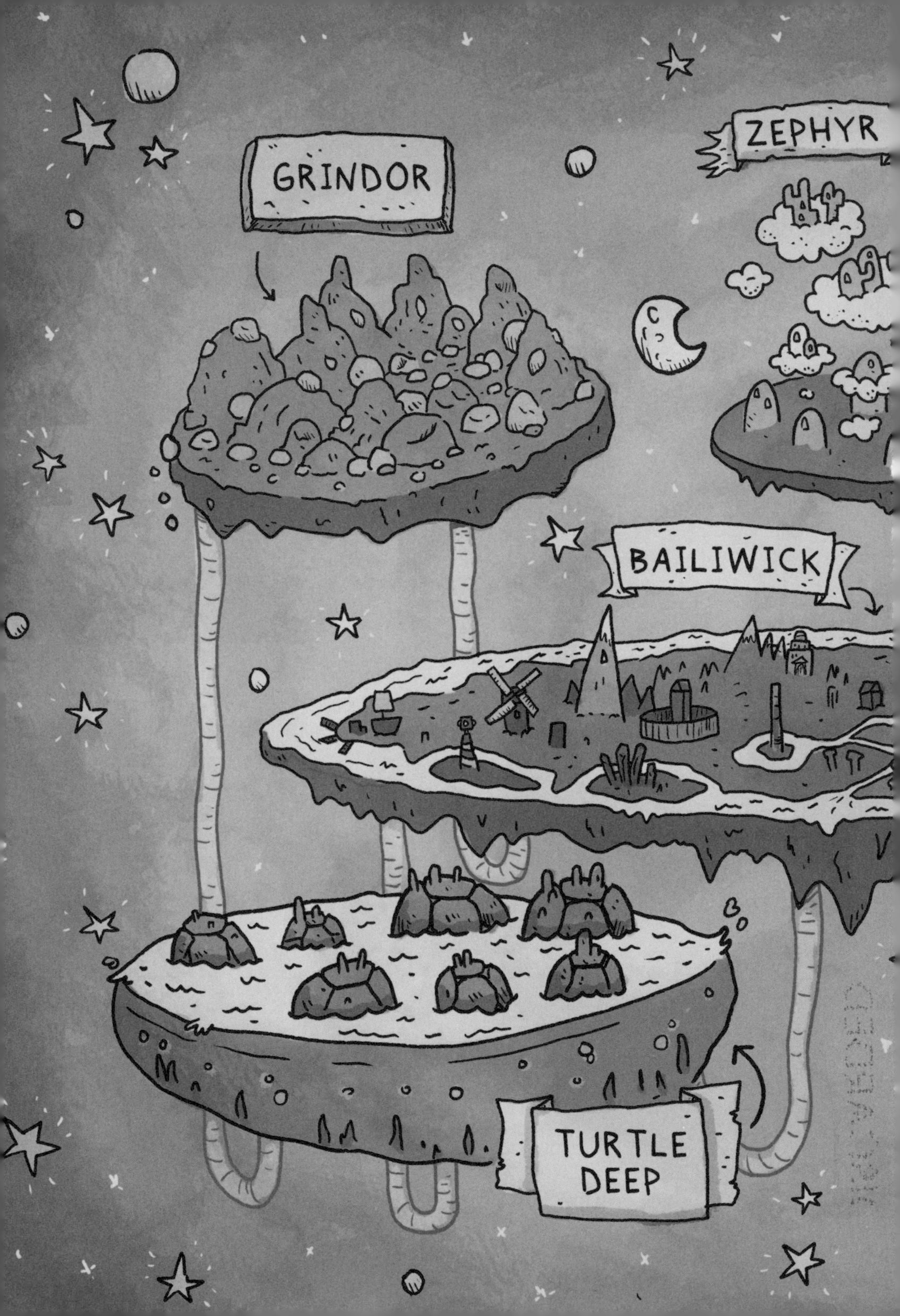
GRINDOR
ZEPHYR
BAILIWICK
TURTLE DEEP